KING JAVAN'S YEAR

Volume II of *The Heirs of Saint Camber*

By Katherine Kurtz
Published by Ballantine Books:

THE LEGENDS OF CAMBER OF CULDI

CAMBER OF CULDI
SAINT CAMBER
CAMBER THE HERETIC

THE CHRONICLES OF THE DERYNI

DERYNI RISING
DERYNI CHECKMATE
HIGH DERYNI

THE HISTORIES OF KING KELSON

THE BISHOP'S HEIR
THE KING'S JUSTICE
THE QUEST FOR SAINT CAMBER

THE HEIRS OF SAINT CAMBER

THE HARROWING OF GWYNEDD
KING JAVAN'S YEAR

THE DERYNI ARCHIVES
DERYNI MAGIC

LAMMAS NIGHT

KING JAVAN'S YEAR

Volume II of *The Heirs of Saint Camber*

Katherine Kurtz

A Del Rey Book
Ballantine Books • New York

A Del Rey Book
Published by Ballantine Books

Copyright © 1992 by Katherine Kurtz
Map by Shelly Shapiro

Library of Congress Cataloging-in-Publication Data
Kurtz, Katherine.
King Javan's year / Katherine Kurtz. — 1st ed.
p.   cm. — (The heirs of Saint Camber ; v. 2)
"A Del Rey book."
ISBN 0-345-33260-1.
I. Title.   II. Series: Kurtz, Katherine. Heirs of Saint Camber; v. 2
PS3561.U69K48   1992
813'.54—dc20   92-53218
CIP

Manufactured in the United States of America

First Edition: December 1992

10 9 8 7 6 5 4 3 2 1

For
Lester del Rey
with affection and gratitude

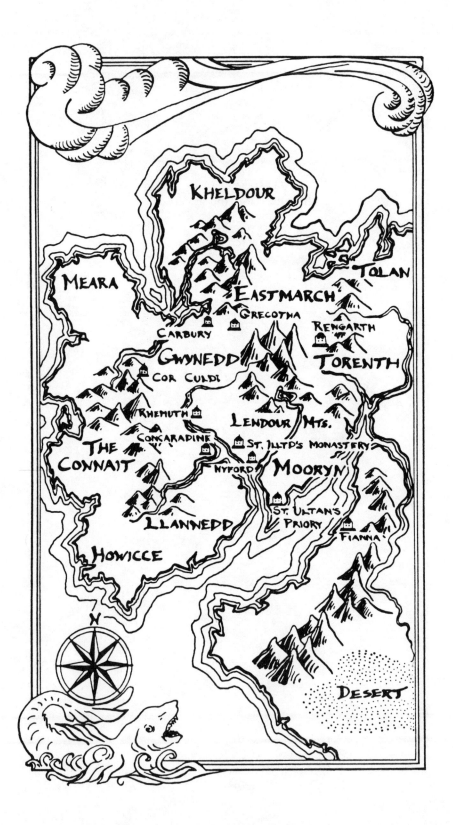

CONTENTS

KING JAVAN'S
YEAR

PROLOGUE

A little past dawn of a June morning already promising uncompromising heat, the dark-haired child whose job it was to check the pigeon roost clambered up the last few rungs of the ladder leading up from the room below and cautiously emerged on the tower's flat roof, keeping low.

The old square stone tower set on this barren hillside was assumed by local folk to be derelict. Twisted shrubs the size of small trees grew from a gap partway up one side, and what remained of the crenellated battlements looked ready to tumble down at the first good storm. In fact, the tower provided cover for a variety of clandestine activities whose scope would have surprised and shocked most of the human folk who lived in this remote area.

Young Seanna MacGregor and the pigeons were a small part of one of those activities. Several dozen of the dark-striped grey birds ruffled and chuckled to themselves behind the roost's restraining mesh of knotted cord as the sun's white disk cleared the eastern horizon. Seanna squinted against its brightness and scooped back sweaty wisps of hair that had escaped from her dark braid. Not a breath of air was moving. Usually no birds came in during the night, but this morning two were sauntering along the edge of the tower's parapet, striped necks bobbing back and forth as they pecked for grain and twittered and cooed to the other birds.

Trying to avoid any too-quick motion that might frighten them, the ten-year-old began creeping quietly toward the nearer of the two pigeons. Practiced little hands soon had the first bird captive against her chest, so that she could pull the curl of vellum out of the little wooden cylinder tied around the bird's leg. Her dark eyes widened as she read the brief message, and after stuffing it in a pocket, she slipped the first bird into the cage with the others and went after the second.

The second message proved to be the same as the first—insurance, no doubt, to make certain that at least one of them reached its destination. Glancing over the tower's parapet to the yard below, Seanna looked for and spotted her favorite brother over by the tumbledown stables, watching a groom lead out a big, rangy bay that looked out of place in such mean surroundings. Not bothering to put the second bird into the cage, she released it onto the parapet again and started back down the ladder, sniffling back tears.

Below in the yard, standing next to a bearded man in a farrier's leather apron, the outlawed son of the outlawed Earl of Ebor turned a critical eye on the mare being trotted back and forth outside the stable. Jesse MacGregor was not a tall man, but his compact frame was muscled and hard. At twenty, he had been a warrior for almost half his life. Flecks of gold stirred in the depths of brown eyes that missed very little. The sun had bronzed his olive skin and put brassy lights in the brown hair tied back in a queue. Over a full-sleeved white shirt of gauzy linen, open at the collar, he wore riding leathers of a dusty cinnamon color, almost the same shade as the callused hand he raised to point at the mare's front feet.

"Look there. Do you see it? She's still favoring the near front."

"Aye, she is," the farrier agreed. "I'll try weighting the shoe one more time, but we won't have any hoof left to nail it to if we don't get it right this time."

"Well, do what you can," Jesse replied. "Thanks, Ned."

As the farrier took the mare from the groom and led her back into the barn, Jesse turned at movement from the direction of the tower and opened his arms to the slight, anxious form in boy's attire who came hurtling across the yard to tackle him around the waist, dark braid flying.

"Hey, Seanna Madonna, light of my life, what's wrong?" he asked as he realized she had been crying.

"Two birds this morning," she said, raking a slightly grubby sleeve across her eyes. "They both had the same message. He's dying, Jesse."

Stiffening slightly, Jesse hugged her closer for a moment, stroking a comforting hand down the dark hair, then took the two slips of parchment and headed back across the yard to the tower and a succession of hidden passages leading downward.

The tower was a gateway to the last bastion of the outlawed Order of Saint Michael, though the Michaelines themselves were long gone as an order. Nearly two decades before, the underground sanctuary had served as headquarters for the Deryni Camber MacRorie and his associates, many of them human, who had ousted the Deryni King Imre of Festil and restored the human line of Prince Cinhil Haldane to the throne of Gwynedd. Since Cinhil's death four years before, it again had become the hub for a combined human and Deryni resistance, this time led by Camber's son Joram.

For King Cinhil's eldest son and heir, not yet twelve when he came to his father's throne, had never managed to shake off the influence of the powerful human lords who had been his regents during his minority. Legislation pushed forward in the very first year of young Alroy's reign had revived old resentments of Deryni privilege and excesses by focusing them through the lens of religious conviction that Deryni and their magical powers were evil. It was that legacy which had forced Joram and Jesse and their colleagues underground and which drove them in their ongoing efforts to see the balance set straight.

"Two birds this morning," Jesse said without preamble as he entered the underground library where Joram was working. "The messages are identical—and not what we wanted to hear."

Joram was already scanning the curl of parchment Jesse had handed him, and allowed himself a heavy sigh as he sat back and looked up at the newcomer.

"I can't say I haven't been expecting this," he said. "Sit down, sit down. I'd hoped we might make it through the summer, but—" He shrugged and shook his head. "Well, we'll just have to move our plans ahead. Will you send the other copy on to Ansel?"

Jesse nodded, wiping a sheen of perspiration off his brow with the back of a sunburned hand. Even in the relative cool of the underground Michaeline sanctuary, clad as he was for the summer heat, the air seemed close and still. He found it mildly comforting to note that even the usually fastidious Joram had loosened the collar of his black cassock.

It still jarred Jesse not to see Michaeline blue when he looked at Joram. Since the suppression of the Order, Joram increasingly had taken to wearing the plain black working cassock of an ordinary priest—not that much was ordinary about Joram MacRorie. Though Joram now was into his forties, with most of his waking hours taken up in the coordination of their various efforts, he still managed to convey the keen, battle-ready image of the Michaeline knight he once had been.

Like the old Michaeline blue, clerical black set off Joram's lean form to perfection, dramatic contrast to the famous silver-gilt hair. It had gone more silvery than gold, perhaps, in the last few years, but he still wore it short-cropped for battle ease, with the small, coin-sized Michaeline tonsure shaven at the crown—a reminder, if primarily to himself, that he remained a Michaeline in spirit. The blue eyes still missed nothing, but a fine network of tiny lines around them told of new stresses that had not been his in the old days, when he had served his famous father as secretary and aide.

Joram heaved a heavy sigh and ran both hands through the silver-gilt hair, then sat back wearily in his chair.

"The timing on this is rotten," he said, "but then, I suppose so is dying."

"Do you think it's time to call in Queron and Tavis?" Jesse asked.

"I'm afraid so. I wanted to minimize any movement that might jeopardize their cover, but we knew this was only a matter of time. Contact Queron and tell him what's about to happen. I don't see how it can be more than a few days. Ask him and Tavis to come as soon as they can do so without arousing suspicion. If it becomes more urgent than that, we'll let them know. At least we'll have gotten our part in motion."

Jesse nodded. "I'll try to get through at midday. It may have to wait until tonight, though."

"Can't be helped." Joram crumpled the curl of parchment into a stiff little ball, then opened his hand to gaze at it sitting on his palm. After a few seconds, it burst into flame with a bright flare and a pop that made Jesse start.

"So, for poor Alroy," Joram whispered as he tipped the burning parchment off his hand. "The king is about to be dead; long live the king. Let's just hope it's the *right* king."

CHAPTER ONE

*And I will give children to be their princes, and
babes shall rule over them.*
                                        —Isaiah 3:4

King Alroy was dying. The Healer Oriel had tried to persuade himself otherwise for days, but the sweat-drenched sixteen-year-old fretting feverishly under even a single layer of limp sheeting was no
longer even conscious much of the time—though there were occasional lucid moments.

It was during one of those lucid moments, earlier in the day,
that Alroy had rallied enough to ask that his bed be moved into
one of the ground-level rooms opening onto the castle gardens,
where the windows might admit a little breeze. A breeze *had* come,
with the setting of the sun, spilling the heady perfume of roses into
the room, but there still was little enough respite from the heat,
even this late at night. Summer had arrived early this year, and
with uncharacteristic harshness. These first weeks of June had
seemed more like August at its worst, the air still and stifling, heavy
with humidity. Even the usually proper Oriel was stripped down to
breeches and a thin linen shirt, open at the throat, the full sleeves
pushed well up above his elbows.

A young squire offered a basin of cool water, and Oriel wrung
out another cloth in it, touching the back of one hand against his
royal patient's cheek before laying the cloth across the brow. Alroy
Haldane had never been robust, and fever had burned away what
little spare flesh there once had been on the boy's slight frame, so
that what remained resembled all too closely the stark planes of
the effigy even now being prepared to lie beneath Rhemuth Cathe-

dral. The sable hair, cut short around his face, was plastered to his skull like a glistening ebon cap.

The king moaned and stirred a little, teeth clenched as if against a chill, even though the fever burned still, and the heat of the summer night as well. The court physicians had given him syrup of poppies earlier in the evening, when even Oriel's feared Deryni powers had not been able to stop a particularly bad bout of hacking that seemed actually apt to end in the king coughing up part of his lungs. He slept now, but his breathing was labored and liquid-sounding; Oriel, like the king's human physicians, knew that the king's illness and his life were drawing inexorably toward their close.

"He—isn't getting any better, is he, sir?" the squire whispered, turning worried eyes on the Healer as Oriel wrung out another cold compress. The boy's name was Fulk Fitz-Arthur, and he was two years younger than the king. His father was one of the lords of state waiting for word in the anteroom outside.

Oriel sighed and shook his head as he changed the compress, pausing then to set his fingertips to the king's sweat-drenched temples. Though he had no doubt what he would find, he sent his Healer's senses deep into the ailing king, reading again what he already knew, to his heart's despair—that the boy's lungs were nearly eaten away with disease and filling with fluid. Court gossip had it that the boy's father had perished of a similar ailment, with Healers far more skilled than Oriel helpless to save him.

Somehow that knowledge did little to ease Oriel's sense of helplessness, of failure, the cosmic injustice that, even given the almost godlike powers that condemned him to the servitude of the lords of state, else he suffer death the first time he used them unauthorized, those powers were not sufficient to save the boy beneath his hands.

Alroy stirred and moaned as Oriel withdrew, the grey eyes flickering and then opening in another of those increasingly rare lucid moments. His pupils were wide from the drugs they had given him, but he made a gallant effort to focus on Oriel, one fragile hand shifting from under the sheet to reach toward the Healer's wrist.

"Oriel, what time is it?" he whispered.

"Near midnight, Sire," the Healer replied, taking the king's hand and leaning closer to hear. "You should go back to sleep. If you talk too much, you'll set yourself coughing again."

"I want to see my brother," Alroy murmured. "Have they called him?"

Setting his lips, Oriel gently chafed the royal hand between his own, knowing that the brother the king's ministers had called was not the brother Alroy wanted to see. The Haldane Ring of Fire shifted under his fingers, for Alroy had refused to set it aside, even in his illness, even though loss of weight had made it loose on his hand and likely to fall off—though somehow, it never did.

"Prince Rhys Michael is without, Sire," Oriel murmured, choosing his words with care, lest young Fulk relay it back to his father as some criticism of the royal ministers' handling of the situation. "Shall I ask him to come to you?"

At the same time, he set the psychic suggestion that Alroy should make his request of Rhys Michael, for Oriel dared not—and Rhys Michael was the one person who might be able to insist that the king's wishes were carried out.

Alroy gave no outward sign that the suggestion had registered, but he gave a weak nod. "Yes. Please. I should like to see Rhys Michael."

Bowing over the royal hand, Oriel pressed his lips to it briefly, then laid it gently at the king's side.

"Stay with the King's Grace, Fulk," he said to the squire, "and continue changing the compresses. I'll summon his Highness."

He braced himself for almost certain unpleasantness as he withdrew, at least pulling his sleeves into place and doing up the wrists before he went into the anteroom outside the king's bedchamber.

Lord Tammaron, young squire Fulk's father, was there, along with Archbishop Hubert and one of Hubert's nephews, Lord Iver MacInnis. Rhys Michael, the king's younger brother, was standing before the dark opening of an empty fireplace, one arm laid along the cool stone of its mantel and chimney breast, and looked up anxiously as Oriel came in.

"How is he?" Tammaron demanded, before the prince could speak.

"He's resting as peacefully as may be expected, my lord," Oriel replied. "However, he's asked to see his brother." He turned his gaze pointedly toward Rhys Michael, three months short of his fifteenth birthday, but already nearly grown to the adult stature his elder brother would never live to achieve. "If you'd care to come with me, your Highness?"

Before any of his elders could forbid it, Rhys Michael was bolting toward Oriel and the door, slicking his sweat-damp hair back over his ears and tugging at a fold of his long, belted tunic of royal blue. The wide sleeves were rolled to his elbows against the heat, and Oriel could see the clean-limbed flash of long, bare legs and sandals through the high-slit sides—sensible attire in the heat, even

for a prince. Archbishop Hubert looked to be stifling in a cassock
of purple silk buttoned right up to his multiple chins, sweat darkening a streak down the center of his chest and extending crescent-
wise underneath both heavy arms.

"Your Highness, please allow me to accompany you," Hubert
began, the edge to his voice quite belying the formal words of courtesy—though he did not manage to set his own bulk into motion
until Rhys Michael was already halfway across the room.

A cringing look of apprehension flashed across the prince's face
at the words, though only Oriel could see it, but Rhys Michael did
not turn until he had reached the Healer's side.

"Actually, I'd prefer to see my brother alone, if you don't mind,"
he said, lifting his chin in an uncustomary show of spirit. "I—may
not have many more chances."

He turned away at that, eyes averted, anxiety for his brother
clouding the handsome Haldane face. Oriel made a point of not
meeting the eyes of any of the others in the anteroom as he stood
aside to let the prince pass—though he expected he would answer
for the defiance later—only following close behind and closing the
door.

The prince was already at the royal bedside as Oriel turned, picking up Alroy's slack left hand to kiss it. The king's eyes opened at
the touch, his grey gaze locking on his brother's as Oriel slipped in
on his other side—unobtrusive as possible, but knowing he must
remain nearby, for Alroy almost certainly would begin coughing if
he said very much. The Healer had no need to resort to Deryni
perceptions to perceive the brothers' genuine love for one another.
The squire Fulk had withdrawn to a side table with the basin of
water and cool compresses, trying not to look as if he were watching and listening.

"Alroy?" Rhys Michael whispered.

The king managed a thin, taut smile.

"You're here," he said weakly. "I'm glad. But where is Javan? I
have to see him."

Rhys Michael swallowed once, the sound almost startling in the
still, heavy night, and ducked his head over the hand he held cradled to his chest.

"He's at *Arx Fidei*, in the seminary," he murmured. "You know
that."

"But he's my *heir*," Alroy insisted, wide, drug-dilated eyes
searching his brother's face. "I'm dying—"

"No, you're not!"

"Rhysem, I *am*," Alroy went on, reverting to the pet name that had developed between them these last few years. "I'm going to die, and there's nothing that the stupid court physicians or even our good Master Oriel can do to prevent it." His eyes flicked briefly to Oriel, who hung his head in helplessness. "Don't you remember how our father went?"

As the king paused to stifle a cough with his free hand, his exertion already stirring up his illness, Oriel let his left hand ease unobtrusively to the royal shoulder, where young Fulk hopefully would not notice, daring to extend his powers just a little to give the king ease. At the same time, Rhys Michael tightened his grip on the hand he held, trying to will strength across the link of their fraternal love. Whether from that or from Oriel's ministrations, Alroy did manage to stop coughing.

"I must see our brother before I die, Rhysem," the king continued, when he had caught his breath. "You must make them send for him."

"But I can't. They'll never listen—"

"They'll listen if you insist," Alroy said. "You're not a child anymore. You're nearly a year past your legal majority. And if they *should* manage to bypass Javan and make you king—as is certainly their intention, if you let them—then they'll have to answer to you in your full authority, without recourse to regents. Remind them of that—and that Haldane memories are long!"

As Alroy had spoken, increasingly fighting to get each word out, a kind of hope had begun to light Rhys Michael's eyes—for he truly did not want the crown that, by rights, should pass next to the king's twin.

"You're right," he murmured. "I *am* of age. They *aren't* our regents anymore. And if I did become king, I could really make them sorry they'd disobeyed me!"

"Whereas, if they send for Javan," Alroy rasped, *"as is my death-bed wish,* the new king may be inclined to be clement, whoever he may be." Alroy coughed again, and Oriel knew he could not control it much longer.

"Go now," Alroy gasped, around another cough. "If a rider leaves now, he can be back by dawn. I don't know that I can last much past then."

As coughing took him again, so that Oriel had to roll him on his side and then into a sitting position, motioning for Fulk to bring more of the extract of poppies, a moist-eyed Rhys Michael gave his brother's hand a final squeeze, then turned on his heels and fled. He drew himself up just before he got to the door, pausing with both hands on the latch and head bowed for just a moment to draw deep breath and gird himself for the confrontation ahead. Then he raised his head like the Haldane prince he was and pushed down the latch, moving through and closing the door behind him before the three men waiting could even get to their feet.

"The king commands that our brother Javan be summoned," he said, his face taut but composed. "This is my command, as well. And before you consider defying the command of a dying king," he added, holding up a hand to still the objection already forming on the lips of young Iver MacInnis, "consider whether you also wish to defy the man *you* desire to have as your next king. For if I *should* ever become king, gentlemen—though that is not *my* desire—I assure you that I shall not forget this night."

As he looked pointedly past Iver at Earl Tammaron and Iver's uncle the archbishop, the rotund Hubert bit at his rosebud lips and made a short little bow.

"The king's wish is our command, of course, your Highness, but is it altogether wise to drag your royal brother from his studies? The king is not yet in danger of death; he has not requested the Last Rites. With all due respect, these final days could drag on for weeks or even months, as was the case for your Highness' sainted father. Time enough, in due time, to send for Prince Javan, if that is still the king's desire."

"It is the king's *command*," Rhys Michael said evenly, fighting back the panic he dared not allow himself to show—for it frightened him that Alroy himself had indicated that he might not last much past dawn. "Furthermore, it is the king's command that our brother be summoned *now*. If you are unwilling to do it, then I shall do it myself. Guard!" he called.

He was already moving toward the door to the outer corridor before any of the three truly believed he was going to do it. Only just in time did Earl Tammaron grab young Iver's arm and stop him from trying to physically prevent the prince from leaving, earning the earl a sparse nod of acknowledgment from Rhys Michael and Iver a raking glance of disdain.

"I suggest that you tread very softly, Iver MacInnis," the prince said in a low voice, as the outer door opened to admit a guard liveried in Haldane crimson. "And if *ever* you dare to lay hands upon our royal person, I promise that you shall not live long to regret the impertinence."

Eyes as cold as only Haldane anger could make them, he turned back to the guard before giving Iver a chance to reply, pushing past when he saw who it was, for he doubted that most of the ordinary guards would take important orders from him without confirmation of one of the lords of state. He needed one of the younger knights.

Quickly he glanced down the corridor outside. In the open passage beyond, which linked this wing of the castle with the next, perhaps a dozen lesser gentlemen of the court were lounging along the arched colonnade that faced the castle gardens, some awaiting word of the king, others simply seeking the promise of cooler air from the gardens beyond. Among them was a man whom Rhys Michael thought certain he could trust.

"Sir Charlan!" he called, raising a hand in summons as the young man rose at the sound of his name.

Nearly three years before, when Javan Haldane had withdrawn from public life to test a possible religious vocation—for so had been the official explanation—Charlan Kai Morgan had been the last squire to serve him. Despite the petty spying required of all the royal squires by the regents—and the squires had been quite open about telling their royal masters what they had been ordered to do—there had been mutual respect and genuine liking between squire and master. Though Charlan had readily accepted his transfer into the king's household for the remaining two years before his knighting, Rhys Michael knew from talking to his own former squire, Sir Tomais, that Charlan still spoke fondly of his former master. Alroy had knighted both young men at the previous year's Christmas Court.

Now, as the young knight approached, blond head bobbing in respect, Rhys Michael wondered whether Charlan would dare to assert, as a man, that old loyalty he had shown to Javan as a squire. The regents were regents no longer, and all answered to a king now two years come into his majority—even if that king was dying.

"You wish something, your Highness?" Charlan said.

"Yes, I do." Rhys Michael pitched his voice so that it could be heard by the others drifting closer, so that there would be witnesses. "What is more important, your king wishes something, on behalf of your future king." Let his other listeners take *that* as they wished.

"The king desires that Prince Javan be summoned to court immediately." He watched Charlan's face light at those words and knew he had chosen the right man. "Therefore, you are to take a dozen knights as escort, mount yourself and them on the fastest horses in the royal stables, and proceed with all haste to *Arx Fidei* Abbey, where you will escort His Royal Highness back to Rhemuth with all possible speed."

He pulled the silver signet from the little finger of his left hand, the seal with the Haldane arms differenced by the label of a third son, and put it in the hand that Charlan held out to receive it.

"This will be your authority to procure whatever is necessary for your journey," he said. "Know that you travel with my goodwill as well as that of the king. And if my brother should question that this is, indeed, my desire—" He faltered briefly as he considered, then reached to his right earlobe. "I bid you give him this."

Quickly he removed the earring of twisted gold, mate to one that Javan himself once had worn—though Javan had been forced to put aside both his earring and his signet when he entered the abbey. Javan would recognize it, though—and that his brother would not part with his unless there were dire cause, for their father had given them the earrings not long before his death.

Charlan glanced at both items, the ring and the earring, then slipped the signet over the end of his middle finger for safekeeping and wrapped the earring in a handkerchief that he tucked into the pouch slung below the white belt of his knighthood. The sleeveless leather jerkin over his full-sleeved linen shirt would take him to *Arx Fidei* well enough, but he was bare-legged and sandaled like many of the men who had been lounging in the breezeway and now drifted closer to see what was amiss.

"I shall be away as quickly as I may, your Highness," Charlan said, joining his hands palm to palm and extending them to the prince, dropping to one knee as he did so. "I give you my renewed pledge, as I gave it at my knighting, that I am the king's loyal man."

He bowed his head as Rhys Michael took the hands between his in the time-hallowed gesture of fealty accepted.

"Not on my own behalf, but in the name of the king who is and the king who shall be, I bid you go, Sir Charlan," the prince whispered. "Javan shall be king next—not me. Go to him now—quickly. Please!"

As Charlan rose and turned away, already summoning those men to his side who would ride with him to *Arx Fidei*, Rhys Michael watched him go. He had asserted himself as a prince and as a man, as was his right and duty, but he felt like an errant schoolboy just the same. He wondered if Archbishop Hubert would have him whipped—and what *he* would do, if Hubert tried it. The archbishop once had had Javan whipped for disobedience—but Rhys Michael was not and never had been under obedience to Hubert the way Javan had been. He didn't think Hubert would dare.

Still, he did not relish the next few hours, or facing the men in the room between him and his dying brother.

CHAPTER TWO

Behold, I come quickly: hold that fast which
thou hast, that no man take thy crown.

Revelations 3:11

Three hours' ride from Rhemuth, the cloister garden attached to the seminary at *Arx Fidei* Abbey was still and silent—no less stifling than at the capital, but the Haldane prince who sought its refuge in the stillness of the summer night at least had fewer immediate concerns than his two brothers. Following Matins, the Great Office of the night, after which every soul under the discipline of the abbey fell under the Great Silence until after Morning Prayer, Javan had passed quietly through the processional door and into the cloister garth rather than returning to his cell via the night stair.

Now he settled quickly on the granite curbing around the carp pool—to meditate, should anyone inquire. It was one of the few indulgences he had gained in his two years here: permission to enjoy the gardens in solitude while the rest of the abbey slept. It had caused its own stir among the abbey's hierarchy, for the abbot, a strict *Custodes Fidei* priest named Father Halex, did not approve of any divergence from the strict discipline and regimentation expected of his seminarians.

Fortunately, Javan was no ordinary seminarian. Even though also a clerk in minor orders, he was also a prince. Royal blood could demand some privileges. Yet even this concession had taken the intervention of the archbishop, and then only after several months of exemplary behavior at *Arx Fidei* and as a grudging recognition of

15

Javan's having come of age and being, therefore, free to leave altogether, if he insisted.

Though what a fourteen-year-old heir presumptive might have done better with his time for the next few years, even Javan had to agree was a moot point. Far better to spend those years between legal and actual manhood as he was doing, acquiring the formal education that would stand him in good stead if he eventually became king, as seemed more and more likely—so long as the lords of state did not manage some trick to bypass him and give the crown to his younger brother, now of age, as well, but who was thought to be less clever and more biddable.

Sighing heavily, Javan pulled off the stiff, hooded scapular that was part of the habit of the detested *Custodes Fidei*, though long training bade him fold it neatly before dropping it on the parched grass beside the carp pool. The black soutane he wore as a seminarian fastened at the right shoulder and down the right side, and he undid enough of the buttons to loosen the standing collar, briefly pulling the opening away from his neck a few times to puff air inside. Then he hiked the garment's hem up above his knees and shifted himself slightly around to the left so he could swing his sandaled left foot up onto the granite curbing and cradle his knee, idly turning his gaze over his shoulder to the water beside him.

The moonlight mirrored on the water's surface, reflecting back the clean-lined image of a pale, serious face surrounded by a close-cut shock of glossy black hair, slightly rumpled from pulling off the scapular. From this angle, he could not see the clerical tonsure his circumstances forced him to wear and was free to pretend that he was the layman and prince he longed to be.

In a rare outward declaration of that pretense—though hardly particularly daring, since no one was likely to see it—he slipped his good left foot out of its sandal and nudged the offending item off the side of the granite curbing, then slid that foot into the water as he bent to unfasten and remove the special boot that supported his misshapen right foot. He smiled as he flexed the toes in newfound freedom, briefly massaging the thickened ankle before shifting around to ease it into the water beside the other.

The mud on the bottom was squishy and cool, and his smile turned to a grin. At sixteen, the occasional stolen pleasures of an all-too-brief childhood still held their own allure, to be relished between the more serious aspects of surviving as a superfluous prince.

And survival was the name of the game. In the nearly three years since placing himself under the obedience of the *Custodes*, Prince Javan Haldane had learned survival skills far beyond the mere academics expected of the future priest and ecclesiastic they were trying to make of him. Along with the dutiful assimilation of cloistered life and the round of devotions that marked every hour of the abbey's calendar, he had also learned the subtler arts of dissembling and subterfuge.

He had learned to keep his own counsel, and to watch and listen far more than he spoke. By seeming to go along with the program of spiritual direction and study mapped out by Archbishop Hubert and the other men who had been the royal regents when it all began, and who now continued as his brother's ministers of state, Javan had gained their guarded approval of his apparent piety, a grudging respect for his academic achievements, and even a degree of freedom to return occasionally to Court—though he was careful to hide the true extent of his accomplishments, and especially not to reveal any hint of the Deryni-like powers stirring ever more deeply within him. Hubert himself, though he did not know it, had felt subtle touches of Javan's influence from time to time—though if Javan chose to exercise that influence to the extent that Hubert began to act out of character, the discovery of Javan's part in it was almost inevitable and almost certainly would cost him his life.

And if Javan himself were not found out, then the blame was sure to fasten on one or more of the few Deryni still at court—the "Deryni sniffers," as they were sometimes called in derision, or the great lords' "pet" Deryni. According to the provisions of the Statutes of Ramos, enacted shortly after the death of Javan's father, Deryni were officially prohibited from holding any office, from teaching, or from endeavoring to seek out any religious vocation, especially the priesthood. Ownership of property was being increasingly restricted. In addition, Deryni were forbidden to use their powers in any manner whatsoever, under pain of death.

The sole exceptions were those Deryni forcibly recruited to royal service and compelled, by threats to their families held hostage, to exercise their powers in behalf of the regents, now the principal lords of state. Not infrequently, their duties required the betrayal of other Deryni, or at least the perversion of their powers for intimidation. At one time, four or five such men had been the regents' personal pawns, with another several dozen attached to various military units.

There were not so many now, for unquestioning obedience was not a characteristic of most Deryni, and the regents' answer to any resistance had been the immediate execution of the offender's family before his eyes—wives and children, even tiny infants, it made no difference—followed by the offender's own slow death by torture. Javan had been forced to witness more than one such outrage, and the memories sickened him still.

The Healer Oriel was most visible of those Deryni still managing to eke out so precarious an existence. As Javan trailed a hand in the water, watching the patterns of ripples in the moonlight, he wondered how Oriel continued to tolerate such a state. It helped, of course, that young King Alroy trusted his Deryni Healer far more than his human physicians, whom he judged to be bumbling incompetents. The former regents had attempted to undermine that trust, but to no avail. At the great lords' whim, the Healer still might be required to turn his Healing talents to betrayal of fellow Deryni at any time, but at least direct royal patronage gave him some measure of protection.

Fortunately for Javan, it was Oriel alone, of all the men at Rhemuth, whether human or Deryni, who even guessed a part of what Javan was achieving on his own, as he bided his time and prepared himself, waiting for the day when he might dare to defy the former regents. It was Oriel who had managed to smuggle out the occasional letter to Javan, here in the abbey, telling him of his brother's gradual decline and the necessity to be ready to take up the crown. Javan had seen his twin just last month, when he was permitted to return to the capital for their joint birthday celebration. It had been clear even then—though the lords of state were at pains to assure him otherwise—that barring miracles, Alroy was not going to last out the summer, never mind the year.

There had been no chance to speak privately with his brother, for the great lords had every hour planned out, and watched all three princes with a solicitude that passed for utter devotion among those who did not know better. But Javan did manage a few minutes alone with Oriel, who was able to pass on a more detailed report in that manner available only to Deryni and those who shared their powers.

Javan was not yet as adept at this as he would like, for his contact and training with his old Deryni mentors had ceased perforce with his taking of temporary vows and subsequent removal to *Custodes* control; but he was far more adept than any human had a right to be—even a Haldane human with Deryni-like powers, which only the king should have, but which Javan had and Alroy did not. Javan knew that his powers had something to do with whatever his father had done to him and his brothers the night he died, but even Joram MacRorie, son of Saint Camber and the only man still alive who had been present that night, could not account for it.

Regardless of *what* had been done, its result could only be welcome, for it might be the one thing to keep Javan alive until he came into his own. He regretted that it had not seemed to help Alroy, whose failing health was of increasing concern. Tonight, during Matins, he had offered up special prayers for his brother's recovery, for throughout the day he had become increasingly aware of a vague uneasiness somehow centered on his brother. The psychic bonding so often noted between twins seemed further heightened in Javan, whose perceptions had been strengthening in all areas as his unexpected powers emerged and matured. Tonight, when most of those around him slept and psychic interference was at its ebb, that impression of dark foreboding connected with his twin was even stronger.

Closing his eyes, Javan tried to bring the perception into clearer focus, ignoring the faint, tickling sensation of several carp come to investigate his feet and to mouth gently at his toes. He gained a greater measure of tranquillity, but no clearer impression of what was amiss. After a while he looked up with a start, his attention recalled to the present by the sound of horses approaching the gate to the yard on the other side of the cloister wall, and a somehow familiar voice shouting "Porter!"

Charlan? The thought came immediately to Javan, as he turned his head to listen more closely and the voice cried out again.

"Porter? Open the gate, I say. Open in the name of the king! I bear a message for Prince Javan!"

It *was* Charlan!

Even as Javan jerked his feet out of the water and set to drying them hastily on the hem of his soutane, other voices were added to Charlan's, along with the sounds of bolts being withdrawn and the clatter of many hooves on cobblestones as a large number of horses entered the yard. The glare of many torches lit the air above the cloister wall, and Javan estimated that there might be as many as a dozen men with his former squire. As the voices died down, Javan realized that someone must have been summoned to speak to Charlan.

But what was Charlan doing here at this hour? It could not be to tell of Alroy's death, for he had demanded admittance in the name of the king and asked to see *Prince* Javan.

Of course, Alroy *could* be dead and Rhys Michael declared king—but surely not even Rhun or Murdoch would have been stupid enough to send Charlan to tell his former master that his crown was usurped.

Which all suggested that Alroy was still alive but failing. As Javan slipped his good foot into his sandal and then set about the more time-consuming process of putting his special boot back on, he decided that could also account for what he had been feeling all day. And if Alroy was failing—

Mince no words, Javan, he told himself. *If Alroy is dying, you're about to have to fight for your crown. You'd just better hope you're ready . . .*

He was fastening up the last buckle on his boot when torches approached from the processional door that led into the cloister from the abbey church. Heart pounding in his throat, he scooped up his scapular and rose, automatically starting to don it before the abbot saw him out of uniform—for Father Halex surely would be the one to bring Charlan to him, the only one with authority to do so.

But then he decided to take the gamble that this was the call he had been waiting for and that he had removed the hated symbol of servitude to the *Custodes Fidei* for the last time. As the torches approached, Father Halex clearly in the lead and Charlan's towhead right beside him, Javan dropped the scapular back onto the grass and contented himself with doing up the throat of his soutane.

Charlan strode out ahead of the abbot as he saw his former master, and Javan drew himself to attention as the young knight drew near and made him a respectful bow, left hand resting lightly on the hilt of his sword. The young knight wore a quilted jazerant over his riding leathers, token indication that this was not a social call, but that seemed to be the extent of his armor. Still, it was a measure of the impact he had made on arrival that Charlan retained his sword and dagger, even within these cloistered walls, though he had not been allowed to bring any of his men with him.

"Your Highness, I bear important news from Rhemuth," Charlan said carefully, obviously as aware as Javan that the abbot and his two attendant monks were taking in every word.

"The king?" Javan asked in a low voice, afraid for what he would hear.

"The king lives," Charlan breathed, "but he commands your presence. The Prince Rhys Michael bade me come, and gave me this as token of his authority."

Without taking his eyes from Charlan's dark ones, Javan opened a palm under the closed fist Charlan offered, glancing then at what lay gleaming in the torchlight. It was Rhys Michael's signet, near mate to Javan's own, which he kept hidden in a small leather pouch under the mattress in his cell.

"*Brother* Javan," the abbot said pointedly, "this is highly irregular. You are under obedience to this Order. And where is the rest of your habit?"

"I mean you no disrespect, Father Abbot, but I am under a higher obedience to my king, who is my brother," Javan replied, ignoring the question of his habit as he glanced back at Charlan. "*Rhys Michael* sent you, Sir Charlan?"

"Aye, my lord, for the king was too weak to make his wishes known outside his sickroom." Charlan delved into the pouch hanging from his belt and produced a folded handkerchief, which he handed to Javan. "As further earnest that this is his personal request, the prince bade me give you this."

Carefully Javan unfolded the soft linen, deliberately angling it so that Father Halex could not see what it contained. The earring of twisted gold wire was mate to another he had been directed to remove prior to making his vows and bespoke the very urgency of Rhys Michael's summons—that this, indeed, touched on the kingship of Gwynedd. He kept his expression neutral as he folded the earring back into its linen nest, deliberately ignoring the abbot as he slipped Rhys Michael's ring onto his right hand and looked up at Charlan again.

"I'll need to boot up and change," he said, handing the handkerchief back to the young knight for safekeeping. "Look after that, will you? And did you bring me a horse, or shall I borrow one from the abbey stables?"

"Now, see here, Brother Javan!" the abbot began.

"It's *Prince* Javan now, my Lord Abbot," Javan replied, rounding on the older man with a look of fierce determination. "And I ride at the command of my king—and your king as well."

The abbot gaped and glanced indignantly at his two monks for support. "But you're under vows. You owe me obedience!"

"My vows are and always have been temporary, my lord," Javan said, quietly but firmly. "They now are at an end. I'm leaving. So unless you intend to take up the matter with Sir Charlan and the other knights waiting in the yard, I suggest you stand aside and allow me to pass. Sir Charlan, would you please accompany me?"

The abbot gave way speechlessly as Javan pressed forward, Charlan at his elbow, and the monks likewise parted to either side, leaving them a clear path across the garden.

"I did bring you a horse, your Highness," Charlan murmured breathlessly as they made for the processional door, away from the now-muttering abbot. "I have a spare pair of breeches and a short tunic in my saddlebag, too, if you're in need of proper riding clothes. It would be a grim ride, bare-legged."

"No, I have what I need in my cell, from my last trip to Rhemuth," Javan said. "Nothing fancy, but it will do the job." He pushed open the processional door and led Charlan briefly into the south transept and around to the night stair. As they mounted the stair, Javan steadying his hobbling gait with a hand on the thick rope swagged up the wall, he glanced back over his shoulder at the following Charlan.

"How *is* my brother Alroy, Charlan? Did you see him?"

"No, sir. Only Rhys Michael. But he said he'd just come from the king, and he looked really worried. I'm reasonably confident we can get you back to Rhemuth in time, but I don't think I'd have been sent like this, in the middle of the night, unless it was urgent. Rhys Michael took a big risk, too, sending me the way he did. It's my impression that it was against the wishes of Archbishop Hubert and whatever other great lords might have been waiting outside the king's chamber."

They had reached the landing now, and Javan led the young knight quickly along the dormer corridor, limping only a little on the flat, ignoring the occasional sleepy head that peered out of a doorway.

"In here," Javan murmured, pausing to take up the night-light set in a niche in the corridor before leading Charlan into the tiny room designated as his monastic cell.

He lit the rushlight in another niche inside, then handed the night-light to Charlan to replace in the hallway while he began unbuttoning his soutane, starting to formulate a plan of action as he did so.

"I hope you don't mind squiring for me, the way you used to do," Javan said as the young knight ducked anxiously back into the room. "You'll find my other boot and my riding things in that chest at the foot of the bed. I want to get out of here as quickly as we can, before the abbot decides that his *Custodes* men are a match for yours."

Grinning, Charlan bent to the task assigned.

"The possibility *had* crossed my mind, your Highness," he said easily, quickly producing the desired boot and then beginning to rummage through the stacks of uniformly black garments. "However, I think the presence of a dozen armed knights in his yard may have dampened the good abbot's enthusiasm for such rash action. Are these the breeches you wanted?" he asked, holding a handful of black aloft by one leg.

Glancing up, Javan gave a nod.

"As for being your squire," Charlan went on, tossing the breeches onto the bed, "I shall always count those months in your service as my honor and privilege. I—hope you'll be gracious enough to accept my continued service, when you are king."

"When I am king—"

Javan had been in the process of stripping the hated *Custodes* cincture from around his waist, and he stiffened and then swallowed before deliberately dropping it onto the bed like a limp snake—the braided cincture of crimson and gold intertwined, whose colors the *Custodes Fidei* had usurped from the Haldane royal house to lend credibility to their mission against Deryni.

"I hope I needn't tell you that being king is the last thing I would have wished, if it meant that harm would come to my brother," Javan said quietly. He shrugged out of the heavy soutane and let it fall in a pool of wool around his feet, stepping free awkwardly to sit on the edge of the bed, now clad only in the baggy underdrawers the monks were allowed.

"I have to face realities, though," he continued as Charlan knelt at his feet and began unbuckling the special boot. "I hope that doesn't sound disloyal. But if he's to die before he gets an heir—"

Charlan shot him an appraising look before returning his attention to the buckles.

"Better you than Rhys Michael," he said shortly, not looking up. "Oh, I have no quarrel with your younger brother, Sire, but *you're* the heir. And *you* have the backbone to stand up to the lords of state—which I don't think your brother does. The king certainly doesn't."

Anger flared in the grey Haldane eyes, and Javan kicked his good foot free of its sandal.

"It isn't Alroy's fault that he's been under their thumb," he said sharply. "He's always been frail. And once the regents had driven Lord Rhys and Bishop Alister from Court, the court physicians had orders to keep him just slightly sedated all the time, even when he was healthy otherwise. I didn't want to believe it at first, but I saw it for myself, the last few times I had a chance to be alone with him."

Charlan freed the last buckle, glancing up as he eased the boot from Javan's crippled foot and rocked back on his heels. "Did Master Oriel tell you that, Sire?"

The question could be taken many ways. That Charlan was even here bespoke a loyalty to all three Haldane brothers that went beyond whatever duty he might feel he owed the former regents; but Javan was not certain he liked having Charlan link him with the Deryni Oriel. It skirted too close to the truth about Javan's own growing talents.

Of course, Javan could use those talents to make sure of Charlan, here and now. Kneeling there at Javan's feet, the young knight could never get out of range in time to prevent Javan touching him and triggering old controls. But if Javan was about to be king and must use those talents to keep his throne, he would rather not force loyalty that appeared to be freely offered.

Careful not to show his concern, Javan pulled the breeches to him and thrust his feet into the legs, standing long enough to pull them up and do up the fastenings. He stepped back into the special boot before sitting back down again, so that Charlan could do up the buckles while he pulled the mate onto his good left foot.

"As a matter of fact, Master Oriel did tell me about it," he said, taking the slight gamble—for he could always seize control later, if Charlan proved treacherous. "He didn't approve, and he thought I should know—as Alroy's brother as well as heir presumptive. As you'll recall, the terms of his service don't permit open disagreement with his 'employers,' regardless of his professional opinion." He cocked his head at Charlan, who was doing up the last buckles.

"What about you, Charlan? You were open enough, when you first entered my service, to confess that you were obliged to report to the regents concerning me. I'd like to think that you told me that out of a personal loyalty that went beyond official duty. But all of that changed when I left Court. You became the king's squire—which means that any oaths you swore to him were essentially to the regents and then the great lords, as well." He drew a deep breath.

"So I guess what I'm trying to ask is, where are your personal loyalties now? I need to know, before I leave here with you."

He was extending his Truth-Reading talents as he asked the question, and to his relief, Charlan's reply was open and guileless.

"Sire, I am *your* man," he said, dark eyes locking fearlessly with Javan's grey ones. "I think I always have been. I suppose I began to realize that oaths were more than mere words at about the time you left Court, and it's become increasingly clear since I was knighted.

"You have other loyal men, as well, that you don't even know about—others of the younger knights, mostly, who served you and your brothers as squires and such, but there are a few of the older men at Court whom you can trust. The ones waiting for you in the abbey yard would all die for you, if need be."

"Indeed," Javan murmured, wide-eyed, for while he had been reasonably confident of Charlan's ultimate loyalty, he had not expected the rest of the young knight's revelation. "Will they *live* for me, though, Charlan? That may be far harder, in these next weeks and months. The great lords have been in power long enough to entrench themselves into the next generation. Some of their *sons* hold high office. If I'm not extremely careful how I ease them out, I could find myself in the middle of a civil war—if I don't find myself dead first!"

Charlan tucked the last strap into place on Javan's boots and gave the left boot a slap in signal that he had finished, but he did not get to his feet.

"There are those ready to do what they can to prevent both options, Sire," he said, looking up at Javan. "We've—taken the liberty, in these past few weeks, of sounding out some of the other knights about specific recommendations in a number of areas that will need your attention fairly quickly, once you're on the throne. There are documents waiting for you, back at Rhemuth, and men to explain them. None of us would presume to tell you what to do, but there's information you'd have no other way of knowing." He swallowed, looking suddenly apprehensive. "You're—not angry, are you, Sire? We only did it to help you."

Javan could only stare at Charlan in disbelief for several seconds, though he knew that every word the man had spoken was the truth. But as the implications began to sink in, he clapped Charlan on the shoulder and rose, shaking his head as a faint smile played on his lips.

"How could I be angry, Charlan?" he said quietly. "You've given me real hope, where it all was theory and wishful thinking before."

Forcing himself to turn to other practicalities—for if they did not get out of there, all the young knight's efforts would be for nought, as well as Javan's own—he moved to the chest at the foot of the bed and pulled out the riding tunic he had worn for his last trip to Rhemuth, the month before. It was black, like every other garment he owned there at the abbey, cut high-collared like a cassock but reaching only to the knee, and slit fore and aft for riding. It would be stifling in the summer heat, for it was a heavier wool than the soutane he had discarded, but that couldn't be helped. He had to look the part of a prince, and this was all he had.

He did not speak as he dressed, and Charlan respected his silence. When he had buttoned the tunic, all but the top three buttons, he pulled a plain black leather belt out of the trunk and buckled it around his waist, then retrieved a small leather pouch from under his mattress.

Inside were his own signet ring, bearing the Haldane arms differenced with the label of a second son, and the mate to Rhys Michael's earring. After slipping the signet onto his left little finger, he gave his hair a few swipes with a comb made of horn, then let Charlan help him thread the twisted wire of the earring through the hole in his right earlobe. He had no mirror to check the overall impression, but he gathered, by Charlan's expression, that he passed muster.

"We'd better ride now," he murmured, glancing around the cell for the last time. "You can brief me more on the way. We'll hope that matters haven't gotten out of hand down in the yard while we tarried here."

As Charlan opened the door, Javan bent down and blew out the rushlight, serene but eager as he followed the young knight back along the dim-lit corridor toward the night stair. He had what he wanted from this place, and he did not look back.

CHAPTER THREE

These things hast thou done, and I kept silence;
thou thoughtest that I was altogether such a
one as thyself.

—Psalms 50:21

Down in the abbey yard, things had not gotten precisely out of hand, but the half-dozen *Custodes* monks and priests initially drawn to the yard by the arrival of Charlan and his men had now been joined by nearly a score of *Custodes* knights. The royal knights sat their horses in a quiet but uneasy knot near the gate, most of them with torches in their hands, two of the men holding extra mounts. The *Custodes* men were drawn up in two precise lines across the front of the abbey steps, many of them also holding torches.

Javan assessed the situation at a glance as he came out the postern door, Charlan at his elbow and the abbot and his two monks at his heels. If it came to an armed confrontation, he did not like the odds. The *Custodes* men outnumbered Charlan's knights by nearly two to one and were better armored as well, with steel greaves and vambraces protecting legs and arms and the gleam of steel at the throats of black brigantines. The royal knights were well mounted and armed, but they wore no real armor—only leather jacks and light steel caps, in deference to the heat. Up on the cloister wall, though Javan could not see them against the torches' glare, he knew there would be at least half a dozen *Custodes* archers, only awaiting the order to let fly.

"Lord Joshua," he called, seizing the initiative by heading directly for the captain of the *Custodes* force. "My thanks for the honor you do me by turning out an additional escort. However,

these good knights who accompanied Sir Charlan on his royal er-
rand are well qualified to accompany me back to Rhemuth."

The *Custodes* captain glanced uncertainly at the abbot, but at
least he made no move toward the sword at his belt.

"Father Abbot was concerned that these men might attempt to
take you from the abbey against your will, Brother Javan," the man
said.

Javan allowed the man a forbearing hint of a smile. "My will is
not a factor in this discussion, Captain," he said easily. "It is the
king's will that I accompany these gentlemen back to Rhemuth.
Do you intend to question *him*?"

The captain's jaw tightened, but before he could reply, the abbot
set his hand on the man's steel-clad arm and moved a step closer.
"My information is that the king is too ill to issue orders, Brother
Javan. Now I beg you to return to your cell and await further official
word from Rhemuth."

"How official must it be?" Javan retorted, thrusting Rhys Michael's ring under the abbot's nose. "My brother, Prince Rhys Michael Haldane, commands me to come, in the name of my brother
the king, who is dying. If some have their way, then that same Rhys
Michael shall be the next king—in which case, he will not look
kindly upon those who have defied his commands. And if the proper
succession is allowed to occur, then *I* shall be king—and I assure
you, I shall not forget those who obstruct me.

"Now, will you stand your men down, or must blood be shed
in these hallowed grounds?"

"You would not dare to raise steel here," the abbot muttered.

"Not I, my lord, for I am unarmed, as you see," Javan replied,
raising his hands away from the empty belt around his waist. "But
the king's men have their orders, as have I. If, by defying the king's
wishes, you compel them to draw steel to enforce the royal command, then be it upon your head, not mine." He drew deep breath,
praying that he could pull this off.

"With respect, then, I bid you good morrow, my Lord Abbot,
and take my leave of you."

So saying, he gathered Charlan to his side with a glance and
turned to press past the *Custodes* captain and down the abbey steps,
heading both of them toward the waiting knights. The men holding
the two extra horses came forward into the center of the yard, several more moving their mounts behind Javan and Charlan to shield
them, turning their backs on the *Custodes* knights with utter disdain—for any show of weakness now could prove fatal.

Only the hollow clip-clop of hooves on cobbles and the soft creak and jingle of the horses' harnesses intruded on the taut, sullen silence. Javan could feel himself trembling as Charlan gave him a leg up onto a tall, well-made chestnut, but he allowed himself no show of fear or even apprehension as he gathered the reins in his hands and turned the horse's head toward the gate, even as the others finished mounting up around him.

His knees continued to tremble as he urged the horse forward, Charlan and another knight falling in on either side of him—Bertrand, who had been his squire before Charlan. To his unmitigated relief, no one tried to stop them. But not until they were through the gates and heading down the hill slope toward the main road, picking up a canter, did he allow himself to relax even a little.

Three hours' ride and a change of horses saw them trotting up the final incline toward the city gates of Rhemuth, just as the first fingers of dawn were thrusting upward from behind the eastern horizon. Even the new horses were spent by then, for they had pushed on at a steady gallop for most of the way. One of the knights spurred on ahead as they approached the awakening city, and the portcullis rumbled upward and the gates swung wide just before the main party reached the city wall. The guards on duty gave Javan royal salute as he rode through the gates, and he squared his shoulders and tried to look confident as Charlan led the band on up the King's Way toward the castle on the hill.

The castle yard was abustle with activity as they rode into it, crowded with horses and liveried servants and armed guards and courtiers all milling apprehensively. The heat was already oppressive. As Javan's party rode into the yard, a wave of somberly dressed lords of various degrees came spilling onto the great hall steps. Pushing through from their rear, accompanied by Sir Tomais, who had once been his squire, was a worried-looking Rhys Michael, set apart by the bright splash of a short crimson cape slung over one shoulder, despite the heat.

The brothers' eyes locked as Javan drew rein and flung his right leg over the pommel to jump lightly to the ground. Charlan was at his side immediately, opening a path for him as he headed up the steps. Bertrand and three more of Charlan's knights followed close behind, gloved hands set casually on the hilts of their swords, though their expressions spoke of a far from casual concern for their royal charge.

Rhys Michael came partway down the steps to meet him, a

guarded look of relief on his handsome face. The crimson cape slipped down onto his arm as he reached out to embrace his brother.

"Thank God you're here!" he whispered fiercely, dropping his forehead to his brother's shoulder for just an instant. "Let me put this on you, before we do another thing," he added, just before the two drew apart. "It's the clearest symbol *I* can think of, for the moment."

Nodding slightly, and more relieved than he could say, Javan let his brother lay the cape around his shoulders, noting the murmuring the action produced, as Rhys Michael also seized his hand and kissed it. He need not have feared on Rhys Michael's account. As they turned to go inside, arm in arm, Charlan taking the lead and the other knights at their heels, Javan pulled off Rhys Michael's signet and passed it back to him.

"How is he?" he murmured, nodding to several lesser courtiers as they headed left across the near end of the great hall and down a short flight of steps.

"Not good. He had a reasonably comfortable night, once he'd had me send for you, but only because of the medication."

"What are they giving him?"

"Extract of poppy." Rhys Michael made a face. "Oh, it makes the coughing stop and eases the worst of the pain. But it also eases him into such a heavy sleep that it's difficult to rouse him. The fever hasn't helped. Most of the time I don't think he's really aware what's going on around him."

"Why do I suddenly suspect that the former regents have been trying to capitalize on that?" Javan murmured.

With a mirthless laugh, Rhys Michael ushered his brother through a short colonnaded passageway that led into a wing fronting the gardens.

"That was the thin line *I* trod, when I took it on myself to send for you. I hope you don't mind that I threatened them with the thought that *I* might soon be king."

"Not at all." Javan's answering smile held the same grim determination. "I used the same argument myself, when persuading the abbot that he oughtn't to try to stop my leaving. But back to Alroy—the drugs do ease him?"

"That depends on your definition of ease," the younger prince replied. "His lungs still fill with fluid; he just doesn't cough it up, or realize that he needs to."

"And Master Oriel concurs with this treatment?"

"Aye. It's probably the one thing on which he and the royal physicians agree. They—" He stumbled and came to a halt, suddenly blinking back tears, and swallowed hard, shaking his head.

"Javan, they say his lungs are nearly gone. All Oriel or anybody else can do is ease the passing. It's a question of letting him literally cough his lungs out or—letting him dream away what little time he has left."

As Rhys Michael knuckled at his bowed forehead, shaking his head despairingly, Javan had to fight back his own tears, grieving already for the elder brother who had never really stood a chance against the circumstances of his position. He had tried to prepare himself for news of this sort, but actually hearing it was far more difficult than he had expected.

"Dear, gentle *Jesu*, it wasn't supposed to be like this," he breathed, trying to get a grip on himself. "He's only sixteen, for God's sake! His life should be just beginning!"

"Sire, Lord Manfred is coming up fast," Charlan murmured, just ahead of him, calling his knights closer with a gesture. "I'd hoped he wouldn't get here so quickly."

Stiffening, Javan forced back his tears and made himself look up, dropping his hands to his sides and raising his chin defiantly to the first of the great lords he must either win over or subdue. His eyes locked with Manfred's as the older man approached, and Javan decided then and there that *he* was not going to be the one to look away first.

"Lord Manfred," he acknowledged tonelessly as the man came within hailing distance.

"Your Highnesses," the cool, clipped reply came, edged with disapproval.

The Earl of Culdi had changed very little since Javan last had seen him: a more faded blond than his brother Hubert and slightly taller, but merely beefy where Hubert was undeniably fat. He held himself like the soldier he was, the blue eyes keen as flint above a sweeping pair of blond moustaches beginning to go grey.

He eyed first Javan and then Rhys Michael with an expression just short of distaste, quickly taking in the crimson cape, the ring on Javan's hand, the twisted gold in his ear—and the six armed knights surrounding him. But whatever his true emotions, his words sounded of careful solicitude, calculated not to cause blatant offense in this new, unexpected, and undesired presence.

"Your arrival is most timely, your Highnesses," he said. "The king is awake and asking for both of you. My brother has had the physicians delay his medication until I could locate you. Please come with me."

He made them both a brisk bow, just short of arrogance, then turned on his heel and headed back the way he had come, not waiting to see if they followed.

They did, of course. Javan pulled off the crimson cape and handed it off to Charlan as they walked, for the heat of the day already was becoming unbearable, even within the insulation of the castle's thick stone walls.

The buzz of voices ahead got louder as they rounded a turn in the corridor and approached the end; there three steps led down into an open colonnade where fifteen or twenty men were lounging. Those seated came to their feet as the royal party approached, a few of them bowing, but whether to acknowledge the royal brothers or the Lord Manfred was hard to tell.

Manfred drew up just before the steps, at the last door on the right. Setting his hand to the latch, he stood aside as he pushed it open. Javan did not like the smile on his face, just before he bowed so that Javan could not see it. As he had feared, others of the former regents were in the anteroom within, chiefest among them Manfred's brother, Hubert MacInnis, Archbishop of Valoret and Primate of All Gwynedd.

The archbishop bestirred himself to stand as Javan entered, Rhys Michael and Charlan following. At Hubert's gesture, Tomais and Bertrand and the other knights remained outside, though not without Rhys Michael's cautious exchange of glances with Charlan, who stationed himself with his back against the edge of the open door, resisting any attempt of Manfred to close it. If the princes called, Charlan and the other knights would come, regardless of what the archbishop wanted.

Hubert himself had grown more mountainous than ever, in only the month since Javan last had seen him; or perhaps it was the sheer expanse of purple cassock, unbroken by the extra layers of episcopal attire with which the archbishop usually was wont to adorn his ample person. A pudgy left hand fingered the amethyst-set pectoral cross hanging around his fleshy neck. The rosebud mouth was set in petulant disapproval. He started to extend his ring to Javan as their eyes met, then thought better of it and clasped the ringed hand to its mate in a pious but distant pose of self-righteous authority.

"Brother Javan. We had not thought to see you here. Do you not have duties which require your presence at the seminary? To quit the abbey without leave is a grievous fault, which I am certain will earn you a severe penance when you return."

From behind him, two *Custodes* priests moved a little closer, so that for the first time Javan became aware of the candles burning in a far corner of the room, flanking a jewelled altar cross and the veiled silhouette of a ciborium. The presence of the Blessed Sacrament outside the king's sickroom confirmed that Alroy's condition was grave indeed.

Glancing around, Javan chose his words carefully. He thought he could control Hubert if he had to, but not in front of so many—and best if he could deescalate this situation with his wits alone. In addition to Earl Tammaron, whom he occasionally almost liked, and Manfred's pimply-faced son Iver, whom almost no one liked, Earl Murdoch's two sons also were present—the randy and devious Sir Richard, who was married to the constable's daughter, and the burly bully Cashel, but a year older than Javan and the king, who was constantly spoiling for a fight and was good enough to win most of them. They were but a few of the new blood the former regents were attempting to insert into the Council of Gwynedd—and would do so, Javan decided then and there, literally over his dead body.

"I have not come to argue monastic discipline with you, Archbishop," he said quietly—but forcefully. "I have come at the command of the king. My duty now is here, at his side, so long as he lives; and to take up his crown when he is gone, as is my birthright."

As the young lords glanced restively among themselves, and Tammaron looked decidedly uneasy, Hubert drew himself up in his full archepiscopal dignity.

"Do you forsake your vows so easily, then, Brother Javan?" he said. "You made promises to me and to God. You cannot simply set those promises aside as the whim takes you."

Javan set his fists on his hips and looked the archbishop up and down.

"I'll not be drawn into argument, your Grace," he said evenly, "and certainly not about temporary vows all but forced upon me while I was underage. I've come to see my brother, who commands my presence and is dying. If there's a drop of Christian charity in your body, you'll stand aside so that I may obey his dying wish."

As he headed past Hubert, Rhys Michael stayed well on Javan's other side, screened from the archbishop's bulk. The speechless Hubert glanced at his compatriots for support, which was not forthcoming, though gloomy looks abounded. By the time Hubert had wits enough to look back, the princes were already disappearing behind the door to the king's sickroom, Rhys Michael pushing the door closed behind them.

Inside, the Healer Oriel rose from his stool at the head of the king's bed. He had been wringing out yet another cool cloth for the king's forehead, but now he replaced the cloth in the basin held by a squire and dismissed the boy with a gesture.

"Wait outside, please, Quiric," he murmured. "I'll call you when I need you again."

When the boy had withdrawn, bowing nervously to Javan and to Rhys Michael, who opened the door far enough to let him pass, Oriel said, "Thank you for coming, your Highness."

Sighing, Javan came around to the other side of the bed, forcing his gaze to move across the still, almost-motionless form of his brother the king, nearly as white as the linen sheeting drawn up just past his waist. Alroy's labored breath still stirred the narrow chest, but the closed eyes had dark smudges beneath them. Perspiration soaked the raven hair, which was slightly longer than Javan's monastic barbering.

Javan started to reach for the slack left hand lying atop the sheet beside Alroy's body—it wore the Haldane Ring of Fire, despite Alroy's desperate illness—then paused to lift his gaze to Oriel instead.

"How long?" he whispered, searching the Healer's eyes.

"However long he has, prolonging his suffering cannot be justified," Oriel murmured, "for he cannot possibly recover. I have his pain controlled for now, and his sleep is one of Healer's crafting, not the drugs he has been taking; but I cannot hold this for very long."

"And if you do nothing?" Javan said.

Oriel bowed his head. "He wanted desperately to see you, my prince—and that he should be able to speak to you a final time without his mind clouded by the drugs that can give him ease. I have promised that I will make that possible—though it means that your final exchange with him will not be entirely private, for I cannot maintain my controls at a distance. I—will try to be as unobtrusive as possible."

Javan swallowed with difficulty. "I—see. And when we have spoken? When he has told me what he wishes me to know?"

"Then I have promised that I will give him ease," the Healer said, not looking at him. "It will not be a fatal dose, for I may not, by my Healer's oaths; but I will give him peaceful sleep until he—until he quite literally drowns in the fluids that are filling his lungs." He swallowed, as if feeling those fluids encroach upon his own lungs. "But he will not suffer anymore. It is the best ease I can offer him, once he has unburdened his soul to you."

Tears were filling Javan's eyes, and he had to blink hard to regain control.

"Has he unburdened his soul to a priest?" he asked quietly. "I saw that they'd brought the Blessed Sacrament outside. Has he received the Last Rites?"

Oriel's lips compressed beneath his faint smudge of moustache as he shook his head. "He said that there is no priest in Rhemuth from whom he will accept them. A few hours ago, while he slept, both archbishops came and anointed him anyway and gave him conditional absolution, but he has absolutely refused to receive Communion from them or any of their priests. Perhaps you can reason with him."

Javan ducked his head, remembering how often he had been obliged to accept Communion from Hubert, loathing the man but forcing himself to separate the man from the Sacrament he dispensed. That Alroy finally was taking a stand on this point spoke much of his moral courage, however belatedly it was being manifest. At least on that point, Javan thought he might be able to ease Alroy's mind.

But first he must discover his brother's mind, on which there were far more pressing concerns than the outward token of a peace with the Maker Whom he very shortly would behold. Drawing deep breath, Javan dared to take Alroy's limp hand in his, pressing its back tenderly to his lips before glancing across at Oriel.

"Wake him, please," he said softly. "And I shall rely upon your holy vows as a Healer to ensure that what passes between the king and myself does not go beyond this room."

Nodding, Oriel passed one hand across the king's closed eyes, withdrawing then to let the fingertips of both hands rest lightly against the bare right shoulder. Alroy stirred at that touch; but as the grey eyes fluttered open, no pain in any part of their regard, they sought only Javan's. The fever-flushed lips parted in a relieved smile, and the hand in Javan's tightened, weak in strength but fierce in joy and thanksgiving.

"You came," he breathed. "Rhysem said he'd bring you, and he did!"

"He did," Javan agreed. "Or actually, Charlan did—though it was Rhysem who was brave enough to send him. Shall I call him over?"

Faintly Alroy's head turned back and forth on the pillow, his eyes never leaving Javan's.

"No, there will be a little time yet for him," he whispered. "Oriel has promised me. But first I wanted to give you our father's ring and the Eye of Rom. They belong to the King of Gwynedd—and I am king no longer."

"No! You *are* king, so long as you live!" Javan whispered fiercely. "I will not take them while you live, Sire!"

Alroy closed his eyes briefly and smiled. "Sire. I shall never be that now, shall I? But *you* must be. Promise that you shall be the king I should have been, that everything we all have suffered will not have been for nothing."

"I promise," Javan whispered, bowing his head over his brother's hand.

"And if you will not yet take the ring—which *I* did not receive until after our father's death—then at least take the Eye of Rom. It would mean much to me, to see you wear it as our father used to do."

To this compromise, at least, Javan could raise no real objection, for Cinhil himself had passed the Eye of Rom to his heir while still alive, just as Alroy now desired to do. Still, Javan's hands were trembling as he gently removed the stone from his brother's ear; and tears were streaming down his face by the time he threaded its golden wire through his own earlobe and fastened it. He had given his own earring to Oriel before making the exchange, indicating that Oriel should fasten it back in Alroy's ear, and the king smiled faintly as he lifted a wasted hand to brush the little hoop of twisted gold wire.

"A prince again," he murmured. " 'Tis better thus." The grey gaze lifted to take the measure of the tawny ruby now gracing Javan's right ear.

"One other thing," he said after a few seconds, when he had looked his fill. "Something happened to us, the night our father died. Did you ever find out what it was?"

Javan dared a quick glance at Oriel, but the young Healer was bowed as if in prayer, at least appearing to be oblivious to what was being said. Anyway, if he could not trust Oriel, his cause was lost already. And he did not want to deny his dying brother what little he knew.

"There was a ritual that night in Father's chapel," he said softly, himself only able to recall scant images of what had occurred. "Tavis drugged us, on Father's orders, but the Deryni were behind it. You knew that Father had magic from the Deryni, didn't you?"

Alroy's eyes searched his brother's face, wanting to believe, but doubtful. "I'd heard rumors, over the years. I know he always seemed to know when we weren't telling the truth. Did he really have magic?"

Javan nodded. "That's what Bishop Alister told me. He was involved with what happened that night. Also Rhys and Father Joram and the Lady Evaine." He glanced down, still unable to connect exactly with what had happened—though Evaine had told him, at their last meeting, that he would remember when the time was appropriate. He wondered if that would be today, once Alroy was gone.

"Anyway, it wasn't their ritual that night; it was Father's," Javan went on. "And it had something to do with—preparing us to receive his power—or at least setting its potential. I—think it was supposed to surface in you, as the heir, once he was dead." He searched his brother's eyes. "But it never did, did it?"

Alroy swallowed and shook his head weakly. "Life might have been a lot easier if it had," he whispered. "If I'd even been able to Truth-Read—"

"I think it was the drugs the regents gave you," Javan said, to shift any sense of guilt away from Alroy and onto the former regents—whose actions might well have prevented Alroy from coming into his magic, for all Javan knew. "If they hadn't kept you drugged all the time—"

Alroy closed his eyes briefly, shaking his head again. "It doesn't matter now," he whispered, stifling a slight cough. "They did, and I didn't. Do you—do you think it will pass to you, once I'm gone?"

Nodding wordlessly, Javan squeezed his dying brother's hand. "Some of it already has," he whispered. "I don't think it was supposed to, but it did. It started soon after Father died. Tavis thought I might have gotten primed for it by working with him for so long. I got accustomed to having him put me into trance when he'd use his Healing to work on my foot. Shields were the first thing we discovered. We found that out the night after his hand was cut off. I didn't know what I was doing, but I wanted to help. I put myself totally into his power that night, to do with me as he needed. And he—was able to pull energy from me, past shields that neither of us had even suspected were there."

"*Shields* . . ." Alroy barely mouthed the word, his grey eyes wide with wonder and a little fear.

"I know," Javan went on. "It all scares me, too. I've gotten much stronger since then. Alroy, I have powers almost like a Deryni. If I'm careful, I can control some humans." He hazarded a quick grin. "I used to do it to Charlan all the time, once I found out how. It's dangerous, though, if anyone found out."

Alroy swallowed hard, stifling another cough, and glanced uneasily at Oriel, still bowed deep in trancing beside him.

"He knows some of it," Javan whispered, answering the unasked question. "No one else does, other than the Deryni working directly with Father Joram."

"What about Rhysem?" Alroy whispered, looking beyond the bed where Rhys Michael guarded the door.

Javan shook his head. "There was no way to tell him. And it only would have made things more dangerous, once I was away from Court."

"But you're back now," Alroy said anxiously. "And you *do* intend to stay, don't you?"

Javan smiled faintly. "I'm not meant to be a priest," he said, "though I think I understand now what Father was giving up in accepting the crown. In any case, the seminary's been a grand place to hide, these past few years—and to acquire a useful education while I gave myself time to grow up. I'd hoped it would all be in aid of helping you rule, as one of your ministers; but I suppose I guessed, deep inside, that it wasn't going to happen. Murdoch and his cronies were never going to let you rule."

"That's why they kept me drugged," Alroy whispered, closing his eyes briefly. "Just enough to take the edge off any resistance or independent thought. I knew, after a while—but there wasn't anything I could do about it.

"I've foiled their plans, though, haven't I? At least I've given *you* time. You're four years older than I was when I became king. You won't need to have regents. And you're onto them. You won't be as gullible as I was."

Javan bowed his head, blinking back new tears. It was senseless to pretend that Alroy was not dying.

"I—hope I'll have better luck," he murmured. "God, how I wish there were something I could do for you."

Alroy swallowed noisily, tears swimming in the shadowed eyes. "You've done it, just by being here," he whispered. "I'm glad it was in time. Oriel has—has promised that I don't have to suffer any more. But stay with me . . . please. Even if I seem to be far, far away before the end, somehow I'll know you're there. It isn't that I'm afraid, though I do wish . . ."

His voice trailed off, and Javan leaned closer to peer into the clouded grey eyes.

"You do wish what?" he breathed.

"It would have been a comfort to receive the Sacrament one last time," he murmured, not looking at Javan. "But I *won't* receive it from Hubert. That would be sacrilege."

The coughing bout that started this time was one that Oriel could not muffle, and he stirred from his Healer's trancing to help

Javan shift the king onto his side, where Alroy still coughed uncontrollably until Oriel sent him plummeting into unconsciousness.

"It will have to be the drugs soon," Oriel murmured, when the coughing had abated and he could at last distract enough attention from his patient to look across at the anxious Javan. "I can bring him around once more, for just a few minutes, but anything beyond that would only prolong his suffering needlessly. If you have anything else you need to say to one another, you'd better make up your mind quickly."

Mind whirling furiously, Javan gave Oriel a nod. From somewhere—he had an impression of Evaine's memory behind it—a compelling image had flashed in his mind. Suddenly bringing a parallel of that image into present reality became all important.

"Master Oriel, can you delay that last time for a few more minutes, in a good cause?" he asked.

"As long as it isn't for too many more minutes, Sire," the Healer replied. "What do you intend to do?"

Javan's thin smile was not pleasant. "Something that will not please the archbishop," he said, motioning for Rhys Michael to join him. "Rhysem, come and stay with him, would you? And pay no mind to any shouting and arguing you may hear from the next room."

Chapter Four

Behold, I have set before thee an open door.
—Revelations 3:8

Beckoning a puzzled Rhys Michael to come and stand beside the royal sickbed, Javan buttoned up the neck of his tunic, then clapped a reassuring hand to his younger brother's shoulder before himself heading toward the door. He drew a deep breath and squared his shoulders as he set his hands on the latch, then opened the door and stepped through, pulling it to, but not latched.

More of Alroy's lords of state had gathered in the anteroom since his arrival. Two of the knights who had accompanied him and Charlan from the yard had taken up stations just inside the door that opened to the corridor, one to each side, casual but alert. Charlan himself still stood easy vigilance with his back to the door jamb, arms folded across his chest, half blocking the doorway to any further entrance or egress. Beyond him, Javan could see Tomais with Bertrand and more of the other knights who had ridden with him, quietly congregated outside.

There were not many seats in the anteroom, for it was not large, but those who were seated came to their feet as Javan appeared, the same question in every pair of eyes.

"The king yet lives, gentlemen," he said quietly, "but the end is drawing near. Archbishop, may I see you, please?"

At the direct address, a flushed and suspicious-looking Hubert drew himself erect and made his ponderous way forward, inclining his head as Javan stepped back into the room with a slight bow and indicated that Hubert should follow.

"I trust this betokens a change of heart, Brother Javan," Hubert said in a low voice as the prince closed the door behind them. "Do I dare to hope that the king has managed to remind you where your true duty lies?"

Javan controlled his growing disgust at the hypocrisy of the man and kept his voice equally low and uninflected.

"Indeed, I am reminded of a Christian duty that takes precedence over any personal consideration, your Grace," he said quietly. "It has always been my brother's wish, as a faithful son of the Church, to receive the full solace of the Sacraments before he dies. I understand that you gave him Unction during the night, but that he has declined to receive Communion. Can you explain why that might be?"

Hubert lifted both hands in a gesture of denial. "The King's Grace is not himself, from the illness and the drugs. I offered him the Blessed Sacrament, but he would not receive it."

"He is ready to receive it now," Javan murmured, adding only in his mind, *but not from you.*

A tiny, self-satisfied smile curved at the archbishop's rosebud mouth. "It will be my privilege, of course. No priest could desire any greater fulfillment than to minister thus to a dying man."

"Then please do so."

"I shall need but a moment," Hubert replied.

Inclining his head in what he hoped the archbishop would take for a sign of conciliation, Javan opened the door to allow Hubert's passage, then closed it behind him and leaned his head briefly against the door jamb, calming and centering himself before he turned back to beckon to Rhys Michael.

"Be ready to follow my lead when he comes back," he whispered to his brother. "And Oriel, please try not to look surprised at anything you may see or hear."

As Rhys Michael approached, both he and Oriel giving Javan odd looks, a quiet rap at the door preceded the turning of the door latch. Touching one finger across his lips in a gesture for silence, Javan drew Rhys Michael to one side with him and turned his gaze attentively to the opening door.

Slowly the door swung inward to reveal two ornate candlesticks held by the two *Custodes* priests, who had donned wilted white surplices over their cassocks and looked very warm. Behind them, reverently bearing the veiled ciborium at his breast, came a sweating and pink-faced Hubert, his already-damp purple cassock now layered under a surplice lavish with lace. In the room behind him, everyone had gone to their knees in respect to the Blessed Sacrament passing among them.

Crossing himself piously, Javan also bent in respect, but only to touch one knee to the floor in a genuflection. Rhys Michael haltingly did the same. As Javan stood, he moved forward with authority to put both hands on the candlestick held by one of the startled *Custodes*.

"My brother and I will serve as his Grace's acolytes today, good Fathers," Javan said to the priests, glancing back to call Rhys Michael forward, then looking beyond them at Hubert when his man did not immediately relinquish the candlestick. "I ask most humbly that you permit this, your Grace. We have served this way before. It would mean a great deal to us—and to the king, I believe."

Though a little taken aback, Hubert hesitated only briefly before nodding dismissal to the two priests. Javan's candlestick was heavy in his hands as he took its weight, inclining his head in a proper ecclesiastical bow.

When the door had closed behind the departing priests, Javan and his brother made Hubert proper bows as well, the candlesticks held carefully aloft, then turned to lead the way over to the royal bed, where Oriel had sunk dutifully to his knees as Hubert entered, though one hand still maintained contact with the unconscious king. Rhys Michael went to Oriel's side; and when Javan had led the archbishop around to the other side, he turned to set his free hand on one of Hubert's wrists, close to where he grasped the ciborium, at the same time using the physical contact to trigger the controls he had set so long ago and so rarely had dared to use.

"Close your eyes, Archbishop," he commanded softly, at the same time holding out his candlestick for Rhys Michael to take. "Close your eyes and hear my words. You cannot resist."

As Hubert meekly obeyed, Rhys Michael took the second candlestick and passed it to Oriel to set on the bedside table, prince and Healer both wide-eyed. Heart pounding, Javan shifted his now-empty hand under the ciborium's veil to cup under its bowl, suddenly aware of the potency of what Hubert held—and that whatever he did would be Witnessed by the sacred energy focused in the Sacrament.

Javan shivered at that realization. He meant no sacrilege, no disrespect. But he must ensure that his brother was allowed to receive that Sacrament in the manner of his choosing, from hands he could respect; and those hands were not Hubert's hands. Trusting that God would understand, Javan took the ciborium away from Hubert and set it on the little table on his side of the bed, then led Hubert back across the room and sat him down on a stool that groaned under his weight.

"My brother will receive Communion now, Archbishop," he said quietly, setting his hand firmly on Hubert's sweating forehead, "but not from your hands. My Holy Orders still are valid, so I shall offer him this gift. You will sit here with your eyes closed and say and do nothing and remember nothing. Sleep deep now and hear nothing until I call you by name. Hear and remember nothing."

The archbishop actually began to snore, so deeply did he sleep. As Javan came back to his brother's bed, Oriel was staring at him in amazement, and Rhys Michael looked very scared.

"Oriel, please help him to sit," Javan whispered as he came and picked up the ciborium.

Gently, tenderly, Oriel eased Alroy onto his back again, then slid one arm under the king's shoulders and lifted him up. Alroy's breathing had changed as the Healer turned him, and rattled faintly with a wet, liquid sound. Supporting him against his left shoulder, Oriel laid his right hand over the ravaged lungs.

"Come back to us now, Alroy," he whispered softly in the king's ear, at the same time easing him back to consciousness and clamping his controls more tightly on the pain and the reflexes that would set him coughing again.

At once the black eyelashes fluttered, no pain showing in the grey eyes that wandered dreamily for a few seconds, then focused on the veiled cup that Javan held. The king blinked once, then shifted his gaze to the one who held the cup.

"The Blessed Sacrament," he murmured in wonder. "But what will Hubert—"

"Never mind Hubert," Javan whispered, shaking his head. "If you want it from someone besides him, it has to be me and it has to be now."

Alroy swallowed hard and nodded, tears welling in the grey eyes, and Javan bowed his head over the cup in his hand, casting back in memory for words he often had heard at *Arx Fidei* when nursing the dying.

"O Lord of Hosts, Heavenly Father," he said, translating from the Latin for Alroy's benefit, "we beg Thee at this moment, above all, to deliver this Thy servant Alroy from all evil and to strengthen him with the Bread of Life, the Body of our Lord the Christ, Who lives and reigns with Thee for ever and ever. Amen."

"Amen" came the hushed response from Rhys Michael and Oriel, mouthed as well by Alroy.

Hands trembling, Javan lifted the veiled lid off the ciborium and laid it aside on the table beside the bed. He had never actually given anyone Communion before, but again he called upon the memories of watching others do it, reverently extracting a single Host from the golden cup and holding it above, where Alroy could see it clearly.

"Ecce Agnus Dei, qui tollis peccata mundi," he murmured, shifting to the traditional Latin. Behold the Lamb of God, who taketh away the sins of the world.

"Domine, non sum dignus . . ." Alroy whispered, echoed by the others. Lord, I am not worthy that Thou shouldst come under my roof. Speak but the word, and my soul shall be healed . . .

With that, Javan made the Sign of the Cross over his brother with the Host, recalling another prayer as he put it reverently on his brother's tongue.

"Receive, my brother, this food for your journey, the Body of our Lord Jesus Christ, that He may guard you from the malicious enemy and lead you into everlasting life. Amen."

"Amen," Alroy whispered, closing his eyes until, after a moment's labored effort, he swallowed.

"Javan?" he whispered weakly then, before Javan could cover the cup. "One thing more—please."

"Yes, what is it?"

"Will—you and Rhysem and Oriel receive Holy Communion as well?" He stifled a little cough. "I know that no one can go with me on—my final journey, but—will you accompany me this far, at least?"

Greatly moved, for he had not expected this, Javan bowed his head over the golden cup again, allowing the others time to prepare as well as himself, then dutifully gave them Communion. By the time he carefully put the cover back on the ciborium, he could hardly see for the tears; and as he set the vessel back on the table beside the bed, Alroy surrendered to a long-suppressed coughing bout.

It curled him onto his side again and left him gasping when Oriel at last managed to control it. The cloth he had jammed against his lips as he coughed came away stained with red. The young king's face was white but composed as he straightened once more in the Healer's arms and cast his gaze first to Rhys Michael, then to Javan, finally laying his right hand atop Oriel's, over his heart.

"I—think it's—time for that cup now—Master Oriel," he managed to gasp out, the breath rattling liquidly in his chest. "I—never was very—brave."

"I have—always thought you *very* brave, my prince," Oriel whispered, reaching blindly for the cup, which Rhys Michael tearfully set in his hand. "But you need not worry about bravery anymore. You have fought the good fight; and God's angels surely await you, to escort you to His bosom."

He brought the cup to the king's lips without wavering, his supporting arm strong behind Alroy's shoulders, suppressing the coughing so that the king could drain it in a few labored swallows. Javan, watching them together, fastened on Oriel's mention of angels, recalling something else about angels, and another cup . . .

All at once other memory came flooding back to him, memory long buried both by his own condition at the time and the design of those responsible—of the long-ago night when their father had died, and the moments just before, when a cup had been prepared in the presence of Beings of such immeasurable power that Javan's knees started to buckle, even thinking about them. He gasped as the returning memory all but overwhelmed him, catching himself on the edge of the bed as Oriel laid Alroy back on the pillows.

As the images flashed before him, Javan knew what *he* must do now, before Alroy slipped into the Nether world and the power never quite uncoiled in him was freed at last in Javan, who was his heir. Clasping his brother's left hand in both of his, he raised it to his lips and bowed his head over it, closing his eyes.

They summoned Archangels to witness what our father did and to escort him through the Gates of Death, Javan thought, fingering the Ring of Fire that so loosely encircled the third finger and sensing Alroy's fading awareness of the contact. *They summoned them for him, and I must summon them for you, dear brother.*

He made his thoughts a prayer as he lifted his entreaty to the powers that had come before, at the behest of the Deryni who had befriended the Haldane line.

Hear me, mighty ones, he breathed. *I know not the form by which to invite your presence, but I ask it now, for the sake of him who soon shall cross to your domain. I summon you, Raphael, Lord of Air; Michael, Lord of Fire; Gabriel, Lord of Water; and Uriel, dark Lord of Earth. Be here, I beseech you, to welcome him who shall pass and to carry him swiftly into the loving presence of the Most High.*

To his utter astonishment, listeners seemed to heed his petition. He dared not open his eyes or even raise his head, but in his mind's eye he seemed to sense the vague forms of other presences suddenly surrounding the bed, broad-pinioned and powerful, surely taller than the room could hold, trailing gossamer robes of fog-grey and flame and palest aquamarine and the cool green-black of winter evergreens.

Startled, he let his eyes open the merest slit. The exhausted and wheezing Alroy had sunk back on his pillows and was drifting into the oblivion of the potion Oriel had given him, no longer fighting the fluid that was filling his lungs and soon would drown him.

Oriel himself knelt at his side, one hand still resting on the king's arm to monitor, his eyes shifting restlessly across the air above the bed, perhaps sensing at least a little of what Javan was perceiving. A trembling Rhys Michael was bowed over Alroy's right hand, cradling it in both of his, but Javan did not think he Saw.

"He shall give His angels charge over thee," Javan whispered aloud, returning his attention to Alroy, closing his eyes then as he reached out toward his brother's mind. "Lord, let it be done according to Thy will. Into Thy hands we commend his spirit."

He could feel Alroy's breathing falter under the trembling link of their clasped hands, growing ever weaker and more labored, but in his inner vision, the spirit essence of his brother seemed finally to rise slowly out of its disease-wracked body to a sitting position, turning its eyes just beyond Javan's right shoulder. In spirit Javan turned as well—and beheld a figure he had not seen in many a year, and never quite like this.

Almost close enough to touch, Javan fancied he could see the regal figure of their father Cinhil, cloaked from shoulder to ankles in a sweeping mantle of Haldane crimson that was cut like a cope. On a head only faintly touched by silver at the temples shone the State Crown of Gwynedd, with its motif of oak leaves and crosses intertwined. He nodded solemnly as his eyes briefly met Javan's; but then all his attention was for Alroy, the expression on his face one of joy and sadness mixed as he held out his arms to his eldest son.

Javan longed to speak to him, but he could not seem to summon up any will to do so. Caught fast in mind and body, he watched numbly as Alroy's spirit rose the rest of the way out of the wasted body and seemed to slide to its feet beside him, laying one spirit hand on his arm and with the other pointing to the physical hand Javan still held—to the ring on the now-relaxing finger.

Then the figure was moving into the embrace of their father and the two images were blurring into one. At the same time, Javan was overwhelmed by the powerful impression of wings buffeting the air around him, stirring to the very depths of his soul, lifting up and away with such force that Javan swayed on his knees, only his grip on Alroy's now-limp hand keeping him grounded to the mortal world. At the very end, he seemed to hear the silvery chime of bells, gradually fading into silence; and when he finally opened his eyes, he had no doubt that Alroy was gone.

Stunned, he forced himself to look around. Oriel apparently had sensed something, for his head was bowed to rest on the edge of the bed, both forearms arched over his head, rocking a little on his knees. Rhys Michael was sobbing unabashedly over the hand he still held.

But Javan dared not spare them any of his attention just yet. One last duty to Alroy remained to be done. Very quietly, and without letting himself think about it too much, he eased the Ring of Fire from Alroy's slack hand and brought it to his lips, bestowing a reverent kiss. Then, silently invoking the witness of Those he had called—Whom he hoped were still there—he slid the ring onto his finger.

A chill shivered up his spine despite the heat, but he felt little else. He wondered if that was all there was to it—though *all*, in his case, might be a very great deal indeed, for he thought that no one else besides a Deryni or a saint could have experienced what he had just experienced. Given the unexpected appearance of his father, he had to wonder that no further memory had returned of what had been done to him—but no time just now to worry overly about *that*.

No, first on the agenda, right now, was to ensure that he was, in fact, to be king; and that involved squaring things—or appearing to square them—with Archbishop Hubert. Time enough, later on, to perhaps reestablish the long-dormant links with his Deryni teachers and see if he could bring his talents to their intended potential.

He slipped the ring back on the dead Alroy's finger and lurched to his feet, intending to go and deal with the sleeping archbishop, but he was hit by such a wave of weariness that he nearly passed out. He jostled the bed as he caught his balance, also rousing Oriel.

"Sire?" the Healer breathed as he raised his head. "Are you all right?"

Swallowing, Javan turned his gaze to focus on the Healer. The moment of light-headedness had passed, but it had reminded him poignantly of his fatigue, already with him when he arrived in Rhemuth and doubtless made worse by what he had just experienced.

"I'll be all right," he whispered. "Too much exertion, not enough sleep—"

"I can do something about that," Oriel said.

Javan shook his head. "No time just now. If I take the time to sleep, I may end up sleeping for all eternity."

"Then let me do something quick and temporary for now," Oriel said, "and I'll come to you later this morning and give you an hour of Healer's sleep." He reached across the bed to touch Javan's wrist and assess his condition. "You do need the rest. I don't think you want to face an Accession Council without it."

A sinking feeling assailed him. Oriel was right. An Accession Council would have to meet as soon as possible. He could delay it for a few hours, but not beyond the afternoon. And there were arrangements to be made for Alroy's lying in state—

"You say you can do something quick?" he said.

Nodding, Oriel came around the foot of the bed and set his hands on the new king's head, thumbs pressing lightly on the eyelids when they closed and fingers cupping up around the temples.

"Relax and think of this as just an ordinary Healing, the way Tavis used to do for you," the Healer said quietly as Rhys Michael looked up dazedly through his tears. "You'll feel it as a wave of warmth. You may feel a little dizzy for a few seconds."

Inhaling deeply and then exhaling, Javan let fall his shields, surrendering to the Healer's ministrations. Restoration came as a flood, not just a wave, and made his knees start to buckle, so that Oriel had to catch him under the arm to steady him. But as he found his feet again, bracing himself on the bed, he could sense a new clear-headedness.

"It's called a fatigue-banishing spell," Oriel murmured, standing back a little to survey him. "Its duration is inversely proportional to the amount of restoration demanded, and it can't be renewed indefinitely. Also, once it wears off, the bottom is going to drop out quite suddenly, and you'll seem to feel even more tired than before I did it. But I'll be back to you by then. This should get you through the next couple of hours."

Javan nodded, feeling more and more restored as he settled into the spell. "Thank you. I'll remember this."

Not smiling, Oriel only glanced pointedly at Hubert, still snoring on his stool on the other side of the room. "Just make certain *he* doesn't, or we're all dead."

Nodding, Javan looked over at the archbishop, then back at Oriel.

"I'll take care of Hubert," he murmured. "Would you blur all of this for Rhysem?"

"Of course."

Squaring his shoulders, Javan crossed to the snoring archbishop. Very little tampering would be necessary, for him or for Rhys Michael.

"Archbishop, listen to what I say to you," Javan said quietly, setting a hand on Hubert's. "You will come with me now. The king is near his end. You have given him the Sacrament, and he received it peacefully. Now he needs only your prayers to speed him on his way."

The blue eyes fluttered open as Hubert roused, and he gave a little sigh with the effort it cost him to stand. Javan led him to the royal bedside, keeping his controls in place as he released Hubert's hand and knelt once again. The archbishop stood close behind him, hands folded piously before him, and Javan gently took his brother's hand and kissed it.

"I will begin the prayers now, Archbishop, and you will join in and carry on," Javan whispered, "remembering only that the king's passing was gentle, and that he died in a state of grace." He drew a deep breath and began.

"Come to his aid, O Saints of God; come forth to meet him, Angels of the Lord, receiving his soul, presenting it to the Most High . . ."

Blinking, Hubert picked up the versicle, his tone more reverent than Javan had expected, even under control. "May Christ, Who has called you, now receive you, and may the angels bring you to Abraham's bosom."

"Receiving his soul," Javan murmured the response, knowing that it already was so, "presenting it unto the Most High."

"Eternal rest grant unto him, O Lord."

"And let perpetual light shine upon him," Javan responded, now joined by Rhys Michael and Oriel.

"From the gates of hell—"

"Save his soul, O Lord," Javan said strongly.

"May he rest in peace."

"Amen."

"Let us pray," Hubert went on, bowing his head over his folded hands. "O Lord, we commend to Thee the soul of Thy servant Alroy, that when he departs from this world, he may live with Thee. By the grace of Thy merciful love wash away the sins that in human frailty he has committed in the conduct of his life. Through Christ our Lord—"

"Amen," the others responded.

Javan, trusting that Alroy was indeed now in the hands of God, slowly got to his feet and, as Hubert looked at him sharply, took the ring once again from his dead brother's hand and slid it onto his own finger beside his silver signet. Before he could do more, Rhys Michael reached across and took the hand, murmuring "My liege" as he bent pointedly to kiss it in fealty. Ducking his head and throwing caution to the winds, Oriel did the same.

Hubert simply looked on in amazement for several seconds— Javan with no idea what he was going to do, for he was no longer controlled—then ducked his head to Javan in what might be interpreted as a bow.

"You have made your decision then," the archbishop said, his blue eyes hard and cold. "You will have an earthly crown rather than a heavenly one."

"I hope that eventually I shall have both," Javan replied quietly. "But in conscience, I could not refuse my duty to my House."

As Oriel quietly drew the sheet over Alroy's face, trying to be invisible, Hubert heaved a heavy sigh and gestured toward the door.

"Very well, then," he said, resignation in his voice. "Come with me, and I shall—announce your accession to the lords assembled outside—Sire. And may God have mercy on us all."

CHAPTER FIVE

For thou hast maintained my right and cause.
—Psalms 9:4

The close oppressiveness of the summer morning was all around Javan as he and Rhys Michael followed Hubert toward the door. Beyond that door lay the first of the great lords who, henceforth, would demand all Javan's attention. His palms were sweating, his pulse pounding in his ears. He made himself take a deep breath as Hubert swung the door wide.

Conversation ceased. The room beyond now held more than a score of black-clad figures, half again the number who had been there before. Robert Oriss, the Archbishop of Rhemuth, had joined the secular lords, along with Constable Udaut and several other officers of the royal household. They stood back as Hubert moved into the room, but their eyes were for the two Haldane princes, one of them now surely their king.

Javan had his hands clasped behind him as he and a very shaken-looking Rhys Michael followed Hubert in, so no one could see that Javan now wore the Ring of Fire—or that his hands were clasped to keep them from trembling—but Charlan noticed the Eye of Rom right away. He would have gone to his knees then and there, but Javan caught his eye and gave him a minute shake of his head, deeming it better to let Hubert make the announcement.

"My lords," Hubert said quietly, folding his hands across his ample waist, "I ask you, of your charity, to pray for the soul of our late sovereign lord, King Alroy." He crossed himself heavily as he said, *"Requiem aeternam dona ei, Domine."*

"*Et lux perpetua luceat ei,*" the others murmured brokenly, dropping to their knees in twos and threes to follow the lead of Javan and Rhys Michael.

"*Offerentes eam in conspectu Altissimi. Kyrie eleison.*"

"*Christe eleison, Kyrie eleison.*"

Hubert led them in a *Pater Noster* then, followed by another exchange invoking eternal rest and perpetual light upon the soul of the departed king.

"*Requiescat in pace,*" he concluded. May he rest in peace.

To which all of them answered, "Amen."

As they all got to their feet again, all attention returned to the two princes—and then shifted to a dark, hook-nosed man in burgundy, wearing a baron's coronet and a chain of minor office, who moved suddenly forward several steps, thumbs hooked in his sword belt, looking predatory.

"Does my Lord Archbishop have a statement regarding the succession?" he said bluntly.

Hubert looked uncomfortable and cleared his throat nervously several times. "Regarding the passing of our late sovereign lord, the High and Mighty Prince Alroy Bearand Brion Haldane, lately our king. It—was his will, and that of his father before him, that if he died without issue, his brother should succeed him."

"That his brother *Javan* should succeed him," the baron corrected, turning to Tammaron. "Is that not so, my Lord Chancellor? Or do the laws of primogeniture no longer prevail within this realm?"

"Now, see here!" Iver MacInnis objected. "Rhys Michael was to be the next king!"

"I do not recall asking your opinion, my lord!" the baron said, rounding briefly on Iver, hand moving to the hilt of his sword. "I have asked the Lord Chancellor, whose place it is to know the laws of this land. I pray you answer, my Lord Tammaron. Do the laws of primogeniture still apply in Gwynedd or do they not?"

Tammaron, obviously wishing anyone else would have dealt with the question, stepped forward and cleared his throat. "It is—true that, by primogeniture, Prince Javan unquestionably is the heir. However, I was given to understand that there was some question of—stepping aside, in light of a religious vocation?"

As he looked hopefully, almost pleadingly, at Javan, the new king made a point of folding his arms on his chest so that the Ring of Fire was clearly visible beside his Haldane signet.

"Let us lay that fantasy aside from the outset, my Lord Chancellor," he said. "As his Grace the Archbishop will surely attest, my trial of a religious vocation has entailed only simple vows, which are temporary. Even were they permanent, such vows can be dispensed, as was done for my father. I am ready to take up my crown."

"And I, to support him!" Rhys Michael cried, seizing Javan's hand and dropping to one knee to kiss it. "The king is dead. Long live King Javan!"

"Long live King Javan!" Charlan responded, echoed by the other young knights, who drew their swords in salute and brandished them as Javan's name became a chant, daring anyone to gainsay them. The baron who had come to Javan's support was among the first to kneel with them, a grim look of satisfaction on his face, followed by the household officers and gradually the great lords who were present, until every knee in the room had bent except Hubert's, who bowed to kiss the royal hand as the chanting died away.

In the silence that followed, Javan inclined his head to the archbishop, raised up his brother, then gestured a little self-consciously for the rest to rise. The Ring of Fire glinted on his left hand, and its sparkle reminded *him* of what he was trying to take on, even if not all his audience were entirely convinced. As they got to their feet, a few of them exchanging dubious glances, he hooked his thumbs in the front of his belt to keep the ring in their sight—and to keep his hands from shaking.

"I thank you, my lords," he said. "In the interests of the heat, and the long night most of us have spent, I shall be brief for now." He drew a deep breath, heartened when no one seemed disposed to interrupt—though he knew it was not over yet.

"First of all, regarding the final disposition of the late king, my brother." He had forced himself to think about this moment on the ride from *Arx Fidei* and had made inquiries of Charlan and some of the other knights when they stopped to change horses.

"I have decided that my brother shall lie at Saint Hilary's until his funeral. The Chapel Royal is too small," he added, to quell the objections several started to raise. "Saint Hilary's possesses sufficient size and dignity for a royal lying-in-state, and was often my brother's favored place of worship. In addition, Saint Hilary's being within the outer wards of the castle, it is accessible both to the Court and to those good folk of Rhemuth city who may wish to come and pay their respects. I shall ask Sir Gavin, who was his squire, to organize a guard of honor to escort his body thence at noon, at which time and place I should like a Solemn Requiem sung for him."

At his somewhat tentative glance at the archbishops, Hubert

gave him a forbearing nod, but Javan suspected he had not heard the last from Hubert MacInnis.

"Following Mass, a vigil guard will be mounted through the rest of today and tonight and throughout tomorrow. I should like the funeral to take place at noon on the following day."

"So soon?" someone murmured in the back of the room.

"For shame!" someone else muttered.

"His *father* lay in state for a full *week*," a surly voice said from the left side of the room.

Javan bit back the sharp retort that almost escaped his lips and took a deep breath instead.

"His *father* died in *February*, when heat was not a factor," he said pointedly to the left side of the room. "Or has everyone forgotten the heat? *I* have not."

"But his Highness apparently *has* forgotten that the day after tomorrow is a Sunday," Archbishop Oriss said blandly. "Of course, if he truly wishes a funeral to be held on the Lord's Day, against custom . . ."

Javan felt a dull shiver of dismay knot in his gut. He had made his first mistake. Not a serious one, but he knew it would be used to fuel further recalcitrance if he did not defuse it right now.

"I thank your Grace for the correction," he said quietly, inclining his head in an attitude of apology. "Not having slept last night, I had lost track of the day. Monday, then. Specific arrangements for the funeral itself can be worked out in the next day or two. I shall value your input in that regard, my Lord Archbishop."

Oriss was too well bred to gloat openly, but others in the room were not. Javan tried to ignore them as he turned his mind to the other topic he must address.

"My second instruction concerns the continuation of government," he said. "To that end, I desire that an Accession Council be convened immediately after Mass. Earl Tammaron, as Chancellor, if you would be so good as to summon the officers of the late king's Council, I shall inform those additional persons I wish to attend."

Tammaron looked worried, but inclined his head in agreement.

"Thank you." Javan drew a careful breath, still scanning them, and decided it was time to make a tactful retreat. "If you will excuse me, then, my lords, gentlemen. I need a bath and some rest. I have ridden hard and slept not at all this past night, to be at my brother's bedside. I shall return before noon to escort my brother's body to the chapel. Should I be needed before then, you may find me in the apartments of my brother Rhys Michael."

He headed for the door without further ceremony, Charlan leading and Rhys Michael flanking him. His audience parted before him, most of them granting him at least token signs of respect, many simply watching with stony resentment.

The baron who had spoken up in his support gave him an inclination of his head and backed off a few paces as their eyes met. Javan could not recall seeing him at Court before. He looked to be in his late forties, clean-shaven, but with grey threaded through the jet-black hair; a powerful man, still in his prime.

Just beyond him, the constable, Lord Udaut, was moving on into the corridor just ahead of the king and his party, surprising Javan as he turned to sketch a perfunctory bow as Javan came through the door.

"Sire, I shan't keep you long," he murmured as Javan looked him up and down. He was known to be a cool-headed professional and a survivor. He had been Constable of Gwynedd since the time of Javan's father, though other officers of the Crown had come and gone. As constable, he was also in charge of security wherever the royal household lodged—which meant that his loyalty could well make the difference of whether or not Javan survived, regardless of the dozen young knights of Javan's earlier escort, drawn up as an honor guard in the corridor behind him.

"Lord Udaut," Javan said cautiously. "What is it you wished to say?"

"Only that I had no part in what went on in there," Udaut replied, gesturing past Javan with his chin. "You are my rightful sovereign and liege. As your constable, I intend to keep your person and this castle secure against any who would say otherwise."

Javan allowed himself a faint sigh of relief and offered Udaut his hand. "Thank you, my lord. Your loyalty is more welcome than you can know."

"My liege," Udaut murmured as he ducked to kiss the royal hand. Then he was setting his hand on the hilt of his sword with a nod and easing his way through the waiting courtiers and knights in the direction of the great hall.

Charlan had stepped aside with Sir Gavin during Javan's exchange with his constable and was relaying the new king's instructions regarding the guard of honor. As Javan moved on into the corridor, Rhys Michael sticking close by his side, he acknowledged the salute of his escort knights with a nod, also summoning Bertrand de Ville to his side with a glance. Two more of the knights accompanied him, slipping quietly but pointedly behind Javan and Rhys Michael to insulate them from the occupants of the anteroom.

"Well, Udaut is with us," Javan murmured to Bertrand, resisting the impulse to look back over his shoulder. "But tell me, who was the baron who spoke in my behalf?"

"Etienne de Courcy, Sire," Bertrand replied promptly. "His lands are in the south, near Mooryn."

"De Courcy," Javan repeated. The name stirred a memory somewhere, but he could not quite pin it down. "What's his function?"

"Chancellor's staff, I think, sir. Something to do with the law. I only know his son." Bertrand paused. "Do you want me to bring him over?"

"No, not now. I really do need to get some rest." Charlan was finishing with Gavin, starting to look as if he were ready to move out, and Rhys Michael had drifted farther into the corridor. "There's something you *can* do for me, though," he said, setting himself to Truth-Read the younger man's response. "I'd like you to keep it as quiet as possible."

Bertrand gave him an eager nod. "You know you can rely on me, Sire."

"Yes, I do. I've asked Master Oriel to come to me as soon as he can break away from here, probably in an hour or so. I'd prefer that Hubert and the others don't know, but I need to see him. My—foot needs some attention," he lied. "I'm afraid I may have overdone a bit, riding here in such haste."

Bertrand gave only a cursory glance at the foot with its special boot as he said, "I'm sorry to hear that, Sire. I'll bring him as soon as I can."

With a nod, Javan returned his attention to Charlan, who now was calling several more of the escort knights to fall in as he turned to lead Javan back along the cloister corridor, heading for the royal apartments.

The exchange had not gone unnoticed. As the king and his party disappeared down the corridor and young Bertrand began working his way into the anteroom, a man already there made it his business to edge closer to the younger man. The door into the room where the king had died was open now. Inside, Etienne de Courcy could see the royal physicians remonstrating with Earl Manfred and the two archbishops. Bertrand seemed very interested in what was going on in there, and glanced up attentively as Etienne touched his forearm, but saw no threat from the hook-nosed older baron who had come to the new king's defense in the matter of the succession.

"Trouble?" Etienne murmured, so that only Bertrand could hear him.

The young knight pretended casual interest in the rest of the room, but answered readily enough. "Not exactly. The king's asked me to take care of something for him—confidentially."

"Ah, I see," Etienne replied, not adding that he saw far more than Bertrand supposed. "Well, I'd best go see if Guiscard has arrived yet. I'm sure he'll want to take a turn on the rota for the vigil tonight. I know I do."

"Aye, most everyone will want a turn, I expect," Bertrand agreed. "You might speak to Sir Gavin before you go."

"I'll do that," Etienne said.

When he had done so, Etienne de Courcy threaded his way free of the hangers-on still lingering outside the king's sickroom and made his way back to the castle's great hall. Guiscard and word of the king's death had already arrived. As Etienne spotted him, the muffled bell of Saint Hilary's began to toll, once for each year of the king's life, and dragged at his spirits as he wove his way among the knots of sober men and sad-faced women. As the tolling ceased, the booming voice of Great George took up the knell, down in the cathedral.

Sir Guiscard de Courcy was waiting by an open panel of one of the wide window embrasures, trying to catch a breath of cooler air. The dark hair and eyes of both men, and the matching hook noses, made it clear the two were related, even if they had not borne the same surname.

The younger man wore dust-streaked riding leathers of a dark, ox-blood hue, his once-white shirt open at the throat. The matched sword and dagger at his hip were serviceable rather than decorative, the weapons of a seasoned fighting man, but inkstains on the first two fingers of his right hand proclaimed him a man of letters, as well. He glanced around surreptitiously as his father stepped up into the embrasure and they moved deeper into it, both of them feigning interest in the gardens below.

"It's over, then," Guiscard said.

The elder de Courcy gave him a weary nod. "Not that the bells leave any room for doubt. It happened about half an hour ago."

Guiscard sighed and gave critical regard to a smear of dust caked with horse-sweat on the inner leg of one of his boots. "We started getting rumors fairly quickly, then. Any trouble over the succession?"

Etienne almost smiled. "Nothing like what I feared. His presence made all the difference—totally unexpected until Rhys Michael sent for him late last night. Whether he can hold on to it remains to be seen. The first test comes this afternoon. He's asked for a Requiem Mass at noon at Saint Hilary's, where Alroy will lie in state for the next three days, with the Accession Council to follow immediately after. That's going to make it almost impossible for you to pass the word and be back by then."

"Can't be done," Guiscard said, shaking his head. "I'll have to go later tonight. Why Saint Hilary's?"

"Javan wanted it. There was no way to advise him otherwise. There's to be a vigil there throughout the night—though at least that gives us an excuse to be there. I've put us on the rota. For this afternoon, however, he's going to have to make it through that Accession Council more or less on his own."

"Can he?" Guiscard said quietly, casting a sidelong glance at his father.

"Good question," Etienne replied. "If he can, then he's worth fighting for. If not, this all may be academic by nightfall."

Back where the king had died, Archbishops Oriss and Hubert had withdrawn into the garden to leave the king's body with those who would prepare it for its lying in state.

"What happened in there?" Oriss asked as they sought the shade of a leafy tree. "What made him change his mind?"

Hubert shook his head. "I can only guess that enough of Javan's religious training made an impression that he persuaded his brother not to neglect the final Sacraments."

"He made a final Confession, then?"

Hubert shrugged vaguely. "He'd received the Last Rites during the night. It was only Viaticum he required."

"Viaticum. Food for the journey." Oriss smiled sadly and shook his head. "Poor lad. His father died the same way, I'm told. But he was so young . . . Was it—a peaceful death, do you think?"

Hubert tried to remember the actual moment of the king's passing, but could not quite focus on it. It had happened while they recited the prayers for the dying . . . Yes, that was it. So it must have been relatively peaceful. The Healer was there, after all. He would have eased any pain.

"I think he—just slipped away," he said slowly. "He'd been given medication, after all. He must have been asleep when it finally happened. One of the physicians told me last night that it would be like drowning." He shook his head. "I don't think he suffered, there at the end."

Oriss gave him a quizzical look, but did not comment.

"Javan surprised me, though," Hubert went on. "I'd really come to believe that he thought that he had a genuine vocation—or at least that he was resigned."

Oriss snorted. "Obviously not. And what on earth made de Courcy come to his defense that way? I thought he was Tammaron's man."

"Apparently he's the *king's* man," Hubert replied. "I shall be very surprised if he doesn't show up at the Accession Council. If he does, and there are many more like him, we can forget about overturning the succession."

"Then Javan's in," Oriss said. "There's nothing we can do about it."

"A temporary setback," Hubert assured him. "We'll give him a chance, since we have no choice, but if he remains a problem, we'll give him a chance to hang himself."

Oriss looked up sharply. "You wouldn't kill him? He'll be an anointed king!"

"My dear Robert," Hubert replied, with a look of astonished affront. "I am not a regicide. The boy has been like a son to me."

"Well, what do we do, then, if he refuses to cooperate?"

"Let's wait until he does," Hubert replied. "If all else fails, there are other ways to ensure a cooperative king."

CHAPTER SIX

*Separate thyself from thine enemies, and take
heed of thy friends.*
                          —Ecclesiasticus 6:13

In Rhys Michael's bedchamber, meanwhile, the new king had stripped down and immersed himself gratefully in a deep wooden tub of tepid water, hastily filled by a parade of earnest and curious servants. The bath was cool and refreshing, and the temporary solitude seductive, once Charlan had shooed everyone out, but Javan knew he dared not indulge the luxury of staying very long in it. Not only were there things to do and people waiting to talk to him, but he truly feared he might fall asleep and drown.

He was saved from this danger by Charlan's return, all too soon. A brisk sudsing revived him somewhat, as did several submersions to rinse the sweat and travel grime out of his hair. His former squire provided further diversion by lamenting the state of Javan's barbering as he toweled the royal head.

"You're fortunate the *Custodes* don't use a full tonsure as some orders do," Charlan said, briefly testing the stubble on the fist-size shaven patch on Javan's crown. "This is going to look bad enough until it grows out. When was it last done? About a week ago?"

"About that," Javan said. "I hate it, too." He stood up to climb shakily out of the tub, unsteady on his bad foot, then wrapped himself in the linen sheeting Charlan offered. He was almost cool for a few minutes, while Charlan went to find him clean clothes, but body heat soon began to reverse the benefits of the dunking, and he had to throw it off.

He would have preferred to stretch out naked on the canopied bed and simply succumb to sleep for about a week. Instead, he dutifully pulled on the clean breeches Charlan brought and hobbled into the outer room to sit in the cool of a shady window, where a faint breeze stirred across his skin and Rhys Michael chattered at him while making his own lesser ablutions.

Very soon Tomais brought him the first of the promised briefing documents to begin reading, after which Tomais and Charlan disappeared for several minutes. They returned with another of the young knights who had fetched Javan from *Arx Fidei*—Sir Sorle Dalriada, who had been the last of Cinhil's squires to be knighted by Cinhil himself and was several years older than either Charlan or Tomais.

"Sir Sorle," Javan said, smiling, as the dark young knight sketched him an elegant bow. "Did you have a hand in this?" he asked, slightly lifting the documents in his hand. "I seem to recall a penchant for the law, back when you used to tutor us."

Sorle grinned and pulled another stool closer, settling on it as the other two did the same. Rhys Michael also joined them, pulling on a loose-fitting tunic of gauzy black linen.

"I wish I could claim total credit, my prince," Sorle said, "but several of your escort today had a hand in it—and some other gentlemen you probably won't remember, but who remember you. Lord Jerowen Reynolds was one; and the de Courcys, father and son. Baron de Courcy was the one who spoke up for you when old Hubert got fuddled on who came next in the succession."

"Yes. I asked Bertrand who he was," Javan said. "The name's familiar, but I didn't recognize him. Have I met him before?"

"Yes, but he's shaved off his beard and moustache since then," Charlan said. "Nor was the occasion particularly auspicious. He gave you and Alroy a rather remarkable Cardounet board at your thirteenth birthday court—but I don't think you ever got to play with it."

Javan closed his eyes briefly, trying *not* to remember that particular birthday. He remembered the board clearly—a splendid thing of ebony and olivewood, with inlays of mother-of-pearl and semi-precious stones set around the edges. The playing pieces had been lavish as well, with real gems set in the crowns of the priest-kings and the archbishops' mitres.

He also remembered the rest of that afternoon, though he wished he could not—when the regents had turned on Duke Ewan of Claibourne, and the Deryni Declan Carmody had broken under the strain—and paid for it with his life and the lives of his wife and two young sons.

"I remember," he said quietly. "You're right; it *was* the missing beard. He's one of the southern barons, isn't he?"

"Aye, from down by Mooryn, where my family come from," Charlan said. "As you may have gathered, he's extremely well versed in the law, as is Lord Jerowen. They've both been functionaries in the chancellor's office for several years. You'd be well advised to retain them—and these two rascals as well! Sir Jason? Sir Robear?"

As he said the last names, two burly figures in the livery of the household garrison stepped into the room, one tall and fair, the other shorter and slightly darker, both of them bearded and going grey. Wide smiles split their beards as they made him respectful bows. The taller one, Sir Robear, had a mass of black fabric draped over one arm.

"I've brought you something cooler to wear, Sire," he said, bending a knee to lay it across Javan's lap. "My wife cut it down from an old one of mine, when it became apparent there was going to be a need for it. The rest of the day will be difficult enough without sweltering in the tunic you wore here—and I don't think you want to continue looking like a seminarian."

"No, I don't. Thank you, Robear," Javan managed to murmur, touched by the man's sensitivity to the situation and heartened by his presence—though not by the prospect of putting on black again. The short, loose-sleeved tunic he held up briefly was made of a nubbly, loosely woven linen, and undoubtedly as cool as anything he was likely to find, but it still was black.

"I've brought you something as well, Sire," the other knight said, dropping to one knee and fumbling in a pouch at his belt, which bore his coat of arms picked out in bright threads and dyes.

All in a rush Javan realized that Robear was wearing a similar pouch and flashed back to the day he and Rhys Michael had bought the pouches for the two knights—and for two more, both dead now: Piedur in a border skirmish a few years back and Corund in the ambush that had claimed the life of Ansel MacRorie's brother Davin.

The memory brought less pleasant images as well, for Tavis O'Neill had lost his hand that day. But it also had been the day when Javan first began to realize that he was not like other humans and that unexpected powers were awakening in him.

He yanked himself back from that memory as Jason delved deep into his pouch and produced a coil of snow-white leather, perhaps three fingers wide.

"I see that your Highness has remembered the pouch," Jason said quietly, shaking out the white leather so that all could see that it was a knight's belt, with a simple gold ring attached at one end. "I regret that this is not the same piece of leather that your Highness bought that day, but I remembered the longing that went with the purchase and telling Master Tavis—though you never knew it— that I doubted you would ever wear the white belt unless you became king."

The older knight's callused fingers caressed the soft leather, and his dark eyes met Javan's squarely. "I am here to tell you, Sire, that you have merited this belt even before this morning's sorrow made you king, by your courage and by the honor you have shown in all your conduct over these difficult years since your beloved father died. I am also here to tell you that we are prepared—all of us present here, and on behalf of many who cannot be present just now—we are prepared to offer you the knightly accolade that goes with this token of that estate, to receive it here and now, for you are surely worthy of it."

Stunned, Javan could only blink at Jason for an interminable instant, hardly able to believe the honor this very senior and respected knight was doing him. Knighthood had been a childhood dream he had long ago put aside in the expediency of survival. He had not let himself think about the white belt for several years, believing it beyond any reasonable likelihood of attainment—and caught up in what he must do for his own survival. To have it now within reach, and offered by a knight of Jason's standing—

Almost trembling, Javan handed off the tunic and his sheaf of papers to Charlan, who was grinning widely. He allowed himself to look at the length of white leather still offered on Jason's hands, but he made himself fold his own hands in his lap, so that he would not touch it.

"Sir Jason, I—am overwhelmed by the honor you do me. But I am as I am." He could not keep from glancing at his clubfoot, exposed there for all to see, and he had to blink back tears as he let his eyes sweep the others as well.

"Please forgive me, gentlemen, but I—would not have you lessen your standards merely to prove a loyalty that need not be proven. I am more grateful than I can say, for your support and the danger you take upon yourselves by championing my cause, but you need not do this."

To his utter amazement, the rest of the knights merely smiled and went to one knee, all of them looking expectantly at Jason, who sighed and leaned forward conspiratorially, one forearm resting on his upraised knee. Rhys Michael had drawn back against the edge of the window embrasure, for he was not one of their company in this, but tears of joy glistered in his eyes as he made happy witness to it.

"Sire," Jason said gravely, "I believe I continue to speak for the rest of my brother knights when I tell you that none of us intend to take another step out of this room or to lift another finger in your service until you agree to accept the accolade."

"You will but make my task the more difficult, gentlemen," Javan whispered. "To appear before the lords of state wearing this"—he gestured toward the belt—"would only provoke those who far sooner would have my brother on the throne instead of me."

"You need not wear the white belt out of this room," Robear replied, leaning closer. "For now, we would be satisfied if you receive the accolade in secret. Later, when circumstances permit the full ceremony to which you, as king, are entitled—and which your subjects will expect—the ceremony can be repeated and this external sign taken up. But it is not *that* which makes a knight." He gestured as Jason held up the belt and flexed the length between his two hands. "*We* will know that our king is one of us, and sealed by our recognition as fit to lead us in battle, if need be."

Trembling, Javan looked around at the five upturned faces, three young and two not so young, awed by their faith in him, then raised his eyes to Jason's.

"Very well," he whispered.

Smiling, Jason laid the white belt over his shoulder and rose, the others also getting to their feet. "Then kneel, Sire. I think we've wasted enough time as it is."

"Shouldn't I at least put on my tunic?" Javan asked as he rose, for he was standing before them in only his black breeches.

Jason shook his head and put both his hands on Javan's shoulders, steadying him as he urged him to his knees. "No time, lad. Besides, it's too hot. Let this be the only time you feel the kiss of steel on bare flesh, and remember it well."

Kneeling there, his face upturned to Jason's, Javan thought it highly unlikely he was ever to forget it. Pressing his palms together in an attitude of prayer, he was aware of the others moving to either side of Jason, two to a side, and of the slither of steel as Jason drew his broadsword and held it flat-bladed before his kneeling king.

"Let this blade stand in the place of the great sword carried by your father, by which blade I was knighted nearly twenty years ago," he said softly. "Swear upon it, that you will be a good and faithful knight and a true king to your people."

Placing his hands flat on the blade over Jason's, Javan murmured, "I swear it, so help me God," and bent to touch his lips to the steel between. Then, as Jason raised the blade before him, himself kissing the cross-hilt before preparing to deliver the accolade, Javan joined his hands again and bowed his head.

"Javan Jashan Urien Haldane," Jason said, as the right hands of the other knights came to rest lightly on his hand that held the sword. "I dub thee a knight, in the name of the Father"—the blade dipped to touch Javan's right shoulder, cold steel against warm flesh—"and of the Son"—the blade arched over Javan's head to touch his other shoulder—"and of the Holy Spirit."

The blade moved a third time, touching the flat to the crown of Javan's bowed head, cold against the shaved circle of the tonsure that could not grow out fast enough to satisfy Javan—though he did not spurn the true Master he had served during his years in seminary, as God's knight; only the humans who had tried to force his compliance to a vocation he did not feel, that they might deprive him of his birthright.

The sword lifted. Tears were glittering in Javan's eyes as he raised them to Jason's and to those of the other four who had laid hands on the sword with which he was knighted. And as Jason sheathed his blade, Javan had to clear his throat before he could whisper "Amen."

"Rise now, Sir Javan Haldane," Jason said, holding out a right hand to him. "And I think that Sir Charlan should be the one to put the belt on him, since he's the youngest among us."

Charlan smiled as Jason pulled the white leather off his shoulder and held it out, but shook his head.

"Nay, Sir Jason, *you* should do it," he said. "Not only are you senior among us, but you made the belt. And you helped him buy the leather for that first belt that never got made."

Robear gave a nod. "He's right, Jason. You should do it."

Sighing, but obviously pleased, Jason raised an eyebrow and glanced at the rest of them for confirmation, then slipped the ring end of the belt around Javan's narrow waist without further demur, drawing the end through the ring to snug it up, then passing the end up behind the belt and down through the loop thus formed. When he had adjusted it to his liking, he went to his knees and took Javan's right hand, pressing its back to his lips in homage before releasing it to offer up his own joined palms in the gesture of fealty.

"My king and liege," he said. "I am your man of life and limb and earthly worship. Faith and truth will I bear unto you, to live and to die, against all manner of folk. So help me God."

The others were going to their knees even as Jason said it, likewise lifting up their hands, and Javan's hands were trembling as he enclosed Jason's between his. In the emotion of the moment, he could not remember the exact words he was supposed to respond, but he knew the sense of what they wanted to hear.

"I receive your faith and truth and I pledge my faith and truth in return," he said. "Insofar as such grace is given me, I promise to be a true liege to all of you, to protect and defend you with all my heart and with all my strength and with all my might. So help me God."

Jason bowed to touch his forehead to their joined hands then. Javan was moving on to clasp Robear's hands when a brisk knock on the outer door shattered the solemnity of the moment.

Instantly Jason was on his feet and moving toward the door, signalling them to finish. Briskly, but careful not to hurry, Javan took the fealty of Robear, then of the three younger knights, lifting one finger to his lips and retreating to his stool as he heard voices in the outer room. Charlan came with him, bending to remove the telltale white belt. He had it shielded behind his body, coiling it up again, when Jason and Bertrand entered, with the Healer Oriel between them.

"I'm told that you asked to see Master Oriel," Jason said carefully. "That your foot was giving you some trouble, after your ride. Bertrand has brought him, as you requested."

Carefully Javan drew breath. After the emotional experience of his knighting, he felt drained—or perhaps it was Oriel's fatigue-banishing spell giving out. The knights had given him their unqualified trust, as one of them. Now, perhaps, it was time to trust them just a little.

"Yes, I did ask to see Master Oriel," he said quietly, restraining a yawn. "He was my Healer after Tavis O'Neill left court, and he risked a great deal to keep me apprised of my brother's condition after I was sent to the seminary. Without his personal courage and support last night, I doubt that Rhys Michael would have had the courage to summon me against the wishes of the great lords."

As Rhys Michael shook his head in agreement, wide-eyed, the knights glanced uncomfortably among themselves, several of them casting covert glances at Javan's foot.

"You must forgive us, Sire," Robear said. "We accept whatever limitations your foot may cause you, but we do not know what they are. I don't believe anyone realized that you needed a Healer's attention."

"I'm afraid I misled you," Javan said, "and for that I apologize. It wasn't really my foot I called him for. A long ride after long absence from a horse will always have its cost, but what I really need is some sleep, before I face the Council. One doesn't get much sleep in a monastery, and you know what last night was like. An hour of Healer's sleep is better than half a night's ordinary sleep. I trust him to do only what I ask of him. Will you trust him as well?"

Sorle, dark and quick and handsome, cast a suspicious glance over the Deryni.

"Is he not the creature of the great lords, Sire?" he said. "Of Earl Tammaron and Archbishop Hubert?"

"Oriel, answer him," Javan said.

Trembling, Oriel locked his eyes on Sorle's, looking very young and vulnerable.

"Those are the masters I am forced to serve, my lord," he whispered, "because my wife and daughter are held as hostage. I have seen the cost to other Deryni who did not do as they were told. When the great lords still were regents, I watched them order Declan Carmody's family killed before his very eyes. Some in this room saw it as well, and how the regents then took Declan's life by slow torture. They will do the same to me and mine if I defy them openly."

"And yet Master Oriel has freely given me aid," Javan said. "I trust his integrity, be he Deryni or not. In return, I will not put him in a position in which he must openly choose between me and those who hold his family hostage. Even coming here now could put him at risk, as the great lords will know that I am conferring with those who support me. Fortunately, they're probably conferring, too, and I hope will not miss him. But I must not keep him overlong and I do need his services."

A heavy yawn took him this time without him being able to prevent it, and he glanced at Oriel and got to his feet. "You'll have to excuse me, gentlemen. Robear, can I ask you to handle whatever arrangements need to be made in the next hour or so?"

"The main thing is who should be asked to attend the Council," Robear replied. "And security arrangements. The great lords may take exception to what you did this morning, once they've had a chance to think about it."

Javan had been slowly heading back toward the sleeping chamber as he listened, making a point of walking as boldly as he could without his supportive boot, hardly limping at all, but the mere sight of the curtained bed in the corner of the room reminded him just how exhausted he was. "I throw myself on your good judgment, Robear. Summon the ones you think will work best for me and make arrangements to secure the castle against whatever kind of internal insurrection the former regents might think to try." He shook his head as a huge yawn claimed his attention.

"I'm sorry. Charlan, wake me when it's time to dress and go back down. And feel free to continue using these rooms. I assure you, I shan't hear a thing."

As Charlan drew the others out of the room, shepherding them back toward the window embrasure, Javan swung his legs up on the bed and lay back on the pillows with a sigh, shifting a little aside so that Oriel could sit on the edge beside him.

"Thank you for coming and thank you for what you said in there," he murmured. "You told them just what you ought to have."

Oriel gave him a taut smile. "I had little choice, did I, after you'd committed me?"

Grimacing, Javan rubbed at the bridge of his nose with a thumb and forefinger. "We all have our charades to play, Oriel. At least if they know you're on my side, for whatever reason, they'll be inclined to protect you. I intend to do what I can, as I promised you several years ago, but I can't be everywhere at once. Especially not for a while."

Oriel allowed himself a resigned shrug. "No matter. For now, it's enough that they mean well by you." He glanced down at Javan's foot. "Is your foot bothering you, or was that really part of the ruse to get me here, as you told them?"

Javan flexed the foot and winced. "As I said, a ride like last night, after so long a time away from horses, does have its price. But I can live with that. You promised me Healer's sleep. I think I can spare about an hour."

Oriel nodded and set his hands to either side of Javan's head, thumbs pressed to the temples. "An hour will certainly help— though two would be better. May I take you really deep?"

Javan drew a deep breath and closed his eyes as he let it out. "Do what you think is best," he whispered.

"Thank you."

Javan could feel the Healer's mind questing at his shields, and he let them fall away, confident that Oriel would not take advantage.

"Let yourself float now," the Healer murmured, pushing sleep before him as his mind came into Javan's. It was like a wave of dark water, cool and all embracing, and Javan let it carry him deep, deeper . . .

"That's right," Oriel whispered. "Rather than set a specific length of time, I'll leave you to sleep on until Charlan rouses you. If he's kind, you could pick up an extra quarter hour or so. And I'll see what I can do with that foot before I leave . . ."

CHAPTER SEVEN

They compassed me about also with words of
hatred; and fought against me without a cause.
—Psalms 109:3

By noon, as Javan made his way downstairs to accompany his brother's body to Saint Hilary's, he found his fatigue much diminished
and his composure considerably restored—though the latter suffered new assaults as he made his way through the great hall among
his new subjects, heading with his escort knights toward the door
to the courtyard beyond. Sir Robear had counseled him and Rhys
Michael not to go back to the sickroom where Alroy had died, but
to await the procession on the great hall porch.

Robear was with them now, along with Jason and Charlan, Sorle,
Bertrand, and Tomais. The six formed a phalanx around him and
Rhys Michael as they moved quietly through the hall, shielding
them from physical danger, but he could feel the eyes upon him,
assessing, calculating. He held his head high and tried to carry himself like a king.

It was not easy in the heat and got harder when he and his party
had gained the great hall porch. The sun beat down on his bare
head and dazzled his eyes, making an oven of even the lightweight
tunic he wore—though at least with everyone else in somber garments, he did not feel as conspicuous as he had before, or that his
own attire proclaimed his former clergy status quite so stridently.
He had been pleasantly surprised to discover that the tunic Jason
had brought him, though black, was cut with a square neck rather
than the standing collar that would have made it so like the clerical
garb he had put aside. The loosely woven linen had felt almost cool

70

against his skin when he put it on, though it was not cool just now, standing there in the sun, with the muffled bells of Saint Hilary's and the cathedral down below tolling out the passing of a king.

He tried to put the heat from his mind as a stir in the hall behind him presaged the approach of the cortege. Some of the courtiers in the hall swept down the steps ahead of it, murmuring among themselves and seeking shelter from the sun in the meager shade of walls, but silence breathed from the hall as the great processional cross from Rhemuth Cathedral emerged from the inner dimness.

It was borne by a crucifer in the full black habit and hooded scapular of the *Custodes Fidei*, the hood drawn up to obscure his face. Boy acolytes from the cathedral flanked him with processional torches, sweltering in cassocks and surplices, and a thurifer walked behind them, trailing a cloud of pungent incense smoke and contributing to everyone's discomfort.

Following them came Manfred MacInnis with the sheathed State Sword held before him, and Earl Tammaron with a crimson cushion bearing the State Crown of Gwynedd—the real one, not the scaled-down version they had made to crown a twelve-year-old king.

And behind the crown came Alroy himself, his bier borne on the shoulders of six of his knights, his pale, wasted body laid out with hands folded on the breast of a plain white robe like an alb—perhaps the very one he had worn for the anointing at his sacring. Covering him from the waist down, they had laid a pall of Haldane crimson worked with the royal arms, supple with silken embroidery and appliqué, spilling off the sides and end of the bier and over the shoulders of the knights at that end. Sir Gavin walked beside the bier, head bowed and sword grasped by the blade like a cross.

The two archbishops followed side by side carrying their croziers, both perspiring in heavy black copes and mitres. They paused as the knights carried Alroy down the steps to the castle yard, allowing Javan and Rhys Michael to join the procession directly behind the bier, as chief mourners. The Court began falling in behind the archbishops as the cortege started across the castle yard, silent but for the continued tolling of the bells.

The basilica was crowded and close, as Javan had known it would be, offering respite from the sun but not from the heat. He had known the service would be an ordeal; but the combination of too many candles, too much incense, and too many bodies confined in a space with too little ventilation far exceeded his expectations, especially when he must deal with his grief and the prospects in store for him at the Accession Council. Sweat plastered his tunic to his body and occasionally ran into his eyes, matting his hair to his skull, and the very air was thick and hard to breathe.

Mercifully, the next two hours passed mostly in a blur, as the tone-deaf Archbishop Oriss labored through the sung Requiem with a hastily assembled choir brought up from his cathedral, and Javan knelt dutifully with his remaining brother and their escort of knights at the very front of the basilica. Unremitting sunlight poured through the clerestory windows, raising the temperature in the crowded church and starkly illuminating the black-draped catafalque and its royal burden, paling the flames of the six massive candlesticks around it to insignificance. At the head of the catafalque, the State Crown rested on its crimson cushion in a particularly glaring ray of sunlight, the incense smoke twining among the crosses and leaves. Up on Alroy's body, though Javan could not see it from where he knelt, Earl Tammaron had laid the Great Sword of Gwynedd atop the Haldane pall, the hilt slipped under the dead king's folded hands.

Somehow Javan made it through the Mass. After, with his six escort knights in tow, he sought temporary refuge in Rhys Michael's rooms again, stripping off his tunic to let Charlan sponge him off with cool water and even dunking his head in a basin to cool it. Robear made him eat some bread and cheese and gnaw on a joint of roast capon—and he knew he needed sustenance before going down to face the Council—but he could not summon up much appetite. He did manage to fortify himself with a cup of ale, while he reviewed the list of knights Jason had summoned to the meeting ahead and Jason briefed him on essentials that must be covered. A brief summary of topics needing future investigation or legislation bore closer examination for the future.

When he had dressed again, suffering Charlan's brief ministrations with a comb, he let Rhys Michael set a coronet on his head that he had never worn before—a golden circlet hammered with a repoussé of running lions, their legs and tails intertwined. It had been Alroy's. He looked into the polished metal mirror that Charlan held before him, at the royal diadem set above stark raven hair and eyes that seemed to have gone almost colorless, then drew a deep breath and squared his shoulders.

"Does that look like a king to you?" he murmured to his brother.

Rhys Michael managed a taut smile and gave him a nod.

"Let's try it on the Council and see what they think."

A full two dozen knights in his Haldane livery were waiting for him and his party outside the doors to the Council chamber, all of them armed and battle-ready. Though he recognized one of Udaut's senior captains among them and apparently in charge, a full third of the men were among those who had accompanied him back from *Arx Fidei*. Standing to one side of them were a silver-haired stranger and the hook-nosed baron who had come to his defense outside Alroy's sickroom, both of them in black, both of them wearing swords and daggers. Among a handful of other knights behind them, who were not wearing livery, Javan noticed another man who looked to be a son or younger brother of the bold baron.

"The older man is Lord Jerowen Reynolds, Sire," Charlan murmured close beside his ear. "The baron is Etienne de Courcy, as you know. And that's his son toward the back—Sir Guiscard."

Javan nodded. "I may owe de Courcy my crown," he said under his breath, studying the man anew. "He's the lawyer?"

"Aye, my lord. So is Lord Jerowen. He and the de Courcys have been working on draft documents to support that summary you looked at while you ate."

Along with the other knights, Lord Jerowen and both de Courcys bowed as Javan drew abreast of them.

"Gentlemen," Javan said quietly, acknowledging their bows with a nod.

Before he could say anything further, Jason touched his elbow.

"We'd best go inside, my liege," he murmured. "You've made the Council cool their heels for nearly half an hour already."

Javan managed a wry grin. "If the process has brought them relief from the heat, then I've done them a favor, haven't I?" he murmured, heartened when most of his audience at least smiled and a few even chuckled. "But you're right. We should go in. Wish me luck, gentlemen."

The liveried knights drew back, for they would remain outside unless needed. At Charlan's signal, Tomais and Bertrand threw open the doors to the Council chamber. The room beyond *was* cooler, breathing a puff of breeze against Javan's face and neck as he started forward—or was it a shiver of apprehension? The low murmur of voices gave way immediately to the sound of chairs being pushed back, wood grating against stone, and the hollow scuff of shoes and boots knocking against chair legs, spurs and scabbards ringing against wood and stone.

Javan refused to let himself be intimidated as he stepped across the threshold. The room was familiar, paneled in golden oak, its vaulted ceiling plastered between the support beams and painted with a starry sky picked out in gilt. A series of deep windows along the left looked out on a vista of sunny garden, with the long table set parallel. To reach the head of the table, he must traverse the full length of the room.

Taking his time and hardly limping at all, Javan made his way deliberately between the table and the windows, so that his adversaries must view him against the glare. Benches had been set up against the long wall on the other side of the table, and most of his small party headed there, though Charlan and Jason followed directly behind him and Rhys Michael made for the chair at the foot of the table. Earl Tammaron and Archbishop Hubert had been sitting to either side of the high-backed chair with the Haldane arms painted on its back, and they bowed as Javan eased in front of it. The sheathed Sword of State lay on the table with its hilt pointed toward the chair: the sword that had been his father's—and his brother's—and was one of the symbols of Haldane sovereignty.

Javan touched the fingertips of his right hand to his lips, then to the crossing on the sword, where the hilt met the quillons. As he sat, gesturing for the rest to take their seats, he directed his gaze appraisingly across the men gathered 'round the table.

It was not as bad as he had feared. Neither Murdoch nor Rhun was here—the two men he had least been looking forward to dealing with. Archbishop Oriss and Lord Udaut were seated beyond Earl Tammaron, along the left side of the table. Rhys Michael was at the other end, with Manfred MacInnis at his right.

But between Manfred and Udaut was a man Javan had last seen more than three years ago, at the institution of the *Custodes Fidei*. Prior to that, "Brother Albertus" had been Peter Sinclair, Earl of Tarleton; but on that day, having resigned his earldom to his eldest son, he had become Grand Master of the *Equites Custodum Fidei*— the Knights of the Guardians of the Faith—a poor substitute for Lord Jebediah of Alcara, who had been Grand Master of the Michaelines.

And across from Albertus sat the man who was directly responsible for the *Custodes Fidei*, its knights, and indeed, most of the organized persecution of Deryni over the last five years: Paulin of Ramos, who had set aside a bishop's mitre to become Vicar General of the new Order, and who had been born a Sinclair, the younger brother of Albertus. Both were Tammaron's stepsons by his wife's first marriage, though nearly of his generation. Javan had no idea how close they were to their stepfather, but the brothers themselves were said to be thick as thieves. He felt a little sick to see them sitting here, for he had not realized that they were on Alroy's Council.

He glanced aside at Charlan, who was settling himself on a stool at Javan's right, as Jason scooted closer on the left and passed him a written agenda, which Javan laid on the table before him.

"I thank you for your prompt attendance, gentlemen," he said, looking down the table. "The Earl Marshal will please convene the Council."

He had expected Manfred to stand, for the marshal's ivory baton lay on the table before him, close by his right hand. But to Javan's dismay, it was Albertus who rose and took up the baton, shifting it from his left hand to his right to salute the king. Only then did Javan realize that Albertus wore his sword on his right and was left-handed. The *Custodes* Grand Master reminded Javan of a great, black bird of prey as he addressed the room in a soldier's voice.

"My lords, I call to order this first Council of Gwynedd following the death of our late beloved King Alroy Bearand Brion Haldane. Let Justice, tempered by Mercy, prevail in all our judgments. So be it."

"So be it," the others repeated as Albertus folded back into his seat.

It had *not* been the prescribed formula. And Albertus' careful wording to avoid mentioning Javan's name betokened a challenge that must be met and disarmed immediately, or all was lost.

"Lord Albertus," he said, though he raised his voice hardly at all, "I was under the impression that Lord Manfred MacInnis was still Earl Marshal of this kingdom. Furthermore, since this is an Accession Council, I believe it is customary to invoke the name of the present king as well as the late one. If I am mistaken in the first instance, pray, at least correct the second."

Slowly and deliberately Paulin, not Albertus, stood, deliberately directing his gaze toward Tammaron, seated at Javan's left. "My Lord Chancellor, until the matter of the succession is properly settled, Lord Albertus may not comply with Brother Javan's request, both of them being under vows of obedience to me."

Javan felt his jaw clench involuntarily. So *that* was how they were going to play it—invoking Tammaron's leadership for the moment and going back to the old question of Javan's "vows." Keeping his anger tightly in check, Javan leaned back in his chair and glanced at Tammaron, ready to Truth-Read what was being said.

"Tammaron, you will not answer him," he said. "Since Father Paulin was not present earlier today, he was not privy to the exchange in which the temporary nature of my vows was discussed. Such Holy Orders as I took are not an impediment to the crown— only to marriage. Such Orders can be dispensed, as was done for my late father. As for the vows I made with the *Custodes Fidei*, ask Archbishop Hubert whether I, at any time, indicated a desire or intention that any vows be permanent."

Bowing slightly from his place, Paulin smiled and gestured in the direction of a shadowed corner behind him, just inside the door.

"My wise and generous patron, the Archbishop-Primate of Gwynedd, need not exercise himself to answer this allegation," he said smoothly. "Anticipating such a change of heart, I have asked Father Marcus Concannon, our Chancellor General in charge of seminaries, to bring along the transcripts of all vows made by Brother Javan since his reception into the *Ordo Custodum Fidei*. Please refresh Brother Javan's memory, Father Marcus. I assure you, my lords, the vows *are* binding, both to celibacy and to withdrawal from the world—and crowns."

The black-robed priest who emerged from the shadows behind Paulin looked harmless enough, tonsured head bent humbly and eyes downcast as he shuffled behind Hubert to hand several sheets of vellum to Javan. But as Javan skimmed the text, appalled to read words he had never spoken, subtle changes that most people would not even notice, Jason was snapping his fingers toward the men seated on the benches against the wall.

"Jerowen, Etienne—"

The pair he summoned were the two who were trained in the law. Jerowen, the senior of them, also had written documents in hand, and came to spread them on the table beside the ones Javan was reading.

"I believe *these* are the vows you made, Sire," he murmured under his breath, pointing out differences. "You had friends present, who made transcripts immediately after the fact. By my honor I swear to you, *there was no possibility of error.*"

No possibility—

"What's that?" Hubert said, straining to hear, as Javan's mind raced over the implications—for unless the witness had been Deryni, or questioned afterward by a Deryni . . . *Was Jerowen Deryni?*

He kept his face expressionless as he tried to order his thoughts, keeping his eyes on the pages but questing out with his mind. No, Jerowen was not Deryni; or if he was, his shielding was very, *very* good.

But the very thought gave Javan an idea how to resolve this. For his Truth-Reading ability also told him that Jerowen was telling the truth and the sanctimonious Paulin of Ramos was not. He dared not reveal this himself, but there was a Deryni he could call upon who *could* expose the lie—or even simply threaten to expose it, at Javan's order—which, in this instance, was just as good.

"Sir Robear," he said quietly, beckoning the knight closer to whisper in his ear.

The knight listened to Javan's instruction, then nodded, expressionless, and went out. Javan, feigning far more confidence than he felt, returned to his comparison of the two sets of documents.

"These are very interesting, Father Paulin," he said, after deciding he would confront the issue directly by engaging the *Custodes* Vicar General's attention. "As Archbishop Hubert will surely confirm, I did a great deal of soul-searching and reflection before embarking upon the trial of a religious vocation. Even the decision of a trial was not lightly undertaken, far less the vows themselves. Is it conceivable that I would have taken such vows without being *precisely* aware of what I was swearing to, especially knowing that my brother was in poor health and might not live to beget an heir?"

Paulin gazed at him with haughty disdain. "You are your father's son, Brother Javan. The fire of vocation burned strong in him."

"Yet he left his beloved priesthood when royal duty called," Javan pointed out.

"Because there was none other to take up that duty!" Paulin retorted. "*You* have another brother."

"Ask him, then, whether I had any intention of stepping aside for him—or he, of superseding me."

Before Rhys Michael could reply, or Paulin could ask him to, the doors at the other end of the room parted to readmit Robear, one hand firmly on the elbow of a reluctant and frightened-looking Oriel.

"Now, see here," Hubert began as Robear marched the Healer along the window side of the room toward the chairs where archbishop and king sat. "Master Oriel is in the employ of myself and Earl Tammaron—"

"His services are required for the common good," Javan replied, sending his instructions to Oriel in a tightly focused burst. "In fact, I may second him to my own service. He *has* been performing the office of royal Healer for some years now. Or do you object, Archbishop? Earl Tammaron?"

Not giving them the chance to interrupt him, he went on. "In any case, for now, it's the truth I mean to get at—nothing more. Father Paulin has questioned my recollection of what vows I made. If a king cannot be trusted to remember what he has promised, and to whom, then he is not fit to be king. Master Oriel, stand here at my right, where Father Marcus and I both can see you, and tell me if he deviates from the truth."

He picked up the sheets of vellum Father Marcus had brought

and hefted them in his hand, looking directly at the now uneasy-looking priest.

"Are these accurate transcriptions of vows I made, Father?" he said. "Before you answer, bear in mind that Master Oriel will know if you are lying and will reveal that lie—for those are the terms of oaths *he* has sworn."

Father Marcus had gone a little pale as Javan spoke, and he glanced nervously at Oriel and then at Paulin before replying.

"I—did not actually make those transcriptions, my lord," he whispered.

Clever man, Javan thought, as he glanced at Oriel and the Healer gave a faint nod. *He knows the limitations of Truth-Reading and how to avoid the direct lie. Let's see if we can get around that.*

"Who did make the transcriptions?" Javan asked.

The priest looked distinctly uncomfortable. "I—imagine that someone who was present must have made them, my lord."

Javan's eyes narrowed. The statement obviously was true, but told him nothing. "Then, who gave you the transcriptions, Father?"

"I—believe they came from the Chancery Office, my lord." Again, the priest had avoided the direct answer that might have perjured him.

"The Chancery Office of your Order?" Javan said patiently.

"Yes, my lord."

"And do you know from *whom* in the Chancery Office? Don't give me a name at this point," he added. "I just want to know if you know."

Defeated, eyes downcast, the priest murmured, "Yes, my lord."

Allowing himself a slight nod, Javan prepared to follow up the advantage.

"Very good. Now, *who* sent you the transcriptions?" he asked, though by now he was almost certain of the answer.

"I—would rather not answer that, my lord."

"No, I'm sure you'd rather not," Javan murmured. "Shall I ask your superior to order you to answer, then, Father?" He swung his gaze at last to Paulin, simmering in his chair near the other end of the table. "Or would that perjure both of you?"

A low gasp murmured through the room, but Javan went on. "How say you, my Lord Vicar General? *You* were present on every occasion when I made vows. Was it you who sent the transcriptions to Father Marcus and ordered him to present them as authentic?"

"You may not ask that question," Paulin muttered.

"Ah, but I *may*," Javan said. "And what can have been your motive? You obviously have been at great pains to keep me from my throne. Do you think my brother more biddable, that you could sway him more easily than I, especially out of gratitude for giving him a crown?"

"You may not require me to answer those questions," Paulin said, his voice deadly low.

"And *you* have not the authority to tell me what I may or may not ask a subject!" Javan stabbed a trembling forefinger at the vellum pages. "You have prepared, or caused to be prepared, false documentation, in an attempt to render me ineligible for the crown. I swear before almighty God and this assembled company that those are not the vows I made."

Coming to his feet, he seized the Haldane sword and drew it from its sheath, handing off the latter to Jason as he kissed the joining of blade and hilt, which contained a holy relic, then reversed it to hold the weapon before him by the blade, like a cross.

"By this sword which was my father's, and then my brother's, by all the line of Haldane kings who have gone before me, by all that I hold sacred—I swear to you that my intention is and has always been to take up my royal and sacred birthright, if my brother Alroy died without issue.

"What I have done regarding the *Ordo Custodum Fidei*, I have done to gain respite from those who would have seen me put aside while still of tender years—and so that I might acquire the learning that befits a king. Thus did I prepare myself both to rule, if called to take up the Crown, or to aid my brother, if he, in fact, survived. I freely confess that I did this under false pretenses, without any conviction that I had a genuine religious vocation—but that is a matter between me and my confessor, and not a subject for this Council. I am willing to comply with whatever administrative procedure my Lord Archbishop may deem necessary to dispense me from my clerical state, that I may eventually take up my dynastic duty to secure the succession"—he glanced pointedly at Hubert—"but I stand before you as your lawful king!"

He spiked the point of the sword hard against the tabletop for emphasis and felt it bite into the wood—and into the fingers of his right hand as it slid a little in his grasp. "Those unwilling to acknowledge that fact have my leave to depart, both from this chamber and from this realm!"

"Well said!" Rhys Michael blurted, springing to his feet as Jason raised a clenched fist and shouted, "God save King Javan!"

The cry was taken up at once by Charlan, Jerowen, and Etienne de Courcy, and then by the knights listening from the benches along the wall—Robear, Bertrand, and Tomais—who shot to their feet in fervent support.

Constable Udaut rose as well, pounding the flat of his hand

against the table in acclamation—the only member of the Council Javan had known he could count on—followed reluctantly by Tammaron, Archbishop Oriss, and then even Manfred. Hubert lumbered to his feet as well, followed most reluctantly by the hitherto silent Lord Albertus, who could not have been too comfortable with so many armed and enthusiastic knights at his back. Paulin finally stood, too, but his face was a mask of cold resentment.

Javan's heart was pounding as the acclaim died away. As he unclenched his fingers from around the blade of the Haldane sword and made to lower it, he saw blood on his right hand, as he had known he would. His fingers stung as he tentatively straightened them, but fortunately the cuts did not look too bad. Already feeling light-headed from the emotion of the past minutes, he made himself lay the sword quietly back on the table, accepting the handkerchief Robear passed him quite nonchalantly. Even then, he used it to wipe off the blade before casually twisting it around his wounded hand, aware that he could ask Oriel to Heal it but knowing that the Deryni element he himself had introduced must be minimized, now that the immediate crisis seemed past.

"Please be seated, gentlemen," he said, himself easing back into his chair.

CHAPTER EIGHT

Righteous lips are the delight of kings; and they
love him that speaketh right.

Proverbs 16:13

The meeting that followed was an anticlimax, after its stormy beginning. While Paulin stewed, Albertus coldly reconvened the Council by the proper formula, acknowledging Javan as king, and all the members of the Council present tendered their resignations as was customary—which resignations Javan neither accepted nor declined for the moment, though he longed to dismiss Paulin and Albertus then and there, preferably into the hands of an executioner, not that he dared to do so.

As for the rest, he knew he was stuck with some of them, at least. The two archbishops held their seats by right of their ecclesiastical offices, so they could not be dismissed. Hubert, though personally despicable, might be controllable in the long term. Oriss pretty much did as he was told, by whomever was in power.

Javan also meant to retain Tammaron and even Manfred, at least for the present, for they had useful skills in governing and had shown themselves able to adapt to Javan's change of their plans with at least a little grace. Besides that, Tammaron generally had been kind to Javan and his brothers, even when Rhun and Murdoch were at their worst; and Manfred had proven himself a reasonably able Earl Marshal—though Javan would want to find out whether any other reason lay behind his replacement by Albertus, other than the clergy contingent of the Council wanting that office in the hands of one of their own.

A more promising retention was Lord Udaut, who had already

81

demonstrated his loyalty. He was able and innocuous, rarely caus-
ing controversy, and had served as constable under Javan's father as
well as under Alroy. And of course Rhys Michael would stay—
automatically entitled to a seat as the heir presumptive and being
now of age to sit in his own right.

That left five Council lords still to be reckoned with, who had
not yet arrived in Rhemuth. Baron Hildred would present no difficulties—a bandy-legged little man far more interested in horses than
in politics, a friend in the past and hopefully to continue as such
in the future.

Nor was Fane Fitz-Arthur likely to cause any trouble. He was
Tammaron's son and heir, but he also had made a brilliant political
marriage with the heiress of Cassan and was only rarely seen at
Court. Under the terms of Prince Ambert Quinnell's original set-
tlement before the marriage, Cassan was to become a duchy under
Gwynedd upon the death of its last prince, with Fane and the Princess Anne to become duke and duchess. A codicil added three years
ago, after the birth of Anne's first son, had shifted the ducal succession directly to the boy they christened Tambert, for his two
grandfathers. Technically, Fane and the boy's mother would become co-regents until Tambert came of age, but in fact Fane would
wield a duke's power during his son's minority. It was almost as
good as being regent for a king.

On a smaller scale, Lord Bonner Sinclair was similarly occupied
with his own affairs, now that he was Earl of Tarleton—though he
would support his father, now known as Lord Albertus, if things
got really bad.

That accounted for everyone except the two *Custodes* men and
Rhun and Murdoch. Javan did not want to end up with any of them
on his Council, though he supposed he could live with Paulin and
Albertus for a time, if he must, judging it better to have them where
he knew what they were doing rather than off plotting and schem-
ing behind his back. They might do that anyway, once they realized
he planned to begin reversing the legislation against Deryni, but at
least he had a better chance of thwarting them if he kept them
under observation. Rhun and Murdoch were an altogether different
proposition, and very dangerous.

Still, that left Javan room for half a dozen appointments of his
own choice—though he must speak with the men in private and
sound them out before making any final decisions. So once he had
established his authority—and released Oriel to return to his duties,
for he knew the old guard would chafe at the continued presence
of a Deryni, with its potential unmasking of the social and diplomatic lies that made a meeting like this at least seem to run

smoothly—he kept the remainder of that first Council meeting short.

The only other matter of immediate urgency was to agree on details of the state funeral on Monday. Alroy's death had not been sudden or unexpected, so much of the general planning was already in place—and Alroy himself had confided certain wishes to Rhys Michael, which Javan stated flatly would be carried out as the late king his brother had wished. Javan managed not to let himself get too caught up in the discussion, or to let Rhys Michael get too upset, so it was the work of less than an hour to resolve the remaining agenda. He flatly refused to discuss even the date of his coronation until the next meeting, which he set for the following Tuesday.

"I must bury my brother first," he told them when Oriss pressed him. "Can you not grant me that, at least?"

It was a tense moment, in which he found himself very close to tears, but Oriss backed down and no one else chose to pursue the issue.

"I thank you, then, for your attendance, gentlemen," he said briskly, hoping he could now make his escape. "I trust you will excuse me if I do not dine with the court this evening, but the day has been long. Anyone desiring to speak with me tomorrow may request an appointment through Sir Jason."

He returned the Haldane sword to its sheath as he stood, aware of them scrambling uncertainly to their feet, and gave them a nod of acknowledgment before retiring with his supporters, the sheathed sword carried casually at his side. The sun was sinking low in the western sky as he made his way this time to Alroy's former apartments, now made ready for his occupancy, where Charlan had arranged for a light supper to be laid in the little presence chamber adjoining the royal bedroom. The room soon became crowded and was still very warm, but no one seemed to mind.

Nor did anyone seem to be particularly interested in eating. A fair amount of wine was consumed, but no one got even mildly inebriated. Without any apparent discussion beforehand, those present made of the gathering an impromptu working session, each man taking a few minutes to introduce himself to the new king, if not already known, and acquaint him with particular talents and resources and family connections that might be especially useful. Javan had Charlan take careful notes, for he knew that the last twenty-four hours were starting to catch up with him. Oriel came to tend his wounded hand at one point, but did nothing to alleviate his drowsiness this time.

"I wouldn't try to stay awake too late, Sire," he said as he pushed aside the basin in which he had washed out the cuts before healing them. "A good night's rest is what you need most. Have them come back in the morning, when you've slept."

The admonition was hardly necessary, for Javan was tiring fast. When Oriel had gone, he picked at some cheese and fruit and drank some well-watered wine, which helped a little, but his yawns were becoming wider and closer together, however hard he tried to stifle them. Still, he managed to learn a fair amount about some of the men who were staking so much on his cause.

Lord Jerowen Reynolds and Baron Etienne de Courcy he found of particular interest, the better he got to know them, and decided then and there that he would have them on his Council. A little later, when Robear began shooing everyone out so the new king could get some sleep, de Courcy lingered for a private word.

"I'll ask only a moment of your time, my liege," he said as the others filtered past him to go their separate ways. "I know you must be exhausted after the day you've had, but it's rather important—and confidential."

Making little attempt to cover another yawn—*everyone* thought that what he had to say was important—Javan took up a candlestick from among several on the mantel and resignedly drew the baron back into the relative privacy of the bedroom, though he left the door open.

"You can see the state I'm in, my lord, so I trust that this *is* important."

The baron smiled, dark eyes hawk-fierce above the aquiline nose. "You are my rightful king, my liege," he murmured. "I and my family wish only to serve you as honestly and as fully as we may."

Javan nodded politely around another yawn and set the candlestick on a small table, wishing Etienne would get to the point. Though his sleepiness was the honest fatigue of an intense day, not the urgent winding down of a fatigue-banishing spell, the end effect was much the same: Bed was calling.

"That is why I come to you with this information, my prince," the baron went on, taking Javan's left hand in his and cupping the other over the Ring of Fire, looking Javan in the eyes. "Sometime tomorrow, I hope—I cannot tell you just when—my son Guiscard will endeavor to bring you a message I believe you are eagerly awaiting—though you may not yet have realized that such a message was possible and so quickly."

Suddenly Javan felt a surge against his shields—not an assault, but an enfolding—the brief feather-touch of another mind on his. As he gasped and started back, instantly wide awake, staring at Etienne in some surprise, the older man smiled faintly and clasped his hands more firmly around Javan's.

"You are in no danger, my prince."

"But—who sent you?" Javan demanded, daring a tentative probe and encountering close-shuttered Deryni shields. "Was it—"

"No names just now, Sire," Etienne murmured, shaking his head, "but Read the truth of what I say. *I know that you can do this.* I am your man to command. I will lay down my life for you if need be—and more, if I must. My son will do the same; you may call upon either of us to do whatever you need done. At this time I ask only that when Guiscard requests an audience, no matter when that might be, you leave instructions to admit him—and listen to what he has to say. It will be well worth your while."

Every word was true. Javan knew that as surely as he knew that he had the ability to discern such truth. And Etienne de Courcy was Deryni—though how a baron had managed to keep that fact a secret, Javan had no idea.

"Your—son will come to me?" Javan murmured numbly, searching Etienne's eyes.

"Aye, my liege. Guiscard." Etienne bent to kiss the hand he held. "Now may God grant you restful sleep, my prince. If you have need of me during the night, you have only to send for me. Sir Charlan knows where I am lodged."

With that he was drawing back to bow, turning to leave. A host of unanswered questions churned in Javan's mind as he watched him go, and he flinched when Rhys Michael came up to him and touched his shoulder in concern.

"Is anything wrong?" Rhys Michael asked, glancing worriedly after the departing back of Etienne de Courcy as he disappeared through the outer door.

"No, nothing's wrong," Javan murmured. "I'm tired, is all."

"What did de Courcy want?"

"Oh, just to assure me again of his loyalty," Javan said vaguely, breaking into another gigantic yawn that he almost feared would dislocate his jaw. "Sweet *Jesu,*" he murmured when he could see properly again. "If I don't get into that bed soon, someone is going to have to carry me there."

Rubbing at his eyes and fighting back a wave of impending sleep, he limped and stumbled over to the great, canopied bed and climbed up on it. Rhys Michael came with him, lending a hand when Javan bent to begin unbuckling his boots.

"Who's staying here tonight, do you know?" Javan asked as he let one boot fall to the floor with a thud.

"Charlan and Bertrand, at least," Rhys Michael replied. "And probably either Jason or Robear. Do you want me to stay as well?"

Javan tried to unbuckle his belt and think about it at the same time, but could not seem to make either brain or fingers engage properly.

"I'm not sure whether that's a good or a bad idea," he said around another yawn as Rhys Michael tugged off the other boot. "I annoyed some powerful men today. If someone decided to be rid of the annoyance, I'm not sure this is a good place to be. On the other hand, maybe they wouldn't try, if you're here. Do you want to stay?"

Rhys Michael nodded, the whites of his eyes glinting in the candlelight. "I'm scared, Javan. There's so much going on. I really don't know whether this is going to work or not. But I *don't* want to sleep by myself tonight."

"Come on up then, little brother," Javan said with a smile, patting the bed beside him. "I don't think I particularly want to sleep by myself either."

When Charlan came in a few minutes later to turn back the bed, he found them both fast asleep already, Javan sprawled full length on his back, looking more unconscious than merely asleep, and Rhys Michael scrunched up in a ball close by his side, with his face half buried in the crook of an arm.

Shaking his head and smiling, Charlan beckoned for Bertrand to fetch in a pallet, himself bringing the Haldane sword to lay across the pegs at the head of the bed where it customarily lay while the king slept. The doors to the balcony were open to admit what breeze there was, and Bertrand unrolled his pallet across the opening; Jason was arranging another in the adjacent presence chamber, and Robear had already taken up a post outside the outer door.

With this assurance that a proper guard had been mounted, Charlan closed the door between the two rooms and set a chair against it, moving then to the balcony doors, where Bertrand was preparing to lie down, naked sword on the floor beside his pallet. Bertrand said, "You don't mind taking the first watch?"

Charlan shook his head. "I used to keep vigil with him in the chapel, when I was his squire," he said, glancing back at the bed where the two brothers slept. "Sometimes I dozed off; sometimes *he* dozed off; sometimes we both did. I won't doze off tonight, though, I promise you."

Bertrand chuckled softly. "He hadn't yet gotten to his pious phase when *I* was his squire. I guess you didn't realize it was all an act, at the time."

"I'm not sure it was," Charlan said thoughtfully. "Not entirely, at any rate. But I'll certainly grant you that at least part of it was in aid of a rather shrewd plan for survival. Where better to spend these last few years than in the safety of a cloister? He's also gotten himself quite an education—in more ways than just from books."

"Hmmm, I suppose he has," Bertrand replied. "I have to say, *I* wouldn't have had the guts to do what he's done—especially not starting at thirteen. He may turn out to be a rather impressive king."

"Aye, he may that," Charlan murmured. "But you'd better get some sleep. I'll wake you in a few hours."

Grunting amused acquiescence, Bertrand lay back and closed his eyes, and was snoring softly by the time Charlan had extinguished all but two of the candles in the room and tiptoed back to take up his post in the chair against the door.

Elsewhere in Rhemuth Castle, in the quarters allocated to Earl Manfred MacInnis when he was in residence, reaction to the day's events had not yet yielded to sleep.

"Udaut has always been a king's man, whoever the king," Earl Tammaron was saying to the other five men crowded into Manfred's solar. Udaut was not among them. "I wasn't really surprised that he went over to Javan. I *was* surprised to see how quickly Javan managed to rally so many of the younger knights to his support. If the boy had really gotten the bit in his teeth, we all could have ended up in custody or worse."

"No one expected him to take such initiative so quickly," Paulin replied. "I confess, it had not occurred to me that he would force the issue of his vows so soon, by bringing in Master Oriel."

"Yes, it does bode ill that his first thought was to summon Deryni assistance when challenged," Hubert said thoughtfully. "He's repeatedly denied ongoing contact with any of the Deryni who used to be his associates, but that may have been as false as his apparent willingness to embrace the religious life. The last two days have proven how wrong I was about *that*."

"Recriminations serve no purpose," Paulin said.

"No, but I fear that my misjudgment of the situation may have complicated the problem beyond what some of these gentlemen are aware," Hubert went on. "For the last three years, we have allowed him to steep himself in the most rigorous intellectual and spiritual discipline we could devise, in hopes that academic challenge and the habits of monastic obedience might permanently wean him away from thoughts of secular involvement. Unfortunately, the same discipline that encourages strong spiritual formation can also encourage the kind of independent thinking that will make him dangerous as king. It was a gamble that seemed reasonable at the time—and might have worked, if Alroy had lived longer."

"Well, he didn't," Paulin said, ever practical. "And in letter of the law, no matter how much we might wish otherwise, Javan *is* the rightful heir. We can work with that for now, while other plans go forward. The formalities of his brother's funeral will occupy much of his attention for the next few days. While he is thus focused, we must make it our business to learn as much as we can of his intentions, his methods, his strengths and weaknesses."

"Well, youth and lack of practical experience should hamper him," Oriss observed. "Intellectually, he may well prove a formidable adversary—as we saw this afternoon—but if it comes to a physical confrontation, he's still only sixteen."

"I've known some reasonably formidable sixteen-year-olds," Manfred muttered. "That array he'd gathered outside the Council chamber today was no mean accomplishment for someone who's been away from Court for three years."

"Yes, and they're mostly under thirty and unseasoned," Albertus said dismissively. "Fortunately for us, this kingdom hasn't had a war recently enough to train up the young ones. He has a few men who know what they're doing—Udaut himself and some of his senior captains, and Sir Jason and Sir Robear—but their numbers are small and their experience somewhat limited."

"As is Javan's," Hubert interjected. "Three years behind a cloister wall may inadvertently have given him the academic preparation for rule, but at least it's kept him from the physical exercise and training that might have made a warrior of another sixteen-year-old. In a word, he is soft; and his clubfoot will continue to be a handicap."

Some of the others nodded and murmured among themselves, but Tammaron muttered, "Don't count on it."

"What was that?" Archbishop Oriss asked.

"I said, 'Don't count on the foot slowing him down much,'" Tammaron repeated, sweeping them with his eyes. "He wasn't limping nearly as much as I expected, even after the hard ride from *Arx Fidei*. In the old days, that could have laid him up for days, even with a Healer's attention. The cloister factor may not be that important."

"Limping less still won't give him the martial training that would make him a real physical threat," Albertus pointed out.

"No, but it was mainly his lack of mobility that ever held him back, when he was still in training," Manfred replied. "Remember that Murdoch and I used to help supervise the princes' training. On horseback—and he's a bold, natural rider—his bladework was more than competent, considering his age—and that was three years ago. He also was better with a bow at thirteen than most of us are *ever* likely to be, whether mounted or on foot."

Albertus snorted. "I'll concede his horsemanship. And obviously he's going to be better at all the martial forms as a man than he was as a boy, once he gets back into training. I still don't see him personally leading any armed movement against us in the very near future. Nor does a bow offer much protection from an enemy who strikes at close quarters, or from behind."

"Here, now!" Tammaron said. "I'll hear none of that. He's the king."

"He is also shaping up to be a very difficult king," Hubert said testily. "But let's not be hasty, gentlemen. Lord Albertus, I'll thank you to restrain such comments in future. Javan *is* the king and he may wake up to the realities of his situation. Things may not be as bad as we fear. Meanwhile, I suggest that all of us might do well to get some sleep. Keeping up with this particular sixteen-year-old may prove far more taxing than it was to keep up with his brother."

But when Oriss and then Tammaron had taken their leave, Hubert gestured for the two *Custodes* to remain. Paulin cast the archbishop a look of puzzled query as Manfred closed and bolted the door.

"There is one other thing of which I wished you and Lord Albertus to be aware," Hubert said quietly, gesturing them back into the room. "Call it a contingency plan."

"What sort of a contingency plan?" Paulin asked, exchanging a glance with his brother Albertus.

"Well, it has occurred to me that if we can't control the new king, perhaps the *next* king will prove more biddable."

"I mean no disrespect, Archbishop," Albertus said, "but I hardly think that allowing Rhys Michael to send for Javan was an impressive demonstration of anyone's ability to control him."

"I grant you that," Hubert said lightly, folding sweaty hands across his ample girth. "So we'll control his son—his *future* son," he amended, at their looks of astonishment and disbelief.

"I confide to you the secrets of the confessional, dear brothers," he went on. "Of late, our redoubtable Prince Rhys Michael Haldane has begun to suffer the first agonized stirrings of adolescent passion. The object of his intense infatuation is none other than my brother's delectable young ward, the Lady Michaela Drummond."

Albertus pursed his lips in an almost soundless whistle and glanced at Manfred, obviously aware of the implications of such a match, but Paulin only shook his head.

"Javan would never approve," he said flatly.

"With luck, Javan will never know until it's too late," Hubert replied. "I've been encouraging the match for more than six months now. Court mourning will put a temporary damper on the actual courtship, but I hope it will also discourage the prince from approaching his brother on the subject of marriage, at least for a while. I've—ah—suggested to Rhys Michael that the idea might not be too well received, that Javan's cloistered life may not have given him an appreciation or understanding of things of the flesh. He might even resent that while he was constrained behind cloister walls, his younger brother has been free to pursue the normal passionate awakenings of young manhood."

Paulin was shaking his head and smiling. "You've coupled all the insecurities of adolescent longing with all the old assumptions that laymen often make about monastic celibacy, when they don't really understand what it's all about."

"Well, Rhys Michael is a layman," Hubert said brightly. "If it keeps him from saying anything to Javan until the subject *can't* be avoided any longer—" He shrugged and smiled. "And under the circumstances, I suspect that neither you nor I would have any qualms about solemnizing royal marriage vows *after* the desired blessed event is on its way."

"He won't be fifteen until September," Albertus pointed out, "and the prospective bride is even younger, I believe. We may have a bit of a wait."

"Aye, but not *too* long," Hubert replied with a chuckle. "They're both healthy youngsters, and I don't think our prince will be found wanting in enthusiasm. He burns for her. He's told me so. He can hardly keep his hands off her—and as a priest, I confess that I have been less than conscientious in insisting that he subdue these temptations of the flesh. May I dare to hope that you will give me absolution, Father Paulin?"

His droll glance in the direction of the *Custodes* Vicar General produced an answering smile.

"*Ego te absolvo,*" Paulin replied.

Albertus snorted and folded his arms across his chest. "I just hope you can pull this off before Javan finds out. You may have convinced Rhys Michael that it's 'better to marry than to burn,' but Javan will be well aware of the implications, once either of them produces an heir."

"So we must keep Javan preoccupied with other matters, until the question becomes academic," Hubert replied. "It's doubtful that anything will happen to prevent him being crowned. It's equally doubtful that he will allow himself to be guided by the wise counsel of his lords of state.

"I hope I'm wrong. I was fond of the boy; I suppose I still am. But if I'm right, then our contingency plan must be to see that one of the princes—preferably Rhys Michael—produces an heir as quickly as possible. Once the succession is secured—well, accidents do happen to impetuous young men, and crowns sometimes pass unexpectedly to infant heirs, who of course must be guided in their immaturity by experienced regents."

He allowed himself a prim smile, his rosebud lips quirking up at the corners in a sly smirk, and as he cast his mild blue gaze over his listeners, the smile slowly was taken up by all three.

CHAPTER NINE

A prudent man concealeth knowledge.

Proverbs 12:23

The heat woke Javan at midmorning on Saturday, several hours later than he had expected. He was sweating, his tunic clammy against his skin, and his hair was matted to his scalp. His breeches were compressing a very full bladder. Rhys Michael was gone from the bed, but the door to the presence chamber was standing ajar, and Javan could hear voices outside, trying to be quiet.

He rolled onto his back and looked around the room. The underside of the canopy above the bed was of pale-yellow Forcinn silk shot with gold, and the heavy hangings tied back to either side were a patterned crimson damask, lined with the same gold-shot yellow. An almost life-size Haldane lion was carved in high relief at the head of the bed, the pegs that supported the Haldane sword set so that it appeared the lion was holding it. He reached up and took the sword by its scabbard, bringing it down into the bed with him to cradle the cross-hilt against one cheek. The metal was only faintly cool against his skin.

I really am king, he thought, one thumb caressing the metalwork at the throat of the scabbard. *And what happens now? Father, what did you do to your sons, that night you died? What did you do to me? I need help. I need to know what to do. Joram's the only one left who was there. I need to see—*

He froze, suddenly remembering the conversation he had had with Etienne de Courcy the night before—Etienne de Courcy, who was Deryni.

His son is supposed to bring me a message! he thought. *That means the son is Deryni, too. Could he be my contact with Joram? Is that how I'm supposed to sort everything out?*

Galvanized into activity by that thought, he sat up and twisted around to put the sword back on its pegs, then inch-wormed himself over to the edge of the bed and off, favoring his lame foot as he got his feet under him. After stripping off his sweaty tunic and tossing it across the foot of the bed, he padded over to the garderobe to relieve himself, then headed for the outer room. Rhys Michael was nowhere to be seen, but Bertrand and Charlan looked up from the remnants of a hearty breakfast at one end of the table, and Robear and Jason were huddled over several stacks of papers with Jerowen Reynolds and Etienne de Courcy at the other end, Etienne making notations on another page. All of them came to their feet as Javan appeared in the doorway.

"Good morning, Sire," Robear said. "I hope you slept well."

"Thank you, I did," Javan replied, suddenly a little awkward to be the center of their obvious respect. "The heat woke me up. Where's Rhys Michael?"

"He's gone back to his own apartments to bathe and change," Charlan said. "I've had a bath brought for you," he added, gesturing toward a tub set in the window embrasure. "It should be about comfortable by now. I didn't think you'd want it too hot."

"I see. Thank you. Ah, has anyone asked to see me?" he said, chancing a glance at Etienne.

Etienne gave a minute shake of his head as Jason said, "No, Sire. We've been refining some of the documents you glanced at yesterday. We have a draft list of proposed appointments to the Council, whenever you're ready to look at it.

"But bathe and get dressed first and have something to eat," Jason went on. "I'd say that your only obligation today, other than in this room, is to pay a visit to your brother down in the basilica. And I'd recommend waiting until tonight for that, when it's cooler."

"Yes, I'll do that," Javan murmured, going over to cut himself a chunk of cheese.

Later, when he had bathed and dressed and filled a suddenly gnawing emptiness in his stomach, he settled down dutifully to read what they had written, asking questions, making suggestions, and fretting inwardly as the hours crawled by. Callers came and went, mostly from among the knights who had escorted him back from *Arx Fidei*, but not the one Javan was waiting for. It was not until midafternoon that Bertrand's summons to the door revealed the hook-nosed visage of Guiscard de Courcy.

Javan watched him as he came into the room and went to his father, bending to murmur something in the older man's ear. Javan affected to still be reading what was in his hands. After a moment, Etienne glanced at him and rose, Guiscard also straightening.

"Sire, might I have a word with you in private?" Etienne said.

"Of course."

Laying aside his papers, Javan rose and led the way into the sleeping chamber, Etienne and his son following. Etienne closed the door behind them, gesturing for all of them to move into the doorway leading onto the balcony.

"Sire, this is Sir Guiscard de Courcy, my son," Etienne said softly. "I don't believe you've formally met."

"My liege," Guiscard murmured.

He looked to be in his early thirties, perhaps a little younger, dark of hair and eye like his father but with the hook nose slightly softened in the son. Javan could not take his eyes off him.

"You have a message for me?" he whispered.

Guiscard made him a little bow, regarding him as well with a hawklike intensity. "Aye, Sire. Tonight, while the castle sleeps, I am to take you to the basilica, to the little study off the sacristy, where you used to go for tutoring from Father Boniface. I'm afraid Father Boniface has died while you were away, but I've already ensured that the new man will give us no trouble. Once we have reached there in safety, I'm to take you to a friend."

"Father Joram?"

"Aye."

Javan had not realized he was holding his breath as Guiscard spoke, and he let it out with a soft sigh, moving out onto the balcony to rest both hands against the stone railing. He had to wonder how much Guiscard and his father knew about him—though if Joram had entrusted the de Courcys to infiltrate the court and Guiscard to bring him, then they must be trustworthy. At very least, they knew he could Truth-Read—and that he had shields and could detect pressure against them.

"How do you plan to arrange things for tonight?" he asked, looking out over the heat shimmer that lay across the city.

Guiscard came to stand closer beside him, leaving his father to block the doorway, in case anyone should come into the sleeping chamber.

"It's appropriate for you to go to the basilica tonight to pay your respects to your brother," Guiscard said quietly. "I shall accompany you. I've arranged for my father to be part of the vigil guard at that hour. He'll be available to help create a diversion, if that's necessary. Do you agree?''

A thunderstorm broke the heatwave later that afternoon, darkening the sky several hours earlier than usual and splitting the heavens with thunder, lightning, and heavy rain. After so long a dry spell, it was respite of a sort, but the humidity soared in response to the downpour. The rain let up for a few hours after sunset, but started up again shortly before Javan made ready to go down to the basilica.

No breeze stirred the gently falling rain, and the air was very heavy and close, but at least the temperature seemed to have dropped a little. It was still too warm for the disguising cloaks Guiscard would have preferred they wear for the night's foray, but the black of their mourning attire would help to keep them unobtrusive.

Javan also had suggested that adding a second attendant would arouse less notice than if he went only with Guiscard, whom he barely knew, so Charlan accompanied them. The young knight's memory could be blurred later, if necessary. Javan had told Guiscard of the controls set in Charlan, but not of their origin. Let the Deryni assume that Joram or one of the others had set those controls; he did not know how much he was supposed to reveal, even to a Deryni apparently sent by Joram.

They made no secret of their trip to the basilica, for as Guiscard had pointed out, no one would think it odd if the king went late at night to pay his respects to his brother, after the crowds had gone and it was cooler. The three of them entered through the main door and passed quietly down the side aisle to kneel just back from the catafalque on the left. By the unsteady light of the tall funeral brands set three on each side of the bier, Javan could just make out the form of Etienne de Courcy among the four knights standing silent vigil there, their backs to the bier, bare heads bowed over greatswords, hands resting motionless on the quillons. The men wore surcoats of the Haldane livery over their black mourning attire, drabbed by wide black sashes swathed across their chests like baldrics.

Of Alroy himself, Javan preferred not to think too much. That was not his brother up there anyway. A sheer veil of black samite now draped the body from head to toe, spilling over the crimson pall and deepening the shadows cast by the candlelight. It made Alroy seem smaller. It also softened the very real visual signs of morbidity setting in, though even the lingering perfume of incense smoke could not wholly mask the faint whiff of decay.

Javan did not stay long, though he made himself go up to the bier and touch his hand to the folded ones under the veil in a final farewell. Alroy would be coffined tomorrow for his final journey down to the cathedral, and Javan would not look upon his twin again.

He was much subdued as they slipped back out the rear doors, but forced his thoughts from the past to the here and now as he and Guiscard and Charlan flattened themselves into the shadows outside and kept silent for several minutes, to be certain they had not been observed. He had resurrected Charlan's old controls as they knelt side by side in the basilica, so that the young knight did not question what they did now.

At Guiscard's eventual signal, Javan drew Charlan with him along the shadows masking the basilica's north side until they came to a slype passage leading around to the east end of the building. The little door there was unlocked, and they passed quietly inside, waiting as Guiscard glided on ahead past the sacristy to disappear through a familiar door. A few minutes later Guiscard poked his head out to beckon them inside.

The little study was much as Javan remembered it, except that Father Boniface's tilted scrivening table was gone and the man lying on the pallet that had taken its place was not Father Boniface. He wore the habit of the *Custodes Fidei*, and Guiscard, after closing and latching the door behind them, went and knelt down beside the man again, laying one hand across the eyes.

"His name is Father Ascelin," Guiscard said. "He's one of the more bastardly of this *Custodes* lot—attached to the office of the Inquisitor General. I'd love to put him to sleep for good, but that might raise suspicion where there isn't any, so far."

Javan swallowed and came closer. It had never occurred to him that a Deryni might actually be able to do that. The thought was sobering. Fortunately, Guiscard mistook his contemplation for squeamishness and gave him a reassuring smile as he rose from his now deeply sleeping subject.

"Don't worry," he said. "It's only a temptation; I'd never do it— not to a helpless man while he slept."

Without warning, his hand shot out to grasp Charlan's wrist, at the same time seizing control. It was not like when Javan had done it in the past. Charlan's knees buckled and he started to collapse, eyes rolling up until only the whites showed, fully conscious one second and profoundly unconscious the next. Between them, Javan and Guiscard caught him and eased him to a sitting position on a stool set close beside the darkened hearth, where he could not be seen easily from the door. Javan was surprised and a little resentful of the Deryni's rather high-handed treatment of Charlan, who hadn't a mean bone in his body, and chose his words carefully as they straightened from their task.

"Was that really necessary?" he murmured, looking Guiscard in the eyes.

"Was what necessary?"

"He was already set up. All it needed was a nudge."

Guiscard raised a dark eyebrow in surprise. "How often have you seen that done?" he asked.

"Often enough," Javan replied vaguely. "It doesn't matter. It's just that Charlan is a friend. There's no need to treat him the way— the way you treated the priest, Father— I'm afraid I've forgotten his name."

"It's Ascelin," Guiscard supplied automatically, then shook his head in disbelief. "I don't believe I'm letting a human tell me how to use my powers—even a king."

Javan looked away. "I used to work with a Healer. He was subtle. I'm not afraid of you, but I'm not used to seeing power used quite so—forcefully."

"Maybe if more of us were forceful, we Deryni wouldn't be in the dilemma we're in today," Guiscard said sharply. "Maybe there wouldn't be any *Custodes Fidei*, to ferret out those of my race and destroy them because of what they are."

"I don't like them any better than you do," Javan whispered, "and I'm somewhat responsible for them, because my brother allowed the Order to be formed. I intend to do something about that, but it isn't going to happen if we stand here arguing all night. Now, will you please take me to Joram, if that's what we're here for?"

Obviously taken aback, Guiscard gave him a guarded nod. "I'm sorry, my prince. But I don't really know Sir Charlan, and I certainly didn't know the extent to which he'd been prepared. I thought it better to be safe than sorry."

With that he moved quickly across the room to feel under the armrest of a *prie-dieu* in the corner. At a soft *snick* sound, a portion of the paneling to the right drew quietly back. As Guiscard moved to enter the tiny cubicle thus revealed, Javan went to join him, stepping in without prompting and turning to stand with his back to the other man, all too aware of their earlier friction.

"I'm told that you've been through this Portal before," Guiscard murmured, setting a hand on Javan's shoulder as he closed them into darkness.

"Yes," Javan whispered, preparing himself for what he did not expect to be a particularly pleasant Portal jump.

"I know that you somehow have shields, too," Guiscard went

on, close beside his ear, both hands now resting on Javan's shoulders. "Dom Queron said I wasn't to meddle—just put you under enough to bring you through. After our conversation about Charlan, however, it's clear you know more than I was led to believe—and that perhaps I *was* too forceful earlier. Any suggestions?"

The tone was utterly sincere and without resentment, an obvious peace offering, and Javan found himself warming slightly to this brusque young Deryni who obviously was risking a great deal to help him. It had been a while, but all at once he was confident he could let Guiscard far enough past his shields to blank him for the time it took to make the jump. He drew a deep breath and let it out, making a conscious effort to relax more heavily against Guiscard's chest.

"I'm sure this will be easier for both of us, once we get to know one another better," he said quietly. "Try it the way you would do if I were trained. They've taught me a little. If it doesn't work, you can put me out whatever way you have to."

"Fair enough," Guiscard murmured. "Whenever you're ready."

Breathing deeply again, Javan closed his eyes and let his head loll back against the other's shoulder. As he did, he rolled back his shields as well, inviting Guiscard's entry to those outer precincts needing access for successful control of a jump. He did not even try to guess their destination, though he had his suspicions.

The other's control was more rigid than what he was accustomed to, but his reaction apparently was enough to Guiscard's liking to make the attempt. The swooping, slightly disorienting instant of vertigo was quickly past, and he opened his eyes to a familiar, stone-faced chamber he knew lay within the Michaeline sanctuary.

CHAPTER TEN

I will teach you by the hand of God: that
which is with the Almighty will I not conceal.
Job 27:11

There were two of them waiting for him: Joram and Bishop Niallan Trey. It gave Javan a jolt to see them both wearing Michaeline blue, so long absent from Court and from his sight. He could feel tears welling in his eyes as he stepped from the Portal, but Joram rescued him from the moment by drawing him into the embrace Javan had longed for but had never hoped to have from the formerly unbending Joram MacRorie.

"Javan, my liege, my dear, brave prince," Joram murmured, enfolding him with mind as well as arms. "I was so sorry to hear about Alroy."

Somehow the words drained away the sadness, made the relief a positive joy rather than a surrendering to grief and fear. Drawing back at last, Javan was able to meet the other's eyes as one man to another, king to loyal ally. He let his arms slip down Joram's to clasp both his hands, glorying in his great good fortune to have such a friend, as Joram, smiling, bent his golden head to kiss each royal hand in wordless homage.

"Father Joram, it's good to see you," Javan murmured, looking into the grey eyes. "It's been too long."

"Aye, my prince, far too long," Joram replied. Remembering himself, he turned to beckon Niallan forward with a glance. "Here is Bishop Niallan to greet you as well," he went on. "We thought to keep the welcoming party small, this first time."

As Niallan, too, bent to kiss the royal hand, Joram cast his glance beyond Javan at the waiting Guiscard.

"How long is it safe to keep him here?" he asked.

"Perhaps half an hour?" Guiscard replied. "I've left Ascelin and Charlan asleep in the study. They're safe enough, unless someone should come—though that isn't likely, at this hour. If you'd rather, though, I can wait with them, just to make sure, and one of you can bring his Highness back through."

"That's probably a wise idea," Joram agreed. "But let Niallan Read you before you go, so we'll have as much background as possible."

At Guiscard's nod of agreement, Joram took Javan's arm and led him out of the Portal chamber and across the corridor to the little octagonal chapel.

"How did you and Guiscard get on?" Joram asked as he closed the door behind them and turned to look at Javan.

Javan shrugged and managed a shy grin. "A little shaky at first, but we'll be fine. He doesn't have the subtlety of you or Tavis or—Evaine." The speaking of her name drew his gaze irresistibly toward the front of the chapel, where several of those who had championed his family's cause had been laid to rest more than three years before. "Is she—"

Joram shook his head. "Not here. Elsewhere. Someday, perhaps, I'll take you there. We moved Rhys there, as well."

"Oh."

Joram glanced at the floor, obviously uncomfortable, then looked up at Javan again. "We daren't take much time tonight. I had—hoped to have this first reunion under less stress. It's been a very long time."

"I know." Javan paused. "And nothing happened when Alroy died, Joram. I was with him, I put on the Ring of Fire—" He held out his hand to display the ring. "But I don't feel any different. Evaine said something was supposed to happen."

Joram drew a deep breath, suddenly solemn. "There are—things that need to be done, to properly trigger what was set," he said. "Evaine had begun to reach that conclusion, while trying to discover why you began developing some of the Haldane powers but Alroy didn't. She left notes."

"Then you know?"

"Not precisely. But over the past two or three years, I've carried on with her research, trying to prepare for this day—and as you know, I'm the only one left who was present when your father set the potential in you and your brothers." He sighed.

"I've let Tavis in on what we did—it was only fair, since he was peripherally involved—and I've also told Queron. They've agreed to assist us in what needs to be done. I couldn't get either one here for tonight, but they'll be here by tomorrow night. I'd like you to come back then, and we'll—see if Evaine and I guessed right."

"To awaken my father's full powers in me?" Javan whispered.

"Yes."

Javan exhaled with a long, soft sigh, then moved distractedly to one side to sink down on one of the stone benches set into the walls. "I faced down the dragons in my first Council meeting yesterday, Joram. I won the first round, but I've got some powerful opposition and nobody very experienced who's totally on my side. How much do the de Courcys know about me? And how have they managed to keep it secret that they're Deryni, in a baronial family?"

Joram smiled and went to sit beside the king. "Etienne's lands are in the south, where people don't pay that much attention to such things, and his family have always had good survival instincts.

"But we really haven't time to go into all of this now—not in words, at any rate. That's why I must ask you for something I've no right to ask at a time like this—except that I'm going to ask anyway, even though I know it's going to frighten you."

Javan stiffened a little, for he thought he knew what Joram was about to say.

"Do you remember the time that Evaine brought you here and did a strip-Read followed by a briefing, and Queron and I assisted?" Joram said softly.

Javan shivered and looked away, focusing on the Presence Lamp above the altar, for he remembered it very well—and the pounding headache afterward. But he had learned from the experience; and the exchange of information had been well worth the temporary discomfort.

"Can you—do it by yourself?" he murmured, after an awkward swallow.

"Yes. And I hope we'll both be better at it this time," Joram said. "I wouldn't ask if I didn't think it was important—for tomorrow night, in specific, as well as the future in general. There are lots of things we both need to know—three years' worth."

Swallowing again, Javan nodded, not daring to look up at Joram. He had always been a little afraid of the cool, controlled Michaeline priest, but Joram *was* Evaine's brother—and Saint Camber's son. "All right. What do you want me to do?"

"The more you can relax, the easier it's going to be for both of us," Joram said, setting a reassuring hand on his shoulder. "Why don't you swing your feet around onto the bench and lean back against me?"

Nodding a little nervously, Javan did as he was told, laying his head in Joram's lap and folding his hands across his breast. He closed his eyes and tried to will himself to relax as the priest's hands curved gently on his brow.

Remember everything you've ever learned from any of us, especially Evaine, came Joram's gentle instruction, directly in his mind. *Try to let yourself go very, very deep—even deeper than you did that other time. I'll do my best not to hurt you, but you need to help me. The deeper you can go, the faster I can draw and the less discomfort you'll have. Relax now, and let it happen . . .*

It had been a long time, but the memory came flooding back of how to do it. He could feel himself sinking with an almost physical vertigo, spiraling deeper and deeper, more and more detached from conscious awareness of anything to do with the physical—and Joram was right with him, close and supportive, gently holding him on a steady course toward the centerpoint, urging him on, lightly pushing him now, deeper, deeper . . .

He hardly noticed when Joram began to draw on the memories, for the pressure was smooth and steady. He flashed on an earlier image of a vessel being emptied; but rather than the contents being sucked out through holes punched in his shields, it was as if his mind had become a sieve, and gravity alone drew all to the lowest point and out, where Joram—absorbed it?

The reversal was no more traumatic—a gentle welling of new material in a vessel now sound once more, perhaps even stronger than before. A growing heaviness came with it, but it was not the burning heaviness of molten lead he had experienced that other time. Rather, it was like the sated fullness that comes after eating well—or perhaps eating just a trifle *too* well, overindulging—but it was small enough discomfort, especially compared to Javan's previous experience.

As Joram brought him back, his heartbeat was steady and his breathing still light. At no time had he been at all afraid or more than mildly uncomfortable. He opened his eyes just before Joram did and caught the instant of undisguised satisfaction in the other's gaze as Joram blinked and focused.

"How do you feel?" Joram asked.

Grinning shyly, Javan heaved himself to a sitting position and stretched, indulging an enormous yawn. Whatever apprehensions he had retained about working with Joram had utterly dissolved away in the aftermath of their rapport, and he sensed a wealth of new information just at the edge of consciousness, ready to be examined and assimilated.

"I think both of us must be getting better at this," he said. "I feel—stuffed, if you can say that about thoughts. But it didn't hurt."

Joram smiled and pulled a tiny twist of parchment from under his cincture, handing it to Javan. "You're going to want a good night's sleep to sort things out, though. Dissolve this in a little wine and drink it just before you go to bed."

"What is it?" Javan asked, trying to read the tiny writing on one of the tails.

"A light sedative, mostly," Joram replied. "I had Niallan's Healer make it up. It will also take care of any vestigial headache that might creep up on you, if any afterreaction sets in. Judging from your condition right now, I don't expect anything dramatic, but you do need a good, uninterrupted night of sleep."

"I'm in favor of that," Javan said around a yawn. "I still haven't caught up from the last couple of days."

"You'd better get back, then," Joram said, rising and helping Javan to his feet. "A lot from what we've just done will become clearer once you've slept. And you need to be rested for tomorrow night. Have Guiscard bring you back at about the same time and tell him to be prepared to cover for about an hour."

Javan cocked his head at the priest. "He's not to know I can use the Portal myself?"

"That's right. Your instincts are good. It's best not to let anyone know too much about what you can and cannot do. He knows you can Truth-Read and that you have shields, because that couldn't be helped—and Niallan will have dealt with any overcurious tendencies when he took Guiscard's report, and any necessary explanation about Charlan.

"Don't misunderstand; Guiscard's utterly loyal and trustworthy, and he and his father really would die for you—but for now, the less he knows, the less he can spill if disaster strikes. Fair enough?"

"I suppose so," Javan murmured. He shivered as they walked toward the door out of the chapel, tucking the twist of parchment into his belt pouch, and Joram laid an arm around his shoulders.

"It's going to be all right, my prince," Joram murmured. "You're doing just fine. Your handling of the Council meeting was nothing short of brilliant. Just take things slowly."

They crossed the corridor back into the Portal chamber, and Niallan rose from the chair where he had been sitting, steel-grey hair and close-clipped beard glinting in the light of a single candle by the chair.

"Is Guiscard all right?" Joram asked as he guided Javan toward the Portal square.

Niallan nodded. "He's fine. He's impressed with our fledgling king and can't figure out about the shields, but he's about convinced that perhaps Truth-Reading and other quasi-Deryni talents go along with the Divine Right of the king. Haldane kings, at any rate. Of course I did nothing to disabuse him of that notion."

"And probably a fair lot to reinforce it," Joram said with a smile. "Which is as it should be, at least for now. So on that note, I suppose we'd best—"

"Before Javan leaves," Niallan said, interrupting with a raised eyebrow, "Jesse's arrived while you were otherwise occupied. He's in the next room. This might be a good time to make introductions."

The look he exchanged with Joram suggested that more than words passed between the two, but Javan could detect nothing.

"Jesse's here?" Joram said. "This *is* fortuitous. By all means, ask him to join us."

As Niallan passed outside, Javan looked askance at Joram. "Who's Jesse?"

Joram smiled. "Someone you should know. He's the son and heir of Gregory, Earl of Ebor—not that the title means much, these days, with most of the Deryni titles being attainted. He used to ride patrol with my nephews, Davin and Ansel. Now he's my liaison with Ansel—and just come from him, I suspect. Ah, there you are, Jesse. Welcome back. How long can you stay?"

The keen-eyed young man at Niallan's elbow looked to be about twenty, lean and graceful, a sword at his side and an open-throated white shirt tucked into tan leather riding breeches. His brown hair was pulled back in a queue, and flecks of gold stirred in the depths of brown eyes that appeared to miss little. He was not much taller than Javan, but he had more muscle to him. Bright white teeth flashed in his suntanned face as he cast a smile in Joram's direction and, recognizing Javan, made him a respectful bow.

"That depends on how long you need me," Jesse said easily. "And this, I presume, is our new king."

"It is, indeed. Javan Haldane, King of Gwynedd, may I present Sir Jesse MacGregor, who should have been Master of Ebor, except that he and his father have been attainted for being Deryni," Joram said.

As Javan extended his hand, Jesse clasping it lightly as he bent in smiling homage, Joram clamped his two hands around their clasped ones and looked Javan in the eyes.

"Jesse is another whose touch you should learn, my prince," he said quietly. "The time is not ideal, but I suggest that a brief rapport would be to both your advantage, since you'll almost certainly have cause to work together in the future. He's very, very good," he added. "And he knows about you."

Javan fought down a momentary panic and exhaled softly, shifting his gaze to Jesse's. Why did Joram keep springing these things on him unexpectedly? Javan knew exactly why, but it was unnerving all the same. At least this Jesse did not *look* as formidable as any of the senior Deryni with whom Javan had been learning to deal.

The young knight had straightened at Joram's words, his hand now clasping Javan's more firmly, even within the encirclement of Joram's two. Brown eyes met grey without guile or demand, simply waiting for Javan to make the next move. As Joram's hands fell away, he and Niallan moving back out of Javan's line of vision, Javan dared to make that move, bringing his left hand very deliberately to clasp over his and Jesse's joined ones, not allowing himself to break eye contact. Somehow, it seemed easier with someone nearer his own age, even though he knew Jesse must be very experienced indeed.

"Jesse MacGregor," he said steadily, nodding slightly in acknowledgment of the other. "I'm not very good at this yet—which no doubt is part of the reason Joram wants me to do it—but I fancy I'm improving. If Joram thinks we should do this, here and now, I'm willing to give it my best effort."

As he wound down, hardly able to believe he had said it and to someone he knew not at all, Jesse smiled.

"You honor me with your trust, my prince," he said quietly. "This needn't be the trial you're obviously expecting, though. Will you allow me to guide you?"

As Javan nodded, for he could not quite bring himself to speak his assent, Jesse added his left hand to the three already clasped between them, setting it firmly atop, encompassing all three. The grasp was strong and sure, the grasp of a seasoned fighting man, but the shields Jesse presented, just at the edge of Javan's awareness, were not at all intimidating.

"Close your eyes and relax, my prince," Jesse said. "We needn't go deep, this first time. Just a gentle, easy rapport. I'll guide, but you control the depth. There's no urgency. I'm here to serve. Relax . . ."

Javan obeyed, letting himself sink in response to Jesse's words,

sighing softly as he felt himself slip back to the centered serenity
he had experienced with Joram. Jesse's touch was silken smooth,
enfolding but not restraining, soothing but also inviting, so that
Javan felt his shields roll back in perfect unison with the other's.

The rapport was utterly undemanding, offering an easy glimpse
of the mind and soul that were Jesse MacGregor and taking up what
Javan offered in return. Without being aware how it happened, Javan
found himself possessed of a fairly detailed impression of a young
Deryni who had accomplished much in the few years of his young
manhood, and much of it in the service of the Haldanes. Jesse asked
nothing in return, but Javan found himself sharing some of the
highlights—and low points—of *his* last three years, sensing instinctively that the other needed to know these things.

When, by unspoken but mutual consent, both withdrew once
again behind their shields, Javan slowly opened his eyes and heaved
a contented sigh. Jesse was watching him, smiling faintly, and
somehow it came as no surprise when Jesse bent slowly and gravely
to kiss the royal hand. The fealty it betokened, however, had already been cemented in far more personal and binding form.

"You underestimate your own skill, my prince," Jesse said,
straightening and dismantling hands. "But I think you have other
duties calling you just now." He glanced beyond Javan at Joram and
Niallan. "Shall I take him back, or would one of you rather?"

"Let's have Niallan do it, shall we?" Joram replied, glancing at
Javan. "Someone has to, so that Guiscard doesn't find out you can
do it yourself. And the more of us you learn to work with, the more
versatile you'll be."

After the workout Joram had given him, and the very successful
rapport with Jesse, the gentle Niallan was hardly likely to be very
frightening. Besides, Javan liked the bishop.

"I have no objection," he said, "though his Grace had better be
warned that I'm still awfully new at this."

Niallan chuckled and went to guide Javan onto the Portal Square,
setting his hands on the king's shoulders from behind. "You really
needn't title me so formally, Sire," the bishop said. "I'm not even
officially a bishop anymore. Why don't you just call me Niallan?
Or Father Niallan, if you must use a title. And it would please me
greatly if I might simply call you my prince."

The warmth of the Deryni bishop was irresistible, and Javan
found himself grinning delightedly back over his shoulder. "Niallan.
Thank you, I like that name. But you'll have to forgive me if I slip
from time to time. I've spent the last three years making sure I
remembered what ecclesiastical titles were due to whom."

"All in a good cause, my prince," Niallan murmured, reaching his right hand around to fold across Javan's forehead. "Close your eyes and relax now, and we'll get this done. You're going to want your bed fairly soon, I think."

The warmth that wrapped itself around Javan's mind was so soothing and reassuring that he was able to slip immediately to that deeply centered state in which controls might be surrendered. He gave himself into the Deryni bishop's guidance, adrift for just an instant, then felt the brief thrill of the energies shifting, the touch of vertigo—and they were back in the Portal cubicle in the study at Rhemuth. He opened his eyes to a different kind of vertigo—a brief fading into the edge of sleep, almost instantly overcome. He fought a yawn, remembering the twist of parchment in his pouch.

"You're fine," Niallan whispered in his ear, steadying him with a quick press of his shoulders and then reaching out for the sliding panel. As it slid back, Guiscard turned from his post by the door, darting forward as Javan staggered a little coming out.

"He's just tired," Niallan murmured. "A bit of sleep will fix everything. Get him to bed as soon as you can."

"Aye, your Grace," Guiscard replied—and took Javan by the arm.

They made their way out of the basilica without incident, leaving the unwitting Father Ascelin to snore on in his bed, with no memory of their visit. Neither did Charlan remember anything of the affair, aware only that the king had spent some time by his brother's bier in prayer and now was ready to return to his quarters. He gave Javan his arm as they trudged back up the cobbled approach to the inner ward, for the footing was slippery from the rainfall, and the king seemed suddenly very tired.

There were steaming horses being walked out in the castle yard as they came back beneath the gatehouse, and weary men bedding down in the hall, who eyed Javan with interest as he and his escort came up the great hall steps and headed through the hall. Javan was too bleary-eyed to get a good look at the men, but Guiscard stiffened as he noted the badges on their surcoats, and Charlan tried to hurry them on toward the stair.

"Murdoch's men," Guiscard murmured, under his breath. "I don't like the looks of this. Why couldn't he have waited until tomorrow?"

They clattered up the first flight and met Bertrand coming down, just at the first-floor landing. The young knight drew them urgently along a back corridor rather than continuing up.

"Lord Murdoch has arrived and he's in a nasty mood," he said, hurrying them toward another stair. "He's in your apartments with four of his men-at-arms, Sire, and he says he isn't leaving until he sees you. Sir Robear explained that you were praying, but he said he was prepared to wait. I was afraid I'd have to come all the way to the basilica to find you."

"Sorry," Javan murmured. "I didn't think anyone would want me this late. Who else is there of ours, besides Robear?"

"Lord Jerowen and Tomais," Bertrand replied, "and I've already sent six men to stand by in the corridor. Baron de Courcy's gone to roust Constable Udaut and see about containing the men in the hall, just in case Murdoch tries something stupid. Tammaron's there, too, trying to calm Murdoch down."

"Shall I see if my father needs any assistance, Sire?" Guiscard said. And in Javan's mind he added, *If you can hear me, my prince, perhaps I ought not to be present at this interview until we're certain Murdoch has no Deryni with him.*

Javan shot a startled look at Guiscard, commensurate with having unexpectedly heard the voice in his mind, but he was also frantically considering his options as they climbed the next stair. At least it was Murdoch rather than Rhun. Murdoch would rant and rave and probably be insufferably insulting, but he was not likely to take direct action; Rhun might well take arms—and certainly had at least one Deryni collaborator working for him, who would be a definite danger until he could be gotten out of Rhun's clutches and convinced that he no longer need work against his own kind.

"Yes, please give Baron de Courcy my compliments and have Constable Udaut take whatever measures are necessary to secure those men in the great hall," he said. "Try to avoid actually taking them into custody if you can; but I want them loyal or out within the hour. Is that clear?"

Guiscard smiled and sketched him a jaunty salute. "It shall be done, my prince. God keep your Highness."

They had reached the top of the stairs. As Guiscard reversed to go back down, Javan paused to draw a deep breath and to tug his tunic more smoothly over his hips.

"Very well, gentlemen," he said to Bertrand and Charlan. "Let's go and see what my Lord Murdoch has to say, shall we?"

There were guards—six of them, wearing Javan's livery—standing attentively outside the door to his apartments. The door was standing slightly ajar, and Javan could hear angry voices disputing inside. The guards snapped to attention as he approached, and the captain gave Javan a nod and loosened his sword in its scabbard before opening the door and preceding him in, hand on the hilt.

Murdoch of Carthane was not a happy man. This was not an

unusual occurrence, for even at the best of times Murdoch managed to find fault with something, but several days in the saddle with little or no sleep had made the tendency a certainty. The narrow, gaunt face with its close-trimmed beard looked thinner still with the shadows of fatigue staining the hollows of his eyes and new lines etching his forehead. The prim, prissy lips were drawn back in a grimace of distaste. Though usually fastidious in his dress, Murdoch's riding leathers were streaked with mud and sweat. He had been berating Tammaron, towering over the chancellor by a full head, and he rounded on the guard captain who preceded Javan with murder in his eye, only checking his anger as he saw Javan himself.

"My Lord Murdoch," Javan said politely, seizing the initiative before Murdoch could. "We are moved by your courtesy, that you should make such speed to pay your respects to the late king our brother—as we ourselves have been doing this past hour. But your salutations to us could have waited until morning. You obviously have ridden long and hard."

"Yes, and I have been to see the archbishops before I came here," Murdoch said, omitting any title of respect. "You seem to have neatly sidestepped your holy vows in order to seize the crown from your brother."

"To seize the crown from my brother?" Javan replied, all wide-eyed innocence. "My brother is dead. To whom should the Crown of Gwynedd go, besides his twin?"

"You were to have set aside that claim when you entered Holy Orders," Murdoch said, and swept a cold glance at Javan's foot in its special boot. "It is not fitting that a cripple should wear the crown. I understood that you had accepted that."

"Then you have *mis*understood," Javan said calmly, raising a hand to cut off indignant responses on the part of his supporters. "Such physical limitation as I may have does not affect my ability to rule, just as it would not have affected my ability to function as a priest. If you have already spoken with Archbishop Hubert, then you will know that it was never my intention to put aside my royal duty. Nor have I done so."

"But Rhys Michael was to be—"

"Rhys Michael is now heir presumptive," Jerowen Reynolds interjected smoothly, "and Prince Javan now is king. Or do you dispute that, my lord?"

The captain at Javan's side had wrapped a gloved hand more resolutely around the hilt of his sword, his eyes narrowed at Murdoch in speculation, and his men were lurking in the doorway. Murdoch's jaws were so tightly clenched that he looked like to shear off his teeth, but he managed to give a grudging shake of his head.

"And you, gentlemen," Jerowen continued, pointedly turning his glance on Murdoch's four men-at-arms. "Will you do reverence to your king?"

He was quite unarmed, as was Javan, but Robear and Tomais wore swords at their sides, as did Bertrand. Charlan wore a dagger. The guards in the doorway carried short spears in addition to swords and poniards, and wore brigandines similar to those sported by the men-at-arms.

The four weighed the odds and the options and obviously decided that compliance was the better part of survival—though they undoubtedly would hear about it from their lord when they withdrew. First one man and then the other three uneasily bent one knee, bowing their heads in homage as Murdoch fumed. Javan breathed a guarded little sigh of relief, motioning them to rise, then turned his gaze back to Murdoch.

"The devotion of a loyal subject is beyond price, my lord," he said quietly, in a double-edged statement that Murdoch could take any way he liked. "However, as the hour grows extremely late, I shall ask you to retire, as I intend to do. You have ridden hard and must be yearning for your bed."

To that, at least, Murdoch could hardly object; nor did he. Favoring Javan with the most scornful of nods, he took his leave, his men falling in behind him in ragged escort. The guard captain went with him, he and his men following at a respectful distance to ensure that Murdoch did indeed leave that part of the castle. As the door closed behind them, Lord Jerowen came around from behind the table, he and Charlan steadying Javan as the king shivered and swayed on his feet.

"I'm all right," Javan murmured, though he found himself reeling under waves of drowsiness now that the crisis was past. "And my especial thanks to you, Lord Jerowen. I wasn't expecting to have to face Murdoch tonight."

"It's my honor to serve you, Sire," Jerowen said.

"And mine, to be served by good men and true," Javan replied, glancing toward his sleeping chamber. "But you'll excuse me now, I hope. After visiting my brother, and then this—" He drew a deep breath. "Bertrand, would you fetch me something to drink while Charlan helps me undress?"

By the time he had climbed up onto the bed and Charlan had pulled off his boots, Bertrand was back with a goblet and a pitcher of wine.

"Shall I pour for you, Sire?" Bertrand asked, moving to set them on the table by the head of the bed.

"No, Charlan can do that, thank you," Javan said, surreptitiously retrieving Joram's twist of parchment from the pouch at his waist. "But bring me some water for it, if you please. It's too late to drink undiluted wine."

As Bertrand retreated, and Charlan picked up pitcher and goblet to pour, Javan stayed him with a hand on his wrist, extending control, and opened the twist of parchment over the cup. A fine, crystalline powder sifted into the bottom, and Javan pressed the parchment into Charlan's hand when he had taken the goblet in his own hand.

"Just a little in the bottom," he murmured, setting it under the lip of the pitcher. "And dispose of that later, remembering nothing of it."

He swirled the wine in the goblet as Charlan put the pitcher aside as if Javan had said nothing at all, and when Bertrand returned with a flask of water, Javan let him top up the wine.

"Thank you both," he said, raising the cup a little in salute before draining it in four smooth gulps. "Wake me if there's anything really urgent," he said, as he handed Charlan the empty goblet, "but otherwise let me sleep as long as I can. Tomorrow shouldn't be *too* demanding, unless Rhun shows up, too." He tried not to think about tomorrow *night*. "Monday is going to be rough, though. And Tuesday, in its way, will be even worse."

He could feel Joram's drug already at work in him as he lay back on the pillows, gentle but insistent, dulling the edge of headache he had started to develop during the confrontation with Murdoch.

"We'll be here if you need us, Sire," he heard Charlan say through a fog of encroaching sleep.

He was oblivious long before they finished laying out their pallets for the night.

CHAPTER ELEVEN

Who coverest thyself with light as with a garment.

—Psalms 104:2

Fortunately for Javan, Sunday proved to be the day of rest it was intended to be. He heard Mass at noon in the castle's Chapel Royal with Rhys Michael and about a dozen of his supporters, went with his brother to pay another official visit to the dead king, then closeted himself with his advisors for the rest of the afternoon to continue going over the briefing documents they had prepared for him. The weather continued to moderate, with thunderstorms again darkening the sky periodically and lowering the temperature each time a new deluge poured down. That evening he dined informally in the great hall with the Court, because it was expected, but he retired early, pleading the need for sleep before the ordeal of the funeral the next day.

He did nap for an hour or two, but just after midnight he betook himself, Charlan, and Guiscard with him to the basilica again, once more using the ruse of going to pray by his brother's body. It had been coffined since his visit after Mass, and he went with Charlan to kneel close beside it, slipping one hand up under the pall to caress the polished wood. Guiscard had lingered behind as they entered.

This is the last chance I'm going to have for a private good-bye, Alroy, he told his brother, trying not to think of him now nailed away in the dark. *I know you aren't really in there, but a part of me is still mourning the loss of that physical part of you—which is in there.*

I'm going to try to be a good king, he went on. *I wish that you had had a chance to be the kind of king you could have been.* He sighed. *But since that wasn't meant to be, I guess I'll just have to make my reign glorious enough for both of us. I'll never forget you.*

He leaned his forehead briefly against the side of the coffin. *I have to go now. I'm finally about to find out what Father did to us that night he died—though I guess you already know. I hope it will make me strong. Because I've inherited a lot of enemies.* He sighed. *Good-bye, Alroy. Pray for me, as I shall for you.*

After a further long moment of wordless general prayer, he sighed again and got to his feet, Charlan giving him a hand up. Guiscard was waiting to fall in silently behind him as he and Charlan headed out of the basilica, not looking back.

But it had never been their intention to go back to the castle yet. After disappearing into the shadows in that direction, they doubled back as they had the night before, along the dark slype passage and through the east door.

In the little study beyond the sacristy, its occupant was sleeping heavily as he had the night before and did not stir as they entered. When Guiscard had closed and locked the door, Etienne de Courcy stepped out from the shelter of the chimney embrasure, motioning to the completely nonplussed Charlan as he went to the bed and lifted up the blanket trailing off the side.

"Under the bed with you, Charlan my man," he murmured, helping the unresisting knight to slide under. "Scoot over to the other side as far as you can and go to sleep until I wake you."

When he dropped the blanket back into place, no sign of the room's extra occupant could be seen. Guiscard, meanwhile, had gone to the *prie-dieu* and pressed the stud that released the door to the Portal chamber.

"We'd better go, my prince," he whispered, holding out an arm to Javan as he backed into the little cubicle. "Etienne, where are you going to be?"

"In there, if I hear anybody coming," Etienne said, gesturing toward the cubicle as Javan stepped boldly in. "Don't worry about me."

This time Guiscard drew the Portal door closed without ceremony, setting his hands on Javan's shoulders very matter-of-factly.

"Give me just a second," Javan murmured, drawing a deep breath and tilting his head back against Guiscard's shoulder.

He was able to let Guiscard take over much more easily this time and felt only a flutter as the other wrenched the energies. He opened his eyes to see Tavis O'Neill standing just outside the haven

Portal. He threw himself into the Healer's arms with a little cry of joy, trembling as he buried his face against Tavis' chest, hardly noticing how the Healer's right hand reached beyond him to touch Guiscard.

"My prince, my prince," Tavis murmured, voice and mind soothing as the hand returned to stroke Javan's hair. "Or should I say my king? My, how you've grown."

Something in his voice made Javan pull back to look at him again. It had been more than three years since their last meeting, and Javan was not the only one who had changed.

The formerly clean-shaven Healer now sported a rather bushy beard with a great deal of grey grizzling the red; the dark-red hair, pulled back in a neat clout at the nape of the neck, had gone silver at the temples. He was wearing a tunic of Healer's green that lit the more aquamarine shade deep in his pale eyes, but there were new lines around the eyes that had not come altogether from exposure to wind and weather. The eyes and the lips were smiling as Tavis slowly sank to one knee, offering his hand and the stump of his wrist in wordless homage, but a weariness permeated his every movement.

"Tavis, what's happened to you?" Javan demanded, taking hand and wrist and urging the Healer to his feet.

Shaking his head, still smiling, Tavis rose. "Someday, when we both have the time and leisure, I shall tell you, my prince," he said quietly. "Let us simply say that I have been doing what I must do, while you have been doing what you must do. We have both paid our prices, I think. But tonight, at least, we both shall learn something of what we have been seeking for—about four years now?"

"What happened the night my father died," Javan supplied, eyes wide and awed.

Suddenly remembering they were not alone, he glanced back at Guiscard, who had not moved. He was startled to see the young knight simply standing there, eyes closed. At his look of inquiry, Tavis simply shook his head and moved a little closer to brush Guiscard's forehead with his fingertips, drawing him then toward a chair set beside the door of the little anteroom from which the Portal chamber opened.

"It isn't that I don't trust our friend," he said quietly, pressing the young knight down to sit in the chair, "but what he does not know, he cannot reveal, even under torture." He passed his hand briefly over the knight's closed eyes, setting controls, then straightened to glance at Javan.

"He's strong, if a bit lacking in finesse. Have you had much opportunity to work with him?"

Javan shook his head. "I only met him yesterday. Did you block him?"

"Temporarily, yes. But obviously I'll restore him before the two of you go back. Did Joram give you any idea what's to happen tonight?"

"Only that we'd try to free up the rest of the powers I'm supposed to have. Why? Don't you know, either?"

Tavis chuckled in genuine mirth and took Javan's arm, heading them toward the door. "I know that it's going to be a formal ritual and that I'm to help set the Wards and call the Quarters. Other than that, it's Joram's game. He and Queron have been closeted for hours, working out the details. We'll be using the chapel."

They were in front of the chapel door as he said it, and he gave the door two quick raps with his stump. After a few seconds the door was opened by Joram, again cassocked in Michaeline blue. Behind him, doing something with candles on the altar, Dom Queron also had made an effort to resume his former habit, cool and serene looking in a spotless white robe with the Gabrilite Healer's badge boldly emblazoned on the left breast. His hair had grown out somewhat, though it was white now, but the Gabrilite braid was only a hand-span long, and Javan had never seen him with a beard before.

Both men bowed as Tavis escorted Javan into the room. The faint sweetness of incense hung on the air, coming from a thurible set on a little white-covered table in the center of the room's Kheldish carpet.

"Father Joram, Dom Queron," Javan said a little nervously.

"Come in and sit down for a few minutes, my prince," Joram said, gesturing toward one of the benches set into the wall at the left as Queron returned to his preparations at the altar. "Tavis, you might as well hear this, too. I'll try to give you both an idea what's going to happen—or what we *hope* will happen."

Javan sat, Tavis settling on his right and Joram on his left.

"Now," Joram said. "What we're going to try to do, because we don't know exactly how Cinhil had actually structured this to work, is to re-create as closely as possible what he did to you and your brothers to set up the Haldane potential. We don't know why it didn't work in Alroy; we don't know why it started working *early* in you. But because it did, you'll be in a position to help it along, now that we want it to manifest completely in you."

"What do you mean, 'help it along'?" Javan asked. "How can I do that?"

Joram shook his head. "I can't tell you that. Not *won't—can't*. Just try to be as open as you can to whatever seems to be happening.

Queron will be controlling this ritual, so all of us will defer to him. If you can achieve a good level of trance on your own, before he even starts working directly on you, that will only be to the good.

"What we hope will happen is that we'll re-create the conditions under which you can open fully to what your father was trying to activate, without the blocks he set in place because you were second in line at the time. When it's all over—if it works—you should have conscious knowledge and control of everything that my father and Evaine and Rhys and I opened up in Cinhil himself, and which he never fully utilized."

"Will I—be like a Deryni?" Javan murmured.

Joram smiled and patted Javan's knee as he got to his feet. "You're already very much like a Deryni, my prince. As for what additional you may acquire—we'll just have to wait and see, shan't we? Come into the center of the circle now, and we'll begin. Tavis, I'll ask you to take your place in the West, please."

The Kheldish carpet was lush underfoot as they moved into the center of the room, Joram leading the king between the little table and the altar steps, on the topmost of which stood a candlestick shaded by sun-colored glass. Queron had been lighting the altar candles, and came down to spoon incense onto the thurible as Tavis took a place to the west of the little altar table. As Joram moved on into the South, crossing himself before bowing his head, Queron picked up the thurible and carried it past Javan to stand facing the eastern candle. Bowing, he saluted the East with three swings, then turned to his right and headed toward another candle shielded in red, tracing the circumference of the circle.

"The Lord is my Shepherd; I shall not want," he began chanting softly. "He maketh me to lie down in green pastures: he leadeth me beside the still waters . . ."

The familiar words gave Javan some reassurance as he watched Queron pass between Joram and the southern candle, pausing to reverence the South with three swings and then moving on toward the West and Tavis. As he approached, Tavis moved forward to the altar table and crouched to take out a white-glazed bowl of water and a sprig of evergreen. He gave Javan a glance of reassurance as he went past him to begin tracing the circle a second time with water, saluting each quarter with three shakes of his impromptu aspergillum.

"Thou shalt sprinkle me with hyssop, O Lord, and I shall be clean," he murmured. "Wash me, and I shall be whiter than snow . . ."

Queron had passed the West and was censing the North. Behind him the incense smoke hung on the still air like a fragile veil. Where

Tavis passed, to the right of Javan, the veil seemed to grow more weighty. Javan squinted his eyes, but that did not change his perception that the veil was thickening.

Queron came before him, his circuit complete, obviously intending to cense him, and Javan slipped automatically into the long habit of his altar training and joined his palms at his breast to exchange bows with the Gabrilite priest, bowing again when Queron had given him the requisite three swings. Somehow it did not seem odd that Queron then gave the censer to him, so that he might cense Queron in turn.

He thought Queron seemed pleased at how he handled the thurible, for the Healer gave him a knowing nod as they exchanged bows again and Queron took the thurible back. Behind him, Tavis was finishing his circuit with the aspergillum and came to asperse Javan as Queron went on to cense Joram. The water felt cool splashing against his face and hands, and Javan readily took the bowl and evergreen sprig from Tavis to do the same for him, watching then as Tavis went on to asperse Joram. It occurred to Javan that the pattern of their movements almost formed a kind of dance, usually at opposite sides of the circle, always spiralling deosil or sunwise.

Queron had finished with the thurible and set it back on the little table in the center, where it continued to send up a narrow thread of smoke; and when Tavis had finished with Joram, they both turned gracefully toward the center of the circle, always turning right, Tavis to continue on to asperse Queron and Joram to withdraw a sword from underneath the table.

The dance continued as Tavis came back to the East, between Javan and the little table, and put the bowl and aspergillum back under the table, while Joram went before Queron and knelt, bowing his head over his hands on the quillons of the sword before him. Queron cupped his hands briefly atop Joram's bowed head, but Javan could get no clear idea what they were doing because Tavis came to him then with a small silver goblet he drew from under the table. He gave Javan a strained, ironic little grin as he held it out.

"You'll recall that we both got to sample some rather interesting wine that night," he said, "and that we spent a lot of time and energy later trying to figure out what was in it." He shrugged and glanced at the cup. "I still have only a vague notion what's in it— except that there's no *merasha* this time, and no specific sedative, because you're meant to be alert. However, Joram assures me that it's a close approximation of what Rhys gave us that night, and Queron confirms that it won't hurt you."

Javan could feel himself starting to tremble, and for just an instant, as Tavis set the goblet in his hand, he fancied that the dark wine held danger.

"Tavis, I'm not sure I want to do this," he whispered.

"My prince, you've been wanting it for more than four years now. Don't lose heart now."

Closing his eyes, Javan brought the goblet to his lips and timidly tasted. As before, it was one of the sweet Fianna varietals. He could appreciate now what the eleven-year-old palate could not, but he gulped it down, trying not to think about what else was in it besides wine.

Tavis only smiled and nodded as Javan opened his eyes and put the empty goblet back in his hand. Joram was on his feet and heading toward him with the sword upright before him, coming to stand beside him facing East, directing Javan to do the same.

"The words you are about to hear," Joram said quietly, fixing his gaze on the golden flame of the Eastern Ward, "are the words your father spoke as he cast the third circle that night before he died. With Queron's assistance, I am able to provide exact recall. You were present in the room when he spoke these words. If you'll center and focus, you'll find that you recall them, too—and other things that happened that night."

So saying, he drew himself to attention for a few seconds, focusing his concentration, then saluted the East with his blade—the East, the source of Light. He drew a breath as he let the tip of the sword sink to point at the floor just to the right of the candle, beginning to speak in a low voice.

"Saint Raphael, Healer, Guardian of Wind and Tempest—" He began to walk slowly to his right, retracing the previous two circles. "May we be guarded and healed in mind and soul and body this night."

He had nearly reached the Southern Quarter, with its red-shielded flame, and he inclined his head in salute as his blade traced on. As he did so, Javan saw Tavis out of the corner of his eye, bowing, and Javan bowed, too.

"Saint Michael, Defender, Guardian of Eden, protect us in our hour of need."

Joram continued on. Where the tip of his blade passed, it laid down a glowing ribbon of silver, misty and substantial at once, perhaps the span of a man's forearm. Javan watched it grow behind Joram, with almost an impression that it took the priest more effort to pull the ribbon behind him, the farther around the circle he got. He could not take his eyes off it as Joram saluted the Western Quarter and he and Tavis and Queron bowed. A part of him knew what Joram was about to say, and he could not even find it in himself to be amazed as blue fire reflected off the polished blade and the words came exactly as he had known they must.

"Saint Gabriel, Heavenly Herald, carry our supplications to Our Lady."

Javan could hear his father's voice overlaid with Joram's now— could almost see a familiar, fur-lined gown of Haldane scarlet superimposed over Joram's Michaeline blue. He resisted the impulse to rub at his eyes as Joram passed on toward the Northern Quarter, with its green-lit candle and the waiting Queron; but he had the feeling that if he closed his eyes, the voice would make the image *be* his father.

"Saint Uriel, Dark Angel, come gently, if you must," Joram said, "and let all fear die here within this place."

Javan could feel himself trembling as Joram continued on around to join the two ends of the circle in the East and then gave salute once more, right beside him. He did not really understand what Joram was summoning—what his father had summoned with those same words, and what he himself had summoned to his brother's deathbed—but he stood in awe of it. The archangels he knew of, both from childhood catechisms and his seminary training, though he had never heard anyone address them the way Joram was doing.

Joram turned, the sword now dangling by its quillons in front of him, and motioned for Javan also to turn toward the center. Javan obeyed, gazing across the circle at a pale and focused Tavis as Joram spoke new words that Javan somehow knew had been Evaine's words before.

"We stand outside time, in a place not of earth," Joram said. "As our ancestors before us bade, we join together and are One. By Thy blessed Apostles, Matthew, Mark, Luke, and John; by all Powers of Light and Shadow, we call Thee to guard and defend us from all perils, O Most High. Thus it is and has always been, thus it will be for all times to come. *Per omnia saecula saeculorum.*"

The "Amen" of the others' response came to Javan's lips all unbidden but wholly proper and natural, and he found his hand making the Sign of the Cross as they did.

Then Joram was bending to lay the sword along the edge of the circle to their right, in the northeast quadrant; taking Javan's arm to lead him closer into the center of the circle to stand before the little altar table. He moved around to Javan's left to return to his proper place in the South as Queron knelt down to bring several more items out from under the table: a footed goblet of glazed white

pottery, partially filled with water, which he set on the table beside
the thurible; a small piece of parchment with something written
on it that Javan could not see; and a little silver dagger, which he
handed to Tavis as he stood.

"I'll ask you for the Ring of Fire now," Joram said, holding out
his hand.

Javan took off the ring and offered it with his right hand. Joram
retained the hand, isolating the thumb and compressing it, but
passed the ring to Tavis, taking the dagger from him in exchange
as Queron read from the parchment in a low voice.

"I will declare the decree," he said. "The Lord hath said unto
me, Thou art my Son: This day have I begotten thee. Ask of me,
and I shall give thee the heathen for thine inheritance, and the
uttermost parts of the earth for thy possession."

"Javan Jashan Urien Haldane, King of Gwynedd," Joram said as
Queron lowered the parchment, "be consecrated to the service of
thy people."

With that he jabbed Javan's thumb sharply against the blade.
Blood spurted, bright and startling, but even Javan's reflexive flinch
was dulled, as if it were happening to someone else. His thought
processes seemed to be slowing down, and he found himself watching with a detached fascination as Tavis rolled the dark stones of
the Ring of Fire through the blood on his thumb and then Joram
pressed the still-bleeding thumb to the parchment Queron held.

The parchment then was laid on the thurible to burn, after which
Queron wiped off Javan's wounded thumb with a bit of linen and
Healed it. When the parchment had curled to ash, he pinched a bit
between thumb and forefinger and sifted it over the water, quoting
again from Scripture.

"Give the king Thy judgements, O God, and Thy righteousness
unto the king's son."

Tavis bent to slip the bloody ring into the cup at that. A little
dreamily, Javan watched the blood diffuse in the water, wondering
what it would taste like—this intinction of blood and ash. Another
part of him seemed to know. His eyes did not seem to be focusing
quite properly. The cup seemed to draw him, so that he swayed a
little on his feet, and Joram set a steadying hand on his elbow.

"Steady," he murmured. "In addition to everything else, you're
feeling the effects of the first cup. Just go with it. Let yourself take
it all in, but don't try to analyze."

Joram gave him into Queron's keeping then, moving around to
take up the sword lying in the northeast quarter of the circle. Tavis
went with him.

"Tavis will leave the circle now," Queron murmured, smiling slightly as Javan's eyes followed the path of Joram's sword-tip, tracing up and across and down, cutting an arched doorway in the circle. "We're about to move on to the dramatic bit. Don't worry; he'll be right outside," he added as Tavis reluctantly stepped though and went to crouch on the altar steps close behind Javan. "He wasn't in the circle that night, so he shouldn't be there now. *I* shouldn't be here, except that I'm part of the process. Joram is the key to this part, since he's the only one remaining who was present and coherent that night."

Joram cast him a wary glance before closing the gate again with three swift strokes of the sword along the floor, replacing it on the floor again before heading back toward his place in the South.

"Now," Queron went on, standing easily at Javan's left, between him and Joram. "In order to re-create as accurately as possible what happened on the night in question, I plan to use a technique Joram has seen me use once before, many years ago. I trust he will not find it as startling this time as he did that other time. You, however, my prince, may find it very startling indeed."

Before Javan could even react, Queron's hand had reached out to touch his forehead, seizing controls as he did, taking Javan several levels deeper into trance than his own efforts and the drugged cup had already carried him.

"Deeply centered and at peace, my prince," Queron murmured.

An even greater stillness seemed to settle around him, and a part of him watched, detached, as Queron turned his attentions to Joram.

Chapter Twelve

In a trance I saw a vision.

—Acts 11:5

Despite his utter faith in Queron, Joram could not help a brief surge of uneasiness as the Gabrilite Healer moved before him and set both hands on his shoulders. Queron had told him precisely what was involved and reassured him that he would retain a detached awareness of exactly what was happening, even as Queron tapped his memory in so dramatic a manner; but the specter of that other time he had watched it done evoked a dread that was totally irrational.

"You can let go of that fear," Queron whispered, sliding his hands up to cup around Joram's neck and the back of his head, thumbs resting on his temples as the dark eyes compelled. "When you saw me do this before, you had cause to be wary. This is totally different."

Relax and open to me, Joram, he went on, shifting to mindspeech as Joram let fall his shields and gave the other access.

Good, came Queron's encouragement. *And now go deeper still, to the memory of that night . . . Standing in the little chapel adjoining Cinhil's bedchamber . . . you and Cinhil and Evaine and Alister . . . And be in that chapel . . .*

Joram was there. A part of him remained detached, well aware that it was but memory he relived, standing a little apart, as if observing from over his own shoulder. But the greater part of his conscious awareness had returned to that night in Cinhil's chapel, standing in the presence of persons now dead. That part saw them already: father and sister and sister's husband and ill-fated king.

But as Queron moved around to his right to stand slightly behind him, retaining contact with a hand on that shoulder, the detached part of Joram's mind began to see them, too. An armspan farther to the right, a slightly dazed-looking Javan stood watching and waiting—and beside him, where memory supplied the likeness of the boy's father, a more solid form began to materialize.

It was not the form Queron had summoned that other time, in the chapter house at Valoret, when his conjuration had unwittingly confirmed the illusion of a visitation by the recently deceased Camber MacRorie—and sealed his sainthood. A variation on that form eventually would materialize as well, but it would be as Alister Cullen, Camber's alter ego, not Camber himself.

Meanwhile, there were the other players to re-create. As Joram watched, the detached part of him utterly fascinated, the figure of Cinhil Haldane slowly took solid shape in the East beside his son, appearing as he had that fateful night he set his Haldane seal on Alroy and Rhys Michael as well as Javan, holding a ghost-echo of the physical cup set on the little altar table before him.

But the young king was staring across the circle at another form beginning to solidify, his joy and surprise evident even through the heavy controls and the drugs. Joram glanced left to behold the likeness of Evaine, graceful form enveloped in a dark cloak, the gold of her hair gleaming from inside its hood.

And across from him began to form the shape and semblance of one whom Joram and Queron both knew in two guises, though it was solely as Alister Cullen that he had appeared that night and as he now appeared, in the purple of his episcopal rank. Joram's immersion in the memory intensified as the figure crossed his arms on his breast, directing his gaze toward the larger altar as he had done that night, and Joram followed suit, watching the oddly solid ghost-Cinhil face that way as well, and raise his ghost-cup in salutation. In that instant Joram truly was back in that chapel adjoining Cinhil's bedchamber in Valoret, reliving the moment as Cinhil seemed to speak.

"O Lord, Thou art holy indeed: the fountain of all holiness. In trembling and humility we come before Thee with our supplications, asking Thy blessing and protection on what we must do this night."

The voice sounded exactly like the dead Cinhil, though a part of Joram knew that the words came from Queron's lips, projected across the space separating them. But as Cinhil turned to face the awestruck Javan, lowering the cup to extend his right palm flat above the rim, fact and illusion blurred and it *was* Cinhil, setting the pattern for the rest of their invocations, summoning the attributes of Air to permeate the contents of the cup.

"Send now Thy holy Archangel Raphael, O Lord, to breathe upon this water and make it holy, that they who shall drink of it may justly command the element of Air. Amen."

As he shifted the summoning hand to help support the cup, a breeze seemed to stir in the East, cycling gently at first but then gathering in intensity, stirring hair and robes, sweeping the hood from Evaine's hair in a shower of golden pins, even buffeting at Javan and Joram—but not touching so much as a hair on Queron's head. Indeed, Queron seemed hardly even aware of what he was calling up, head half bowed, eyes half closed, left hand still resting quietly on Joram's shoulder.

The storm condensed into a whirlwind that sucked at a blue-tinged curl of smoke spiralling upward from the thurible which, in reality, was hardly smoking at all anymore. It swirled above the ghost-cup in Cinhil's ghost-hands and tightened down, faintly stirring the surface of the water and then dying away.

The Cinhil figure closed his eyes briefly and passed the cup across to Joram. To Joram's senses, melded of reality and recall, the ghost-cup seemed to have real weight and substance in his hands. He held it beside the entranced Javan and extended his right hand flat over the rim as he had done that other night, repeating the same words, and with the same intent.

"O Lord, Thou art holy indeed: the fountain of all holiness. We pray Thee now send Thy holy Archangel of Fire, the Blessed Michael, to instill this water with the fire of Thy love and make it holy. So may all who drink of it command the element of Fire. Amen."

He moved his right hand a little aside from the cup as he had done before, cupping the palm upward, but the fire that grew to egg size in the hollow of his hand was not of his own crafting; rather, it was spun from the memory that Queron invoked, yet as substantial as if Joram had conjured the flame it represented.

He tilted his hand above the cup and watched the fiery sphere float slowly downward, steam hissing upward as fire permeated the water, lingering as a cold blue flame that frosted the surface and played about the white-glazed rim. With no less reverence than he had that first time, Joram turned to offer the ghost-cup to the image of his sister, standing at his left. She shook her wind-tousled hair back off her face in a graceful and fondly remembered gesture and took the cup. Their fingers brushed as it passed—warm and alive!—and Joram found himself staring at her as she bowed her head over it for a moment, then raised it in supplication.

"O Lord, Thou art holy indeed: the fountain of all holiness," she seemed to say. "Let now Thine Archangel Gabriel, who rules the stormy waters, instill this cup with the rain of Thy wisdom, that they who shall drink hereof may justly command the element of Water. Amen."

Joram could feel the tension rebuilding as it had that long-ago night, and he flinched a little as lightning crackled in the air above their heads and thunder rumbled, and a small, dark cloud began to take shape above the cup. Power smouldered in Evaine's blue eyes, contained yet potent; and as the thunder spoke again, more softly this time, the little cloud gave way to a brief thundershower. Most of the rain fell into the cup, but some of it ran down the sides and a few drops splashed on those watching. The drop that hit Joram's upper lip had been real that other time; and as he tasted of this one, it was just as sweet as he remembered.

She lowered the cup, and Joram watched her pass it to the Alister Cullen figure, who was their father. He watched Camber-Alister raise the cup to eye level with both hands, the sea-ice eyes fixed on a point above, and *knew* the coming of the One he called.

"O Lord, Thou art holy indeed: the fountain of all holiness," the familiar voice murmured, wrenching at Joram's heart. "Let Uriel, Thy messenger of darkness and of death, instill this cup with all the strength and secrets of the earth, that they who shall drink hereof may justly command the element of Earth. Amen."

The earth did not really tremble under their feet this time, but a part of Joram was convinced that it did. He seemed to hear the dull rattle of the altar candlesticks and the chains of the thurible, as he had before, and the light tinkle of the Ring of Fire vibrating at the bottom of the white-glazed cup in Camber-Alister's hands.

But as he watched and listened, another part of him became convinced that he was hearing the actual ring vibrating at the bottom of the actual cup on the little altar table. He looked at it sharply, and it stopped as quickly, as the Camber-Alister figure lowered the ghost-cup in its hands.

But now events diverged from memory. Where before Camber-Alister had passed the cup back to Cinhil for the culmination of the ritual, he now turned his sea-ice gaze upon Queron, who had not been present that night, raising the cup to him in bidding and compulsion.

Joram could feel his heart beginning to pound as a sense of immanent Presence seemed to surge over him like a wave. Queron obviously realized that events were diverging, too. Still sunk in his own deep trancing, but impelled now by direction not of his crafting, the Healer let his hand slip from Joram's shoulder and moved forward to pick up the physical cup from the little table. Joram could see him quite clearly, but could do no more than watch, struck motionless and dumb.

Queron straightened, holding the cup in his two hands, and turned his face slightly toward the right, toward the Cinhil figure. The figure wavered, then dissolved into a disembodied mist that flowed over and enveloped him like a cloak, transparent yet substantial, giving his face a very near likeness to Cinhil's. That face was expressionless as he continued across the circle toward the North and held out the physical cup to that quarter's representative. Bowing slightly, the Camber-Alister figure set his ghost-cup over the real one, so that the two merged into one.

"The cup is ready, Sire," the Camber-Alister figure said. "What remains is in your hands."

Gravely Queron bowed to him, turning then to approach the wide-eyed Javan, still trembling where he had been left. From his expression, Joram guessed that the boy now was seeing Queron as his father. As Queron lifted the cup between them and spoke, the voice was certainly Cinhil's.

"Javan, you are my son and heir," he said, paraphrasing slightly, for the words he recited had been for Alroy that first time. "Drink. By this mystery shall you come to the power that is your Divine Right, as king of this realm; and even so shall you instruct your own sons, if that should some day come to pass."

Under the compulsion of his father's eyes, Javan lifted his hands to rest on the hands that held the cup, tipping it to drink. Joram could hear the Ring of Fire tumbling along the side of the cup as Javan drained it, and he found himself moving in to take the cup as Javan's hands fell away. He moved behind Javan when he had set the cup down, catching him under the arms when the king began to sway on his feet, an odd expression on his face as he stared at his "father."

Then he saw the reason for Javan's expression. For beyond Queron-Cinhil, who now slowly raised his hands to clasp them to Javan's head the way Cinhil had done, the Camber-Alister figure had now become wholly Camber, pale eyes serene and compassionate, quicksilver hair gleaming in the candlelight as he glided in beside Queron to set his hands atop the Healer's, just as they made contact with Javan's head.

Javan reacted as if he had been bolted, body going rigid and then buckling at the knees, eyes rolling upward in their sockets. Joram, bracing the king from behind, had to shift his own balance to keep both of them on their feet. He gaped at the familiar figure, so near and yet so far, shrinking back a little in fear as, after a breathless heartbeat or two, the figure lifted the hand nearest him to touch it briefly to his brow.

The touch was not quite physical, but the touch of the other's mind was exquisitely real.

You need not fear, the familiar mind spoke in his. *Well have you wrought this night's work.*

Joram reeled under the touch, for the mind that spoke to his undoubtedly was his father's.

Father, will he keep his crown? he asked. *Will what we have done be enough?*

That knowledge is not given me, Camber returned. *Many enemies will seek his life. Pray that the vessel bears no hidden weaknesses, and bid him remember that kings kin to those of our blood can die just as easily as humans, if sword or arrow take their toll.*

With that the hand withdrew and the voice faded from Joram's mind, the figure also vanishing. In that same instant Javan went completely limp, and Queron as well, so that Joram had to shuffle quickly to ease both to the floor.

"Joram, what's happened!" he could hear Tavis calling, on his feet now on the other side of the circle, shading his eyes to squint past the veiling.

"Javan's fine," Joram muttered, after a cursory pass of his hand over the king's brow—for he had anticipated that the boy might pass out in the intensity of his experience; he had before. He had not expected it of Queron.

He checked Queron next, pressing his fingers hard against the carotid pulse and probing with his mind. The pulse was steady, Queron's unconsciousness apparently of the sort that often followed the conclusion of a profound inner working.

"They've both just fainted," Joram said, scrambling to his feet and staggering none too steadily over to the sword, which he swept up and across and down to cut a doorway.

Tavis was past it as soon as it literally was possible to do so, darting in first to check Javan, then shifting to Queron, who was starting to stir. Joram reclosed the gate and went to join them, kneeling anxiously at Queron's side as the elder Healer opened his eyes with a flutter, clearly startled to find himself lying flat on his back.

"What happened?" he demanded, dark eyes flicking first to Tavis, whose hand was on his brow, then to Joram.

"You—ah—got into the ritual more than I think you planned,"

Joram said, choosing his words carefully, since Tavis was listening. "After we'd re-created the charging of the cup, you came into the center of the circle and picked up the physical cup. Do you remember that?"

"Aye." He started to sit up, but Tavis' hand stayed him. "Then you—assimilated the Cinhil-figure," Joram said, sending him a mental image of what he had seen.

Queron nodded. "Preparing to take that role, so that the real cup could be offered to Javan," he said. "I remember that."

"Do you remember taking the ghost-cup from the Alister-figure after that?" Tavis asked, as Queron again made an attempt to sit up and this time was allowed, even assisted, by the younger Healer.

"I remember that it seemed to have weight," Queron said. He cocked his head as he gazed unfocused past them. "Odd—somehow it seemed like more than just the weight of the physical cup in my hands. You know, I'd always planned to do that part of the re-creation—reciting Cinhil's words before giving Javan to drink. But *after* he'd drunk . . ."

His voice trailed off, memory apparently eluding him of the most important part of what had just happened.

"It was *somebody else* who put his hands on your hands, Queron," Joram prompted, looking at the elder Healer and willing him to a tight link that Tavis could not overhear.

But Tavis nodded his head anyway, clearly having seen exactly what Joram had seen.

"I'd been expecting you to take on the Cinhil façade," Tavis said, awed. "We'd all agreed that was necessary, to maintain the illusion for Javan. But this was after that—and after you'd taken the cup overlay into the physical one. The Alister image followed you over to Javan while he was drinking, and then it—changed. Just before it touched him, it changed."

He glanced in question at the Michaeline priest, but Joram was saved from having to answer by a faint whimper and a twitch from Javan. At once recalled to his duty, Joram reached behind him to pluck the Ring of Fire out of the white-glazed goblet, hastily drying it on the hem of his cassock.

Javan breathed a little sigh and opened his eyes.

"I saw my father," he whispered, his gaze flicking to the other faces to see if they had seen it, too. "It was just like that other time. I remember everything now. It didn't hurt this time, though. He put something into my head, but it didn't hurt me."

Trembling, Tavis brushed his hand across the king's brow, almost a caress, and set his stump lightly against his neck.

"Do you remember *what* he put into your head, my prince?" he whispered. *"Think!"*

"I think this will help," Joram said, displaying the ring and reaching for Javan's left hand. "The original mandate that Cinhil set in you and Alroy and Rhys Michael was meant to be triggered by putting on this ring, after he was dead. We'll probably never know why it didn't work for Alroy; but after what's just happened, I'd be surprised if it doesn't work for you." He poised the ring at the tip of Javan's left ring finger. "Are you ready?"

As Javan nodded, eyes wide and trusting, Joram slid the ring onto the finger and shoved it home.

CHAPTER THIRTEEN

Surely thou hast spoken in mine hearing, and I
have heard the voice of thy words.
                                        —Job 33:8

It was like waking from refreshing sleep, or opening a door onto sunlight. In one instant Javan was still bewildered, uncertain whether he had at last attained his father's legacy; in the next, in less than a blink of the eye, knowledge was upon him. He stiffened momentarily as he realized it had happened, relaxing then as he briefly allowed himself to explore the deeper awareness suddenly made his. He was aware of Joram and Queron and Tavis watching him, waiting, and he allowed a slow, lazy smile to come upon his lips as he sat up and looked at them.

"This is the legacy that you and Evaine and Rhys and your father gave to *my* father, isn't it?" he said to Joram, flicking open a mind link directly to the priest and grinning as Joram, pleased, took up the link and sent tentative congratulations. "It's really quite extraordinary. I can see now that it's been here all along; I just didn't know how to tap it. Or—I was starting to learn, but this took away whatever was holding me back: the strictures placed because Alroy was supposed to have it first."

He glanced around him at the shimmer of the circle still enfolding them, and what he could now see beyond it—vague shadow-shapes of the Watchers they had called to Ward the place. They brooded at the four Quarters—he had the impression they were looking directly at him, though he could sense no eyes. He felt awe before them, but no longer any fear.

"I understand what all of this was about, too," Javan went on

130

softly. "I know who you called, and why. I'm aware that I still have limitations, but now I have the knowledge to make full use of what I do have." He shook his head and sighed. "I see, too, why my father was reluctant to use his power. He didn't understand. With God's help, maybe I'll have the wisdom to use mine, though. It may well be the only way I'll survive."

To demonstrate his newfound talents, Joram had him direct the closing of the circle then. The king's performance was flawless, coolly mediating all excess energy into the earth beneath them and then dismissing the Quarters with unruffled courtesy. When he had taken up the sword to conclude the rite, symbolically cutting across the arcs of the circle in four places and saluting the East a final time, he turned to give the blade back into Joram's keeping— and staggered as a wave of exhaustion hit him.

"Steady!" Joram admonished, catching him under one arm as the sword fell from his fingers in a clangor of steel against stone steps. Tavis caught him under the other arm, and as they eased him to a sitting position on the bottom step, Queron grasped one hand to monitor.

"He's all right," the Healer murmured. "I'd have been a bit surprised if he *hadn't* had a bit of backlash. You're going to need another good night's sleep, my prince," he said, crouching down to look Javan in the eyes. "You should be able to access a fatigue-banishing spell now. Can you?"

Javan blinked and nodded, still breathing a little hard and definitely looking less certain than he had before.

"What you're experiencing is quite normal after a working like you've just been through," Queron reassured him. "Would you like me to take you through the spell, so you'll know how to do it next time?"

"That might be a good idea," Javan agreed.

"All right. First I want you to put your head between your knees for a few seconds, to get rid of the light-headedness." He set his hands to either side of Javan's head and guided him, urging him to straighten after a moment. "Now close your eyes and cup your palms over them, with the fingers overlapping—that's right— and center on the spell. You've got it. Now draw a deep breath to trigger it . . ."

After a few seconds Javan drew a second deep breath and dropped his hands, opening his eyes with a surprised and slightly sheepish grin.

"I did it," he murmured.

"And did it very well, too," Queron said, smiling as he glanced at Tavis. "You'd better take him back to the Portal now. The longer he's here, the more chance there is of him being missed and dangerous questions being raised."

"But—when shall I see you all again?" Javan asked, even as he got to his feet to go with Tavis.

"That will have to be worked out in the days and weeks to come, my prince," Joram said, also rising. "Displacing the Deryni from Court was not accomplished in a day, and restoration of a balance will not be possible overnight, either, however good all of our intentions. Etienne de Courcy and Guiscard will give you guidance on some of the legislative revisions needed. In the meantime, we have in mind that a new Portal somewhere in the castle would be the most useful immediate thing we could do for you, to expedite further communication. The one you've been using will become too dangerous, if it's used very often."

"A new Portal—where?" Javan breathed.

"That's what you'll need to decide," Joram said, motioning Tavis to go on ahead. "Think about it for a few days—and keep in mind that we'll have to smuggle in a Deryni or two to actually set it up."

"How about in my apartments?" Javan asked.

Queron shook his head. "If it's to be as secure as it must be, it will require several days' preparation to do it right, Sire. How would you keep nonessential personnel out of the royal apartments for that long? No, better some other room—easily accessible to you, but not in particular demand for any other purpose. Give yourself time to think about it. You have other things to worry about for the next few days. Joram will endeavor to get a message to you in a week or so via Guiscard—who will be waiting for you, by the way."

Javan nodded, taking it all in. "What *about* Guiscard?" he asked. "I can't think that you want him to know about everything I—ah—accumulated tonight."

Joram smiled. "I think you'll find that Tavis has taken care of that," he said. "You'd best go now, my prince."

"Not without a proper Deryni blessing," Javan retorted, eyes shining as he thumped to both knees at Joram's feet and folded his hands before him. "Then I'll go," he added in a whisper.

Tears glinting suddenly in his grey eyes, Joram likewise clasped both hands before him to collect his intent, then raised both above the king's head.

"The compassing of God and His right hand be upon you, my prince," he murmured, touching his hands lightly to Javan's bowed head. "Father, Son, and Holy Spirit." He made the Sign of the Cross in the air between them, then brought his hands back to his breast in a bow. "Amen."

"Amen," Javan responded, repeating the gesture.

Then he was on his feet and turning to flee through the door Tavis had left ajar, not looking back. When he had gone, Queron cast an appraising glance at Joram.

"That *was* who I thought it was during the ritual, wasn't it?" he said, his tone making it no question but a statement. "Do you think Javan saw him?"

"Only for a few seconds," Joram replied, "and I doubt he knew what he was seeing. He was only an infant when my father was 'killed,' after all—less than a month old. He couldn't possibly remember what he looked like."

"He's seen paintings," Queron ventured.

"Not the same. Besides, he wouldn't have been expecting to see a 'saint' in our ritual."

"What about the night Cinhil died?" Queron persisted. "Could he have seen anything then?"

Joram shook his head. "No. Camber never shifted from his Alister form. *Cinhil* saw the truth—but that was something different, at the moment he passed over. None of us knew about that until Camber told us. The princes couldn't have known."

"Then it's just Tavis we have to worry about," Queron said. "*He* saw Camber tonight—and he may well have known who he was seeing."

"We'll just have to hope the full implications don't sink in for a while—and be ready to deal with the situation when they eventually do."

He did not want to consider, as he turned to begin gathering up the accoutrements of their night's work, just what *he* thought about his father's unexpected and very mystical reappearance.

The next day dawned sunny and bright again in Rhemuth, but not as hot as it had been. The black-clad procession that accompanied the coffin of the dead king down from the castle to the cathedral was more sombre than Cinhil's had been, four years before, for the new king was an unknown quantity to most people. Though physically he resembled a taller and more robust version of his twin who had died—except for the clubfoot that made him limp as he walked behind his brother's coffin—he had been absent from Court for most of the past three years. Thanks to the careful campaign of the former regents, even before the late king's health entered its final decline, most folk assumed that Javan's call to the religious life had been a genuine one and found themselves uneasy that he should be walking behind the coffin as his brother's heir, wearing the full Haldane achievement on his otherwise sombre tunic.

But he was an adult by law; this time Gwynedd need not be governed by regents until the king reached his majority. What *kind* of a king he would be was another question. Having spent the last three years in seminary training, he would be well educated to rule; but what would God say about a king who set aside his Holy Orders to take up an earthly crown? Granted, the father had done so; but the father had not known who he was until called from his monastery; Javan had known before he even entered.

And even so, God had punished the father for renouncing his holy vows. The first Haldane son had died at his baptism, poisoned by a Deryni priest turned renegade. And why else should one twin be born clean-limbed and whole, if sickly, the other with a twisted foot that made of him a cripple?

Nor was it a question of no other Haldane being available. Prince Rhys Michael, the engaging youngest son, had endeared himself to the ordinary people since his first exposure to them, at the funeral of the late king his father. Since then, his pleasant disposition and growing interest in and aptitude for the activities of the weapons yard had made him easily the most popular prince to come along in many a year. Many folk had thought it long settled that Rhys Michael should reign if Alroy died without heir. Why, then, was he not wearing the accoutrements of the heir?

Not that Rhys Michael seemed to mind. Fondly attentive, he walked at his brother's side and a pace behind and showed every evidence of being exactly where he wanted to be, if one must march in a funeral procession at all. And Javan comported himself with a kingly dignity that did not go unnoticed, despite his limp—which was far less than most folk remembered. The long walk to the cathedral would have its price, for Javan was far less accustomed to walking long distances than he had been four years before, when he followed his father's coffin. But though his newfound abilities had enabled him to put aside the discomfort without recourse to outside assistance, he knew he would need Oriel's services by the end of the day, to repair the very real damage he was doing by blocking the warning signs of pain.

They would not mistake him for a priest, though. He had been determined about that, within the bounds of propriety. The bright Haldane shield emblazoned on chest and back made the black tunic bear no resemblance to clerical attire; and to minimize the visual reminder of his tonsure, only just beginning to grow out, he wore a cap of maintenance with his chased-gold coronet—black velvet and sable, which blended with his hair. Rhys Michael wore one as well, under his silver circlet, so the ulterior reason for Javan's would not be so obvious.

A mounted escort led the procession, all on black horses, wide black baldrics partially masking the Haldane surcoats they wore, black plumes nodding in the horses' headstalls. The coffin was borne on the shoulders of six young knights, for Alroy had died a young king. Sir Gavin, his last squire to be knighted, walked at the coffin's left, as captain of the coffin detail, drawn sword carried before him at *present arms*, either perspiration or tears running down his face.

The stiffened black pall covering the coffin was adorned with escutcheons of the Haldane arms, three to each side, and fell well over the shoulders of the knights beneath, so that only the first two could see Lord Albertus leading the late king's charger just ahead of them—the tall albino stallion Alroy had ridden to his coronation, caparisoned in crimson, with the king's boots reversed in the stirrups. Atop the coffin, the State Crown of Gwynedd glittered in the sunlight, gold and silver leaves and crosses intertwined, rich against a pillow of crimson velvet, with Earl Tammaron to walk beside it and watch it did not tumble.

Behind the coffin came the new king and his brother, with an honor guard of young knights directly at their backs, four abreast, and the rest of the Court ranged behind, also in fours—peers and officeholders and a rear guard of mounted escort. Muffled drums beat out the cadence, and Great George tolled the final passing of the king.

Two archbishops met them at the doors to the cathedral, and the full choir of Saint George's began a psalm as the ecclesiastical procession formed up and then began processing slowly inside. The air was close and the heat oppressive, but no worse than many other times Javan had been forced to endure—and certainly more bearable than that first Requiem sung the morning of Alroy's death.

Javan set himself to go through it a little detached—he had done his mourning for Alroy several days ago. He went forward for Communion at the proper time, forcing himself not to mind that it was Hubert's hand from which he must receive it. And when the final prayers had been said for the repose of Alroy's soul, and the coffin had been carried down into the undercroft where the royal vaults lay, he watched impassively beside his brother as the plain wooden coffin underneath the pall was shifted into the sarcophagus prepared for it. It was cooler down in the crypts, and he and Rhys Michael lit a final candle for their dead brother as the heavy lid was slid onto the sarcophagus and Great George slowly tolled again—sixteen times, once for each year of the king's life.

They emerged from the crypt when the last leaden toll had died away, moving toward the cathedral doors in less formal procession to a sung *Laudate*. Horses were waiting for him and Rhys Michael as they came out, Alroy's white stallion for Javan and a chestnut for Rhys Michael. As they mounted up, additional mounts were brought up from among the waiting escort, for Charlan and the other three young knights who were their personal bodyguard. Javan kept his head high as they rode, knowing that on horseback, at least, he looked every inch a king.

He maintained the façade all the way to the castle; and the respite for his lame foot, while riding, enabled him to make his entrance into the great hall without limping very much. There, as he moved informally among those come to pay their respects, even those most inclined to look for fault in the new king could find little to complain about.

The ladies of the Court undoubtedly applied different criteria from their menfolk in sizing up the new king. Other than servants, women had been little in evidence during the first few days after Javan's return, while the Court was in deepest mourning, but the prospect of an unmarried king come to the throne had brought the ladies out in force. They reminded Javan of doves, fluttering and cooing among themselves in their gowns of quiet blacks and greys. A few called to mind more predatory birds.

One of the more obvious of these, because Javan knew who she was and exactly what she was after, was the daughter of Rhun of Horthness by his first marriage—Juliana, a bold, dark-eyed beauty about a year older than Javan whose name had been mentioned more than once in the past three years as a potential queen for Alroy. Such a match would have been the ultimate achievement for Rhun, whose own brilliant second marriage to Murdoch's only daughter had given him a powerful political alliance with his fellow regent, in addition to the son and heir denied him by his first wife.

Unfortunately for Juliana and for Rhun, Alroy's declining health had made it less and less likely that any woman would ever be his queen. Javan liked to think that Rhun himself, by condoning the regents' policy of keeping Alroy biddable by constant medication, had perhaps contributed to the failure of any match to take place. Rhun undoubtedly would renew his quest for a crown for his daughter now that Alroy was dead, but he could campaign until hell froze over, so far as Javan was concerned. Of all the former regents, Javan probably detested Rhun the most—though Murdoch ran a very close second.

He counted himself particularly fortunate that Rhun had been absent from Court for the all-important Accession Council, even if his luck had not extended to keeping Rhun from returning in time for the funeral. Rumor had it that he had brought along Sitric, his tame Deryni, but to Javan's very great relief, Sitric did not make an appearance with his master. In fact, the earl seemed to be on his good behavior when he approached to pay his official condolences—though he did make a point of formally presenting his daughter as well as his wife. Other courtiers found opportunity to introduce their eligible daughters and sisters as well. Javan kept Charlan and Sir Jason close beside him, and prayed for the hour when he might decently take his leave.

But the afternoon seemed interminable, even when servants began laying out a light collation and the wine began to flow. After an hour or so, Rhys Michael wandered off in the company of some of the younger denizens of the Court—Cathan Drummond, who was his junior squire, and Quiric and Fulk Fitz-Arthur, the sons of Lord Tammaron, all of whom were slightly younger than the prince. A little later the four had become part of an animated cluster of other youngsters, among them a bevy of chattering young girls. Glancing across the room at them as he pretended to be interested in the droning condolences of a baron from Desse, Javan was amazed to see how the girls he had known from childhood were turning into women. For some, the changes were not entirely for the better.

Udaut's pretty daughter Lirin, wed to Murdoch's son Richard when she was only twelve, was now a slightly dowdy though animated matron of fifteen, the hub of a flutter of adolescent chatter that also included an attractive, dark-haired girl with slightly haunted eyes whom Javan suddenly realized must be Richeldis MacLean, now MacInnis. Political maneuverings shortly before Javan left Court three years before had left Richeldis' elder sister mysteriously dead in her sleep, and Richeldis herself sole heiress of Cassan and the reluctant bride of Earl Manfred's elder son. Rumor had reached Javan of a daughter born to the pair sometime last year, and she looked to be carrying another child now, one hand curving protectively over a gentle bulge beneath her grey gown. He could only hope and pray that Richeldis' children would provide her some consolation for having been sacrificed on the altar of political expediency.

Cathan's sister Michaela was another who could probably look forward to such a fate. Several years older than her brother, she was turning into quite an attractive little thing, with her bright blue eyes and waves of tawny hair cascading down her back. She would bring no spectacular dowry to her marriage, for James Drummond, her father, had only been a younger son of the gentry; but the Drummond blood was old. She also was a distant cousin to Richeldis, and like Richeldis, her line had been proven untainted by an infusion of Deryni ancestry far back in their pedigrees. Javan would never forget the day the regents had tested all three children with *merasha*, that first time the doomed Declan Carmody had begun to crack under the strain of forced collaboration.

Since then, rather conveniently, James Drummond had been killed in a skirmish with highway robbers while on a mission for one of the regents. The children's mother, once married to the slain son of Saint Camber whose name was borne by their son, had retired to a convent near Valoret—probably not entirely at her own instigation. But by then both Michaela and young Cathan had been fostered at Court, Michaela to the household of Manfred's countess and Cathan as Rhys Michael's squire. Javan was pleased to see the two apparently flourishing despite what had happened—and even more pleased when he could finally take his leave and quietly retire.

Oriel was waiting in Javan's presence chamber when he and Charlan at last returned to the royal apartments. The Healer looked professionally concerned, and brought a rushlight closer as Javan sank down wearily in a chair beside the window embrasure and Charlan knelt to begin unbuckling his boots, starting with the right.

"How did the foot hold up?" Oriel asked.

Javan took off his coronet and cap of maintenance and set them aside, running his fingers through his sweaty hair and permitting himself a sigh of relief as Charlan pulled the boot off his crippled foot.

"Well enough," he said. "Better than I expected." He dropped a hand onto Charlan's head and gently exerted control. "Relax, Charlan," he murmured. "Remember nothing of what you're about to hear unless I tell you to."

Charlan hardly missed a beat as he turned his attention to the other boot. Oriel, after observing him for a moment, said, "That's twice I've seen you do this sort of thing in the last few days. I hope you don't make a habit of it."

"Only when there's need," Javan replied as Charlan pulled off the other boot. "Charlan, you can bring over a basin of water now, if you would. My feet could do with a bit of a wash before Master Oriel works on me."

As Charlan went to fetch the requested water, Javan leaned a little closer to the Healer.

"Before you start lecturing me, you should know that Lord Rhun is back, as from today," he said quietly. "That's primarily my problem, but they're saying he's brought Sitric with him. From what I hear, Master Sitric is rather more resigned to his work than most Deryni in your position. We're both going to have to be careful."

Oriel gave a little shudder as Charlan returned, a towel over one shoulder, and knelt to set a basin and ewer on the floor at Javan's feet. When he had lifted out the ewer, Javan shifted his feet into the cool basin, wiggling his toes contentedly as Charlan poured water over them.

"He's a dangerous man, is Sitric," Oriel murmured, watching the operation. "He's ambitious—and Rhun knows just how to feed that ambition without actually conceding anything. Fortunately, he isn't half the man that Declan Carmody was—God rest his soul— and he isn't nearly as well trained."

"What can he do, Oriel?" Javan asked. "Obviously he can Truth-Read, or Rhun wouldn't have kept him. Can he read minds?"

"Aye—and rip them, if there's resistance," Oriel said bitterly. "He hasn't much finesse—but then, Rhun doesn't demand that, does he?"

"No, he doesn't," Javan agreed. "But perhaps that will be to our advantage." He touched a hand to Charlan's shoulder and gave a silent command, retaining the towel as the knight rose and retreated to a nearby chair, there to close his eyes and lapse into light snoring as his head came forward on his chest.

"Tell me about Sitric's limitations," Javan went on, pretending not to notice Oriel's raised eyebrow at what he had just done. "What's his range? How much danger am I in, if I'm merely in the same room with him? How careful do I have to be?"

Recalling himself to the questions, Oriel took the towel from Javan and drew a stool under himself, laying the towel across his lap and lifting the crippled foot, dripping, to rest it on his knees as he began his examination.

"If he's Truth-Reading, you'd better remember everything you've ever been taught about avoiding the direct lie, because he'll catch any deviation from the literal truth," Oriel said, gently probing the misshapen ankle. "Of course, kings are allowed a certain amount of lying—diplomatic half-truths and such—but if you lie about anything important, you can be assured that Sitric will tell Rhun—if not then, certainly at the very earliest opportunity. Your foot isn't too bad, considering how far you had to walk," he added, clasping the ankle close between his two hands. "Just give me a minute here."

Javan could feel the Healing already radiating like warmth from Oriel's hands. Closing his eyes, he let himself bask in the bliss of it as the stiffness melted away and overstressed muscles relaxed. When Oriel had finished, bathing the foot again before drying it, Javan wiggled his toes luxuriantly and sighed, forcing his mind back to the original question.

"He can Truth-Read me, then," he murmured, collecting his thoughts. "And probably will."

"I think we must assume that as a given," Oriel agreed. "It takes very little effort on his part, for a potentially great return, if he does catch you in an important lie. But that's nothing you didn't know before."

"No." Javan lifted his good foot out of the basin and let Oriel dry that one, too. "What else do I have to worry about?"

"The biggest danger would be direct physical contact," Oriel replied. "Given his level of training and ability, he'd need that for any actual Reading, or for trying to force the truth—but I don't think he'd dare lay hands on you unless Rhun ordered it. Of course, if you were careless enough to let Rhun and his cronies get you alone—"

"I plan to avoid that," Javan assured him. "If I couldn't, though, would my shields protect me?"

"Probably," Oriel conceded. "At least until they got some *merasha* into you." He grimaced. "I'm assuming that if you have shields like a Deryni, you'd probably react like a Deryni to the drug. And that would *really* raise the hue and cry."

Javan swallowed, suddenly less sure of himself than he had been only minutes before. He had seen all too graphically what *merasha* did to Deryni and had no idea whether it would affect him or not.

"I've got to be sure I don't give them cause to try that, then," he murmured. "Either to have Sitric try to Read me or to dose me with *merasha*. Is there anything it *is* safe to do, if Sitric is around?"

Oriel cocked an eyebrow thoughtfully. "I think you're safe enough to Truth-Read in his presence—so long as you don't try to Truth-Read *him* and you don't let it be known what you're doing—but if you tried anything else, he might detect that. Of course, I don't know what else you might be able to do."

"Neither do I," Javan said a bit sheepishly. "And it looks as if I'd better be very careful while I learn."

Oriel nodded. "We both must be careful. And what of Sir Charlan?" he asked, nodding in the sleeping knight's direction. "How much does he know?"

"If he could remember it all," Javan said with a sickly smile, "probably enough to send me to the stake several times over, king or not, if the *Custodes* had anything to say about it. As it is, he just thinks he learned years ago to catch the odd catnap while waiting for his somewhat eccentric master to tire of all-night prayer vigils and forays to obscure scholars to talk about undoubtedly boring manuscripts."

"Does he really?"

"Well, I think that was how he'd explained it to himself when he was my squire," Javan said with a grin. "From the very beginning, though, he's always been absolutely loyal—far beyond whatever duty he owes me. I—suppose he must be the closest thing I've got to a friend, with Tavis gone away—at least with someone who's near my own age." He sighed.

"It's been very difficult, not intruding on his trust any more than I had to. The worst was once I started my campaign to get sent off to seminary, because then I had to protect both of us. It can't have been easy for him, knowing he had to spy on me and report back with a Deryni present. I expect you were the Deryni, at least some of the time."

Reluctantly Oriel shrugged and nodded. "I never guessed a thing, though, or had to risk a false Reading. You covered your tracks well."

"I had to." Javan looked down at his hands, at the Ring of Fire. "Now that I'm back, though, I'm trying not to interfere any more than absolutely necessary. It seems ungrateful, at very best, to compel a loyalty that's already freely given. I—*have* made memory adjustments a couple of times, as I did just now, to protect both of us, but I'd like to think he wouldn't object, if he knew why. He took a huge personal risk by coming to fetch me out of *Arx Fidei*. I suppose I've put my life in his hands more times than I'd care to count—and doubtless will do so again."

Oriel glanced over at the sleeping Charlan, then back at Javan.

"He has no idea about any of this, then," he said softly.

Javan shook his head. "It's safer if he doesn't know, for both of us."

"May I?" Oriel asked, gesturing toward the knight.

Swallowing, Javan lowered his eyes. "If you can detect who else has controlled him in the past week or so, you'd better not," he said. "I've—been to Joram twice since I got back. And I had help."

"And if I don't know from whom, I can't reveal it, even under interrogation by Sitric," Oriel agreed, nodding. He closed his eyes briefly. "That means there are other Deryni about, whom even I don't know about." A hopeful light came into his eyes as he looked again at Javan. "Does it also mean that perhaps my family may soon be free?" he dared to whisper.

Javan shifted uncomfortably. "I can't promise anything right away," he said quietly. "There are a lot of details to be worked out first. But I hope at least to let you see them before too long. I know how hard it must be for you."

"If only you knew, my prince," Oriel breathed, shaking his head softly. "Not seeing Alana for these three years and more has been bad enough. But Karis, my little girl . . ." His voice choked up a little as he went on. "She was only a few months old when they were taken hostage. She was just a baby. I try to imagine how she's growing, how she must look like a tiny version of her mother, or maybe a bit like me. She'll be a little person now—walking, *talking* by now—and I've missed all these years . . ."

"I promised you I'd do what I could," Javan murmured, "but it's going to take some time. Are they still being held in the same place?"

"Aye, so far as I know."

"And the other hostages?"

Oriel nodded, pulling himself together. "Sitric's mother and sister, Ursin O'Carroll's wife and son—and Ursin himself. They're said to be comfortable enough, if it weren't captivity. But I'm told that Ursin has been in solitary confinement since they brought him back from the Baptizers and that the *Custodes* test him periodically with *merasha*, to be certain his powers haven't come back. God, how they must fear us!"

Javan, having been subjected to the constant harangues of the *Custodes* for nearly three years on the evil of the Deryni and how they must be isolated from all decent folk, could only agree.

CHAPTER FOURTEEN

And why stand we in jeopardy every hour?
                              —I Corinthians 15:30

Javan managed to avoid any confrontation with the dangerous Sitric in the first days that followed, but the same could not be said of Rhun, his master. Possibly on the advice of Murdoch and the others who had been faced down in earlier encounters, even Rhun dared not make open defiance of the new king—not yet, at any rate—but his staunchest advocates could not have called him cooperative. He offered his resignation dutifully enough, when the Council met on the morning after Alroy's funeral—knowing Javan dared not accept it—but criticism and obstruction were to become regular features of his activity within the Council context. Keeping him on the Council rankled, but Javan really had no choice.

Far more pleasing was the return of Baron Hildred, Alroy's former Master of Horse, who also had arrived just in time for the funeral. Hildred had no part of politics and wanted none; his focus was horses and those who rode them well. All three Haldane princes had begun their experience in the saddle under Hildred's tutelage. The appearance of another friend at that first Council meeting after the funeral brightened an otherwise taut day for the new young king.

Javan was grateful as well for the briefings that Jerowen and Etienne had been giving him over the past few days. For as soon as Hildred and Rhun had made token resignation of their offices—and Bonner Sinclair, who had missed the funeral but arrived in time for the meeting—Earl Tammaron produced a letter from his son, Fane Fitz-Arthur, the sole member of the Council yet to turn up.

"My son begs you to pardon his absence, Sire," Tammaron explained as he unfolded the letter Fane had sent. "A bereavement in his wife's family requires his continued presence in Cassan—though he intends to be present for your Grace's coronation and to present his compliments at that time."

"I am sorry to hear of his bereavement," Javan said, immediately guessing what Tammaron was about to tell him and very glad he had paid attention to his various briefings. "His wife is the daughter of the Prince of Cassan, I believe?"

Tammaron gave him a formal inclination of his head, as if surprised that Javan remembered.

"She is, Sire," Tammaron replied. "Alas, it is her father who has passed away—Prince Ambert Quinnell. He had been ill for some time. However, under the terms of treaties drawn up during the reign of your late father—"

"Why so modest, my lord?" Javan said, schooling himself to a taut, slightly ironic smile; for if he played this right, Tammaron's vanity would have him eating out of the royal hand. "Under the terms of the bridal contract that *you* negotiated, your son's marriage to the Princess Anne set in place an irrevocable covenant by which Cassan devolves to Gwynedd upon the death of her father, he having no sons. I thank you for Gwynedd's new duchy, my lord."

"Well, I—"

"It was brilliantly done, my lord," Javan went on, keeping up the momentum. "Would that I may have someone as shrewd as yourself to negotiate on my behalf when I eventually wed. You have done Gwynedd a great service, and I shall not forget."

"You—*are* aware, I trust, that Fane is not to be the first duke," Tammaron said tentatively. "That was the original provision, but it was changed after the birth of Fane's son, Ambert's grandson."

"Yes, young Tambert," Javan said easily. "I was so informed. Named, I believe, for both his noble grandfathers."

At Tammaron's look of astonishment, Javan allowed himself a faint smile. The thought of a long regency for one of his vassals was not particularly appealing, but having the jump on Tammaron was exquisitely satisfying.

"I thank you for conveying your son's message, my lord," he said, reaching out to take the letter Tammaron still had not managed to read to the Council. "Baron de Courcy, I shall ask you to send an appropriate reply to Cassan. Say that I shall be pleased to acknowledge my new duke when he arrives for my coronation and to receive his homage and fealty through his most excellent regents.

"Say also to Lord Fane that, as he now has a duchy to administer, I excuse him from further obligations as a Council lord and shall accept his resignation when he offers it, for I would not have his old obligations interfere with his new responsibilities as regent for his young son. Please assure him that his seat shall remain vacant until a worthy replacement can be chosen to succeed him."

So couched, no one could find any reasonable cause to object without sounding deliberately contentious. Tammaron even nodded his agreement, for the logic of Javan's decision was inescapable; the regent of a faraway duchy the size of Cassan could not possibly give useful service to the Council as well. Not even the volatile Murdoch raised an objection, though glances were exchanged among several of the other former regents.

Grateful that he seemed to have avoided yet another potential disagreement with his balky Council, Javan refrained from mentioning his other duke just then, for Graham, the young Duke of Claibourne, was an extremely sore point with the former regents, Murdoch in particular. He allowed the discussion to move on to the subject of possible coronation dates, finally settling on the last day of July, but when they finally adjourned, he held back Jason and Robear with Charlan after the others had left.

"I wasn't going to mention it during the meeting, but no one has yet said anything about my *other* duke," he said, "and no one has mentioned him in any of my briefings thus far. Are the Kheldour lords going to show up for the coronation?"

The three knights exchanged guarded looks, both Robear and Charlan deferring to Jason.

"I'm afraid the Kheldour situation has not improved during your absence, Sire," Jason said. "If anything, it's deteriorated. No one from Kheldour has been seen at Court since young Graham and his uncles came to have his title acknowledged as Duke of Claibourne and his regents sworn in. You were still here when that happened, I believe."

Javan nodded agreement as Jason continued.

"Since that day, so that no one can say they've violated the letter of their feudal obligations, Claibourne and the Earls of Eastmarch and Marley have continued to send their taxes and minimum levies for royal service—but nothing beyond what the law requires. Even that has slipped in recent months."

"How so?"

"Well, young Graham would have reached his majority earlier this year—which means he should have come to Rhemuth to have his coming of age confirmed and his regency officially ended. Need I say that he didn't come?"

"I can't say I blame him," Javan murmured, "when the man responsible for slaying his father still sits on the royal Council and has never been held accountable. I'm not sure I would have come, in his position."

"The question is, will he come to *you*, once he learns that your brother is dead?" Robear retorted. "If he doesn't—if he and his uncles fail to appear at the coronation, if they decline to acknowledge you as their overlord and do homage for their Kheldour holdings—reasonable men could justly construe that Kheldour has withdrawn from the alliance that brought Kheldour to Gwynedd in the first place. If that should happen, you're in no position to attempt bringing them back into the fold by force. Any war you fight in the next few years almost certainly will have to be against a Festillic pretender trying to invade from Torenth and regain what he regards as his throne."

"I'm aware of the Festillic danger," Javan murmured. "I know I can't afford to fight with Kheldour." He paused a beat. "You really think they won't come?"

Jason snorted. "I'm almost more afraid that they *will* come and decide that this is the time to renew their quarrel with Murdoch."

"Murdoch was responsible for the death of the boy's father," Javan said sharply. "And what he did to Declan Carmody and his family—I'll never forgive him for that!"

All three men looked distinctly uncomfortable, for all had been present at that terrible birthday court three years before, forced to witness the cold-blooded execution of Declan's wife and young sons and the cruel tortures inflicted on the former Deryni collaborator until he finally died.

"Ewan did attack Murdoch first, Sire," Robear said uneasily.

"Yes, after Murdoch provoked him!"

"Yes, but it wasn't perceived that way by the Court," Jason said, "and your witness would be judged faulty because you were a minor at the time. If you try to reopen the case after this long, you will be perceived as being either soft on Deryni or escalating a personal vendetta against Murdoch. I don't think you can afford either perception."

Javan sighed heavily, knowing Jason was right—yet another burden of the crown he was struggling to keep.

"I hadn't in mind to go after Murdoch," he finally said. "At least not now. Back to the Kheldour lords, though—do you think they'll come?"

"I believe Etienne has sent notification north to inform them of your brother's death, Sire," Robear said. "Also, official summons to appear at the coronation. Whether or not they comply remains to be seen—and the consequences, whichever way they go."

Which was all anyone could say, at this point. Shaking his head in resignation, Javan picked up the Haldane sword and got to his feet.

"Thank you, gentlemen. You've given me yet another thing to worry about. It isn't your fault," he added, flashing them a tight smile. "It simply means I'm walking a sword-edge rather than a mere tightrope. Let's go down to the great hall and get something to eat."

He thought about how to ease the situation while he ate a light midday meal with his knights, vaguely distracted from their easy banter. The prospect of a secession in Kheldour, not to mention possible war against a Festillic invader, had brought home the very real military challenges he might have to face, in addition to the more insidious threats he had already anticipated from the former regents. By the time they had ridden out for an afternoon's light exercise, galloping along the long, straight stretches beside the riverbank, he decided that part of his personal preparation for either eventuality lay in making himself better physically fit for the job he had inherited. After even this short jaunt, his thighs ached.

"I want you to put me back in training," he told Robear and Jason as they rested their horses in the shade of a stone bridge that spanned a stream just above the city. "I haven't had a sword in my hand in three years, other than to cut myself at the Accession Council, and I'm not sure I even remember how to draw a bow."

The latter certainly was not true, and all of them knew it, for Javan's skill at the archery butts had been better by age twelve than most of the men in the Haldane Archers Corps. Jason himself had encouraged it, for archery was a martial art not dependent upon agility of foot.

Swordplay was another matter entirely, however. And it *was* true that three years of mostly sedentary pursuits at *Arx Fidei* had not exactly provided the opportunity for ongoing physical development of a king who might need to lead men into battle, much less defend himself against rebellious subjects.

"You'll give us free rein?" Robear said, casting him one of those sidelong glances that Javan knew meant he was going to have to work, and work hard.

"I wouldn't have asked, if I didn't mean to do it right," Javan replied. "I'm not expecting it to be easy. I need you to make a proper knight of me, though, if I'm to live up to the pledges we exchanged a few days ago."

"Are you willing to make the regular commitment of your time?" Jason asked. "It can't be done overnight, or slapdash."

"I'm well aware of that," Javan said. "You can have my mornings, when it's still a little cooler; I'll keep other businesses to the afternoons, at least until we're well started. I want you to push me as hard as you think I can stand, and then some. I know it's going to involve a lot of sweat and not a little pain. I'm not looking forward to that. But I've got to do it. Next time one of the Council lords tries to defy me, I may need more than a glib tongue to get me out of it."

A glib tongue continued to keep Javan's opponents off balance in the next few weeks, as concern turned increasingly to planning for his coronation, but thereafter his days began in the practice yard, alternating between weapons drill, riding, and weapons drill while riding. He spent hours striking at the pells to begin building up his shoulders again and sparring with one or another of his knights. He spent more hours at the archery butts, quickly regaining his accuracy but appalled at how light a bow he had to use at first to do it.

On alternate days, training shifted to the breaking yard, where Baron Hildred endeavored to bring his riding skills back up to their previous level. Javan had been a bold and brilliant rider before leaving Court and remembered everything he had ever been taught; but getting disused riding muscles to obey him again was a humbling experience. Hildred took him back to basics for the first week or so, putting him up on a smooth-paced, reliable palfrey at the end of a lunge line and making him circle for what seemed like hours at the trot and canter, going over low jumps, deliberately falling off—all without stirrups.

Later, when he began to get legged up again, the arena sessions alternated with the tilting yard, working with lance or spear, and sword drill from horseback. Once he could draw one of the powerful little R'Kassan recurve bows again, there was shooting from horseback as well. It was all very hard work; but in this as in all the other disciplines he had resumed, Javan was pleased to find that his body performed far better at sixteen than it had at thirteen.

Mornings usually ended with a gallop down to the river again, where he could relax a little and pretend that he still enjoyed riding. Sometimes, when he got down from his horse at the end of a morning's training, his legs would hardly support him for their trembling—and it had nothing to do with his weak foot. His shoulders ached almost continually, for most of the skills he was reinstating made use of upper body strength, to compensate for his lessened mobility on foot.

Noonday sessions with Oriel after a bath became a regular feature for those first few weeks, the only way Javan could revive himself enough to face his afternoon obligations—for meetings seemed to multiply weekly, sometimes with the Council, increasingly with various commissions and assize courts, sometimes with staff from the earl marshal's office regarding plans for the coronation, now definitely set for the thirty-first of July.

One rather more pleasant if bittersweet accomplishment of those first few weeks was to arrange Oriel's longed-for reunion with his wife and daughter. It did not last long, and Javan had to reinforce his demand to the *Custodes* guards with the threat of Charlan and Guiscard lurking at his back, hands on sword hilts; but at least until one of the men summoned higher-ranking reinforcements, Oriel's joy was uncontained. While his own men barred the open doorway, Javan watched moist-eyed as the Healer wordlessly embraced his wife and then knelt to entice a tousle-headed toddler from behind her mother's skirts, to meet the father of whom she had no memory.

But all too soon, a well-armed *Custodes* captain was striding up to the doorway to end the scene of domestic happiness. With him came half a dozen more *Custodes* knights who looked even less inclined to be swayed by royal whim or sentiment.

"Sire, this must end at once," the captain said, courteous but single-minded. "I have standing orders that the Deryni collaborators are not to be granted access to their families. My authority comes directly from Brother Serafin as Grand Inquisitor, as set out in the Statutes of Ramos. Master Oriel will have to come away immediately."

Javan considered arguing the point, for he doubted that the *Custodes* commander's orders extended to laying hands on the king, but Charlan and Guiscard were not immune. Furthermore, current law did give Serafin the right to issue such orders—and further time stolen in defiance of the increased *Custodes* presence clearly would be of little worth.

"I had forgotten those were your orders," he said quietly, reluctantly beckoning for Oriel to come away. "Master Oriel has been a steadfastly loyal servant of this Court for many years now and had not seen his little daughter since shortly after her birth. It seemed a harmless kindness to repay him for his services."

"The Grand Inquisitor does not deem it harmless," the captain replied, watching Oriel like a cat fixed on a mouse as the Healer tearfully disentangled his daughter's arms from around his neck and gave her back into the arms of his wife, unable to look at them as he returned to the king's side.

Javan said nothing as he shrugged and turned to go, but he would never forget the look of despair on Oriel's face as the door closed behind them, the Healer's hand outstretched in final farewell to the weeping woman and the rosy-faced toddler who was blithely waving good-bye to him, wide-eyed and innocent beneath a tangle of red-gold curls. The incident left Oriel bound to him even more firmly and made Javan all the more determined that he must do whatever he could to reverse this blight that the former regents had set upon his kingdom.

To do that, he needed to survive; day-to-day survival depended partly upon domestic stability to bolster his efforts. His personal household began to take shape during those first few weeks, as his schedule became more fixed and some routine began to emerge. He had not yet dared to dismiss any of the officers of the previous reign, but the Court slowly began to include men of his own choosing. He named Lord Jerowen Reynolds to the seat being vacated by Fane Fitz-Arthur and appointed him Vice Chancellor. Baron Etienne de Courcy became his confidential secretary, and Guiscard became one of his aides.

The appointment he broached to the Council at a meeting in mid-July, however, had more personal implications, for it touched on a more personal need. And unlike the other appointments he had made, he must gain permission for this one—and from the *Custodes Fidei*. It represented a backing down from the adversary stance he had been forced to assume against the Order while securing his throne, and it rankled—but keeping Paulin and Albertus totally on their guard would only make things more difficult. Paulin was already annoyed over the Oriel incident.

"One last item this afternoon, gentlemen. I should like to make a personal request of Father Paulin," Javan said, forcing himself to keep a suppliant's face as he addressed the *Custodes* Vicar General, "but first, to offer him an apology."

"An apology, Sire?" Paulin looked dubious.

"Yes, Father. I formed my decision to leave Holy Orders in good conscience, and after sober reflection, but I regret that the manner of my leaving may have left ill feelings—with my abbot, in particular, and with you, Father. I also regret any disrespect I may have seemed to show to you, Archbishop," he added, casting his glance at Hubert. "I learned much under your tutelage and I am grateful for it. I am also grateful for the grace with which you have handled my dispensation from Orders."

Hubert nodded, and Paulin inclined his head cautiously.

"Your Highness mentioned a personal request," the latter said.

"Yes, Father." Javan drew a deep breath. "I desire to appoint a personal chaplain. The confessors I used when last I lived at Court are no longer available. Father Boniface has died, and his Grace has other duties that take him often from Court—as is only proper, for he has other sheep to tend besides this rather black and wayward one." He essayed a glance at Hubert and saw the archbishop was covering a faint smile with one pudgy hand.

"Perhaps his Highness would care to avail himself of my offices," Archbishop Oriss said, looking slightly affronted. "I believe that my auxiliary, Bishop Alfred, has occasionally confessed him."

Javan shook his head as if distracted, returning his attention to Paulin.

"I thank your Grace, but I have found a less busy priest I think would better serve my needs," he said. "One nearer my age, who knows something of my past few years. He is a *Custodes* priest, Father General, whose wisdom and counsel I came to respect while resident at *Arx Fidei*."

"One of my priests, Sire?" Paulin said, uncertain whether to be pleased or suspicious.

Javan kept his expression bland and guileless as he made himself meet Paulin's eyes. "His name is Father Faelan. He was not my confessor at the abbey, as you must know—only one of my tutors— but it is clear that his superiors must count him a worthy representative of his Order, else they would not have kept him there after his ordination, to train up more like him. If you have no objection, I would ask that he be transferred to my household, to serve as Chaplain Royal."

"Faelan, you say?" Paulin murmured, glancing across at Albertus, who shook his head minutely—but in nonrecognition, not disapproval.

"Yes, Father. I don't believe I ever heard his surname, but I found him gentle and pious—and sensible. I believe he could provide responsible guidance without being stodgy—no offense to any of my previous confessors, of course."

"Of course," Hubert murmured, no longer smiling, though Paulin almost was.

"Very well, Sire," Paulin said, jotting the name on the edge of a paper. "I make you no promises, but I shall inquire regarding this Father Faelan; and if he is deemed suitable, you shall have him, as a gesture of goodwill on my part—and for the sake of your immortal soul."

Javan inclined his head in what he prayed Paulin would take for humility. "I thank you, Father. I shall await your decision."

He hoped, as they moved on to other topics, that he was not putting the kind young Father Faelan into an uncomfortable position, for Faelan was not any part of Javan's intrigues. He had been a friend, though; and Javan had a desperate need of friends.

CHAPTER FIFTEEN

Surely I will keep close nothing from you.
—Tobit 12:11

In the days that followed, others besides Paulin of Ramos made inquiries touching on the king's business. One evening, with the coronation less than a fortnight away, Guiscard lingered after supper in Javan's apartments when everyone but Charlan had gone.

"I've found you a site for the Portal," he said when Javan had sent Charlan off to the cellars for a new flask of wine. "It's on the level just below us, next to that room where the new library's being assembled."

Javan scowled, trying to picture it. "I thought it had to be at cellar level," he said. "Doesn't the floor need to be natural rock or earth?"

"That *is* the floor requirement," Guiscard replied, grinning. "But you don't really want to go skulking around the cellars to get to it, do you? Kings who do that are apt to arouse some suspicion."

Remembering the difficulties surrounding a now-blocked Portal in the cellars of Valoret Castle, then disguised as a garderobe, Javan had to agree.

"Aye, I'll grant you that. But most of these rooms have wooden floors. This one does." He drummed his heel twice against the floor to make his point. "In fact, I think this whole wing does."

Guiscard smiled, obviously pleased with himself.

"The room I'm talking about is just above the cellar vaults," he said. "Do you know what's between the curve of a stone vault and the floor of the level above?"

"No, I'd never really thought about it."

"It's filled in with earth," Guiscard said. "Good, solid earth, right underneath the flagstones in that room."

"Ah."

"And a king doesn't need any excuse to use his library at odd hours—or to slip into a disused guest chamber right next to it."

"No, indeed. We'll still have to be careful, but it's brilliant. Where did you say it was again?"

"Actually, you may never have seen the library the way it is now," Guiscard said. "Restoration on that part of the castle probably began after you left Court. I had the impression it was all quite new when I came to Court last year."

Javan nodded. "I seem to recall talk of a library, the few times I've been back in the last couple of years, but I was always closely watched on those visits home—and before that, after the Court moved here from Valoret, we weren't in residence for very long before they packed me off to the abbey."

"I'll take you down to see it, once I've gotten the go-ahead from Joram," Guiscard said. "We don't want too much traffic through there, but a tour of the new library and environs with the Master of Works wouldn't be amiss. It's your castle now, after all."

"Hmmm, I suppose it is," Javan murmured. "Once Joram approves the site, what happens next? He said something about needing five or six people to actually do it."

"Well, you've got de Courcys for two of them," Guiscard said. "Not that either of us has ever even seen a Portal set up, much less participated in the process. He says that doesn't matter, though. Whoever's directing the work will bring all the participants into proper focus."

"Joram won't be doing that, then?" Javan asked.

Guiscard shook his head. "He's too recognizable, if anyone saw him infiltrating the castle. Actually, I don't think he's decided who *will* be doing it."

"Ah." Javan cocked his head at the older man. "Who else for participants, then?" he asked. "You and your father and I only make three."

"Oriel," Guiscard replied. "But you're not to tell him until closer to the night. No sense increasing his risk before we must. From there, we'll have to fill in with humans. He suggests Charlan, to round out the complement."

Javan pursed his lips. "I'd hoped to avoid that. Charlan doesn't know anything about any of this."

"I know. But he can be blocked afterward."

"Again." Javan rose and moved into the window embrasure,

looking out at the deepening night. "I don't like *using* him, Guiscard. And this wouldn't just be like erasing his memory of escapades he shouldn't see, so he can't reveal them under questioning."

Pursing his lips, Guiscard went into the window embrasure with the king. "You've been doing it for years, Sire. A king cannot afford the luxury of sentimentality."

"No, this is different. I've tried not to do that since I've come back as king. Back when he was my squire, I had no choice. But he's a knight now. He's *my* knight now. I'm obliged to protect and defend him and to deal honestly with him. I've already violated that obligation to a certain extent, in taking him to Saint Hilary's with us those two times. It was necessary, I know, but I—don't know if I can stretch that necessity to cover what we'd ask of him in helping set up the Portal."

"If you won't just use him, would you consider levelling with him?" Guiscard asked quietly. "He's a good man; I'd stake my life on that—we're *all* staking our lives on that. You could give him the protection he needs, with his permission."

Javan nodded. "I've been thinking about that. Unless I'm totally wrong about him, I think he'd help me willingly in this and agree to any measures necessary to protect both of us. And if he—had any misgivings, I suppose I could still erase his memory of the entire encounter and put things back the way they were before, so far as he was concerned."

Guiscard smiled and shook his head. "You're worried about interfering with his free will, but if his will doesn't turn out to be the same as yours, you're prepared to interfere even more with his free will." Javan looked up sharply. "That *is* what you're proposing, you know."

Sighing, Javan sank down on one of the stone benches in the window embrasure. "I have to survive, Guiscard," he whispered. "But I don't want it at other people's cost, any more than it has to be."

"I see." Guiscard's dark eyes were unreadable in the gathering darkness. "You realize, of course, that by implication, you've told me rather a lot more about yourself than you perhaps meant to do. Your abilities run to considerably more than shields and Truth-Reading, don't they?"

"Yes."

"But you aren't Deryni. How is that possible?"

Javan gazed back out the window, making the decision to share with Guiscard just a little of what he was, though he would gloss over any mention of Camber and his kin.

"It has to do with being Haldane, I think," he said softly. "The power came upon my father after he'd made his pledge to take up his crown. They say he used its full potential three times: the first time, to destroy a traitor who had poisoned his firstborn son; the second, to stand against Imre of Festil. The third was an unwonted act of retaliation against an enemy by then helpless, before he had been on the throne a year.

"After that, other than to Truth-Read occasionally, he never really used his powers again until shortly before his death, when he bequeathed their wielding to his heirs. The powers never quite manifested in Alroy; they came early in me. Rhys Michael shows no sign of the inheritance, though it's supposed to pass to him if I should die without issue."

Guiscard had sat very still during Javan's recitation and now slowly nodded. "What you've just told me explains a lot," he said. "Frankly, I find myself uneasy that you should have told me. You may not be technically Deryni, but if Paulin and the *Custodes* got hold of this information—"

"Why, do you intend to tell them?" Javan asked, eyeing the Deryni knight with bitter irony.

Blanching, Guiscard slid to both knees before Javan, a dagger suddenly lying across one open palm, but pointed at his own heart.

"Slay me now, if you doubt my loyalty, Sire!" he whispered fiercely, also rolling back his shields and offering full access to his mind. "Read me." He took one of Javan's hands with his free one and pressed it to his forehead. "Rip my mind if you find one trace of treachery! I am not afraid of my king, and would gladly die for him, if need be, but I *am* afraid of what the *Custodes* would do to me, if they found me out for what I am. I am Deryni, Sire, but I entertain no delusions about my abilities. Disabled with *merasha*, Sitric or someone like him could break me utterly; I know this."

Sighing, for he had been Truth-Reading Guiscard throughout this emotional outburst, Javan withdrew his hand from the knight's forehead and took the dagger from his palm, reversing the weapon to offer it back.

"I have never doubted your loyalty, Guiscard," he said. "And God knows I'm aware of the danger from the *Custodes*. I've lived with them for nearly three years, after all. What will make you feel more secure? What do you want me to do?"

Guiscard rocked back on his heels as he made the dagger disappear, eyes lowered, shaking his head softly. "I don't know what you *can* do, Sire," he whispered. "If you simply blank my memory of this conversation, as I suspect you could do, I'm of no use to you. I—hadn't expected that things would get this complicated."

"Nor had I," Javan said with a smile. "Get up; I hear Charlan coming with that wine. Let me think on the problem, and just be very careful for the next few days."

By the time Charlan came to hand each of them a cup of wine, Guiscard had recovered his composure and was seated opposite the king again.

"Thanks, Charlan," Javan said easily. "Pour yourself a cup and join us. I was just lamenting the weight of the robes I'll have to wear for the coronation, in this heat, and Guiscard allowed as how, if we had snow brought in from the Lendours in b-i-i-i-g chests . . ."

The three of them sat companionably in the window embrasure for another hour, concocting ever more outrageous ideas for keeping the king cool on the day in question, until Guiscard glanced out the window at what was now full dark and reluctantly excused himself.

"I suppose I'd best be getting back to my quarters, Sire," he said after draining the last of his wine. "My father has some documents he wants me to read over—drafts that you'll see in a few days— and I ought to attend to some correspondence as well. Oh, shall I try to set up that session with the Master of Works for sometime tomorrow?"

"Yes, that would be fine," Javan said, recalled to their earlier conversation. "Thank you, Guiscard."

"It's my pleasure to serve you, Sire. Sleep well," Guiscard said, withdrawing with a bow.

As Charlan followed after to bar the door, Javan considered whether he wanted any more wine. He didn't—but the pretense of another companionable cup might provide an easier introit for what he needed to explore with Charlan. The young knight had taken up a candlestick from the mantel and was lighting it from one of the rushlights set on the table in the center of the room, obviously thinking in terms of the king being ready to retire.

"Hold off on that for a while yet, Charlan," Javan said from the semidarkness of the window embrasure. "There's something else I wanted to discuss with you. Come and have another cup of wine, if you'd like."

Curious but smiling, Charlan came and set the candlestick on the bench opposite Javan, then went on into the embrasure to sit farther along the bench, where the wine flask and empty cups were set on a silver tray.

"Thank you, Sire. Perhaps I *will* have just a little." He picked up the flask. "May I pour more for you?"

"Just a little for me, as well," Javan said, illustrating with a thumb and forefinger. As Charlan complied and handed him the cup, Javan sighed with evident satisfaction and leaned back against the cushions, also stretching out his lame foot to rest on the opposite bench—and hemming in Charlan from any ready withdrawal.

"Guiscard's an interesting man," he said after sipping from his cup and savoring the taste of the wine. "Would you be shocked to learn that he's Deryni?"

Charlan, just taking a swallow from his own cup, nearly choked on it, his eyes wide and astonished as he set his cup aside and wiped at his mouth with the back of a hand.

"This—doesn't seem to distress you, sir," he managed to murmur after a few seconds.

With a droll smile, Javan leaned his head against the stone behind him and pretended to study the rim of his cup.

"I gather that it doesn't distress you either," he said easily. "But then, you've become accustomed enough to dealing with Master Oriel, these past few years, that perhaps you've decided for yourself that all Deryni are not the evil that Paulin and the *Custodes* would have everyone believe."

Charlan swallowed uncomfortably. "I've been—given to understand that those were your sentiments as well, my prince. I'm— afraid I can't believe Master Oriel is evil, despite what the Church may say. I don't know Sir Guiscard all that well, but he certainly seems to have only your welfare at heart. If you feel differently, if I've misjudged—well, you might as well just turn me over to the *Custodes* right now, because I've consorted with both of them, quite willingly, and would do so again. I thought I was doing it for my prince."

As he ducked his head, apparently anticipating utter ruin, Javan quickly set aside his cup and sat forward, moving close enough to reach across and lay both hands on Charlan's shoulders.

"Charlan, Charlan, forgive me," he said. "I haven't been entirely honest with you. You haven't misjudged. And from the very first day we met, you were honest and straightforward. You told me you were bound to report back to the regents when you were my squire, and we both knew you had no choice."

He withdrew his hands and looked out the window past Charlan as he went on, sensing that despair was giving way to amazement, and thanking God for it.

"Fortunately, after a while, I had the means to use our situation to my advantage," he went on softly. "You know I'm not Deryni,

Charlan, but I—can do a few of the things Deryni do. I'd rather not explain how, just now. I swear to you, though, that I've never done anything to your harm and never would."

He chanced a glance at Charlan then, but the young knight's face was still with guarded shock.

"You didn't have any choice in those days, from me or the regents," Javan went on hopefully. "But when you risked everything to come to me at *Arx Fidei*, you *chose* to do it. You gave me your assistance and loyalty freely, but I've repaid your loyalty by compelling it twice since we got back. I've used you, Charlan, and I need to use you again. But I'd like it to be with your consent from now on."

Charlan's face in the candlelight had taken on an edge of apprehension mixed with overwhelming confusion.

"I—don't understand, Sire," he breathed. "How have you—*used* me, and what else is it that you want me to do for you, that you don't think I'd agree to do?"

Leaning back in his seat again, Javan chose his words carefully. "Do you remember how you always used to fall asleep when you had to accompany me on one of my all-night vigils, or on those dreary visits to Father Boniface?"

"Yes."

"I know you never thought it odd enough to report it to the regents, but did you ever wonder about it?"

"I—just thought I was catching up sleep, or storing it up for the future," Charlan whispered. "A squire's day starts early and sometimes it goes really late."

Javan allowed himself a faint smile, amazed at how efficient he had actually been, back when he was still feeling his way so cautiously into his growing powers.

"That's true," he said gently. "Let's try another angle. You've seen Oriel put patients to sleep."

"Of course."

"Well, I can do that."

"You can?" Charlan's jaw dropped for just an instant, but then challenge lit in the dark eyes. "Show me."

"You're even braver than I thought," Javan replied with a smile. "Charlan, go to sleep."

He didn't even have to touch the knight for that command to be obeyed. The dark eyes closed as they had so many times before, Charlan settling against the cushions with a sigh as Javan pressed him back with a hand set on his forehead. Going briefly into the young knight's mind, he brought back to conscious memory what he had done before, and why, knowing now that Charlan would accept it all, grateful that he would not have to *force* Charlan to accept it.

"When there is need, you will be able to remember all of this when alone or in my company," he whispered, setting his safeties in place, "but you will be unable to speak of it or communicate it to any person in any way unless I am present and give you leave. This is for your safety as well as my own. Do you agree?"

From deep trancing, Charlan whispered, "Yes."

"Then wake up," Javan said, dropping his hand. "In future, I'll do what's necessary to protect both of us, but I'll always try to give you a choice—even if it's only to do willingly what you would really rather not do but has to be done."

After a few seconds, the dark eyes fluttered and then opened, unfocused at first, then flicking fearlessly to Javan's grey ones.

"I thank you for trusting me enough to tell me, my prince," the young knight murmured. "I'm—deeply honored to be a part of what you're doing and that you should think me able to help you." He nervously cleared a throat gone dry with emotion.

"You—mentioned earlier that there's something else you need me to do for you," he said. "I'll do it, of course—there was never any question of that—but may I know what it is?"

Javan sighed and picked up his cup of wine again, handing Charlan his. "This is something more directly to do with Deryni," he said, "and *I* don't even know everything that's involved. What I haven't told you before, because I didn't want to put you in a position where you might have to lie and be caught in it, is that my association with Deryni didn't end when Tavis O'Neill left Court. He and Joram and a few of the others who were so loyal to my father are part of the reason I'm able to be sitting in this room talking to you tonight, and part of the reason I'll be able to keep my crown—if, indeed, I do manage to hang on to it. You know the kind of men I'm up against."

Charlan nodded, wide-eyed and avid.

"For my Deryni allies to be of much use to me, though," Javan went on, "I have to have access to them, and they to me. Infiltrating the Court with secret Deryni like Guiscard and his father helps, but their usefulness is limited, since they don't dare let themselves be discovered—and they aren't that highly skilled as Deryni, or they'd be known for what they are. The most useful ones are also the ones best known; and obviously, my former regents—and, in particular, the *Custodes Fidei*—are not going to be inclined to tolerate any of them.

"All of that means that a Transfer Portal needs to be set up here in the castle. Do you know what they are?"

"Yes."

"Well, setting one up takes Deryni—more than several and at least one of whom knows precisely what he's doing. The de Courcys don't, though they'll help; and I'll help, to whatever extent I can—though I also know next to nothing. That doesn't really matter, because the extra bodies merely provide the energy sources that the principal operator draws upon to establish the Portal. We can import an expert for that, for one night, and get him out via the Portal we establish—provided everything works—but we need one more person to be sure there's enough energy to call upon. I don't want to risk that many Deryni in the same place, only to have us fall short and have to try again later—or worse yet, get caught."

"Can't Oriel help?" Charlan said, trying not to look as if he suspected what Javan was really driving at.

"I'm already counting on his support—though I don't intend to tell him about it until closer to time. It was probably a tactical error to let him see his wife and daughter before this was settled. That may have put him under closer scrutiny, especially now that Sitric is back at Court. I'm sure that Rhun will have the two Deryni sniffers spying on one another. As for what I need, the other person doesn't have to be another Deryni."

"How about your brother, then?" Charlan ventured.

Javan shook his head. "He doesn't know anything about any of this. Besides, if something should go wrong—well, I daren't risk my heir."

He would not look at Charlan. He knew that Charlan knew what he was suggesting. And when Charlan finally said, very softly, "How about me, then?" Javan allowed himself to breathe a faint sigh of relief.

CHAPTER SIXTEEN

Let us examine him with despitefulness and
torture, that we may know his meekness . . .
—Wisdom of Solomon 2:19

They spoke for another quarter hour as Javan tried to explain to Charlan what he thought would be involved.

"I can't tell you exactly, because I don't know myself, but I've been assured you won't come to any harm. If it's any consolation, I don't know what will be done to me, either."

"You don't need to justify yourself to *me*, Sire," Charlan said. "And you don't really need to explain—especially since it's clear you can't, since you don't know, either. It may be anybody's guess which of us will be more terrified, on the given night, but I would never shrink from my duty to my prince, just because I was afraid. What kind of knight would do that?"

"Not your kind, that's obvious," Javan said, smiling as he clapped a hand to Charlan's shoulder. "Thank you, Charlan."

"It is truly *my* honor, my prince," Charlan whispered, his eyes not leaving Javan's. "Could I—ask you one favor, though?"

"Of course."

"Well, I—don't want you to think I have any doubts, either about you or myself, but could you—make me forget all of this we've spoken about tonight, until it's time to actually do it?"

Closing his eyes briefly, Javan smiled and nodded. "Of course. I only wish someone could do the same for me."

Before either of them could change his mind, Javan laid his hand on Charlan's and went into his mind, making the required adjustments and inserting memory of another conversation he had been meaning to have with him anyway.

"So I'm going to be appointing you as my principal aide," he said as he brought the young knight back. "That's been your function anyway; you should have the recognition. And much as I appreciate the fact that you've been squiring for me these past few weeks, we really should think about a proper squire to do the drudge work part of it, at least. Any suggestions?"

Charlan picked up his cup and sipped from it thoughtfully, not missing a beat.

"Well, you don't want any of the sons of the lords who want your guts for garters," he said candidly. "That eliminates the obvious choices, like Cashel Murdoch or either of Earl Tammaron's boys. I think Lord Jerowen has a grandson about the right age. Or how about young Cathan Drummond?"

"Hmmm, not a popular choice."

"Only because he isn't the son of one of the great lords."

"Perhaps."

"They say he's a bright lad," Charlan went on. "He was a bit young when he started, but he's been functioning as a junior squire for several years now, mainly for Rhys Michael. I think he must be coming twelve by now, so he's about ready for a proper appointment. And his pretty sister's a maid-in-waiting to Tammaron's countess. By the way, did you know that your brother fancies her?"

"Michaela?" Javan said, astonished. "Pretty? Rhys Michael?"

When Charlan only cocked an eyebrow at him and shrugged, smiling, Javan said, "You're not joking, are you? Of course you're not. Good Lord, I saw him near her after the funeral, but that's ridiculous. They're both still children."

"Think again, Sire. She's thirteen. Your brother will be fifteen come Michaelmas. He's been legally of age for nearly a year. I know that *you're* aware of the potential danger if either of you should produce an heir before your reign is stabilized, but that may not have occurred to your brother—and I'm sure none of the great lords have pointed it out to him. Politically, I'm afraid the prince is a little naive."

"I still can't believe it." Javan paused a beat. "What exactly do you mean when you say he 'fancies' her? He hasn't done anything improper, has he?"

Charlan grinned and shook his head. "If you mean, has he lured her into his bed, or wheedled his way into hers, I'd guess that he hasn't. Someone would have noticed, and servants gossip. But he's certainly old enough to be thinking about a wife—a fact of life that may have slipped your mind, whilst vowed to celibacy."

Javan could feel himself going scarlet and looked away in some embarrassment. "It hadn't slipped my mind," he said softly. "It isn't that celibates don't know about passions of the flesh, Charlan. It's that they don't indulge them. There's a—discipline they allow in many abbeys to subdue those passions—fairly common, I understand. They call it *minution*. It means that they bleed you—and then they let you stay in the infirmary for two or three days to recover, with dietary restrictions and fasting set aside. It keeps the blood low, in more than just the literal sense. An abbot who permits it four to six times a year is considered a great benefactor."

"I suppose that's one way to subdue the 'passions of the flesh,' " Charlan said gravely, nodding. "And—ah—how often did the Abbot of *Arx Fidei* permit it?"

Javan allowed himself a sheepish laugh. "Oh, he was a *very* great benefactor," he said. "Every six to eight weeks—though I suspect its purpose was as much to keep general resistance down as to subdue the flesh. The *Custodes* don't much approve of independent thinking. Fortunately, that particular discipline wasn't mandatory—other than once, to experience its 'benefits.' "

"They did that to you?" Charlan asked, amazed.

"Just the once. The Rule required it. I suppose it's also one of the first serious tests of the vow of obedience. I'd just turned fourteen." Javan leaned his head against the stone behind him, trying to distance himself from the memory.

"They open a vein in your arm. I'm told they hold you down if you try to resist. They let you bleed into a special bowl with an indentation in the side to accommodate your arm. They take quite a lot—though some of the other seminarians told me later that the first time is always the worst. I wouldn't know about that, but the one time was bad enough."

"Did they hold you down?" Charlan asked.

"No." Javan picked up his cup and looked at it distractedly. "Fighting it wouldn't have made any difference. I suppose I valued my princely dignity too much to give them that satisfaction. I came near to fainting, though, near the end. If they'd wanted to, they could have been rid of one inconvenient prince right then and there, and there wouldn't have been a thing I could do about it. I think they wanted me to know that. I spent a week in the infirmary, recovering. At least the food was good."

He tossed off the rest of his wine then, drawing a deep, shuddering breath as he set the cup aside and wiped his sleeve across his mouth, suddenly weary.

"Anyway, that's past now," he said, getting to his feet. "Just another instance of how something meant to be benign can be misused." He sighed. "I suppose we both ought to think about getting some sleep. Thank you for the recommendations on squires—and the caution about Rhysem and Michaela. I'll give both matters serious thought."

To Javan's surprise, considering the fears and the memories he had stirred up in his conversations both with Guiscard and with Charlan, he slept as soon as his head hit the pillow and did not dream. The next morning, after early Mass in the Chapel Royal, he submitted to final fittings for his coronation robes while he wolfed down a light breakfast on his feet, then spent the remainder of the morning riding with the royal lancers who would provide his mounted escort on Coronation Day. The pleasant gallop along the shady riverbank provided welcome distraction from the increasing strictures on his freedom, but he found no opportunity to speak to his brother in private.

Noon found him back in the great hall, standing in one of the wide window embrasures with Charlan, Jerowen, Robear, and several more of the younger knights, most of them in various stages of finishing off a midday repast, as the king was doing. Rhys Michael was sitting on one of the stone benches, crunching on an apple—in royal blue today, rather than black, for official mourning was over, the coronation hardly a week away.

The knights' talk was of formations and harness and a critique of the lancers they had just left, Jerowen questioning some minor point of protocol regarding order of march on coronation day. Robear expressed doubt about the fitness of one of the men who was reported badly hung over. A bit bored by it all, Javan found himself wandering over to gaze down at the rose garden, a tankard of ale in one hand and the last of a chunk of cheese-smeared bread in the other. He was restless, despite having just returned from his ride.

At least he felt more like a king today. He supposed he might even be starting to look like one. Being still uncrowned, it was not yet appropriate for him to don Haldane crimson, but the full-sleeved white tunic belted over dark-grey breeches at least broke him away from funereal or clerical black. His leather hunting cap was black, but worked with gold embroidery around the crown to suggest a coronet—and covered up his still growing out tonsure. His belt was the same plain black one he had worn from the abbey, but the handsome pouch and hunting dagger hanging from it declared him a young man of some substance. Since they must ride back down to the cathedral in little more than an hour for a rehearsal, he still wore spurs.

He sighed as the conversation behind him shifted to horses, and

favorable comments about a new stallion Baron Hildred had just
brought in from the Forcinn and planned to ride in the coronation
procession. He tried not to think about the rest of the day—about
keeping an even temper as he dealt with Hubert and Oriss, and
probably Paulin and Albertus as well, down at the cathedral.

After that, there was a required appearance at supper in the great
hall that evening, informal but still requiring him to be on show.
And Rhun and Murdoch and their cronies were almost certain to
be present, still smouldering in their resentment at having been
outmaneuvered by a stripling king, watching him like hungry
vultures.

Gazing down at the serenity of the castle gardens as they shimmered in the noonday heat, Javan found himself recalling the sweet
seclusion of the cloister. For all the fear and danger of his days at
Arx Fidei, the nightly retreats to the garden had provided a spiritual
oasis. He popped the rest of his bread into his mouth and washed
it down with a swig of ale, then set the tankard aside and moved
farther into the embrasure, dusting crumbs off his hands before
pushing one of the mullioned windows wider. The fruity-sweet
scent of roses and honeysuckle came tumbling over the windowsill
with the breath of breeze the opening admitted, and he inhaled of
it with delight.

"Have you been down to the gardens since your return, Sire?"
Robear asked, noting his longing. "You do have time to go down
for a few minutes if you wish."

"Do I?" Javan breathed. "I think I will, then. God, I'd forgotten
how beautiful they are."

Smiling indulgently, Robear gave Charlan a faint nod. "Then
go, by all means, Sire. I think we can spare you for—say—half an
hour. Take Charlan with you."

"I'll come, too," Rhys Michael said, setting aside his apple core.

"No, stay and tell me about that new cob you were riding this
morning," Robear said. "I don't believe I've seen him before. I think
your brother wants a little time apart, before plunging back into
the day's activities."

"Oh, all right," Rhys Michael murmured.

"Another time, Rhysem," Javan said, smiling gratefully as he
clapped his brother on the shoulder in passing. He still wanted a
private word with his brother about Michaela, but it could wait
until later. "I'm not even going to let Charlan stay with me, other
than to lurk nearby and make certain nobody else wants me to
solve some problem."

The others chuckled at that, for Javan himself was smiling, and he and Charlan had nearly made their escape into the stair at the end of the hall when Guiscard emerged from it, accompanied by a slight, grey-haired man in grey fustian.

"Sire, this is your Master of Works, William of Desse," Guiscard said as the little man swept off his cap and sketched a deep, nervous bow. "You asked that he be presented at the earliest opportunity."

"My Lord King," the man murmured.

"Ah, yes. Thank you for interrupting your work, Master William. I understand that I have you to thank for the ongoing restoration work here in the castle."

"I pray that the work may meet with your approval, Sire," the man said, ducking his head.

"Oh, I'm sure it will. Sir Guiscard tells me that one of the projects involves fitting out a library, somewhere underneath the royal apartments. I wondered if you might show it to me. I fancy I've acquired a scholar's appreciation of books during my years in seminary."

The little man's face lit up. "I would be honored, Sire. Perhaps your Grace would care to see it now?"

"I'm afraid I couldn't do it justice right now," Javan said, glancing at Charlan, who shook his head. "How about later this afternoon, after the rehearsal? Have I got time then, Charlan?"

"Perhaps an hour, Sire," the young knight replied. "Your presence is expected at supper this evening, and you'll wish to dress for it."

"Yes, of course. Still, I want to see that library. Would that be convenient for you, Master William? Late this afternoon, about the time of Vespers?"

"It will be my honor, Sire," the little man murmured as he bowed again, clearly thrilled.

Javan's spirits were much restored as he and Charlan continued on down the stair, Guiscard following shortly behind. He hoped that so prompt a presentation of the Master of Works meant that Guiscard had secured approval of the Portal site the night before, which meant—

Actually, Javan found he preferred not to think about what that meant, because the whole notion of being part of setting up the Portal was more than a little intimidating. He lingered at the entrance to the gardens until Guiscard caught up with them, searching the older man's face.

"The site's approved?" he asked.

"Aye. Two nights from now. What about—"

He jerked his head slightly in the direction of Charlan, who had wandered a few yards away and was bending down to inspect a particularly fine rose. Inclining his head slightly, Javan murmured, "He asked not to remember, but he's in."

Guiscard nodded. "Brave lad." He looked out at the garden. "Am I interrupting something?"

"Actually, I'd come down here to get away from everybody for a few minutes, before we have to go off to the cathedral and face down ecclesiastical dragons. Do you mind waiting with Charlan?"

"Not at all, Sire."

As Guiscard bowed his acquiescence, sitting then in one of the arched openings of the cloister colonnade, Javan moved on into the garden, inhaling the perfume of the roses and heading toward the fountain that marked the crossing of two gravelled paths. It was a more formal fountain than the one at *Arx Fidei*, with water spilling down from a stone jar held over the shoulder of a kneeling statue of a woman, slightly larger than life size. She was kneeling on a plinth in the center of the fountain, her averted face shaded by the folds of her veil. Javan liked to imagine that she was beautiful.

In fact, she had no face at all. He and Rhys Michael had climbed up to look, one sunny summer afternoon a lifetime ago, only to find the face sheared off—whether from exposure to the elements or a more deliberate destruction, no one knew. Javan had questioned the gardeners about her, but all they could say was that the statue was very old; no one remembered how ancient.

Smiling at the memory, Javan waggled the fingers of one hand in the cool water—there were no fish—then set aside his cap and wet both hands to wipe across his face and into the open neck of his tunic. The crunching of footsteps on gravel behind him warned that this brief respite was about to be interrupted, but he spared another sluicing of cool water over his hair and down the back of his neck before turning to see two figures in *Custodes* black approaching.

Squinting against the sun—and resenting the intrusion, especially by *Custodes*—Javan scooped up his cap and put it back on. The wide crimson sash and the crimson-lined mantle flaring behind the first of the intruders identified him as Paulin—which explained why Charlan and Guiscard were following meekly behind and doing nothing to stop them—but the other wore the monastic dress of an ordinary *Custodes* priest, hands tucked into the flowing black sleeves. The man's head was bowed in the shadows of the hood pulled up from a stiffened black scapular like the one Javan had left beside another fountain at *Arx Fidei*. They were almost up to him before Javan realized the priest was Father Faelan.

"I have brought the king his new confessor, as requested," Paulin said without preamble, though he favored Javan with a slight bow, hands clasped behind him. "Make your duty to his Highness, Father Faelan."

Not looking up, the priest dropped heavily to both knees on the sharp gravel. Javan almost winced as he offered the priest his hand. What he could see of Faelan's face looked pale and drawn. "You are most welcome to my household, Father."

"I am your servant, your Highness," Faelan whispered.

His hand was trembling as he took Javan's briefly to brush it with dry lips. In that instant of contact, Javan sensed fear underlying an apprehension almost approaching dread. He covered his own surprise and would have helped Faelan to his feet, but the priest pulled away and lurched back to his feet on his own before Javan could do anything about it, eyes still downcast.

"I am certain that Father Faelan will prove a most satisfactory spiritual director," Paulin was saying. "Naturally, he remains under the jurisdiction of the Abbot of *Arx Fidei*, and will be required to make retreat among his old community for three days each month, but this should prove no great inconvenience for your Highness."

Faelan had thrust his hands back into his sleeves, but Javan could see that the man was still trembling. Something was very wrong. Javan wondered what could have happened to make the priest so afraid. He dared not address the question in front of Paulin, but he was going to find out before he left this garden.

"I thank you for bringing me my new chaplain, Vicar General," he said. His tone was neutral, but brooked no interruption. "I believe that Father Faelan and I will walk in the garden for a few minutes and renew our acquaintance. I'm aware that I have a rehearsal very shortly. Sir Charlan will escort you back to the great hall, where we'll join you momentarily. Guiscard, wait here, please."

Without waiting to see whether Paulin was going to take exception, Javan took the young priest's elbow and led him around the fountain and on along the main path that led farther into the heart of the garden. After a few seconds, retreating footsteps on the gravel behind told of Paulin and Charlan departing. Javan glanced at Faelan, but the priest was walking beside him with eyes still averted, gaze fixed on the gravel at his sandaled feet.

"I'm glad you're here," Javan said quietly after a few more steps, still wondering why the priest was so afraid. "It's good to have another friend close by."

"You are a dangerous friend to have, Sire," Faelan whispered. His voice almost broke in a sob.

Startled, Javan darted another look at the priest, then drew him into the shade of a flowering tree—and also somewhat screened from observation from the windows of the great hall, where he was nearly certain Paulin would be watching.

"All right," he said, hooking his thumbs in his belt and facing Faelan squarely. "Paulin's gone. No one can overhear us. You're in *my* household now, and I'll protect you. What's happened, to make you so afraid? You can't be afraid of *me*? Forget I'm the king. We were pupil and mentor, not so very long ago. We were *brothers*."

Jaws clenched to try to stop their trembling, Faelan raised tear-filled eyes to gaze past Javan at something only he could see, arms clenched hard across his chest, hugging himself against an inner chill. Javan was appalled at the change that had come over the man he remembered as serene and unshakable.

After a deep breath, Faelan said, "They made me swear on holy relics to report back to them, on everything I see and hear. That's—why I have to go back to the abbey once a month."

"I see," Javan said.

But there was more to it than that. That Faelan should have been ordered to spy on him was almost a given. Surely the priest would have realized that. And telling Javan certainly removed any personal responsibility from Faelan. Why, then, was he so cowed?

"Faelan, the fact that you've been ordered to spy on me is no betrayal on your part," he said softly. "I expected it. It isn't your fault. But I didn't expect that you'd be afraid of me. Did they threaten you?"

Choking back a sob, Faelan pushed back his hood and ran shaking hands through tonsured brown hair. Then he pressed his clasped hands to his lips, searching for words.

"You've—lived at the abbey, Sire," he said haltingly. "You know about some of the less gentle disciplines. I think I—experienced them all, in the week or so since you asked for me."

"Faelan, I'm sorry!" Javan murmured, wide-eyed. "I didn't know."

"Of course you didn't. How could you? Father Paulin wanted to know why you'd asked for *me*, what the basis of our friendship had been, everything we'd ever talked about. He didn't believe me when I told him I hadn't known you planned to leave when your brother died, that you intended to take up the crown, that you'd never discussed your vocation with me." He lifted dark eyes to gaze at the trunk of the tree they were standing under.

"Father Paulin said I was rebellious and disobedient. To bring me 'round, he started with the fasting and the long vigils prostrate in the *disciplinarium*, the days and nights without sleep. There were daily trysts with the 'little discipline'—enough to raise weals, but not to draw blood. That came three days ago."

"Dear God, they didn't *bleed* you?" Javan whispered, aghast.

Faelan hung his head, his voice faltering. "I wasn't telling them what they wanted to hear. They'd about lost patience with me. They—took me into the infirmary in the middle of the night, into that little room that's set aside for minution."

"But you'd submitted to minution as a novice," Javan objected. "They can't require it a second time. That's against the Rule."

"Then I suppose they suspended the Rule," Faelan said a little sharply. "Four strapping monks I'd never seen before were standing by to hold me if I struggled, while another one opened my vein. It was the assistant inquisitor asking the questions by then—Father Lior—and he kept asking me, while the blood ran down my arm and gradually filled the bowl."

A little sob caught in his throat as he went on. "They made me watch. I honestly thought they were going to let me die—and for *nothing*. It's one thing to die for *something*, but I hadn't anything to hide . . ." He paused to swallow, one hand easing up inside the opposite sleeve to gently finger what Javan guessed must be the physical legacy of that ordeal.

"Anyway, I passed out after they'd taken away the first bowl and I saw they meant to go on. When I came around, Father Paulin himself was sitting at my bedside, and the Grand Inquisitor of the whole Order was with him—Brother Serafin, he's called. *He* even dosed me with *merasha*. He told me what it was. Maybe he thought I was some new, insidious kind of Deryni, to be able to resist their questioning for so long. At least I got some sleep, after that." He swallowed painfully.

"They—questioned me again the next afternoon, after the drug had worn off. The morning after that—yesterday, I suppose it was— Paulin told me to get cleaned up; that I was coming to Rhemuth to be your new chaplain."

Javan was shaking his head, utterly appalled at the story Faelan had told him—and what the priest had suffered for his sake. At the same time, something in the back of Javan's mind suggested an omission—though he had detected nothing but truth in what Faelan *had* said.

What could it be? What would Faelan have neglected to mention, whether or not it was of his own choosing? Suddenly Javan was struck by the similarity between the instructions to Faelan and the old practice of setting the squires spying on the princes. At least the regents had been quite open about what they did.

Good God, could *that* be it? Was it conceivable that the *Custodes* now had a Deryni in their employ, as the regents had done, but in secret? Was that what Faelan had omitted to mention? It might explain the use of *merasha*.

"I'm very sorry about what you had to go through, Father," he said. "If you'd died, it *would* have been for nothing. And it would have been my fault. I deliberately avoided discussing my plans with you, because I didn't want to put you at risk—though that doesn't seem to have been much help. I'm appalled that Paulin would resort to such measures, and against a member of his own Order. Who else did you say questioned you? Paulin and Father Lior and—?"

"Brother Serafin," Faelan supplied.

"Ah, yes," Javan murmured. "Brother Serafin. Anyone else?"

"No, Sire."

"Just the three, then," Javan replied, though he knew that the last answer had been false—and that raised the question of why.

Chilled to the bone despite the heat, he made himself put the thought aside, still feeling for Faelan, who was caught up in Paulin's intrigues, whatever they were, whether or not he wanted to be.

"Well, I'll keep that in mind," he murmured. "I wish I could undo what's been done, but I can't. You don't have to stay here if you don't want to, though. Would you like me to send you back? I could tell Paulin you weren't suitable after all."

With a tiny, stifled sob, Faelan shook his head. "If you did, they'd probably punish me for having displeased you—and then they'd put some other priest through what I've suffered. And I—don't even know that I can be much use to you. As a Mass priest, yes. But a confessor . . ."

Another chill raced down Javan's spine, worse than any so far. From far, far away, he could hear footsteps crunching along the path, from the direction of the fountain—probably Guiscard.

"Are you saying that they might require you to violate the seal of the confessional?" he asked. He had thought he was almost beyond shock by now.

Faelan glanced down at his clasped hands in shame and would have colored if he hadn't been so debilitated from his recent ordeal.

"It—was never mentioned specifically," he whispered, "but the implication was there. I didn't dare ask. I—suppose it depends on whether they think you might confess something they could use against you." He swallowed and looked down.

"Sire, I've never, ever betrayed the seal, and I never would." He swallowed again. "A good priest is supposed to die rather than reveal information received under the seal. Is that—what you want me to do?"

"Let's not worry about that for now," Javan murmured, setting his hand on the priest's shoulder and easing them both back out onto the path, to head toward the approaching Guiscard. "For the present, let's assume that I'll give you permission to reveal what I've confessed, if that's required of you.

"Meanwhile, I'm due down at the cathedral for a rehearsal, so I'm going to have one of my aides take you to your quarters. They're very near mine; he'll show you where. While I'm gone, I want you to lie down and get some rest. I'll send my Healer to you later on, to see if any really serious damage was done."

"A Healer?" Faelan said, stiffening. "A Deryni?"

"He's been *my* Healer for about four years, off and on," Javan assured him, wondering at the reaction. "If it's any reassurance, he's also Archbishop Hubert's pet Deryni—so I think you can assume he's safe."

"But I—"

"Relax, Father. He won't hurt you. But if you prefer, I'll wait to send him until I can come with him," Javan said. They came up to Guiscard, who turned and fell into step with them as they continued back around the fountain.

"Guiscard, I'd like you to take Father Faelan up and show him his quarters. See that he has whatever he'd like to eat—and a bath, if he wants one. After that, he's to rest for the afternoon. Be sure that he does. I'll meet you in my quarters after the rehearsal, and we'll make that inspection with the Master of Works."

"Very good, Sire."

They continued on into the shade of the cloister colonnade and headed for the stair, but just before entering the stairwell, Javan paused to bend and fidget with a buckle on his boot.

"Give me a hand with this, would you, Guiscard?" he said.

When Guiscard crouched to see what the problem was, Javan straightened to catch his balance on the knight's shoulder, fingers brushing against the bare flesh of Guiscard's neck and using that physical contact to send a brief but cogent message.

Keep a sharp eye on this one until we know more about him, he sent. *I have an awful suspicion that Paulin may have had a Deryni at him whom no one knows about. Hands off, though, be-*

cause I don't know yet what might have been done to him that might be detected.

As Guiscard straightened, dusting off his hands, his eyes met Javan's over Faelan's bowed head and he gave a nod. At least somewhat reassured, Javan headed on up the stairs to rejoin Charlan and the others, not at all looking forward to the next few hours.

CHAPTER SEVENTEEN

For the hand of the artificer the work shall be
commended.

—Ecclesiasticus 9:17

In fact, the rehearsal went far more smoothly than Javan had feared, though Paulin seemed distinctly annoyed that the king had not brought his new chaplain with him.

"Well, he seemed exhausted," Javan remarked, when asked where Faelan was. "I expect it was the heat—or maybe the unaccustomed ride. I know *I* was exhausted after making the same journey last month. I told him to lie down for the rest of the afternoon. If he isn't looking better soon, I may have Master Oriel see him."

Paulin gave him a long, appraising look and then a slight inclination of his head. "I'm told he had been feeling poorly, this last week or so. In fact, I believe he was bled to relieve the ill humours. No doubt he'll recover quickly, though."

"Hmmm, no doubt," Javan murmured. "Excuse me, Father," he added as Tammaron beckoned for him to move to another position farther up the cathedral aisle.

When the rehearsal finally ended and Javan could return to the castle, he and Charlan found Guiscard waiting to escort them to the chosen Portal site as planned.

"How is Father Faelan?" Javan asked as the three of them headed down a back stair to the next level.

"Asleep" was Guiscard's reply. "He had a light meal, he all but fell asleep in the bath, then roused himself just long enough to dress and stagger to his bed, where he passed out. He hasn't moved since, though I've checked to make sure he hasn't died. I didn't try to probe further, because of what you told me, but I'd say he's had a rough time of it."

"Later tonight I'll tell you *how* rough," Javan murmured. "Did you leave a guard outside his door?"

"Of course. Do you think he's a spy for Paulin?"

"Oh, I'm certain that's Paulin's intention. Whether it will hold remains to be seen."

They came out on a landing and turned left at Guiscard's gesture. Javan knew that both he and Charlan were dying to know more, but this was not the time. For now he must turn his attention to the potential Portal site. So far he liked the proximity and approach.

The corridor walls were newly whitewashed, with pine-knot torches set in cressets to light the way where daylight from other landings and open doors did not reach. New-laid black and white tiles as wide as the length of a man's forearm paved the floor underfoot, set diagonally in a chequerboard design.

Outside some of the open doors, stocks of timber and nails and carpenters' tools vied with buckets and brushes for space, everything layered with a fine sheen of chalky dust. The clean aroma of newly planed wood mingled with the sharper lime scent of the whitewash and the tang of pine resin from the torches. As they ventured farther along the corridor, the sounds of hammering and sawing and the rhythmic ring of steel on stone grew gradually louder, coming from an open doorway ahead and on the left, where a fine haze of dust shimmered on a slanting beam of late-afternoon sun.

"Your library will be in here, Sire," Guiscard said, indicating the open doorway and standing to one side as they came abreast of it.

As Javan stepped into the opening, shading his eyes against the glare of sunlight, the sounds of men at work fell off almost immediately. Scaffolding overhead creaked alarmingly, and Javan instinctively ducked his head as he glanced up and continued into the room until he was clear of it. Charlan and Guiscard followed close behind him, and Master William materialized out of the haze to the left, mallet and chisel in dust-streaked hands.

"Sire, you honor us," Master William said with a bow. "Pray, pardon the disarray."

"Nay, 'tis I who should pray pardon for interrupting your work," Javan replied, already looking around appraisingly. "And it is you who honor me by your fine craftsmanship. I had no idea such progress had been made. But please, have your men continue."

"As you wish, Sire."

As the men resumed work, Master William lingering nearby in case the king should have a question, Javan moved farther into the whitewashed brilliance of the room and allowed his gaze to range around it, squinting less as his eyes adjusted to the glare. It was a fine, large room, well suited for a library, with two tall, wide window embrasures in the wall opposite the door that spilled an abundance of afternoon sunlight over the flagstones of the floor. Walking over to one of the windows, Javan stepped up into its alcove to see the view, but there were only the stable yards below. A beefy, sunburned man was fitting thin slabs of greeny-grey stone to the windowsills, and gave a companionable nod as Javan bent to inspect his work.

"That's unusual color on that stone," Javan said, peering more closely at the sill and touching a fingertip to an edge. "What is it? It looks like slate, but I've never seen green before."

"Och, ye won't see the green around here, milord, 'cept in the very finest buildings," the man said easily, smiling as he ran a mortar-roughened hand lovingly along one of the joins. "Lord Tammaron ordered it. Comes from a quarry down by Nyford—not nearly as common as the blue and grey ye get locally, but it do make up pretty, don't it?"

"Aye, it's lovely."

Nodding to himself in satisfaction, Javan moved back out of the embrasure to survey the rest of the room. Carpenters were building shelves and pigeonholes across the wall now to his left, and a stonecutter was chiseling at something on one of the supports of a massive fireplace dominating the other end wall. Crouched on the scaffolding above the doorway, a painter was laying down color in the outlines of a bold interlace design dominated by blues and greens, joining it in with work already twining upward along either side. Seeing Javan's interest, Master William came nearer.

"We plan to repeat that design around the windows, Sire," he volunteered. "The greens will tone with the green of the slate. We've been told to set slate on the floor, as well, but just in the window embrasures. It's—ah—rather expensive."

"So I gathered," Javan said. He glanced at Charlan and Guiscard, waiting patiently just to one side of the scaffolding, and nodded as the latter indicated it was time to go.

"Well, thank you, Master William. I'm very pleased. I've other engagements now, but I'll have a quick look at a few of the other rooms on my way out. Good day to all of you."

"Sire," the man replied with a bow, the other men also stopping work briefly to tug at forelocks as he went out.

"Most of the rest of the rooms on this level will be set aside as guest chambers," Guiscard said rather more loudly than he needed to, shepherding them left as they went out the door. "If you'll come this way, Sire, I'll show you a typical one."

The door to the next room was closed, but Guiscard pushed it open and led the way in. Like the library, it was plastered and whitewashed over the stone, but hardly a third the size, with a single window embrasure in the wall opposite the door, deep enough for one person to sit on either side.

The window itself was mullioned, with lead cames holding lozenge-shaped panes of glass in the lower half and wood shutters closing off the upper. To the right of the window, occupying the corner angle of the room, was a tiny fireplace with a nicely carved hood. The floor was paved with smooth square and rectangular flag-stones set in a random pattern.

"Very fine," Javan commented, for the benefit of anyone who might be listening in the corridor. "Are they all to this standard?"

"They are," Guiscard replied, stepping very deliberately onto a square flag in the center of the room—the only one both square and in the center—and turning to look pointedly at Javan. "No garde-robes in rooms this small, of course, Sire, but they'll be quite comfortable, nonetheless—especially these that catch the afternoon sun."

"Yes, I can see that." Javan stepped briefly into the window embrasure to peer out the window. Like the library windows, this one also overlooked the stable yards. Dusting off his hands, he stepped back down and eyed the square where Guiscard was still standing.

"Well, I've seen enough," he said, moving toward the door. "We'd better get back. I want a bath before I have to face a public supper."

Guiscard pulled the door shut behind them—it already had its inside bolt, Javan had noted—and the three retreated down the corridor in silence, each alone with his thoughts of what the room would mean the next time they entered it.

Supper, fortunately, was not the ordeal Javan had feared. All of his enemies were there, but so were his friends; and everyone seemed determined to put on congenial faces, now that court mourning was ended and things were gearing up for the coronation, but three days away.

Still eschewing Haldane crimson, Javan wore a long, tawny green-gold tunic of raw silk, discreetly jewelled at cuffs and standing collar but open at the throat, belted with a girdle of bronze plaques set with amber. The dagger at his hip was a border dirk set with a water-pale cairngorm in the pommel, like sunlight on peat in a highland stream. By careful combing of his hair, he was able to wear the hammered gold circlet of running lions without a cap of maintenance—no technical pretense of crown, but more than a prince's coronet. The Eye of Rom gleamed in his right earlobe and the Ring of Fire winked on his left hand beside his signet.

The end of official mourning had brought the ladies out again— the wives and daughters of the great lords in residence and a few early arrivals for the coronation to come. The pastels and muted hues of their raiment were welcome relief from the blacks and greys of strict mourning, even though bright colors or too-gaudy adornment were still to be eschewed until coronation day itself. Still, the feminine presence lent an air of gentility to what had been largely an all-male enclave during those first few weeks. The fare was simple but plentiful, the wine ample, the music soothing and unobtrusive.

It was a night for circulating rather than sitting still, at least for everyone but the king. Somewhat to Javan's surprise, unlike any other public banquet of his experience, the guests came to him. Either Charlan or Guiscard was always at his back, ready to answer his questions, prompt him on the names of guests, or simply bring him what he needed. Rhys Michael started out sitting at his right, cool in the royal blue of the heir, but soon after eating, he asked to be excused. Later, Javan noticed him in one of the window embrasures off to the right, with Cathan Drummond and the two Fitz-Arthur boys again, talking animatedly to several pretty girls, one of whom was Michaela.

"Charlan says that my brother fancies Michaela Drummond," Javan said to Guiscard during a lull between courtiers and their ladies come to offer greetings. He sipped at a cup of ale as he noted the pert profile and the sweep of a thick, bronze-gold braid falling past her waist. "Is that your impression, as well?"

"If he does, he has good taste," Guiscard replied, "but I can't say I've noticed anything in particular. She's a fine-looking lass, though, and well regarded. She'd make a better royal bride than many I could name who're campaigning for the job."

"I don't intend that there should be *any* royal brides for a while," Javan said quietly, giving Guiscard a sidelong glance.

Guiscard shrugged and allowed himself a wan smile. "Then you'll open yourself to yet another pressure from the Council," he said. "It's generally expected that a king should wed fairly young."

"It's also generally expected that a king should not have to be on guard against his own ministers, who might arrange a convenient 'accident' for said king once he produced an heir," Javan replied. "Unfortunately, we've already got a ready-made cadre of men who've tasted the power of a regency. The prospect of another, longer regency might be too tempting to resist. I think I'd prefer a few years to consolidate my position, before having to worry about being ousted in favor of my son."

"The same argument applies for your brother, then," Guiscard said. "I hadn't really thought about that aspect of things, but if he marries before you and secures the succession in the junior line, you *both* might provide tempting targets."

Javan nodded. "That's why I'm appalled at the thought there might be something between him and Michaela. I fear I shall have to speak to my brother." He sighed and set his cup aside. "But not tonight. I think we have more immediately pressing matters to attend to, as soon as we can decently break away."

It was several more hours before that could be done. Charlan and Guiscard continued to take turns attending him, ready to carry messages, identify people, and generally see to the king's comfort. Throughout the evening, most of the members of his Court came to him in twos and threes to pay their respects.

Those conspicuous by their distance were the ones he would have expected—Murdoch, Rhun, Manfred—who paid their dutiful calls on him once but did not stay. Both Paulin and Albertus stayed rather longer, the former obviously fishing for further information on the condition of Father Faelan, wondering how much Javan knew.

"He was sleeping peacefully when I left to come down," Javan said ingenuously. "I'm sure he'll feel better after a good night's sleep."

It was late by the time Javan could withdraw to his apartments with a few close intimates, calling Guiscard and Charlan to remain after the others had gone; later still when he summoned Oriel to join them, there to impart to the Healer what Faelan had told him that afternoon.

"We haven't dared to touch him," Javan whispered, when the Healer had read all that he or Guiscard knew about Faelan's condition. "It may just be my own suspicions of anything Paulin has a hand in, but I do think that someone questioned him besides Paulin, Lior, and Serafin. If it was a Deryni we don't know about, he could present complications we don't need. Have you heard anything about someone working for the *Custodes*?"

Oriel shook his head, troubled. "Nary a word, Sire. Sitric certainly hasn't let on. But he might not know, either, especially if a new man is working for Paulin voluntarily."

Charlan's eyes were huge. With his memory unfettered in this select company, he was absorbing the new information with horrified fascination.

"What kind of man would willingly sell out his own kind?" he whispered. "And to corrupt a priest—"

Javan snorted. "It's a measure of *Custodes* zeal, the depths to which they'll stoop to achieve their aims, to annihilate those responsible for outrages that are long past. Faelan's in their obedience, so they feel justified in doing whatever they must to use him as their tool. If that means setting him up to spy on me and using a Deryni to make him more efficient, they'll do whatever's necessary." He sighed.

"Of course, we don't know that they did that. We don't even know for certain that there's another Deryni involved. We need to find out, Oriel. And you're the only one who has the legitimate excuse to Read him."

Oriel shivered. "It's dangerous."

"For you, personally? Not unless there *is* another Deryni, and he's set some kind of trap, to guard against tampering with his tampering. Correct me if I'm wrong, but that would take someone pretty powerful—probably far more powerful than the *Custodes* would risk, for fear he might turn on them.

"For anything else, though, you have the perfect justification: I was worried about his health and asked you to see him. If he's clean, no problem; and *we* can set up a few safeguards to keep him from becoming a liability."

"And if he *isn't* clean?"

"I suspect that's going to depend on degree. If there's something really blatant, then you get out and you report back to Hubert immediately. Tell him that you think someone has tried to plant a Deryni spy in my household. We'll put it all on him to figure out how to get out of it. Areas of grey, we'll judge once we know."

Guiscard was nodding, a faint smile on his rugged face. "You're getting very good at this, Sire."

Javan managed a strained smile in return. "Being very scared makes you very good or very dead. But thanks for the vote of confidence. I was thinking about this all through the rehearsal and all through dinner."

"Well, it was thinking well spent." Guiscard glanced at Oriel. "Are you willing to try it?"

Shrugging, Oriel got to his feet. "I don't suppose it's any worse than a lot of the things I've had to do these last few years—and a far sight better than many. And *Faelan* isn't Deryni." He darted a quick look at Javan. "We do know he isn't Deryni, don't we?"

"Of that, at least, I'm sure," Javan said. "Let's go look in on him. Charlan, you can come; I'd be expected to have an aide with me. Guiscard, you'd better stay; no need to risk your cover on this."

A few minutes saw them approaching the modest quarters set aside for the king's confessor, just down the corridor from the royal apartments. A man-at-arms in Haldane livery was standing guard outside and snapped to attention as the king and his party approached.

"At ease," Javan murmured. "How is Father Faelan? Has he stirred?"

"No, Sire. Sir Guiscard said I was to look in on him every hour, but he hasn't moved."

"Well, I've brought Master Oriel to have a look at him," Javan said, gesturing for the door to be opened. "See that we aren't disturbed."

With a nod of agreement, the guard obeyed. Ushering Oriel and Charlan inside, Javan followed and pulled the door closed behind them.

The room was similar to the one next to the library, but with an arched doorway opening off to the left into a tiny oratory lit with a red votive candle. Just to the right of the door, another light burned in a niche at the head of a low bed, vaguely illuminating the figure of a black-clad man curled onto his side and facing them. A large trunk loomed at the foot of the bed, a heavy fustian curtain beyond it screening a garderobe. A chair and a writing table took up most of the rest of the room, the table pushed against the wall between the oratory and a small fireplace set in the far left angle of the room.

Without saying anything, Oriel went to the writing table and fetched a candle in a stand, lighting it from the rushlight at the head of the bed and then handing it to Javan. Charlan stood with his back against the closed door, watching. The Healer crouched down beside the bed and studied its occupant for nearly a minute before reaching out a hand and laying it lightly across the sleeping man's brow.

Utter silence reigned for several seconds, stirred only by the slow, somewhat labored breathing of their subject. Then Oriel sighed and withdrew his hand briefly, rising long enough to shift himself to a sitting position on the edge of the bed.

"Well, that's something," he murmured, closing the man's wrist in his hand. "He definitely isn't Deryni, by any test I know to apply, and there's no overt sign of tampering. He's certainly exhausted, though. Let's find out why."

Retaining the wrist, he set his other hand on the priest's forehead again and bowed his head, as Javan eased nearer the head of the bed and crouched to hold the candle closer. After a few minutes Oriel shook his head and rolled Faelan onto his back, pushing back the sleeve on the wrist he held until his questing fingers found the bandage at the elbow. As Javan leaned forward on his knees to watch, and Charlan, too, moved closer, Oriel unwound the bandage to reveal the angry, barely healing wound of Faelan's blood-letting. The Healer's lips tightened as he turned the arm to the light.

"Well, at least we can do something about this," he murmured. He probed lightly at the hurt, gently rolling the vein above and below it, then pressed his fingers over the wound and went into Healing trance. Javan found himself fingering his own arm as Oriel worked, remembering another wound and another blood-letting, recalling the sinking despair as he realized he was totally in their power, helpless to prevent his life draining away if they chose to let it happen . . .

"Let's have a look at his back now," Oriel said, his words jarring Javan from his reverie. Faelan's arm now was clean, the injury gone as if it had never been. "Sir Charlan, would you give me a hand?"

Javan helped, too, showing them how the hated scapular and its hood came off, watching Oriel untie and pull off the cincture, helping them raise the limp Faelan to a sitting position so Oriel could reach down the neck of Faelan's habit to check his back.

"Hmmm, the weals are still nasty—some bruising. No wonder he was sleeping on his side."

"Do you want the habit off, sir?" Charlan asked.

Oriel shook his head, reaching deeper. "Not necessary. I think I can manage from here."

His eyes had gone a little glazed again, indicative of Healing trance. After a few more seconds he sighed and withdrew, letting Charlan help him lay the priest back on the pillows. Javan was watching him, wide-eyed, and shot Charlan a pained glance. They both knew about weals on backs, too.

"We could have used Master Oriel's services that other time, eh, my prince?" Charlan whispered with a strained smile.

"Aye."

At Javan's whispered reply, Oriel looked up sharply, gasping as Javan sent him the quick, painful image of his own encounter with the "little discipline," at Hubert's order.

"They dared to do that to *you*, Sire?" he whispered.

Javan swallowed and made himself push back the memory. "That's past now," he said. "And I *did* defy Hubert. In that sense, I suppose I deserved my stripes. Faelan didn't deserve his, though. And the other—the minution—it was never meant to be a torture or a threat." He sighed. "One more thing the *Custodes* have to answer for. How can we minimize Faelan's part in this, Oriel? He doesn't *want* to be a part of it. Is there anything we can do to protect him—and us?"

"Perhaps." Oriel sat back with his hands on his thighs and stared at Faelan for a long moment, then looked at Javan. "The safest thing, of course, is simply to avoid letting him know anything that it would be dangerous for the *Custodes* to know."

"And erase anything potentially dangerous before he goes off for his monthly debriefing," Javan agreed.

Oriel nodded. "So long as we know precisely when he's to go, that might suffice. It wouldn't protect him from Sitric, though—or from a Deryni in Paulin's service."

"*Is* there one?" Javan asked. "You still haven't said for certain."

"I don't *know* for certain," Oriel replied. "And before I try to find out, are you sure we want to get further involved? So far, I haven't gone beyond what might be expected of a Healer in the line of duty. But if I probe and find what you suspect, we're committed. At very least, I'll have to cover myself; and if I can't, we have no choice but to go to Hubert."

"That may not be our only choice," Javan replied. "If you just patch things for now, will it hold for a few days until we figure out what else to do?"

"It should, if no one gets his hands on him in the meantime."

"Let's bring him around, then, and see what he has to say for himself," Javan said, rising from his knees to change places with the Healer. "I'll ask the questions. I'm the only one of us he knows, and he wasn't too keen on having a Healer examine him."

Holding the candle so he would be well illuminated when Faelan woke, Javan waited until Oriel had taken up a position behind him, then glanced back at the Healer and nodded. Without speaking, Oriel leaned forward briefly to touch the priest's hand, giving the command. Faelan's eyelids fluttered as the Healer straightened, eyes opening uncertainly and then darting in alarm first to Javan, then to Oriel, to Charlan, and back to the king.

"You're perfectly safe, Father," Javan said. "This is Master Oriel, and that's Sir Charlan, one of my aides. Are you feeling better?"

"I—" All at once, Faelan's hand darted to his sleeve, feeling for the wound that was no longer there. Simultaneously he realized he was lying on his back without pain—and immediately guessed what had happened.

"He—already did it," he whispered, fearful eyes meeting Javan's in shocked betrayal. "I didn't think—"

"You weren't in any condition to think," Javan said quietly. "Nothing can be done about the blood you lost other than to feed you up and give you time to recover, but there was no point to enduring the rest. I'm very sorry you had to suffer that for my sake. The least I could do was to have you healed."

Swallowing audibly, Faelan turned his face to the wall. "That— doesn't solve the ultimate problem, Sire," he whispered. "Father Paulin is looking for any excuse to discredit you. Anything you say or do that might help him, I'm sworn to report. And even if I broke my oath, he'd—know."

"Oh, *he* wouldn't know," Javan said confidently. "But his new Deryni might know—mightn't he, Father?"

Faelan froze, alarm and consternation pinching the man's sharp features.

"I didn't tell you that," he whispered.

"No, you didn't. In fact, it was precisely what you *didn't* tell me that first tipped me off. I know you aren't responsible," he added, at Faelan's growing look of confusion and fear. "Oriel, let's get to the bottom of this."

Before Faelan could draw breath to cry out, Javan had set his hand on the priest's forehead and seized control, sending him plummeting into unconsciousness. Oriel swooped in right behind him, delving deep as Javan withdrew. Charlan had surged forward as he fathomed Javan's intention, fearing physical resistance or an outcry on Faelan's part, but now he retreated to the door again at the king's gesture.

After a moment Oriel raised his head, smiling as he opened his eyes.

"Sire, you must be the luckiest man in all Christendom," he murmured. "I can't speak directly for the talents of Paulin's Deryni, but he didn't spend too much time on this one. There are traces of one fairly superficial Reading—and of course nothing awkward showed up, because Faelan didn't know anything. There was also a definite compulsion set to prevent him speaking of that part of his 'discipline.' But no attempt was made to block the memory. Cocky bastard. I suppose he thought it wasn't necessary—or maybe that it would just reinforce the intimidation."

"Can you undo it?" Javan asked.

Oriel nodded. "I could. I don't think it's necessary, though. The less tampering, the better. It's enough that I'll have to cover tonight's work. Before, there was nothing interesting to Read. I can't say that now."

"Well, cover it, then," Javan said. "But don't hurt him. I want an ally, not a victim."

"Just give me a few minutes," the Healer said, kneeling to lay both hands on the sleeping man's forehead.

After a few minutes he withdrew, shifting one hand down to lightly encircle Faelan's near wrist.

"Truth-Read him when I bring him out," he murmured. "I think that's taken care of things."

Faelan was silent and still for several seconds more. Then he stirred and opened his eyes, all the fear gone, not seeming to notice Oriel's touch.

"Sire," he murmured, lifting his eyes to Javan. "I must have fallen asleep. Pray, pardon me. I should have been more vigilant."

Javan shook his head slightly and smiled. "You were very tired after your ride. The rest was good for you. Were you asleep long?"

"Since midafternoon, I think," Faelan replied, looking beyond them at the darkened window embrasure and frowning. "It must be very late. I intended to rise and say the Vesper Office. Now it's—"

"Well past Compline," Javan supplied. "You remember nothing of the past little while, do you?"

Faelan looked at him quizzically. "Should I, Sire?"

For answer, Javan merely glanced aside at Oriel, who bowed his head briefly over Faelan's hand. All at once Faelan gasped, remembering all. Javan could see the flood of returning memory in the priest's eyes, shocked and stunned, the realization of his body's healing, the significance of the hand still clasped to his wrist—and the reaction gradually giving way to guarded hope.

"I—couldn't remember any of this," Faelan breathed.

"No," Javan said. "And if you can't remember something, you can't tell a lie about it."

"But—wouldn't *he* be able to detect what you'd done?" Faelan whispered, now addressing Oriel directly.

"Not by simple Truth-Reading," Oriel replied. "Probably not even by direct probe, unless anyone had reason to suspect there'd been tampering. And I don't intend to leave you with any memory of what's happened here tonight."

Faelan swallowed. "They'll know you healed me."

"Paulin will expect it," Javan said. "He told me quite blatantly that you'd been bled to relieve ill humours, that you hadn't been feeling well lately, and I told him I was going to have Oriel take a look at you. But he doesn't have to know that we know the true circumstances. You won't remember telling me, and I'll pretend not to have guessed. You'll simply take up your duties as my chaplain—saying daily Mass in the Chapel Royal, hearing confessions, accompanying me at Court functions when appropriate—the usual things."

"But—"

"None of this will require any effort on your part," Oriel assured him. "You won't retain any memory of this conversation. All you'll remember is that you have a kind and honorable master who has never been observed to do anything to which his critics might take exception. When you go for your monthly sessions at the abbey, you'll have forgotten anything you may have seen or heard that shouldn't be passed on."

Faelan swallowed, suddenly apprehensive again, and turned his face slightly toward the wall.

"Sire, I don't want to betray you," he whispered. "Can he make me forget the fear, as well? That's the worst—knowing that they could kill me any time the fancy took them. If they bleed me again—"

Javan set his hand briefly over Oriel's, clasped on the priest's wrist. "You know I can't promise that they won't," he said quietly, "if only as a token reminder of how totally you're in their power when you're there at the abbey. But they *aren't* going to take as much as they did last time—they *can't*, on anything like a monthly basis, and still have you able to function as they want. Unfortunately, we don't dare tamper with that memory. You're going to have to live with that one."

Faelan closed his eyes briefly and made himself take a deep breath, reluctantly resigned to the logic.

"You'll have to expect that Paulin's Deryni probably will be present at future debriefings, too," Javan went on, "but since you'll be utterly open and sincere in your reporting, it shouldn't be anything like before. If all he does is Truth-Read you, you won't even be aware of it. Once we've established that you intend to cooperate, we might even manufacture an occasional tidbit for you to feed them, just to reassure them that you're keeping your eyes and ears open in their behalf. Naturally, I don't expect these trips back to the abbey to be pleasant—they'll certainly be frightening at times—but I hope that the worst they'll do is threaten. I wish I could offer you something more positive, but I can't."

"He should rest now, Sire," Oriel said quietly, when it was clear that further discussion was only going to further fuel Faelan's fears. "I'll make this as quick as I can."

He had already seized control as he spoke, so Faelan could only flash the king a look of helpless trust just before unconsciousness claimed him.

"Set that I'd like him to begin saying daily Mass in the Chapel Royal directly after Prime," Javan said, withdrawing his hand as Oriel prepared to delve deep. "To cover our conversation in the garden this afternoon, say that I inquired concerning his health—about which he was noncommittal, save that the ride from *Arx Fidei* exhausted him—and that I then merely outlined his expected duties and sent him off to rest. That's essentially what I told Paulin. We can make up the rest as we go along."

Oriel nodded as he closed his eyes. "It shall be done, Sire," he whispered.

CHAPTER EIGHTEEN

Forget not thy friend in thy mind . . .
—Ecclesiasticus 37:6

All was still and silent as Javan and Charlan made their way back along the short stretch of corridor separating the priest's quarters from the royal apartments. Oriel, his task quickly completed, had been released to return to his own quarters, lest his absence be noted and remarked upon. Two senior serjeants came to attention as king and aide approached the door, one of them reaching aside to raise the latch and push the door open. Charlan pulled it closed behind them. Guiscard was waiting in one of the chairs beside the trestle table set in the center of the room, a rack of candles at his elbow, and came to his feet as the two entered.

"All's well?" he said quietly.

"Aye." Javan sighed and flopped into a chair opposite. "Apparently Paulin does have a tame Deryni out at *Arx Fidei*—or did, as recently as a few days ago. Faelan's going to require careful handling, but I think it can be managed. Until we know more, I don't want anyone but Oriel touching him."

"You'd best fill in your visitor on what you've learned, then," Guiscard said, glancing pointedly toward the door to the sleeping chamber, which Javan suddenly realized was closed. "You didn't tell me to expect him this early, so I very nearly had heart failure when I opened the door and saw him. He's disguised as a *Custodes* monk."

Slowly Javan got back to his feet.

"He's already *here?*" he whispered.

189

"Aye, waiting for the pair of you," Guiscard replied, moving toward the door and beckoning them to follow. "He's already put me through my paces—sort of a trial run for tomorrow night."

He threw open the door to darkness; only a single rushlight burned beside the great, canopied state bed. Guiscard stepped inside, waiting for them to join him. Javan did so warily, standing his ground as a shadow detached itself from the murky darkness near the garderobe entrance, and Guiscard pulled the bedroom door closed behind them. Beside him, Charlan had one hand on the hilt of his dagger, though steel would have been meager defense against any of the men Javan was expecting.

"Who's there?" the king found himself whispering.

"It's Jesse, Sire," said a voice he had heard before, as familiar shields flared and briefly brushed his and a Deryni aura brightened around the face of a figure in *Custodes* black.

Despite the reassurance, Javan had to look twice to be sure. Jesse looked nothing like the other time Javan had seen him, brown hair now cut close around his ears and tonsured at the crown, warrior's erect form looking almost a little stoop-shouldered in the stiffened scapular and pushed-back cowl of a *Custodes* monk.

"I'm afraid I gave Guiscard a bit of a scare," Jesse said with a faint smile, "for which I apologize. He tells me you may have gotten wind of a new Deryni collaborator—working for the *Custodes*, of all things. Can you add anything to that?"

"Well, it's confirmed that the *Custodes* do have a Deryni working for them," Javan replied. "We don't know anything yet about him personally—I'll let you and Joram sort that out—but Oriel has taken remedial action that should hold, for the time being. Father Faelan—"

"Guiscard gave me the priest's background," Jesse said. "Maybe I'd better just Read the details. It won't take long."

"I hardly had any contact myself," Javan began. "Oriel—"

"Just lay your hands on mine and close your eyes," Jesse said, smiling and upturning his palms to receive Javan's. "I know you're still nervous about this sort of thing, but practice will make it easier, believe me. Drop your shields and focus on the contacts you've had with Faelan—no need to be anxious. Allow me to guide the process. If there's any physical sensation at all, you'll feel this as a faint tickling sort of sensation just behind your eyes, nothing more."

Javan obeyed. For a brief, interminable instant, time seemed to stand still. A vague sensation not unlike vertigo accompanied a profound stilling of everything not connected with the hapless Faelan. He felt the deft whisper of intrusion as his shields were breached, but by then he could not bring himself to care.

After a moment Jesse released him, glancing briefly beyond him at the watching Guiscard—and at Charlan, standing quietly beside Guiscard and now controlled by him, in this potentially frightening situation.

"You were right not to let anyone but Oriel touch your priest, until we're sure what we've got," Jesse said, returning his gaze to Javan. "If he's clean, as it appears, we can take steps to keep him that way. If he isn't—well, it doesn't appear that Oriel's done anything that can't be explained by usual Healer procedures. And if necessary, we'll simply have to deal with Faelan."

Javan shivered. "You mean kill him."

"If it becomes necessary," Jesse replied, "but you know we'll try to avoid that. Meanwhile, I'd like to use both him and Oriel in tomorrow night's working. It will give me a chance for a close look at both of them—and I can call in reinforcements, once the Portal's set, if extraordinary measures prove necessary."

Like killing him, Javan thought, closing his eyes briefly. But he said, "Do you think it will be possible to save him?"

"Sire, that's a question I can't possibly answer yet," Jesse said. "I'll certainly do what I can for him. It will be tricky, because any tampering on our part has to stand up to direct Deryni scrutiny on a regular basis." He cocked his head at Javan in question. "I don't suppose there's some other priest who could serve as your chaplain, who would be less prone to *Custodes* meddling?"

Javan grimaced. "Joram or Niallan or Queron are hardly available—or suitable, by current legislation. And just about any priest I name from my own experience of the last few years is going to be a *Custodes* priest and subject to the same kinds of scrutiny as Faelan. Any priest who's acceptable to me is going to be suspect."

"I take your point," Jesse said, nodding. "Very well, we'll see what can be done with Father Faelan. If he's clean, the whole matter becomes academic. We won't worry about the alternative for now. We'll use him to pull power for setting the Portal, and then, while we've got him under, I'll simply do a general tidying up and bury some extra safeguards. Neither he nor Paulin's Deryni will ever know."

Javan blinked at him in amazement. "You can do that? I mean, it's that easy?"

"Well, doing what I just suggested takes more time than just the telling," Jesse said with a grin, "but it isn't *difficult*, if you're dealing with humans. Speaking of which, let's have a look at your Charlan," he said, gesturing to Guiscard to bring him over. "I don't anticipate any problem, since you've already been working with him, but we need to be introduced. Guiscard, give control over to Javan, if you will. I'll take it through him, when I'm ready."

Wordlessly Guiscard brought the entranced Charlan to stand before the king, drawing back as Javan brushed the young knight's wrist and took control. At Jesse's direction, Javan brought Charlan back to normal consciousness.

"Sir Charlan, meet Sir Jesse," he said quietly. "He'll be directing the setting of the Portal tomorrow night."

"Hello, Charlan," Jesse said.

Charlan blinked once, his gaze flicking over Jesse's Deryni aura, then turned his attention back to the king, an odd little smile curving at his lips.

"This is amazing," he said softly. "You're blocking my fear, aren't you?"

"Yes. But there really *is* nothing to be afraid of," Javan said.

"I know that," Charlan agreed, nodding. "At least it's easy to *say* that, standing here like this."

Smiling, Jesse stepped within touching distance of the young knight. Dark and fair, they yet were two of a kind, seasoned warriors both, very near in age. The two studied one another for a long moment, measuring, weighing, after which Jesse nodded and very deliberately folded his hands behind his back.

"In future, I hope it will be easy to say that without the controls," he said. "I'd like to show you what will happen tomorrow night, so you don't need to be afraid. May I?"

Charlan drew a cautious breath. "You're asking my permission?"

"Of course. You're an ally, not an enemy."

"All right."

Slowly, casually, Jesse brought his hands back into view.

"It will all begin by having Javan take you to a deeply relaxed state, exactly as he's done so many times before. Then I'll set up a preliminary link like this." He clasped his hands lightly to Charlan's head, thumbs resting on the temples. "You may feel a—sort of a sticky sensation just at the top of your head. That's the connection being made. You see, it isn't frightening at all. And if I need to draw, this is what it will feel like."

Nothing outward happened except that Charlan's eyes widened momentarily and then fluttered closed. After a moment he opened them again, looking slightly bemused, and Jesse took away his hands, apparently pleased.

"You did that very well," he said. "When we actually do the

deed, you might lose consciousness briefly, but it would only be for a little while. That doesn't frighten you, does it?"

Charlan blinked and stared hard at Jesse, glanced briefly at Javan, then looked back at the Deryni.

"No, it doesn't," he said just a little defiantly.

"Which is not *entirely* true," Jesse said with a smile, "but you've proved admirably that you can function even *with* your fear—which is rare enough in any man, human or Deryni. Sire, you've taught him well."

Javan snorted. "He's taught *himself* well. Up until about a week ago, he didn't have any choice in the matter. But I've already apologized for that."

"You didn't need to apologize," Charlan said. "You did what you had to do. I'm only glad I managed to be a help rather than a hindrance, whether or not I was aware of it at the time." He glanced at Jesse.

"Is that all? Because if it is, his Highness really should get some sleep. *All* of us should get some sleep. It sounds as if we're going to be very busy about this time tomorrow night."

In fact, they were busy all the next day, the last but one before the coronation. The morning began with Mass in the Chapel Royal, celebrated by a Father Faelan who seemed much recovered from his condition of the day before. In sheerly physical terms, the improvement would have been marked; but he seemed also to have put aside the concerns that had him quaking and cowed the day before. The homily he preached was short but fitting for a king soon to be crowned, speaking of rendering unto God and Caesar. The two pages serving at the altar were a little stiff, as was normal when adjusting to the preferences of a new priest, but the Mass proceeded with acceptable decorum and only one minor fumble when the younger page nearly dropped the great silver lavabo bowl. For the first time in weeks, Javan was able to receive Communion from a priest whom he respected as a man as well as for his office, and he prayed that ways would continue to be found so that Faelan could exercise his office in good conscience. Paulin slipped into the back of the chapel just as Mass was beginning and grilled Faelan in the sacristy after, but he and Faelan both looked satisfied with the interview when Paulin left a few minutes later.

"Was there any problem with Father Paulin?" Javan asked the priest as Faelan joined him and Guiscard and Charlan to go down to the great hall for a light breakfast before exercise.

"Not at all, Sire," Faelan replied. "He merely inquired after my health and asked if I was recovered from the fatigue of my journey. I assured him that a good night's sleep had much restored me and that I looked forward to taking up the full range of my spiritual duties in the royal household. He gave me his blessing and left.''

And that was precisely all that had passed between them, as both Javan and Guiscard could attest. And since Paulin most assuredly was not Deryni, there was no chance that anything else had transpired of which neither they nor Faelan were aware. As the day went on, with morning exercise extended in favor of extra time in the tilting yard, as preparation for the tourney that would take place the day after the coronation, Javan was able to put most of his worries out of mind, at least for a few hours.

After a bath and light repast at midday and final fittings for his coronation robes, the afternoon was occupied with archery practice, which enabled him to focus much of his concern about his great lords at the center of the straw butt that was his target. When Sir Radan commented on his particular accuracy as the afternoon wore on, Javan did not tell him it came of envisioning the faces of Murdoch and Rhun in the center of the target. Late afternoon saw the arrival of the expected entourage from Cassan—Fane Fitz-Arthur with his wife and their three-year-old son, who now was Cassan's duke—and arrangements were made to receive them at a special court the following day at noon.

Supper was early and simple, in his apartments, with Rhys Michael, his aides, Robear and Jason, Etienne de Courcy, and a handful of the other young knights not occupied elsewhere. It was a congenial gathering, but Javan did not let it last much past dark, pleading fatigue and the need for a clear head on the morrow, the last day before his coronation.

Gradually the supper guests filtered out, some of the men to take up nighttime duties, others to return to their families. Etienne was among the first to leave—he would join them in the Portal room later. But though the others soon followed, Rhys Michael lingered until only he and Charlan and Guiscard remained, the latter two supervising the squires who were clearing away the last of the debris from their meal.

The prince had put away copious amounts of wine with dinner, and Javan had hoped that gentle inebriation would encourage his brother's early departure with the rest. Instead, as the last of the squires took their leave, Rhys Michael moved into the window embrasure, pushing one of the glazed lower panels wider to admit more air. The evening was still and balmy, just on the edge of being too hot, and both brothers were in their shirt sleeves.

"Are you scared about the day after tomorrow?" Rhys Michael asked, turning back to him, his face barely discernible in the light of a candle by Javan on the table.

Javan brought the candle nearer and set it just inside the embrasure, stepping up to stand beside his brother.

"Not scared, exactly," Javan said. "A little apprehensive, maybe. It's a complicated ceremony."

"That isn't what I meant," Rhys Michael said. "You'll be an anointed king. That's—almost magical. You'll be set apart. You'll never be the same again."

Javan sank down on one of the cushions to consider. Father Faelan had mentioned something of the sort in his homily this morning. Javan supposed the sacring of a king *was* magical, in the same sense that a priest's anointing set him apart for a special kind of service. Most assuredly, he would not be the same when it was over; but he already would never be the same as he was before Joram and the others had unleashed the Haldane powers in him.

"I'll still be your brother," he said, suspecting that this was what was really troubling Rhys Michael. "Nothing can ever change that. Did you think it would?"

Rhys Michael looked away, swaying a little on his feet. "I dunno. It changed something in Alroy once he became king. I hardly ever got to see him. He was always busy doing king things."

"Well, it wasn't exactly by choice," Javan replied. "And with none of us being of legal age when it all started, the situation was hardly typical. Things are going to be different now, though. I hope you'll be able to help me with a lot of the 'king things,' as you put it. After all, until I marry and start producing heirs, you're the heir presumptive. You need the training, just in case."

Rhys Michael wobbled down onto the seat opposite Javan. "That's something I've been wanting to talk to you about—marrying, not the training. I'm not too keen on books, y'know. Maybe this isn't the best time, though. I think maybe I've had too much to drink . . ."

It was *not* the best time. The subject certainly needed airing, but not with Rhys Michael in his cups and looking to go maudlin any minute, and not tonight. The work ahead brooked no prolonged discussion on any topic. Sending a quick command to Guiscard, Javan leaned back in his seat and made himself chuckle.

"I hope this is theoretical rather than practical," he said lightly, to the sound of liquid being poured elsewhere in the room. "Princes obviously are expected to marry eventually, but you aren't even fifteen yet."

"I *will* be, in another couple of months," Rhys Michael said indignantly.

"Oh, I'm well aware of that. I'm also aware of the almost irresistible urges that probably are starting to stir by now. You've plenty of time, though." He cocked his head, choosing his next words for their shock value. "Or is there some urgency I don't know about? Rhysem, you haven't gone and gotten some poor serving wench pregnant, have you?"

"Me? Oh, no! I never—I mean, I—"

As Rhys Michael stammered and stumbled over his own tongue, spared the open blaze of his blushes by the dim light in the embrasure, an impassive Guiscard approached with a pair of small silver goblets, bowing blandly and withdrawing as Javan took them with a nod of thanks.

"Well, that's a relief. Here, try some of this Rhennish brandywine and tell me what you think of it."

As he handed one of the goblets across to Rhys Michael and their hands touched, he tried to reach across the bond of their flesh to trigger sleep—and was brought up short by shields!

The rebound did not hurt, but it made Javan gasp. To cover his astonishment, he managed to fumble the goblet in his other hand and drop it. It struck the stone flags in a silvery clangor, splashing his boot with brandywine, and he leaped to his feet with a yelp.

"Yipe, that was clumsy of me! Guiscard, get a cloth to wipe this up, will you?"

"Coming, Sire."

As Javan pretended to root at his feet for the errant goblet, his mind was reeling. How could Rhys Michael have shields? When could it have happened, and how? His immediate suspicion was that the shields dated from the moment of Alroy's death, when Rhys Michael had moved that much closer in the succession. Maybe exposure to the energies surrounding Alroy's passing had stirred up part of the Haldane potential set in him the night their father died. Javan didn't think it was meant to work that way, but who knew? No one had expected *his* powers to start developing spontaneously while Alroy was still alive—but they had.

Not knowing the extent of his brother's awakening, Javan decided not to risk sending directly to Guiscard again, lest Rhys Michael detect it. But when the young knight came near, taking the goblet from Javan and crouching to look for the spill, Javan decided he had to risk a contact rapport.

"Better get it off the boot first, before it stains," he said, grabbing Guiscard's hand to guide it to the boot—and to establish the necessary physical contact.

Guiscard, he has shields. I don't know how or when he got them. I couldn't put him out.

Did he feel the attempt?

I don't think so. What now, though? We've got people waiting.

Leave it to me, Guiscard returned. "That's got it, I think," he went on verbally, shifting his attention to mopping up the floor. "Can I get you something else, Sire? I'm afraid that was the last of the brandywine."

"A pity," Javan murmured, glancing at Rhys Michael, who was downing his with obvious relish. "At least Rhysem got to taste it."

"Mmmmm, it really is good, Javan!" his brother said archly, lifting his goblet in jaunty salute. "It's a sin to waste it. You'd better mention that, the next time you go to confession!"

"I guess I'm more nervous than I thought," Javan allowed with a sheepish grin. "Guiscard, how about one of those sweet Fianna varietals? Rhysem would probably like the one we were drinking last night, if you and Charlan didn't finish it off."

"I think there's some left in the other room, Sire. I'll go and see."

As he withdrew to get it, Javan shifted his attention back to Rhys Michael, who was tossing off the last of his brandywine.

"This *was* very good," the prince said, setting his empty goblet aside with a smirk. "Sorry you didn't get any. Serves you right for that cheeky remark. I don't consort with serving wenches."

Allowing himself a halfhearted chuckle, Javan sat back in his seat, hoping Guiscard would hurry.

"It might almost be better if you did," he said, determined to keep his brother off balance while Guiscard dealt with this new complication. "Even if the worst happens, you can't be made to marry one. Royal bastards might be an embarrassment, but they aren't a threat to the crown—at least not until they're grown."

"It isn't like that!" Rhys Michael began.

"No? I'm glad to hear it," Javan went on. "Because if you play around with a girl of 'suitable' breeding and you get *her* pregnant, her father—by definition—is going to be highly enough placed to put a lot of pressure on you to marry her. And if you do, and she bears you a son, that could be all our enemies need as an excuse to eliminate both of us and help themselves to fourteen more years of regency. After that long in virtually absolute power, do you really think they'd be willing to step back from that power and let your son take up his crown in any meaningful way? He'd be a puppet, Rhysem, the same way Alroy was!"

"Alroy wasn't a puppet, and they'd never do that," Rhys Michael said sulkily as Guiscard came back into the room with a new pair of goblets. "You've broken the back of the old regency. You'll have your own men in place in a matter of weeks. Besides," he muttered under his breath, "her father is dead."

"Whose father?" Javan said as Guiscard delivered one of the goblets to his brother.

"It isn't important. Nothing's going to happen," Rhys Michael said, and took a fortifying gulp from his cup.

Javan, reaching for his own, knew immediately who his brother was talking about.

"It's Michaela Drummond, isn't it?" he said.

Don't drink that, came Guiscard's warning as his hand brushed Javan's.

Rhys Michael took another deep pull from his cup and glanced out the window, not noticing that Javan set his cup aside untasted.

"What if it is?" he declared, sullen and closed. "I like her. After you left Court, she was one of the few friends I had. She's suitable."

"Yes, and she's the ward of Manfred MacInnis, fostered to his lady's household. I'll bet that he and the Lady Estellan have made it very easy for the two of you to be together, haven't they?"

Rhys Michael was starting to droop visibly, his head nodding over his cup, but he took another deep swallow before answering.

"You don't unnerstand," he whispered, his speech starting to slur. "It isn't like that. Besides, we—haven't done anything. And even if we had, and she—Well, I—can't believe the regents would do what you're suggesting. It's—monstrous."

"Yes, that's a good word to describe it," Javan agreed. "And they've never done anything monstrous before, have they? Their hands are spotlessly clean—unless you count the Duke of Claibourne, and Declan Carmody and his wife and sons, and little Giesele MacLean, smothered in her bed."

Rhys Michael had drifted into sleep somewhere during this recitation, and Javan reached across to take the goblet from his relaxing fingers. At once Guiscard moved in from the shadows, shoving his fingers hard against one of the carotid pulse points in Rhys Michael's throat.

"Is he all right?" Javan whispered.

"He's fine," Guiscard said, sinking down beside the sleeping prince and reaching across for Javan's untouched goblet. "Let's get a little more of this in him, and then we'll see if we can't get far enough past those shields to tidy up any memory of this."

As Javan watched wide-eyed, Guiscard tipped back the prince's head and set the goblet to his lips, tilting the wine through the parted lips. To Javan's surprise, his brother began swallowing—a succession of halting contractions of his throat, almost yielding to coughs, but enough to drain the cup by half before Guiscard relented.

"That should do it," the Deryni knight said, handing the cup off to Javan. "Swallowing is a reflex, when someone is unconscious. Fortunately, shields don't interfere with triggering that reflex—not that his shields are particularly strong. They aren't even complete. I've gone ahead and dealt with what little memory might have aroused suspicion later on, but I gather that you hadn't expected this turn of events."

Javan shook his head. "It's part of the Haldane legacy. It has to be. Maybe Alroy's death triggered something." He sighed. "We can't worry about this now, though. Will he sleep all night?"

"Oh, yes. There's no immediate problem—other than his apparent infatuation with the Drummond girl. Charlan, come and give us a hand getting the prince to bed," he added in a slightly louder voice. "Fortunately, the coronation should keep him sufficiently occupied with official duties that he won't have time or energy to dig himself in deeper with his lady-love. Once you're safely crowned, though, it might be wise to find an excuse to get her away from Court."

As Charlan approached, Guiscard was already easing around to the prince's other side and pulling him to his feet, setting a shoulder under his arm as Charlan took the other.

"Poor Rhysem," Javan murmured as the two half dragged and half walked him staggering into the other room. "I expect he's going to have quite a head on him in the morning."

"Maybe less than you might think," Charlan said, "unless Guiscard's potion makes things worse than usual. He's acquired quite a capacity while you were away from Court, Sire."

Shocked at the implication, Javan glanced at Guiscard. "Is that true?"

Guiscard grimaced as he and Charlan hefted the prince onto the great canopied bed. "Well, I won't go so far as to say that his Highness has an outright problem with drink, but he does manage to put away far more for his size than one might imagine. That isn't the issue right now, however. Let's get him undressed and bedded down. People are waiting for us."

"Aye, of course."

Javan watched a little stunned as they stripped his brother of his boots and outer garments and installed him in the state bed. By the time they finished, the king had forced himself back to something approaching equilibrium.

Minutes later Charlan was heading down for their rendezvous

next to the incipient library, while Javan and Guiscard diverted to
Father Faelan's quarters. Their knock at the priest's door produced
a somewhat rumpled-looking Faelan. In the heat, and not consciously expecting visitors this late, he had put aside his hooded
scapular and opened the throat of his habit, which he hurriedly
began doing up again as the king's presence registered. In the little
oratory beyond, a breviary lay open on the armrest of the *prie-dieu*,
illuminated by a fat yellow candle in a black wrought-iron candlestick.

"I've disturbed you at your prayers, Father. I'm sorry," Javan
said. Laying a hand on Faelan's wrist, he triggered light controls as
he and Guiscard moved Faelan back into the room and Guiscard
drew the door closed behind them. "I require your services for an
hour or so this evening. Will you come?"

Faelan blinked, surprise and apprehension damped heavily by
Javan's controls, then gave a dazed jerk of his chin.

"Aye, my lord," he whispered.

"He'd better put the rest of his habit back on before we go, Sire,"
Guiscard murmured, holding up a mass of black. "I know you dis-
like it, but questions would be asked, if he should be seen without
it."

He was right, of course. With a curt nod, Javan turned away to
close Faelan's book and extinguish the extra candle in the oratory
while the priest drew the offending garment back over his head,
Guiscard preparing to open the door. Faelan was still adjusting his
garments as he headed out of the room, Javan and then Guiscard
following—and all but collided with two men wearing black habits
that matched his own.

CHAPTER NINETEEN

*Observe, and take good heed, for thou walkest
in peril of thy overthrowing.*
—Ecclesiasticus 13:13

Of all the men Javan would have preferred not to meet just then, members of the *Custodes Fidei* ranked among the very least desirable.

"Why, Father Faelan, were we planning some late-night assignation?" the taller of the two said coldly, at first noting only that Faelan was accompanied, but not by how many and by whom. He did not see Guiscard melt back into the shadows behind the door.

"Actually," Javan said, moving farther into the light, "the good Father's 'assignation' was to accompany me back to my apartments. This close to my coronation, I felt the need of spiritual guidance—which is precisely why I have a personal chaplain."

"It's the king!" the second man murmured.

Stepping back a pace, the taller one eyed Javan impassively, then favored him with a formal inclination of his head.

"Your Highness."

As the man straightened, and as Javan got a better look at him and his companion, his heart sank. Scarcely could this meeting have been more ill-timed. The tall, gaunt monk occasionally haunted Javan's nightmares, as he surely must haunt Faelan's, for Brother Serafin was the Grand Inquisitor of the *Custodes Fidei*. The priest accompanying him was Father Lior, his assistant, equally dangerous. Peripherally, during his years in seminary, Javan had dealt with both men; both had been involved more recently and more directly in Faelan's interrogation-*cum*-torture.

201

"So, may I ask what brings you abroad this late, gentlemen?"
Javan said pointedly, sending to Guiscard to keep out of sight but
be ready to act—for if Javan could not divert the two, and quickly,
other measures would be necessary.

Clasping his hands behind his back, Serafin gazed down his long
nose at the king. "Father Faelan may be your chaplain, Sire, but he
is still a member of the Order you chose to abandon. Having heard
that he was indisposed when he first arrived here yesterday, our
superior—and his—instructed that we inquire regarding his health.
We anticipated that a late visit would least incommode your Highness. Obviously we misjudged."

"Yes, you did."

Faelan, meanwhile, had been standing mute in the midst of this
exchange—still sufficiently controlled that his anxiety did not
show, but increasingly aware of his danger, if the two tried to take
him away for any intense interrogation.

"Sire, there is no need to vex yourself over this interruption,"
he said to Javan. "And Brother Serafin, Father Lior, I assure you, I
am well recovered. It was a fatigue of the journey, nothing more."

"Were you seen by the Healer Oriel?" Serafin asked, gimlet eyes
fixed on the priest.

"He saw me briefly, yes," Faelan said truthfully. "I did not request it, but his Highness thought it prudent."

"Perhaps his Highness will not mind if we have a few words in
private," Serafin replied, boldly seizing Faelan's arm and propelling
him toward the still-ajar door, as Lior simultaneously pressed between them and the king. "If you'll excuse us, Sire. We'll send him
on to your quarters in a few minutes."

Javan could not stop him. The captive Faelan was already nearly
through the door, Serafin at his side and Lior right behind them—
and Guiscard was on the other side of the door!

Take Serafin as soon as he's inside, he sent to the Deryni knight.
I'll see to Lior.

He moved in on Lior even as the startled Serafin was suddenly
jerked into the room by one arm. While Javan clapped one hand
hard over Lior's mouth from behind, his other arm reached around
for a choke hold. He was not heavy enough to take the priest down
on sheer physical strength, but at least he was able to keep him
from crying out as he sought either a pressure point or a control
that would produce unconsciousness.

Lior struggled manfully for a few seconds, lifting Javan right off
his feet as he twisted and bent sharply forward in an effort to throw
off his assailant, but then he went limp. He and Javan collapsed in

a confused heap, fortunately mostly inside the room. As Javan hurriedly scrambled to his feet, breathing hard, an appalled Father Faelan grabbed several handfuls of Lior's habit and helped drag him the rest of the way in, nudging the door closed behind them. Guiscard had subdued Brother Serafin rather more easily and was standing astride the supine figure, bent with one hand clasped across Serafin's throat.

"God *damn*, this man's a nuisance!" he murmured. "Not to put too fine a point on it, but now we've got them, what do you intend to do with them?"

He straightened, wiping his hands against his thighs in distaste, and stepped clear of his unconscious captive.

"Well, I didn't *want* them, but the situation was escalating," Javan said, making sure Lior was not going to stir. "I didn't need this, on top of the business with Rhysem." He sighed. "I suppose we're going to have to doctor their memories and let them go."

"Mmmm, tricky, making sure both sets of memory match," Guiscard replied. "Are *you* up to it? I'm not sure I am."

"Then we'll have to take them down to Jesse," Javan said impatiently, keeping his voice low. "What else was I to do? Serafin's the Grand Inquisitor, for God's sake. I don't know how I would have explained you being here, and I couldn't have him sniffing around before we've at least got a bolt-hole."

"Sire," Faelan interrupted, "he knows who Paulin's Deryni is."

"What?"

"I said, he knows who Paulin's Deryni is. Both of them must know. They were there when I was questioned." He paused a beat, looking at Javan intently. "Can you make them talk, Sire?"

Javan glanced at the two unconscious *Custodes*, considering briefly, then nodded. "I probably could, but I think I'll let experts handle it. This is getting entirely too complicated. Guiscard, bring Serafin. I'll get Lior."

Sufficient control to get the two downstairs was easy enough. Fortunately, no one else was abroad in the king's corridor at that hour, or on the next level down, as they quietly made their way to the room beside the library. An astonished Etienne de Courcy admitted them, Oriel coming immediately to take the frightened Faelan in tow as Javan and Guiscard shuffled their unresisting charges inside.

Jesse had been crouching in the center of the room, chalking an octagon on the flagstones around the square space where the center one had been pried up and leaned against a wall. He rose as they entered, dusting off his hands, and Javan went to him fearlessly, holding out his hand in an invitation to make contact and Read details of what his words sketched.

"Serafin and Lior," he said by way of explanation, jerking his chin in their direction. "They picked a bad time to try to interview Father Faelan. I had no choice but to bring them. It may be all to the good, though. Faelan thinks they might know who Paulin's new Deryni is."

Jesse drew more detailed information from Javan in the space of only a few heartbeats, then turned a hard-eyed gaze on the entranced Serafin, standing quiet under Guiscard's hand.

"I'll deal with them after we've set the Portal," he said coldly, disdain hardening the usually congenial features. "Meanwhile, we'll use them. If I had the same kind of scruples they have, I'd derive a great deal of satisfaction from just draining them dry. As it is, I'll satisfy myself with a little light irony, redirecting some of the power that's normally turned against us."

He glanced around the room, at all of them apprehensively awaiting his direction.

"All right, I'm reshuffling a few of the pairings, since we now have a surfeit of bodies," he said. "Charlan, I'll ask you to keep watch outside with Guiscard, with one or both of you ready to come in if we need more. Etienne, I'll give you Serafin; Oriel, you take Lior. Father Faelan, you'll work with his Highness, since you know him best. If you'll all begin setting up your links, I'll finish the other necessary preparations and we'll get started."

To spare Faelan any more anxiety, Javan put him under quickly, drawing him to a seat in the little window embrasure and taking him deep, reassuring and soothing. As a consequence, he missed some of what Jesse was doing in the center of the room. When he had time to look up again, he was able to see at least the outward evidence of Jesse's preparations.

He had noted the chalked octagon on entering, about as large across as the height of a man. It was not complete, he now noticed, for Jesse had not yet drawn in the final facet to the north, though the piece of chalk lay right beside the northwestern end. Fat, fist-size yellow candles were set at each of the angles of the octagon, though they were not yet lit. The room's sole illumination came from another candle in a holder, set on the empty hearth of the little corner fireplace.

To keep that light from being seen outside, someone had hung a cloak from the top of the shutters in the window, covering the faceted windowpanes, and another cloak had been twisted into a long, narrow roll and laid across the doorsill after everyone was on the proper side of the door. Guiscard and Charlan had disappeared, one of them probably to take up a lookout post in the library next door and the other, perhaps, to circulate elsewhere in this wing, watching for more intruders like the hapless Serafin and Lior. Those two were seated on the floor to either side of the window embrasure, each with his minder, heads lolling forward on their chests, totally oblivious to what was going on.

And in the center of the room, Jesse was crouching over a pile of what looked like odd black and white dice, separating out four white ones to set them in a square. The black ones that were left he set at the white square's four corners, rocking back on his hunkers then to survey what lay before him.

Javan slowly eased to his feet, for from deep in untapped memory came knowledge of what Jesse was doing, the Haldane legacy asserting itself in useful fashion as Jesse touched a forefinger to each of the white cubes that made the square and softly spoke their names. Javan could not hear those names, but his memory supplied them, *"Prime, Seconde, Tierce, Quarte,"* as Jesse touched each of the four in turn.

When he had done, the four glowed softly from within, a pure, milky white glow. As Javan continued to watch, rapt with interest, Jesse drew a deep breath and repeated his fourfold invocation for the black cubes, again whispering names that Javan could not hear with his ears but knew from deep within: *"Quinte, Sixte, Septime, Octave."*

As each black cube was named, it seemed to kindle from within, in an opalescent, blue-black glitter like magpies' wings. Javan's breath caught in his throat as Jesse glanced up at him, flicked a wordless query in his direction, then signalled with a nod that Javan should join him.

"You've never seen Wards set this way before, have you?" Jesse whispered as Javan knelt opposite him. "And yet you know what's happening."

"I—do and I don't," Javan replied. "The words come, when you name the cubes, but it isn't anything I've consciously known before."

"You don't have to explain," Jesse said, picking up the white cube in the upper left corner of the white square and poising it above the black cube diagonally closest. "Joram told me about the Haldane powers. Have a closer look while I complete this. Say the words with me, if you want. You ought to have this information at conscious levels, not just lurking at the back of memory somewhere."

Drawing another deep breath, Jesse returned his attention to the cube in his hand and the one below it. As he set the white cube on the black and whispered its cognomen, the name came to Javan's lips as well.

"*Primus.*"

Just before the two cubes touched, the black cube seemed almost to jig upward just a little to meet its white counterpart, the two touching with a distinct *click* and melding to a single oblong unit, glittering grey-black. Smiling as he glanced up at Javan, Jesse set that oblong aside and picked up the next white cube, holding it above its black counterpart.

"*Secundus,*" he murmured, with Javan in almost perfect unison, as the process repeated.

Tertius and *Quartus* followed in rapid succession, each cognomen producing another of the silvery oblongs. When Jesse had finished, he instructed Javan to set the oblongs at the cardinal points of the octagon, just outside, at the same time summoning Oriel and Etienne to join them in the center.

"All right, it's usual to stand, but I think we'll sit tonight, since none of you have ever done this before. I don't want anyone keeling over if the draw gets heavy. Sit cross-legged here in the center," he said, sinking down, directing Javan to his right hand, Oriel to his left, and Etienne opposite. "Stay within the boundaries of the octagon, but try to keep clear of the center square. We'll eventually focus there, but for now, I want you each to settle down and make certain your link with your secondary is secure."

Jesse's back was to the open side of the octagon, and as the others settled, he reached behind him and chalked in the remaining side. Javan closed his eyes briefly, reaching out for the link with Father Faelan—still, serene, static potential—then looked up again as movement stirred, of Jesse's hand raising between them to point to each of the tiny Ward towers in succession, invoking Wards Major.

"*Primus, Secundus, Tertius, et Quartus, fiat lux!*"

And there *was* light. It flared upward in a gently shining canopy of luminance generated by the four rectoids at the quarters. Oriel and Etienne seemed nonplussed and probably had seen such warding dozens of times in the past, but for Javan the experience itself was all new, even though that tantalizing scrap of surfacing memory declared this quite ordinary and expected. Equally ordinary, though not expected, was the way Jesse then passed his hands over the candles nearest him to light them, gesturing for Etienne to do the same on his side.

"Master Oriel, I'll bring you into the master link first," he said then, laying his left hand palm upward on his knee and inviting Oriel's contact. His voice seemed to have taken on new authority as he spoke, potent as the flash of restrained anger that had surfaced when first confronting their unwelcome captives, but untainted by any hint of rancor. No longer the intent but easygoing young knight of Javan's earlier acquaintance, he was now the master magician coolly crafting his sorcery.

Oriel set his right hand on Jesse's left and closed his eyes, drawing a deep breath and exhaling softly. Fascinated, Javan watched the Healer's face relax, noting the telltale signs as he slipped into trance. Beyond Oriel, the two *Custodes* slumbered on, but Javan knew that Father Lior, at least, was now bound into the linkage. Javan could sense it, like a faint flavor of heightened potential in the air, focusing around Jesse, and watched in fascination as Jesse calmly shifted his attention to Etienne.

"Etienne?" he said softly, holding out his right hand.

Drawing a deep breath, Etienne reached across the space separating them and gave his right hand to Jesse, closing his eyes as he exhaled heavily. Javan could almost see the linkage this time, knowing what to look for, and perceived the potential channeling through each man as strands of blue-white light clasped lightly in Jesse's hands. Jesse bowed his head momentarily, apparently consolidating his control, then brought Etienne's hand to Oriel's, lightly retaining both right hands in his left as he turned his attention to Javan. In the light of candles and warding circle, a nimbus of faint white light seemed to play about Jesse's head.

"Are you following this?" he said softly as he held out his right hand. "If you like, I'll keep you conscious in the link for as long as I can, so you can see how this is done."

Drawing a steadying breath, not taking his eyes from Jesse's, Javan set his right hand in Jesse's and nodded.

"I'd like that," he said. "And don't think you have to hold back for my sake. I'm not afraid."

"I know that," Jesse said with a slight smile. "Nor need you be. Close your eyes now, and we'll go subvocal. There won't be anything to see, anyway. Not with eyes, at any rate."

Javan obeyed, rolling back his shields and feeling the gentle insinuation of Jesse's controls creep softly into place behind them, testing and teasing at the link with the slumbering Faelan, drawing out the strand that was the combined energy source of Javan and Faelan, shifting now to bring that strand into hand with the two from Oriel and Etienne.

Jesse began plaiting the energies then. Javan knew that was not *really* what Jesse was doing, but it was the closest analogy he could envision to describe the way Jesse began his slow draw, out the top of Javan's head, and then seemed to intertwine that strand with the ones he was pulling out of Oriel and Etienne.

After a few seconds he could feel it up through his spine and all the way up from the tips of his toes, the pressure increasing until it was almost a sensation of being turned inside out—somewhat disturbing, but not altogether unpleasant. Nonetheless, as the pressure increased, he felt his awareness telescoping down to only the knot of energy Jesse was now weaving with the plaited skein he had made.

He was aware of Jesse's focus now, centered on the square of bare earth bracketed by their four sets of splayed knees. Instinctively he braced himself for a final push as Jesse centered the knot of power, symbolically contained in the locked link of their four right hands.

The release, when it came, was accompanied by a flash of light that dazzled him even behind closed eyelids, the wash of power around him momentarily stunning all perception. He recovered to find himself slumped slightly sideways, collapsed over Jesse's right knee, still gripping his hand. Still a little dazed as Jesse disengaged himself and banished the Wards, directing Oriel to douse the candles, Javan quickly recovered enough presence of mind to get his feet under him and stagger over to where Father Faelan lay very still. Reducing the candles from nine to one seemed to plunge the room into darkness at first, but Javan found his eyes quickly adjusting as he bent over Faelan. Oriel and Etienne were likewise returning to their charges, and Jesse was lurching to his feet on the patch of earth.

"Did it work?" Javan whispered with an anxious glance at Jesse as soon as he had ascertained Faelan's well-being.

But Jesse vanished even as Javan spoke, to a sigh mixed of awe and relief from Oriel, as Etienne moved to the door to summon his son and Charlan.

CHAPTER TWENTY

For there are certain men crept in unawares . . .
—Jude 1:4

Within five minutes, Javan was aware of at least five different things happening simultaneously in the little chamber beside the library. Joram and Niallan had been brought back through the new Portal and were conducting comprehensive Readings on the two *Custodes* captives. Jesse had taken Oriel aside to tighten his defenses, should he come under the scrutiny of Paulin's Deryni—and also to set controls that would prevent him using the new Portal without authorization. Charlan and Guiscard were resetting the center flagstone and removing other physical evidence of the night's work. Etienne was guarding the door. Javan sat in the window embrasure with a groggy and largely oblivious Father Faelan, waiting to see what his allies had planned for *him*.

After about ten minutes, Joram went over to them, nodding amiably to the bewildered Faelan as he took control from Javan and sat down. He had not introduced himself, but he wore a plain black cassock such as any priest might wear. Let Faelan draw his own conclusions—though he hardly could have failed to surmise that most of those in the room must be Deryni.

"You're a very brave man, Father," Joram said quietly. "If it will ease your mind a little, your fellow *Custodes* over there have no idea you're involved in any intrigue. What was done to you, they would have done to anyone his Highness asked to have in his service. You weren't singled out, and I doubt you will be—though I'm afraid Paulin's pet Deryni will continue to be a threat."

"Did you find out who he is?" Javan asked as Faelan merely blinked.

Joram inclined his head slightly. "We now know a little about him," he conceded. "But there's no need to expose Father Faelan to information that could put him in further danger." His eyes caught and held Faelan's.

"Forgive me if this seems high-handed, Father, but I'm going to ask you to go over to Jesse and Oriel now. Someday I hope that we'll be able to explain to you what we're doing and why, but for now, I must ask you to trust that what we require is for the protection of the king and of Gwynedd. Go now."

Faelan obeyed without demur, submitting first to Jesse's quick assessment and then to Oriel's more detailed ministrations, under Jesse's supervision, since the Healer would continue to have contact with him in the future. Priest and prince observed in silence for several seconds before Joram shifted his gaze back to Javan.

"You needn't worry overly about Faelan," Joram murmured. "He *is* a brave man and he'll be fine."

"I know that," Javan said. "What did you find out about our *Custodes* collaborator?"

"Not as much as we hoped," Joram said frankly, "though Niallan is still digging. It seems Paulin doesn't confide much in his minions—which is hardly surprising, I suppose, in an autocratic command structure like that of the *Custodes*. Those two only know the man as Dimitri, or Master Dimitri—no last name—which may or may not be his true identity."

He sent a tight-focused image of the man—dark eyes above a neatly trimmed beard and moustache of a mousy brown flecked with grey, greyer hair cut just below his ears, one of which—the right—was pierced through the lobe by a slender golden hoop the diameter of a man's thumb. His high-collared tunic was black, buttoned at the shoulder like a soutane, but it was not a cleric's attire—not with all that heavy silk braid lavished across collar and cuffs and shoulders. The design was nothing Javan could precisely place, but it had a foreign feel to it—eastern, perhaps. Somehow, Javan found that disconcerting.

"He looks—self-confident," he said to Joram, filing the image away for future reference. "How skilled do you reckon he is?"

Joram shrugged. "That's difficult to say. It's a given that he can Truth-Read, and we know he did a reasonably thorough probe on Faelan. In addition, Lior has seen him do several forced Readings and possibly rip a mind. Not that Lior really knows what that means, but that's what Niallan and I surmise, from the condition of the subject afterward.

"The resourceful Dimitri also knows a fairly wide range of drugs to make his work easier, whether it's humans or Deryni he's dealing with. It was his idea to give Faelan *merasha*—as much for the terror factor as from any real need, though most sedatives will take the edge off resistance. Secondhand, just from what Lior and Serafin know, it's hard to be certain whether he's a high-level practitioner or just a trained inquisitor, but whatever his abilities, he's working for pay. There's no coercion involved."

"He's a hireling, then," Javan said, contempt in his voice. "He's selling out his own kind for *money!*"

"What worries me more," Joram replied, "is that maybe he *isn't* selling out his own kind."

"What do you mean?"

"Just this. You noted the vaguely foreign flavor to his attire. Suppose he has other paymasters besides Paulin? Eastern ones, perhaps even Torenthi ones. Paulin's only human. It wouldn't be difficult to hide that from him."

Javan fought down a sick, queasy churning in the pit of his stomach.

"Sweet *Jesu*," he murmured. "You mean, Torenth could have a Deryni spy within the *Custodes Fidei*?"

"It's a possibility. And Paulin's made it clear to Lior and Serafin that Dimitri's status is to be kept secret—which could be coming from Dimitri himself. Hubert may not even know about it. You might try to find out whether he does, if you can do it unobtrusively. If he doesn't know, that's an indication that someone is playing a double game—either Paulin, perhaps preparing to make some sort of power play, or Dimitri, as part of some larger scheme."

Feeling almost light-headed, Javan turned half away. Aside from any personal danger, which came with the crown he would shortly don, Torenthi interference in Gwynedd's affairs was the ultimate outside threat he could conceive. All his life, he had lived in the knowledge that a Festillic Pretender was sheltering at the Torenthi Court, almost exactly Javan's age, biding his time until he should attain sufficient maturity and support to make a bid for the throne his parents once had held.

"Do you think this Dimitri *has* been sent by Torenth?"

"I don't think we can exclude the possibility until we're sure," Joram replied. "Whatever his ultimate loyalty, he certainly isn't working in your behalf—not if he sets your confessor to spy on you. And even if he *is* simply Paulin's 'tame' Deryni, keeping the *Custodes* 'pure' and working to prevent *you* from bringing Deryni back into favor—he's still a problem that eventually will have to be dealt with.

"It's going to be tricky, though, because you can't let on how you've found out about him. Unless you mean to go after him directly, and simply have him taken out before he can give a warning, it almost has to be a setup involving Oriel—or possibly Sitric, but that's even more dangerous, because he doesn't know about any of this and might not want to take the risks associated with playing both—"

He broke off at a sudden stirring around the supine form of Serafin, as Niallan lurched abruptly to his feet and came quickly toward them, leaving Jesse and Oriel bent anxiously over the unconscious monk. Guiscard had joined them at some point and was kneeling near Serafin's feet, looking worried. Father Lior was still sitting nearby with his back against the wall, head bowed, deep asleep, as was Father Faelan on the other side of the room. Charlan had withdrawn to stand by the door.

"Joram, you'd better have another look at Brother Serafin," Niallan said. "Apparently Dimitri's far more clever than we thought. We just found a telltale that Guiscard must have triggered when he took him out—no fault of Guiscard's, but Dimitri will know there's been tampering, the first time he Reads Serafin again. It was deep. We all almost missed it."

Swearing softly under his breath, Joram came to his feet and pushed past Niallan to crouch by Serafin's head, Javan following anxiously, for it seemed some of their worst fears were already being realized. Guiscard would not look at either of them. Both Jesse and Oriel were engaged in deep Readings, and Joram waited until they had finished before laying hands on Serafin's forehead and conducting his own. If anything, he looked even more serious as he came out of trance and glanced around at all of them—though pointedly not at Javan.

"All right," Joram said quietly, "what are the options?"

Niallan gave a perplexed sigh and sat back on his heels. "Thanks to Dimitri, I very much fear that Brother Serafin has run out of options. It was a subtle piece of work—which does, indeed, tend to confirm that Dimitri is more than just a trained inquisitor. Guiscard's blaming himself, but he couldn't have known. Probably none of us could have caught it in time to pull out and avoid triggering it."

"What about Lior?" Javan asked, for he had been the one to put the priest out of commission.

"Fortunately, he appears to be clean," Niallan said. "Now that we know what to look for, we'll check again, just to make sure. Serafin, though—we were able to blur the trace enough that Dimitri wouldn't know *what* has been done, or by whom, but there's no way he can miss the signs of tampering.

"That means tampering by another Deryni—which puts Oriel at the top of the list of suspects, as soon as Dimitri finds out," Niallan went on. "And if he starts wondering whether other Deryni might be close to the king—"

"Say no more. It's clear what has to be done," Joram said, turning his gaze on Oriel, who had gone absolutely white. "Oriel, relax. We'll continue to protect you and your family, but you've got to help us. Give us a Healer's assessment of Serafin's general health. Does he have any problems we can amplify?"

Oriel looked like he was going to be physically ill. "You're going to have to kill him, aren't you?" he whispered. "Please don't ask me to be a part of it. They've made me do murder for *them*. Don't ask me to do the same for you!"

"It isn't murder; it's an execution," Joram said mildly. "And it mustn't look like either—which, unfortunately, precludes the quick dose of steel Guiscard would like to give him in a dark alley."

Guiscard grimaced and looked away, obviously still feeling responsible, though there was no cause.

"Oriel, no one's asking *you* to kill him," Joram went on. "If the specific offense may not seem to warrant a death sentence—falling victim to whatever scheme this Dimitri's set up—keep in mind that he has plenty else to answer for, besides what he had done to Faelan. Just answer me this one question: If his heart stopped in his sleep, would your suspicions as a Healer be aroused? More to the point, would a human physician be suspicious?"

As Oriel wrestled with the question, Javan forced himself to pull his own dismay up short, knowing Joram was right yet still feeling for Oriel—and even the luckless Serafin. The Healer was trembling as he laid hands on the unconscious man, swallowing hard before beginning his appraisal.

"S-sometimes, when he gets very angry, he has fainting spells," he said haltingly, after a moment. "His—blood is high, and he—has himself bled regularly, to keep it down. That's where he—got the idea to use blood-letting as a threat, a control within the Order, even a torture—the—the way he had done to Father Faelan."

Pulling away with a shudder, he glanced over at the sleeping priest—as did Javan, remembering his own ordeal. But this was not about vengeance or even retribution, but survival. And if Serafin survived to betray them to Dimitri, Javan knew that some of the men in this room were almost sure to die.

"Oriel, it doesn't really matter what he's done or why," he heard himself saying. "You don't kill a mad dog because it's bitten someone; you kill it to prevent it biting again. It's clear what has to happen. And if it has to be done, best make it as clean and quick as possible, and with minimal danger to any of us. I don't like it any more than any of the rest of you, but I accept its necessity— just as I accept ultimate responsibility for it, because that's a part of being king. So I'll repeat Joram's question. Would it be out of character for Serafin's heart to fail?"

He had taken them by surprise, he knew. Joram, at least, probably had expected him to be squeamish and had thought to spare him the necessity to take an active part in what was being decided. As he waited for Oriel's answer, he could feel their eyes upon him, weighing, calculating, but he knew in his heart that what he had said, he honestly believed; and for the first time since returning to Rhemuth, he found that he actually *felt* like a king, and that he had some control over what was unfolding.

The moment persisted for only a few heartbeats; then everything was racing along again as Oriel said, "No, no one would suspect."

"All right, then," Jesse said, picking up as if nothing unusual had just happened. "He's staying down at the archbishop's palace with the other *Custodes* dignitaries. I'm already dressed to go calling, so I'll follow him down and take him while he sleeps." He made a fist and shook it once. "Quick, clean, and untraceable. He simply doesn't wake up. And no one is going to notice another *Custodes* monk coming and going, two nights before the coronation."

"But if they do, and you're caught, you're dead," Joram pointed out. "We can't take that risk. No, the method's right, but I think it happens en route. I think you accompany our two *Custodes* brethren about as far as the gatehouse—where the unfortunate Brother Serafin collapses from the heat and overexertion and simply doesn't get up again."

"Except that *I'm* the one who does it," Guiscard said, finally speaking. "Jesse's already had a full night. He can't guarantee he's at peak efficiency. It's my call, Joram. I got us into this mess."

Niallan laid a hand on his and shook his head. "Guiscard, you're not to blame and you don't need to expiate any guilt by doing this— but I do agree that Jesse's done enough. Furthermore, Jesse would still have to make his escape from a largely unfamiliar area, whereas you're free to go where you wish in the castle precincts without arousing suspicion. Joram?"

Javan could almost hear Joram's thought process, looking for flaws in the scenario, but he knew, as did Guiscard and Niallan, that it was a good plan. He even knew the spell to which they'd been alluding, against which the human Serafin would have no defense. Almost, he felt sorry for the monk—until he made himself recall the deeds for which Serafin must answer, of which Father Faelan's torture was one of the less odious.

"Very well, I'll accept that reasoning," Joram said after a few seconds. "In this instance, I think Guiscard *is* better suited. Jesse, go ahead back to the sanctuary. You've done enough for one night. Niallan and I will follow when we've finished tidying up."

The order brooked no disagreement. Nodding, Jesse clapped a hand to Guiscard's shoulder and rose. As he moved off toward the Portal square, Joram murmured, "All right, let's get him up."

Without further ado, he and Niallan guided Brother Serafin to his feet, Javan and a benumbed Oriel looking on in sober silence. Then Lior, too, was roused, he and Serafin standing docilely to either side of Guiscard with eyes closed. As an afterthought, Joram brought Father Faelan around as well, summoning Etienne to take charge of him as they opened the door for Guiscard and his pair to pass.

"I suggest you restart the scenario with Serafin and Lior leaving Faelan's quarters, having concluded a short but satisfactory interview," Joram said to Guiscard, one hand on Etienne's wrist to send him the gist of what had happened and what was planned. "Be careful, both of you—and may God have mercy on *his* soul."

His hand sketched the Sign of the Cross over Serafin, just before Guiscard moved them out, final dismissal of the man being sent unwitting to his death. Etienne followed with Faelan, Charlan remaining outside to guard. Joram, when he had closed the door again, stood for a long moment with his hands resting on the latch, head bowed against the wood, before finally turning to glance wearily around the room.

Jesse was gone. Niallan had drawn Oriel into the window embrasure and was deep in conversation with him, both hands resting on the Healer's shoulders. Javan had been watching the departure from near the Portal square, and met his gaze fearlessly as Joram came over to him.

"Joram, I want Dimitri," the king said quietly. "At this point, I don't *care* whether he's a Torenthi agent or not. I want him gone, and in such a way that Paulin won't try the same thing again. In fact, if Paulin can also be taken out, so much the better. I want the *Custodes* gone, as well, but I'll settle for a new Vicar General, as an interim step. I can't imagine the Order could survive in its present form for very long, once Paulin's out of the picture."

Joram pursed his lips, considering. "You do realize that we're talking about more killing?"

"Vermin control," Javan murmured, himself surprised at his own cold-bloodedness. "Do *you* see any other way?"

"No," Joram said. "It's going to take some doing, though. We've already discussed the difficulties of going after Dimitri without your sources coming to light. It will require a *very* careful setup."

"Then we'd better start planning," Javan replied. "I don't expect overnight results and I certainly don't want to stir up further problems before I'm safely crowned. But we daren't let this drag on, either. Dimitri is dangerous, no matter who he's working for, and Paulin is warping religion for his own ends. They've got to be stopped."

"Let me see what else I can find out," Joram said. "We'll first want to see whether Serafin's death generates any suspicion. It shouldn't, but the timing could have been better, with Faelan less than a week arrived at Court. I hope, though, that any connection they might make will get lost amid all the normal upheavals of the next few days. It's vital that you get through your coronation without incident."

"I can't argue with that," Javan agreed. "Incidentally, did Jesse tell you why we were late—besides being delayed by our *Custodes* guests?"

"Yes, spontaneous shields in Rhys Michael and intimations of matrimony with Michaela," Joram replied. "Someone thought your job wasn't difficult enough already."

Javan did not even try to restrain his ironic chuckle. "I've always heard that God moves in mysterious ways. Frankly, I'd be happier with a bit less mystery. I don't suppose the shields are exactly a surprise, though. The timing is awkward, but he hasn't got a Tavis to help him figure out what's happening—and *I* don't intend to tell him. Marriage just now is out of the question, too—to *anybody*. I may have to send one of them away from Court, until his ardor cools."

"I'd also check to see whether someone else isn't actively encouraging this grand passion," Joram said, gesturing toward the Portal square. "It's possible he thought of it himself, but I wouldn't put it past any of the former regents. But we'd better have a look at your night's work now. I want to be certain you can use it. After that, Niallan and I must be off."

Nodding, Javan crouched down beside the square, trying to put his other concerns out of mind as he laid his hands flat on it, aware of Joram's scrutiny above him. Other than a moistness of new mortar sealing the square to the other flags surrounding it and a faint dampening where someone had wiped out the chalk lines with a wet cloth, no physical sign remained of their presence here tonight.

Not so the reason for their presence, though even that was subtle, confined to the area bounded by the single flagstone and undetectable until one actually touched it—and only a Deryni or one Deryni-gifted would detect it even then. Javan sensed its telltale tingle under his hands and closed his eyes to better savor it—though having helped create it, he could never have mistaken this spot on earth for any other. He gave himself a few seconds to let its knowledge settle into every fiber of his consciousness, then exhaled with a satisfied sigh and got slowly to his feet.

"I can make it work," he said to Joram.

"Good. Then suppose you demonstrate by taking me back to the sanctuary for a few minutes," Joram replied, stepping onto the Portal square. "Niallan will stay with Oriel while you're gone."

Javan restrained a start of surprise, for the Michaeline priest had never before invited such a contact as he was now suggesting. In all their previous interactions, as in the night's earlier decision, Joram had always taken charge—self-possessed, competent, faintly distant. Never had he offered to give up control to Javan. That he did so now bespoke a subtle change in their relationship, a powerful trust, not only in Javan's abilities but in his judgment and self-restraint; for even the most powerful Deryni was vulnerable when placing him- or herself in another's hands to make a Portal jump.

Hardly missing a beat, Javan stepped in boldly beside Joram and took his wrist. He dared not look at Joram for fear of losing his nerve, so he drew a breath and closed his eyes, centering and then reaching out tentatively for the consciousness beside him, wondering whether he needed to talk Joram down the way Joram usually did for him.

But Joram was already still and centered, and at Javan's touch rolled back his shields without hesitation. Even as Javan sought out the control points, Joram was offering them to him—passive receptivity, unequivocal and unreserved, awaiting Javan's bidding. With a fierce surge of gratitude and pride and perhaps even love, Javan took Joram's mind to his, poised on the brink, and reached out to warp the energies.

The jump was a good one, as smooth as Javan had ever made. His own and Joram's satisfaction flared around the pair of them like a mantle as he stabilized them both at the other end and released the priest. Joram wore a wry smile of approval as he opened his eyes, and he shifted his arm around Javan's shoulders in a gesture of almost paternal camaraderie as they moved off the Portal square in the Michaeline sanctuary. The shift of place had caused a shift of mood as well.

"Well done indeed, my prince," Joram murmured. "You've learned *all* your lessons well."

Javan managed a grim ghost of a smile and dared to look up at Joram, knowing he was not speaking of the Portal jump at all.

"I suppose I truly came of age tonight, didn't I?" he said. "I lost my innocence. I ordered a man's death and then I asked for more deaths. I never expected . . . It was—it was—"

"It was done exactly as it should have been, my prince—all of it," Joram said quietly. "You are my king, and you must be master in your house and master of those who serve you. You know the weight as well as the power of the crown you shall wear. When you are crowned on Monday, you will be king in a way that no man has been king for many generations. I pray God may grant you the wisdom to wisely wield the power you shall bring with you, as you approach His altar. Your challenge is great, but so are the rewards—for you and for all of Gwynedd, if you prosper."

Listening, Javan found he had tears in his eyes, but he would not take his gaze from Joram's.

"I wish you could be there to crown me, Joram," he said softly. "Your father crowned *my* father—not in the cathedral, but in a way that mattered far more, when he had defeated Imre and won his crown by his valor. I fear Hubert's hands will profane the rite."

Joram looked a little taken aback, but his answer was what Javan might have expected.

"You know that isn't true, my prince. For all his human failings, Hubert was duly consecrated for the holy office he will perform for you. His unworthiness cannot tarnish the crown you shall wear, or diminish the rite by which he places it upon your head."

Javan swallowed awkwardly, hanging his head a little. "I keep reminding myself of that," he whispered. "I suppose I'll endure it the same way I've endured receiving Communion from his hands and from *Custodes* priests, knowing that the Sacrament overshadows its instrument. I still wish you were doing it—or even that you could simply *be* there. I've sought this, because it's the duty I was born to, but it isn't a burden I take up lightly."

Joram had begun to watch him with a new intensity as he spoke, and now he slowly set his hands on Javan's shoulders, searching his eyes, a gravity come upon him of someone older, even more awesome than Joram at his most powerful, almost a physical presence that made Javan want to kneel before him.

"Javan, I was present when my father placed the crown on your father's head," Joram said quietly, his voice a little flattened as if in trance. "I sense his presence, and his willingness that you should receive a like crowning from my hands—and his. Is this your will as well?"

Javan had no idea how Joram proposed to accomplish this, but a new power was in the priest, coursing through him and tingling through his hands where they touched Javan's shoulders. Almost without his own volition, Javan felt himself sinking beneath those hands, to kneel at Joram's feet as he sensed his father had knelt before Camber, his own hands clasped wonderingly at his breast as he gazed upward.

Joram's face had changed. It both was and was not his own. Lifting his hands from Javan's shoulders, Joram joined them before him for just an instant, head bowed in prayer, then lifted them parted above Javan's head and fixed his gaze on the space between them. As both of them watched, neither daring to breathe, the air shimmered and then solidified in the likeness of Gwynedd's State Crown of leaves and crosses intertwined. A faint breath of awe escaped Javan's lips as Joram curved his hands around the ghostly image and seemed to raise it higher above both their heads. The voice that whispered from Joram's lips was not quite his own.

"Javan Jashan Urien Haldane, thine ancient line is continued, to the great joy of thy people," Joram said, though it was not only Joram who spoke as he lowered the crown to rest on Javan's head. "Be crowned with strength and wisdom for all thy days. And may the Almighty grant thee a long and prosperous reign, in justice and honor for all thy people of Gwynedd."

No crown but Joram's hands touched Javan's head in that instant, but the weight was as real as any diadem of metal and jewels and the moment as sacred as if Javan had knelt in the cathedral. As Joram's hands curved in gentle caress and he bowed to rest his forehead against Javan's for just an instant, Javan sensed another presence enfolding him in fierce protection and affirmation, so potent that he swayed under its power, faintly disoriented.

Then Joram was drawing a deep, shuddering breath, straightening, sliding his hands to Javan's shoulders to help him rise, and the moment was past. Javan pulled back a little as he staggered to his feet, almost afraid to look at Joram again, but the priest appeared almost as bewildered as Javan felt.

"Who—"

Joram gave an uneasy shake of his head. "It—felt like my father," he murmured. "He—made an appearance the night we stirred
up your powers, too."

"You didn't tell me," Javan whispered, accusation in his voice.

"It—didn't seem appropriate, at the time," Joram said. "And
later, the opportunity didn't arise. Does it bother you that a saint
takes a personal interest in your affairs? It does me, and he's my
father."

"I don't know," Javan said carefully. "I'll have to think about
it." He paused. "Joram, was it *really* Saint Camber?"

Joram flashed him a taut, uneasy grin. "Oh, yes. Of all the doubts
I have about a great many things, that is not one of them.

"But you'd better go back now. Try to avoid being seen going
back to your apartments. After the coronation, I'd install some
trustworthy person in the Portal room as soon as possible. Perhaps
one of your knights—one you'd have reason to visit reasonably often and who can be easily directed."

Javan nodded. "I already have someone in mind."

"God go with you, then, my prince."

Javan was not altogether satisfied with Joram's answer about
Saint Camber, but it would have to wait for another time. Squaring
his shoulders, he backed onto the Portal square again, never taking
his eyes from Joram's until he had seized the energies and was actually beginning the jump.

He opened his eyes to see Niallan waiting for him, just off the
Portal square. Charlan and a drowsy-looking Oriel were standing by
the door. He longed to tell Niallan what had just happened, for
Niallan had been there when Saint Camber made his other appearance, that night they had confirmed his Haldane powers, but there
was no time now. Niallan must be away, and Javan must see that
Oriel got back to his quarters safely and that everyone else had
ended up where and how he was supposed to be. He tried not to
think about the doomed Serafin, perhaps already lying dead in the
darkness.

"I've taken the necessary measures to safeguard them, my
prince," Niallan murmured, touching his shoulder in reassurance
as they changed places on the Portal square. "Unless you permit it,
they'll remember nothing of tonight's work. God keep your Highness."

"Thank you," Javan whispered.

With a nod and a smile, Niallan was gone, leaving Javan to
direct his charges back to their respective quarters. It was accomplished without incident. When he and Charlan had gained the

safety of the royal apartments, he checked on Rhys Michael—still dead asleep and snoring, reeking of wine—then sent Charlan to bed down on his accustomed pallet by the door. Once crowned, Javan intended to move his aides into quarters across the hall, near at hand yet retaining his privacy, but for now he was glad of their company—even if the oblivious Charlan retained no knowledge of Guiscard's dark mission, which weighed so heavily on Javan's mind.

He took his time preparing for bed, but Guiscard still had not returned by the time he was finished. Beginning to get a little anxious, he pulled on a cool night robe and went into the outer chamber to wait. He had extinguished all the lights but one candle on the trestle table and was sitting in the darkened window of the outer room when Guiscard finally came in, after another quarter hour.

"Guiscard, I'm over here," he whispered as the Deryni knight closed and bolted the door.

Guiscard stiffened for just an instant, then came reluctantly across the room to set one foot on the step up into the window embrasure where Javan sat.

"I was hoping you hadn't waited up," he said quietly.

"I had to know," Javan replied. "It's finished?"

Guiscard nodded and turned to sit wearily on the step, clasping his arms around his knees.

"It shouldn't be that easy to kill a man," he murmured after a long moment.

Javan closed his eyes briefly, then drew his night robe more closely around him and stood, going down to sit beside Guiscard.

"I don't like this part of being king," he said.

"It isn't my favorite part of serving a king, either," Guiscard replied, "but sometimes it has to be done. If it's any comfort, he never felt a thing, beyond the first twinge."

"I suppose that's something," Javan said. He heaved a great sigh and put it out of his mind. "No point dwelling on it, though. It's done now. I suppose I ought to try to get some sleep. I suggest you do the same. We're likely to need all our wits about us tomorrow."

"Aye. God keep your Grace," Guiscard murmured.

As Javan crawled into bed, careful not to disturb the sleeping Rhys Michael, he feared he might not sleep at all, but fatigue washed over him like a wave before his head could even hit the pillow. In those few seconds before sleep claimed him, he made himself put aside speculation about a party of *Custodes* monks

probably even now bearing the body of their stricken brother to
Saint Hilary's or the archbishop's palace.

Instead, he turned his last conscious thought to what had happened between him and Joram, and was not surprised that he
dreamed of Saint Camber that night—and of hallowed hands lifting
up a shining crown above his head.

CHAPTER TWENTY-ONE

He that delicately bringeth up his servant from a child shall have him become his son at the length.

—Proverbs 29:21

Javan had hoped to sleep late the next morning, the last before his coronation, but he found himself drifting into consciousness shortly after dawn. He kept his eyes closed against the glare coming from the balcony doors—open to admit of a faint breeze—and tried to recapture some of the blissful escape he had attained in sleep, resolutely putting aside both his satisfaction at the setting of the new Portal and his remorse at having been obliged to order another man's death. Both had been necessary for survival. He must not dwell on what he could not change.

Having acknowledged the darkest aspect of this day he must face, he directed his further attention to the more positive aspects of his situation. Today, for example, because of Sunday morning obligations and the special Cassani Court at midday, he was excused from the rigorous schedule of physical training he had ordered Jason and Robear to set for him—and which certainly was accomplishing its purpose.

In fact, he had never been so fit and strong. A month of very determined work had added breadth to his shoulders and chest, trimmed an already slender waist, and even put muscle onto his legs such that his limp was less pronounced. The process had been gruelling in the heat, and in so short a time, but as he stretched lazily in bed, he could take satisfaction in the knowledge that he even stood a few fingers taller now—though perhaps that was as much from increased self-confidence as from any real increase in height.

Stretching brought one foot into contact with a warm body—Rhys Michael's—and Javan cracked an eye open to gaze across thoughtfully at his sleeping brother. Hardly unexpectedly, Gwynedd's heir presumptive was looking decidedly fragile this morning, even asleep. Javan's cautious probe confirmed what promised to be a rather spectacular hangover, as soon as Rhys Michael woke—and also the hitherto unsuspected shields.

Feeling only slight remorse over his part in his brother's incipient misery, Javan turned his gaze vexedly to the underside of the canopy above him and considered what to do about him—besides let him sleep as long as possible this morning. The previous night had produced several unwelcome revelations about Rhys Michael Alister Haldane.

Shields aside—and Javan supposed they were really an inevitability of being a Haldane heir—he had not intended to have to deal with Rhys Michael at all last night, and certainly not concerning the very delicate subject of marriage. Nor had he expected the insinuations by both Charlan and Guiscard concerning Rhys Michael's drinking habits. The prospect of his heir becoming a drunkard was not at all appealing.

Even less appealing was the prospect of his heir wanting to marry, at least in the very near future. The alcohol question was sufficiently serious to bear closer observation, though it probably could not be assessed reliably in the context of festivities accompanying a coronation; but Rhys Michael's apparent intentions regarding the fair Michaela could well become a prelude to disaster. Javan wondered if his brother really did not understand how the premature provision of additional heirs could put the present heirs' lives in danger.

Or perhaps the younger prince, the darling of the regents during his formative years, simply did not want to believe that, to regain the influence they had lost when the regency ended, such men might well resort to murder. Once the coronation was out of the way, Javan knew he was going to have to set his younger brother straight on more than one fact of life.

Feeling vaguely like a spoilsport—for that was probably how Rhys Michael would view the interference with his romance—Javan got up and padded over to use the garderobe, then set about his morning ablutions. On impulse, while he washed, he decided to see about sneaking in a quick gallop before he had to deal with the noon Court. Charlan stirred while he was dressing, sitting up blearily on his pallet.

"You were going to sleep in," he said. "What are you doing up so early?"

"I thought I'd roust Father Faelan for an early Mass and then have a quick ride before it gets too hot," Javan replied, tightening a spur strap. "One last burst of freedom before I have to settle down to 'king things,' as Rhysem so aptly put it last night. If you want to come, you'd better get dressed."

He left Guiscard to see that Rhys Michael made it out of bed in time for Court. He and Charlan heard Mass privately in Faelan's little oratory, then betook themselves down to the stables like a pair of errant schoolboys to saddle two of the faster horses of the royal menage.

Charlan wore a sword at his side and was turned out in riding leathers that would see him through the Court scheduled for later in the day, but Javan rode in shirt sleeves that morning, perhaps the last time he would be allowed to venture forth so informally, and unarmed as well. This early, and with Charlan at his side, he was safe enough; the troop of Haldane lancers who trailed them at a discreet distance were armed to the teeth. Pounding along the north road that paralleled the river, the wind on his face and the feel of good horseflesh beneath him, Javan was almost able to put out of mind the concerns he must face when he returned to the castle.

But as he and Charlan walked their horses back up the cobbled approach to the gatehouse again, into a castle yard far more congested than when they had ridden out, it was clear he must be a king once more. His principal courtiers were waiting for him on the great hall steps, taking advantage of the slight breeze. Most of them swept before him into the hall as he and Charlan dismounted and came up the steps, heading in the direction of the withdrawing room behind the great hall dais. For smaller Courts like the one scheduled for today, Javan far preferred its intimacy to the vastness of the great hall, which was in the process of being set up for the morrow's coronation banquet.

Jason and Robear and a few more of his intimates fell in beside him as he and Charlan strode through the great hall. Guiscard and a squire were waiting for him just outside the withdrawing room, armed with the royal accoutrements that would make of a wind-burned royal escapee some semblance of a king: a fresh tunic, simply cut from white linen but embroidered around neck and hem and cuffs with little crimson lions; the Haldane sword, though Javan must carry it rather than wear it until he was crowned; and hooked over one of Guiscard's wrists, the hammered coronet of golden lions intertwined, set with rubies.

He stripped off his horsey-smelling shirt and towelled down, then pulled on the long Haldane tunic, holding the coronet while Guiscard fastened a belt of silver plaques around his waist and the squire haltingly applied a comb to his sweat-plastered hair. Jason thrust a goblet into his hand, and he gulped it down gratefully. The wine was well watered but very refreshing, chilled in snow brought down from the mountains by Cashien.

The combination of fresh clothing and cool drink made him feel cooler, even though he knew it would not last for long. Squaring his shoulders, he cradled the sheathed sword in the crook of his left arm, the hilt extending like a cross above his left shoulder. Just as Guiscard was setting the coronet on his head, Rhys Michael and Tomais joined them, the prince decently garbed in a royal-blue tunic and silver circlet but looking as if he wished he were anywhere else, particularly in bed again.

"Rhysem, are you going to be able to get through this?" Javan asked, genuinely concerned for his brother's condition.

Though paler by far than was his usual wont, Rhys Michael nodded. "It'll be all right. Just don't let anyone make any loud noises."

"I'll do my best." Turning to Tammaron, who had just emerged from the withdrawing chamber, Javan asked, "Are they ready inside?"

"They are, Sire," Tammaron said. He was wearing the Chancellor's gilt collar of linked Haldane H's over a long robe of forest green. "This way, if you please."

The outward informality of those assembled in the withdrawing room belied the importance of what was about to take place. Public affirmation of today's actions would be made tomorrow, during the coronation, but the kernel of the matter was this: that the Princess Anne Quinnell, sole heiress of the ancient principality of Cassan, should present unto Javan the decrees of her late father's will, formally setting in motion the procedures that ceded Cassan to Gwynedd and made of her son Cassan's first duke.

Conversation ceased as Javan entered the room. Moving casually toward the chair of state prepared for him, pleased that his limp was hardly noticeable, he could see the ducal party gathered in one of the back corners. He recognized Tammaron's son Fane, husband of the Cassani princess. To either side of Fane were a veiled, richly coronetted lady in murrey and gold, who must be the princess herself, and an older woman in black, also wearing a coronet—perhaps the dead prince's widow?—holding the hand of a bright-eyed, blue-clad boy of three or four.

Also assembled, in addition to Javan's personal household and the expected lords of state—Manfred, Udaut, Rhun, Murdoch, and Hubert, who would witness on behalf of the Church—were various other members of Tammaron's family: his other two sons, Fulk and Quiric; their mother, Nieve; and her sons by her first marriage, Albertus and Paulin. The latter looked preoccupied, and even more grim than usual—as well he might, Javan thought, having just lost his Inquisitor General.

"My lords and ladies, the King's Grace," Tammaron said as Javan reached the state chair.

They had hung a great tapestry of the Haldane arms behind the chair since he last had been in the room, with a rich canopy of state above it. In that instant, as he turned to face the men and women assembled, Javan was aware of the connection with all his Haldane ancestors. His subjects bowed as he made to sit. Settling, he laid the sword across his knees and waited for his aides to take their places behind and to either side of him, Rhys Michael to sit at his left, before turning expectantly to Tammaron.

"My Lord Tammaron, I believe you have business to bring before our Court?" he said.

"I do, Sire," Tammaron said, bowing. "It is my very great honor to present my daughter-in-law: her Royal Highness the Princess Anne Quinnell of Cassan, daughter and sole heir of the late his Royal Highness the Prince Ambert Quinnell, Sovereign Prince of Cassan. My son Fane I believe you know."

Tammaron's eldest son brought his wife forward—the slender figure gowned and veiled in murrey silk. As both of them knelt before the king, the princess folded back her veil over coils of jet-black hair, then handed forward the scroll her husband had carried.

"May it please the King's Grace, I bring greetings from far Cassan and this testimony of my father's last will concerning the disposition of his lands," she said. Her voice was low and melodious, her dark-lashed eyes a clear blue-grey in the pale perfection of her face, and Javan found himself thinking what a lucky man was Fane Fitz-Arthur.

"As your Grace will have been informed," she went on, "it was my father's wish that, having no sons, Cassan should pass through me to my eldest son, who comes now before you to acknowledge you his sovereign overlord and asks to be granted tenure of Cassan as a Duke of Gwynedd in perpetuity for himself and his male issue. May I present him to your Highness?"

"Please do," Javan said, handing off the scroll to Charlan and beckoning the two to rise. Only reluctantly did he turn his gaze toward the boy and the black-clad woman who brought him forward—for Anne of Cassan was breathtaking.

At the prompting of the black-clad woman, the little boy knelt at Javan's feet, head ducked shyly over hands folded as if in prayer but peeking out from under a shock of dark hair with wide eyes that missed little, eliciting a faint smile from Javan. The woman in black remained standing.

"Sire," Anne said, "my mother, the Lady Duvessa Sinclair, Dowager Princess of Cassan."

The Lady Duvessa inclined her head at the introduction, and Javan returned the salute, wondering whether she was related to Paulin and Albertus, whose family name also was Sinclair.

"My lady, you are most welcome," he said. "May I offer my condolences on your loss and my wish that this merging of our lands may prove as prosperous for all our peoples as your late husband dreamed. I shall cherish your grandson as if he were my own son."

A faint smile curved Duvessa's lips. "You are most gracious, Sire," she murmured. "The boy is bright. He is all one might have wished in a grandson. Would that his grandfather could have lived to see him grow to manhood."

"I share your sorrow, madame, having lost the opportunity for my own father to see *me* grow to manhood," Javan replied. "When the time comes, and if it pleases you and his parents, it would be my pleasure to have him fostered here at Court, to learn the ways of rule. Cassan is far away, and I shall need to rely on my loyal Duke of Cassan to uphold my law—as I know his regents shall do, during his minority. I believe that the three of you are to be constituted his governors?" he said, gesturing toward Anne and Fane as well.

"That was my father's wish, Sire," Anne said, moving closer to set her hand on her son's shoulder. "It is ours as well, if it please your Grace."

"It pleases us very well, indeed," Javan replied, glancing aside at his waiting clergy, and at Hubert in particular. "My Lord Archbishop, are you prepared to witness an exchange of oaths?"

"I am, Sire," Hubert said, moving forward in cope and mitre, a deacon following him with a richly bound Gospel book.

"Very well," Javan said. "Which of you shall speak for—Tambert, is it?"

"It is, my lord, and I shall speak for him," Duvessa said, coming to stand behind her grandson, as his parents knelt to either side and each placed a hand on his shoulders.

Young Tambert, who had been watching all these proceedings wide-eyed from around his folded hands, essayed a bright smile as Javan leaned forward, over the Haldane sword, to clasp the joined little hands between his two.

"Hello, Tambert," he said softly, engaging the boy's eyes and smiling. "My name is Javan. Shall we be friends?"

At Tambert's earnest nod, Javan flicked a glance up at the boy's grandmother to proceed.

"We, the regents for Duke Tambert Fitz-Arthur Quinnell, heir to all of Cassan, do pledge the following on his behalf," she said. "That the said Tambert of Cassan does become your liege man of life and limb and enters your fealty, doing homage for all the lands of Cassan formerly held of the last sovereign Prince of Cassan, his grandfather. Faith and truth will he bear unto you, to live and to die, against all manner of folk. This is our pledge as well, so help me God."

Javan had been Truth-Reading as she spoke—she meant what she had said—and he briefly turned his talent on Anne and then on Fane, whose murmured repeats of "So help me God" bore no hint of deception. Drawing breath, Javan returned his gaze to young Tambert, who was gazing up at him with rapt fascination.

"This do I hear, Tambert of Cassan and the regents for his Grace," he said. "And I, for my part, pledge the protection of Gwynedd to you and all your people, to defend you from every creature with all my power, giving loyalty for loyalty and justice for honor. This is the word of Javan Jashan Urien Haldane, King of Gwynedd, Lord of Meara and Mooryn and the Purple March, and Overlord of Cassan. So help me God."

So saying, Javan released Tambert's hands and turned toward Hubert to lay his hand on the Gospel and kiss its jewelled cover, after which Hubert offered it to Duvessa, Anne, and Fane to do the same. The archbishop was turning to give it back into the hands of the deacon who had brought it when Tambert tugged urgently at the edge of Javan's tunic, which was all he could reach.

"Me, too!" he whispered, in a *sotto voce* that reached every corner of the room, producing an amused chuckle from several present.

"You, too?" Javan said, leaning down gravely to Tambert's eye level. "What do you want to do? Kiss the book?"

Tambert nodded sagely.

"Ah, I see," Javan said, staying Hubert with an upraised hand when he would have continued to hand the book away.

"But, Sire—"

"No, stay. Let's see how much he understands," Javan murmured, leaning back toward the boy. "Tambert, do you know what that is?"

"God's word," Tambert said, quite emphatically.

"That's right, it is," Javan said approvingly. "Do you know what it means, when you kiss the Book of God's word?" he asked.

Tambert looked uncertain.

"It means," Javan said, "that a promise has been made in front of God. Did you make a promise today, Tambert? I did. I promised to be your friend and to take care of you and all the other people who live back at home in Cassan. Will you promise to be *my* friend, in front of God?"

Tambert's face had lit up as Javan explained, and he clapped his hands enthusiastically and nodded.

"Friends!" he crowed.

Only partially restraining a droll grin, as others around him tried less successfully to keep their chuckles smothered, Javan held out his hand for the Gospel Hubert was still holding. Hubert relinquished it without a word, watching in amazement and grudging respect as Javan took it between his hands, one at each end, and brought it down to where Tambert could see it.

"Here is God's word, Tambert," he said, hefting the book. "You know and I know that God hears everything we say. When I kiss the Book that has God's word in it, that means that I know He has heard what I promised. I promise, before God, to be your friend, Tambert."

He could feel Tambert's eyes on him as he bent solemnly to kiss the Book again. Being friends was a gross simplification of the oaths he had exchanged with Tambert's guardians, but it was the crux of what Tambert might be able to understand. Apparently he did, for as Javan straightened, Tambert's little hands were creeping up to touch the jewelled cover, the eyes of sunlit blue turning to his in a child's pure trust.

"Friends," he said simply. And as he leaned forward to plant a loud kiss on the Book, a murmur of amused approval rippled through the room.

Laughter was in Javan's eyes as well, but he kept his face solemn as he whispered, "Thank you, Tambert," and handed the Book back to Hubert. He had not planned any further ceremony, with Tambert being so young, but now he beckoned the boy's mother nearer.

"My lady, your son has demonstrated amply that he understands what this is all about," he said in a low voice, the sword resting on his knees between them. "Under the circumstances, I think it would be slighting him to withhold the rest of the formality that confirms him in his title—unless you think he might be frightened by a drawn sword."

She looked surprised as he lifted the sheathed sword slightly between them, but then she smiled tentatively.

"Do you mean to dub him, Sire?" she asked.

"Unless you would prefer it otherwise."

Clearly pleased, she bent to whisper to her son, who listened avidly and then nodded. As she settled back to her knees beside him, shifting a glance to husband and mother likewise to kneel, Javan slowly rose, carefully unsheathing the sword as he did so and handing off the scabbard to Guiscard. He brought the blade to his lips in salute, both hands on the hilt, then looked down at Tambert, smiling reassurance.

"Tambert of Cassan, I confirm you in your rank and title as Duke of Cassan," he said, bringing the flat of the blade down lightly on the boy's right shoulder and then the left. "We'll do this again when you've come of age and can claim your title in your own right," he went on, touching the blade lightly to the top of the boy's head. "And then, in about fifteen years, I hope to do this once more, when it's time for you to receive the accolade of knighthood."

The boy's gaze was one of awe and pure hero worship as Javan passed the sword to Guiscard to sheathe, and he broke into a sunny smile as Javan then bent to take Tambert's two hands in his.

"Rise, most excellent Duke of Cassan."

Tambert scrambled to his feet and, to Javan's surprise, threw his little arms exuberantly around the royal knees, laughing delightedly. His parents looked mortified, though the grandmother was barely containing her smile, and Tambert's mother came forward immediately to rescue Javan.

"I do beg your pardon, Sire," she murmured. "He isn't usually this demonstrative."

"No, it's all right," Javan replied, himself now chuckling as he bent to lift Tambert onto his hip. "It isn't often that a king gets such an enthusiastic show of affection from one of his dukes. Why, thank you, Tambert," he said as the boy threw his little arms around Javan's neck and planted a wet kiss on the royal cheek. "Tambert and I are going to be great friends, aren't we, Tambert? And he's going to grow up to be a very fine duke."

Softening a little, the boy's mother smiled. "Methinks he shall serve a very fine king as well, Sire," she murmured. "I thank you for your kindness. You are—not what I expected."

"Oh, and what did you expect?" Javan said easily, looking into the blue-grey eyes.

"An awkward boy, unskilled in the ways of statecraft," she said bluntly. "I see that I was mistaken."

To Javan's surprise, she then sank in a deep, formal curtsey, far more profound than duty required. Struck again by her beauty, Javan let the boy back down to the floor and took the mother's hand to raise her up, keeping it in his for just a trifle longer than protocol demanded.

"I thank you, my lady," he murmured, bringing it to his lips in salute. "I look forward to watching young Tambert grow into gentle manhood, as must surely happen, with so gracious a lady for a mother."

The whole exchange could not have taken above a few seconds. As he released her hand, things began moving again, Fane coming forward to retrieve his son, daughter and mother making their bows as they prepared to return to their places. A proud and beaming Earl Tammaron came forward to usher them out, turning back to Javan as the immediate area before the throne cleared.

"I thank you for your kindness to my grandson, Sire," he said. "This being the only business to come before you this morning, may I dismiss the Court?"

"Certainly," Javan said, taking back his sword from Guiscard.

"My lords and ladies," Tammaron said, moving slightly to the side and turning to face the room, "his Highness gives you his leave."

As the Court made their ragged obeisances and slowly began escaping to the larger and cooler confines of the great hall, Hubert came closer to delay Javan's departure. Guiscard and Charlan drew back slightly, ready to rescue their royal master, if need be. Paulin and Albertus had paused just outside the door but still in sight of Hubert, obviously waiting for him to come out as they conversed quietly together.

"It was well done, what you did for the boy, Sire," the archbishop said grudgingly as the room slowly emptied. "God grant that he remembers this day when he comes to manhood."

Javan favored Hubert with a nod. "I intend that he shall, Archbishop," he said. "Would that my other duke loved me half so well. I take it there's been no word, as yet, whether Graham and the other Kheldour lords intend to attend the coronation?"

Hubert looked distinctly uncomfortable. "Alas, Sire, there has not. But most of the rest of the expected baronage have arrived. Also, a fair number of representatives from our neighboring kingdoms, who will present their credentials and felicitations tomorrow, after the coronation. Which reminds me—Lord Udaut bade me inform you that a Torenthi delegation is expected to arrive sometime later today. Rumor has it that the Torenthi king is sending one of his brothers as his personal envoy."

Javan pursed his lips. "A Torenthi prince in Rhemuth. Who authorized *that*?"

Hubert made a grimace of distaste. "The practice is not of *my* making, Sire. It is ancient custom that a new king's coronation be witnessed by representatives of neighboring kingdoms, so that they can testify as to the legitimacy of the reign. We are not at war with Torenth, after all."

"No, they're only harboring the pretender to my throne," Javan said.

"Well, no one expected that King Arion would be so bold as to send one of his own brothers as witness."

"Foreign Deryni at Court, then," Javan said neutrally, watching Hubert's expression and thinking about the mysterious "foreign" Deryni currently in Paulin's employ. "I don't like that. What precautions are being taken to ensure that our Torenthi visitors remain within the bounds of good guestship?"

Hubert pursed his rosebud lips in annoyance. " 'Within the bounds of good guestship,' all is being done that *can* be done, Sire. The Lord Constable will provide an appropriate guard of honor." He smiled primly. "And I believe that Lord Rhun has arranged for Master Sitric to be among them. I've also ordered that archers be strategically deployed, with orders to watch for any sign of treachery. If you wish, I can have them dress their arrowheads with *merasha*."

Javan gave the archbishop a sour look. "I hardly think we need go that far." He sighed. "Very well. Is there anything else I should know about?"

A shadow flitted across Hubert's usually open expression. "Nothing else affecting tomorrow, Sire," he murmured. "Ah, there *is* one other bit of news you may not have heard yet, since you rode early this morning. Brother Serafin collapsed and died last night— his heart, they think. Father Lior was with him and was able to give him the Last Rites. Needless to say, Father Paulin is greatly shocked. This will be a great loss to the Order."

"Indeed," Javan murmured, feigning appropriate surprise—and somewhat relieved to learn that Serafin had not gone unshriven into death. "Why, he wasn't that old a man. Still, the heat and all . . ."

Hubert nodded. "He was not yet fifty, I believe. His blood was high, though. I am told he availed himself of minution on a regular basis—which seemed to help, but—" He shook his head. "It gives one pause. We were nearly of an age, he and I. May God have mercy on his soul."

"Amen to that," Javan murmured, crossing himself as Hubert did the same. "It is a sobering event with which to enter my coronation festivities. I confess, I had no personal fondness for the man, but I shall ask Father Faelan to include him in the prayers at my private Masses for the next month."

All of which was true. He could not honestly mourn Serafin, but praying for him was the least he could do, having been responsible for his death. And most fortunately, the death did not seem to have generated unwelcome suspicion, at least on Hubert's part.

He saw Guiscard trying to catch his eye and gave Hubert a slight bow. "I beg you to excuse me, Archbishop. Additional matters apparently require my attention, and I also feel the need of nourishment before heading down for the final rehearsal. Tomorrow will be upon us all too quickly."

When the king had gone out with his two aides, nodding silent acknowledgment to the waiting Paulin and Albertus, Hubert followed more casually. Most everyone else from the Court just concluded had filtered out into the great hall, where the open windows admitted a breath of faintly moving air, but Paulin drew Hubert into the relative seclusion of a stairwell entrance.

"What was the anger about?" Paulin demanded.

"The Torenthi delegation," Hubert answered mildly. "You'd hardly expect him to be happy about it, would you?"

Snorting, Paulin shook his head. "No one is. How about the news of Serafin's death? How did he react?"

Hubert gave a noncommittal shrug, though his expression perhaps reflected a faint dissatisfaction.

"How did you *think* he would react? He offered no false regret over the news, but that's hardly surprising, given his antipathy toward the *Custodes*. Nonetheless, he said he would instruct Father Faelan to include Serafin in his prayers for the next month and affirmed my prayer that God might have mercy on Serafin's soul. It was all entirely proper."

"Then why do you look like the exchange left a sour taste in your mouth?" Albertus demanded.

Hubert looked sharply at the *Custodes* Grand Master. "What is that supposed to mean?"

"Simply that we have an interesting coincidence here—if coincidence it is. At the express request of the king, a particular priest is brought to Court to be his personal chaplain. He has been thoroughly vetted by his superiors and instructed to observe and report on what occurs in the king's household. But only a few days after his arrival, one of the men who vetted that priest is dead."

Hubert rolled his eyes heavenward and folded pudgy hands over his ample waist. "Next you'll be suggesting that Faelan somehow had a hand in it, or the king. Serafin's heart simply failed."

"I'm not disputing that," Paulin muttered. "But what if it were *helped* to fail?"

"Ah, then you're insinuating that Oriel had a hand in it—or maybe Sitric. They're the only Deryni left at Court, and it would take a Deryni to do what you're suggesting."

"Or maybe a Haldane," Albertus said quietly. " 'Tis said that the king's father once slew a would-be assassin without touching him."

"I never heard that," Hubert said.

"I have," Paulin replied distractedly. "It was early in his reign. A number of Deryni are said also to have been present, chiefly of the redoubtable MacRorie clan. Camber himself was among them, I believe."

"Then Deryni obviously were responsible, if in fact the incident occurred," Hubert stated flatly. "I don't believe it, though. And I don't believe that Javan *or* secret Deryni infiltrators of the Court somehow murdered Serafin by magic. It's absurd!"

"You're probably right," Paulin said, reluctantly backing down. "Still, I'm going to question Father Lior again, since he was there when Serafin died. And in a few weeks, when Father Faelan comes for his monthly debriefing, we'll inquire of him as well. I'm still uneasy as to why Javan should have requested him, in particular."

"To throw us off the scent," Hubert said sourly. "To lull us into a false sense of security because we have one of *our* confessors in the royal household. That's all it is. That's all it *can* be."

"I hope you're right," Paulin said after a taut pause. "I do hope you're right."

Chapter Twenty-two

*For thou, O God, hast heard my vows; thou
hast given me the heritage of those that fear
thy name.*

—Psalms 61:5

No incidents or accusations marred the final rehearsal for the coronation. After Javan's inspired handling of young Duke Tambert, a significant proportion of those who had been present seemed inclined to grant him more respect than might have been forthcoming before. When king and courtiers finally declared themselves mutually satisfied with preparations for the upcoming ceremony, Javan dismissed all with his thanks and retired back to the castle, there to take a quiet supper in his quarters with his intimates and make an early night of it. He slept soundly and could not remember whatever dreams he had.

Coronation day dawned bright and clear, a little cooler than previous days, but promising sultry heat before noon. Javan rose with the sun again and spent nearly an hour on his knees before the little shrine he had asked to be set up in one corner of his sleeping chamber. Earlier in the week, from a box of boyhood treasures he had left in Rhys Michael's keeping before going off to seminary, he had retrieved a little Saint Michael medal given him by Evaine. He dared not wear it for his coronation, where hostile eyes might see the badge of the outlawed Michaeline Order, but he clasped it close in his hand as he prayed for the strength and wisdom to take up his crown worthily and asked God's forgiveness for condoning the killing of Brother Serafin. Just after he heard Saint Hilary's bell ring Prime, Charlan came in to inform him that his bath was ready in the outer room.

Those closest to him were waiting to assist him—Guiscard and his father, Robear and Jason, Bertrand, Gavin, and Sorle. Father Faelan was there as well, to read him the day's Psalms while he soaked in his tub and a barber trimmed his hair and the senior knights laid out the robes he would wear for his sacring. Just before he got out of the bath, Oriel turned up briefly to examine his bad foot and put what he could of strength upon it for the day's demands. Javan would ride to and from his coronation, but the rest of the day would be spent mostly on his feet.

They dressed him in silence when he had finished towelling off—reverent service that underlined the solemnity of the day's undertaking, each garment placed upon him with care, every lace and button done up with fastidious attention. Over the traditional alblike garment of fine linen next to his skin they placed an outer robe of white slubbed silk, embellished at the collar and cuffs and down the front with bold embroidery of gold bullion. White breeches encased his legs, since he must ride, and supple new boots of white leather had been made as well, under Sir Jason's direction—too light for any hard use, but more than adequate for the sedate procession to and from the cathedral, with the right one artfully designed to disguise his thickened ankle and give him the extra support that foot required. He grinned as he tried the boots' fit, striding back and forth several times under the eyes of his knights and hardly limping at all.

"They wouldn't do for everyday wear," Jason allowed, "but your faithful black workaday ones would have glared against all this white. Besides that, these will be cooler. You're going to be warm enough, under all these layers, without having your feet die as well."

Javan chuckled delightedly and pivoted again, then went to let them lay the mantle around his shoulders. "You'd best have a care, or I'll be appointing you royal bootmaker, Jason. Thank you."

"You're very welcome, Sire."

The mantle itself was a vast, featherweight wonder of white silk damask woven with a self-pattern of crowns and lion faces, heavily embroidered down the fronts and around the border but lined with supple white samite rather than the heavy fur that had adorned Alroy's mantle five years before at a May coronation. As Charlan fastened its jewelled clasp over the stiff standing collar of the overtunic and Guiscard shook out its folds and spread its length behind him for the others to admire, Javan could hardly feel its weight.

"Magnificent!" someone murmured.

"Fit for a king, Sire!" another one quipped.

He hefted it on his shoulders as Guiscard and his father gathered up masses of it in their arms to keep it from getting soiled when they made their way downstairs to join the procession forming up, suffering Charlan to give his hair a final combing. The barber's ministrations had left it rather shorter than the fashion, but his grown-out tonsure now was all but disappeared unless one looked very closely. As Javan glanced into the polished metal mirror that Robear held up for him, he could see a lean, solemn face that put him in mind of a Roman statue. With the Eye of Rom winking in his ear above the stiff tunic collar and the mantle's clasp, it was a king who looked back at him. He straightened on an intake of breath, squaring his shoulders, and all of them sank to one knee around him.

"God save the king!" Robear said boldly, right fist going to his chest in a salute that was echoed by the others.

Tears were prickling at Javan's eyelids as he motioned them to rise, and he did not dare to speak for the lump in his throat as they formed up around him to escort him down to the castle yard. Rhys Michael and Tomais joined them en route, the prince clad head to toe in crimson, with the Haldane lion emblazoned on chest and back in appliqué and embroidery, differenced with the label of a third son. A silver circlet confined his sable hair, and he flashed Javan a grin as they embraced briefly and continued together out to the yard.

Those who would attend the king were waiting for him, friend and foe alike, most bedecked in the richest raiment that finance and the heat allowed. The composition of the coronation party was not exactly as Javan would have liked, but he had managed to intersperse most of his intimates among those jealously clinging to offices exercised in the past.

First in the procession, and only awaiting the order to move out, came a full score of black-clad *Custodes* knights—hard-eyed men capped with steel and mounted on jet-black steeds, apparently oblivious to the heat in their full black mantles faced with scarlet. Twenty black surcoats bore the Order's red moline cross charged with a haloed lion's head, and swallow-tailed pennons fluttered from steel-tipped lances in twenty mailed fists—black, charged with a red moline cross. They made a proud display, but Javan hardly spared them a second glance, for the scarlet fringes on the white sashes of their knighthood seemed to him to profane the very concept of chivalry, just as the braided cincture of Haldane crimson and gold encircling each left shoulder profaned the colors of Javan's House.

Far more pleasing in his sight was the elite guard of ten Haldane lancers in the crimson livery of Gwynedd, drawn up behind the *Custodes* knights and waiting for Jason and Robear to join them. They dipped their lances in brisk precision as Javan appeared on the great hall steps, fully as smart in appearance for being half the *Custodes'* strength. And just behind them, holding the horses Rhys Michael and Tomais would ride—

"Well, will you look at that, Sire?" Charlan murmured, touching Javan's elbow to direct his attention.

Relief warred with apprehension as Javan looked where Charlan indicated, for the Kheldish lords—at least the Earls of Eastmarch and Marley—had, indeed, decided to grace the coronation with their presence, but so accoutred as to cause serious uncertainty about their intentions. Eschewing court silks for the leather and tweed of the far north, their hair clubbed back in fat border braids, the two sat a matched pair of piebald border ponies, incongruous among the sleek steeds of the lancers and Rhys Michael's leggy chestnut. Javan's quick scrutiny of the surrounding area did not immediately discover the whereabouts of their nephew, Graham, but he guessed the young duke must be there somewhere.

"Oh, my," Rhys Michael muttered. "Look who's here. You don't really expect me to go down there with them, do you?"

Javan kept his face impassive, for he had seen the object of the two earls' unwavering interest—Murdoch, the chief instigator of their brother's slaughter, standing farther along in the line of march with the royal banner, just ahead of the horse waiting for Javan himself.

"I—ah—don't think they have any quarrel with *you*, Rhysem," he said softly. "I would *not* want to be in Murdoch's shoes, though— especially not later today, when everyone's had a bit too much to drink and is off his best behavior. But go ahead down, and give them my greeting."

He continued slowly down the steps as Rhys Michael and Tomais went on ahead, speaking amiably to everyone, friend and foe alike, but keeping his eyes on Rhys Michael and the earls. The earls bowed as Rhys Michael came among them to mount up, Tomais watchful at his side, but their deference was grudging, minimal.

It was then that Javan finally spotted Duke Graham, closer toward the foot of the great hall steps and more conventionally mounted on a compact little mouse-grey mare, an unadorned tunic of the same shade only drawing further attention to the ducal coronet gracing his fair head. The boy would not have thought of the gesture on his own, but he obviously had been well coached by his uncles. Even without this sartorial statement, his very presence was blatant reminder to all that border justice had not been served by that of the former king's regents. If Graham chose to demand the justice previously denied him and his family, as a condition of his continuing homage for the lands he held for the king in the north, Javan would have no option but to respond. He almost hoped Graham would.

He caught young Graham's eye and nodded greeting as he reached the yard and went past him to head for his own horse—the same tall albino stallion that he had ridden from his brother's funeral, and the same that had carried that brother to his own coronation five years before. Tammaron and Rhun were holding the animal, both glittering like princes in their jewelled silks and coronets, and Tammaron, at least, gave him a respectful bow as he approached.

"Good morning, Sire," Tammaron said.

"My Lord Tammaron, my Lord Rhun," Javan replied neutrally.

With a leg up from Charlan, Javan settled into the padded red saddle, gathering up the reins and adjusting the skirts of his tunic as Charlan and Guiscard spread the white and shining mantle back over the horse's rump, to hang nearly to the ground all around. When it was arranged to their satisfaction, they mounted up on matched blacks being held by pages and paced themselves to Javan's either side. More of the young knights who had helped Javan seize and keep his throne thus far fell in behind as the procession moved out of the yard and started down toward Rhemuth Cathedral, to a trumpet fanfare from the castle battlements.

The heat grew more oppressive as they made their descent, especially once they came off the castle's hill to wind through the town. Rhemuth had not seen the coronation of a Haldane king in more than a century, for both Cinhil and Alroy had been crowned in Valoret, where the Festils had kept Court. The streets were lined with people, curious for a proper look at their new king. They had known him but briefly as a boy, during those few months between relocation of the Court to Rhemuth and his own departure to seminary, and had caught but a glimpse of him at the late king's funeral. Opinion continued to vary on whether the fledgling cleric should have returned to take up his brother's crown.

But mounted on his tall milk-white steed, resplendent in glittering gold and creamy silks, none could deny that the limping boy of most folks' memory had taken on at least the appearance of an able-looking king. Certainly his twin, the ill-fated King Alroy, had never cut so fine a figure on horseback. Nor had anyone ever seen

a look of such cool determination in Alroy as that displayed by
Javan. Vague rumor had it that the new king might be contemplat-
ing important reforms in Gwynedd, some of them aimed at clipping
the wings of certain former regents, some of whom were said to
have used their offices to enrich their own coffers.

Such speculations were natural enough, with a new king come
to the throne after an ineffectual predecessor and a regency before
that, especially when the new king was young and still naive in the
realities of governing. Somewhat more disturbing was the suggestion that he had tolerated Deryni around him for some months after
his father's death, and shown a marked squeamishness for the measures applied to Deryni who came under the full penalties of the
new laws.

But that had been before he went to study with the *Custodes
Fidei*, who were noted for their adherence to orthodox doctrine regarding the evils of Deryni magic, and whose Vicar General had
been responsible for the Statutes of Ramos that were putting Deryni increasingly in their place. Few knew much about Javan's ca-
reer with the *Custodes*, but surely three years of their indoctrination
would ensure that earlier tendencies toward leniency were eradi-
cated along with Deryni themselves.

Such was the reasoning running through many a mind of those
watching Javan ride to his coronation that last day in July of 921.
As the procession approached the cathedral and the crowds grew
larger, their acclaim grew as well, so that an enthusiastic welcome
met King Cinhil's second son as he drew up before the cathedral
steps and dismounted.

A new procession awaited him now, set to convey him into the
sacred precincts for his king-making. Instead of the choir monks of
Valoret's cathedral chapter to sing him in, a black-clad assemblage
from the *Ordo Custodum Fidei* waited to perform this honor—for
he *was* one of theirs, even if he had set aside his vocation to take
up a crown. Eight boy altar servers dressed in white would follow
the choristers, drawn up by twos behind them, each carrying a processional torch in a silver-gleaming holder, each looking most uncomfortable in the heat.

Next came the bishops' procession, a thurifer preceding a deacon
bearing the great Rhemuth processional cross and then all the bishops of Gwynedd, by twos—six itinerant bishops and then the titled
ones, Dhassa and Grecotha, Nyford and Cashien, Marbury and Stavenham. Rhemuth's archbishop followed them, glittering and majes-
tic in heavy golden cope and mitre, accompanied by his chaplain.
Then came the processional cross of the Primate of All Gwynedd;

and behind it, the primate himself, Hubert MacInnis, looming like a walking mountain in his vestments all of white and gold, crowned like a king with the jewels of the precious mitre on his head and with his crozier in his hand, flanked by his chaplain and another deacon.

Bishop Alfred of Woodbourne and Paulin of Ramos were waiting to escort Javan himself—Alfred all in white, Paulin in the full, sweeping black robes of the Vicar General of the *Custodes Fidei*, mitred as well, for when he resigned his bishopric to found the Order, he had but exchanged his bishop's mitre for that of an abbot. As part of the procession ahead of Javan continued on into the cathedral, the two came to flank Javan, each extending him an arm, black and white.

Javan paused while Guiscard and Charlan arranged his mantle behind him and a golden canopy moved into place before the cathedral doors, borne by four young knights rather than four earls' sons as had been done at Alroy's coronation—Sorle, Gavin, Bertrand, and Tomais. Then he set his hands lightly on his escorts' arms and mounted the steps into the welcome shade. Charlan and Guiscard fell in directly behind him and slightly to either side, lest they tread on his train, followed by Father Faelan as King's Confessor.

Then came the bearers of the royal regalia: Lord Albertus as Earl Marshal, with the State Sword; Murdoch with the Haldane banner, golden lion lifting and shimmering on the faint breeze against a field of crimson silk; young Duke Graham bearing the sceptre on a crimson cushion, slender ivory encrusted with gold; Rhun with the Ring of Fire on a silver salver; and Tammaron bearing the State Crown of leaves and crosses intertwined. Behind them came Rhys Michael, still escorted by his Kheldish earls, followed by other nobility entitled to a place in the coronation procession.

Javan held his head high as he proceeded down the aisle to the choir's introit, *Laetatus sum. I was glad when they said unto me, let us go into the house of the Lord.* As he went he was mindful of every eye upon him, weighing him, trying to decide what kind of a king he would be—this bold young man who had asserted his rights and taken up the crown most had thought destined to pass to his younger brother. Now, it seemed, this second son of King Cinhil had developed a mind of his own and intended to assert it—to what end, no one yet knew. He *looked* the king, though—hardly even limping in new white boots that made it difficult to see his handicap.

The assembled congregation bent in homage as he passed, following his progress into the choir, to the foot of the sanctuary steps, where the white-clad figure made a graceful reverence and then moved to the right to kneel at a faldstool. The sable head bowed in prayer as the singing went on and the rest of the procession continued filing into the cathedral to take their places, regalia being placed upon the altar, the archbishops praying silently at the foot of the altar steps, until all at last were present and ready.

This spectacle was observed with general interest by most of the congregation gathered to witness the rite now beginning, and with rather more analytical intent by diplomatic envoys from several other neighboring lands—Howicce and Llannedd to the southwest, Meara, Mooryn, and Torenth.

Representing Arion, King of Torenth, was his brother Miklos, but a year older than Javan himself—tall and graceful for his years, fair-haired and light-eyed, languid eastern manners masking a quick comprehension of all about him, quietly aglitter in tawny eastern silks. Sitting in a seat of honor along with other foreign dignitaries massed along one side of the choir, accompanied by the obviously high-born young aide who was his companion for this excursion, Prince Miklos watched with detached curiosity as the two archbishops went to raise up the young king and lead him into the center of the choir to be presented to his people. When his brother Arion was crowned some three years before in Beldour, Miklos had been quite old enough to know what he was seeing, and found it interesting to compare that rite with the one now unfolding.

"All hail Javan Jashan Urien, our undoubted king!" the Archbishop-Primate of Gwynedd announced, he and the other archbishop raising the king's arms to the East. "Be ye willing to do homage and service in his behalf?"

"God save King Javan!" the thundering response came, echoing in the vaulting of the great cathedral.

Thrice more the archbishop asked the question, turning Javan to the South, West, and North in what Miklos knew was a magical invocation of the angelic entities who ruled the Quarters, even though the humans of Gwynedd had no comprehension of such matters—nor wanted to, especially since the restoration of the Haldane line, at the expense of the Deryni Festils.

But now, having called the Four Quarters to witness—who *were* present, Miklos had no doubt—the archbishop was drawing the young king before the altar itself, where the great Book of Holy Writ lay open. From beside it he took up a sheet of parchment already prepared.

"My Lord Javan, are you now willing to take the coronation oath, sworn by your ancestors in times past?" he demanded.

"I am willing," Javan replied in a clear, steady tenor.

As Miklos watched, idly preparing to Read the truth of the king's oath, Javan boldly mounted the altar steps and laid his right hand on the open Book, the archbishop setting his left atop it and reading from the parchment.

"Javan Jashan Urien, here before God and men declared and affirmed to be the undisputed heir of our late beloved King Alroy, will you solemnly promise and swear to keep the peace in Gwynedd and to govern its peoples according to our ancient laws and customs?"

"I solemnly promise to do so," Javan replied.

"Will you, to the utmost of your power, cause Law and Justice, in Mercy, to be executed in all your judgments?"

"I will."

"And do you pledge that Evil and Wrong-Doing shall be suppressed and the law of God maintained?"

"All this I pledge," Javan said.

As the archbishop laid the parchment back on the altar, Javan moved closer to sign it, lifting it up when he had done so and laying his right hand on Scripture again as he turned to face the people.

"That which I have here promised," he said loudly, "I will perform and keep, so help me God."

So saying, he laid the oath back on the altar and bent to kiss the Book, then retreated back down the altar steps to the center of the sanctuary, where he turned to face the archbishop once more.

Watching him, Miklos nodded slightly to himself. Javan Haldane had spoken the truth, at least of his intentions, but it remained to be seen whether he could keep his oath. As king, he had sworn to suppress Evil and Wrong-Doing. But if, as Gwynedd's Church taught, Evil and Wrong-Doing were personified by Deryni, then the king either must turn away from his former friends who were Deryni, or be forsworn. Except as an item of intellectual interest, that mattered not at all to Miklos, for Javan was not his king, but it mattered a great deal to the dark-haired boy sitting beside him.

"Javan Jashan Urien Haldane," the archbishop said, "having given your sacred pledge before God and this holy people, now must you humble yourself by setting aside the trappings of worldly glory, that through us, the servant of the Most High, you may be prepared and brought before Him as a holy oblation."

As he spoke, two *Custodes* priests came forward to take away the white mantle and the silken overrobe, leaving the king to stand in the plain white underrobe of fine linen, so like a priestly alb. In this he sank gracefully to his knees and then laid himself prostrate at the archbishop's feet, resting his forehead on the backs of his hands rather than spreading his arms in the cruciform attitude Miklos would have expected—though perhaps this was a small display of independence. Miklos had been privy to certain privileged information regarding Prince Javan Haldane's years in seminary—all but a prisoner, some said, with only feigned espousal of a priestly vocation. Small wonder, then, if he chose to distance his sacring just a little from too-close comparison with a priestly ordination.

The archbishops and other assisting clergy went to kneel around the king, all of them facing the altar, and at a signal from the Master of Ceremonies, the congregation likewise went to their knees. Then, after a moment of utter silence, the choir began to sing the *Veni Creator*, whose melody, written by a Bremagni king centuries before, was familiar even to the eastern-trained ears of a Torenthi prince.

"*Veni Creator Spiritus, mentes tuorum visita, imple superna gratia, quae tu creasti pectora . . .*"

The choir sang a full four verses, after which the second archbishop censed the altar and the oblation with brisk efficiency while the corpulent Archbishop MacInnis intoned a sacring prayer. At its conclusion, the congregation were allowed to sit and the choir began a new chant: an unfamiliar setting for a familiar coronation formula, used even in Torenth.

"*Zadok the priest and Nathan the prophet have anointed him king in Gihon and they are come up from thence rejoicing . . .*"

As the anthem ended, two priests went to set a chair before the still-prostrate king, then helped him rise to his knees as the archbishop sat in the chair and the four knights bearing the golden canopy moved into place once more. Miklos could not hear the archbishop's words as he anointed the kneeling Javan on head, breast, and hands, for knowledge, valor, and glory; but he knew it for the most solemn moment of the sacring, whereby an anointed king became more than man but not quite priest, sealed unto his divine office by the unction of the sacring oil. He had sensed that moment of ineffable magic at his brother's coronation, and he sensed it anew as Gwynedd's anointed lord rose to be clothed in the garments of kingship.

Over the priestly robe of white linen went a new tunic of cloth of gold, stiff with bullion and laidwork and scarlet-winking jewels, ablaze in the summer sun that beat mercilessly through the stained glass windows. Around the king's narrow waist the archbishop fastened the white girdle of chivalry studded with jewels, while two of his knights fastened the golden spurs upon his heels. Though not yet old enough for formal knighthood, he was now the fount of honor for his kingdom, whence knighthood and all other nobility derived. Only a handful of those present knew that the delivery of these symbols to the king betokened no mere potential but a right already earned, by right of his own knights' election.

And over all, the great crimson mantle of earthly majesty—damask silk reembroidered with the Haldane lions in a darker shade of crimson and set with gems for eyes, lined with cloth of gold rather than fur for this summer rite, but no less rich, with a wide band worked round the hem in stiff bullion and gems, as wide as a man's two hands.

So adorned, his mantle spilling down the steps behind him, the king now was invested with more of the regalia of his office: first the State Sword, placed briefly in his hands to be kissed and then returned to the tall, gaunt man in black—who, according to Dimitri, was the Earl Marshal of Gwynedd as well as Grand Master of the new Order that had replaced the Michaelines.

As the man carried the sword back to the altar, there to lift it briefly in black-gloved hands before depositing it with a bow, a tight-lipped man in emerald and ultramarine carried forward a silver salver bearing a dazzle of red and gold—a ring, for the archbishop placed it on the king's finger with an admonition Miklos could not hear. Following that, a noble, fair-haired lad in grey, wearing an ornate but not royal coronet, brought forward the sceptre, an ivory rod encrusted with gold, which the archbishop set in the king's hands briefly, then returned to its keeper.

For now it was time for the crowning itself, the outward culmination of all this rite. Bowing to the king, the archbishop and his assistant took him by both his hands and led him across the sanctuary almost to the steps of the altar, where a kneeler had been set a short pace out and the king now knelt, hands clasped and head bowed. Solemnly, reverently, the second archbishop approached the altar and took up the crown, bearing it before him in gloved hands as he rejoined his fellow and gave it over. Javan lifted his head to gaze at it, blazing bright-gold in the sunlight, as Gwynedd's primate raised it above his head and likewise raised his prayer to heaven.

"Bless, we beseech Thee, O Lord, this crown, and so sanctify Thy servant, Javan, upon whose head Thou dost place it today as a sign of royal majesty. Grant that he may, by Thy grace, be filled with all princely virtues. Through the King Eternal, Our Lord, Who lives and reigns with Thee in the unity of the Holy Spirit, God forever. Amen."

He set it on the king's head as the echoed "Amen" rustled through the cathedral and a trumpet fanfare announced the accomplishment to those without as well as within. The Deryni Prince Miklos of Torenth caught his breath to see a blur of subtle power briefly surrounding the king's head like a nimbus of light—though, looking around, no one else seemed able to see it, with the possible exception of his companion, who had watched the entire ritual in tight-lipped concentration. It was rumored, and had been for many years, that the new king's father had somehow wielded magic in the time of the other's father, and that the latter had taken his own life rather than accept defeat at the hands of such a man. Certain it was that the other's mother had perished in battle with the new king's father . . .

Miklos gave the king another careful look, extending his powers to try to fathom more of what he had seen; but it was gone, and King Javan of Gwynedd merely human once more. During the homage and fealty that followed, and then the Mass, whose form differed slightly from that to which Miklos was accustomed, he used the focused concentration in the great cathedral to try to Read the new king more clearly, but shields seemed to surround him—either from the natural warding produced by the structure of the liturgy or from King Javan himself, Miklos had no way of telling.

He was quietly thoughtful, his young companion tautly silent, as they made their way up to the castle afterward for the coronation feast and its informal Court. He wondered how King Javan would react when Miklos presented his brother Arion's compliments and requested a coronation boon of the newly crowned king.

Chapter Twenty-three

Deliver him that suffereth wrong from the
hand of the oppressor; and be not faint-hearted
when thou sittest in judgment.
— Ecclesiasticus 4:9

It was midafternoon as Javan's coronation procession wound its way back up the hill to Rhemuth keep, through cheering throngs lining the streets. A faint breeze stirred outside the packed cathedral, but the sun was still blazing down. Javan was soaking wet beneath the thin silks of his coronation robes, and endured the slow ride back to the castle largely by anticipation of stripping everything off and collapsing for an hour or two before going back on display. Having fasted since the night before, he was also ferociously hungry, with a nagging headache pulsing just behind his eyes that owed to the heat as well as the hunger.

He was unhooking the clasp of his mantle even as he rode beneath the gatehouse arch of the inner ward, letting the crimson silk and cloth of gold slip from his shoulders as soon as he had drawn rein before the great hall steps. Waiting squires rescued the garment, to install it at his place in the hall for the festivities to follow, and Javan gathered his intimates to him with a weary gesture and headed directly for his quarters.

Once there, jewelled girdle and tunic of gold and underrobe of linen were likewise discarded before he plopped down on a stool. He guzzled two cups of cool water in quick succession while he let Charlan sponge him down, then just sat quietly in the faint breeze of the open window for a few minutes, eyes closed and thinking of nothing, while Jason and Robear removed the golden spurs and then the white boots.

"I've brought you some light refreshments, Sire," Guiscard said, breaking in on his reverie to set a tray on the trestle table. "You haven't eaten since last night, and you should have something in you before you start on wine this evening."

Nodding his agreement with a sigh, Javan moved back into the room to sit at his accustomed place. The time was sufficient for a quick debriefing while he ate. The others were drinking watered wine in the heat, but mostly saving their appetites for the banquet to follow.

"All right, let's start with the most startling development of the day," Javan said as he attacked part of a cold joint of chicken. "The Kheldour lords were rather conspicuous by their presence. Does anyone know what they're planning? Am I going to have any unpleasant surprises at Court this evening?"

Etienne de Courcy leaned back in his chair, affable and easy even in the heat. "The situation, as you know, is very precariously balanced, Sire. It's encouraging that they didn't have to be coerced to offer you fealty, but the border attire was a blatant statement of separation, if they choose to make it so."

"What about young Graham?" Javan asked. "He swore in his own right, so I suppose that confirmed that he's officially of age now. And while he wasn't exactly dressed for a coronation, it was a step up from riding leathers and northern tweeds. Any indications what kind of a man he's turning out to be?"

Jerowen Reynolds came to lean on the table beside Etienne. "Levelheaded, Sire—which is remarkable, considering that it was his father's death that started the quarrel."

"He wasn't there; his uncles were," Javan said with a snort, gesturing with his chicken. "*I* was there, and *I* find it difficult to keep a level head regarding those responsible. What do you think will satisfy them? What are they going to ask?"

"No one knows," Etienne replied. "We weren't even certain they were going to show up, as you know. I'd expect a request for a private audience, at very least—and God knows what they'll demand."

"*Demand?*" Robear said. "Since when do subjects *demand* something of their king?"

"They'll demand," Javan said simply, washing down a swallow of chicken with wine. "*I'd* demand. And I would've demanded, three years ago, if I'd been able. Most of you weren't there. You didn't see what was done to Duke Ewan—and then to Declan Carmody and his wife and sons. I've never forgiven Murdoch for that and I never will. Now that I'm king, if the Kheldour lords demand justice, I'm going to do my best to give it to them."

"Just don't underestimate Murdoch and his friends," Jason said.

"Your position is much stronger than it was even a few weeks ago, but you aren't ready for a showdown with the former regents as a group. And they *will* stick together—you can depend on it!"

"I'll keep that in mind," Javan said. "Now, what other potentially tricky negotiations have I got to get through? Jerowen?"

The law lord consulted a written itinerary. "Hmmm, the usual delegations from various of our neighbors. You *are* aware, I assume, that Torenth has sent an official observer."

"Yes, Hubert told me yesterday." Javan set down his cup. "One of the king's brothers, I hear."

Jerowen nodded. "Prince Miklos, he's called. He's not much older than you are. Said to be charming, brought only a small entourage. And of course, he's Deryni, like all the rest of the House of Furstan."

"I see. And?"

Jerowen shrugged. "He and his men have behaved impeccably thus far, Sire. The Earl Marshal had archers stationed in the galleries at the cathedral, and there will be more on call tonight. Would you like Oriel or Sitric available as well? At least you'd know if Miklos was lying—and he'd know that you knew."

Javan had gone very still, his mind racing furiously. Knowing what he did about the possible Torenthi links of Paulin's Deryni, the renewal of diplomatic relations with Torenth suddenly seemed suspiciously convenient. And an interview with a Deryni prince meant that Javan dared not even have Guiscard or Etienne attend him at the audience, lest Miklos detect another Deryni where none should be.

But perhaps he *could* have Oriel attend him. The presence of a Healer at the king's side could hardly be questioned, and might discourage any Torenthi trickery, if they thought he was under Deryni protection.

"Y-e-e-e-s," he said, slowly drawing out the word. "I believe I *will* ask Master Oriel to be present. And I believe Lord Rhun had already infiltrated Sitric among the guards assigned to 'escort' our Torenthi visitors. Tell me, though, is the Torenthi Court still harboring the Festillic Pretender?"

"Well, not officially," Etienne replied. "Mark of Festil is believed to have gone into Arjenol to continue his schooling. It remains to be seen what kind of support Torenth will give him, once he's ready to make his move."

"So we wait," Javan said. "And meanwhile, we entertain Torenthi princes at our Court."

Robear shrugged. "We're not at war, Sire. Haven't been for some years. And maybe he's brought an interesting gift."

"Interesting—it could well be that." Javan drummed his finger-tips on the table for a few seconds, then shook his head.

"Well, gentlemen, it looks as if I begin my lessons in foreign diplomacy right near the top. Have those archers continue to stand by, will you, Jerowen? Unobtrusively, of course, but just in case. I'm told that for speed, an arrow is far quicker than a spell."

Nervous laughter rippled among them at that, after which Jason resumed his briefing. A little later, when they had finished, Oriel came to examine his foot, which was fine, and to guide him into deep, refreshing sleep for an hour, while the others also changed their coronation finery for cooler attire.

An hour later the newly crowned king was rousing himself, somewhat restored, to don a long, sleeveless tunic of crimson silk over a thin white shirt of cotton gauze—not as elegant as his earlier attire, but it was infinitely more appropriate to the heat and looked kingly enough with the jewelled white girdle and the Haldane sword and the boots with the golden spurs and the State Crown. He was almost comfortable as he made his way down to the great hall to receive the official congratulations of his subjects and guests.

The entire atmosphere of the festivity was different from that of Alroy's coronation five years before. Then the order of the eve-ning had been to amuse and entertain a preadolescent king and his younger brothers—and to show off the wealth and the power of the young king's regents. King Javan was already two years a man, how-ever, at least in law. Accordingly, the protocol had been expanded to include more adult interests and diversions.

Chiefest among these, besides the necessity to receive the offi-cial greetings of foreign emissaries, was the inclusion of far more members of the fair sex than Javan remembered from five years before—though he had to admit that active notice of such things would not have occurred to him at age eleven. Perhaps his present awareness came of having his blood stirred so thoroughly the day before by the fair Anne of Cassan—whose presence even now, standing with her husband at the far end of the room, made his stomach do pleasant, flip-floppy things every time he looked at her.

There were other lovelies aplenty, too, some of them potential political disasters, like Rhun's dark-eyed daughter Juliana or—already a danger to Rhys Michael—Michaela Drummond. He lost track of the number of other young ladies of "suitable breeding" who were presented to him and his brother between their arrival and the first course. Blond or raven-tressed, titian or chestnut, they ranged in age all the way from hopefuls of nine or ten to more mature beauties approaching thirty. Their gowns were a veritable nosegay of summer flower colors—azure and rose and violet and buttercup—with scents to accompany in dizzying variety.

Javan had heard of such parades for the marriage mart, but he had hoped not to be subjected to one so soon. He watched with grudging appreciation, his attention occasionally caught briefly by a tossing curl or a twinkling eye, but he schooled himself to polite neutrality. His relief was profound when he and Rhys Michael at last could retreat to the more remote public display of merely sitting at the center of the head table.

With Rhys Michael to his right and Hubert to his left, he was soon tucking into the banquet's first course, sampling from fresh-baked venison tartlets, a clear soup with tiny dumplings floating in it, a salad of fresh garden vegetables in a mint vinaigrette, and skewered bits of fish roasted with an almond sauce. Everything was good, but Javan ate sparingly, both because of the heat and his earlier snack and because he knew there were at least five or six more removes.

Between the first and second removes, he received the emissaries of Llannedd and Mooryn in the withdrawing room behind the dais. Rhys Michael and Guiscard accompanied him, along with Hubert and Tammaron and several others of his senior ministers. Felicitations were presented, along with gifts—a leather pouchful of balass rubies from the mountains of Mooryn and ingots of ruddy gold from Llannedd—and then all returned to the great hall for the second remove.

It was during the interval between the third and fourth removes, as the sun was slanting long rays through the western windows of the great hall, that Javan prepared to receive the emissary of the King of Torenth. Oriel came to join him, quietly dressed in a dull-green tunic that suggested but did not proclaim his healing function, for the wearing of the old "official" badge of the Healer's call was now prohibited by law. His presence should discourage any too-close scrutiny on the part of their Deryni visitor.

And if Miklos did perceive more than he should, at least Javan could fall back on the precedent of being a Haldane, which line was already known to have acquired from somewhere the power to deal with Imre of Festil. Good manners probably would prevent the Torenthi prince from mentioning that, if he did notice anything.

Having taken all the precautions he could then, Javan contented himself with having his brother seated at his left, Charlan holding the Haldane sword between the two of them, and Jerowen Reynolds standing to his right to advise him as they took their places in the withdrawing room. Master Oriel he had stand directly behind his chair. More of the knights whose loyalty was beyond question were ranged informally toward the front of the room—Jason and Robear, Sorle, Bertrand, and Tomais—and he knew that the half-dozen guards at the back, Sitric among them, had bows and arrows stashed nearby.

Also present, being disinclined to risk missing anything important that might spring from an official communication with Torenth on so important a day, were most of the rest of his Council. Tammaron was there, along with Manfred, Rhun, and Murdoch, and also Archbishop Hubert and Albertus—though not Paulin, interestingly enough. Javan had to wonder whether the latter's absence meant anything.

The room stilled as Javan settled in the chair of state, now draped with the gold-lined mantle he had worn from the cathedral. When he had checked his crown to be sure it was straight, turning to his brother for confirmation, he signalled the guards at the door to proceed. As they threw the doors wide, a Torenthi herald announced his ambassador's style and titles.

"The emissary of the King of Torenth—His Serene Highness, the Prince Miklos von Furstan."

A Torenthi escort of six led the princely party, conical helmets bright-polished, cuirasses gleaming from beneath eastern silks in the same shade of tawny orange as the background of the banner their captain carried just behind them. The white roundel that covered most of the banner was charged with the leaping black hart of the House of Furstan, the ribbands and cordons of past battle honors streaming from the head of the staff to cascade over the captain's white gauntlets.

The escort saluted by twos as they came within a few paces of Javan's chair, white-gloved fists snapping to chests as helmeted heads inclined precisely enough to render respect but not subservience. As each pair made their devoirs, they parted to either side so that the banner-bearer approached through an honor guard of three on each side. He bowed his head briefly but did not dip the Torenthi banner, only stepping to the left and turning slightly to permit the approach of a strikingly blond young man in tawny silks, the jewelled diadem across his brow proclaiming his rank.

A curved sword hung at the Torenthi prince's side, its golden scabbard and hilt heavily carved and set with pearls and citrine. A squire or aide accompanied him, younger than himself, bearing something perhaps the size of a man's forearm wrapped in more of the tawny silk.

Javan sensed just the faintest prickle of shields surrounding prince and man—entirely expected—but no hint of probing from beyond those shields, which was well. His own shields he kept close and low, lest his visitors detect them, and he could feel Oriel's shields behind him, slightly extended to include him as well.

"Javan of Gwynedd," the prince said, making him a mannerly bow that, like the salutes of his escort, could not be mistaken for deference or arrogance. "On this, your coronation day, I bring felicitations from my king and brother, Arion of Torenth. Although in the past our fathers and, indeed, our two kingdoms may have harbored profound differences, my lord wishes you to know that he bears you no personal ill will and prays for you a most fruitful and peaceful reign. To that end, he asks me to present unto your Highness this small token of his regard, as one Christian prince to another."

He turned briefly to his attendant, who laid the silk-wrapped package across both his hands.

"Since rumor of your Highness' scholarly interests has reached even to Torenth, it was thought that this might become a worthy addition to your Highness' library," the prince went on, folding back the wrappings to reveal a rather aged-looking scroll. "It is an account of the life of an ancestor of yours, the blessed Saint King Bearand Haldane. I am told that it was begun during his lifetime, when his exploits were still fresh in the minds of those who record such matters, and finished not long after his death. The writing style, alas, is not to my personal taste, but the illuminations are far above the average—if I may be permitted to show your Highness?"

As Miklos partially unrolled the scroll to display a lavishly illuminated panel, Javan sat forward with interest, then signalled his assent for the prince to come closer. Miklos did so, easing down upon one knee on a cushion beside Javan's chair, there to spread the scroll across Javan's lap and the arms of the chair.

"You see, here, the spectacle of Bearand's coronation—much as we witnessed today," Miklos said, pointing out the scene. "And here, embarking upon the great venture of the Southern Seas. Here, the great sea battle with the Moorish host—you can see the admiral who later was instrumental in founding the late lamented Michaeline Order. And here, several of the miracles later attributed to Saint Bearand . . ."

By no word or action did the Torenthi prince transgress the conventions of guestship; and he was careful never to touch his host. But as the two of them scrolled through the yellowed parchment roll, the account of a Haldane king more than a century dead, Javan could feel the faint brush of the other's shields against his. He kept his own shields soft—though hard enough to keep Miklos out—and met the prince's gaze squarely as Miklos finished showing the scroll and began winding it up again, still on one knee beside the chair of state.

"I trust that your Highness will find the scroll of interest," the prince said blandly. "The Haldane line is a fascinating one."

Javan gave the prince a faint smile, well aware that Miklos was not referring to the scroll at all.

"Yes, it is a great honor to be part of so noble a lineage," he said. "Please convey my thanks to King Arion, your brother, for his kind gift, and say that I shall endeavor to find it a worthy place in the library I am assembling here at Rhemuth. As well, I thank your Highness for honoring me with your presence at my coronation. I am glad to know that matters may stand at peace between our two kingdoms. Unlike many of my predecessors, I am not minded to take my country into war, unless no other option remains. I hope that his Highness of Torenth shares these aspirations toward peace."

"He does, indeed, Sire," Miklos said, rising gracefully to his feet and backing off a few paces with a bow. "To that end, and because our two countries *are* at peace—and have been so for several years now—my lord now ventures to request a boon of your Highness, sovereign to sovereign, on this, your coronation day."

Javan allowed himself a faint smile, though a murmur of misgiving rippled among the rest of those present. He had been half expecting something beyond the mere presentation of a gift, though what it was remained to be seen.

"If it be not to the detriment of my kingdom, I will consider it, my lord. What is it the King of Torenth desires?"

Miklos made a disparaging motion with both hands and smiled as well. "Indeed, gracious prince, the matter reeks of ancient history, for you and I and even my brother were but infants when it occurred. My lord would know the fate of certain Torenthi hostages taken by Gwynedd during the reign of the late king your father— distant kin to our House, as it happens."

"Indeed?" Javan said, holding up a hand to silence uneasy murmurings among his lords of state. "Perhaps your Highness would be so good as to identify these hostages."

"Lady Sudrey and Lord Kennet, the niece and nephew of Lord Termod of Rhorau, Sire," the prince replied with a bow. "As children, they were placed in the wardship of Duke Sighere's son Ewan."

Whether or not it was intentional—and Javan suspected Miklos knew exactly what he was doing—the prince's request produced instant consternation, for everyone present knew that the man responsible for Ewan's death was in their midst, and that Murdoch of Carthane would not welcome the summoning of the dead man's brothers, who alone could shed light on the fate of the hostages in question. The Kheldour lords had arrived in Rhemuth spoiling for a fight, looking for an excuse to take up their quarrel with Murdoch again. Javan had hoped to keep them from even being in the same room. But perhaps it was time for the inevitable confrontation.

"You have brought us a most intriguing question, my lord," Javan said noncommittally, watching Murdoch in his side-vision. "As you have rightly pointed out, this matter occurred outside our memories. Furthermore, both Duke Sighere and his son Duke Ewan are dead."

"News had reached us of their passing," Miklos murmured. "May their souls and the souls of all the faithful departed rest in peace."

He crossed himself piously as he said it right to left in the eastern fashion, and Javan and the rest followed suit in the western manner. Hubert looked decidedly uncomfortable.

"Happily for us all, however," Javan went on, "both of Duke Ewan's brothers were in attendance today—though not present in this room. I am confident that they will be able to provide enlightenment regarding your query." He raised his glance slightly to catch Tammaron's eye. "My Lord Chancellor, please be so good as to request the presence of the Earls of Eastmarch and Marley."

As Tammaron bowed and then made his way from the room, Prince Miklos inclined his head in thanks and drew his men to one side to make way for the expected earls. Casually, while they waited, Javan reached back and took the Haldane sword from Charlan, to rest it sheathed across his knees—for this exchange of diplomatic courtesies had changed into something that had all the earmarks of a political incident in the making.

A few minutes later the doors at the other side of the room opened and Tammaron came in, preceding the earls and their rather puzzled looking nephew. Young Graham looked sober enough, but both Hrorik and Sighere had the high color and faintly unsteady gait that spoke of imbibing well progressed. The two flanked Graham, the three of them making Javan dutiful-enough bows. Hrorik's eyes strayed to the side as he straightened, lighting on Murdoch, who was doing his best to be invisible. Before the northern lord could put his foot in the situation, Javan cleared his throat to recall their attention.

"I thank you for attending me, my good lords," he said easily. "Allow me to make you acquainted with his Serene Highness the

Prince Miklos of Torenth, brother of King Arion. His Highness has made inquiries concerning certain hostages entrusted to the late Duke Ewan some fifteen years ago. Their names again, my Lord Miklos?"

"Lord Kennet and Lady Sudrey of Rhorau, Sire."

Hrorik went white, and Sighere glanced uneasily at his older brother. Graham looked astonished.

"I gather that the names are familiar to you, my lords," Javan said quietly, wondering at their reactions and setting himself to Truth-Read. "Perhaps you can tell his Highness of their fate."

Hrorik swayed on his feet, looking resolutely at the floor, and Sighere, after another glance at his brother, looked squarely at Murdoch.

"Best ask the Earl of Carthane what became of Lord Kennet, Sire, for his men *murdered* him, the same way they murdered our brother Ewan!"

"That's a lie!" Murdoch declared, half drawing his sword, though he was kept from it by Manfred and Rhun. "Ewan of Claibourne was a foul traitor, and attacked *me* when I sought to make him answer for it! Besides that, it was the Deryni who killed him, in the end—that devious, defiant—"

"And I say *you* lie, Murdoch of Carthane!" Hrorik bellowed, yanking a dirk from his belt but restrained by Sighere and a horrified Graham. "You slew Kennet of Rhorau the same way you slew the others of my brother's men. If it was not your hand on the dagger, it was your order—"

"*Liar!*"

As Hrorik bucked and struggled, hatred blazing in the blue eyes, Murdoch wrenched free of Manfred and Rhun and drew his sword at last, launching himself toward the grappling Kheldour lords with a mindless cry of rage.

"Hold!" Javan shouted.

Even as Murdoch moved, Javan was out of his chair with enough force to overturn it, whipping the Haldane sword clear of its scabbard with a mighty snap of his wrist and thrusting the blade upward to block Murdoch's.

"Hold, I say!" he repeated, as the blades clashed. "Murdoch, drop it!"

Charlan and Udaut were already in motion as well, tackling Murdoch as he drew back for another swing—this time aimed at the king—and wrestling him to the ground, wrenching the sword from his hand. Rhys Michael had thrown himself to one side, out of harm's way.

More of the knights were swarming around Hrorik and Sighere and Graham, both to shield them and to prevent their further participation, more still with hard hands on Rhun and Manfred to stay them from joining in.

Murdoch flailed and twisted in his captors' hands, screaming wordless rage and even kicking at Javan's knee, only subsiding as the cold steel of the king's blade pressed hard against his throat and the men holding him shrank back to give Javan room—though they did not loosen their grip on Murdoch.

"Give it up, Murdoch!" Javan ordered. "Or better yet, *don't*. Guards, come and take charge of this fool before I have to kill him! And *you!*" He pointed the sword at the still-struggling Hrorik. "Leave it to me, or you're no better than him!"

Standing there straddling the supine Murdoch, sweeping the room with his gaze as he likewise swept it with his sword, he must have looked far more impressive than he felt. They were all staring at him, mouths open, apprehension and surprise and even admiration writ across their faces. Two of Javan's knights had hustled Prince Miklos and his aide into the safety of his own men at the first sign of trouble and now stood wary guard before the lot of them.

Javan saluted the prince with his sword, then stepped back from Murdoch, who had become quite docile in the hands of the guards who came to take over from Charlan and Udaut. From beside him, Archbishop Hubert hesitantly held out the scabbard he had retrieved from the floor. Javan took it, but he did not sheathe the Haldane sword.

"All right, I still want to know the answers to some questions," he said, gesturing with it toward Murdoch. "You, on your feet. One more outburst like that, and you're in a dungeon to cool off. You watch it, too, Hrorik."

He reached down to right the State Chair that he had kicked out of the way when he launched himself, nodding thanks to Rhys Michael for his assistance, then sat.

"Now," he said, laying the naked blade and its scabbard across his knees. "We were talking about Kennet of Rhorau. Murdoch, Sighere says you killed him—you or your men. Do you deny it?"

"Of course I deny it!" Murdoch said, all but spitting as he glared at Sighere.

"Thank you, that's enough. Sighere, Murdoch denies it. Would you care to provide details that, perhaps, will jog his memory? Perhaps tell us how Kennet came to be at Court that day?"

Sighere turned a look of pure venom on Murdoch and shook off the hands still laid lightly on his sleeves.

"I'll no jump on him!" he said contemptuously. "The Laird Kennet was fourteen when he an' his sister came intae Ewan's wardenship. She was thirteen. The terms o' the wardenship said that they were to be kept in honorable confinement, so Ewan made Kennet his squire."

He drew a deep breath, then went on, not looking at any of them. "He was a braw squire, once he settled down, an' he became a bauld sword—sae guid that when he was twenty, Ewan knighted him, even though he shouldnae hae done, because Kennet was a hostage. But by then, it didnae matter, because Ewan had come tae love Kennet like his own son."

Miklos had come closer as Sighere spoke, and nodded quietly as the earl went on.

"In time, Ewan became duke. Kennet was one o' his captains by then, an' naebody even remembered he'd started out as a hostage. He came wi' Ewan tae that birthday Court, three years ago. An' when that man stole Ewan's office an' his men attacked ours"—he pointed at Murdoch—"Kennet was one o' the first Claibourne men tae fall, defendin' his liege! He was a guid man an' a braw knight, an' *that man* is responsible for his death!"

Murdoch had folded his arms across his chest, his face dark with outrage. "I know nothing of this. My men were defending me from a traitor. Some of Claibourne's men died. That's all I know."

"An' *I* know," Hrorik said, finally speaking out to Murdoch, "that ye were responsible for our brother's death, and for Kennet's and for the deaths of every other man wha' fell that day! I call ye to account for yer crimes, Murdoch! I call ye tae mortal combat, tae prove yer innocence upon yer body!"

Taking a step forward, he yanked rough border gauntlets out of his belt and flung them at Murdoch's feet.

"If ye be innocent o' his blood, then may I perish as terribly as did m' brother. But if ye be guilty o' contrivin' his death, then may ye writhe out yer life the way ye wished for him! As God is my witness, Javan Haldane, King o' Gwynedd, I accuse this man o' the murder o' Ewan Duke o' Claibourne, an' stand ready to prove my accusation upon my body!"

The room had grown ever more still as Hrorik unfurled his challenge. All eyes shifted from him to Murdoch and then to the king as Hrorik set his thumbs in his belt and gave a final "Humph!"

"Sire, this is an outrage!" Murdoch muttered. "Am I required to answer this madman's claim? You were there. I murdered no one."

"Yes, I was there," Javan said quietly, fingering the hilt of the Haldane sword. "That is why I will not permit myself the satisfaction of judging this case. Hrorik has made an accusation and called you before God's Court to answer. If you refuse, I shall have you banished from *my* Court as a craven."

"And if I accept, and I prevail, shall I have your apology, *Sire?*" Murdoch said through clenched teeth. "You need not answer that. I see that you are determined to permit this travesty of justice."

"There shall be no travesty, my lord," Javan said, sweeping them with his eyes and watching as they backed down, almost to the man. "All shall be done according to the law. Your accuser has declared his grievance in open Court. He has the right to see your innocence tested—and to put his own life in the balance."

"This is no justice," Richard, Murdoch's son, said. "You've always hated him. Now the crown is on your head, you think you can have your revenge!"

Javan took the scabbard of the Haldane sword and jammed it onto the blade, not looking at Richard.

"The sword is sheathed, gentlemen," he said. "The king's justice has naught to do with this affair except to see that proper protocol is carried out. Murdoch of Carthane, Hrorik of Eastmarch has issued you a challenge. Do you accept?"

"I do," Murdoch said, his voice full of hate as he threw off his guards' hands long enough to bend and scoop up the gauntlets Hrorik had thrown. "I say that Hrorik of Eastmarch lies and I shall prove it upon my body, upon the field of honor, at whatever time and place the King's Grace shall decide."

Glancing at Hrorik, he flung the gauntlets backhanded across the space between them, to strike Hrorik's chest. The earl caught them before they could fall and made Murdoch sardonic salute with them, a nasty smile curving his lips.

"On the field, to the death, Murdoch," he murmured. "I hae waited for this day these three years."

When both men had been escorted from the room, Master Oriel moved a little closer to the king as Prince Miklos again drew near, his aide at his side, and cast an appraising eye over both of them.

"Your Healer, I surmise," he murmured, folding his hands behind his back and favoring Oriel with a slight nod. "Very prudent. I wish to offer apologies to your Highness for precipitating this unfortunate turn of events. While I had anticipated that my inquiry might possibly provoke hostility or even embarrassment, I had not expected a brawl. Alas, it appears that both gentlemen honestly believe that they are in the right—as I am certain Master Healer will confirm. Your Highness is aware, of course, that the Healer could extract the truth without the bloodshed you plan to allow on the morrow?"

"The methods you suggest are not encouraged at my Court, my lord," Javan said coolly. "I will thank you not to interfere in such matters."

Miklos smiled and inclined his head, apparently not offended. "If I may return, then, to matters in which my interference is appropriate, my lord. It appears that Lord Kennet, though he died, yet came to a noble end. Dare I presume to inquire further concerning what became of the Lady Sudrey?"

The question brought Javan up short, for in the confusion it had quite slipped his mind that Sudrey's fate was yet unknown. With a nod to Miklos, Javan raised a hand to catch young Graham's eye and beckoned him to join them, his uncle Sighere following.

"Prince Miklos has just reminded me of a question still unanswered, gentlemen," he said. "Whatever became of the Lady Sudrey?"

Graham glanced at Sighere, looking apprehensive, but Sighere only gave him a grim smile, eyeing Miklos with something akin to defiance.

"The lady is well, m'lord," he said, "but I dinnae think she will abide returning tae Torenth. She is lady an' wife tae my brother Hrorik. They hae one daughter, Stacia, who becomes Countess of Eastmarch if her father falls tomorrow. An' her guardianship falls tae me an' tae her cousin, Duke Graham."

"Indeed?" Miklos was heard to murmur, as Javan lamented yet another convolution in the political balance he had inherited.

"Very well, I believe further speculation is pointless until tomorrow is decided," Javan said, calling Charlan to his side with a glance. "Earl Sighere, Duke Graham, we shall speak more on this matter before your return to Kheldour. Prince Miklos, I hope you will pardon me if I return now to my other guests in the great hall."

"Of course, your Highness," Miklos purred. "I, too, look forward to tomorrow's outcome with great interest."

He favored Javan with a courtier's bow and watched as the king and the rest of his retinue filed out of the withdrawing room and back into the great hall. When they were gone, and his own men had assembled in the doorway, ready to go out, Miklos turned to his young aide, who had remained silent throughout the past hour's exchanges.

"Well, cousin, your education progresses," he said softly. "You've seen your opposition now, and the turmoil surrounding him. I suspect you only need be patient. By the time you yourself are ready to make your move, Javan Haldane may not even be a factor."

Nodding, the younger man turned his gaze to the great tapestry of the Haldane arms hanging behind the canopied chair of state. There had been a time when his own family's arms had hung in this hall and in others all over Gwynedd. Among his Torenthi kin he was reckoned no less a prince than Miklos, and of late had taken to using the Torenthi form of his name, which was Marek. But his baptismal name, given him by his mother when she also named him true heir to the throne of Gwynedd, was Mark—Mark of Festil.

CHAPTER TWENTY-FOUR

I said in mine heart, God shall judge the
righteous and the wicked.
—Ecclesiasticus 3:17

No fanfare greeted Javan's arrival in the tilting yard the next morning, where the accoutrements of the tournament had been dismantled to make room for more deadly combat. In contrast to the previous day's ceremony, today was stark and grim, pared down to barest essentials, for of the two contenders presently arming in the shade of pavilions erected to either end of the field, only one would survive.

Javan reviewed the justification for the coming trial as he, Rhys Michael, Charlan, and Guiscard moved along the edge of the field, Javan nodding wordless greeting to those they passed. Earlier, the four of them had heard an early Mass in the Chapel Royal, because a man was to die today. Javan fervently hoped that it would be Murdoch of Carthane.

He told himself that what he was allowing to take place this morning would answer the justice long denied in the case of Ewan of Claibourne's slaying, but he knew that this trial by combat also answered his own desire for vengeance in the matter of Declan Carmody's death. He would not allow himself to think about what he would do if Hrorik died instead, and Murdoch was acquitted before all the Court.

Now, as Javan moved along the yard, he could see how the trial had polarized the Court; Murdoch's supporters stood at one end of the yard, Hrorik's at the other. Gathered around the pavilion at Murdoch's end were the expected hard-liners of the old regime:

Rhun and Manfred and Murdoch's sons, Richard and Cashel. At
Hrorik's end were Sighere and Graham, of course, but also several
of the younger nobles who, hitherto, had not particularly taken Javan's side: Lord Udaut the Constable and Fane Fitz-Arthur, who
had taken a princess to wife.

To either side of the king's box, which lay midway along one
side of the area being laid out for the confrontation, stood those
who could not afford to be seen blatantly choosing sides: Chancellor Tammaron, both of Gwynedd's archbishops with Paulin of Ramos; and Jerowen and Etienne, Sir Robear and Sir Jason, and the
other knights of Javan's immediate companionship.

Javan noted how they deferred to him as he passed, in many an
eye respect where little had been before, perhaps a legacy of the
way he had handled himself the previous night. He looked like a
very different sort of king today, with the Haldane sword girt about
the waist of a light-grey tunic with the Haldane badge emblazoned
on the breast. His crown was a hammered circlet of gold studded
with rubies the size of a man's thumbnail, its gems ablaze in the
unremitting glare of the morning sun, an almost primitive piece of
work well suited for presiding over a trial by combat. As he and
Rhys Michael took their seats under the shade of the royal box, he
immediately turned his gaze down the field where battle chargers
were being readied for their riders.

Drums rolled, brisk and commanding, and guard details from
the castle garrison came to attention outside each pavilion to escort
the contenders and their banners onto the field. Murdoch was preceded by the black aurochs of Carthane on a crimson field; Hrorik
followed the Eastmarch standard, golden suns and a silver saltire
on blue. The two wore gambesons of quilted leather under embroidered surcoats that repeated the devices on the banners, and greaves
and vambraces of boiled leather, but no true armor. They would
don steel caps and mail coifs later on, but helmets would not be
permitted. Both carried swords and long poniards at their belts.

Trailed by the Earl Marshal and the banner-bearers, the combatants approached, eyeing one another sidelong. Hrorik went at once
to his knees when they had reached the barrier between field and
royal enclosure, head bowing in homage, but Murdoch gave Javan
a long, cold look before slowly sinking down, arrogance in every
line of his body. Javan met Murdoch's glare without flinching, resting his left hand on the hilt of the Haldane sword as he stood.

"Hrorik of Eastmarch and Murdoch of Carthane," he said, "you
have come upon this field of trial by combat, accuser and accused,
and agreed to do battle to prove the right of your claims. I charge

you, before God, to conduct yourselves according to the terms of such combat. Battle shall commence on horseback and proceed until mortal injury is done to one of the contending parties. All weapons are allowed. No quarter shall be asked, and none given. Having heard these charges, have you any questions?"

When only silence answered him, Javan turned to Hubert, waiting in cope and mitre to bless the two. The archbishop's pudgy hands were trembling on his pastoral staff, for if he had not sanctioned Murdoch's actions that other day, neither had he forbidden or even discouraged them. As a clergyman, he could not be called out on the question, but his guilt would be indicated clearly enough if Murdoch fell, even if Hubert himself was never made to answer in this life. The archbishop looked queasy and restive as he raised his right hand in the formula of blessing.

"Benedicat vos omnipotens Deus, Pater, et Filius, et Spiritus Sanctus. Amen."

The two crossed themselves and got to their feet, Hrorik bowing again to Javan, Murdoch merely inclining his head. Then they were striding back to their respective ends of the field where warhorses and weapons waited. The Earl Marshal retired to mount up, then rode to the center of the field. Below the royal box, a *Custodes* battle surgeon and a priest slipped quietly into place beside a court physician. Oriel was standing behind Javan again, for Prince Miklos and his party occupied a pavilion directly opposite the royal box.

Silence descended as the two now-mounted combatants turned at the ends of the field to face one another, barely curbing increasingly fractious mounts, shields glinting in the sun, lances at the ready—not the lightweight, breakaway lances of the tournament field but shorter, heavier war lances. The jingle of harness and the creak of saddle leather were the only sounds besides the snorting of the horses. Albertus, watching them, turned toward Javan and bowed low in the saddle, then straightened to back his horse deftly to the other side of the field, baton raised. When he had reined in, he glanced toward Javan once more, caught the royal nod, and brought the end of the baton down sharply.

Suddenly given their heads, the battle chargers bolted, whinnying defiance as heavy hooves pounded down the sun-parched footing of the battleground. Lance tips winked in the sun as they dropped, just before the two engaged, but deft shieldwork deflected both blows, splintering Hrorik's lance full along its length and spinning Murdoch's out of his hand.

Both men dragged their mounts' heads around to make another

pass, Murdoch fumbling for his sword, Hrorik heaving the remnants of his shattered lance directly in the path of Murdoch's charging steed. The angle was just right to tangle the lance between the grey's heavy forelegs. The horse screamed as it went down in a tangle of thrashing hooves, and Murdoch was pitched over the animal's shoulder.

He managed to keep hold of the reins as he tumbled in a twisting somersault—incredible, for someone still clutching sword and shield—but he somehow accomplished a three-point landing on both hands and a knee, sword still in his fist and shield intact. He was already scrambling back into the saddle as Hrorik made his turn and came around for another pass, drawing a battle ax from his saddlebow.

Squealing its rage, the grey lurched to its feet with Murdoch aboard and went for Hrorik's bay as the two closed. Murdoch only barely managed to retain both seat and sword. The grey got its teeth in the other stallion's throat and the two reared up, screaming, but Hrorik's ax was already singing forward and down, smiting the grey between the ears, splitting its skull and severing the bridle strap to leave Murdoch with a handful of reins connected with nothing at all as the bit dropped out of the grey's gasping mouth.

Only barely did Murdoch manage to block Hrorik's next blow, catching the haft of the ax on the quillons of his sword with a bone-jarring impact. As the grey sank to its knees, dying, and Hrorik maneuvered for another blow, Murdoch frantically threw himself to one side to avoid being pinned.

The tip of his blade was coming up, though, even as he rolled clear. He braced the hilt against the ground as Hrorik's bay reared again, struck out with steel-shod hooves, then came down—full onto Murdoch's sword.

The horse screamed with pain; Hrorik screamed in rage. Roaring his glee, Murdoch twisted his blade as he wrenched it free, opening the animal's belly and spilling its guts to tangle in its flailing hooves. Now it was Hrorik's turn to bail out of the saddle, desperate to be clear of a thrashing, dying horse, using his shield to block Murdoch's blade as he kicked free of spur-tangled stirrups and scrambled for his footing.

Combat now settled down in earnest, sword and shield against ax and shield. Most of the spectators had come to their feet as the first exchange of blows went sour and horses started being cut from under riders. Javan and his immediate attendants remained seated, maintaining the required decorum, but Javan's hands were clenched in a death-grip on the ends of the arms of his chair. He had groaned for the horses' fate, and now he flinched at nearly every blow, wondering how long it must go on. The crown seemed to burn into his brow, and each clash of steel on steel seemed to pound at his brain.

The two fought more than a score of exchanges, parry and riposte, thrust and counterthrust, attack and counterattack, before the scales began to swing. In the beginning, once the two had won clear of the encumbering bulk of dead horseflesh, they had seemed quite evenly matched, settling down to cool-headed, almost logical exchanges—a dance of death, but almost beautiful in its horror. Gradually, however, Hrorik's slight advantage of age began to tell.

It began with a cut to Murdoch's right shoulder, shallow but bloody, answered by a thin graze along Hrorik's forehead. First blood seemed to break the impasse, though; and before long, Murdoch was bleeding from half a dozen wounds, painful enough to slow him down, but none yet serious enough to give his opponent the victory he sought. Hrorik was bloody, too, but all of his wounds were superficial.

The glittering upward arc of the telling blow was almost off-handed. Surely it was moving far too slowly for Murdoch not to get out of the way in time.

But Murdoch did *not* move fast enough, and Hrorik's already bloody ax cut a deep, clean gash across Murdoch's lower belly, right through crimson surcoat and quilted leather padding.

Its import was not immediately apparent. The blood was not readily visible against the surcoat, and Murdoch clutched at his belly and staggered back with hardly a louder cry than many another he had made. After throwing his shield at Hrorik's head with a roar of defiance, he launched another savage sword attack, left hand now pressed to his belly as the right hand wove a deadly net of steel before him. The burst of aggression got him through Hrorik's defenses enough to lay open his ax arm just above the elbow.

Bellowing with outrage, Hrorik fell back and also threw aside his shield, shifting his ax to his other hand and wading into another attack. This one caught Murdoch behind the right knee, hamstringing him. As he fell groaning, clutching at this new wound—but never relinquishing his sword—the extent of the previous wound was revealed at last: a gaping gash as wide as a man's hand, through which could be seen the bloody bulge of entrails. His free hand shifted back almost immediately in futile attempt to press back what was sundered, but blood was leaking from between his gloved fingers.

A groan passed among the assembled witnesses as the gravity of the wound registered. As Murdoch staggered, Hrorik pulled up short, ax still upraised—then slowly straightened and let the weapon sink to his side, a wolfish grin curving his lips.

"Welcome tae hell, Murdoch!" he said softly, breathing hard, gesturing toward the belly wound with his ax.

The Earl Marshal and Richard Murdoch were already running onto the field, soldiers of the garrison preventing anyone else from following. Richard's face contorted with horror as he flung himself down beside his father and made futile motions to staunch the bleeding. Albertus bent dispassionately over the fallen man, coolly noting the dirt already befouling the wound, the grey gleam of entrails exposed, then turned expectantly to Hrorik.

"The victory is yours, my Lord of Eastmarch. Finish him."

"Let someone else finish him," Hrorik replied, casting the bloody ax at Murdoch's feet.

Richard Murdoch looked up in shock, as if unable to comprehend. Javan had come to his feet at Albertus' words, straining to see and hear, and signalled the guards to let Sighere go to Hrorik.

"According to the agreed terms of combat," Albertus said calmly, "battle was to be to the death, with no quarter given. Until he is dead, you have not won."

"I hae won," Hrorik said contemptuously, as Sighere came to throw an arm around his shoulder and Murdoch at last rallied enough to open his eyes and look up, panting with the pain. "He cannae recover, no more could Ewan recover from the hurt done tae *him*. But I will gie ye better an' ye gave my brother, Murdoch o' Carthane!" he said, pointing a shaking, bloody finger at his vanquished foe. "I dinnae demand the rippin' o' yer mind—an' I willnae deny ye the coup. But *I* willnae do it. Upon my soul, I willnae."

As he turned to walk away, leaning heavily on his brother, others were pouring onto the field: Rhun and Manfred, Hubert, a surgeon, Murdoch's wife, and his other son—and Javan himself following more sedately, accompanied by Rhys Michael, Charlan, Guiscard, and Lord Jerowen. Hubert went to the wounded man immediately, easing his bulk to his knees, the surgeon crouching to examine the belly wound. Elaine, Murdoch's wife, was restrained from coming too close by her younger son Cashel. As Javan approached, he heard Hubert say to his brother Manfred, "Get Oriel over here!"

Manfred was gone before Javan could gainsay it, returning almost immediately with a pale-looking Oriel, one burly fist locked tightly on the Healer's bicep. Oriel bit back a sob as Manfred flung him to his knees beside Hubert and the wounded Murdoch, who was panting with the pain.

"Help him!" Hubert commanded.

"My lord, I—"

"I said, *help* him!" Hubert repeated, with a vicious backhand across Oriel's face that cut his cheek with his bishop's ring. "Defy me, and your family shall pay the consequences, I swear it, Oriel!"

"Archbishop, enough!" Javan said, seizing Hubert's wrist to prevent another blow. "You may not compel him to do that!"

Hubert jerked his hand away and glared at the king.

"How dare you!" he whispered, under his breath but loud enough for Javan to hear. "I may command my servant to do whatever I please!"

"My lord, you may not compel *anyone* to give aid to a man dealt a mortal wound in trial by combat," Javan said quietly. "I will permit mercy freely given, but never compulsion. Furthermore, Master Oriel is no longer your servant. From this moment hence, he is part of my own household, and I give him the right to decide whether he wishes to grant mercy to one who has so greatly wronged him."

"And how has my father wronged *him*?" Richard demanded. "He is Deryni. He has no rights to *be* wronged!"

"He would dispute that point, I think," Javan said. "But did you truly think it was only Ewan's kin who had quarrel with him? Even if Murdoch did not himself slay Ewan—and I believe it was *his* dagger buried to the hilt in Ewan's gut—his direct order was responsible for the deaths of at least four other persons, one of them under circumstances so excruciating, I hope you cannot imagine."

"They were Deryni!" Richard said contemptuously.

"Aye, they were—three of them: a woman and her two young sons, gentle and harmless. Oriel was able to do nothing to ease the plight of Declan Carmody and his family that day, nor was I; but I will not raise a finger to force any man to give ease to Murdoch of Carthane. Master Oriel, you are free to help him or not, as you choose, and will suffer no punishment, whatever your decision."

Trembling, not meeting any of their eyes, Oriel slowly extended his hand above Murdoch's wound, though he did not touch it. After a long moment, he returned his hand to his lap to clasp with the other and looked up impassively at Hubert.

"I think you must know that the Healing of this wound is beyond my skill or any other's, my lord—saving, perhaps, a miracle," he said quietly. "Unfortunately, Deryni such as myself are not often granted such grace."

"But you cannot simply let him suffer!" Hubert began.

"I can and will block the pain, if Lord Murdoch requests it of me, my lord," Oriel replied. "So much my Healer's Oath requires, in the name of humanity."

The wounded man snorted, contempt mingled with his pain. "As if humanity were a Deryni trait!" he gasped. "You'll not hear me beg to the likes of you! I'll see you rot in hell first!"

Oriel turned his pale gaze directly on Murdoch. "My Lord Murdoch may, indeed, see me in hell, for that surely is *his* destination," he said quietly. "For myself, I commend me to the mercy of the Most High God, to Whom all shall surely answer on the day of judgment."

"Careful, Healer!" Hubert warned. "You skirt dangerously near blasphemy."

"I mean no disrespect, my lord," Oriel murmured. "I seek but to do my work in peace, wishing harm to no man."

"And what of my father?" Richard demanded. "*There* is your work, Healer."

Slowly Oriel shook his head. "I can give no false hope, my lord. Lord Murdoch must understand that his wound is fatal. If it runs its course, death will not come easily or quickly. The bowel has been breached, and the wound will rot from within. I can block the pain, but I can do nothing about the rot, especially in this heat. The end could be days in coming—perhaps even weeks."

Murdoch had gone even paler as Oriel spoke, and now turned his face away, choking back a sob.

"Perhaps," Oriel went on more coldly, "Lord Murdoch may take comfort from the knowledge that he will have ample time to repent of his sins—a luxury he did not allow Duke Ewan or his other victims. I suggest you shrive him quickly, my Lord Archbishop, before the pain becomes too great—for I see he will not bear a *Deryni* to touch him. And then, best pray for someone else to do him the office that Declan did for Duke Ewan."

Hubert closed his eyes briefly, for while the Church did not officially condone the *coup de grace*, no one could deny its existence—and its preference to the prolonged agony that Murdoch now faced.

"Then you must perform that office, Master Oriel," Hubert said suddenly. "In the name of mercy, I beg you. You have the means. You can make the passing easy."

Boldly Oriel met Hubert's gaze. "I *can*, but upon my soul, I *will* not," he said. "As Healer, it is my office to *give* life, not to take it. Let some other perform that office."

"But—"

As Hubert turned his entreaty to Javan, the king merely shook his head and signalled to Oriel to join him. "Do not appeal to *me*, Archbishop. This is not my argument; but if you *make* it my argument, I, too, have recollection of deeds for which Murdoch is responsible, and must count the balance not yet paid, even were he six months in the dying."

So saying, he gathered his party to him and turned to follow Hrorik and Sighere off the field, leaving Murdoch groaning on the ground and his sons and friends pondering what to do.

CHAPTER TWENTY-FIVE

And another dieth in the bitterness of his soul . . .
—Job 21:25

An hour later Murdoch of Carthane lay taut and pain-wracked on what he knew would be his deathbed, teeth locked in a grimace against the burning in his gut, hurting with every breath he drew. Beside him, his wife of more than twenty years kept dabbing at his brow with cloths wrung out in cool water, but he found her ministrations increasingly more annoying than soothing. She meant well, and he loved her for her devotion even to this bitter end, but it would take more than water to quell the fire that was eating at his life.

And it would only get worse as the hours wore on. Already the agony had been unspeakable. Lord Albertus' battle surgeon and a court physician both had offered him syrup of poppies before beginning their grisly work—for even cutting away his armor and clothing had been excruciating—but Murdoch had declined, setting his teeth in a strip of leather to keep from screaming as they began treating his wounds.

They had done their best to be gentle. Even so, he had passed out from the pain long before they got to the belly wound—which was as well, since all they could do for that one was to gently bathe the protruding parts with warm water and press them back inside him, there to be secured with a pad of clean linen pressed close against the opening and many turns of wide white bandage wrapped tightly around his belly. It was no attempt at repair, but at least the bandaging gave him some support. In other times, they would have afforded his leg wound more thorough treatment than mere bandaging, perhaps even trying to suture the severed muscles, but being crippled for life was the least of Murdoch of Carthane's worries today.

He regained consciousness at about the time they finished what little they could do for him medically, as they washed the last of the blood and dirt from his mangled body and gently clothed him in a cool white robe that, all too soon, would become his shroud. He had known it, and they had known it, but they had gone through the motions nonetheless—as if anyone could do anything other than to prolong his agony. The pain in his gut was still agonizing, a burning that never abated but only shifted intensity, but at least his reason was not blurred by drugs. He had never been one to shirk his duty as he saw it, and there was much he still must say to those gathered around him.

He pressed his less injured left arm hard against the bandages binding his belly and signalled Rhun with his eyes.

"Help me to sit up," he whispered, gasping as Rhun obeyed, bruising his benefactor with the strength of his grip as his fingers dug into the other's forearm.

Richard, his son and heir, helped arrange pillows behind his sire's back, assisted by his ashen-faced young wife. Cashel, Murdoch's younger son, also came near. Archbishop Hubert had given the wounded man the Sacrament before they began working on him and stood resignedly behind the *Custodes* battle surgeon. The Church and the *coup de grace* had reached an understanding long ago.

"Now listen to me, all of you," Murdoch demanded, his breathing quick and labored from the pain. "Our headstrong boy-king has got the bit between his teeth. I warned you there would be trouble, but you spinelessly let him take the crown."

"Could Rhys Michael have stopped Hrorik from making the challenge?" Richard demanded. "I very much doubt it."

"A different king might have been induced to forbid the challenge," Murdoch retorted. "Javan has always hated me, since those first days of the regency. And after the deaths of Duke Ewan and the Deryni Carmody, it was clear that his hatred had found a focus."

"Would that such hatred might focus on the Deryni," Hubert muttered. "And now, to have taken Oriel directly to his service—"

"That can be remedied, in time," Rhun observed. "Perhaps it's time we eliminated all Deryni at Court—and I say that as one who has a Deryni still usefully in my employ, though I would slay him

with my own hand if I thought it was in the kingdom's best interests. But Sitric knows his place. *He* would not have dared to refuse
his services the way Oriel did."

Murdoch snorted, wincing at the pain it cost him. "Do you really think I would have let him lay a finger on me?" he said contemptuously. "The very touch of a Deryni is defiling! No, you have
the right of it. 'Tis time, indeed, that the taint was removed from
Court."

"Such action will require extensive changes to the law," Hubert
pointed out. "We went to considerable trouble to justify the use of
collaborators in the first place. Rhun, you're free to do with your
own Deryni as you see fit—have him strangled in his bed, if it suits
you—but I no longer have that option where Oriel is concerned.
Their families, of course, are another matter."

Richard's young wife froze. "You surely don't mean to butcher
their families," she whispered in a rare show of spirit.

"That doesn't concern you, Lirin," Richard snapped. "Archbishop, are you suggesting that we simply do away with all Deryni
collaborators, even the Healers?"

"We have few Healers left anyway," Hubert muttered. "And
Oriel was the least controversial. We did without Healers in the
past and we can do without them in the future."

Murdoch grimaced as he tried to find a more comfortable position, gasping as the movement sent pain shooting through his body.

"I would advise that you tread very cautiously," he whispered,
motioning for his wife to remove one of his pillows. "Remember
the example of Declan Carmody. Not all of them will go docilely
to their fate." He closed his eyes and shook his head, letting out a
heavy sigh.

"Forgive me, I can bear no more. You who remain must decide
what is to be done about the king, because you must bear the consequences. Would that I might remain with you to carry on the
fight, but Hrorik has decreed otherwise." He grimaced against new
pain, then turned his gaze to the court physician.

"Please take the women out of here, Master James," he said
evenly. "This will not require their witness."

"No," Elaine whispered. "I want to stay."

"Not this time, my heart," he rasped, shaking his head. "Take
Lirin and go. You, too, Archbishop, though I ask your final blessing.
Only my sons and my friend Rhun and this good surgeon shall stay.
Fear not. I shall be brief."

Weeping quietly, Elaine laid her arms around the shoulders of
the stunned Lirin and let the court physician lead them out of the

room. Hubert, after bowing his head briefly in a final prayer for the man about to die, signed him with the Cross and then turned to follow. As the door closed behind them, the battle surgeon was already straightening Murdoch's left arm at his side, looping a length of leather thong around it above the elbow and tightening it down.

"A moment," Murdoch rasped, setting his free hand atop the surgeon's to stay what he was doing.

The movement hurt him, and he groaned against the pain.

"Rest easy, my lord," the surgeon said in a low voice, catching the hand and bidding Rhun take it. "You need not bear this any longer. Soon there will be no more pain, I promise you."

"It isn't that," Murdoch gasped, shaking his head. "I do not fear death. Nor do I question your skill, good brother, but I—would have my friend's hand release me."

Rhun stiffened, and Murdoch's sons both glanced at one another helplessly.

"Murdoch—" Rhun began.

"No, hear me," Murdoch said, his voice tight and hoarsened by pain. "A stranger's hand gives but cold comfort—I mean you no offense, Brother Surgeon. My sons I cannot ask. But no one will question if you act for me in this. Will you do it?"

Rhun's lean face was oddly lit by emotion rarely shown.

"We have faced many battles, old friend," he whispered. "In heat of combat is one thing, even friend to friend—steel to throat, when speed must propel the hand of mercy, but—"

"My lord, we have a gentler way," the surgeon said quietly. "If Lord Murdoch permits, I will guide you."

Murdoch's eyes closed in relief. "It is agreeable to me, if my friend finds it so. Forgive me, Rhun, for laying this burden upon you."

"I forgive you," the other whispered.

After several taut heartbeats of silence, Rhun tore his gaze from the face of his friend and glanced at the surgeon, who had upturned the arm he had bound and was fingering at the bulge of the veins, first at the elbow and then at the top of the wrist.

"Rest you easy, my lord," the surgeon murmured to Murdoch, stroking the arm as he passed a sharp scalpel across to Rhun, shielded behind his hand so Murdoch would not see it. "You have already lost a great deal of blood. This will be very quick. You need not fear."

★ ★ ★

When it was over, Rhun lingered to compose himself while the battle surgeon and Murdoch's sons made the body seemly to look upon, for the sake of the women waiting outside. He left when the women were admitted, not daring to meet their eyes as he passed, retiring to an adjoining room where Hubert had withdrawn. Paulin and Albertus had joined the archbishop while he waited, and the three clerics crossed themselves dutifully as Rhun entered the room. His expression left no doubt as to Murdoch's passing.

"A grim business, Lord Rhun," Paulin murmured as the earl pulled out a chair beside the table and folded into it, gratefully accepting a cup of wine Albertus offered him. "Unfortunately, such things are sometimes necessary."

Rhun tossed off the wine and held out his cup for more.

"He requested my hand rather than the surgeon's," he said quietly, rubbing at his eyes. "I have—often performed the office in the field, but never—like this. This was—a gentle mercy, but—too calculated." He took another deep pull from the cup. "I would rather not speak of it further."

Hubert turned away, retreating to a nearby window to stare out at the afternoon sun, and Paulin sat down opposite Rhun.

"What will you do now?" he asked gently.

Rhun set down his cup and sighed. "Go back to Carthane with Richard. He's shattered, as you can well imagine. Taking on all of his father's responsibilities so young will not be easy. I've offered to travel with the family and help with the burial arrangements—and after."

"When will you leave?"

"Sometime tomorrow. With his temper, he'll not want to risk staying long in Rhemuth until his anger has cooled. The summer heat puts further urgency upon matters." He closed his eyes and shook his head briefly. "I don't want to think about it. I do intend to insist that he delay long enough to present himself before the king, to be confirmed in his titles. Given the king's acquiescence in what almost amounted to judicial murder, young Richard will not find this an easy task, but I shall do my utmost to ensure that he says and does nothing that might jeopardize his confirmation. Time enough, later on, for thoughts of vengeance."

Paulin nodded. Hubert had come back over while Rhun spoke, and exchanged a guarded glance with the *Custodes* Vicar General as he eased himself into another chair beside him.

"I shall keep in mind the new Earl of Carthane's desire for vengeance," Paulin said carefully. "May I assume that Rhun of Horthness also harbors a—resentment of what has taken place?"

"We'll speak more of it when I return from Carthane," Rhun said. "But, yes, I think you could certainly say that both Richard and I harbor a 'resentment.' "

They said nothing as he stood to take his leave, but when he had gone, Paulin glanced meaningfully at his two associates.

"Thank God that man is an ally," he said.

"Aye, thank God," Hubert replied. He glanced at the amethyst on his hand, then back at Paulin. "And what of you? Will you still go back to *Arx Fidei*, as was your intention before this Murdoch thing came up?"

Paulin allowed himself a scowl. "My Inquisitor General still is dead, my lord. We should have left this morning to take him home for burial." He worried at a hangnail on one long thumb, then eyed Hubert again. "Have you thought any more about what we discussed the other day, concerning Serafin's death?"

Hubert shot him a sour look, a frown furrowing the smooth skin between the baby-blue eyes. "When did I have time?" he replied. "And what does Lior say? You said he was with Serafin when it happened."

"Yes, he was. And I've since recalled that I thought he and Father Lior intended to visit Father Faelan that night. Lior never mentioned it, though."

"Faelan," Hubert said thoughtfully. "Well, I'm sure you aren't going to find that *he* had any part in Serafin's death. It still escapes me why the king wanted him in the first place. Have you asked him about it? Serafin, I mean."

Paulin shook his head. "Not yet, but it can wait. It's only a few weeks until Faelan is due for his monthly debriefing. Meanwhile, I'll question Lior further. He may remember more than he thinks he does."

Hubert heaved a heavy sigh and lumbered to his feet. "Well, I wish you well of it—though I still think you're grasping for straws. If I could, I'd lend you Oriel. Unfortunately, the king has taken that option out of my hands.

"But you must pardon me now. Pastoral duties call. The bereaved family will wish a Mass said for the repose of Murdoch's soul."

CHAPTER TWENTY-SIX

*Go not after thy lusts, but refrain thyself from
thine appetites.*

—Ecclesiasticus 18:30

Word came to Javan that evening that Murdoch was dead.

"It's done," Guiscard said, reporting to the king shortly after
dark. "Apparently he asked Rhun to do the actual deed. Hrorik is
resting comfortably—exhausted, of course, and he lost a fair amount
of blood from his combined wounds, but he'll be fine. Oriel's been
to see him."

Javan nodded slowly. He was sitting in the window of his presence chamber in a lightweight linen tunic, bare-legged, Charlan silent across from him. The night was sultry and still—not a good
night for dying, or for being the instrument of someone's death,
even that of an enemy.

"I wish I could say I regretted Murdoch's death," he said after a
moment. "But I honestly believe that justice was done, and seen to
be done. A Higher justice—not mine." He sighed heavily. "It still
gives me great personal satisfaction to know he's dead." He sighed
again. "Did he—die well, do you know?"

"I really couldn't say," Guiscard said. "I'm told that he received
the Sacraments from Archbishop Hubert. I believe his sons were
present at the end. All things considered, his passing was probably
far gentler than he deserved."

The hard note in Guiscard's voice caused Javan to look up
sharply, somewhat relieved to know that he was not the only one
who did not mourn Murdoch's passing. When the Deryni turned

away, moving back into the room to lean both hands on the trestle table, Javan got slowly to his feet.

"So, what are the first repercussions we'll have to weather?" he asked, coming to pour wine for Guiscard and pushing the cup across the table to him. "How is Richard taking it?"

Guiscard took a long pull from the cup before sinking down in the nearest chair, for once unmindful of the protocol that should have kept him standing until the king sat.

"Richard has asked that you receive him formally as the new Earl of Carthane in the morning, after which he requests leave to take his father home to Carthane for burial," he said wearily, rubbing at his eyes. "I believe Rhun intends to accompany him, to assist with the practicalities of the funeral and assumption of local governance."

Nodding, Javan wearily turned back toward the window embrasure, where it was cooler. Charlan had risen when the king did and remained leaning against the window's center mullion, arms crossed on his chest, quietly listening.

"I can't refuse, of course," Javan said, sinking back down on the bottom step of the embrasure. "He's done nothing to merit attainder. It's no crime to loathe the man you believe responsible for your father's death. I don't much like him, either, if only because he's his father's son.

"If the loathing turns to treason, that's another matter; but until and unless he demonstrates treachery, the law says there's nothing I can do to him. So I suppose, for now, we play out our designated roles as king and new liege man. He may go to Carthane, and good riddance; and I will acknowledge him in his title before he leaves."

Guiscard gave him a little nod. "Shall I so inform him, Sire?" he asked. "He will not be abed yet."

"Please do so," Javan replied. "Say that I shall be pleased to convene Court after Mass in the morning and that his petition will be favorably received at that time." His expression hardened as he gazed out the window at the sleeping city, and he glanced back at Guiscard.

"Tell him also," the king went on, "that I shall brook no continuation of the quarrel that led to his father's demise. So far as I am concerned, the matter is closed. If he insists on keeping old wounds open, I cannot answer for the consequences."

"Words that strong, Sire?" Guiscard asked, as Charlan also looked at him askance.

Javan allowed himself a grim, wolfish smile. "I must assert myself, gentlemen. Murdoch's death will have provided a rallying point for some of my enemies. I must pray that strength and justice will provide a rallying point for those who would be my friends."

If Javan had hoped for an immediate sign of some such polarization in his behalf, he was doomed to disappointment. His supporters were there in full force the next morning to witness the new Earl of Carthane's reception, but they were fewer in numbers and in political weight than those who had sided with the departed Murdoch.

Nor was the Court gala or at all glittering, despite the recency of a coronation—other than Prince Miklos, quietly resplendent in his tawny eastern silks. The heat was partially to blame, but most folk of either political persuasion instinctively chose quiet attire for a Court of such potential explosiveness—for no one really knew what Richard Murdoch planned by way of any public statement about his father's death. Nor did they know what further action might be taken by the king.

Out of deference for the feelings of the women of Murdoch's family, even Javan returned to the semimourning he had worn before his coronation—a deep-grey tunic, open at the throat, relieved only by the belt of silver plaques that carried the Haldane sword. Since this morning also was very much an official function, he also wore the State Crown of crosses and leaves intertwined, with the Ring of Fire on his hand.

He convened Court in the great hall this time, for the recognition of an earl—especially this earl—was of sufficient gravity to attract observers who otherwise might not make the effort to attend. Archbishop Hubert stood at his right as witness for the Church, with Father Faelan holding the Book on which the oaths must be sealed. Rhys Michael sat on Javan's immediate left, with Charlan just beyond him. Oriel again stood behind the king, since Prince Miklos was present, but he looked uneasy at having to be so near Hubert, and did not appear to have slept well.

Mercifully, or perhaps ominously, the *Custodes Fidei* were but little in evidence, Paulin and his party having left Rhemuth at first light to escort the body of Brother Serafin back to *Arx Fidei* for burial. Albertus had remained, since the Earl Marshal's presence was desirable for witness of Richard's oath, but Guiscard had told Javan that the *Custodes* Grand Master was expected to ride out immediately after court to catch up with his *Custodes* brethren.

Into a hall already taut with suspicions and uncertainty came Richard and his wife, his younger brother, and his widowed mother, all in deepest mourning, along with the various other members of Court who had supported Murdoch. Some there were among Javan's supporters who feared that Richard might even refuse to put his hands between those of the king and swear him fealty; but Richard was too canny for that. Whatever plans he might be hatching for revenge could be engineered far more easily by the lawfully recognized Earl of Carthane. And whatever resentment he harbored for this particular King of Gwynedd, he had respect for the royal office and for the grave responsibilities he assumed with his father's title as earl.

"I, Richard, Earl of Carthane, do become your liege man of life and limb," he said softly but distinctly, with his joined hands clasped firmly between Javan's. "Faith and trust will I bear unto you, in living and dying, against all manner of folk, so help me God."

He was not lying—which only meant that, as yet, Richard Murdoch had not formed any conscious or certain intention to betray the oath he had just given to his young king.

Nonetheless, Javan detected a note of uneasiness underlying the words, which continued to reverberate as he repeated his own affirmation of the oath, learned by rote for the coronation two days previous and rehearsed so many times that day.

"This do I hear, Richard of Carthane. I, for my part, pledge the protection of Gwynedd to you and all your people, to protect and defend you against every creature with all my power. This is the word of Javan Jashan Urien Haldane, King of Gwynedd and Kheldour, Lord of Meara and Mooryn and the Purple March, Overlord of Carthane. So help me God."

He bent to kiss the Book when he had released Richard's hands, and Richard followed suit, but Javan wondered, as the new earl was invested with the other symbols of his office—the coronet, the golden belt, the sword, the banner, the cauldron—how long either of them would be able to keep the oaths they had just sworn. Carthane lay to the south, in the angle formed by the Lendour River and the great estuary that extended up from the Southern Sea. Nyford, its principal city, had already been the scene of anti-Deryni riots and purges in the past decade. Would Richard be able to hold against that kind of pressure? Would he even try?

These were questions not readily answerable, and Richard and his party did not tarry for further exploration of such questions. As soon as the barest courtesies had been exchanged, Richard took his leave and departed the hall, his supporters following to see him off. Very shortly, while Javan moved informally among those remaining

in the hall in the aftermath of the morning's business, Guiscard
came to tell him that Rhun had ridden out with Richard's party.
Sitric had gone with them, Rhun perhaps fearing that the king
would steal him as he had stolen Oriel. Javan could not say he
would miss any of them. Sitric gone left one less danger at Court.

He prepared to quit the hall, intending to retire for the hottest
part of the day and relax for an hour before plunging back into
business with a Council meeting that afternoon. Charlan was with
him. Guiscard had gone to see where Oriel had gotten to, for Prince
Miklos was heading in Javan's direction. With Etienne prudently
keeping his distance, Javan was on his own for this encounter with
the Deryni prince.

"My good Lord Javan," Miklos said, making the king a graceful
gesture of deference. His young aide accompanied him, quiet and
solemn in dark brown shot through with gold, but with dark eyes
that missed little.

"In light of what has happened these last few days, I think it
best I take my leave of you as well," Miklos said. "I do regret
having been the catalyst for so unfortunate a set of circumstances
as has marred your coronation festivities, and hope that you will
bear no enmity toward me or toward my sovereign liege. My brother
Arion desires only peace between our two Houses."

"That is my wish as well, my lord," Javan replied.

"It is the wish of all men of goodwill," Miklos agreed. "But I
trust that your Highness will agree that inquiries needed to be made
regarding the fate of Lord Kennet and Lady Sudrey." He cocked his
head wistfully. "Might it be possible to see the Earl Hrorik before
I leave? A firsthand assurance from Lady Sudrey's husband would
do much to alleviate my brother's concern for the well-being of our
kinswoman."

Javan eyed the Torenthi prince appraisingly. He wondered at the
continued interest in Sudrey and her Kheldour connections, and
decided then and there that the Deryni prince was not going to see
Hrorik again. The earl's debilitation from the day before would
make him more than ordinarily vulnerable, if Miklos had some
Deryni trickery in mind.

"It is my impression that Lord Hrorik's physicians have prescribed complete rest for several days, my lord," Javan said, careful
to keep every word literally true. "I do not believe that visitors are
recommended."

"Indeed," Miklos replied. "I had been led to believe that his
injuries were not of a serious nature. If your Healer needs assistance—"

"I am assured that Master Oriel has Lord Hrorik's condition well in hand, my lord," Javan replied with a smile, brushing off what appeared to be a second attempt on Miklos' part to get at Hrorik. "Exhaustion and a substantial loss of blood from his wounds make it advisable that the earl spend several days resting quietly, building up his strength again, but at no time were his injuries life-threatening. No assistance is required."

Miklos made a gesture of disavowal with both hands. "Forgive me, Sire. I meant no belittling of your Healer's skills. I merely hoped that, if you had no objection, I might ask the Earl Hrorik to convey my respects to his lady wife and request that she send reassurance to her kinsmen of Torenth, that we might be persuaded of her safety and happiness."

Javan sighed. If he had thought that the tension occasioned by Hrorik's confrontation with Murdoch had ended on the combat field the day before, or even at Court earlier today, he obviously was mistaken. Again he wondered why the sudden interest in Lady Sudrey, who had not been heard from in fifteen years.

"I can appreciate your concern, my lord. I shall certainly so inform Lord Hrorik and ask that he convey your Highness' respects to his lady. Whether it is appropriate for her to respond is for her and her husband to decide. I do feel reasonably confident, however, that Hrorik would permit his lady to receive letters from her kinsmen."

"The situation *is* delicate, is it not, my lord?" Miklos said with a sympathetic sigh.

Javan allowed himself a cautious nod. "As you yourself observed, my lord, this situation is none of our making—not mine and not King Arion's. Hence, the untangling of it must be by those most actively involved in it. If the Lady Sudrey wishes to communicate with her Torenthi kin, I have no objection; nor will I force her to do so, if she does not wish it. I trust that this is acceptable to you, sir?"

Miklos gave him a little bow that mostly shielded an almost feral smile. "I thank you, my lord. It is acceptable," he murmured. "I shall so inform my brother and see that the appropriate letters are sent. To that end, and well knowing the sorts of business that require attention after a coronation, I beg to take respectful leave of your Highness. My men have made the appropriate arrangements, and a ship awaits us at Desse."

"At Desse?" Javan said, almost without thinking.

Smiling, Miklos gave him another little bow. "We came by ship, your Highness," he said softly. "At this time of year, it is by far the most comfortable way to travel. We are to call at Fianna and several other of the Forcinn States on our way home."

What he did not say, nor did Javan, was that going by ship via Desse would take him all along most of the long coast of Carthane, where a young earl with good reason to hold a grudge against his new king was even now taking his father home for burial. If the Torenthi prince's ship called at Nyford before continuing around the long horn of Carthmoor, what thing more natural than to visit with the local nobility—and perhaps fuel resentment that might eventually be to the advantage of Torenthi interests?

But there was nothing Javan could do to stop him. Even were Miklos of Torenth not Deryni, he was a king's brother, protected by the protocols of guestship, royal envoy of a sovereign prince with whom Javan was not at war. So as gracefully as possible, he gave Miklos leave to go, bearing messages of felicitation to the king his brother, and brooded on what the future might make of this day as he headed back into the castle after bidding the prince farewell in the castle yard.

As an afterthought, he dispatched Robear and Gavin to ride on to Nyford by a different route, carrying official warrants to observe and report back on the status of Haldane ships in that port, so that at least he would know if Miklos stopped there.

By the end of that week, Robear was able to report back that the Torenthi contingent apparently had made ship in Desse and sailed on without the feared diversion to Nyford. Local gossip also had it that Lord Murdoch of Carthane had been properly buried and his family had gone into seclusion. Rhun was believed still to be with them, and Sitric as well.

Meanwhile, most of the rest of Javan's coronation visitors wound up their business and also departed from Court. The day after Robear's return, even Hrorik was strong enough to head home with Duke Graham and Earl Sighere, taking their border retinue with them and eliciting sighs of relief from more than just Javan.

One thing Javan did at once, the very evening he sent Robear on his mission, was to take immediate measures for Oriel's continued safety. Knowing how ruthless Hubert could be, he did not fully trust that the archbishop would meekly allow the poaching of "his" Deryni without a fight.

To reduce the temptation to drastic action, Javan moved the Healer into quarters adjacent to the loyal Sir Sorle, who was not afraid of Oriel, and gave that knight the full-time responsibility for

Oriel's physical safety. He also bade Oriel keep himself well out of the public eye, to further avoid putting himself in a situation where one of the king's enemies might decide to simply eliminate the potential problem of the king now being the sole possessor of a Deryni in his employ—at least until Rhun brought Sitric back.

That week also saw the relocation of Etienne de Courcy into the newly restored room next to the library, ostensibly to be nearer the growing collection of books and manuscripts being assembled there, but also to become guardian of Javan's new Portal. The king had no opportunity to use it himself during those first days after his coronation, but he had Etienne go through and make a full report to Joram and the others concerning what had happened at it and immediately after. Henceforth, Etienne became the regular go-between to keep Javan's Deryni allies apprised of developments.

The departures of many of the great lords from Court left the king with a core of working advisors, some dependable and some not, and the breathing space to begin exploring some of the legislation he hoped to present when the Court reconvened at Christmas. With Manfred set to leave at the end of the month for his customary autumn visit to his lands in Culdi, only Tammaron and Hubert would remain of those formerly serving as regents—at least until Rhun returned. The temporary respite lulled him into a false sense of growing security, so that he was largely unprepared when an old danger suddenly re-emerged.

The day had been long and warm, but the heat was beginning to break. Dusk had brought sufficient relief that some dared to hope that summer was nearly done, though a full month yet remained until the autumn equinox. It was already quite late when Javan at last sought his bed, but sleep eluded him despite the respite in temperature.

After half an hour of staring at the canopy of his bed, he decided that a moonlight walk in the gardens might be just the distraction to lull his busy thoughts and turn his mind toward sleep. Pulling on a light night robe, he moved across a slash of moonlight to open the door to the next room, eschewing footgear, for he planned to dabble his feet in the garden's fountain.

Guiscard had already retired to the new quarters he and Charlan shared, across the corridor from the royal apartments, but Charlan was stretched out on a pallet near the door, since he was duty aide for the night. Javan was reluctant to rouse him, even though that was what Charlan was there for, but he knew it was not wise to go out unaccompanied, especially unarmed and vulnerable without his special boot. He cleared his throat to give Charlan slight warning before bending down to touch his shoulder, but Charlan was already shifting onto his elbows to look up.

"What is it, Sire?" he murmured.

"Nothing's wrong," Javan reassured him. "I can't sleep, is all. Sorry to wake you, but I thought a walk in the garden might help me unwind. I knew you'd be far more annoyed if I *didn't* wake you."

Charlan grinned and swung his feet under him to get up.

"It's no annoyance," he said amiably, catching up the sword ready beside him. "It's my job to be available when you need me." He had been sleeping fully dressed, and paused only to belt on the sword before following Javan toward the door.

Going slowly to allow for Javan's foot, they made their way down a back stair and headed along the garden colonnade. The stone was cool underfoot, and as Javan came to the arched entryway to the garden, he trod cautiously on the soft grass that skirted the gravel paths, careful for stones. Charlan hung back to give him privacy yet stayed close enough to still be within call.

The moon was near full, so that by its light Javan was easily able to find his way toward the center of the garden, as he headed toward the fountain with the lady. The perfume of jasmine and roses was on the air, reminding Javan of the last time he had come here. When he came to the fountain, he sat on the wide edge and swung his right foot up and over, into the water, then lay back flat on his back and folded his arms across his chest while he gazed upward past the sparkling stream flowing from over the lady's shoulder, wistfully trying to fathom the face that was not a face.

Gradually his thoughts drifted to more carefree days, when he and his brothers had played in these gardens and the burdens of ruling had lain on other's shoulders. He had thought to contemplate such remembered pleasures that other time, when Paulin's intrusion had jolted him so rudely to more serious considerations. At least tonight, he had found the peacefulness and seclusion denied him that day.

He sighed and stretched out his right hand to trail in the cool water, willing his thoughts to float and tumble with the stream pouring from the lady's ewer, not minding that his sleeve trailed in the water as well. Gradually he could feel himself starting to unwind, the tension draining out of his shoulders and neck. After a few minutes he closed his eyes, for the peaceful bubbling of the falling water was beginning to make him drowsy—which was what he had hoped would happen.

Yawning, he stretched his arms expansively to either side, arching against the stone beneath his back, and thought seriously about going back upstairs. Or perhaps he would wade in the fountain, as he had done as a boy. But as he rose up to a sitting position, still straddling the side of the fountain, and glanced idly behind him to see where Charlan had gotten to, he became suddenly aware that the whisper of falling water was briefly overlaid with a soft burst of girlish laughter, punctuated by a quick series of shushing noises and then more smothered giggling.

The sound froze him in his place, head turning to catch the sound suddenly gone to silence. Romantic assignations were common enough in the castle gardens, especially in summertime, when lovers sought relief from the heat, but something in what Javan had just heard made his blood momentarily run cold. Casting out with his senses, quickly focusing deeper into the garden, he soon located the source of his dismay—and launched himself from his fountain perch to charge along the path heading in that direction, heedless of the gravel underfoot. Charlan was right behind him and quickly gaining, sword halfway out of its scabbard.

He got to them in time—or at least he prayed it was in time. In the bright moonlight, he caught just a glimpse of ivory flesh and pert little breasts as Michaela Drummond struggled to a sitting position and half turned away from his shocked gaze, her rosy lips a taut O of surprise as she hurriedly tugged her bodice back into place, tawny hair tumbled loose and wild over her shoulders.

And emerging from amid a tangle of her skirts was Rhys Michael, his tunic ruched up bare legs nearly to his waist, looking as shocked and frightened as Javan had ever seen him.

CHAPTER TWENTY-SEVEN

A brother offended is harder to be won than a strong city.

—Proverbs 18:19

Neither Rhys Michael nor Michaela made a sound, but from behind Javan, Charlan's choked gasp said enough for all of them.

"And just *what* do you think you're doing?" Javan demanded, setting his hands on his hips.

Rhys Michael drew a deep breath, then scrambled boldly to his knees and began tugging his tunic into place with a nonchalance that bordered on arrogance. At the same time he managed to shield Michaela, who was peering fearfully around him at Javan from behind the curtain of her hair. Somehow, even with bare legs still gleaming from beneath his tunic as he got one foot under him, Rhys Michael managed to convey a reasonable sense of dignity.

"I should have thought it was very clear what I was doing," he murmured, insolence turning his voice to silk as his eyes met Javan's. "But then, I don't suppose monks are taught such things in the monastery, are they? A proper man—"

Before Javan could stop himself, he had taken one step forward and backhanded his brother across the mouth with such force that Rhys Michael tumbled over sideways. Michaela let out a little squeak and shrank back as Javan turned on her, grey Haldane eyes blazing, but Charlan was beside him by then, catching at his sleeve in alarm.

"Sire, no!"

Forcing himself to breathe deeply, Javan shook off Charlan's hand and drew himself erect, shifting his gaze to his brother as Rhys Michael cautiously raised his head.

"Sir Charlan," Javan said softly, "please escort his Highness to my quarters and wait for me there. You're to use him kindly, but he *will* go with you. Do you understand?"

"Aye, my liege," Charlan murmured, wide-eyed.

"And you," Javan said, turning his gaze on his brother, who was nursing a trickle of blood at one corner of his mouth. "Do *you* understand?"

Sullenly Rhys Michael gave a nod, casting a fearful glance at the cowering Michaela. "Don't hurt her," he said. "It isn't her fault."

Javan gave his brother a look of utter disdain as Charlan came to offer him a hand up. "If you think I would lay violent hands on a woman, you truly do not know me," he said coldly. "Go now. I'll join you both directly."

He waited until Charlan and Rhys Michael had disappeared from sight, the latter casting repeated anxious looks over his shoulder as they went, then moved closer to Michaela. She and Rhys Michael had been lying on a dark cloak spread on the grass, and she pulled it around herself as he approached, shrinking back when he would have helped her to her feet.

"Don't touch me," she murmured. "I want no hand of any kind laid upon me by you."

"Mika, I'm sorry," he said, reverting to her childhood nickname. "I knew he was fond of you. I didn't know it had progressed to this point."

"Obviously not. And don't call me Mika. Rhysem was right. What does a monk know about love?"

Eyes closing briefly, Javan made himself draw a calming breath. The possibility of having to deal with this eventuality had been upon him for several weeks now, but he had hoped to postpone it until the winter, especially knowing that Manfred would soon be off to Culdi. He had kept an eye on his brother whenever Michaela was in the vicinity, but if Rhys Michael had been continuing to press his suit since the coronation, he had been remarkably discreet—up until now. And did his brother *really* think that Javan knew nothing about such things?

"You're right," he said quietly. "I know nothing about it. But I'm afraid I'm going to have to forbid you and Rhysem to learn anything else about it either, at least for now. He's too young to marry yet, Mika—Michaela," he added, at her glare of anger.

"Believe me, he isn't too young," she muttered under her breath. "If you hadn't come along—"

"Yes, I can quite imagine what would have happened if I hadn't come along," Javan said. "Thank God I did. You don't understand what else is at stake here."

"I understand that you're jealous of what you don't have," she said bitterly. "You couldn't even give us tonight. Two days hence, my guardian takes his household to his country estate and I'll be gone for *months*."

As she bit back a sob, Javan grimaced, feeling like an ogre. Of all the girls he might have chosen for his brother to love and wed— eventually—Michaela Drummond was probably at the very top of the list. But at least with her about to leave Court in a few days, that removed this particular threat—for the present. All he had to do was keep the two of them apart until then.

"Your leaving Court is probably the best possible resolution any- one could recommend in this situation," he agreed. "God knows, it's nothing against you personally, but I can't allow Rhysem to get involved with anyone just yet. Maybe in a year or two—"

She snorted and drew herself up taller, tossing the tawny hair back onto her shoulders, her cloak clutched around her like a queen's mantle. "A year or two from now, we could all be dead! But you're the king. You have the power to forbid our love."

"That's right, I do," Javan said quietly. "And I have the power of life and death, too. So you'd best go back to your quarters now. Promise that you won't cause trouble, these last few days you're here—that you won't see Rhysem alone—and I won't tell Manfred or Lady Estellan about this."

Michaela dropped her gaze petulantly. "All right," she agreed. "Can—can I ask one favor?"

"Of course. And I'll grant it, if it be not to the harm of my kingdom."

She sighed and dared to glance up at him again. "You—you won't hurt him, will you?"

Rolling his eyes heavenward, Javan had to grin. "Mika, he's my brother. Of course I'm not going to hurt him."

A little while later, as he faced an angry Rhys Michael across the table in his presence chamber, Javan wondered whether he was going to be able to keep that promise.

"You're just jealous!" Rhys Michael shouted. "You've got what *you* wanted. You've got the crown. Can't you let me have what *I* want?"

"Sit down," Javan said, sending to Guiscard to enforce the order if Rhys Michael did not obey. The Deryni lord was standing directly behind Rhys Michael's chair, summoned by Charlan when he brought the prince back to Javan's quarters. Charlan himself had taken up a post with his back against the door, to listen for any approach from outside. Fortunately, the walls in this part of the castle were very thick, but if the prince kept shouting, someone was sure to raise an alarm.

"*Sit down,*" Javan repeated. "I will not ask a third time."

To Javan's intense relief, his brother did sit without Guiscard having to lay a hand on him. Javan was trembling inside as he, too, sat, but he made himself lay his hands quietly on the chair arms to either side of him, leaning back slightly in the cushions.

"Now, suppose you explain."

"What is there to explain?" Rhys Michael muttered after a taut few seconds. "We *will* marry eventually. You can't stop us. We're both of age and we're betrothed."

"You're *what?*"

"I said that we're betrothed," Rhys Michael repeated, raising his chin defiantly. "There's nothing you can do about it. A betrothal is legally binding. You can keep us apart, but you can't force either of us to marry anyone else."

"It isn't a matter of *forcing* you to marry *anyone,*" Javan retorted. "Don't you understand? I can't *let* you marry anyone. Not for a very long time. Who witnessed the betrothal?"

"I won't tell you."

"Was it Hubert?"

"No."

"Oriss?"

"No. And that's all I'm going to say."

"Well, it doesn't matter anyway," Javan said. "I'll get it dispensed."

"The way you had your vows dispensed? Oh, no. You can have your own vows dispensed if you want to, but not mine. Mika and I made vows before God. I'm *going* to marry her!"

"And I forbid it!"

"Oh? And what will you do if I defy you? Disinherit me? Lock me away? Until you decide to marry and get an heir of your own, Javan, I'm all you've got!"

"I could lock *her* away."

"You wouldn't dare. She's done nothing wrong. Besides, Lord Manfred would never stand for it."

"Then I'll *send* her away," Javan retorted. "Come to think of it, Manfred's already doing that for me. Thank God for *that!*"

Rhys Michael glanced down in utter frustration at his hands clasped tightly together in his lap. "They told me this would be your reaction," he murmured. "It's only for a few months, though. She'll be back at Christmas."

"Then at Christmas we'll talk about this again," Javan replied. "And *who* told you this would be my reaction? Hubert? Manfred?"

Rhys Michael shook his head, but Javan knew he was lying. He had been Truth-Reading since the start of their interview, but delving beyond that was impossible with Rhys Michael's shields.

"It has to have been Hubert, at least in part," Javan said. "He's probably the one who put it in your head in the first place. Am I right? When did it happen?"

Rhys Michael only stared down at his folded hands, suddenly gone sullen.

"Well, it doesn't really matter," Javan said, "because you can't convert it to marriage without the banns being read—and I won't countenance that. Not right now, at any rate." He studied his brother for a long moment, then drew a deep breath.

"All right. There's the matter now of what to do with you. Give me your word that there'll be no more of these illicit meetings with Michaela between now and when she leaves—that you'll not see her alone—and I'll try to forget we've had this conversation."

"You'd like that, wouldn't you?" Rhys Michael muttered sullenly. "What if I won't agree?"

"Well, I suppose I could lock you in a dungeon for a few days to cool off," Javan said breezily. "That could prove embarrassing for both of us, but I'd do it, if I thought it was best for the kingdom."

Rhys Michael snorted. "It might prove more than embarrassing," he said. "I have friends, too, you know."

"Yes, I do know. Another option is for you to go on a colossal drunk for a few days, thus rendering you incommunicado. I understand that this is not nearly as much out of character as it once was. In fact, I fear that no one would even remark on it. I'll concede that, under the circumstances, you probably wouldn't be nearly as enthusiastic about drinking yourself into oblivion as you have been in the past, but believe me, your intake can be assured by force, if you insist."

"I don't drink that much," Rhys Michael murmured.

"I hope I'm wrong, then," Javan replied. "My third option is for you to become ill for a few days. I can arrange that, too," he added as his brother looked up in shock. "There are drugs, so much more subtle than what the physicians were giving Alroy, that would cause such a raging fever that you probably wouldn't even remember any of this conversation we're having. Shall I summon Master Oriel to explain in further detail?"

"You're threatening me," Rhys Michael whispered. "You're actually threatening me—your own brother and heir. You wouldn't really do that, would you?"

At Javan's minute signal, Guiscard dropped his hands heavily on Rhys Michael's shoulders. The prince started around in alarm, craning his neck to look back and up, but Guiscard's face was impassive. Javan knew that the Deryni was poised to punch through any gap in his brother's shields, but the shields apparently held. Rhys Michael seemed unaware of any of this and was very subdued as he turned his face back toward Javan.

"You're actually serious about all of this, aren't you?" he whispered, like a little boy who suddenly realized he was not playing with other children but with adults. "Javan, I never meant—"

"Do you give me your word that you won't try to see her in these last few days before she leaves for Culdi?" Javan said, slowly standing at his place.

Rhys Michael was trembling under Guiscard's hands, but to Javan's surprise, he raised his chin and then very deliberately shook his head.

"I don't see why I should make you that promise," he said shakily.

Javan could feel the power stirring deep within him, along with cold fury that his brother should continue to defy him, and he had to consciously relax his fists, which had already begun to gather the strands of magic to lash out. Suddenly he understood the pressures that had led his father to use his power but a few times and then set it aside for the rest of his life.

Cinhil had had that option, being surrounded by powerful Deryni to protect him while he learned to deal with his enemies by the more conventional power of the crown, but Javan did not have that luxury. Caution was essential, for with very few exceptions, the men surrounding Javan while he learned those same lessons were not Deryni, and would surely destroy him if they learned he shared any part of a power like that wielded by the Deryni. Perhaps it was time to acquaint Rhys Michael with these realities. Having shields, he shared the danger, not only of being eliminated in favor of a younger heir.

"Given what I observed tonight in the garden," Javan said softly, "if I were to let you marry Michaela, she almost certainly would present you with an heir within a year or two. This could be all that our enemies need to justify eliminating both of us and to help themselves to a further fourteen years of regency. Since I seriously doubt that you would be willing to espouse the celibacy you seem to abhor so in me, I cannot permit you to marry Michaela or anyone else, because I cannot risk that another heir might be forthcoming before I am ready to deal with that complication. We *have* had this conversation before, you know. You just don't remember it."

Rhys Michael looked at him oddly. The abrupt shift from the argument he had been anticipating to a new topic altogether had set him slightly off balance, as Javan intended. Behind him, Guiscard was looking startled, clearly uncertain just what Javan was going to do.

"What are you talking about?" Rhys Michael whispered. "I didn't even know you knew about Michaela before tonight. I kept meaning to bring it up, but I never quite got around to it."

"Ah, but you did," Javan said. He came around the table to lean against the edge beside his brother's chair. "Don't you remember how you came to me a couple of nights before the coronation? We started on Rhennish brandywine and then moved on to a Fianna vintage."

Rhys Michael glanced away, wringing his hands together. "I drank too much. I had a splitting headache in the morning."

"That's true," Javan agreed. "But you also told me about wanting to marry Michaela. Oh, not in so many words, but it eventually came out. You—ah—did not mention the betrothal, which is why I reacted the way I did earlier."

Hanging his head, Rhys Michael murmured, "It hadn't happened yet. I was going to tell you, though. I knew you'd find out eventually."

"I did find out something else that night," Javan went on, sending to Guiscard to be ready. "I found out that you and I are more alike than I'd thought."

"I don't know what you're talking about."

"I know you don't. That's why I'm going to tell you about it. I don't know how much you remember about the night our father died, but something happened to both of us. Something magical. It had to do with Father's power as a king. It was supposed to awaken in Alroy first, but somehow it never did—maybe because the regents kept him drugged all those years.

"But it started to stir in me. It's been useful over the years, and it gets more useful all the time. For a long time, I was able to use it on you—to see if you were telling the truth, to help you go to sleep, sometimes to make you forget I'd done anything. It even helped me deal with the regents in those early years."

Rhys Michael had gone very rigid as Javan unfolded his confession, and he glanced uneasily at Guiscard's hands on his shoulders, suddenly reminded that he was held from retreat.

"What are you saying?" he whispered. "Do you have some kind of power, like your old Deryni friends?"

In answer, Javan let his shields flare around his head in a visible aura, a vaguely crimson glow of sparkling luminance. Rhys Michael recoiled at the sight, his face going white, and wilted under Guiscard's hands.

"No," he managed to whisper. "You aren't Deryni. You *can't* be Deryni. Because if *you're* Deryni—"

"You would be, too," Javan supplied. "But we're not." He conjured handfire in his right hand and held it out to Rhys Michael, a gently glowing sphere of crimson light. "Some of the powers are similar," he murmured, dispelling the light with a snap of his fingers. "Some of them are very subtle, such as being able to recognize whether a person is telling the truth. That was one of the first things I learned to do.

"But one of the most useful talents, especially in the beginning, is having shields the way the Deryni do. It means that no one can get into your mind to control you—not a Deryni and not someone who has powers like a Deryni."

Without warning, Javan set his right hand to his brother's forehead and surged his mind out across the bond of flesh to wash against the resistance of shields Rhys Michael had not known he had. Rhys Michael gasped and made a halfhearted attempt to twist from under Guiscard's grasp, but the Deryni held him steady for Javan's continued probe—physical restraint only, but not needing to do more as Javan focused on putting his brother's shields to a fairly rigorous test.

The younger prince's initial panic shifted rapidly through frantic uncertainty and then into growing discomfort as he became aware of the unaccustomed sensation of pressure against his shields. Just when he thought he must cry out from the pain, it stopped, Javan dropping his hand and sitting back on the table edge with a perplexed sigh.

"Well, you'll know it if anybody tries to get past *those*," he murmured, cocking his brother a crooked little grin. "It isn't likely that anyone will try—*I* won't, now that I know how strong they are—but if I were you, I'd still try to avoid the notice of Sitric or any other tame Deryni the great lords might bring to court. Oriel is safe—he knows about me—but if anyone else even suspects you have shields like that, you're dead."

"I—don't understand," Rhys Michael whispered, still a little dazed.

"I don't, either," Javan replied, which was mostly true, though at least he knew what had finally focused his powers. "I do know

that whatever abilities you might eventually develop to go along
with those shields, they aren't apt to be much help if the opposition
decides you're Deryni-tainted. Just remember Declan Carmody, if
you start to get cocky."

Rhys Michael shuddered, suddenly looking a little sick, and
Javan had to concentrate to push back the images he had conjured
in his own mind.

"It's quite a quandary, isn't it?" he said after a moment. "Somehow, I've been given the power to make a great deal of difference,
but I don't much dare use it, because if anyone finds out I have this
power, they'll try to destroy me—and call it divine justice, because
the Church has managed to convince nearly everyone that Deryni
are evil, that their powers come from the devil. It doesn't matter
that I'm not Deryni—and I'm afraid I don't know exactly where my
powers come from, though I'm reasonably sure it isn't from the
devil. They'd still damn me in the same terms they damn Deryni.
Talk about a double-edged sword."

"Go back to Declan," Rhys Michael whispered, staring up at
him fearfully. "They gave him *merasha*, so he couldn't fight back.
They gave it to Cathan and Mika, to see if they had Deryni powers.
Javan, what if *we* got dosed with *merasha*? Would they think we
were Deryni?"

A queasy roiling stirred in the pit of Javan's stomach. He had
wondered about it before, but the implications now were even more
staggering. He glanced at Guiscard, seeking reassurance, but the
Deryni could give none. Clearly, he did not know either.

"I honestly don't know, Rhysem," Javan said slowly. "It might
be a good idea to find out, but I'd rather it didn't happen at the
hands of the *Custodes* or someone like them. We *should* react as
human, but—I just don't know."

Rhys Michael heaved a defeated sigh, then glanced wearily at
Guiscard's hands still on his shoulders.

"I'm not going to do anything stupid," he murmured. "Does he
have to keep his hands on me?"

"Guiscard, you can wait in the other room," Javan said quietly.
"Thank you for your assistance."

As Guiscard withdrew, Javan glanced over his shoulder at
Charlan, still guarding the door, then back at Rhys Michael. "Do
you want Charlan to leave, too?"

At Rhys Michael's nod, Javan gestured with his chin for Charlan
to join Guiscard. When the door had closed between the two rooms,
Javan looked back at his brother.

"Well," he said quietly. "This evening didn't quite go as either of us had planned, did it? Returning to the subject that prompted this rather painful discussion, do I have your word that you won't pursue this matter of marrying Michaela for a while? You do understand, I hope, that it isn't just the petty jealousy of your celibate brother that's asking this."

Rhys Michael lowered his eyes, twining his fingers in his lap and staring at them sightlessly. "I do love her, Javan."

"No one said you didn't. It's clear that you do, and that she loves you. I wish you joy of one another—but not yet. All I'm asking is that you wait until I think it's safe."

"But that could be years," Rhys Michael said. "I wasn't cut out to be celibate, Javan. You might be, but I'm not. I *need* her."

"Do you think I don't have needs, too?" Javan replied, trying not to get angry all over again. "You may *need* Michaela, but you and I both *need* to stay alive. That comes first. If you marry now, you seriously reduce the chances that either of us will ever live to see our sons grow old."

"I can't believe they'd really do what you're saying," Rhys Michael said. "They couldn't kill us both. People would suspect."

"But we'd still be dead," Javan pointed out, "and the legitimate heir would be a minor, to be governed by a regency until he or she came of age. The old regents have tasted that kind of power before, Rhysem. They want it back. And the only way they can get it is to see us dead."

Rhys Michael sighed and shook his head wearily, covering a yawn. "You may be right. I don't think you are, but I suppose it's possible. Can I go to bed now? I'm suddenly very tired."

"You haven't yet given me your word about Michaela," Javan said quietly. "You aren't leaving until I have it—unless you'd prefer one of those other three options I outlined earlier this evening."

"Oh, all right!" Rhys Michael replied, giving an exasperated sigh. "You're taking this whole thing entirely too seriously. I understand about Michaela and I won't pursue the matter for now. Is that what you wanted to hear?"

"Only if you mean it. Do you?"

Rolling his eyes heavenward, Rhys Michael raised his right hand in oath. "As God is my witness, I swear to you that I will not pursue the matter of Michaela for now."

"You won't see her before she leaves, or attempt to write to her while she's gone?" Javan insisted.

"I can't even write to her?"

"I think it will only make it more difficult for both of you, if you do."

Rhys Michael heaved an exasperated sigh. "All right, I swear it. I won't give her up altogether, though."

"I'm not asking that," Javan replied, satisfied that his brother had spoken the truth when he made his oath.

After Rhys Michael had gone, though, Javan worried about the understandable bitterness behind the oath, and found himself considering what other fruit this night's work might bring.

Chapter Twenty-Eight

*Mine enemies reproach me all the day; and
they that are mad against me are sworn
against me.*

—Psalms 102:8

To no great surprise on Javan's part, Rhys Michael did not appear
for Father Faelan's weekday Mass the next morning, though he often omitted to attend, and sent word as Javan was preparing for
their morning ride that he was not feeling well and would spend
the day in bed. Somewhat dubious, though he knew his brother had
gone straight to his room after their conversation of the night before, Javan decided to practice his lance work in the tilting yard
instead of riding out, sticking close to home, and had Guiscard and
Charlan take turns at keeping Rhys Michael's quarters under casual
surveillance throughout the day. Earl Manfred was in Council that
afternoon but gave no indication that anything was amiss in his
household, so Javan had to conclude that Michaela had not told her
guardian about the previous night's misadventure.

That evening, to Javan's surprise and relief, his brother duly appeared for supper in the great hall, apologizing for his absence of
the day and declaring himself much recovered from his earlier malaise. That much, at least, was true. For the rest of the evening,
charming as only Rhys Michael could be, he stayed close to Javan
and contrived to comport himself as the most proper of princes,
attentive and gracious, neither seeking out Manfred and his household nor avoiding them. Since Michaela was not present, Javan
thought this probably was not difficult, but he was glad to see his
brother at least going through the motions of compliance. When

299

the Court at last retired, he sent Charlan to keep watch outside the prince's apartments, with orders to apprehend any nocturnal wanderings. At midmorning the next day, Manfred and his household rode out of Rhemuth, Michaela meekly among them, with no further contact apparent between his ward and the king's brother.

Javan informed Joram of the incident with Rhys Michael that very night, using the outward excuse of several bottles of good Fianna wine to seek out the company of Guiscard's father in his new quarters, with Guiscard and Charlan accompanying him. Not that Javan got any of the wine. He left the others to enjoy it, himself standing alone on the Portal square and giving them nervous salute before bending the energies to his will.

Half an hour later he had conveyed every detail to Joram, Niallan, and Jesse in a little study not far from the Portal chamber in the Michaeline stronghold. They were sitting around a little table, the room lit by candles in sconces on the walls, and it was cooler by far than in Rhemuth.

"I suppose I overreacted a bit," he said when they had returned to verbal communication. "With those shields, though, I couldn't force compliance. I figured that maybe the shock value of finding out about our powers would make an impression where mere logic couldn't. He also can't very well expose me out of spite without putting himself in danger. And what about *merasha*? Are we vulnerable?"

Joram steepled his fingertips against his chin, resting his elbows on the chair arms. He and Niallan both were wearing Michaeline habit tonight, Joram with the white sash of his Michaeline knighthood gleaming in the dim-lit room.

"That's something we've never gotten around to finding out," he said. "There was *merasha* in what Rhys gave you the night your father died, but that was before any powers were set. Your faculties were certainly disrupted that night, but there were several other drugs as well as other factors that could have been responsible. We specifically omitted *merasha* for your own rite, precisely because we didn't know how you'd react."

"Well, with the *Custodes* going around using it to ferret out Deryni, don't you think I ought to know? They used it on Father Faelan, just as a sedative. They already knew he wasn't Deryni."

Niallan sighed and leaned back in his chair, the hand with his bishop's ring lightly caressing his close-cropped grey beard.

"It's very fortunate that they didn't use you the same way, my prince, when they bled you at *Arx Fidei*," he said. "Otherwise, we might not now be having this conversation."

"Then you think it *will* affect me?" Javan whispered.

"I should think it highly likely. However, if we test you and you do react, there's a disadvantage you probably haven't even thought of."

"Which is?"

"Well, simply not knowing is one thing. But if you do know and *merasha* does affect you, apprehension could color your behavior before anyone even thought seriously of testing you, and perhaps make the testing more likely."

"I can see that possibility," Javan agreed. "I still think I'd rather know. What's a safe way to find out?"

"In your present situation, there *are* no safe ways," Joram replied. "If we dose you with it, and you react, you're going to be out of commission for half a day and shaky for the best part of another day after that. Covering the first period is easy enough, if you start early in the evening. You can always complain of a headache earlier in the day and say you're taking a physick to knock you out for the night. But a king is expected to function every day. Imagine the worst hangover you've ever had, and then multiply it tenfold. That might begin to give you an idea what it could be like."

"I wouldn't expect it to be pleasant, judging from what I've seen in the past," Javan said, "but I still think it's something I ought to know for sure."

"Some of the effects *can* be fought," Jesse said, speaking for the first time. Javan still could not get used to the *Custodes* tonsure Jesse had affected for his visit to Rhemuth to set up the Portal, though Jesse was wearing lay attire tonight and the tonsure was starting to grow out. "You have to learn *how* to fight, and that can only come from experience, but the effects can be diminished—not well and not for long, but it might save you if you only got a light dose. There are also drugs that can ease some of the discomfort in a training situation. If one can't avoid *merasha* entirely, the best remedy still is simply to have another Deryni standing by with a walloping strong sedative to put you out for the duration."

"Guiscard could do that," Javan said. "Or Oriel. Wouldn't it be better to have a Healer do it anyway?"

"It's too dangerous for Oriel," Jesse said, pushing back his chair to stand and begin slowly pacing before the empty fireplace. "You've been having him keep a low profile, and that's good, but I wouldn't want him in your quarters for any length of time unless you're ill; and if you're ill, a royal physician almost has to be called to give an opinion. That would be too difficult to fake, with *merasha* in you."

Javan shuddered and gave a nod, wondering how much Joram knew about a time when another Healer had made someone appear to be ill—and the consequences had led to a death for which Javan still partially blamed himself. Tavis had been the Healer then, and Javan the "patient," but it was the Healer Rhys Thuryn who had died.

"I think we'd better just use Guiscard," he said, "and forget about trying to fake an illness. I'm not often disturbed in the middle of the night, once I've retired. I'm sure he and Charlan can handle anything that comes up."

"Let's hope so, if you're determined to do this," Niallan replied. "We'll want to give Guiscard some special instruction beforehand, because of the importance of getting you through this as quickly as possible, if you do react; but Joram and I will work out the details and pass on our instructions through Etienne. I'll have Dom Rickart prepare the *merasha* and the necessary medications. I'd prefer to have *him* supervise the testing and any aftermath, but it's just too dangerous. Meanwhile, let's keep a close watch on your brother. The last thing you need is a rival heir, whether it's a child of his by Michaela—or Rhys Michael himself."

Javan walked warily for the next few days, but Niallan's fears appeared to be ill-founded. Rhys Michael scrupulously avoided any mention of Michaela and seemed to throw himself enthusiastically into the work of becoming an adult and contributing part of Javan's Court. Gradually Javan began to breathe a little easier, though he still took the precaution of setting up a watch to ensure that his brother did not try to smuggle out letters, in violation of his oath.

But Rhys Michael truly seemed to have put immediate thoughts of his beloved behind him. To encourage his newly adult behavior, Javan decided to give him increased responsibility, to involve him increasingly in the business of government—and also ensure his familiarity with the process of rule, in case Javan should misjudge too badly and get himself killed for his pains. Very soon after Manfred's entourage departed from Rhemuth, Javan had his brother begin working with Lord Jerowen in the chancery office, and making daily forays into the scriptorium to check on progress of the warrants being drafted for commissioners about to be sent out regarding land holdings. It was Rhys Michael himself who conveyed the warrants to Javan in Council for final approval.

"It is well begun, my lord," Javan told the Council, more than a week after Manfred's departure, when he had signed the warrants and seen them sealed with his great seal. "Lord Udaut, these warrants are to be dispatched immediately. If the work of the commissions progresses on schedule, I hope to see the first returns in time for Christmas Court."

The Council pronounced itself satisfied with the plan, and Javan gathered his determination for his next inquiry.

"The next thing I should like to explore is the codification of all laws promulgated since the Restoration of my House," he said tentatively. "Lord Jerowen has begun compiling an index that covers most of my father's reign, but he finds that records of legislation enacted by my late brother appear to be rather sparse, especially during his regency."

Rhun muttered something under his breath that Javan could not hear and glanced darkly at Lord Tammaron, but the chancellor only cleared his throat self-importantly and shuffled a sheaf of documents on the table in front of him.

"Sire, I believe my office can supply all the information you require in that regard," he said a little peevishly. "I don't know who has told you otherwise, but careful records were kept during the late king's minority."

"No doubt I have been misinformed, then," Javan said. "I'm very pleased to hear that."

"I am certain you will find everything in order, Sire."

"Excellent," Javan said, flashing a disarming smile around the table. "I do believe it's important that these records be accessible, don't you? A comprehensive index to the laws will help to ensure that they are applied uniformly—which is part of the essence of good government, as I'm sure everyone will agree. Please see that Lord Jerowen is given access to those records, would you?"

The request seemed reasonable, but Javan's next line of inquiry made the established lords considerably more edgy, especially the clergy, for he began to ask questions regarding the work of the ecclesiastical courts at Ramos regarding Deryni.

"I realize that this is a delicate subject, gentlemen, but I know that I am very young, and I am trying to understand. What, precisely, triggered this extraordinary convocation besides the zeal of Father Paulin? Can anyone tell me? And what was the theological basis for determining that Deryni are evil, in and of themselves? You might expect that I would know this, having been educated largely in the cloister, but I find it an area of my education that seems woefully lacking."

"Sire," Hubert said coolly, "I regard this query as extremely ill-timed, when you know that Father Paulin is not yet returned to answer these questions."

"Well, I should think he's had ample time to bury his dead and get back," Javan replied, not adding that he was beginning to be nervous about precisely why Paulin had not yet returned. The previous week had brought the time for the first of Father Faelan's required monthly "retreats" at *Arx Fidei*. Javan had delayed sending the priest for several days, fearing for Faelan's safety, but he finally had been forced to trust that he and his allies had done all they could to protect Faelan. Even allowing for a late departure, though, the priest should have been back two days ago, or surely yesterday.

"You know, it really does make it difficult to conduct the business of this Court when those I need to question are not here," Javan went on a little peevishly. "If I'm to be properly informed on the state of my kingdom, I must ask these questions that pertain to previous reigns, especially when they greatly affect my own. Why has Father Paulin not yet returned? Do you know? Does anyone know?"

Hubert looked distinctly uncomfortable. "Sire, I should imagine that he had business of his Order to conclude, necessitated by the untimely death of Brother Serafin."

Which certainly was at least part of the truth, but Javan had known that without benefit of his powers. What he did not know was why Hubert looked so uneasy about the question, though he could make some shrewd guesses.

"I see," he said. "And I assume that Lord Albertus' absence is likewise necessitated by business of his Order? No man can serve two masters, my lord. I like it not that my Earl Marshal is not regularly present in Council."

In truth, he liked it just fine, for in no way was Albertus his choice for Earl Marshal. But he was hoping Hubert might volunteer information that Javan did not already have.

"Your Highness must remember that this is an extraordinary circumstance," Rhun said instead. "I am certain that both Lord Albertus and Father Paulin will return as soon as they are able."

Which was obvious from anyone's perspective and still told Javan precisely nothing that he had not known before. He decided to drop the issue for the moment, for it would only anger Paulin when he did return—he hoped with Father Faelan, as well. He could only pray that the delay came from practical considerations rather than disaster, and that the priest was waiting—or being made to wait—merely so that all the *Custodes* party could travel together when Paulin and Albertus eventually did decide to return to Court. To leave the Council on the focus of some other topic, he allowed Lord Jerowen to take up the rest of the afternoon reviewing what he was setting out in his indices.

That night Javan had Rhys Michael to supper in his apartments, for his brother had commented on the exchanges in Council that afternoon regarding discrepancies in the records of the regency, and also the Ramos queries. Javan, in turn, hoped to ferret out some inkling of his brother's feelings about their last private encounter, now that Michaela had been gone from Court for more than a week. He also had decided it was time to acquaint his brother with the bare bones of the Faelan story, so he would understand at least that aspect of Javan's growing hostility toward Paulin.

He told Rhys Michael about Faelan over a supper of roast fowl and meat pasties, with cheese and fruit to follow—how the innocent Father Faelan had been interrogated and even tortured at *Arx Fidei* before coming to Court, for no other reason than the hope of winkling out information about his friendship with Javan and why Javan should want this particular priest as his confessor. Rhys Michael found it inconceivable that monastic disciplines should have been applied for the purpose of intimidation, to force Faelan's betrayal not only of that friendship but of the seal of the confessional.

"They were going to bleed him to death?" Rhys Michael asked, unable to believe what he was hearing.

"They made him think they were." Javan took a sip of wine. "Believe me, there are few more helpless feelings in the world than watching your life-blood pump out of your veins and knowing that if it suits them, those in authority over you have the power to forbid a halt."

"But surely they wouldn't actually do it," Rhys Michael whispered.

"That depends on what they had to gain. In Faelan's case, certainly they stopped short. They wanted to set him up to spy on me. They didn't stop with the minution, though. After they'd weakened his resistance, through fasting, scourging, and then blood-letting, they drugged him and let a Deryni have a go at interrogating him."

Rhys Michael's eyes got very round. "They have a Deryni?"

"Paulin does," Javan said uneasily. "This is a recent development. I don't know much about him except that he's called Dimitri. Fortunately, he doesn't seem to have done much to Faelan besides Truth-Read him during questioning by Lior and Serafin. But even if there weren't a Dimitri, there's still the threat of the other things they can do to him. As you can imagine, it isn't a situation Faelan was eager to go back to. But he went—out of loyalty to me. And now he's late coming back."

Rhys Michael swallowed hard and sat back in his chair, obviously thinking about what Javan had just told him. He was going easy on the wine tonight, apparently still sobered by his last interview with his brother and what had been said about his drinking. After a few minutes he reached across to pull a grape from a bunch on a pewter tray, popping it distractedly into his mouth.

"It's beginning to sound as if the *Custodes* are your real enemies, rather than the former regents," he said thoughtfully.

Javan raised an eyebrow and sat back, toying with the stem of his goblet. He, too, was watching his intake tonight, to be certain he kept his edge for this conversation. Other than an initial cup to start the meal, he had been drinking his wine well watered, the same as Rhys Michael.

"I wouldn't be too sure of that," he said. "Unfortunately, there's a fair amount of overlap. Hubert is still on the Council and will support the *Custodes* in whatever they do. Regardless of what else happens, I'm stuck with him until he dies, because the Archbishop-Primate of Gwynedd *has* to sit on the royal Council. With Albertus as Earl Marshal, that gives them another powerful voice. I could get rid of him, but the hard fact is that I don't have any other senior military commander who's as good. Rhun probably is, but I'd rather have just about anybody as Earl Marshal besides him. I'll not soon forget what he did to the Gabrilites four years ago. Besides, he was one of the regents.

"Oriss is also part of the old Council, even though he wasn't a regent, and he's subordinate to Hubert—and hence, biddable by the *Custodes*. Thank God Murdoch is no longer a factor. Tammaron's basically a decent sort, but he's only one man. I haven't got anybody among my hand-picked men who are as senior as any of the men I've mentioned."

He deliberately had not mentioned Manfred and felt his heart sink a little when Rhys Michael noticed and mentioned it.

"You don't trust Earl Manfred either?" his brother said.

Javan shrugged. "He's Hubert's brother. If it came down to a choice, to whom do you think he'd give his loyalty? Not to me, I can assure you."

Rhys Michael broke a small bunch of grapes off the larger bunch and used his teeth to casually pull off an individual grape.

"That's another reason you were glad to see him leave Rhemuth, then, isn't it?" he said. "It got you rid of two problems in one fell swoop."

"Are you trying to get me to reconsider about Michaela?" Javan said, certain that was exactly what his brother intended.

Rhys Michael sucked another grape into his mouth and crushed it against the roof of his mouth.

"I really don't think that issue is a part of all this," he said. "I'll

grant you that the *Custodes* are turning out to be far more dangerous than anyone ever dreamed—"

"Not more dangerous than *I'd* ever dreamed," Javan muttered.
"I knew they were trouble from the day they were instituted."

"Well, they aren't Michaelines," Rhys Michael conceded. "Not
that the Michaelines didn't occasionally cause trouble, too."

"Never like this," Javan said. "Whatever else anyone may say
about them, they were never anything but loyal to the Crown."

"But some of them were Deryni," Rhys Michael said uncomfortably.

"Yes, and I know of only one Deryni Michaeline who ever betrayed a Haldane—and he was forced to it."

Rhys Michael cocked his head in question. "Who was that?"

"A priest named Humphrey of Gallareaux. Tavis told me about
him once. It was before our father had taken back his throne. King
Imre broke this Humphrey utterly and set his own compulsions on
the poor man. When our eldest brother was born—the one before
Alroy—this same Humphrey contrived to be at his baptism, assisting the presiding priest. The baby's name was to be Aidan Alroy
Camber."

"I thought he'd died at birth," Rhys Michael said.

"No, he was almost three weeks old. The baptismal salt was
poisoned. Shock at Aidan's death somehow triggered our father's
powers, and he *knew* who was responsible. It was the first time
he ever used his powers, and he used them to kill his son's
slayer." He drew a deep breath. "It wasn't Humphrey's fault,
though. Just as it wasn't Faelan's fault the *Custodes* tried to use
him."

Rhys Michael was shaking his head.

"Our enemies do use the innocent, Rhysem. Don't think they
don't," Javan went on. "It doesn't matter whether those enemies
are human or Deryni. Evil men have no qualms about sacrificing
anything and anyone who will serve their purpose, whether it's
good priests like Humphrey and Faelan or even more helpless victims—women and children, even infants.

"Think of Declan's wife and sons—innocent lives snuffed out
with no more thought than you or I would snuff out a candle. Or
Gieselle MacLean, who I'm virtually certain was put to death at
the regents' orders, so that her sister could be married off to one of
the regents' sons. And they're using Michaela to try to get an heir
from you, after which you and possibly she, as well, are quite likely
to end up the same way as Gieselle or Declan's wife and children
or our little brother Aidan."

Rhys Michael stared at Javan in silence for several stunned seconds, then gave a low, nervous laugh.

"Your imagination is running rampant," he murmured. "You're trying to scare me, so I'll give her up."

"If all I wanted to do was scare you," Javan replied in a very calm voice, "I could come up with something to turn your hair white and probably make you wet yourself." He held out one hand and let lightning crackle between his fingers. "Do you want me to have a go at it?"

Rhys Michael swallowed audibly, shaking his head as Javan lifted the hand higher and the vague suggestion of *something* started to materialize above the upturned palm.

"That's all right. I believe you," he whispered, exhaling softly as Javan lowered his hand and the fire died away. "But do you really think Paulin has done something to Father Faelan, and that's why they haven't come back?"

"I suppose we'll just have to wait and see," Javan replied. "For obvious reasons, I can't inquire too closely. I don't even want them to know how much I know of what they did to him that first time. But if they've killed him . . ."

Chapter Twenty-nine

*How long shall they utter and speak hard
things? and all the workers of iniquity boast
themselves?*

—Psalms 94:4

Fortunately, Javan did not have to decide what he would do if Faelan
was dead, for Paulin and his party returned the very next day, a
quiet and timorous Faelan among them. Rhys Michael gave his
brother an I-told-you-so glance as soon as the message of the arrival
had been announced.

It was not until that evening, after Solemn Vespers in the Chapel
Royal, that Javan could contrive an excuse to speak to his chaplain
in private. Paulin had taken himself off with Hubert immediately
after the close of the afternoon's Council meeting, but Father Lior
had taken it upon himself to attend Faelan's service that night.

"Father, I should like you to hear my confession," Javan said,
pointedly raising his voice slightly when Father Lior would have
approached from where he had been kneeling in the back of the
chapel.

Lior immediately backed off, and Faelan stood meekly aside to
let the king go ahead of him into the chapel's sacristy. The faithful
Charlan took up a casual watch just outside, and Guiscard remained in the chapel as well, kneeling humbly to one side with his
arms folded on his chest and dark head bowed in one hand, apparently deep in prayer but actually keeping an eye on Lior.

As had become a pattern over the past month, Faelan went immediately to a little stool beside the *prie-dieu* where he usually
knelt for his own devotions before and after saying Mass, and where
he often heard confessions. Javan knelt in the suppliant's position,

to keep up appearances if anyone should get past Charlan. Until he had heard Faelan's account the way the *Custodes* intended it to be told, he did not intend to intrude anything of his true relationship with Faelan.

"Bless me, Father, for I have sinned," he whispered. "Are you well?"

Faelan had clasped his hands in his lap and bowed his head, as if he had actually intended to hear Javan's confession, but he did not raise his head, only twining his fingers tightly together.

"They—did me no physical harm this time, Sire," he murmured.

Without replying, Javan clamped one hand over Faelan's joined ones to prevent retreat and slid the fingers of his other hand up first one and then the other sleeve of Faelan's habit, checking for signs that he had been bled. Faelan stiffened but allowed it, not relaxing until Javan returned his hands to the *prie-dieu*'s armrest between them. The priest's expression was bleak and troubled as he raised his face toward the king.

"I do not know whether I can continue to serve you in this way, Sire." The words were whispered, unsteady.

"What did they do to you?"

Faelan returned his gaze to his clasped hands, bracing his courage with a slow intake of breath.

"The—physical discipline was much relaxed this time," he said. "Which was almost as frightening as if they had actually done anything. The threat was always in my mind—and the memory of—last time."

"What did they actually do to you?" Javan repeated.

"For the first two days, I was ordered to keep vigil in the disciplinarium," Faelan said steadily, "made to fast on water only and to observe certain spiritual exercises. There was little opportunity for sleep. I was not permitted to attend Mass until the third day, just before the abbot called me to his solar. Father Paulin and Brother Albertus were present, as well as Father Lior and a lay scribe to take down the answers to their questions."

"Go on."

"They—only asked about you, Sire: what I had observed, what we had discussed, what I had seen and heard of other members of your immediate household. And your confessions. At least you had—given me permission to divulge their contents. Not that there was anything remarkable in them. And since I have observed nothing at all out of the ordinary, of course I could tell them nothing of that, either."

The statement certainly was the literal truth as Faelan remembered it, but Javan knew that the *Custodes'* questioning must have gone beyond what Faelan had indicated—and that he himself had blocked certain memories surrounding events just before the coronation, including the night of Brother Serafin's death.

"Lean closer, Father," he whispered, setting his hand across Faelan's forehead as the priest obeyed. "Now tell me *everything* that happened at the abbey."

Faelan tensed at the touch, half trying to turn his face away, but Javan clasped his other hand behind the priest's head to prevent his retreat, entering the other's mind to find a casual inhibition set against volunteering details of what had transpired in the abbot's study. It was easy enough to release, though; and what Faelan began to reveal startled Javan, though it hardly surprised him.

"Tell me in your own words, Father," he whispered, slipping his hands down to Faelan's shoulders. "You'll find that you can remember it all now."

Faelan spoke slowly and as if in a daze, dark eyes gazing through and beyond the intent Javan.

"That 'lay scribe'—someone referred to him as Master Dimitri," Faelan whispered. "They asked me about the night Brother Serafin died, and Dimitri kept watching me rather than writing down my answers . . ."

Down in the cathedral precincts, in the quarters Archbishop Hubert occupied when he was resident in Rhemuth, Paulin of Ramos was relating another part of the story to his superior.

"So the circumstances surrounding Brother Serafin's death do appear to be exactly as presented at the time," he said. "I have little doubt that his heart did fail. Only Father Lior was anywhere near him when he was stricken, and it had been very hot that day."

Hubert had been listening almost indulgently, still convinced that Paulin's efforts had been wasted—for surely Serafin's death had been from natural causes—but he dutifully offered the next logical question.

"Only Lior was near him," he repeated. "I don't suppose there's any chance that Lior had any part in it?"

"None whatever."

"Very well. Is it possible that Serafin could have been poisoned, or drugged in some way to make it *look* like simple heart failure?"

Paulin shook his head. "He had eaten and drunk nothing for several hours, and he shared his meal then with several other brethren including Lior—and they shared common vessels. There's nothing to suggest that kind of interference."

He drew a breath, as if considering whether to speak further, and Hubert cocked his head at him.

"Does something suggest some other kind of interference?" he asked.

Paulin had been toying with one of the fringed ends of his crimson sash, and brushed it idly against his other hand as he considered the question. "That's what continues to bother me. As you might expect, Lior was questioned very thoroughly about that night, both at the time and after we returned to the abbey with Serafin's body. It had not come out in earlier interviews, but under closer examination he—seemed to recall something about a visit to Father Faelan, earlier in the evening. I believe I told you it had been their intention to interview him in the next day or two, but nothing was said of it in Lior's first accounts of their movements that night."

"Are you implying that it was a deliberate evasion?"

Paulin shook his head. "No, just an understandable omission of what was a very minor event in the context of what else happened that night. There was something else, though. A—" He glanced at Hubert and sighed. "Very well. To tell you about this, I also have to tell you about something else. When I spoke of closer examination, I meant precisely that. Some months ago, I took a Deryni into my employ."

"You did *what*?"

"Don't worry. I've employed all the necessary safeguards. He calls himself Dimitri. A party of my knights returning from the Forcinn encountered him and his brother on a ship outbound from Fianna. The brother, Collos, was gravely ill with a fever, so one of our battle surgeons attended him."

"I don't believe I am hearing this," Hubert muttered from between clenched teeth.

"Just listen, before you presume to judge. Once the crisis was past and it was clear that Collos would live, it emerged that the two were Deryni, and that Dimitri, the other brother, had been an undersheriff in Vezaire, allegedly deposed for malfeasance and misappropriation of funds. He, of course, maintains that he was framed—which may or may not be true. The ship's crew seemed to think it was."

Hubert rolled his eyes heavenward as Paulin continued.

"Be that as it may, the two were destitute. Collos almost certainly would have died if my battle surgeon hadn't intervened—which he probably wouldn't have done, had he known at the time that the two were Deryni. Nonetheless, Dimitri let it be known that while he eventually hoped to return and take revenge on those who had accused him falsely, his gratitude to those who had saved his brother's life impelled him to offer them his service—for pay, of course, since he must eventually finance his return, but he possessed certain skills of interrogation which he had acquired while serving in Vezaire. He had heard that Gwynedd occasionally employs such skills, under certain very controlled circumstances. He readily demonstrated his skills on several crewmen, some willing and some less so."

"I'm sure he did," Hubert muttered. Paulin ignored him and went on.

"As you can imagine, the prospect of willing service was tempting, but my knights still were wary. However, when it was suggested that Dimitri provide some surety for his loyalty to his potential employers, he and his brother readily agreed that the brother should be held as hostage. I feel confident that we have taken ample precautions to protect ourselves."

Hubert was aghast by the time Paulin had finished his story.

"I cannot believe that you recruited a Deryni without consulting me," he said.

Paulin drew himself up in uneasy defense. "*You* have had the benefit of Deryni assistance until recently."

"Yes, but—" Hubert wrung his hands. "I suppose his motives *could* be as he presented them. You're sure this brother really is his brother?"

"I'm sure that he is Deryni," Paulin replied. "He was tested with *merasha*. So was Dimitri. Both of them went into rather spectacular convulsions."

Hubert nodded. "Then he has at least put one of his own kind at risk, if he plays us false and we find out. How extensively have you used him?"

"Don't worry. I've been cautious. I kept them in Carthmoor for the first few months while I applied small tests. Collos is still there, recovering his health, but I had Dimitri brought to *Arx Fidei* when Father Faelan was being vetted for the king's service."

"He read Faelan?"

"Not a probe. I was not yet sure of him. Only Truth-Reading. But Faelan's resistance had been lowered by—other means."

"I'd guessed as much, from his condition when he first arrived. Was Javan told?"

"He knew Faelan had been bled, but I told him it had been for reasons of health."

"Suppose Faelan told him otherwise?"

"If he did, it will only have confirmed to Javan that he himself will place Faelan in further danger if he attempts to subvert him from his duty to the Order," Paulin said. "It's yet another threat to keep the king in line."

Hubert nodded, caressing his bishop's ring with his other hand. "Returning to Serafin's death. Did you have this Dimitri question Faelan about that?"

"I'll get to that," Paulin replied. "After Serafin's burial, my first priority was to question Lior in finer detail, with Dimitri present. Besides, Faelan had not yet arrived. Lior could offer no insights from his conscious recollections of the night Serafin died, but I asked if he would consent to have Dimitri conduct a probe on the night in question. I could have ordered it, of course, but Dimitri tells me that results are generally better if the subject is willing."

"And Lior agreed to this?"

"He did. Both he and Serafin had become accustomed to working with Dimitri in Carthmoor. During Dimitri's questioning, Lior did indeed recall further details of a conversation in Faelan's quarters that night, but it was as unremarkable as one might expect, given Lior's earlier failure to remember it. He and Serafin left after only a short time. The rest of that night you know. The interesting thing is that Dimitri said there was something else brooding underneath the surface—a vague impression that Javan himself might have been present at some point. Or maybe the three of them were simply talking about the king. Dimitri could not be certain."

"Curious," Hubert murmured.

"Shortly after that, Father Faelan finally arrived," Paulin went on. "After his previous interview, I wanted it to be as benign as possible, but I also wanted to find out what he knew about Serafin's death. I let his own imagination supply the apprehension for the first two days, encouraged by fasting and little sleep. After Mass on the third morning, when he was brought into the abbot's parlor for questioning, he was already a little light-headed from the fast and the Communion wine on an empty stomach."

"An effective preparation," Hubert agreed.

"It did seem to have the desired effect. I reinforced his apprehension by suggesting that if he did not give strict attention to Lior's questions, suitable encouragement could be employed to loosen his tongue. Since Albertus was handling a rather blood-stained length of leather thong at the time, Faelan understood the threat precisely—though the abbot somewhat diminished its effect by observing that one month was really too soon to bleed him again."

Hubert snorted. "Abbot Halex still has much to learn of our methods."

"Indeed. The same cannot be said for Dimitri, however. Were he not Deryni and also an adherent of the eastern strain of our faith, I might almost be induced to recruit him for our Order—though he serves well enough, as he is."

"Go on with the account of Father Faelan," Hubert said a little impatiently.

Paulin inclined his head. "I'll skip the details. The crux of the matter is that Father Faelan could add nothing to Lior's earlier account of the interview by himself and Serafin, and knew nothing of any appearance by the king. I had Dimitri probe him to make certain. Nor could Faelan supply anything else in the behavior of either Javan or any of his close retainers in the past month to suggest anything at all untoward regarding Serafin's death."

"Then it sounds as if this was a dead end," Hubert said after a moment. "I always thought it was a long shot that Faelan was somehow involved. He'd only been back at Court for two days when it happened, and he'd been Truth-Read not a week before. And then this hint of Javan's involvement—" He shook his head. "I know how the coincidence must prey on your mind, Paulin, but I don't see how there could be any connection."

"Very well. I'll drop the notion for the moment," Paulin agreed. "Now that you know about Dimitri, would you like me to bring him to Court? With his true status unknown, of course."

Hubert looked at him sidelong. "We'd already talked about eliminating all Deryni from service. You propose to add one to the problem?"

"This one is ours, Hubert, and a willing servant."

"Perhaps he is," Hubert murmured. "Perhaps he is." He toyed with his pectoral cross, running it back and forth on the center of the chain.

"Let me think on the problem for a few days," he said after a moment. "We do have at least one other Deryni available at Court, if we really need one. Not Oriel anymore, of course, but I'm certain Lord Rhun would let us borrow Sitric. Granted, he lacks finesse, but perhaps the time for subtlety is past. We shall see what the next little while brings—and *next* month's report from the exasperating Father Faelan."

"Then the man called Dimitri brought me a cup of wine," Faelan was saying to Javan. "He said that I was weakened from my fast and wasn't thinking clearly. I probably shouldn't have drunk it on an empty stomach. It went right to my head. I remember feeling dizzy, and I—think Dimitri put his hands on my head. The next thing I knew, I was in the infirmary, and one of the brothers was feeding me hot broth." He blinked and refocused on Javan's face.

"I—don't think I told him anything, Sire, but he's—Deryni, isn't he?" he whispered. "He—must have Read my mind while I was unconscious. I—don't think I can face that again. The other was bad enough, but—"

He started to shake then, and Javan had to take control, blurring the disturbing memories and forcing calm upon the priest. Faelan's fear was understandable, but Javan would have a month to reassure him that he could indeed go on. This month's interview apparently had done little harm, other than to terrify Faelan again with the prospect of what they could do to him any time they chose.

But there was no time to pursue this further just now. With Lior lurking outside, Faelan must not appear to have done anything besides his sacramental duty when they went out of here—which must be soon, else they risked arousing curiosity about what Javan had needed to confess that took so long.

Quickly he did what needed to be done. A few minutes later, as the two of them emerged from the sacristy, the priest's face was bland and serene, the king's expression suitably thoughtful and contrite. Sending to Guiscard to come and also make confession to Faelan, to further reinforce the illusion covering the past quarter hour, Javan knelt at the altar rail and recited a *Pater Noster* and three *Aves* as self-imposed penance for the necessary deception, then rose and left with Charlan. Ten minutes later Guiscard also joined them in the king's quarters.

"Everything's all right," the Deryni knight said softly, when he had closed the door behind him. "I had a bit of a mental scurry to come up with something minor to confess on the spur of the moment, but Lior seemed almost bored by it all, when Faelan and I came back out. I kept an ear cocked while I did my penance, but Lior only exchanged a few words with Faelan before he left. Faelan's gone to his room now."

"Then at least everyone's safe for the time being," Javan breathed. "Ask me again in about a month, though. It's going to be increasingly difficult for Faelan to keep going back. They didn't bleed him this time, but next time it will have been more than two months. Between the terror factor of not knowing if they're going to do it again and the very real danger if they do, I can't say I'd blame him if he didn't want to go—which presents yet another set of problems. Incidentally, it's also now certain that Paulin has that Deryni we've been worrying about."

In the next few days, though, Paulin gave Javan more immediate problems to worry about.

"I am given to understand that questions have been raised about the Ramos Statutes, Sire," he said the next afternoon, as soon as the Council had been called to order. "Perhaps your Highness would care to direct those questions to someone better acquainted with their intricacies. I believe you wished to be instructed on certain points of theology regarding Deryni."

The ensuing diatribe—for by no means could it be termed mere instruction—went downhill from there, with Paulin launching into a two-hour disputation on the evil of Deryni and their magic, followed by an almost equally lengthy defense of the actions of the Council of Ramos. By then it was time to adjourn, and Javan had a headache.

Nor was Paulin satisfied to drop the matter the next day. He spent the first hour of the next meeting reiterating what he had said the day before, hardly even slowing down when Javan backed down entirely from theological arguments and insisted that he really had only been asking about questions of procedure.

Even that seemed to elicit hostility from some, especially those who had been personally involved in the Ramos Convocation. It soon became clear that any significant inroads into easing the draconian legislation against Deryni would be over Paulin's dead body—and very possibly over Javan's dead body as well, if he persisted in his inquiries. Paulin stated unequivocally that he had the support of Gwynedd's Primate and all her bishops as well as his Order—a statement in which Hubert and Oriss immediately backed him. After a frustrating and increasingly tense afternoon trying to shift to almost any other topic, Javan adjourned the meeting and went off for a vigorous gallop with Rhys Michael and his aides and some of his younger knights, returning only when it was nearly dark.

The next day Javan asked Rhys Michael to open the meeting with a brief presentation concerning the index on which he and Lord Jerowen had been working. The prince was articulate and well informed and actually succeeded in arousing some enthusiasm for the inquiry currently in progress. So positive an impression did he make that Javan was not at all surprised, the following day, to hear Lord Udaut suggest that the king's heir presumptive might benefit from taking on additional responsibilities.

"These are times of peace, so a military exercise is hardly suitable for his Highness' further tutoring," Udaut concluded, "but since the prince has shown a penchant for administrative work, perhaps he might accompany one of the commissions currently gathering information in the countryside—sit on a few baronial and county courts, hear a few cases to interpret the laws he has been reading about. It surely would prove a worthwhile apprenticeship and might well be useful to the King's Grace."

The logic could hardly be faulted, and several of the commissioners were only now leaving Rhemuth to take up their duties. Among others, a levelheaded western lord named Ainslie was due to leave for Grecotha in less than a week, with Sir Jason to escort him thence. The area was peaceful, there on the borders with Rhendall, and far from Culdi and Michaela, and Javan knew he could rely on both Ainslie and Jason to keep a headstrong prince focused on business.

In addition, Rhys Michael's absence from Court would materially reduce the chance that he might run afoul of Sitric or even the mysterious Dimitri. If either Deryni discovered that Rhys Michael had shields, which only Deryni were believed to have, further inquiry almost invariably would lead to the discovery of Javan's even more damning abilities. Somehow, he doubted the *Custodes* would make fine distinctions between Deryni powers and the powers of a Haldane king.

"What say you, Sir Jason?" Javan asked, raising an eyebrow in the senior knight's direction. "Do you think Lord Ainslie could use another good head?"

Jason rose and made Javan a slight bow. "His Highness has always been a quick study, Sire," he said, "and I have heard nothing but glowing reports from Lord Jerowen on his diligence and grasp of the law. If his Highness would like to join Lord Ainslie's commission, I am certain his assistance would be most welcome."

"Brother?" Javan said, turning his gaze toward Rhys Michael and containing a droll smile. "How say you?"

Rhys Michael's answering grin was like a ray of sunlight at the other end of the table. "Could I really? You'd let me go to Grecotha?"

"With appropriate reservations, certainly," Javan replied, forcing himself to keep at least a somewhat decorous expression. "You may be a prince, but Lord Ainslie is my royal commissioner and he has the last word. Under the circumstances, I would appoint Sir Jason to the commission as well. If you're willing to abide by his direction, with no argument or discussion, I'll commission you as *his* deputy."

"But it would still be my first commission!" Rhys Michael could hardly contain his excitement. "I can hardly believe it."

His exuberance drew sour looks from Rhun and Hubert and a few of the other Council lords, and after the meeting adjourned,

Tammaron drew Javan aside privately to express doubts about the prince's maturity for such an assignment. Albertus also looked dubious, but Rhys Michael's delight was so infectious that Javan determined to proceed anyway. After all, his brother would turn fifteen in another two weeks. In law, he was already a man. It was time to begin taking on some of a man's responsibilities.

That evening, after confirming that Lord Ainslie had no objection to the addition of two more deputies, Javan had Lord Jerowen draw up the necessary warrants—first the official ones naming Sir Jason and the Prince Rhys Michael Alister Haldane as deputy commissioners for Grecotha; then a third, private one, he hoped never to be used, charging Sir Jason with the prince's safety and giving him absolute authority for anything short of capital force to keep said prince in line. Javan hoped and prayed that the latter document would never be needed, but he knew he must take precautions to protect his only heir. He also would miss Jason's company and counsel in the next few months—but at least he knew his brother could not be in better hands.

Almost before Javan realized, the next week was past and Rhys Michael was away. To ensure that the prince did not take advantage of his greater freedom to send or receive letters from Culdi and Michaela, Javan decided at the last minute to send along Sir Tomais as his brother's aide, since the young knight had served previously as the prince's squire and knew all his patterns for mischief.

"I'll keep an eye on him, Sire. Don't you worry," Tomais assured him.

Actually, Javan became far more worried as he watched them ride out—but not about Rhys Michael. As they headed out that bright September morning, led by Tomais bearing the princely banner, Rhys Michael was in prime Haldane form, straight and proud in the saddle, gaily clad in the royal blue of the heir, flanked by Jason on one side and Lord Ainslie on the other. A party of scribes and clerks made up nearly a dozen more, with a score of household cavalry to escort them.

And behind them rode Paulin of Ramos with a half dozen of his *Custodes* knights, ostensibly summoned to attend on a dying brother at *Arx Fidei*. For the extra safety afforded by numbers, the two parties would ride together as far as the abbey, after which the princely party would continue north toward Grecotha. Javan was glad to see Paulin go—and even more glad when he received the first message from Jason after passing *Arx Fidei*, confirming that Paulin's party had turned off at the abbey without incident, and the rest of the royal commission were proceeding on their way.

CHAPTER THIRTY

But a sore trial shall come upon the mighty.
—Wisdom of Solomon 6:8

Within a week, word had come of the safe arrival of Lord Ainslie's party in Grecotha, with assurances from Sir Jason that Rhys Michael's behavior was a credit to his House. At home, Javan allowed himself to relax a little, as the dog days of summer encouraged lazy afternoons and a general slowing down of the work of the Council.

Meanwhile, once he had heard that Rhys Michael's situation seemed to be well in hand, Javan decided that the time had come to resolve the *merasha* question. Guiscard had been ready for some time, only awaiting the king's instructions. On the evening they selected, Javan quit supper early with the pretense of the headache Joram had recommended, sending for one of the court physicians to bring him a strong sedative.

The man left a few minutes later, convinced that the king had drunk it down and was sleeping peacefully. In fact, the cup still containing the sedative was pushed to the back of a little table beside the royal bed. Javan was sitting in the middle of the bed, boots and belt removed and his feet tucked under him, watching Guiscard empty the contents of a twist of parchment into a second cup he had filled from a pitcher set close beside it.

As he stirred it with a finger, Charlan came in from the other room with a silver goblet and filled it as well. Guiscard's father remained in the outer room, ostensibly working on documents that the king required for the morrow, but actually to ensure with a Deryni's skills that no one intruded on the king's sleep.

"That must not be the *merasha*," Javan said, scrunching closer as Guiscard finished stirring the second cup and sucked the drips off his finger, making a sour face.

"Nope, the sedative. Ugh, that's bitter! But a proper Healer concocted this, because I don't know exactly what our eager court apothecary put into that one." He indicated the rejected cup. "And aside from the fact that *merasha* is a liquid, not a powder, I'd never, ever stir it with my finger. It works fastest if it's introduced directly into the blood—from a Deryni pricker, a sword-edge or arrowhead, whatever—but even getting it on the skin can be dangerous." He reached into the pouch at his belt and pulled out a small brown glass vial stoppered with cork. "This is the *merasha*."

Javan stared at the little vial in Guiscard's hand, wondering that something so small could bring all a Deryni's dread powers to naught.

"Do I—drink it?" he whispered.

"In wine," Guiscard replied, handing the vial to Charlan. "But first you're to experience it the way the *Custodes* usually administer it."

At his nod, Charlan carefully removed the cork to reveal two slender slivers of silvery metal stuck into the underside, close beside one another. One pale droplet shivered between the needles where the points nearly met.

"Is that supposed to be a Deryni pricker?" Javan breathed.

"Dom Rickart says it will do the same job," Guiscard replied.

Unsmiling, he sat down on the king's right and reached across to take his left hand, turning the palm upward as Charlan got a better grip on the needle-tipped cork.

"You've seen this done before, Sire," Guiscard murmured as Charlan dipped the needles into the brown vial again. "The discomfort will be minimal, at least from the needles. I've asked Charlan to do this, so I don't risk dosing myself as well."

"It's that potent?" Javan whispered.

"It is for Deryni—and maybe for Haldanes."

With that, before Javan even realized what was happening, Charlan also grasped his hand and jabbed the needles hard into the palm. Javan gasped at the sharp bite of pain, remembering other needles stabbing into flesh beside a pool where a holy man offered cleansing to those touched by the Deryni taint.

He tried to keep his breathing steady and calm as Charlan pulled the needles out and Guiscard closed his hand to contain the blood and the drug and the pain, but after only a few breaths he began to feel vague tendrils of chill radiating up his arm.

"Guiscard?" he whispered as a wave of dizziness made him reel, suddenly disoriented. At the same time, the chill in his arm spread rapidly to the rest of his body, beginning to fuddle all his perceptions.

"*Damn,*" Guiscard muttered under his breath, enfolding him with one arm and setting his other hand across Javan's forehead. "I'd hoped this wouldn't happen. Give me whatever control you can and let me try to show you how to channel this."

His mind surged across the bond of flesh even as he spoke, and Javan could not have stopped it even if he wanted. He could feel his shields disintegrating, falling away in tatters, new waves of dizziness and even nausea engulfing him so that he could hardly bear Guiscard's touch. He tried to reach out for his powers, but only chaos met him. A roaring filled his ears, blocking out all other sound, and the room seemed to begin undulating around him. He closed his eyes to block it out. He dared not imagine how anyone could actually function while enduring this.

You can level out some of it, came the thought, unbidden, in his mind. *Turn the energies this way. You can survive this!*

Somehow he realized what he was being told and thought he almost understood how to do what was being asked. But another part of him was gibbering with terror and knew that if his enemies did this to him, he was doomed.

"All right, I think that's the best we can do," he heard a voice saying, though he had to concentrate on every word to make sense of it. "We might as well get on with the worst of it. Charlan—"

Through the roaring in his ears, he could hear the dim *clink* of glass against metal. Then his head was being tilted back and metal pressed against his lips.

"Drink it down, Sire," he heard Guiscard's voice murmur. "That's it. Just one more swallow. Try to remember the taste at the back of your tongue. That's a distinctive characteristic of *merasha* when it's taken by mouth."

If he had thought the first dose was bad, the second was indescribable. He had taken only about three swallows, but the drugged wine lay in his stomach like molten lead. He wanted to retch it up, but even that seemed to require too much effort. Pressure had focused behind his closed eyes, churning, throbbing, passing quickly through mere discomfort into true pain that curdled and boiled just beneath the top of his skull.

The agony of it made him want to scream, but a hand across his mouth prevented it. His body began to arch against the hands restraining it, his limbs going into spasms. He kept thinking it could not possibly get worse—but it did. And worse beyond that.

Some distant part of his body that really belonged to someone else finally began swallowing, gulping great swallows of something that slid down his tortured throat like molten snow. He choked and coughed, but someone commanded him to keep swallowing, and he could not disobey.

But then, far too slowly, the anguish was receding under ever-darkening waves that brought a gradual sinking, though oblivion was laced with flashes of nightmare shadow that persisted for many lifetimes. Finally, mercifully, he slipped into utter emptiness.

Consciousness returned some time later to the accompaniment of a throbbing in his head and a sick, queasy stirring in his stomach. Candlelight beating at his closed eyelids intensified the pain, and he moaned as he raised one arm to lay across his eyes.

The sound summoned someone to sit down beside him on his right, slightly depressing whatever he was lying on, tilting him slightly downward on that side. Even that slight movement intensified the pain throbbing behind his eyes and set new nausea churning in his empty stomach. As he curled onto his side, reflexively clutching at his gut with the arm that was not shielding his eyes, he could feel a strong arm shifting under his head, lifting it slightly. The movement severed the last shred of control that was keeping him from throwing up, and he found himself retching into a basin that somehow was exactly where it needed to be.

A soft cloth was wiping across his mouth when he was done, the basin somehow removed. And as he collapsed weakly onto his back again, he forced his eyes to open and focus on his benefactor—and recoiled in an instant of sheer, mindless panic as his eyes beheld the black habit and haloed lion-head badge of a *Custodes* monk.

"Easy!" a somehow familiar voice said, though Javan could not quite seem to put a name to the tanned face with the short-cropped *Custodes* tonsure. "It's Jesse. You're going to be fine. Unfortunately, you seem to have acquired a Deryni aversion to *merasha* as well as an affinity for handling Deryni powers."

Javan's relief that it was Jesse washed through him like a wave of comfort, leaving him weak and helpless. He could not remember ever feeling so miserable before, even that time Tavis had made him ill to lure Rhys to them. A part of him decided that he deserved to suffer thus, that he was being punished for his part in Rhys' death.

"Here, now," Jesse murmured, brushing a tanned hand across his burning forehead and obviously able to Read exactly what was going through Javan's mind. "Don't do this to yourself. That wasn't your fault. You did what you thought you had to do. Rhys' death was an unfortunate accident."

Somehow, though he had told himself otherwise for nearly four years, Javan began to believe the poised young Deryni who kept whispering reassurance and easing thoughts with the words, past shields still hopelessly in tatters. He let the man raise him long enough to give him something cool to drink, swallowing obediently, letting the other's mind enfold his and soothe his pain. Eventually he slipped into blessed sleep.

He woke again at midmorning to a golden flood of sunlight pouring through the open balcony doors of his sleeping chamber, still feeling fragile but with his headache now diminished to a dull ache behind his eyes. Jesse was gone, and Charlan was laying out fresh clothing. The young knight smiled as he saw that his master was awake, nothing in his expression indicating that he was aware of anything untoward having occurred during the night. Javan decided that Guiscard must already have made the necessary adjustments to their human ally's memory, now that the crisis was past.

And it did seem to be past. Javan closed his eyes briefly and tested first at his shields, then at his ability to cast out with his senses, and found all intact, if a little stiff, like sore muscles after too strenuous a physical exertion, if mental abilities could be likened to the body.

He opened his eyes and sat up slowly, stretching carefully and glancing out the window as Guiscard also came into the room.

"How late is it?" Javan asked.

"Nearly noon. You had a rough night of it."

Javan snorted. "Somehow I knew that." He blinked again, bracing himself before swinging his legs over the edge of the bed to cool the soles of his feet against the stone floor.

"You know, I think it might have been better to wait until winter to try this," he said to Guiscard. "I thought I was burning."

"You could have done it in a snowbank and it wouldn't have helped," Guiscard said, handing him a goblet.

"What's this?"

"Just water. I'd advise drinking a lot of it in the next day or two, to flush the last of the drug out of your body. I've also drawn you a cool bath in the next room. If you think you're up to it, an appearance downstairs probably wouldn't go amiss. Etienne's managed to come up with a query regarding those documents he was working on last night that makes it pointless to have the Council meet this afternoon, so you don't have to face that prospect. You might try a few rounds at the archery butts, if the thump of the arrows wouldn't bother your headache too much."

As Javan grimaced, Guiscard added, "I don't think you really want to ride with that head. And you certainly don't want anyone bashing you on a practice helmet or clanging swords in your vicinity."

"Archery," Javan agreed, heading for the garderobe. "Guiscard," he called from inside, "was I dreaming earlier, or did a *Custodes* monk really come to visit me during the night?"

"Oh, you had a lot of nightmares last night, Sire," came the cheery reply, "but I don't think he was one of them. Actually, he said you did very well."

As Javan came out, he gave Guiscard a doubtful shake of his head. "If that was well done, I'd hate to be at the bottom of the class." He sighed. "Well, one more thing to worry about. But where's this bath you promised?"

Javan survived his stint at the archery butts, though he shot rather more poorly than he had in months. A few of the younger knights inquired about his headache of the previous evening, and he admitted having had a restless night despite a court physician's ministrations, but he assured them he was feeling better now.

He retired early that night, allowing Guiscard to assist him into sleep, and woke largely recovered the next morning. A brisk ride along the river did much to restore him further, and only a vague feeling of malaise lingered through the Council meeting that afternoon. After another good night's sleep, this time without Guiscard's help, he counted the incident past, though he found himself wondering when and whether he ought to warn his brother of what he had discovered.

In the weeks that followed, regular letters from Jason continued to reassure the king that he been right to send his brother into the field. A report from the usually sober Lord Ainslie, of the prince presiding over his first local Court, was almost effusive in its praise.

The prince was gracious but single-minded, giving careful consideration to all evidence presented, no matter the witness be highborn or low, Ainslie wrote. *He has a good ear for nuances of testimony. I think your Highness would be proud of him.*

Auguries closer to home were not so favorable. Javan had expected a relatively quiet autumn, once Rhys Michael left, and other than his bout with *merasha*, it was. But when days stretched into weeks without the return of Paulin, Javan began to worry that it might be all too quiet.

Not that he particularly wanted Paulin back in Rhemuth, but he wondered what plots the *Custodes* Vicar General might be hatching with his Deryni agent at *Arx Fidei*, especially with the time fast approaching for another of Father Faelan's debriefings.

When he inquired of Lord Albertus about the delay in Paulin's return, the Earl Marshal indicated vaguely that he thought it had to do with the lingering illness of one Brother Georgius, a boyhood friend, whose passing was expected at any time. His phrasing left Javan uncertain whether Brother Georgius even existed, but it was nothing he dared pursue, lest he arouse unwanted suspicion.

Whatever the true motivations behind Paulin's continued absence, it was seen with increasing dread by Father Faelan. As the month wore on, he made it increasingly clear to Javan that he really did not want to go back to *Arx Fidei* again.

The priest's reluctance was certainly understandable, if inconvenient. Since he had survived the first return engagement, Javan was confident that Faelan probably was not in danger of being forced to divulge anything damaging to either Javan or himself, even if deeply probed by Paulin's Deryni agent. Javan also had been careful not to expose the priest to anything else in the ensuing month that he did not want Paulin to know about. If possible, he wanted to let Faelan slip solely into the role of royal confessor, with no further involvement in intrigues of the sort necessitated just after his arrival. After a few months of totally innocuous reporting, Javan hoped that the *Custodes* would lose interest in Faelan and let him get on with being the ordinary priest he longed to be.

That mattered not a bit to Faelan, who had no conscious knowledge of how Javan was trying to protect him. His dread of being put through a repeat of his first interrogation at the abbey only increased as the appointed time for his departure drew near. Given the real possibility that *Custodes* whim might cost Faelan his life on any given return, it did not seem appropriate that Javan should force his compliance, even though he could have done it without him being any the wiser. As Faelan had told Javan when he first arrived at Court, it was one thing to die for *something* . . .

Javan did insist that Faelan consider the possible consequences if he did not go. He could grant Faelan physical protection and even try to persuade Paulin that Faelan's failure to return came of Javan's own refusal to let him go; but at best, it would raise new questions about what he or the king might have to hide. And if perceived as willful disobedience on Faelan's part, it could bring suspension as a priest, expulsion from the Order, and even excommunication.

Michaelmas came and went—Rhys Michael's birthday, celebrated with a modest feast at which king and Court drank the prince's health in absentia—and the following Monday, the appointed day for Faelan's departure. That afternoon, Father Ascelin came up from Saint Hilary's, for he was Faelan's designated replacement when the priest was scheduled to be away; but Faelan did not leave. Two days later, just after midday, Paulin himself arrived back at the capital with only a pair of *Custodes* knights for escort, all of them on well-lathered horses. Very shortly, Javan was summoned for an immediate and urgent audience on behalf of the *Custodes* Vicar General.

CHAPTER THIRTY-ONE

For their heart studieth destruction, and their
lips talk of mischief.

—Proverbs 24:2

"Sire, I wish to inquire why Father Faelan has not yet presented himself at *Arx Fidei*," Paulin began, coming right to the point. He had not even taken the time to change from his dusty riding clothes. "He is expected on the first Monday of every month, as you well know. When he did not appear after two days, I began to be concerned. Am I to understand that Father Faelan has not yet departed Rhemuth?"

"That is correct, my lord," Javan replied. He had received Paulin informally in the little withdrawing room behind the dais of the great hall, attended only by Charlan and Robear. He was wearing the Haldane sword and the coronet of running lions with a red Haldane tunic. Lord Albertus accompanied the *Custodes* Vicar General, looking altogether too menacing in his black leathers and the mantle of the Order. Like everyone except Paulin, he, too, wore a sword at his side, close by the red-fringed white sash of his *Custodes* knighthood.

"Father Faelan has *not* departed Rhemuth," Paulin repeated incredulously.

"That is my understanding."

"Might one ask why? I thought I had made it clear that his monthly retreats were one of the conditions of his appointment to the royal household."

Javan leaned back carefully in his chair of state, measuring Paulin with his eyes.

"My lord, it is barely three weeks since Father Faelan's return from *last* month's retreat," he said boldly, neglecting to mention that his own delay of Faelan's first trip had added to Paulin's delay letting him return. "Already I begin to find such absences intrusive. I should think quarterly would be sufficient. It certainly was not convenient that he be away from Court again so quickly at this time."

"With all respect, Sire, the convenience of this Court—"

"The convenience of the king's Court is essential to the king's peace of mind," Javan went on. "To maintain that peace of mind, a king needs the regular services of his confessor. Or would you dispute that, Vicar General?"

"No one would dispute the need for regular confession, Sire," Paulin muttered. "But a confessor who himself needs confessing can be of little use to your Highness."

"Perhaps Father Faelan has availed himself of other confessors in the city, if he felt the need," Javan observed. "Not that such a man can have much to confess. His attention to his duties has been exemplary—which comes as no surprise to me, having known him at *Arx Fidei*. His gentle piety continues to be an inspiration to all with whom he comes in contact. I can think of no higher praise for any priest."

"You suggest he has confessed himself to priests outside his Order?" Paulin said sharply, ignoring the praise. "That is a blatant breach of the Rule, as you well know, Sire. No doubt the temptations to relax proper discipline are far greater at Court than in a monastic setting—which is precisely the reason I stipulated monthly retreats as a condition of his assignment."

Javan allowed himself an almost indolent shrug, wishing he had not mentioned other confessors. "I do not know that he has transgressed thus, my lord. Nor is it my place to comment, no longer being of your Order."

The oblique reminder of Javan's defection did nothing to mollify Paulin's growing anger.

"Whether or not he has availed himself of a foreign confessor," he said coldly, "Father Faelan's failure to present himself for the required retreat is a breach of his vow of obedience. If you had forbidden him to go, he would have been obliged to inform Father Ascelin, which he did not do.

"Therefore I must conclude that this is Faelan's decision, at least in part—though I find it appalling that so exemplary a priest should suddenly throw away everything he has achieved in his years with our Order. If he is truly set upon defying the instructions of his superiors, I shall be obliged to recall him to his community for discipline."

"I have not forbidden him to go," Javan said coolly. "Nor shall I command him to do so. I *have* made it clear that I shall support him in whatever decision he makes in this matter."

"I see," Paulin said. "You have encouraged him in this—"

"Here, now!" Robear rumbled, no longer able to keep silence.

"I wish to hear this folly from Faelan's own lips," Paulin said, ignoring Robear. "I fear that his exalted status as the king's confessor may have gone to his head. In part, I must blame myself for that. He was far too young to be burdened with such a weighty responsibility. Spiritual direction is all the more urgent, to assist him in recognizing the error of his ways. I shall go to him immediately."

"You shall go nowhere unless I give you leave," Javan said sharply. "If you wish to see my confessor, you may do so in my presence, unless he himself requests otherwise."

"Sire, this violates numerous points of canon law," Paulin muttered.

"Nonetheless, it is my decision. Sir Robear, please ask Father Faelan to attend me, if he wishes to do so. Inform him of the identity of our guests, and say that I do not command his presence. However, if he intends to address Father Paulin's inquiries at all, as I think he must do eventually, I suggest it might be best done here."

"You take entirely too much upon yourself, Sire," Paulin muttered through clenched teeth, as Robear made a brisk bow and went out. "How dare you presume to dictate how I shall deal with *my* priest? Faelan will do as I command. He comes and goes at *my* bidding. If I say that he *dies*, then he dies!"

"You have not that authority," Javan stated flatly. "You are *my* subject, and I will not brook defiance from you or any other subject. Now, mind your tongue, if you wish me to oblige you by allowing this interview with Father Faelan."

He knew, as soon as Faelan came into the room, that both he and the priest had made a mistake. As was his usual wont, Faelan was immaculately turned out, his black habit neatly brushed, his cowled scapular falling in precise folds, his tonsure gleaming newly shaven on his bowed head.

But gone was the gentle diffidence that had marked his first few weeks at Court, as he came out from under the shadow of his arrival, and before his first return to *Arx Fidei*. Cowed apprehension was in his every movement, in the very set of his shoulders, as he first bowed to the king, then came to bend his knee before his religious superior. Paulin permitted him to touch his lips to the abbot's ring on his hand, but stayed him from rising when Faelan would have gotten to his feet.

"I am surprised to see you here, Father," he said coolly. "It was my understanding that you should have reported to *Arx Fidei* some days ago, for your monthly retreat."

"It—was not convenient that I leave Court at this time, your Grace," Faelan murmured, eyes miserably downcast.

"And is the Court's convenience any reason to shirk your religious duty?" Paulin replied. "Did the king forbid you to go?"

"N-no, your Grace. It was my decision."

"It was your decision to be willfully disobedient to your superiors," Paulin said. "That is a grave sin, Father."

Closing his eyes, Faelan drew a deep breath. "I—could not face the prospect of—what transpired before, your Grace."

"Why, whatever can you mean, Father?" Paulin purred, warning in his voice. "Were you ever used other than for the good of your immortal soul?"

"I—am certain that was the intent, your Grace," Faelan said lamely.

"But you presume to judge otherwise?" Paulin asked. "That is the sin of pride, Father. I fear you have fallen far short of the mark. Disobedience and pride are grievous sins. For the good of your immortal soul, I order you to return to *Arx Fidei* for a period of fasting and reflection, that you may come to see the error of your ways and find contrition in your heart. Personally, I have always held that obedience presents even more of a challenge to most young priests than chastity. Fortunately, both these virtues can be reinforced through appropriate discipline and—"

"I would rather die," Faelan whispered, his words almost inaudible.

"What was that, Father?"

"I said I would rather die than go back!" Faelan repeated, his head jerking up with a start, the dark eyes wild and frightened. "I will never submit to that again. Never! I would rather—"

"I did not ask what you would rather do," Paulin said coldly. "I ordered you to—"

"You order no one in my hall, my lord!" Javan said, finally having heard enough. "Father Faelan has made it clear that he does not wish to return to *Arx Fidei*. The subject, therefore, is closed."

"If he does not go back, then he places himself outside the protection of the Order," Paulin said. "Furthermore, such willful disobedience by a priest toward his superior is grounds for immediate suspension. If he defies the suspension, excommunication will follow. Is it worth it, Father?" he said, rounding on the quaking Faelan, who had collapsed onto his haunches, face buried in his hands. "Is your loyalty to a secular king who has forsaken his own holy vows and would lure you from your own, or to the Order to which you willingly gave the care of your immortal soul?"

"That's enough!" Javan said, coming to his feet to interpose himself between Paulin and the trembling Faelan, one hand upflung to warn Albertus against intervening. "It becomes increasingly clear that your real quarrel isn't with Faelan; it's with me. Believe me when I tell you that Father Faelan had no part in my decision to leave your Order. He was and is a good priest, but you have driven him to this. Most reluctantly, he finally told me what was done to him before you let him come to Court. I find it appalling that you would sacrifice so good a man merely to get at me."

Paulin drew himself to his full height and looked down his long nose at Javan, Albertus sidling closer, one hand on the hilt of his sword—and Charlan and Robear fingering theirs—then exhaled on a long sigh.

"I see that the situation is even more serious than I imagined," he said quietly. "Rot, quite obviously, is at the very root of this Court." He turned a disdainful gaze on Faelan, still cowering at his feet.

"I offer you one remaining chance to save your immortal soul, Father," he said. "Submit to the authority you swore to uphold when you made your holy vows to the *Ordo Custodum Fidei*. Come away with me now and let Brother Albertus take you back to *Arx Fidei* for spiritual counseling. From this moment, because I greatly fear for your spiritual health, I relieve you of your priestly duties, until such time as your superiors may judge you fit to resume sacerdotal function."

Faelan's body recoiled as if struck a physical blow, but he did not raise his head.

"If you refuse this most generous offer," Paulin went on, his voice drawing out the phrase in dreadful anticipation, "I shall take immediate steps to excommunicate you." He turned on Javan. "And if, in defiance of suspension and excommunication, Father Faelan attempts to exercise any part of his priestly office, I shall ask the archbishop to place the entire Court of Gwynedd under interdict. He will do this and impute the blame to you, since you personally would be responsible for allowing Faelan to defy the bans of suspension and excommunication in your Court, he having been your confessor."

"I will appeal to the archbishop myself, Vicar General," Javan said coldly. "There will be no interdict."

"No *Custodes* priest will serve you, until you make your peace with the Order," Paulin warned.

"There are other priests, other Orders," Javan said. "I will temporarily seek another confessor from among them."

"You are free to seek, but you will not find."

"Be that as it may," Javan said, though he felt less certain than he hoped he sounded. "I take Father Faelan under my personal protection. He has transgressed no civil law. If you believe he has defied canon law, I require that you present concrete evidence as to his error. Other than declining to return to a place where grievous hurt was done to him without cause, I find no fault with him. Nor would any honest man."

"That is not for you to judge," Paulin said. He planted his hands behind his back and glared down at Faelan. "Be aware, Father, that your own willfulness has brought your fate upon you. At the setting of the sun, you will be declared excommunicate, with all the opprobrium that can be focused upon so pitiful a sinner as yourself, but it is you who have already separated yourself from God and His Church. When you eventually come to your senses and repent of your errors, Mother Church will joyfully receive you to her bosom, but until that time, you have consigned yourself to outer darkness. I also remind you that, should you die without having sought reconciliation, you approach the throne of heaven already damned." He made Javan a curt nod. "Sire."

With that, he turned on his heel and stalked from the room, Albertus at his heels. Robear looked ready to charge out after him— and did—and Charlan was glaring murder in his eyes, but Javan's concern was only for Faelan.

"Father, I'm sorry," he murmured, sinking to his knees beside the huddled priest, slipping an arm around his shoulders. "Don't worry. I'll protect you. I shouldn't have asked you to come here. I should have realized that Paulin would know how to cut you to the quick without even drawing steel."

He was appalled to find that Faelan was weeping silent, choking tears, his head weaving back and forth in anguished denial.

"It isn't your fault, Sire," he managed to choke out. "I have failed in my vocation. I should have held my tongue when I first came to you and simply served you as best I could. I should have borne my burden silently. And yet—"

"And yet?" Javan whispered.

Faelan sniffled miserably and raised his chin, but he could not bear to look Javan in the eyes. "And yet, it did give me joy to offer up the Mysteries in your behalf, Sire. At the abbey, when first we met, I cared for you as I cared for any of my brethren, but as your tutor, I also came to treasure the intellect you brought before me to be trained. I never had a finer or more eager student."

The raw emotion pouring from Faelan almost overwhelmed Javan, and he had to blink back tears.

"That should have been enough for me—I know that now," Faelan went on haltingly. "Perhaps it *was* pride that led me to answer the summons when you became my king and sent for me. I should have realized, when they put me to the question—" He shook his head.

"But I have failed you. As your confessor, it should be my role to help you in your work. Instead, I have become an occasion of contention between you and the Order to which I had offered up my heart and soul. That they should turn against you, and ask me to do so as well—" He shook his head. "I—do not know if I can bear this, Sire. To lose my priesthood and to be excommunicated, barred from all solace of the Sacraments—"

"Keep heart, my friend," Javan murmured, himself sick at heart. "You have a refuge here for as long as you need it, and you are still a priest forever, regardless of what Paulin may say. While, as king, I cannot allow you public exercise of your office until this is resolved, you are free to celebrate in private, within your own quarters. If it causes you no distress, I would also be pleased if you would continue to celebrate Mass privately for me there, with selected members of my personal staff."

"And risk interdict, Sire?"

"Someone would have to find out first, wouldn't they?" Javan retorted with a grim little smile. "But come. I don't *need* to hear Mass until Sunday. Maybe this will be resolved by then. Meanwhile, why don't you go back to your quarters and lie down? Sleep would do you good."

"I couldn't sleep," Faelan said miserably as Javan helped him to his feet. "I will never find peace until this shadow is lifted from me—and Father Paulin will never relent."

"I agree that the shadow needs to be lifted," Javan said, reaching out with his senses, "but I think you'll find that you can sleep." He touched controls at the edge of Faelan's mind and sent a wave of drowsiness rolling briefly over his consciousness, bracing his arm around Faelan's shoulder as the priest swayed on his feet.

"Shall I help you sleep, Faelan? Just briefly, you can remember all that you have been to me besides my confessor. Will you let me help you in this?"

He saw in Faelan's eyes when the memory surfaced, in a blink and a brief unfocusing of the dark gaze. Then those eyes were turning to him again in fearfulness but also in trust and in full knowledge of what Javan was and what he could do, Faelan's taut shoulders relaxing against his arm.

"Aye, my liege," he whispered. "Sleep would be a mercy. I place myself in your hands."

"Good man," Javan murmured, setting his free hand across Faelan's eyes as they closed. "Deep sleep. And remember none of this."

A moment only it took to set the controls. Then he was giving the priest into Charlan's hands to walk him back to his quarters. He went with them as far as the door. Outside, the fuming Robear had been watching Paulin and Albertus retreat down the great hall, the two of them pausing occasionally to speak to other black-clad *Custodes* before disappearing through the doors at the far end. Robear turned as Javan emerged, casting a look of query after Charlan as the younger knight led Faelan away by another route.

"Is he all right?" Robear murmured.

"He will be, after he's slept a bit."

Robear shook his head, folding his arms across his chest. "Paulin was rough on the priest. What did he *do* to him, before they let him come to you?"

"Assorted tortures, in the name of religion," Javan said briefly. "You don't want to know details."

"Probably not. Will Paulin really excommunicate him?"

"I expect so. Would you place me an observer or two and see if he does?"

Robear nodded. "I'll see to it. He said sunset. You'll be in your quarters, when I have something to report?"

"Aye."

Without further word, Robear sketched him a salute and headed off down the great hall. Javan, after watching him for a few seconds, went off in the direction Charlan had gone with Faelan.

An hour after sunset, Archbishop Hubert joined Paulin of Ramos in the sacristy of Rhemuth Cathedral, as the latter was taking off the vestments he had worn to pronounce Father Faelan's excommunication. It was Paulin who had presided over the ceremony, but Hubert and Archbishop Oriss had been in prominent attendance, as were several dozen *Custodes* brethren and most of the cathedral chapter. Albertus and one of his knights stood guard outside the sacristy door, for Paulin had not been at all certain the king would permit the excommunication to take place.

"My Lord Archbishop," Paulin said formally as Hubert came

into the sacristy. Father Lior was just lifting a black cope from his shoulders from behind. "Thank you for attending. The presence of yourself and Archbishop Oriss ensures that the excommunication will be heeded. I confess myself still somewhat amazed that the king permitted it to proceed."

He was left wearing a very plain alb over his black *Custodes* habit, with black stole and cincture stark against the snowy white. Hubert likewise was funereally clad in a plain priest's cassock rather than his customary purple, relieved only by his ring and pectoral cross. The expanse of black made the archbishop look less ample than usual, but only just, as he gave Paulin an indolent shrug.

"Despite his defiance of canon law in this particular instance, the king understands it well enough," Hubert said as Paulin pulled off his stole and handed it to Lior. "Faelan, by his own actions, had already excommunicated himself. It would have served no purpose to stop the formal declaration of that excommunication. Besides that, I do not believe the king wishes to force any public confrontation with your Order at this time. He has enemies enough at Court. Open warfare with so powerful a faction is hardly in his best interests."

"Perhaps not, but he *has* declared war on us," Paulin replied. "He certainly has declared war on me."

He had been pulling off the black cincture cord from around his waist, and now looped it around both his hands and tugged it taut, as if he wished it were around a royal neck. "The insolence—"

"He is yet young," Hubert murmured, calmly taking the cincture from Paulin and starting to coil it up. "I will try to reason with him. There are those of us he *cannot* eliminate from the circles of power, and he must be made to realize that it is in everyone's best interests to reach an accommodation. This business of Father Faelan is not in anyone's best interests, as it will further polarize the Court—especially if the disciplines imposed on Faelan should become general knowledge."

"Laymen don't understand the nuances of monastic discipline," Paulin muttered from inside his alb, which he and Lior were endeavoring to pull off over his head.

"That's true," Hubert agreed. "In particular, they wouldn't understand about minution, especially as it was applied to Father Faelan—and to the king. Of course, Javan was only the heir presumptive then."

Stony-faced, Paulin emerged from under the folds of white linen and pushed the garment roughly into Lior's hands. "Thank you, Father, you may leave us."

Smooth as silk, Lior bowed and laid the alb across a chair back, then quietly withdrew. When he had gone, Paulin turned away from the archbishop and began putting on the wide crimson sash that marked him as Vicar General.

"Mind you, I'm not criticizing your methods," Hubert said with a droll grimace, moving in to help Paulin wrap the sash around his waist. "I'm certain minution made the desired impression on Father Faelan at the time, just as I'm certain the king will never forget his experience of same. You must admit, however, that by lay standards, Faelan's interrogation before he came to Court could be viewed as excessive. It could reflect badly on the Order, if he were to make his experience generally known."

"No one would believe him," Paulin said.

"Well, the king *could* allow Faelan to make his statement before Oriel or Sitric and bid them confirm whether or not he was telling the truth . . ."

Paulin moved a bit farther from the door, closer to the little vesting altar, finishing the knot of his sash with a vicious tug.

"Our wayward prince is getting entirely out of hand," he said softly after a moment. "I'm not sure you're as able to control him as you think you are."

Hubert pursed his rosebud lips and mildly surveyed his *Custodes* counterpart.

"Thus far, I'm confident he can be brought to heel," he said. "I think it's premature to begin considering the sorts of things I suspect are going through your mind. If something were to happen to the king, I'd feel much more at ease if I knew the succession were a bit more secure. I still believe Rhys Michael can be led far more easily than Javan—but then, virgin minds are always easier to guide."

Snorting, Paulin slung his *Custodes* mantle around his shoulders, bending his head down to fasten the clasp of haloed lion-heads. "Speaking of virgins, what of the Drummond girl? Is she still?" he asked.

"I don't know," Hubert said thoughtfully. "She went off with Manfred's household several weeks ago, as we knew would happen, but I had no opportunity to speak to Rhys Michael after that. He was notably aloof, those last few days, for a young man betrothed to a lovely girl who's about to go away for several months."

"Does Javan know about the betrothal?"

"I don't know that, either. I do have a plan for reuniting our young lovers, however. If we can make the official match a *fait accompli* before the king realizes what's happened, so much the better. Let me work matters in my own time, though."

"Very well."

"Meanwhile," Hubert went on, "you will keep me advised regarding Father Faelan's further reactions regarding what has been set in motion. I should not like to have to place the royal household under interdict. It would considerably increase the tension already hampering my attempts to guide the king in Council."

"Perhaps Faelan will submit."

Hubert nodded. "I hope so. Disobedience is a grievous fault in a priest." He sighed. "Most inconvenient."

"Indeed."

After Hubert had gone, Paulin considered a variety of resolutions concerning the increasingly inconvenient Father Faelan. Later he passed on certain orders to his brother, to be carried out at Albertus' discretion, when general reaction to Faelan's excommunication had somewhat died away.

CHAPTER THIRTY-TWO

Let us condemn him with a shameful death.
—Wisdom of Solomon 2:20

Javan felt as if he were walking on eggshells for the first few days after Faelan's excommunication. Though Faelan himself seemed to bear up well enough, once he had gotten a good night's sleep, Javan had to face Paulin, Albertus, and Hubert in the Council the next day. The three were civil enough, and Paulin even inquired about Faelan's state of mind, coolly but correctly solicitous for the excommunicant's spiritual welfare.

"I couldn't really comment on that, my lord," Javan said neutrally. "He was very distressed last night, as you can well imagine. No doubt you will have been informed that he did not appear for Mass this morning."

"That must have been inconvenient for many of the faithful who customarily attend that Mass and were wont to rely upon his guidance," Paulin observed.

Javan inclined his head. "No doubt it was. I wish circumstances were otherwise. But you must understand, my lord, that I had no choice but to support Father Faelan in his decision. I have a sworn duty to protect those of my household, and it was not my place to force Faelan to go against his conscience."

Paulin simply nodded, and Archbishop Oriss deftly turned the Council's discussion to an inquiry regarding progress on Lord Jerowen's index of the law, with special attention to the elusive records of Alroy's regency.

"I believe Lord Tammaron has made notable progress in that regard, Sire," he said. "Is that not so, my lord?"

"It is," Tammaron agreed. "A large number of the records have been located, and I hope to deliver them into Lord Jerowen's custody as soon as we have finished sorting and arranging them in some comprehensible form—perhaps as soon as tomorrow."

"We find that a goodly number of them date from Duke Ewan's tenure on the Council," Rhun added sourly, as Tammaron passed a few sample documents along either side of the table. "Unfortunately, men like Ewan often lack administrative skills."

Whether that was true of Ewan or simply Rhun taking the opportunity to further tarnish Ewan's good name, Javan did not know. He found it interesting that Rhun had framed his comment in such a way that even being Truth-Read, he could not be caught in an outright lie. He wondered if Rhun suspected him or had simply developed the skill from working with his own Deryni, as a further defense against what he himself was quite willing to have used on others.

Javan did know that in the two months since he had first raised the question about the regency records, Tammaron and his staff had spent long hours working late in the chancery offices—though whether they were searching for the missing records or fabricating new ones was not at all clear. Whatever the source, Tammaron did indeed deliver the records to Lord Jerowen that very night.

Javan suspended official meetings of the Council for the remainder of the week. It took that long to make sense of the records and begin to see how they fit into the overall picture emerging of the state of Gwynedd's laws. He found it difficult to concentrate on administration when he was worried about Faelan, but he made himself spend time with Jerowen, learning what he could.

Meanwhile, a *Custodes* priest named Father Daíthi quietly took up the day-to-day duties attached to the Chapel Royal, so that the pattern of Mass and daily Offices resumed even in Father Faelan's absence. Javan visited Faelan regularly in his quarters and tried to convince him that submission was probably the better part of valor—Paulin would never relent until the priest had made his peace with the Order—but Faelan was tearfully adamant that he would not. Daily Father Daíthi was sent on behalf of the Order to plead with Faelan to reconsider, for the sake of his immortal soul; daily Faelan heard the plea and shakily declined.

It was nearly a week after Faelan's excommunication that Lord Albertus decided it was time to carry out the orders Paulin had given him. Toward midnight, the Grand Master of the *Equites Cus-*

todum Fidei and three of his knights made their way quietly up a back stair to the quarters of the king's former confessor, approaching from the opposite end of the corridor from where the king's apartments lay. Albertus' quiet knock brought Father Faelan to the door almost immediately, wide-eyed and instantly apprehensive when he saw who it was.

His apprehension was well founded, for two of the knights manhandled him back into the room without preamble, one of them clapping a hand over his mouth before he could cry out and the third binding his hands behind with brisk efficiency. Albertus said nothing while the prisoner was secured, merely pulling the door gently closed behind him and then casting his gaze dispassionately around the room.

The setting was quite to his liking, just as he had envisioned it. Faelan had been at his devotions, his breviary lying open on the armrest of the *prie-dieu* in the little oratory. Beside it burned a fat yellow candle in a holder of black wrought iron, its light all but overpowering the subtler glow of the Presence Lamp flickering behind red glass farther back in the oratory. Beyond the *prie-dieu*, between it and the narrow window embrasure, was a small writing table with a chair behind. One of the knights pulled out the chair and set it in the center of the little chamber, where his fellows deposited their prisoner without ceremony.

The motion shifted Albertus' attention back to the object of their midnight visit. As one of the knights came to stand with his back against the door, leaving the other two to keep their prisoner under control, Albertus moved a few strides closer to the quaking Faelan, saying nothing as he gazed down at him in disdain. Faelan had been thoroughly gagged, with fabric stuffed hard into his mouth and a wide band tied around his cheeks.

"Good evening, Father," he said softly.

Faelan looked terrified and was, pale as whey against the stark blackness of his habit, which was open at the throat. This late, he clearly had not been expecting further visitors. As was his custom, he had put aside both his hooded scapular and the braided cincture of Haldane crimson and gold before kneeling down to read the final Office of the night. The scapular, with its crimson lining and the haloed lion's head of the Order emblazoned on the left breast, lay neatly folded in prescribed fashion on the chest at the foot of his bed, with the cincture coiled atop it. Albertus smiled as he returned his gaze to his captive, but the smile was cold.

"I see that some of the discipline of the Order remains, Father," he said quietly, his voice barely above a whisper. "Perhaps that means there is still hope for you. I am instructed to ask you a few questions. It would be inconvenient if you were to draw attention to our conversation, and I do not know that I can trust you not to cry out, so I shall leave you gagged and phrase my questions so that you may answer yes or no by the appropriate motion of your head. Do you understand?"

Faelan was nearly retching with terror behind his gag, but he managed to nod yes.

"Good," Albertus said. "Now, I understand that you resent the discipline that was given you before you were brought to be the king's chaplain. I wonder, was it the scourging or the minution to which you most objected?"

Eyes widening, Faelan made a futile attempt to struggle free, cut short when one of his captors cuffed him sharply on the side of his head.

"Here now, Father, that's hardly appropriate behavior when these good brethren are merely trying to restrain you for your own good," Albertus purred. "They haven't drawn blood, though. I think that's what frightens you most, isn't it, Father?"

As Faelan wilted in his captors' hands, gone white with fear, Albertus smiled.

"I thought so," he said. "Perhaps a short discourse is indicated, for your instruction." He folded his hands behind his back.

"The efficacy of minution is twofold. First, it is granted as a grace to assist brethren in maintaining the spiritual serenity appropriate to a celibate life. In all candor, I have never heard report that the vow of celibacy was difficult for you, Father, so it must be the second application that distresses you. As a discipline, minution is intended as a test and a reinforcement of one's vow of absolute obedience. That is why we require it once of every member of the Order, whether clergy like yourself or laymen like myself and these good brethren." He indicated the knights with a sweep of one hand, then let that hand rest lightly on the hilt of the dagger at his waist.

"Occasionally we require it again, Father," he said softly, "especially when there is some suspicion that the pupil has forgotten his lesson from the first time 'round. If the pupil continues to forget, it sometimes becomes necessary to keep repeating the lesson, until the pupil either learns or . . ."

As he let his voice trail off suggestively, Faelan shook his head again, horrified. Unaffected by his victim's terror, Albertus glanced at one of the knights holding him. At his nod, the man wrenched Faelan forward so that his fellow could pull back first one sleeve and then the other, examining his arms for the scar of the previous minution. There was none, for Oriel had healed it. Faelan closed his eyes briefly as they made their inspection, whimpering a little in his throat and trying to look away, but Albertus seized his chin and turned him face-on again as the knights yanked him back in the chair.

"Why, Father Faelan, we can find no scar to prove that you have ever undergone minution," the Grand Master said softly. "You allowed Master Oriel to heal it, didn't you?" He shook his head. "Could you not bear to retain one little scar to remind you of the obedience you owe your Order? Or perhaps, when you came to Court, you chose instead to offer your obedience to the king, far beyond what was required of you as his confessor.

"Yes, I fear we have come upon the truth now, Father. You rejected the discipline of the Order, just as the king rejected it. Besides the pride and disobedience that led to your suspension and excommunication, I think you have broken your vows to the Order and made yourself the king's man instead of God's man. Did you really think that your betrayal could remain undiscovered?"

Faelan was sobbing now, shaking his head in terrified denial, as Albertus casually reached over to the foot of the bed and caught up the *Custodes* cincture of Haldane crimson and gold.

"You have disgraced this token, Father," Albertus said softly, uncoiling the doubled length of silken cord, knotted and intertwined together. "You have chosen loyalty to the colors of the House of Haldane over the unity of holy and secular law that this cincture symbolizes. So be it. You shall not be asked to wear these colors again as a member of the *Ordo Custodum Fidei.*"

He wrapped several turns of the cincture around each of his hands, leaving a span between them slightly narrower than his shoulders, then glanced at the two knights holding the captive and gave a nod. Helpless as they braced their hands to hold him, Faelan closed his eyes and tried to gasp out a prayer around the gag already choking him, now well aware that it was not minution that was to be his death.

When Father Faelan did not answer the summons of the priest who came the next morning to deliver his now-customary plea for a return to the fold, the man tried the door and found it locked, then went and told the guard outside the entrance to the king's apartments. The guard reported it to Sir Guiscard, who was duty aide that morning.

Inside, the king was dressing for weapons practice, Charlan helping him buckle on leather body armor. Both Charlan and Guiscard were already similarly attired. The guard's report raised immediate apprehension in the minds of all three men, for it was not at all like Faelan to sleep so soundly or so late, especially this past week.

Exchanging worried glances with his aides, Javan told the guard to make certain the priest did not leave, hurriedly strapping on the Haldane sword over his practice leathers while Guiscard briefly disappeared to his quarters across the hall to fetch a slender length of brass rod, sharply bent at the end. Wordlessly Javan led the way to Faelan's quarters, Father Daíthi trailing wide-eyed behind in custody of the guard. A knock at Faelan's door produced no response.

"Father Faelan?" Javan called, knocking again. "Father Faelan, are you in there?"

Again, no response. As expected, the door latch did not move when Javan tried it, so he stepped back to let Guiscard crouch down with his bit of brass.

"Do you think he's gone out?" Javan asked softly as Guiscard probed at the lock. He could sense no living presence beyond the door. "He hasn't left this room since the excommunication, but maybe he decided to submit. Maybe he went down to the chapel to pray."

The lock yielded with a quiet, well-oiled *click*, perhaps helped along by Guiscard's powers, and the Deryni tucked his pick into a belt pouch as he rose, one hand on the latch.

"Let me go in first, Sire," he murmured, pushing the door just slightly ajar and moving between Javan and the door.

Javan found his right hand dropping to rest on the hilt of his sword. He sensed no danger, but nonetheless he let Guiscard go first, dread suddenly fueling his apprehension rather than personal peril.

As Guiscard cautiously pushed the door open, Javan's eyes were dazzled at first by the bright sunlight streaming through the open shutters on the window, harsh after the near darkness of the corridor. Shading his eyes with his free hand, Javan sidestepped left into the room behind Guiscard, keeping his back to the wall and trying to pierce the brightness as Charlan surged in behind him. Guiscard was already around the door to the right and checking the bed, which was empty, signalling with a hand gesture for Charlan to close the door behind them, shutting out the guard and the priest.

The room appeared to be deserted. Faelan's breviary lay in its customary place on the armrest of the *prie-dieu*, neatly closed, but there was no candle in the candlestick beside it. Shifting his gaze to the little writing desk, Javan spotted what was left of the missing candle beside several sheets of vellum fanned out to nearly cover the surface, the burnt-out stub just visible in a congealed puddle of wax that extended very near one of the pages.

"That's odd," Javan said, moving closer. "He'd never go off and leave a candle burning on the bare wood. It might have started a fire. Does that mean he got called away in such a hurry that he couldn't put it out, or—"

"It means," Guiscard said in a tight, quiet voice, "that he *couldn't* put it out."

He was walking very slowly toward the heavy curtain that covered the entry to the garderobe opposite the foot of the bed. Mystified, Javan followed with his eyes. The dark-green fustian was suspended from wooden rings on a sturdy iron rod, the rod hinged to a heavy iron staple at one end and resting on a second staple at the other. At first Javan could not imagine what Guiscard was looking at; but then he noticed that one of the curtain rings did not appear to be wooden at all, but a loop of plaited cord of crimson and gold. The significance registered just as Guiscard reached the curtain and briskly drew it back.

"Oh, God!" Javan gasped, as the motion set the body of Father Faelan gently turning, hanging by the *Custodes* cincture around his neck.

Beside him, Charlan crossed himself and whispered, "Sweet *Jesu,* they've driven him to suicide!"

"Cut him down!" Javan ordered, already starting forward to do just that.

But Charlan caught him by one shoulder even as Guiscard whirled to glare at him, one arm outstretched to block his approach.

"It's too late for that!" Guiscard snapped. "He's been dead for hours. The most important question at this point is, did he do it himself or did someone else help him along? We may not be able to find out, if you barge in and disrupt evidence."

Javan's resistance ceased immediately, and he made himself blink back hot tears as Charlan released him.

"*They* killed him, didn't they?" he whispered, staring hard at Guiscard. "Faelan would never have taken his own life."

"I tend to agree," Guiscard said quietly, "but let's examine the evidence before we jump to any conclusions either way. Charlan, lock that door."

As the younger knight moved to obey, Guiscard turned to look more closely at the body hanging from the curtain rod, moving slightly to one side as Javan approached as well.

Faelan's end had been neither painless nor quick. The familiar, earnest face was darkly suffused, the protruding tongue black, the dark eyes staring, bulging in their sockets. There appeared to be little question that he had died of strangulation, but whether before or after he was hanged might be another story. At the foot of the bed, the overturned chair from the writing table told of possibly having been kicked from beneath him by Faelan's own volition, but it just as easily could have been placed there after the fact.

Javan tried not to imagine Faelan being hoisted by the neck to strangle there, perhaps with hands bound so he could not resist, could not reach up to catch his weight on the curtain rod and save himself. What did seem certain was that Faelan's own cincture had been the instrument of his death—the doubled and intertwined cords of Haldane crimson and gold.

Turning away, unable to look at him anymore, Javan stumbled blindly over to the little writing desk and found himself gazing at the top sheet of vellum through his tears. If the deed had been Faelan's, he might have left a message.

Words written in a shaky hand he could not be sure was Faelan's told of his despair at his suspension and excommunication, his inner torment, his growing despondence. But when Javan picked up the page in shaking fingers, not wanting to believe what he was reading, he gasped at the flash of many silver coins spread on the sheet beneath. Suddenly he knew, without counting, that there would be thirty of them.

"The *Custodes* did it," he said softly, his voice like a whisper of dry leaves. "They've named him a Judas."

Both Charlan and Guiscard had turned at his words, and Charlan came to stand close by Javan and gape at the coins in shock.

"Thirty pieces of silver," he whispered. "But he didn't really betray the Order. He just couldn't bear to be tortured again."

Guiscard had come to stare as well, dispassionately setting himself to counting the coins, shifting them in pairs from one side of the vellum to the other.

"The only thing we can do is to pretend that we believe it was suicide," he said quietly. "Of course it wasn't, but any other response that we make could put us under closer scrutiny. It's possible that they suspect something—or Faelan may simply have become inconvenient, too much of an embarrassment. Perhaps this was a test, to see how we'd respond—"

"And it cost a good man his life!" Javan began.

"Yes, it did," Guiscard retorted. "And it could cost other good men *their* lives—among them, a good king, if you overreact. You can't accuse the *Custodes Fidei* of murdering one of their own, Sire, even if he was technically excommunicate. You have to at least pretend to accept that Faelan's death was indeed suicide, brought about by the pressure of his assignment."

"That's certainly reassuring," Javan muttered. "Serving in the royal household drives otherwise sane men to take their own lives." He ducked his head, again trying to blink back tears, though less successfully this time. "He was a good priest, Guiscard—and a very brave and loyal man. And now he—can't even be buried in consecrated ground."

"If that's what's worrying you, I'll see about getting it consecrated after the fact," Guiscard said sharply. "I'll ask Joram to endanger his life, if that's what it takes! You don't really think that matters, do you? God isn't going to hold it against Faelan that he was murdered by men who tried to make it look as if he killed himself."

Drawing a deep, sobering breath, Javan made himself take hold of his emotions. Guiscard was right. Faelan could not be damned through the treachery of others. God surely would take note of the circumstances of his death and receive him to His bosom. He had died excommunicate, but that, too, was undeserved.

Still, he found the tears running unabashedly down his cheeks as he and Charlan lifted up the limp body and Guiscard cut the cincture that secured Faelan to the rod. They laid the body on the bed then, and Guiscard went to summon representatives of the *Custodes Fidei* to come and deal with their own, while Javan and Charlan kept watch.

So it was that Hubert and Paulin found them half an hour later, when Guiscard brought them back with a pair of guards, Charlan standing watch beside the door and Javan sitting quietly on the edge of the bed beside the body, his tears now dried.

"Sire, what has happened?" Hubert said.

"That's all too clear," Paulin said before Javan could reply. "Sire, you have driven him to this."

"Paulin, please!" Hubert snapped, before Paulin could go off on a rampage.

Javan glanced in the direction of the garderobe curtain, glad for the excuse to turn his face from the two.

"We found him hanging by his cincture," he said quietly. "The chair was overturned nearby. He must have—kicked it out of the way. He left some writing that doesn't make much sense, but—"

He bit off the rest of his sentence, afraid that if he continued, he was going to start letting his anger overshadow his sorrow—and good sense. Hubert apparently believed him, for he came to set a hand hesitantly on the royal shoulder, while Paulin crossed brusquely to the table to read what had been written. In picking up the vellum, he disturbed some of the coins, glancing at them contemptuously.

"You pay your chaplain well, Sire," he said. "Perhaps this explains another reason he took his life. I hardly need remind you that the Rule requires all monies received by brethren of the Order to be remitted to the Order forthwith."

"I gave him a regular stipend for charitable works in my name," Javan said steadily, determined that Paulin should not further besmirch Faelan's name with the charge of embezzlement. "I imagine that he had been saving it toward some special purpose."

"Then the money is yours," Paulin said, sweeping the coins off the table into his hand and holding it out to him. "Perhaps you would do better to attend to such charitable works yourself. Come, Sire. Take it. 'Tis a sizable amount for charity."

Controlling his disgust, Javan held out his cupped hands and let Paulin drop the money into them. Charlan looked stunned, and Guiscard quickly moved in to offer a pouch from his belt.

"Here, Sire. Let me take charge of that for you. I'm sure a good use can be found for it."

As Javan let the silver flow through his fingers into Guiscard's pouch, he thought he could devise several good uses for it, all of them involving dire consequences for Paulin and whoever had done this. He forced himself from dreams of vengeance back to practicalities as he rose and glanced down at Faelan again.

"He'll not be able to receive the rites of the Church, will he?" he said quietly. "I'm sorry for that. He was a good priest."

"*Good* priests do not take their own lives," Hubert said primly.

Biting back the retort he longed to make, Javan merely bowed his head and murmured anyway, *"Requiescat in pace."*

So saying, he turned and led Guiscard and Charlan out of the room, knowing that there was nothing else he could do for Father Faelan.

CHAPTER THIRTY-THREE

*Thou hast put away mine acquaintance far
from me.*

—Psalms 88:8

That very afternoon, the body of Father Faelan was laid to rest without ceremony or sacred rites in a potter's field at the edge of the city, for as suicide and excommunicate he could not be buried in consecrated ground. As further sign of his disgrace, those preparing his body for burial had stripped him of the habit of his Order and shaved his head to remove all vestige of his clerical tonsure. He was allowed no coffin, but only the rudest of rough-spun winding sheets to shield him from the earth. Lay men-at-arms under the direction of the *Custodes Fidei* saw to the burial, but no actual member of the Order attended.

Not even Javan was present, though he longed to be. As king, he dared not make an official appearance at the interment of an excommunicate, even though Faelan had been his chaplain. But toward dusk he rode out along the river with Charlan and Guiscard, accompanied by a dozen of his lancers for protection, and timed his return to be passing by the potter's field just as twilight was settling over the city.

He left Charlan with the lancers, holding the horses, while he and Guiscard made their way over the rough ground to the dry, unmarked mound of earth. He dared not kneel to show his respect, for the lancers were watching, but he bowed his head in silent prayer for the repose of Faelan's soul as a cool breeze off the river whipped at his hair. After a moment he had to look up again, for that was the only way he could blink back the tears that were welling in his eyes.

"I shouldn't have let him stay," he said to Guiscard, gazing unseeing into the sunset. "I could have made him go. He never would have known it wasn't his choice."

"And if you *had* made him go, and they'd decided to bleed him to death, he'd be just as dead, and you'd be blaming yourself just as much," Guiscard replied. "It wasn't just your decision at work here. It was Faelan's and Paulin's and whoever actually killed him."

"But he died for *nothing*! Even if he'd gone, they couldn't have gotten anything out of him. He didn't ask to be involved in any of this. All he wanted was to be a good priest."

"And wasn't he?" Guiscard said softly. "Isn't there something in Holy Writ that says something about the good shepherd laying down his life for his sheep?"

"But they hanged him, Guiscard, like a common criminal! Like Judas. They even left him thirty pieces of silver!"

"That's what they did," Guiscard agreed, "but it isn't why Faelan died."

"What do you mean?"

"I think Faelan died because he chose not to risk letting himself be intimidated into betraying *you*. *That's* why he wouldn't put himself into the *Custodes*' hands again. He wasn't afraid for his life—don't you understand? He'd surrendered that to God long before you and he ever met. Don't you suppose his killers came to realize that? And once they knew he couldn't be bought, even by fear, that he wouldn't risk betraying *you*, they decided they'd at least take out their spite for betraying *them*."

"He's still dead," Javan murmured. "And he's still lying here in unconsecrated ground, with only a pauper's shroud around him. I know *he* isn't here, Guiscard, but it isn't right that anyone should be able to do this to an innocent man. Who'll be next? Are they going to start whittling away at everyone I care about who tries to remain loyal to me?"

He asked Joram the same questions later that night, when he had relayed all the events of the past few days. Guiscard had come with him this time and sat sympathetically at his side as Joram and Niallan and Jesse digested what the king had told them.

"I certainly share your grief over Father Faelan," Joram said after a moment. "And I think you're right to fear that this may be only the beginning. If they'll kill a priest and make it look like suicide, they certainly wouldn't hesitate to go after others close to you. I'd worry for Oriel's safety first. If they've got their own Deryni again, especially a willing one, they won't want rivals at court potentially to undo his work."

Javan gave a sharp, bitter laugh. "Short of locking him up like his family, what do you suggest I do? I moved him physically closer to my quarters, where Hubert or the others can't get at him as readily, and I've got one of my sharpest knights assigned essentially as a full-time bodyguard. Unless I personally send one of my own men for him, Oriel doesn't stir out of his quarters except with Sir Gavin to escort him."

Joram nodded. "You've probably done all you can, then. Of course, if Rhun brings Sitric back, the picture changes yet again. With *Custodes* backing, I suspect even the rather pedestrian Sitric could become formidable."

"So, what do I do?" Javan demanded. "Send Oriel from Court? He won't go, so long as his family is held hostage—and Paulin's men aren't about to let them leave."

"No, they aren't," Joram agreed. "But there may be another way to approach that problem. Guiscard, how many hostages are still at Rhemuth?"

The young knight raised an eyebrow. "Maybe half a dozen, counting Oriel's wife and daughter."

"Who are the others?" Niallan asked.

"Well, there'd be Sitric's family—a mother and sister, I think—and Ursin O'Carroll and his wife and son, of course. I guess that's actually seven."

"Only seven?" Niallan sighed and shook his head. "I remember when there were several dozen. May their souls all rest in peace." He crossed himself with a heavy hand, and the others followed suit. "But it could be worse, I suppose. I assume the survivors *are* all Deryni? Not counting Ursin, of course."

Guiscard made a grimace, considering. "Actually, no. I think Ursin's wife may be human—which also makes the son problematical. He would have been very young when the hostages were first taken, perhaps even an infant in arms, so they wouldn't have tested him with *merasha*. I do hear that they test Ursin regularly, just to be certain his powers haven't come back."

"Lord, how they do fear us!" Niallan sighed again. "But that's nothing new. But something has occurred to me that just might work. Sire, you know how Ursin lost his powers. You know about Master Revan, out by Valoret."

Javan cocked his head quizzically at the bishop. "Of course I do. I was *there*."

"Yes, indeed," Niallan said with a faint smile. "Now, here's what I propose . . ."

It took more than a fortnight and several return visits to the Michaeline sanctuary before the plan took final shape, for parts of it must be approved by men not resident there. It was a bold scenario that Niallan proposed, but it might actually result in getting the hostages out of Rhemuth by the following spring. To begin paving the way, Javan even swallowed his pride and pretended to make his peace with Paulin over the Faelan affair, so that a new chaplain might be appointed and the royal household could settle into a regular routine again.

Unfortunately, Javan was given no opportunity to begin implementing his plan, for the very day he had intended to start laying the groundwork for it, very early in November, an exhausted courier arrived in Rhemuth demanding to be taken to the king.

Javan was in the great hall, observing a routine session of the local assize court, when a guard brought the man in. Guiscard and Charlan were sitting behind and to either side of him at the left of the dais, Lord Jerowen actually presiding over the court. Most of the several dozen others present were either functionaries of the court or suppliants. In anticipation of the Council meeting scheduled for later in the afternoon, Lords Albertus, Rhun, and Udaut were huddled around a charcoal brazier in one of the window embrasures, for the weather had turned in the past week. Aside from them, however, not one of the other lords of Council had chosen to attend. It was a very minor Court.

Lord Jerowen stopped speaking and Charlan and Guiscard got to their feet as the messenger staggered down the length of the great hall, heavily supported by a worried-looking guard. With a little moan, the man collapsed to his knees before the king and pulled a creased and travel-stained packet from inside his tunic, offering it with a trembling hand. The bright vermilion seal proclaimed the sender to be Lord Ainslie, with whom Rhys Michael was currently serving in Grecotha.

"Get this man something to drink," Javan commanded, breaking the seal across with his fingers when it would not lift from one side. "Did you bring this from Grecotha?"

"Aye, Sire. Four days ago . . . Hunting party went wrong," the man managed to gasp out, swaying on his knees. "Prince Rhys Michael abducted . . . Sir Jason dead, Lord Ainslie very bad . . . Brigands . . . I rode as quickly as I could."

He pitched forward then, but Guiscard was already bending down to catch him under one arm and ease him to the floor, snapping his fingers in the direction of several squires, who were scurrying for wine and a cup. Javan had gotten to his feet at the news, all the color draining from his face.

"Get Oriel," he said to Charlan, fumbling at the letter to unfold it and learn the rest of its grim news.

As Charlan dashed from the hall, and Lord Jerowen quickly hurried across from where he had been presiding, Albertus and Rhun drifted to the edge of their window alcove to see what was amiss, apparently not having heard the messenger. Javan skimmed the letter with growing alarm. The messenger's garbled words had only just made sense, but the words on the page leaped out at him in uncompromising confirmation of disaster. The hand was that of Sir Tomais, who had ridden out with Rhys Michael and Jason barely six weeks before.

> *Grecotha, the Feast of All Saints*
>
> *Unto Javan, King of Gwynedd, from Sir Tomais d'Edergoll, with Lord Ainslie's commission in Grecotha.*
>
> *I regret to confirm what the messenger will have told your Highness in brief already. The Prince your brother has been taken captive by persons unknown. His present whereabouts or condition is likewise unknown as I write this. Several witnesses believe he may have been slightly wounded in the skirmish. Sir Jason died bravely, in defense of his prince, and Lord Ainslie was sorely wounded. Four other men died, and several more sustained wounds. Whether Ainslie will live or not is in the hands of God. He is lying now at Grecotha, in the palace of Bishop Edward MacInnis.*
>
> *The incident took place yesterday at about midafternoon. I have spent the remainder of that day and all of today combing that area with all the men at my disposal, assisted by a sizable troop of Bishop Edward's men, but thus far have been unable to find any clue regarding the prince's fate. It is Lord Ainslie's impression and that of most others present that the attackers definitely intended to capture the prince rather than kill him.*
>
> *I do not recommend that your Highness should join me at this time, for I do not know the extent of the plot and cannot guarantee your Highness' safety. Also, if the prince has been abducted for ransom, as many here believe, the demand surely will come to you in Rhemuth. However, I would welcome additional troops to assist in our search, for each day increases*

the distance his abductors may have carried him. I regret that I cannot send your Highness more positive information. I remain your obedient but miserable servant, Tomais d'Edergoll, Knight.

Stunned, Javan handed off the letter to Albertus, who had come down from the window alcove with Rhun and Udaut, bidding the latter clear the hall. Guiscard was coaxing wine down the throat of the fallen courier, urging him to drink, but the man clearly was exhausted. Udaut had succeeded in clearing the hall by the time Charlan returned with Oriel, he and Jerowen now exclaiming anew over the letter Albertus and Rhun had already read.

"My brother's been abducted," Javan said as Oriel and Charlan approached. "Find out whether this man was present and whether he knows anything besides what he's already told us."

The others congregated around the king stirred uneasily at the command, but Oriel did not bat an eye as he sank to his knees beside the now-snoring man and lightly laid both hands on the man's forehead. He closed his eyes and was silent for several seconds, then looked up at the king, his expression grave and troubled.

"Neither he nor Sir Tomais was present on the actual hunt, Sire, but he heard Tomais question Lord Ainslie afterward. The attackers were well armed and well disciplined. There can be no doubt that their objective was to capture the prince. Bowmen struck from ambush first, but they carefully shot wide of him. That was when Sir Jason fell—a single arrow in the back. Lord Ainslie took an arrow in the thigh and another in the arm, but actually fell to a sword thrust. The surgeons were working on him even as Tomais questioned him and had given him drugs to ease the pain, so his account grew increasingly less lucid."

"What of my brother?" Javan said impatiently.

"Lord Ainslie saw the prince giving good account of himself, sword in hand, but he himself fell at about that time, so he did not actually see them take him captive. Another man reportedly saw the prince overwhelmed and thought he had not been injured to that point, but he, too, was sorely wounded and could do nothing to stop the abduction."

The same morning that the news of Rhys Michael's abduction reached his brother's Court, Rhys Michael himself was making a princely though largely ineffectual effort to remain alert—though after several days of captivity, he had learned little more about his captors than he knew when they first took him. From the outset, there had never been any chance of escape, or any doubt that he was their target.

Shooting from ambush, the attackers had taken out fully a third of his escort with archers, including the loyal Sir Jason. Then lightly armored horsemen had swept in, more than a score of them, half a dozen heading right for him while the rest fought off those who would have died—and many did—to defend him. He drew his sword and tried to fight back, and thought he had given at least a few of his attackers wounds to remember him by, but they overwhelmed him by sheer numbers, one of them grabbing his horse's reins, another cracking him in the temple with a sword pommel, while yet another one threw a great voluminous cloak over his head to blind him and entangle his sword.

Even sightless and half stunned, flailing dazedly under the weight and bulk of the cloak, he tried to throw himself off his horse, figuring that his own men had a better chance of rescuing him from the ground than if the attackers got him away. Unfortunately, before he could kick free of his stirrups, someone grabbed him in a bear hug over the cloak while someone else nearly broke his fingers wrenching away his sword.

He kept trying to fight, but others wound a rope several times around his shoulders and waist to pinion his elbows at his sides, also binding his wrists. Still kicking and squirming, he was then thrown back into a saddle ahead of someone much larger, who reached powerful leather-clad arms around him and kicked the horse into a gallop.

All he could do, trussed like a pig for market, was to duck his head and hang on to the horse's mane for dear life as it leaped forward, raked by his captor's spurs. He kept trying to scream, to call his men, for they had not managed to gag him before engulfing him in the cloak, but a sharp cuff to the side of his head connected hard enough to make him see stars inside the smothering darkness and make his nose bleed.

For the next little while, half fainting with pain and fear, he made himself concentrate on clinging numbly to the horse's neck and *not* falling off, because they were going far too fast down a rugged slope that made the horse lurch and stumble, and he feared he might break his neck if he went off blind and without being fully able to break his fall.

After what seemed like an eternity of mad scrambles punctuated by short stretches of hard galloping, his captors drew rein long enough for someone to dismount and lash his feet under the horse's belly, after which they bound his wrists in front of him with leather straps and exchanged the smothering cloak for a proper blindfold and gag. At no time was he permitted a glimpse of his abductors. Within minutes they were riding out again, and he still had not a clue who his captors might be or what they wanted of him.

His situation got more frightening as the afternoon passed into evening and then into night. More than once, during those first interminable hours, his captors pulled up to wait in silence while troops of other horsemen passed nearby. The first of those times, the minder riding behind him slid a leather-clad arm around his throat from behind and caught the pressure points in the angle of his elbow, murmuring "Not one move or sound, Haldane, or you're out."

His jaws ached from the gag so that he could hardly breathe, much less cry out. Any attempt at defiance was pointless under the circumstances. In token of his submission, he tried to make himself relax against his captor's chest. Even so, the pressure did not relent. As the hoofbeats drew nearer, the blackness swam behind his blindfold so that he reeled and nearly did pass out. Dull nausea stayed with him for some time when they eventually set out again.

He thought it must have been well after midnight by the time they finally stopped to rest and water the horses, still without giving him any indication of what they wanted other than to see him unrescued. When asked if he would give his oath to keep silent if they removed his gag, he shakily agreed, for further discomfort served no purpose. Mere shouting was not going to get him free.

They removed the gag, but he was not surprised that the blindfold remained in place. His throat was dry and parched, as much from fear as from real thirst; and when they had sat him down on a smooth rock, he timidly asked if he might have something to drink.

To his relieved surprise, a flask was set to his lips. It was only water, but it tasted like nectar after the day he'd had. A few minutes later they put food in his hands as well—heavy journey bread and pungent cheese. Eating was awkward with his hands bound, and it did not help that his fear made swallowing difficult, but his stomach welcomed even this humble fare. They even gave him wine at the end, which he gulped down gratefully.

Soon afterward, to the sounds of horses being led to water, his keeper took him by the elbow and led him a few paces off from the rest.

"If you need to take a piss, now's your chance," the man said bluntly. "We're going to be in the saddle for a lot of hours, once we mount up again."

The man's grip on his arm released, but that was all. With a sinking feeling, Rhys Michael realized that he now was expected to perform. He could not remember when he had felt so vulnerable or humiliated, but his bladder was not going to get any less full unless he did something about it. When he had finished, his minder wordlessly took his elbow again and led him back to their horse.

He seemed to stumble a lot along the way. When he was hoisted up into the saddle again, unaccustomed vertigo made him cling to the pommel to make the world stop spinning behind his blindfold. By the time they were moving out again, the vertigo had become waves of drowsiness threatening to engulf him every time they stopped or even slowed to a walk. Gradually it dawned on him that they had drugged him, probably in the wine, but the dawning also brought a dull awareness that there was absolutely nothing he could do about it.

He did not remember them stopping to sleep that night. He knew he had dozed in the saddle, but he had no idea how long. The next time they stopped to eat, he attempted to decline the wine, but his keeper made it clear that this was not an option. He decided he would rather drink it than have it forced down his throat.

He was never even aware of being put back on a horse that time. At some point they took his signet ring and earring. Kept in darkness behind his blindfold, all time slid together anyway, and the drugs kept him perpetually disoriented and drowsy, even when he was conscious.

Several times he thought he overheard the name Ansel mentioned, and eventually it occurred to him to wonder whether they meant the outlawed Ansel MacRorie. It frightened him that his captors might be Deryni like Ansel, but there was nothing he could do about it. Mostly they simply packed him onto his horse and continued on, with him drifting in and out of disturbing dreams in the leather-clad arms of his keeper.

He was not certain how long this pattern continued before the rescue. He thought it might have been several days. They had just stopped to feed and water horses and men when a cry of alarm precipitated sudden activity. He could hear the sounds of heavy hoofbeats approaching fast, low-muttered oaths from his captors, swords being drawn, the jingle of harness and weapons—and then fighting broke out all around him.

He stiffened as his keeper crushed him against his chest with his left arm, instinctively ducking his head and starting to squirm as the man's other arm stretched back for the poniard he wore in the back of his belt, out of Rhys Michael's reach. All around him were the clash of weapons, the squeals of horses, the cries of men being wounded.

His own horse was plunging under him, his keeper fighting to control it, and he clung to the pommel to keep from being thrown to his death—though death was riding right behind him as well.

"Don't fight me, Haldane!" his keeper commanded.

He felt the man's knife arm whipping forward, flinched from the flat-bladed caress of steel against the side of his neck. With a strangled cry he lurched to the other side and doubled up, trying to claw at his blindfold so he could at least see death approaching. He heard voices shouting his name, even closer, but he did not know if they would reach him in time. At the same time, his keeper was trying to wrench him upright, fighting both him and the snorting, plunging horse. He tried to fend off the man's leather-clad wrist with his bound hands, cringing from the blade he knew the man held.

"To the prince!" someone shouted. "They'll try to kill him!"

He hardly needed anyone to tell him that. He was squirming for his life, trying desperately to guess where his keeper's hand was, with its deadly blade, until a sharp rap at the base of his skull ended all further resistance.

Afterward, when he finally came around, they told him he had been unconscious for the better part of two days, though the black-clad battle surgeon changing a bandage above his left knee assured him that part of his grogginess had been caused by sedation they gave him so they could move him more comfortably.

"You were very lucky," the man said, finishing a neat knot on the bandage. "This just required a little suturing, but the man who had you in the saddle with him came *this* close to sending you to meet your Maker."

He indicated a short span between thumb and forefinger, then touched the right side of his patient's neck, just short of the carotid artery. The spot was sore, and Rhys Michael winced. His head ached, and when he flexed his neck experimentally, a tenderness at the back made him gasp.

"Where am I?" he whispered.

For answer, the battle surgeon turned to beckon another man closer. Rhys Michael attempted to pull the man's image into focus, but even trying was almost too much effort.

"How are you feeling, my prince?" a vaguely familiar voice murmured.

"My head hurts," Rhys Michael whispered. "Who—"

"It's Manfred MacInnis, son. You're in Culdi. You're going to be just fine."

Enough of the words registered that Rhys Michael was able to make his eyes focus. After the past few days, a familiar face was more welcome than he could say.

"Lord Manfred," he murmured. "But how—"

"Do you remember being abducted?" Manfred asked gently.

Rhys Michael nodded weakly, but the movement made his head swim again. "I think they may have been working for Ansel MacRorie," he whispered. "They kept me drugged most of the time. A lot of it is real fuzzy."

Manfred's face hardened. "I suspect it is. Well, don't you worry. We took a few of them alive. I'm sure none of them's MacRorie, but I have no doubt they'll be telling us all they know by the time my experts have had a chance at them for a day or two. I'm just thankful you weren't hurt any worse than you were. Patrols have been looking for you for more than a week."

"Has it been that long?" Rhys Michael asked.

"I'm afraid so. And it took the best part of a day to get you back here. That was yesterday. Tomorrow is Martinmas."

Closing his eyes briefly, Rhys Michael tried to make himself think. His body seemed numbed to pain, but his head still felt as if it were stuffed with cotton wool.

"I can't seem to think straight. Are you keeping me drugged, too?"

"It's mainly something for the pain, your Highness," the battle surgeon replied, "though it does have something of a sedative effect as well. You took a nasty crack to the back of your head. Now that you're back with us, we can begin easing off on the medication."

The explanation seemed entirely plausible. Rhys Michael did remember getting hit, and his head was very tender where it rested on the pillows.

He yawned and returned his attention to Manfred. "Maybe I'll feel better after I've slept some more," he said drowsily. "Does Javan know I'm safe?"

"He does—or will, as soon as the messenger reaches him, probably tonight or early tomorrow. Just don't you worry, your Highness. Master Stevanus will have you on your feet before you know it. For now, sleep is probably the best thing you could do to speed your recovery."

* * *

Meanwhile, in Rhemuth, the king and several of his lords of Council were arguing over how to respond to a letter received early that morning. It had been delivered by a peasant messenger who obviously knew nothing of the contents of what he carried, even had he been able to read it. Daily reports from Sir Tomais in the preceding week, while assuring the king that Lord Ainslie now was expected to recover, had been able to offer no revelations concerning the fate of Rhys Michael. Until receipt of this first communication from the prince's abductors, he might have disappeared into thin air. In part, the letter read:

> To ensure that you meet our demands, we have taken your Highness' brother to hostage, and will keep him in close confinement until these demands are met. As proof that we do, indeed, hold the prince, I enclose a certain item belonging to him and remind your Highness that I could have enclosed the ear as well.

The item in question was the earring of twisted gold wire that Rhys Michael always wore, unmistakably his. The price demanded for the prince's safe release was an immediate repeal of the Ramos Statutes, with restoration of all rights and privileges of Deryni. The demand was signed and sealed by Ansel MacRorie, Earl of Culdi in exile.

The Council reacted with predictable outrage, clergy and laymen alike. Javan's outrage was tempered with fear for his brother, underlined by the threat accompanying the earring in his hand. To give serious countenance to a Deryni ransom demand was out of the question—but so was refusal, when the heir's life was at stake.

"Couldn't we at least make some token concessions while we continue trying to find him?" Javan asked, staring at his brother's earring. "Maybe relax the ruling on land ownership. That's innocuous enough."

"No accommodation to terrorists or Deryni!" Hubert declared, as even the laymen on the Council nodded their emphatic agreement. "We will not be intimidated by traitors!"

"But it's my brother's life that's in the balance."

"The prince should feel honored and humbly grateful if called to a martyr's crown," Paulin replied coldly. "Suppression of the Deryni is ordained by God Himself, for the salvation of His people and the greater glory of His Church on earth. We will make no concessions to the enemies of God!"

In the face of such arguments, Javan could offer no further rebuttals. Later that evening he mulled the dilemma in the privacy his own quarters, with only Charlan and Guiscard for company. They were waiting for the return of Guiscard's father, who had gone to inquire of Joram regarding the demand. Javan knew that his Deryni allies were chafing increasingly under the tightening strictures against those of their race, but he could not imagine that they would really threaten the life of their king's brother.

"There's no reason for Ansel to do this," Guiscard said as the minutes stretched into an hour and Etienne did not return. "It will only increase ill will toward Deryni, especially if they harm the prince. Doesn't he realize that any changes made to the law under duress would only be reversed yet again, once the prince was safe?"

"The desperate act of a desperate man, perhaps," Charlan offered. "Maybe the opportunity came up to abduct the prince, and it seemed like a good idea at the time, but then he didn't know what to do after that."

Javan shook his head. "That wasn't the impression I got from the letter Tomais sent. The attack was well planned. They knew exactly who—"

A knock at the door brought Guiscard bounding to his feet to admit his father. Etienne was shaking his head as he came into the room and pulled up a chair at the table where the others sat.

"You aren't going to believe this," he muttered, including them all in his glance. "Joram doesn't know anything about this, and *neither does Ansel.*"

"What?!"

"Oh, Ansel certainly knew that the prince had been abducted—Joram got word to him as soon as *he* was told—but that's all Ansel knew. He was nowhere near Grecotha when the abduction took place—though he's been combing that area since, trying to find some trace. He's still out there, but the others were meeting about it when I arrived: Joram and Jesse and Bishop Niallan and his Healer, Dom Rickart. When I showed Joram the letter, he went a little pale, then passed it around the table for the others' inspection. They all agreed that it wasn't Ansel's signature or seal."

"Then that means—"

"It means that *someone,*" Guiscard said, before the king could finish, "is trying to further discredit Deryni, and fueling the attempt with the threat to your brother. I have several shrewd guesses who that might be. Oh, it's clever. Just the sort of thing I might expect your enemies to come up with. What do you want to bet that Paulin somehow is behind this?"

"But Jason and several other men were killed in the attack, and Ainslie was nearly killed," Javan protested. "Surely, even Paulin—"

"Would Paulin have your personal supporters killed?" Etienne said. "Why not? Especially if it could be made to look like the work of Deryni. It would certainly strengthen his campaign to ensure that the Ramos Statutes are not altered. And I hardly need remind you of Father Faelan."

"But—surely it isn't possible," Javan murmured, shaking his head. "Dear God, you don't think they'd kill Rhysem, do you?"

When no one answered, Javan stood abruptly and went over to the window. It was raining hard, and he set one hand flat on one of the thick windowpanes, staring into the darkness beyond.

"We don't know for certain that Paulin is responsible," he said after a long moment. "But Rhysem *has* been taken hostage. We know that's true, because they sent back his earring, and he never takes it off.

"So the question is, who *is* holding him?" he whispered. "Where is he now? And what are they going to do to him?"

CHAPTER THIRTY-FOUR

He shall direct his counsel and knowledge, and
in his secrets shall he meditate.
—Ecclesiasticus 39:7

Even as Javan asked the questions, a messenger bearing at least some of the answers was making his way through the streets of Rhemuth, though his information was not intended for Javan. The same man had discharged the first part of his commission earlier in the day by entrusting a sealed missive to a peasant for delivery to the castle—the very missive now giving the king such cause for concern. Earlier he had travelled in the unadorned harness of an ordinary man-at-arms, but before leaving the inn where he had spent the afternoon and evening holed up, he donned the red-fringed white sash and the black surcoat charged with a red moline cross and haloed lion-head that were the uniform of a *Custodes* knight.

It was raining hard. Wearing a plain black mantle over all to shield him from the weather, the man aroused little notice as he made his way up the cobbled street to the cathedral precincts and the archbishop's palace adjoining it. Within minutes of presenting himself, he was being shown into the presence of his superior, Paulin of Ramos, who had quarters permanently set aside in the palace for his use. The Vicar General's apartments adjoined those allocated to the Archbishop of Valoret when he was resident in Rhemuth. The two had been sharing a flask of good Fianna wine in Paulin's dayroom, speculating on how the king would eventually respond to the ransom demand.

"Ah, Lord Vantry, is it not?" Paulin said as the knight approached and bent one knee to kiss his ring.

363

"Aye, Vicar General." The man rose, inclining his head to Archbishop Hubert, who was sitting just beyond Paulin, close beside the fire. "Your Grace."

"I hope you have brought news from Lord Albertus," Hubert said as the man drew a sealed packet from under his surcoat and handed it to Paulin.

"Aye, my lord, but I fear there is little to report. The prince has not yet been found. I have a missive for the king as well, but Lord Albertus bade me deliver this one first."

"You will wait while I read this," Paulin said, gesturing toward a chair as he broke Albertus' seal and unfolded the stiff parchment. "I may wish to send an additional message to the king. You have been with the party still searching for the prince?"

"Aye, my lord."

"Sit, sit."

Despite Paulin's urging, the messenger waited until his superior had sat before perching gingerly on the edge of the chair he had been offered, not nervous at what his superior might read but clearly anxious to be on his way. No salutation headed the missive, but the hand was familiar to Paulin.

> The man who carries this letter is utterly trustworthy, but knows nothing of its contents. I am reliably informed that the rescue went entirely according to plan. The prince now lies at Culdi, recovering from his injuries, which were slight. He suspects nothing. His host will do all in his power to ensure that further developments proceed as planned. Meanwhile, let us trust that the king's energies will be well occupied pondering the contents of the letter he will have received earlier today. The additional message he is shortly to receive will do nothing to alleviate his fears. I respectfully suggest that you burn this when you have read it.—A.

Paulin suppressed a smile as he passed the letter to Hubert. To Lord Vantry, the exchange would appear to confirm sober concern for what was unfolding.

"Thank you, Lord Vantry. You may go. Say to the king that I regret that Lord Albertus' efforts have thus far been unsuccessful, but assure his Highness that the Order will continue to do all within its power to locate and free his brother."

"I will, my lord," Vantry replied, coming to his feet to kiss his superior's hand again.

When he had gone, Paulin took the letter from Hubert, read it again, then consigned it to the flames, where it curled and crackled as it began to burn.

"With the king still having access to a Truth-Reader," Hubert said softly, "it was prudent of Albertus to send a messenger who can tell only what he has been told to say and believes it to be true. Realistically, however, how long do you think the truth can be kept from the king?"

"Almost indefinitely, so long as Manfred is successful at intercepting any letters the prince may try to send from Culdi," Paulin said. "But frankly, my lord, I hardly think the prince will be over-eager to leave, once he realizes what forbidden charms Culdi has to offer."

Prince Rhys Michael Haldane began to discover those forbidden charms the very next morning. He woke to the sound of his bed-curtains being pushed back on either side and the glare of sunlight streaming through the single window in his room. Someone moved across the sunlight, momentarily casting a shadow across his face, and he squinted against the returning brightness, raising a hand to shade his eyes.

"Who's there?" he whispered, through a parched throat.

"Master Stevanus and a new nurse," a voice said from the other side of the bed, as the caster of the shadow bent to put down a tray on a bedside table. "You'd best draw that drape a bit, my lady," the battle surgeon's voice went on. "He won't be quite up to bright light for a day or two."

Rhys Michael turned his head heavily from side to side, trying to follow what was going on. He thought he felt better this morning, though he was very weak. As he squinted toward the sunlight, trying to discern the identity of the lady Stevanus had addressed, she retreated to adjust the drape. With the bright sunlight blocked, his sun-dazzled eyes could just make out a slim, elegant back in a blue damask gown. But as she turned to come back and his sight adjusted, his face lit with surprise and pleasure.

"Mika?"

Smiling, she came to take his hand and press it to her lips, then held it clasped in both her hands. Her tawny hair was plaited in a fat bronze braid that hung over one shoulder and fell nearly to her waist, and the blue eyes were filled with tears above the soft, rosy lips.

"They wouldn't let me see you until this morning," she whispered. "Rhysem, I was so worried!"

"So was I," he managed to reply.

Stevanus cleared his throat at that, and Michaela raised her head.

"I don't wish to intrude upon this obviously happy reunion," the surgeon said with an indulgent smile, "but I would ask that we at least mingle your priorities with what *I* am charged to do. How are you feeling this morning, your Highness?"

"Weak," he admitted, gazing back fondly at Michaela, "but much better than I did a few minutes ago."

"Yes, I can see that," Stevanus murmured, setting a hand to the prince's free wrist, then shaking his head. "Well, there's no point to checking your pulse with a lovely young lady in the room, I suppose. How's the head?" he went on, shifting to slip his hands under Rhys Michael's neck and probe gently where he had been hit at the base of the skull.

Rhys Michael tensed and winced as Stevanus made his examination, not relaxing until the battle surgeon had removed his hands.

"I suppose it feels about the same," he murmured. "I must have quite a bruise."

"You do," Stevanus agreed. "The leg was bruised worse, though. You lost a fair amount of blood, too. You can have a look a little later, after you get some food in you. Meanwhile, if you promise not to let yourself get overexcited, the young lady may stay to help you eat. Do you think you can sit up?"

With a little help from Stevanus and Michaela and half a dozen pillows, he managed to end up sitting partially upright. He felt dizzy, but that might have been as much from Michaela's presence as from his throbbing head, as she settled on the edge of the bed and fed him hot broth and morsels of bread and cheese. They spoke little, for he was too weak to chew and talk at the same time, but their eyes conveyed what lips could not. It was chilly in the room and starting to cloud over outside, but her very presence warmed him—though perhaps the cup of hot mulled ale she gave him to finish the meal also contributed to his sense of drowsy well-being.

Stevanus made her leave after that, so that he and a squire could bathe the prince and change the dressing on his leg. Lord Manfred came in while they were at it, greeting the prince and then watching silently. The one glimpse Rhys Michael got of his leg, as they turned him this way and that to wash him, was enough to make him a little queasy—sutured neatly enough with perhaps a dozen bristling black silk stitches, but surrounded by yellow-purple flesh that Stevanus assured him was only bruising, not massive infection. Before they had finished, Rhys Michael had drifted off again.

After he was asleep, Manfred drew the battle surgeon into an outer room.

"You're sure that isn't festering?" he asked in a low voice.

Stevanus only smiled and shook his head as he dried his hands on a rough linen towel. "His 'rescuers' knew what they were doing, my lord. One can be fairly precise about the placement of bruises when one's 'patient' is unconscious. And his 'wound' came from a surgeon's knife, not a sword. The sutures are for show."

A sly smile of understanding slowly crossed Manfred's face.

"I see," he murmured. "Then the head injury?"

"Oh, he got whacked in the head, all right. It wouldn't have done to have him take too close a notice of the details of his rescue. A calculated risk, but again, his rescuers knew what they were doing. They also bled him right after they took him—that slight wound on his neck, where I told him yesterday he'd nearly met his Maker. The blood loss will help to keep him weak for a few days, and I'm helping the headache along with medication—which also keeps him a little drowsy. But unless he should start to question the situation, which is highly unlikely, I believe we can discontinue everything except plenty of good food and his nurse's company within the next few days, with him none the wiser."

Manfred gave a low, pleased chuckle. "Then I gather that none of this presents any impediment to encouraging nature to take its course where the young lady is concerned."

"On the contrary, my lord, it presents an ideal opportunity for the two of them to spend long hours together with one of them already in bed and naked," the battle surgeon replied archly. "In fact, I'll be very surprised if you can keep them apart until the banns are read."

"Why, Master Stevanus, I thought you *Custodes* chaps paid no notice to such things," Manfred said, grinning.

Stevanus shrugged and smiled. "I wasn't always under vows, my lord, and I found my vocation late in life."

"Well, then, that explains it. Thank you, Master Stevanus," Manfred said. "I shall be watching developments with great interest."

Back in Rhemuth, in the days that followed, Javan's anxiety continued to increase. His Council had made it clear that no possible relaxation could be made of the Ramos Statutes, pressed Javan to increase the efforts already being expended to hunt for his brother's abductors, yet would not permit him to go to Grecotha to see for himself how the search was progressing, lest his interference increase the risks to the captive prince—and also endanger his own safety.

Jason's body came back to Rhemuth for burial after the first week, along with word that Lord Ainslie was sufficiently recovered to take over direction of the search from his sickbed, but neither his nor Albertus' troops could uncover any clues. Rhun even informed the Council that he had sent Sitric north under heavy escort to join Albertus' patrols, in hopes that a Deryni might be able to help discover Deryni abductors.

All that this apparently accomplished, other than to increase royal frustration, was to annoy the abductors. Another letter arrived after about a week, this time accompanied by the prince's signet ring and what appeared to be a little toe—and a statement that the senders had no wish to maim the prince by cutting off a finger, but would do so next time, if the king did not begin complying with their demands.

Receipt of the toe sent Javan into anguished panic. He knew that the abductors were not who they claimed to be, but could not reveal that he knew so. Nor had he any real idea who they actually were—though his imagination supplied ever more unpleasant possibilities as the days wore on. Whoever they were, they were torturing his brother, and Javan could neither find them to stop them nor accede to their demands.

His Deryni allies tried to ease a little of the tension by throwing the uncertainty into public light. Within a few days of the arrival of the second demand letter, the real Ansel MacRorie sent a statement disavowing any connection with whomever had sent the demands and reiterating his continued loyalty to the House of Haldane, even from exile. He also assured the king that though he had been nowhere near Grecotha at the time of the prince's abduction, he had his men working there now, looking for the real abductors of the prince.

Hubert naturally dismissed this as specious, declaring that of course Ansel would claim that, after the fact, when he realized that his threats were not going to get him what he wanted. That made as much sense as any other explanation, at least to the rest of the Council, but it pleased Javan not at all. Hostility toward the Deryni Ansel increased dramatically after the receipt of his letter, and several members of the Council even suggested that the Ramos Statutes should be tightened even more and dragnets put out to find the impudent Ansel and finish him, once and for all.

More days passed, and Javan became increasingly convinced that Paulin and Hubert knew more than they were letting on. Both men assured him of their concern and a desire to help, and he never caught either of them in an outright lie, but both sometimes went to great lengths to avoid answering precisely the question he had asked.

They were hiding something, but he dared not accuse them. He knew it was too risky to try to press Paulin for information he was determined not to give, especially when the extent of the Vicar General's relationship with the mysterious Dimitri was unknown. He might be protected. Archbishop Hubert, though hardly without risk, was a much more likely prospect. Javan had meddled before, where Hubert was concerned. The trick was to get Hubert alone and in a frame of mind such that he would suspect nothing.

It took the better part of a week for Javan to find his opportunity, after several days of laying careful groundwork. He could do little else, so long as he received no new demands from his brother's abductors. On a Sunday late in November, when Javan knew that Hubert and not Oriss would be officiating at solemn Vespers and Benediction down in the cathedral, the king put on a suppliant's face and betook himself to divine services there, closely cloaked and hooded both against the cold and casual recognition and accompanied by Charlan and Guiscard as was his usual wont.

The congregation was small, for winter was settling in with a vengeance. A moderate snowfall earlier in the week, followed by rain, had left the streets a quagmire of mud and puddles now turning to icy patches, for new snow had been flurrying as Javan and his companions made their way down from the castle mound. To his relief, Paulin was nowhere in evidence either before or after the service, and what few worshippers had been present did not linger once the participating clergy had withdrawn to the sacristy.

The great cathedral grew very quiet as the last of the altar candles were extinguished and the responsible acolyte retreated. Hubert was still in the sacristy. Javan could see its only door from where he remained kneeling far back in the choir, his hood pulled up. Eventually Hubert appeared, turning to give some final instruction to someone still inside.

Drawing a fortifying breath, Javan rose and headed toward him, Charlan and Guiscard trailing at a discreet distance. Hubert looked up at their approach, one hesitant hand on the sacristy door, not pulling it closed until Javan pushed back his hood to reveal his identity.

"Your Grace, may I speak with you?" he said.

"Oh, it's you, Sire," Hubert said coolly. "If this is in the nature of official business—"

Javan shook his head and bowed it as he sank to one knee.

"It's personal," he whispered, hoping Hubert would extend his ring to be kissed. "I—have need of a priest."

"I believe a new royal confessor has been appointed, Sire," Hubert said. "Has your Highness found him to be unsatisfactory?"

Abandoning the ring ploy as an excuse to touch Hubert, Javan got to his feet, keeping his head slightly bowed over folded hands.

"I'm sure he is admirably qualified for his position," he said. "This matter—touches on older concerns with which you are already acquainted." He swallowed nervously before offering the next persuasion. "You gave me good counsel then, and I didn't heed it. I've done a great deal of soul-searching in these past few—could we go somewhere private? Your quarters, perhaps? I can't really discuss this, standing out here."

The archbishop inclined his head, the blue eyes unreadable in the cherub face, and gestured toward a side door.

"Very well, my prince. The accommodations are modest, but they serve my purpose well enough—a place to lay my head at night, which even the Son of man hath not."

Catching the allusion, Javan promptly responded, "Saint Luke," and chanced a faint grin at Hubert, knowing the archbishop would not have expected him to pick up on the reference. "Shall I give you chapter and verse as well?"

To his relief, Hubert responded with a pleased if slightly wary chuckle, leading him through the door and along a polished corridor. Charlan and Guiscard followed silently behind.

"Now, I wonder," Hubert said. "Is that the bluff of a man who wants me to think he remembers the full citation, so that I won't ask for it, or do you really know?"

"Saint Luke, chapter—nine, I think." In the old days, when Javan had been under Hubert's instruction prior to entering seminary, it had been an intellectual exercise they both had enjoyed. *The foxes have holes, and birds of the air have nests; but the Son of man hath not where to lay his head.*

"Not that an archbishop really has to worry about a place to lay his head," he added, as they approached a polished door with the episcopal arms of Valoret painted on it. "You know, this would be far more impressive if the arms were carved, like the door back at Valoret."

Hubert smiled and pushed the door open without looking. "Why this apparent effort to make me recall old times, Sire? I had great hopes for you. I was greatly disappointed."

As they went through, Charlan and Guiscard took up posts to either side, their backs to the wall, exchanging apprehensive glances. Inside, through a small vestibule, Hubert led the king into a small, cozy parlor with a fire blazing cheerily in a modest fireplace. An elderly priest had been mulling wine in an earthen pot set on the hearth and went at once to fetch another cup when he saw that the archbishop had company.

Not speaking, Hubert lowered his bulk into the largest of the three chairs set before the fire and pushed his fur-lined cloak back off his shoulders, gesturing for Javan to take the chair beside him. Javan laid his own cloak over the back of the other chair, then moved the remaining one a little closer to his host. Until the old priest had come and gone, he dared do nothing more overt.

"Thank you," he murmured, settling into the chair. "I'm sorry I've been such a trial to you. May I—make what I have to say to you in the nature of a confession?"

"*Is* it a confession, my son?" Hubert asked quietly.

"In a manner of speaking, I suppose it is—or may become one," Javan replied, falling silent as the priest came back in with an extra cup and knelt by the hearth once more, to ladle mulled wine into both.

"Thank you, Father Sixtus, you may go to bed now," Hubert said when the priest had delivered the steaming cups. "I shan't need you more tonight."

Bowing, the priest withdrew through another door and closed it. Hubert sipped at his wine and said nothing, gazing distractedly into the fire until the sound came of another door closing, farther away.

"Very well, Sire. Father Sixtus will not disturb us further," the archbishop said at last. "You may assume that the purple stole is about my shoulders and that what passes between us shall be held under the seal of the confessional. What did you wish to discuss?"

Sighing, Javan set his cup aside and shifted forward in his chair, resting his elbows on his knees and letting his hands dangle between them as he intertwined his fingers. He needed to get at Hubert for a proper probe concerning his part in Rhys Michael's abduction—which was far more difficult than the simple control and blurring of memory he had imposed on the archbishop the morning of Alroy's death. For one thing, Hubert was paying close attention tonight—if no longer quite suspicious, then certainly curious about why Javan had sought him out.

Further, the control required for a proper probe required physical contact—and that could turn dangerous, if Hubert somehow guessed what was happening and tried to offer physical resistance. Javan did not know whether a cry for help would carry beyond his own men waiting outside the door, but he did know that in sheer physical bulk, he was no match for Hubert.

"These last few weeks have made me think quite a lot about

what it means to be king," he said softly, a vague enough opening that was certain to get Hubert's attention. "I thought I was ready to handle it, but when they sent me Rhysem's toe—"

He shivered and buried his face in one hand—the hand farthest from Hubert—but also leaving cracks between his fingers so he could see.

"I'm afraid, Father," he whispered. "They're going to kill my brother. They've demanded that I do something I can't do, but if I don't—"

"My prince," Hubert murmured, leaning forward. "You mustn't lose heart. We'll find him in time. You'll see."

Shaking his bowed head, Javan let his shoulders shudder in a feigned sob, at the same time *willing* the archbishop to reach out to him.

"I know you have to say that," he whispered. "I know it's meant to be comforting, but—"

In that instant, as Hubert's hand reached across to pat Javan's shoulder in sympathy, Javan shifted to cover Hubert's hand with his, surging controls across the bond of flesh.

Hubert blinked as Javan raised his head to look into his eyes, held by the grey gaze as well as the hand grasping his. Alarm flickered briefly across the cherubic face, disappearing utterly as Javan raised his free hand to touch Hubert's forehead between the closing eyes.

"Thank you, Archbishop, we'll make this quick," the king said, slipping to his knees at Hubert's feet, just in case Father Sixtus came back after all. He took both of Hubert's hands in his, resting them on the archbishop's purple-covered knees, then settled onto his haunches to bow his head over the joined hands.

Thus poised, he sent his mind into Hubert's to query regarding his brother—and gasped at the scope of the plot so revealed, hatched primarily by Paulin and Albertus but fully endorsed by Hubert.

Of having Rhys Michael abducted by disguised *Custodes* knights who let it be assumed that they were Ansel's. Of engineering the prince's "rescue" by more players in the plot—Manfred's men, who had taken the freed but injured prince to Culdi to recover.

And the plot had not really been about Deryni presumption or smearing the name of Ansel at all, though that had been a convenient side benefit. The real goal had been to accomplish Rhys Michael's marriage with Michaela Drummond. Apparently, the former regents really were thinking in terms of controlling a future heir, if they could not control Javan or Rhys Michael. It was very long-term planning, but what else could they do, without risking outright civil war?

And Rhys Michael had been an innocent dupe throughout. Even now the prince had been safe at Culdi for several weeks, recuperating from his "ordeal," blissfully unaware that neither his own letters nor any supposedly sent by his host had reached Rhemuth to inform the king of his brother's safety. Perhaps occasionally he wondered why no word came by return, no royal explosion to forbid resuming the courtship cut short by his darling's departure from Court two months before—though Rhys Michael carefully avoided mentioning Michaela in his own sparse letters.

But the snows were beginning to fall, and travel was slower, and there in Culdi, it was easy to put unpleasant possibilities from mind and resume his single-minded wooing of the object of his desire, cheerfully encouraged by a solicitous and cooperative host. "Besotted" was the word Albertus had used in his last letter to describe the prince—and he had not been referring to wine.

The information stunned Javan. Even in his joy at learning of his brother's physical safety, his heart sank; for there was no way he could act on what he knew, even if he were in time to prevent the marriage—which could take place at any time, if it had not already. It was treachery of a most insidious sort, and he could not prevent it. When the conspirators finally decided it was time for Rhys Michael to be "rescued," Manfred would return to Court in triumph, with the rescued prince now wed to the childhood sweetheart who had nursed him back to health after his ordeal—a romantic tale to wrench the hearts of any who heard it. After that, any further opposition on Javan's part would only make of him an ogre.

Approaching footsteps warned of the feared return of Father Sixtus. Startled, Javan rose back onto his knees and shifted his hands to clasp between Hubert's. At the same time, he went quickly back into Hubert's mind to erase any awareness of what he had done and insert more diverting memories—of a brief chat by the fire and a halting, red-faced confession by the king of vaguely "impure thoughts" regarding several young ladies of the Court. It was the only thing he could think of on such short notice that might begin to balance out the implications of what he had learned about Rhys Michael.

In particular, Hubert would recall mention of one Juliana of Horthness, Rhun's daughter, whose naming had shifted Hubert's hopes firmly to the possibility that Javan, too, might eventually be induced to marry as the lords of Council directed. The scenario was repugnant to Javan, for never would he even consider joining his blood to Rhun's detested line, but he hoped the sheer audacity of the notion would tend to confirm that Javan really had confessed it.

He had hoped for time to implant more complex controls for the future, which would not require physical touch for their triggering, but the footsteps were approaching too quickly for that—could Father Sixtus really walk that fast? Just as the door opened, he withdrew with a final command for Hubert to give him absolution, keeping his head bowed over tight-clasped hands until Hubert had pronounced the prescribed formula. To his horror, as he looked up, it was Paulin and not Father Sixtus who had come striding into the little room, clearly as surprised as he.

"I do beg your pardon, Sire, your Grace," Paulin murmured. "I did not realize . . ."

"No harm," Hubert assured him, giving Javan a hand up. "His Highness and I were just finishing. I give you leave to perform your penance in the Chapel Royal, Sire. 'Twill be a cold ride back up to the castle. Think upon your sin as you ride, offering up your discomfort to God. But the sin is a small one, and easily transformed into a virtue. Remember that."

"I will endeavor to do so, your Grace," Javan murmured, bowing formally to the archbishop and then inclining his head toward Paulin. "Vicar General."

Then he was fleeing from the archbishop's quarters, shaking in afterreaction once he had reached the safety of Guiscard and Charlan and was on his way out of the episcopal precincts.

"Paulin came in, just at the end," he murmured as they went into the cathedral close to mount up. "I don't think he suspected anything, but it was a near-run thing. I'll tell you more when we get back to the castle. And then I think we'd better go and visit your father, Guiscard."

Paulin, meanwhile, was by no means devoid of suspicion.

"What did he want of you?" he demanded, sitting down in the chair next to Hubert's.

"Absolution," the archbishop replied blandly, but with an arch little smile. "It seems that the king's brother is not the only one who burns for want of a lady's favors."

"Javan?" Paulin murmured, incredulous.

"Yes. So much for *Custodes* discipline of the flesh." Hubert smiled. "It's clear he hasn't succumbed as yet, except to impure thoughts, but one may entertain fond hopes. Would you like to know who has inspired such an occasion of sin?"

"I can't imagine," Paulin replied, clearly intrigued—and dubious.

"Would the name Juliana of Horthness surprise you?" Hubert returned. "He mentioned several others as well, but Rhun's dark-eyed daughter seems to be the one who troubles him most."

"Yes, she *would* trouble him—a bewitching creature—though one must wonder whether the troubling has more political origins than carnal ones, in Javan's case." He looked at Hubert closely. "Are you sure he was sincere about this? He couldn't have been making it up, to test how you'd react?"

"You're suggesting that he'd fake a confession, sully the Sacrament?" Hubert said. "Not Javan. He may have forsaken his vows, but I can't imagine that of him. No, I think he's simply a healthy young man beginning to discover his own passions. That's becoming in a king. I hold great hopes for him, Paulin."

And that same night in Culdi, assured of privacy by his indulgent host, another healthy young man reclined in a pile of sleeping furs pulled onto the floor in front of a cozy fire, a fair, tousled head cradled against his shoulder. In the near dark, the king's brother almost could not see the thin red scar of the healed wound just above his left knee. Master Stevanus had removed the sutures nearly a week ago, and most of the bruising had faded. He was pleased at how quickly he had healed.

As if reading his thoughts, his comely companion snuggled closer and reached a slender hand across to stroke lightly up the scar and then on to tease at his manhood. He chuckled at that, stretching languidly, and then rolled over to enfold her in his arms again. It mattered little to him that on the morrow, the Church would set such formal blessing upon their union as to make her his princess, for she had come to him some days ago as his bride. So far as Rhys Michael was concerned, he and Michaela Drummond were already husband and wife.

CHAPTER THIRTY-FIVE

He shall serve among great men, and appear
before princes; he will travel through strange
countries.

—Ecclesiasticus 39:4

The next morning, while Rhys Michael and his princess-to-be made preparations for their formal nuptials, the bride's guardian was scanning over a letter long prepared and now ready to be sent, purporting to be a follow-up to an earlier missive telling of the prince's safe rescue from his abductors and his imminent return to Rhemuth. Since the first letter had never been sent, it most certainly had never arrived.

Further to my letter of three days ago, Earl Manfred had written, in consultation with Lord Albertus and several of his knights, who had paid an incognito visit to Culdi soon after Rhys Michael's arrival.

> *I continue to thank God that the prince's injuries were not*
> *of a serious nature. Though exhausted from his ordeal, he is*
> *resting comfortably and making daily progress, but my battle*
> *surgeon has determined that it would be best if he lies here at*
> *Culdi for perhaps another week before embarking for Rhemuth.*
> *Regarding the prisoners taken when his Highness was res-*
> *cued—interrogation is proceeding, with the valuable assistance*
> *of Master Sitric, who confirms that MacRorie was their com-*
> *mander. I still regret that he managed to elude capture. One of*
> *the prisoners was Deryni, and died of his wounds; another died*
> *when Sitric attempted to force a Reading. The ones remaining*

*are human, but we are proceeding with caution, as one has
already tried to commit suicide.*

*I shall bring the Prince Rhys Michael back to Rhemuth as
soon as I may, and shall bid him write to you again as soon as
he is able. He still finds this very tiring, because of recurring
headaches caused by a blow to his head. These are abating.*

*Since Christmas Court approaches, it is my present inten-
tion to return with my entire household as soon as his Highness
is fit to travel, for I know that you will wish to reassure yourself
of his safety in person, as soon as may be practicable. I remain
your Highness' most loyal subject, Manfred MacInnis, Earl of
Culdi.*

Smiling, Manfred folded the missive and sealed it, handing it
and a second sealed missive to a knight standing by in Culdi livery,
waiting to take it away.

"The second dispatch is to be forwarded to Lord Albertus," he
said, rising to move with the man toward the door. "The messenger
will find him lying at Grecotha, headquartered at the bishop's palace. Ask him to convey my greetings as well to my son, the Bishop
Edward, and say that I look forward to visiting him in Grecotha
after Christmas."

As the man bowed and withdrew, Manfred smiled contentedly
and headed downstairs to where his wife was helping his ward dress
for her wedding to a prince. He had waited long for this day.

And in Rhemuth, Paulin of Ramos also was sealing a letter, though
it was intended for his principal abbey at *Arx Fidei* rather than any
royal or episcopal palace.

"Say to Father Lior that I urge him to use all speed in executing
these instructions, but also great care," he said to the *Custodes*
knight he entrusted with the letter. "We enter into ever more delicate aspects of our negotiations. God go with you."

As the man bowed and withdrew, Paulin pondered the events
he had set in motion, hoping he was wrong, but prepared to respond
if his fears proved well founded.

Javan received Earl Manfred's letter as he sat at supper with his
Council four days later, in the little withdrawing room behind the
dais in the great hall. Out of deference to his brother's continued
captivity, he had resumed the wearing of semi-mourning grey,

though relieved by the belt of silver plaques that carried the Haldane sword. The coronet of running lions was on his head, now actually serving some purpose besides denoting his rank, for his hair was growing longer and beginning to fall in his eyes if he did not restrain it under a circlet.

He held up a hand for silence as he recognized the livery on the man one of his guards escorted into the room. A letter from Manfred was no more than he had expected, knowing of the plot from his interview with Hubert, but as he read it, he found himself reacting as if the information were new, a part of him undeniably impressed at the finesse with which his enemies had carried it off.

Manfred covered himself in the very first line by alluding to another letter supposedly sent some days ago. It was so well done that Javan almost had to laugh, suppressing the impulse by momentarily burying his face in one hand and emitting a great, shuddering sigh that he hoped his listeners would take for relief.

"My brother is safe," he announced as he passed the letter to Tammaron to read aloud. "Apparently an earlier letter went astray. Lord Tammaron, if you please."

While Tammaron read out the text, to the apparent astonishment and relief of everyone present, Javan was weighing all the new implications. No earlier letter had gone astray—not from Manfred or from Rhys Michael. Most assuredly, the alleged earlier letters had never even been sent. Alluding to a previous letter also obviated the need to go into specifics of the "rescue" at this time, since that would have been reported before. If Javan pressed for particulars later on, Manfred could always plead that the passage of time had blurred some of the details; and anyway, the prince's return now was far more important than how he was rescued.

That left the question of Michaela. Manfred's letter made no mention of his ward, but Javan had no doubt that her romance with the recuperating prince was being actively encouraged—and that a sympathetic priest could be found to marry the young lovers without the dreary inconvenience of posting banns. If the two were not already wed, they soon would be—certainly before Manfred brought them back for Christmas Court.

Oh, Rhysem, Javan found himself thinking. *Don't you see how they're using you!*

He wondered about the captured prisoners, too. He was certain that whatever Sitric "discovered," it would only support the "Deryni plot" theory that had been part of the point of this exercise. Certainly none of the prisoners would ever reach Javan for questioning. Not with Oriel at the king's beck and call.

". . . as soon as his Highness is fit to travel," Tammaron was reading, "for I know that you will wish to reassure yourself of his safety in person, as soon as may be practicable. I remain your Highness' most loyal subject, Manfred MacInnis, Earl of—but this is most welcome news, Sire! After so long, I confess I had begun to lose hope. But he is rescued, and relatively unharmed!"

"Aye," Javan said weakly. "It will be—interesting to see what Earl Manfred manages to learn from the captured abductors."

It was what they would expect him to say, under the circumstances, and it *would* be interesting—interesting to see how they played out the charade. Meanwhile, he was not certain how long he could maintain his own charade of pretending to be surprised as well as relieved.

"Gentlemen, you will forgive me, I hope, if I beg leave to retire early," he went on. "I—will have letters to write back to Culdi, seeking further news of my brother's condition and word of when we might expect his return. Words cannot express my relief. Meanwhile, I would count it a great favor, Archbishop Oriss, if you would arrange for a solemn *Te Deum* to be sung at the cathedral tomorrow morning, in thanksgiving for my brother's safe release."

He really was fighting back tears as he stumbled blindly to his feet and made his escape, though the tears were as much of frustration as of relief. Charlan and Etienne fell in behind him, but Guiscard remained a few minutes, ostensibly to exchange comments with Lord Jerowen but actually to gauge the Council's reaction after Javan's departure.

"Virtually everyone seemed surprised and relieved at the news," he reported half an hour later. "Paulin and Hubert were a little weak in the 'surprise' category, but we knew that, of course."

"That's as may be," Javan murmured. He had laid aside his circlet and thrown himself into a chair in front of the fire with a cup of wine. His hair was disheveled, and his hands moved with ill-disguised uneasiness, caressing the sides of the cup. "Now we have to try to guess what they'll do next."

"Well, 'confirmation' that Deryni abducted the prince and tried to use him for bargaining won't help the Deryni cause," Guiscard said. "And of more immediate concern, it's more than likely that your brother will return in the next week or two with a bride. Once he's got her pregnant," he went on bluntly, "the odds for a fatal accident involving one or more Haldane princes increase dramatically." He glanced around curiously. "Where's my father?"

"Gone to report to Joram," Javan murmured. "I didn't dare go myself, after what's happened. No telling who will want to see me after they think I've had a chance to catch my breath."

"There's never any respite, is there?" Charlan muttered, shaking his head. "Why can't they leave you alone?"

"Loyal Charlan," Javan said bleakly. "They can't leave me alone because I keep reminding them that I'm not and never will be their puppet. But there's no help for that. If Rhysem has gone and married Michaela, we'll just have to muddle on from there. I don't intend to go down without a fight, though. Once some of the dust of the last month has settled—probably not until Rhysem is actually back—I still intend to proceed with what we were going to do before all this started. Maybe I can still salvage something from this mess I've made of being king."

"Sire, that isn't true," Guiscard murmured, sitting forward in indignation.

"Certainly not," Charlan agreed. "No one could ask for a better or braver master."

"Yes, but will bravery be enough?" Javan quipped. Smiling wearily, he drank deeply from his cup, then leaned back in his chair, resting his head against its back. "It might be different if I dared to unleash the powers I think I have at my disposal. It certainly might be different if I dared to call old allies back to Court. I know now that most of the Deryni who served my father were honest, upright men and women—though you'll never convince our enemies of that. But sometimes I do wish . . ."

As he closed his eyes and his voice trailed off, his two aides exchanged troubled looks, one a Deryni and one human, drawn together by their common love and loyalty for the third man in the room, who embodied perhaps the best of both races. Whether the enemies of such a man could allow him to retain his crown remained to be seen.

The man conversing earnestly with the Archbishop-Primate of All Gwynedd had determined that it should not be allowed. Paulin of Ramos had taken many gambles to bring him where he was tonight, and now prepared to take yet another, if his companion proved at all cooperative.

"There's someone you should meet," he told the archbishop. "He arrived last night, but I wanted to wait until today's news arrived."

Hubert was sipping a cup of mulled cider in the rather spartan dayroom that connected his parlor with Paulin's quarters, here at

Paulin's invitation after leaving the aborted supper party up at the castle. The *Custodes* Vicar General had been nursing some secret satisfaction all the way back. His eyes were almost feverishly bright as he searched his superior's face for any warning to back off.

"Why are you acting so strangely?" Hubert muttered, taking another swallow of cider. "Who is this you want me to meet?"

For answer, Paulin went to the door that led into his sleeping chamber and threw it open. Father Lior was waiting behind it, standing beside a middle-aged man with greying, mousy-brown hair cut just below his ears, one of which was pierced by a gold ring. The eyes were averted, but a neatly trimmed beard and moustache framed a sensuous mouth. Under a hooded black mantle, completely unadorned, he was wearing an ankle-length robe that gave the vague impression of religious attire, but without the hooded scapular or braided cincture that would have made of it a *Custodes* habit.

"You know Father Lior," Paulin said as the two moved into the room and Lior came to kiss Hubert's ring, "but you've not yet met Master Dimitri."

The man looked up as his name was spoken, piercing black eyes catching and holding Hubert's as he continued forward. Hubert gasped, drawing back his hand from Lior, staring as Dimitri sank gracefully to his knees at Hubert's feet and bent forward to touch his forehead to the floor. As he straightened to sit back onto his haunches, small hands resting easily on his thighs, the black eyes reengaged Hubert's.

"My suspicions were aroused when I came in last week and found the king at your feet, your hands in his," Paulin said, sitting easily in the chair beside Hubert's. "Something bothered me about it. I know you were just giving him absolution after confession," he said, raising a hand as Hubert started to protest. "But after he'd gone, and you told me what he'd confessed, that didn't ring true, either."

"What are you suggesting?" Hubert said, unable to take his eyes from Dimitri's.

"I'm getting to that. Javan has been very careful to avoid romantic entanglements with any of the eligible young ladies of court. It may well be that occasionally he has found himself entertaining lewd fantasies regarding any or all of these ladies. He's a red-blooded young man like any other of his age.

"But given the less than cordial relationship you and he have enjoyed since his return to Court, do you really think it likely that he would have confessed such intimate failings to you? And certainly not about Juliana of Horthness, whose father he despises.

Even if the young lady in question *had* aroused such passions, and he felt the overwhelming urge to confess it, there are many other priests to whom he could have made confession anonymously, and without mentioning the lady's name. Names are not necessary, as you know, and are usually discouraged."

"He did tell me, though."

"Yes, I'm certain you believe that he did," Paulin said lightly, keeping a casual eye on Dimitri, who had not moved. "I can't begin to guess *how* he might have persuaded you of that," he went on, "but I begin to suspect that it may not have been any ordinary persuasion.

"Now, who would be capable of that? A Deryni, of course. Master Oriel comes to mind immediately, but I should think his involvement rather unlikely, if only because he's so obvious. Besides that, his movements have been severely restricted since becoming part of the king's household.

"That leaves several distressing possibilities. Some other Deryni working secretly for the king, perhaps? Or is it possible that the king himself has somehow acquired the power to alter your memory?"

"That isn't possible!" Hubert whispered, at last dragging his eyes from Dimitri's to stare aghast at Paulin. "He's human! I know he is!"

"Is he?" Paulin said softly. "His father is said to have withstood every magic that King Imre could raise against him. That doesn't even begin to explain how he blasted a Deryni Michaeline named Father Humphrey, who had poisoned the salt used at the baptism of Cinhil's firstborn son. Were you even aware that there was an infant prince before Alroy and Javan?"

Hubert shook his head.

"I thought not." Paulin went on. "I can't verify the story about standing up to Imre, but I did manage to gain access to Archbishop Anscom's official register of baptisms and deaths. It was Anscom who presided over the little prince's baptism and then administered the Last Rites. Interestingly enough, the very next entry refers to one Humphrey of Gallareaux, priest of the Order of Saint Michael, who also received the final Rites of the Church on that date. I'd say that tends to confirm the other story I'd heard that Cinhil somehow called upon incredible powers to kill the man who had murdered his son."

"Dear *Jesu*," Hubert said after a few seconds. "But even if it were true, that doesn't mean his other sons inherited such powers. Alroy certainly didn't have any magic, and you'd think Javan would have used his by now, if he had any."

"I think perhaps he has," Paulin said quietly. "That's why I asked Master Dimitri to join us this evening. This doesn't mean I think Javan has the high magic his father occasionally tapped," he added, at Hubert's look of horror, "but I think, perhaps, he wields the subtler magics. Of all the princes, Hubert, he would have been the one most likely to be corrupted by Deryni influence. The Healer Tavis O'Neill was his constant companion for several years before being driven from Court."

"This is preposterous," Hubert began. "He can't possibly—"

"What if he Truth-Reads?" Paulin insisted. "What if he can compel people to tell the truth? Tavis might have taught him how. Maybe he even learned how to make people forget, after he'd plied his wicked work. What do you suppose you and Javan might have talked about *before* he confessed stirrings of lust for a girl he's always studiously avoided? Can you remember? What kinds of questions do you think he might have asked regarding what you *really* know about Rhys Michael's abduction?"

Hubert's eyes had been getting wider and wider as Paulin piled suggestion upon suggestion, and he was pressing tightly clenched hands to his rosebud lips as Paulin finished, the baby-blue eyes wide and frightened.

"Dear God, how can we know?" He breathed. "How can any—"

He broke off as his darting eyes met Dimitri's again and could not move on, his body going rigid as he realized what Paulin had been leading up to. Faintly smiling, Dimitri raised up onto his knees and laid his hands palm-up on Hubert's knees, his eyes inviting Hubert's touch but no longer compelling.

"Is this familiar, Hubert?" Paulin's voice whispered, close by Hubert's side. "What was Javan really doing when I came in that other night? How many times has he done this before? Is this, perhaps, why you believed him, years ago, when he told you he had a vocation and asked to go into the abbey? I've always wondered how he managed to beguile you so easily; you're usually far less gullible than that."

"It wasn't like that," Hubert found himself saying. "It can't have been. I surely would have known."

"I believe Master Dimitri can show you how surely you would have known," Paulin purred. "There's only one way to find out. All you have to do is lay your hands on his."

Hubert's heart was pounding in his chest, apprehension immobilizing him, but gradually anger began to supplant the fear—anger that perhaps he had indeed been used. He remembered Javan's confession clearly, but if it had never really happened—

Trembling, he forced himself to lower his clenched fists to his lap, staring at Dimitri's upturned hands. Then, timidly drawing a breath, he made himself unclench his fists and set his hands on the Deryni's, every muscle tensed.

Nothing happened. In the first shocked seconds of contact, Hubert could not believe it. After half a dozen heartbeats, he let himself exhale. As he slowly drew another breath, Dimitri glanced casually at their joined hands, then slowly closed his thumbs inward, not to catch Hubert's hands but to stroke gently along their backs.

"I shan't hurt you," he said softly, speaking for the first time. His voice had a melody to it, the accent recalling eastern climes. The eyes seemed to have depths to them that called to Hubert, inviting him to drown in blissful nothingness.

"Rest easy, my lord," the voice urged, as waves of relaxation now began to wash into Hubert's mind. "This need not be difficult for either of us. Just relax . . ."

The next thing Hubert knew, he was jerking back awake in his chair, surprised to see a bearded stranger kneeling at his feet, hands folded piously at his waist. Paulin was sitting in the chair beside him. For some reason, Father Lior was perched on the granite curbing that edged the hearth behind the stranger, his arms wrapped around his knees. And all of them were looking at him expectantly.

"Do you remember anything of the past half hour?" Paulin said quietly from beside him.

Hubert whipped his head around to stare at the *Custodes* Vicar General. "What are you talking about?" he said. "Who is this man?"

For answer, Paulin nodded to the bearded man, who calmly reached out to brush his fingertips across the back of one of Hubert's hands. Memory came flooding back so abruptly that Hubert gasped. He could feel himself blanching with shock as he looked first to Master Dimitri, who had done it, then over at Paulin, who had ordered it.

"Javan *did* tamper with my mind," he whispered. "How could I not have known?"

"Your Grace is fortunate that the Haldane had not time to finish well what he started last week," Dimitri said, rocking back to sit on the hearth curbing beside Lior. "I cannot say for certain what was the subject of his inquiry, for he left no trace of that, but I think he never made you confession."

"But I remember it—"

"Because you were instructed to remember it," Dimitri replied. "I cannot say exactly how he was able to accomplish this, but I believe your Grace must assume that he knows, at very least, that the abduction of his brother was a sham—and why. Most likely, he is also aware that both you and my Lord Paulin were party to the deception—though he dare not confront you lest he betray how he learned it. Had my Lord Paulin not interrupted, he might have succeeded in hiding all trace of his night's work."

"Did he—tamper before?" Hubert dared to ask. "Is that how he made me believe he had a genuine vocation?"

Dimitri shrugged, an eloquent gesture of graceful shoulders moving beneath his black robe. "I cannot say. He is young to have such skill, even if he were Deryni, and was younger still at that time. Any 'tampering,' as you put it, would have been relatively simple and very cautious. Nothing so blatant as what he did last week—though that was well enough done. Had he been given another moment or two, I might not have been able to detect the seams in his work."

"This is incredible," Hubert breathed. "I can't believe this of Javan. Are you certain that Master Oriel had no part in it? I've used his services on occasion. Maybe *he* did it."

"Master Oriel—the Healer, yes? I think not. You would have taken care not to let him touch you without witnesses present. Under such circumstances, it would have been very difficult. No, it was the king who touched your mind last week, have no doubt."

"Is he Deryni, then?"

"No, but something similar and just as dangerous, if you do not stop him."

The words hung on the air, neither Hubert nor Lior daring to breathe, until Paulin calmly stood and gestured for the two crouching men to rise. "Father Lior, you and Master Dimitri may retire now. Please remain in your quarters. For now, I would prefer that your presence in Rhemuth not become known."

When the two had gone, Paulin turned to lay one arm along the edge of the mantel, glancing back over his shoulder at Hubert.

"What now?" he said softly. "Or would you prefer to sleep on it? We've not increased our danger by what happened here tonight. We simply know now far more than we did before. The king doesn't know that we know—and even if he did, there's nothing he dares do without betraying himself. I'd like to see just how far he thinks he can take this, now that he's failed to prevent his brother's marriage."

"Aye, but we don't dare take any really serious action until there's another heir," Hubert muttered. "I shudder to think what might have happened if one of your men had thumped the prince just a little too hard, or an archer had been just a little off target."

"Don't waste energy worrying about might-have-beens," Paulin replied. "All we have to do now is maintain the status quo until Michaela whelps—perhaps as soon as late summer, if her prince has done his job properly."

"Maintain the status quo," Hubert repeated, snorting. "And what if the king decides to launch a further investigation into his brother's abduction in these long winter months that are now upon us?"

"We'll give him some bodies to reinforce the official version of what happened," Paulin replied. "One body is like another, when it's been dead for a week or two."

"But aren't Deryni supposed to be able to do something called a Death-Reading?" Hubert asked. "What if he has Oriel examine the bodies?"

"Master Dimitri assures me that nothing can be read from a body that long dead," Paulin replied. "Meanwhile, I've already ensured that the men actually responsible are kept far from Court for the next few months. Other than ourselves, no one else has all the pieces of the puzzle."

"Suppose he gets to us, then?" Hubert said. "Even if he didn't risk it himself, *Oriel* could make us spill everything."

"Then we'll have to see about eliminating Oriel, won't we?" Paulin said. "And as for the king—so long as neither of us permits a private meeting, without witnesses, we're safe. He has to touch us to influence us. And I mean to have Master Dimitri do some touching on our behalf. Be patient, Hubert. These next few weeks and months could prove very interesting."

CHAPTER THIRTY-SIX

Marriage is honourable in all, and the bed
undefiled.

—Hebrews 13:4

"Interesting" was not precisely the word Javan would have used to describe the days that followed. The next morning, before departing for the cathedral with his household for the *Te Deum* service, he dispatched Sir Robert with letters to Culdi written the night before—an anxious one to his brother, begging for assurance that he was indeed recovering, and a sterner one to Manfred, complaining that he had *not* received any previous letter and demanding details of the rescue and prisoners.

He met with his great lords in the afternoon. Udaut questioned how Ansel was continuing to elude capture. Hubert wondered whether Master Oriel ought to be sent to Culdi to attend the prince as Healer—which made Javan wonder whether his brother's injuries were more serious than he was being told. He longed to ride north to meet Manfred's party, if only partway, but Tammaron rightly pointed out that, since Ansel and his band were still at large, such an action could only expose the king to needless danger.

The advice was no more than prudent, if Ansel had indeed been involved in the abduction of Rhys Michael—which, of course, he had not. That Tammaron believed it tended to suggest that he, at least, had not been a part of the plot. To ignore his counsel and go anyway would only make the king appear reckless, prone to taking needless chances. Besides that, the weather was worsening.

Accordingly, Javan made himself bide his time as the days passed, though he fretted over the delay and made certain his Council was aware of it. Further letters arrived almost daily—from Manfred, from Tomais and Robear, from Lord Ainslie, and eventually several short ones from Rhys Michael himself—reassuring the king that his brother was indeed safe and making a good recovery. Like Manfred's letters, those from the prince suggested that earlier ones had never reached Rhemuth. After nearly a week came word that Lord Manfred expected to depart any day now.

This latter message arrived in the company of a band of *Custodes* knights, several of whom had assisted Earl Manfred's men in the prince's rescue. They brought with them five bodies alleged to be those of abductors taken during Rhys Michael's rescue, who had since died of their wounds or under torture. An accompanying letter from Lord Albertus regretted that so little information had been extracted from the men beyond their mere involvement with the outlawed Ansel, but assured the king that he and Rhun were redoubling their efforts to run down more of the men.

Meanwhile, the dead "abductors" were unknown to anyone at Court—as Javan had been almost certain would be the case. Paulin had the bodies laid out in the castle yard the afternoon they arrived and bade all men at Court look at them with an eye toward identification, but no one recognized any of the faces. Oriel also passed among the bodies, pausing briefly by each to test with his powers, but he and Javan had known before he started that it was a futile exercise.

But the exercise did not end there. The next morning, despite Javan's personal distaste for such measures, Constable Udaut ordered the bodies beheaded and quartered. It was a variation on the traditional sentence of hanging, drawing, and quartering usually meted out to live traitors and served at least part of the same deterrent function. By noon, portions of the bodies would be en route to most of the major cities of Gwynedd, with orders to display them at crossroads and above town gates as a warning to other Deryni who might consider treachery against the Crown of Gwynedd.

The fact that none of these men might actually have been Deryni would never now be proven. Nor was it even certain they had been involved in any way. One thing Oriel did note, in his inspection of the bodies, was that several of the men bore calluses more in keeping with farmers than with fighting men.

"I'm sorry to say that it wouldn't really surprise me if they simply rounded up a handful of peasants and killed them appropriately, just to provide some bodies," he had confided to the king. "Needless to say, I can't prove anything."

Nonetheless, the law required Javan to be present at the beheadings—though he excused himself when the further butchery began. The entire thing brought back all too vivid memories of another judicial mutilation of the dead, in the person of Ansel's brother Davin; and under the regents' governance, Javan had been forced to watch more than one live victim subjected to this form of execution. The very notion made the gorge rise in his throat.

Fortunately, no one could require Javan to stay and watch it, once the formal beheadings were accomplished. But even the awareness that it had been done set a sour note on the next few days, until word came that Earl Manfred's party lay half a day's ride north and would arrive on the morrow.

Javan decided not to ride out to meet them. Snow was falling, the arriving party was large, and adding the king and a suitable escort would only compound the confusion when they entered the city. There was also the added awkwardness of knowing that Michaela would be with Rhys Michael. He wondered how his brother intended to make the announcement of his ill-advised marriage.

A rider came to warn of their approach just before noon the next day. It was the Tuesday after the beginning of Advent. Javan assembled the Court on the great hall steps to await their arrival.

He had taken great care in his dress, to make certain he conveyed the desired impression on his brother as well as the watching lords of state. The rich mantle of Haldane crimson that muffled him against the cold was lined with black fox. The crimson tunic underneath was emblazoned with the Haldane lion full across the chest, the Haldane sword buckled around his waist. A matching cap of maintenance graced his head, supporting a band of hammered gold chased with celtic interlace and studded with cabochon rubies—not the familiar circlet of running lions, but not the State Crown, either. The image was relaxed but also official. There must be no doubt in Rhys Michael's mind just who was in authority.

The cavalcade that began winding up the cobbled approach to the castle mound well befitted the homecoming of a prince. After an escort of nearly threescore *Custodes* knights, led by Albertus, came several dozen of Earl Manfred's men, followed by Sir Robear and Sir Tomais riding side by side and then Manfred himself with the prince beside him, mounted on a fine white horse. Following the pair came the women of Manfred's household and another twenty mounted men-at-arms, these in the livery of Rhun of Horthness.

The *Custodes* knights split to either side in a guard of honor as the first of their number reached the castle gates, allowing Manfred's men and then the earl himself to pass through with his precious charge. Rhys Michael looked pale and a little tense as the procession came into the castle yard, but he seemed steady enough in the saddle. Snow powdered his sable hair and frosted the shoulders of a vast blue cloak lined with grey squirrel.

The king broke into a grin and raised a gloved hand in greeting as his brother came into sight, gathering his furs closer around him as he headed down the great hall steps.

"Brother, at last!" he called as Manfred and the prince came even with the great hall steps and drew rein.

"Javan!"

Rhys Michael had dismounted by the time Javan could reach him, and buried his face against Javan's shoulder as the two embraced.

"My God, Rhysem, I thought I'd never see you again," Javan murmured as they drew apart. "Are you all right? Did they hurt you much? Nobody was ever very specific about your injuries."

Rhys Michael gave him a sickly grin and shook his head, his words tumbling out in nervous relief. "I didn't want to scare you. It wasn't really too bad, all things considered. I've got a new scar to show you, on my leg." He gestured vaguely in that direction. "And they said I nearly got my throat cut when I was being rescued. I'm okay now, though. I got whacked on the head a couple of times, and I still get headaches—but not as bad as before. I suppose it was a really stupid thing to do, to get myself kidnapped."

Javan snorted as he chuckled. "If I thought you'd enjoyed putting either of us through this, I'd finish you off myself! It wasn't your fault."

"Well, at least it didn't turn out too badly," Rhys Michael replied, looking sheepish. "After Earl Manfred's men rescued me, I thought I'd died and gone to heaven." He flashed Javan a sickly smile, then ducked his head and started to turn away. "Wait here a minute. There's something you need to know."

Javan hardly needed to guess what his brother was talking about. As Rhys Michael moved quickly back along the line of riders now starting to dismount, Javan could see Manfred helping another blue-cloaked figure alight from a little grey palfrey.

Resigned, he moved back onto the great hall steps, out of the mud, to stand between Charlan and Guiscard as Rhys Michael turned to lead the figure toward him. He could not see her face inside the shadow of her hood, but it obviously had to be Michaela. Hubert and Oriss had come forward while he was down with Rhys Michael, coped and mitred to welcome the prince home, and Paulin stood a little behind Hubert, like a great, dark bird of prey. Javan knew they must be gloating.

Javan braced himself to receive his brother. Just before the pair reached the bottom step, Rhys Michael paused to turn and fold back his companion's hood. The close-wrapped white coif of a married woman covered Michaela's glorious tawny hair, a jewelled circlet binding its veil across her brow. Its severity obviously was intended to convey an impression of greater maturity, but it only emphasized the spray of freckles across her fair cheeks and the wide, apprehensive gaze of a very frightened young girl.

"I hope you won't be angry, brother," Rhys Michael said, turning to meet Javan's eyes squarely as he led her forward, her hand enclosed in his. "Michaela nursed me back to health, and we realized that our love was too strong to be put aside. I've married her, Javan, and we ask that you give us your blessing."

As he finished, he and Michaela both dropped to their knees on the bottommost step, both heads ducking in anticipation of a royal explosion. Javan knew they certainly deserved one, but he also knew that any protest he made now would only be seen as begrudgery by friend and foe alike. Nor would it reverse what had already been done.

"Of course I give you my blessing," he murmured, coming down to lay his hand on their joined ones and raise them up. "Michaela, I welcome you as a sister and pray that you find only happiness as a member of our family." He gave her a chaste kiss on both cheeks, then turned to embrace his brother.

"And congratulations to you, Rhysem," he murmured, dropping his voice to add, whispering, "we'll talk more about this later. But you do understand, I hope, that it isn't the marriage I object to—just the timing."

As they drew apart, Javan caught one of his brother's hands in his, reached out for one of Michaela's, and turned them both to face Hubert. "My Lord Archbishop, my brother informs me that he and the Lady Michaela have wed. Will you grant them your blessing? We must also arrange for a proper Mass of thanksgiving, in which the lady may be officially recognized in her new rank."

As he joined their hands and stepped back, bowing to Hubert, the pair knelt for Hubert's blessing, after which the watching courtiers broke out in spontaneous applause and cheers. It was difficult for Javan to maintain the required façade of brotherly indulgence, but somehow he managed, only succumbing to a fit of shaking when he had reached the privacy of his quarters an hour later.

"I knew the marriage was a foregone conclusion," he told Guiscard when he had regained a degree of composure. "That still didn't prepare me to actually deal with it. I don't know whether I found Manfred or Rhun more insufferable. I don't want to believe that

Rhysem connived with them to set this up, but it's very tempting. I've got to find out how much he knows about what's happened to him in this last month. Later this evening, once the banquet is well under way, I want you to arrange for Oriel to be brought down to the withdrawing room behind the dais. I'll find an excuse at some point to get Rhysem alone there for a few minutes."

He found his opportunity a few hours into the banquet, while singers were entertaining the Court with a medley of madrigals in honor of the royal couple. To no one's surprise, Rhys Michael had been partaking liberally of the wine on offer at the feast and had excused himself to seek out a garderobe. About then, Juliana of Horthness came up to the high table to gossip with Michaela, which also made it a good time for Javan to flee.

He waited a few minutes after Rhys Michael had disappeared behind the dais before following with Charlan. They were waiting for the prince when he emerged from the garderobe, drawing his mantle around him against the cold.

"Rhysem, I need to talk to you for a few minutes," Javan said, taking his brother by the arm and steering him toward the door to the withdrawing room. "I promise it won't take long. It's either now, or keep you from your bride later tonight; you choose."

Rolling his eyes heavenward, Rhys Michael let himself be propelled in the direction Javan was taking him, the wine keeping him amiable.

"I didn't think I was going to get off that lightly," he said good-naturedly.

He faltered a little as they entered the room, for Charlan closed the door behind them and bolted it, and Guiscard and Oriel were waiting beside the fireplace.

"First of all, I want to satisfy myself about your injuries," Javan said, fingers digging into his brother's arm as Rhys Michael started to balk, suddenly sobered. "I want you to tell Master Oriel about each and every injury you can remember."

"Good Lord, you'd think I faked the whole abduction," the prince muttered as Javan sat him down on a stool in front of Oriel. "I told you, I was hit in the head several times, and I had a nasty cut above my knee. Ouch, yes, it's still tender!" he objected, as Oriel ran his fingers through the sable hair and Guiscard bent to remove his left boot to get at the knee. "This is ridiculous."

"I read two distinct head injuries," Oriel murmured, his eyes going unfocused as his fingers probed at the base of the prince's skull. "This one's fairly well healed; probably accounts for the recurring headaches you mentioned, but they should diminish fairly quickly. The other one—" He shifted to finger the right temple, then moved on to examine the nearly healed wound in the prince's neck.

"The second blow's nothing to worry about, but how did you get this?" he asked. "It nicked the jugular."

Rhys Michael squirmed as the Healer fingered the spot, straightening his now-bootless left leg so that Guiscard could push up the leg of his breeches to expose his other injury.

"I—guess it must have been worse than they wanted me to know," he murmured, shrinking from the Healer's touch. "When they rescued me, I was riding ahead of one of the abductors. I was blindfolded, and my wrists were bound. The man who had me was about to cut my throat when they got him. Earl Manfred's battle surgeon said it was really close."

"I'll say," Oriel murmured, laying his fingers flat over it. "You've got to have lost a fair amount of blood from this. Relax now, and I'll heal it properly."

"No, don't. It's all right—" the prince began, panic lighting his eyes.

Javan was already catching his wrists and sending to Oriel to do what was necessary, watching dispassionately as the Healer's hand shifted to compress the twin pressure points on either side of his patient's neck, the other hand pressing to his forehead. The combined onslaught of physical compulsion and a command to sleep overcame the prince's shields long enough for Oriel to work his healing magic. He was probing the leg scar that Guiscard had exposed as Rhys Michael fought his way back to consciousness, Guiscard now standing behind the prince with his hands on the royal shoulders.

"Now, this *is* interesting," the Healer was saying, prodding at the faint pin-dots of red that marked the former suture line. "The wound was certainly sutured, but there wasn't any need for it. The cut was very superficial. Quite a lot of bruising, though. Most of it has been reabsorbed by now, but I find evidence of a great deal more trauma than is consistent with the extent of the wound." He glanced at Rhys Michael. "What did they tell you about this injury, your Highness?"

Rhys Michael laid his head back against Guiscard's chest and drew a deep breath. "What are you saying? That I wasn't really injured? I assure you I was."

"No one is saying that you weren't," Javan replied, watching him closely. "What we're suggesting, however, is that your

wounds were quite premeditated, for effect, as was your abduction."

The prince stiffened, then sat forward incredulously. "What do
you mean?" he whispered. "Who would do that? Of *course* I was
abducted."

Without specifying the source of his information, Javan briefly
told his brother of the *Custodes* involvement in the kidnapping,
and how the affair had been engineered with the dual purpose of
reuniting Rhys Michael with Michaela and further discrediting Ansel MacRorie.

"It all worked, too, didn't it?" he finished. "Even once you'd
been 'rescued,' you never suspected a thing—perhaps partially because you didn't want to, by then. You didn't even write to tell me
you were safe. The first thing I knew of it was a letter from Manfred
alluding to some earlier one that never arrived."

"But I did write, as soon as I was able," Rhys Michael said, wide-
eyed. "And Manfred assured me he'd written as well. I didn't tell
you about Michaela because I wanted to tell you in person, but I
must have written half a dozen times."

"Well, none of the letters arrived until the one that came with
the first of Manfred's to get through," Javan replied, knowing that
his brother had spoken only the truth. "That should tell you something. But there isn't time to sort this out now. What's done is done,
and we're going to have to live with it. Which brings us to an important question: What do you intend to do about Michaela?"

"What do you mean?" Rhys Michael asked, suddenly apprehensive.

Gesturing for Oriel and Guiscard to join Charlan by the door,
Javan crouched down at his brother's feet, resting one hand on his
knee.

"Think back to the reason I was against this marriage, Rhysem,"
he murmured. "Especially right now, another Haldane heir might
provide just the impetus to push my enemies to drastic action. Are
you sleeping with her?"

"Of course I'm sleeping with her. We've only been married a
fortnight."

"Do you think it might be a good idea to abstain for a while,
until we get this sorted out?" Javan said patiently.

Rhys Michael started to make a sharp retort, then thought better
of it and ducked his head to study his hands.

"You don't *really* think that's what the great lords are waiting
for, do you?" he whispered.

"You weigh all the evidence and tell *me*."

A heavy silence fell between them for a moment, and then Rhys Michael stirred uneasily.

"Let me think about this," he murmured. "I'm confused. I've drunk too much wine, and I can't think straight right now. Besides, we've got to get back to the banquet."

Javan nodded, getting to his feet. "I agree with everything you've said. Do think about it, though. I'll try to protect you; I'll try to protect all of us. But don't trust anything you're told unless you test it and find it's true."

He hoped Rhys Michael would read the second meaning in his last words and learn to tap an ability to Truth-Read that Javan was confident would develop in conjunction with his shields. Meanwhile, it *was* time to return to the banquet before someone came looking for them.

"Let's go back in together," he said, offering his brother a hand up. "That way, it will be clear we got to talking while we were away. Guiscard, you can escort Master Oriel back to his quarters. Thank you, Oriel. Charlan, let's make this look like an appropriately jolly escapade on behalf of two princes who should know better. Rhysem, are you game?"

By the time they reentered the great hall, the two brothers were laughing and joking, arms around one another's shoulders to hold each other up. The singers had finished, to be replaced by jugglers, and a wine-mellow Michaela greeted both brothers with kisses as they settled to either side of her. Javan even allowed himself to appear flustered and a little flattered when Juliana of Horthness boldly asked if she might partner the king when the dancing began. Archbishops Hubert and Oriss were seated to Javan's left, the former of whom immediately offered the king more wine. Beyond Rhys Michael and his bride, a beaming Manfred and his countess basked in the satisfaction of being seated at the high table, in lieu of the bride's parents.

The royal brothers' short disappearance seemed to have aroused no untoward notice, especially given their obvious good humour when they reappeared. The penultimate course was presented—tiny tartlets filled with quince and nuts, and fragrant cheeses with toasted slivers of bread—and Javan gradually began to relax a little. Later, he danced with the bride and then with several ladies of the Court, including the dark-eyed Juliana.

It was only later on, while he caught his breath during another musical interlude between sets, that he noticed a new addition to the Court, as he cast his casual gaze over the throng now dispersed mainly along the edges of the hall. He should have expected it, but he was still a little shocked. The quick little man pouring wine for Rhun of Horthness and wearing his livery had not been seen since shortly after the coronation, but the pockmarked face was unmistakable. That Rhun had brought the Deryni Sitric back to Court meant that Javan must now exercise even greater caution, if he wished to maintain the delicate balance between survival and disaster.

CHAPTER THIRTY-SEVEN

*Live joyfully with thy wife whom thou lovest
all the days of the life of thy vanity . . . for that
is thy portion in this life, and in thy labour
which thou takest under the sun.*
—Ecclesiastes 9:9

Sitric's return kept Javan even more wary, though the Deryni was little seen in the days and weeks that followed, and Javan was reluctant to ask Rhun about him. He bade his key personnel be alert for any appearance by Sitric, even those who knew nothing of his own more esoteric machinations, and warned them never to venture forth from their respective quarters unattended, for casual probing by Sitric became less likely when a potential witness or witnesses must also be dealt with. The directive helped fuel uneasiness of Deryni in general, but Sitric was one Deryni who definitely merited such uneasiness. Javan tried not to think too much about what might have become of Paulin's Deryni, though he kept an eye out for the face.

Charlan, in particular, the king kept ever by his side, for he dared not risk Sitric getting his hands on him. It had become obvious some weeks before that the young knight could function at full efficiency in his master's behalf only if he retained full awareness at all times—but that was dangerous, if someone like Sitric should get hold of him. To minimize the danger, Javan reinforced the safeguards he had set before, which should protect Charlan from casual inspection by Sitric or his like; but anything more was apt to invite more serious inspection.

Meanwhile, the business of the Court resumed, with the full Council meeting daily during the two weeks prior to Christmas to rehash what was known about Rhys Michael's abduction. Much time was spent commending the efforts of those who had brought about his rescue, but in the final days before Christmas, most serious considerations of the Court ground to a standstill.

An island of serenity in the midst of more festive events was the solemnity of the Vigil of Christmas, kept in the hushed final hours of Christmas Eve in a cathedral ablaze with candles and attended by virtually everyone who was anyone at Court. Javan treasured the magic and the stillness as midnight approached, kneeling reverently in the royal stall with his brother and sister-in-law, with Charlan and Guiscard close by.

As Archbishop Oriss celebrated the first Mass of Christmas, assisted by Hubert, Javan could almost make himself believe that even Hubert was not entirely beyond redemption—for surely the mere handling of the sacred Elements on this holy night conferred a grace that transcended petty human failings. When he received the Sacrament from Hubert's hands, it was the first time in many months that he did not feel sullied by the experience. Such, he reflected, was surely part of the miracle of Christ's Mass.

The principal activity scheduled for Christmas Day itself was a hunt given for the younger members of the Court. Javan gathered the hunt at midday and led a brisk chase out across the new snow with festive good humour, giving his brother the honor of taking up the lead, once the great stag hounds picked up the scent. Michaela rode at her husband's side, tawny hair flying in the wind, looking more like a wayward girl than the princess set to be acknowledged on the morrow in the first of the great formal ceremonies set for the season. Her brother also rode with the hunt, along with most of the other squires and the young men ready to be knighted at Twelfth Night—and the daughters of the Court, sent forth by doting parents in hopes of catching a suitor's eye.

Javan had no intention of being lured into matrimony any time soon, but since learning of Rhys Michael's marriage he had decided that perhaps its potential danger might be at least partially defused if he himself appeared to be thinking along similar lines. He had set the stage, he realized, by choosing to leave Hubert with the impression that he had felt lustful stirrings regarding Juliana of Horthness. So he decided to reinforce that impression by riding with Juliana for a time, feigning the reluctant interest he had already intimated to Hubert. When the pack lost the scent and pulled up to regroup, Juliana pouted prettily and avowed that she cared little for stag-hunting anyway; it was the thrill of the chase that amused her. As she toyed with the end of a glossy dark braid and turned smouldering glances in his direction, Javan pretended to be amused—or was it bemused? But that night he retired early, and alone.

The morrow saw a show of pageantry almost rivaling his coronation—Saint Stephen's Day, as the king led Rhysem and his bride down to the cathedral in festive procession and there witnessed their renewed nuptial vows. Javan could certainly understand his brother's passion. With her tawny hair coiled close at the back of her head and crowned with a wreath of holly and ivy, Michaela was a vision to stir the loins of any red-blooded male as she moved serenely down the aisle on Manfred's arm, gowned in the same royal blue as her waiting prince.

She held her head like a queen as she knelt beside Rhys Michael, and the two repeated the vows they had exchanged in Culdi. After Hubert had confirmed them husband and wife, laying the end of his stole across their joined hands to pronounce the blessing, she remained kneeling as Rhys Michael rose and turned to remove the wreath of holly and ivy, giving it into her hands while he pulled out the pins that held her hair in place—for it was time-honored custom that queens and princesses came to their crownings with hair unbound, regardless of their married status.

Her brother now brought forward the silver coronet on a cushion of royal blue, kneeling before Hubert so that he might cense and asperse it in blessing. Then Hubert was offering it to Rhys Michael with a bow, the prince turning with pride and joy to place it on her head and raise her up with a ceremonial kiss on each cheek and then a more loverly one on the lips.

Afterward, the pair presided at another banquet in their honor, with Javan yielding pride of place to the bride. There was dancing that afternoon and into the night, and Javan made a point of partnering nearly every lady present. Though he hated himself for it, he continued to feign special attention toward Juliana of Horthness—who flirted outrageously, to the guarded approval of her doting father.

Increasingly aware what a dangerous tightrope he was walking, Javan decided to back off just a little. The next morning he made a point of seeking out the new confessor Paulin had designated for the Chapel Royal, and again repented himself of entertaining lascivious thoughts where Juliana was concerned. A fleeting touch of the unwitting priest's mind ensured that the confession would find its way back to the ears for which it was intended. Within a few days, Rhun's attitude softened markedly, and even Hubert seemed a trifle more indulgent—though Paulin continued to be aloof.

The whirl of holiday festivities continued for the next fortnight, with hunting in the daytime, feasting at night, and occasional informal Courts in between. Daily came new arrivals, as the great lords from farther away gathered in preparation for Twelfth Night, the most important Court of the year.

The day dawned cold but clear, with new snow on the ground. For the formal Court at noon, Javan wore the State Crown of leaves and crosses intertwined, and cream-colored wool heavy with gold embroidery under a scarlet mantle lined with ermine. Rhys Michael and Michaela sat at his left, regally coronetted and in royal blue, and both archbishops stood at his right in golden copes and mitres as the Court paid their respects.

One of the more welcome offerings of the day was the assurance of loyalty from far Cassan, both the formal greetings of the Princess Anne and Fane Fitz-Arthur and the shakily lettered missive from the four-year-old Duke Tambert, declaring *Friends—Tambert and Javan.* The boy's obvious hero-worship and affection elicited an indulgent chuckle around the great hall when Javan read it out, for many had been present when the king received the boy before his coronation. The letter also helped lift Javan's spirits when the time came to knight Cashel Murdoch and several other senior squires of the Court, mostly relatives of the great lords. He far rather would have withheld the accolade altogether, for these young men were not of his choosing or in his trust, but he knew he dared not risk offending the men's relatives. At least Robear's hand was on the sword with his when he dubbed them, distancing him a bit from responsibility; for since he was not yet of an age for official knighting himself, and only a handful present knew of his private knighting the day he returned to claim his crown, he might not confer the accolade alone.

"Next year you will be the first, my prince," Robear murmured in a private aside as the first candidate approached the throne to be presented. "God knows you've more than earned your spurs."

Even far Kheldour was heard from, at that gala Twelfth Night Court. Duke Graham sent his respects and duty to the king in this new year, as did his uncles, but Earl Hrorik sent a further missive a few days later, advising the king that letters had been received, as expected, from the King of Torenth. He enclosed the letters, along with fair copies of Lady Sudrey's reply and his own comments.

> *Some there may be who would claim that love blinds me, Sire, but even those of the most suspicious nature could find no fault with my lady's faithfulness or loyalty, either to her hus-*

band or to the king whose justice extends even to these far northern climes. I believe that your Highness may safely put aside any further concerns regarding my Lady Sudrey, for there is no possibility that she would ever return to Torenth or provide information to her Torenthi kin that might damage her family in Kheldour or Kheldour's rightful liege. I am and beg to remain your Highness' loyal subject, Hrorik, Earl of Eastmarch.

At least Kheldour seemed to be back in the fold. Would that those lords closer to home were as loyal. Javan still had not decided how to deal with the treachery of Paulin and Hubert in engineering his brother's abduction.

And the plot was bearing fruit already. Javan tried not to let his imagination run rampant the first few mornings Michaela declined to join him and Rhys Michael hunting, but toward the end of January, he had Guiscard make quiet inquiries among the servants who looked after Rhysem and his bride—though none of them would ever remember being questioned on the subject.

"I'm afraid your suspicions are confirmed, Sire," Guiscard said as he helped the king undress for bed a few nights later. "One of the royal laundresses had some fascinating insights into your brother's domestic details. It seems that the new princess has twice missed her monthly courses now, and for the last several weeks has been increasingly unwell in the mornings. If you ask your brother about it, I'm sure he must be aware."

"Damn!" Javan breathed softly. "I'd hoped he'd restrain himself."

"In all fairness to the prince, it may already have been too late when you had your little talk with him," Guiscard replied. "And once he knew she was pregnant, there was no real reason for further restraint, was there?"

"But isn't there some danger?" Javan asked. "Though if there were, I suppose I should be glad. Maybe she'll miscarry." He closed his eyes briefly and shook his head. "No, I don't wish her that. And it's out of the question to ask Oriel to do something about it."

"I'm afraid so," Guiscard said. "But don't you think you ought to confirm this with Rhys Michael?"

The next morning, when he and Rhys Michael returned from their ride—again without Michaela—Javan confronted his brother. They were rubbing down the horses, a task both princes liked to do for themselves if no other duties intruded. Baron Hildred, who had been their riding master when they were boys, had once said something about the outside of a horse being good for the inside of a man.

"So, when is she due?" Javan said, watching his brother sidelong as he curried at the mud on his horse's flank with a plaited twist of straw.

They were standing between the horses, and Rhys Michael stopped in midstroke, turning sheepishly to glance at his brother.

"Who told you?" he asked in a low voice.

"That doesn't matter. Is it true?"

Rhys Michael sighed and leaned one arm over his horse's back, playing nervously with a wisp of mane. "I suppose it is. We didn't plan it this way, though. I swear we didn't. I—suppose she was already pregnant in early December, when we came back to Rhemuth. It—ah—could have started as early as mid-November."

"I see. That means an August or September baby." Javan sighed. "You haven't given me much time, have you?"

"I still think you're overestimating the danger," Rhys Michael muttered, throwing down his twist of straw. "Besides, now that you're wooing Juliana—"

"That's all sham, and you know it," Javan replied. "And if Rhun finds out, I'm *really* dead."

"But it's still turned speculation from me to you," Rhys Michael pointed out. "Even if you're right, I'm sure they'd much rather have an heir from you than from me."

"How reassuring," Javan said dryly.

The prince did agree to keep his wife's pregnancy quiet for as long as possible. Javan's own ongoing attentiveness to Juliana helped to improve the general atmosphere in the Council. Though Rhun's attitude could never be described as friendly, he did became more indulgent of what Javan had to say, and even seemed to develop an interest in the results of the land inquests being gathered by Javan's commissioners.

After about a month of reasonably civil interaction in a Council somewhat diminished by winter absences of some of its members, Javan at last decided to take up the project he had put aside at word of his brother's kidnapping. Increasingly he had become aware that the Deryni question would have to be approached indirectly, perhaps on a case-at-a-time basis in the beginning. One of the more obvious places to begin was the plight of the families of Deryni collaborators like Oriel.

"Gentlemen, I've been doing some thinking about the Deryni situation, in light of their involvement in my brother's abduction," he said as they settled down for an afternoon session on a particularly gloomy March day. "I concede that I was mistaken when I asked the Council to consider relaxing the Ramos Statutes. Obviously, the Deryni problem is far more complex and insidious than I wanted to believe."

His listeners exchanged glances with one another, uncertain whether to be suspicious or pleased. The scatter effect of the statements stirred vague resentment at Deryni being mentioned at all, yet hinted that the king's attitude was not altogether in favor of the Deryni presence.

"The Deryni involvement has also reminded me that we still have several Deryni held hostage here, in addition to Master Oriel and your Master Sitric, Lord Rhun. And my Lord Archbishop," he said to Hubert, "I apologize again for having complicated matters when I allowed Oriel to see his wife and daughter."

Hubert inclined his head. "Your Highness has a kindly heart. Unfortunately, kindness toward Deryni is misplaced."

"I don't know that I would agree with that," Javan replied uncomfortably. "I render kindness to my horses and my hounds; they serve me better for it, even if we were not so instructed in Scripture, to deal gently with our servants.

"Yet I *am* cognizant of the potential danger that a continuing Deryni presence in Rhemuth may pose," he went on. "Oh, I know we must keep the hostages necessary to ensure the continued obedience of Oriel and Sitric, so long as we choose to retain their services, but what of those whose service is past, like Ursin O'Carroll? While losing his powers may have been of benefit to his Deryni soul, it also made him quite superfluous for the purposes of his former employment. After three years, I should think it clear that his powers are not likely to return."

" 'Not likely' is not good enough!" said Hubert with a vehemence that startled Javan. "Oh, I have seen him tested repeatedly, and his wife as well, and I *know* the drug was potent—but what if his powers *did* come back?"

As the others muttered among themselves, Javan scanned around the room. These were the core of the Council, all of whom he must win if he hoped to make this work. His own people would follow his lead, but Hubert, Paulin, Albertus, Rhun, Manfred, Tammaron—all of these were of the old guard and were already suspicious.

"Gentlemen, it seems to me that perhaps it's time to reevaluate this situation," Javan said when he had called them back to order by rapping his knuckles on the table. Jerowen and Etienne were seated at the other end of the table, flanking Rhys Michael, and Javan had their notes on the table before him. "Am I to understand that Ursin *and* his wife continue to be tested, and that they both test human?"

"The wife *is* human, Sire," Tammaron conceded, looking uncomfortable. "There's never been any question of that."

"Yet she's been kept prisoner, even after Ursin lost his powers—"

"Because she married a Deryni, Sire!" Paulin declared. "And she bore him a brat who may be Deryni!"

"Who *may* be Deryni?" Javan said. "You mean you don't know?"

"The child was an infant when his parents were taken into custody, Sire," Hubert said impatiently. "With only one Deryni parent, it's possible the child was spared the curse. Furthermore, I'm reliably informed that the effect of *merasha* on the very young, whether human or Deryni, can be erratic. I should think you would count it a mercy to spare a possibly fatal reaction in a child who could well be human. For now, the boy is better off with his mother, who is human, even if it means they must remain in custody."

Javan scowled. If he persisted, he was likely to get the boy tested with *merasha*, regardless of the danger. But Oriel had also told him that regular doses of the drug, even in humans, could have a cumulative effect. He did not know how often constituted "regularly" in Hubert's book, but Oriel's indications were that anything more frequent than every eight to ten weeks might begin to do irreversible damage, depending on the concentration. He did not want to force a premature testing of Ursin's young son, but that might become necessary, if he hoped to relieve the plight of the boy's parents.

"I'd like to see Ursin," he said. "I haven't seen him since that day."

The clergy fidgeted among themselves, though his own men had been expecting it.

"Sire," Hubert said, "with all due respect, you were cleansed of Deryni contamination that day, if you believe that Ursin was also cleansed. You already risk recontamination by continuing to use Oriel's services. Do you wish to compound that risk?"

"Ursin isn't Deryni anymore," Javan replied, ignoring the remark about Oriel, almost wishing he could tell Hubert just how contaminated he was. "You've just told me that he's been tested repeatedly and that he shows none of the signs. Surely, if he were Deryni, he would have managed to escape by now."

"Deryni or not, if he *did* escape, he knows what would happen to his wife and child," Albertus pointed out.

"Yes, I suspect that would be your preference, in any case," Javan replied.

"In fact, it is, Sire," Albertus said, to Javan's shock. "If you wish, the problem can be eliminated entirely, once and for all. Neither Ursin nor his family need suffer continued captivity, once they lie in their graves."

"I won't have him murdered!" Javan snapped. "He's done nothing to warrant that."

"He is Deryni," Paulin retorted.

"He *was* Deryni," Javan replied. "He can't help what he was born. But when ordered by his lawful superior to submit himself to a devotional practice already demonstrated likely to remove the Deryni stigma"—he looked pointedly at Hubert—"he complied. You yourself had him tested on that day, my Lord Archbishop. And since that day, he has continued to react only as a human would. What further proof do you need?"

"The 'proof' is based on the actions of a self-proclaimed prophet and miracle-worker whose motives we do not know, Sire," Hubert said. "You were there. You experienced whatever it is that he does."

"Yes, but I am not Deryni," Javan replied. "Ursin was, and after encountering the Master Revan, he was Deryni no more. Father Lior tested him. If you trust him and his drugs, then you must trust that they proved Ursin is no longer Deryni."

"I would be most loath to release him, your Highness," Hubert murmured. "Despite the drugs, we can never be sure, where Deryni are concerned."

Javan nodded slowly. He had the beginning of a plan, but its shaping must be done slowly and with great care.

"I wish to interview Ursin O'Carroll," he said, standing. "I also wish to see him tested for myself."

As the others also stood, Paulin and Hubert exchanged guarded glances.

"Your Highness," Hubert said, "I do not recommend this. What do you hope to prove, or to gain?"

"A reassessment of this particular facet of the Deryni situation," Javan said. "Now, will one of you accompany me to Ursin's quarters or shall I make my own way?"

CHAPTER THIRTY-EIGHT

Now therefore perform the doing of it.
—II Corinthians 8:11

The senior clergy were quick to volunteer their company, once they saw he meant to go regardless. Paulin and Hubert flanked him as he left the Council chamber; Father Lior and Lord Albertus fell in with the king's ever-present aides. Down the main stair they trooped, through the great hall and across the garden, then on through a covered passageway and into an inner courtyard overlooked by lesser buildings than the main castle block.

Across this courtyard and up a tower stair Hubert led them, wheezing by the time they reached a landing guarded by two *Custodes* knights, who snapped to attention at the sight of episcopal purple and their own *Custodes* colors on Paulin, Albertus, and Lior. As the party accompanying Hubert spread onto the landing, a few still standing in the stairwell, he beckoned to a liveried warder with a large ring of keys.

"We will see the prisoner Ursin O'Carroll," Hubert said to the man, gesturing toward a stout-looking door just into the corridor that led from the landing, also guarded by a *Custodes* knight.

At Paulin's confirming nod, the warder bowed dutifully and headed toward the indicated door, selecting a large key from his ring. The lock turned almost soundlessly, the door swinging inward on well-oiled hinges. Paulin and Lior preceded Hubert and Javan in, Lior bearing a torch one of the guards had handed him. The others watched from the corridor outside.

Three years had changed Ursin O'Carroll. He still could not yet be thirty, but ample grey threaded the temples of the mouse-brown hair, grown long and tied back in a queue, and Ursin's beard had grown longer since Javan had last seen him. He was clean and tidy enough, clad in a bulky robe of brownish-black wool, with strips of the same stuff wrapped around his feet, but the once-proud shoulders slumped with the hopelessness of his situation. Bitter but resigned before, yet willing to collaborate to survive, now even the spirit seemed to have gone out of the man.

But of course, Javan reasoned, nothing had happened in the last three years to indicate that the rest of Ursin's life was likely to be anything other than an endless succession of days and nights in captivity, kept largely in solitary confinement, periodically drugged to senselessness for no good reason, and condemned to a living death by a law that allowed no leeway and no mercy.

Ursin had been sitting in the room's single chair when the door opened, enveloped in a thick mantle that was more like a piece of rug than actual fabric and huddling over a charcoal brazier not nearly large enough to heat the entire room. The chamber was similar in size and appointments to the one Father Faelan had occupied, but without the little oratory opening off it.

The faint light coming through the barred window at this hour was bleak and grey, matching Ursin's expression as he came to his feet and then sank quickly to his knees, head bowed, upon seeing the array of high-ranking clergy. From his reaction, Javan guessed that Ursin might not have seen him, wrapped in a grey mantle over his Haldane crimson today. It occurred to Javan to wonder whether Ursin even knew that Alroy was dead and a new king crowned.

"Ursin, the king wishes to speak with you," Hubert said.

Slowly Ursin raised his head, the hazel eyes flicking apprehensively among the clergy as they parted slightly to let Javan ease forward. Lior had passed his torch to Albertus and was already fingering a long, narrow metal tube the length of his hand, ready to administer the requisite dose of *merasha* when instructed. Ursin glanced at the priest with ill-masked dread, but as he turned his gaze dully to the figure in crimson, the hazel eyes widened in surprise.

"Prince Javan?" he murmured.

"Silence, unless you're spoken to!" Hubert warned, raising the back of his hand to Ursin.

Instantly the man cringed closer to the floor, instinctively protecting his head with his arms. The reaction suggested that physical abuse probably was a regular part of officialdom's dealings with the unfortunate Deryni hostages.

"That's enough!" Javan said sharply, moving between Ursin and the archbishop. "Ursin, look at me. You've done nothing wrong, and I won't allow you to be mistreated. Straighten up, man, and look me in the eyes."

Remaining on his knees, Ursin slowly obeyed, carefully folding his hands before him with the fingers intertwined in entreaty—or in illustration that he was helpless to give physical resistance—before he dared to look up. Javan made a quick probe for shields, but there were none, and no hint of anything to suggest that the man once had been Deryni.

"That's better," he said quietly. "How long has it been, Ursin, since we both went down into a pool near Valoret and received cleansing of the Master Revan?"

"More than three years, Sire," Ursin whispered.

"And has the taint ever returned?" he asked.

Gravely Ursin shook his head, his expression mixed of resignation and sorrow. "No, Sire."

Breathing a perplexed sigh, Javan glanced aside coolly at Lior. "I would see him tested, Father."

Ursin's head jerked up with a start, dull betrayal sparking in his eyes for just an instant, and several of the men with Javan murmured among themselves. An expression of smug self-righteousness was on Lior's face as he almost sauntered over to where Ursin was kneeling, unlimbering his Deryni pricker from its vial of *merasha*. The twin needles glistened with the drug, a shimmering droplet caught between them.

Stoic resignation writ across his bearded face, Ursin sank back on his heels and pushed back one loose sleeve, extending his bared arm to Lior and turning his gaze away. The needles were slender, and not very long, but Ursin bit back a gasp as Lior plunged them into the tender flesh of the inner forearm. He made no attempt to pull away, though, perhaps having learned from three years' experience how to avoid any needless further discomfort.

When Lior had jerked the needles out, Ursin let fall his arm and mechanically pulled the sleeve back down, obviously schooling any show of his emotions before raising his eyes. Though Javan had known generally what must happen in response to his command, he had not expected the sheer inhumanity of it; and realized now, by Ursin's resigned compliance, that this indignity must have been a regular part of the man's life for all these three years past.

"What are you feeling?" Javan asked, watching Ursin closely as they waited for the drug to take effect. He thanked God that no one had thought to use it on him when he was at *Arx Fidei*, the way they had used it on Faelan. It also occurred to him how vulnerable he was right now, if Lior were suddenly to turn the Deryni pricker on him.

Ursin's eyelids were already starting to droop over dilating pupils, the tension leaving his taut shoulders as his head started to loll forward, and then he caught himself. He was displaying the usual sedative effect of *merasha* on humans, but none of the symptoms one would expect of a Deryni.

"Ursin?" Javan said. "What are you feeling?"

"I feel—dizzy, Sire," Ursin said haltingly, in response to Javan's question. "Waves of sleep . . ." Then, whispered almost against his will: "Dear God, how many more times . . ."

As he buried his forehead in one hand, Javan briefly clasped a comforting hand to his shoulder. After a few more seconds, the king glanced at the others, then back at Ursin.

"All right, that's what I was expecting," he said. "Now I think it's time we resolved the matter of his family. Ursin, your wife is human, is she not?"

Ursin lifted his head in dull incomprehension, then nodded yes.

"And what about your son?"

He watched Ursin's reaction closely, for he remembered that Tavis had identified the man as a "failed Healer." Javan did not know precisely what that meant, but it certainly meant that Ursin had been fairly well trained and ought to have been able to tell whether his own son was Deryni. Javan hated putting him on the spot this way, but there was no way that Hubert and Paulin were even going to consider what he had in mind, without knowing for certain about Ursin's son.

"What's your son's name, Ursin?" he asked quietly.

Even drugged, Ursin obviously guessed where at least a part of this conversation was headed—and that there was nothing he could do to stop it.

"His name is—C-Carrollan, Sire," Ursin managed to whisper. "He is named for his grandsire."

"And do you know whether he's Deryni?" Javan asked. "Ursin, I know you've had a good deal of training. I'm sure you've evaded this question before, to protect him, but I have to know. If Father Lior tests the lad with *merasha*, is he going to react as a Deryni?"

Ursin's head bowed, shoulders slumping in dejection, and then he slowly nodded. His apparent betrayal by the new king swept away any remaining resistance he might have offered.

"He was—only a baby when—when last I saw him, Sire. But the

signs were there. I was to have been a Healer, but the—gift failed in me. I lacked the ability to focus it properly. I—had hoped it might be perfected in my son. But now I wish I had passed on no part of my powers at all."

His sob held both fear and sorrow as his head sank lower on his chest, and Javan had to strain to hear his next words.

"He would not have been much of a Deryni," he murmured. "And now—" He sighed and seemed to wilt even more. "Now, it seems less and less likely that he will even grow to manhood . . ."

As the distraught voice trailed off, Javan turned to Charlan, waiting expectantly in the doorway.

"Fetch Master Oriel," the king said. "And have him bring his medical kit."

As Charlan bowed and withdrew, Hubert regarded Javan suspiciously, and Paulin looked decidedly indignant.

"I had assumed that Father Lior would test the child," Paulin said.

"Oriel can give the lad a lighter dose of *merasha* than can be administered with Lior's Deryni pricker," Javan replied. "The lad's only four or so. An adult dose could kill him."

"And if he doesn't react?" Paulin said. "Oriel *could* substitute something else, you know, once he learns what you intend. He's Deryni. There's nothing he might not do, to protect one of his own kind."

Javan shot the Vicar General a withering look. "The boy's father has admitted that he believes his son to be Deryni! That means he'll react. If he doesn't, I'll—I'll have Oriel drink from the same cup as the boy, to prove that it was indeed *merasha*. Will *that* satisfy you?"

Grudgingly Hubert and Paulin agreed, Lior standing silent and sullen, not daring to contradict his superiors. When Oriel arrived and was told what Javan wished him to do, his agreement was even more grudging. The appalled and drug-dulled Ursin listened in despair, knowing that his cooperation had committed his son to face a dreaded trial that could only end in his condemnation and aware that there was absolutely nothing he could do to stop it.

Numbly he held out his wrists for the shackles that Paulin required. It placed him even more at their mercy, but at least it appeared he was to be permitted to be present when his son's fate was decided. That softened the betrayal a little.

It was even a victory of sorts. For more than three years, Ursin had not been out of his quarters save for the times they retested him with *merasha*. On those occasions, he was drugged and then shackled before being moved to another room nearby, exactly like the one he had left.

Javan caught the memory as he came to check Ursin's shackles after the warder snapped them in place. For three long years, Ursin had endured this treatment on a regular basis, lent strength to carry on only by the hope that his son might be spared even a little longer—though he had never known for certain whether the boy was even still alive. After a few hours, though still groggy, he was always dosed again before being brought back to his own quarters, which had been cleaned during his absence. Usually, but not always, he made it back to his own bed before passing out from the second dose added to the first.

Javan glanced at the room as they passed it now, heading on along the corridor and around a bend at the end, where the warder bent to another heavy lock with his great ring of keys. Now radiating from Ursin's mind was another memory of the room they had passed. Cautious queries over a three-year period had confirmed it to be the former lodging of Declan Carmody's wife and two young sons, whom Ursin—and Javan—had seen strangled before the entire Court, that awful day that Declan himself had been horribly tortured and killed.

A fragment of Ursin's drug-fogged memory of that day triggered unwelcome and clearer recall in Javan's mind—images of the once-proud Declan stretched spread-eagled before the throne at the regents' command, writhing in his own blood, his screams only gradually growing weaker as the executioners dragged his entrails from his belly and dragged out his death.

The *snick* of the lock broke the flow of awful memories, and Javan shook himself free of them to gaze beyond Hubert and Paulin as the door swung inward.

The woman sitting in the barred window should have been pretty still—she could not be more than twenty-five or so—but three years of confinement had dulled whatever brightness she once might have possessed to a premature aging. She rose as the door opened, her shoulders slightly stooped as she stood silhouetted against the grey of the afternoon, her russet gown hanging baggy and shapeless around her thin figure. Her hair was bound under a wimple of the same sort of rusty-black wool as Ursin's robe, so Javan could not see what color it was, but the besmocked child kneeling behind her in the window, peering at a pair of grey-striped pigeons on the outside sill, had a tousled shock of dark hair that glinted reddish in the waning light.

In that instant, the woman saw Ursin standing behind Hubert

and Paulin. One hand went to her throat as her eyes widened. Taking charge of the situation, Javan stepped alongside Paulin and spoke.

"I think we'll let Ursin tell his wife what's planned," he said quietly, but in a tone that brooked no defiance, setting a hand on Ursin's bicep and propelling him toward the woman before Paulin could object. "There's nothing either of them can do that would present a danger. But don't take too long, Ursin. We wouldn't want anyone getting more nervous than they already are. Oriel, prepare to do what you came for."

As Oriel moved briskly into the room and set down his Healer's satchel on the single table, Paulin and Hubert shuffled uneasily apart. Ursin moved like a man in a trance, his eyes locked on the woman's, hers on his. Tears were now glittering in her eyes—and in his. The boy had stopped playing, his light eyes flicking uncertainly from his mother, to the men in the doorway, to the bearded and manacled stranger now approaching who made his mother cry.

Javan watched as the two came together, casting out for any trace of Deryni interaction between them, but there was none. He could sense rudimentary shields in the boy, however. As Ursin raised manacled hands to encircle his weeping wife, he moved with her farther into the window embrasure, urgent whispers already trying to explain what was happening. Javan went over to the table where Oriel was carefully measuring tawny drops of *merasha* into a cup he had half filled with water from a roughly glazed pitcher.

"Can you have something ready to cancel out some of the effects of that?" he said in a low voice, jerking his chin at the cup. "We already know he's going to react."

Oriel nodded toward another cup already containing a layer of fine white powder in the bottom. "I'm one step ahead of you, Sire," he murmured. "Would you fill that about halfway with water?"

"What are you doing?" Father Lior asked, pushing his way between them. "What is that?"

"An anticonvulsant. It's also a strong sedative," Oriel replied. "We already know the boy's Deryni. At least his father says he is. I've never given *merasha* to a child this young, but all the texts warn about the effects being amplified, because absolutely no resistance has been developed this early. Once everyone is satisfied that he reacts as expected, I intend to put him under—unless you have some overweening desire to see a child convulse and possibly die right before your eyes."

Lior picked up the discarded packet that had contained the pow-der, read the notations penned on the parchment, then dropped it on the table beside the cup. Even he knew that Oriel could have had no opportunity to prepare for treachery.

"Very well. Proceed when you're ready."

CHAPTER THIRTY-NINE

Therefore let us lie in wait for the righteous,
because he is not for our turn, and he is clean
contrary to our doings.

—Wisdom of Solomon 2:12

The woman froze as Oriel turned toward her son, suddenly comprehending what they intended.

"Please, no," she whispered, ducking out of her husband's arms and gathering the boy to her, pale eyes pleading. "Ursin, don't let them . . ."

Ursin only closed his eyes despairingly, slowly shaking his head. Even heavily sedated, he knew exactly what was happening and why, and that only cooperation would minimize the terror of what must occur—the fear even now communicating itself to the boy cowering behind his mother's skirts, tearful and anxious as he shifted his gaze from the stranger who was his father to the strangers approaching.

"My darling, we can't stop them. You know that," Ursin said softly. "Let Master Oriel do what he has to do. I promise you, it's better this way. The dose is low. There's a sedative waiting. It's the boy's best chance. Would I risk my only son if I did not believe that?"

She was not listening. Ursin knew she was not listening—and what the approaching Oriel proposed to do about it. As the Healer came almost within touching distance, Ursin seized his wife's wrists and turned her back to Oriel, nodding acquiescence as the Healer's hands came up to clasp either side of her head from behind. Resistance went out of her instantly, her eyelids fluttering and then closing.

"It will be least upsetting if she helps reassure the boy," Oriel said, looking past her at Ursin.

Bleakly Ursin nodded, caressing her hands in his as Oriel set the command. When the Healer's hands dropped away, she slowly opened her eyes and turned toward where her son had fled to huddle fearfully in the farthest corner of the window embrasure. Ursin stayed where he was, weaving slightly on his feet and setting a shoulder against the wall to steady himself.

"Why, Carrollan, my love, what foolishness is this," she chided gently, "to weep and hide when your papa comes to see you?"

As the boy blinked up at her, letting her move in to sit beside him, Oriel turned to take the first cup from Lior, warning Javan off with a glance.

"And here is Master Oriel, your papa's friend, come to bring you something nice to drink," she went on, not looking at Oriel as she held out her hand. "It's nice—you see?" She sipped from the cup, then offered it to him. "Drink it down like a good boy now, and show Papa how big and brave you've grown."

Fearful but trusting, the boy tasted what was in the cup, then began drinking. Each swallow seemed loud in the silence of the room. Ursin had sunk down to sit on the edge of the window embrasure, turning his face away.

"There's my brave boy," his wife whispered when the cup was empty and the boy gave it back to her, smiling. "Papa, are you not proud of your son, who has drunk down the medicine so bravely?"

Ursin looked up again at that, dull despair giving him the appearance of a man of twice his years. Little Carrollan was searching both their faces, puzzled by his mother's calm and his father's apparent sadness. But then an odd, frightened look came across his face.

"Mummy?" he whispered, just before he reeled, eyes wide and frightened, and then crumpled across her lap.

In a matter of seconds, his breathing shifted abruptly to irregular gasps that shook his entire body, and instead of subsiding, he began to shudder.

"Very well, you have your answer," Oriel said, staying Ursin with a raised hand and a shake of his head when he would have come to comfort his son. The mother merely sat back with eyes closed. "May I give him the other cup now?"

"Not yet." Lior pushed past Oriel and bent to turn the boy's face to the light. The pupils were wide and fixed, the boy's skin clammy, his breathing rapid and irregular. Even to the uninitiated, there could be little doubt that young Carrollan was exhibiting all the classic symptoms of a Deryni reacting to *merasha*.

"Let me give him the other cup, Father. *Please*," Oriel said.

"I'm not sure," Lior replied, though the boy was beginning to twitch, his breathing now coming in gasps.

"Lior, he's about to go into convulsions!" Oriel snapped. "For God's sake, let me give him the other medication. He's just a boy."

As he turned his entreaty on the others—Ursin was looking more and more alarmed—Javan seized the initiative and the second cup, carrying the latter up into the embrasure with Oriel.

"Here, Oriel. Give him this. I think everyone's seen enough. And I think I see a possible solution to this problem, now that we know what we're dealing with. Lior, come down with the rest of us."

As Javan took the priest's arm and physically propelled him down out of the embrasure to stand before Hubert and Paulin, Lior murmured, "This is highly irregular—"

"It's irregular to keep harmless folk imprisoned for no good reason!" Javan retorted, releasing Lior's arm. "And yes, we now know that young Carrollan is not harmless—or might not be, once he's grown. But now that we know that, I think I see a better way of dealing with this—one that should satisfy even the most scrupulous among you."

Behind him, Oriel had enlisted Ursin's assistance to get the contents of the second cup down young Carrollan's throat, and the boy was now slumped unconscious in the Healer's arms, his father tenderly caressing a limp little hand. Lior glanced back at them, clearly still suspicious, but Hubert recalled his attention with a cough.

"Enough, Father."

"But the Deryni are treacherous," Lior muttered.

"Yes, four-year-olds are treacherous," Javan said breezily, "but not to the point that they should frighten grown men. Archbishop, I have a proposition for you," he said, moving Hubert and Paulin back into the room, farther from the embrasure. "Please don't say no until you've heard me out. Oriel, stay with your patients, please."

He could feel the suspicion of the clerics surrounding him as he moved into their midst, but also the support of his own people, still watching from the doorway.

"Just what is it you have in mind, Sire?" Hubert asked.

"Simply this: a second half to the experiment you've been carrying out with Ursin, who used to be Deryni but has been free of the taint for more than three years now. It was an experiment, wasn't it, when you sent him down to Master Revan?"

"Yes."

"I'd like to extend the experiment, but in a more controlled manner."

"Go on," Hubert said, clearly suspicious.

"I'd like to take Ursin's wife and son to Valoret—to present themselves to Master Revan, the way Ursin did. The boy may be Deryni, but he has no knowledge of what he is, absolutely no training, and no hope of getting any. Let Revan cleanse him. If it works as well for him as it did for his father, he won't be Deryni anymore either. And you've condemned Ursin's wife for marrying a Deryni and bearing him a child—let her seek purification at Revan's hands as well."

"And what after that?" Paulin asked. "You surely don't propose that they merely be released—especially not the boy."

"Well, you could let his mother enter a convent," Javan said, "though there's no reason *she* couldn't be set free. And the boy could—could be given to a monastery as an oblate, if you're determined to maintain some control over him. But none of them would have to live in captivity any longer. You don't need them to guarantee Ursin's obedience. For that matter, he could be sent to a monastery as well. I believe he reads and writes. Can't the abbeys always use another competent scribe?"

For a full ten heartbeats, not a sound stirred the silence in the little room. Javan could sense Ursin's shock and prayed that he would go along.

"An interesting proposition," Hubert admitted grudgingly, after cautious reflection. "The question of Master Revan does intrigue me still. Before, there was not adequate time for preparation. What you propose could be controlled. It also would be an opportunity to test Revan and his disciples—to determine, once and for all, whether what they do is valid. I still am not wholly convinced that there is not Deryni subterfuge at work there."

"You still believe that?" Javan said, contempt tinging his voice. He sighed and shook his head, then looked again at Hubert.

"Very well, Archbishop. I have no objection if you make it a test for Revan and his folk as well. My concern is for the lady and her son. Will you allow them to go to Master Revan?"

Hubert glanced at Paulin, then inclined his head. "I will consider it. Your proposal is—interesting."

"And Ursin?"

Hubert glanced askance at the captive, who had been trying not to look as if he had been listening. "*Do* you read and write, Ursin?"

Bewildered, Ursin gave a careful nod.

"Very well." Hubert clasped his fat hands behind him and strode closer to the embrasure where Ursin sat. "I shall ask you this once and once only. Knowing what fate is proposed for your family—which is far better than you could have hoped for, without his Highness' bold championing—is it your desire to withdraw from the world and enter the religious life as a lay brother, where you might lead a useful existence and perhaps gain God's forgiveness for what you have been?"

Blearily Ursin stared at the archbishop. With no prior call to a religious vocation, the prospect could hardly be very attractive in a general sense, but after more than three years of virtual solitary confinement, even a cloistered, celibate existence must have its appeal. Javan knew he was gambling with Ursin's life, for all too many fatal accidents might await an ex-Deryni, once beyond the king's immediate scrutiny; but Javan did not intend that Ursin should stay in the cloister forever. The chances of arranging his escape from a monastic setting were far better than for getting him out of Rhemuth Castle any other way—if he could stay alive long enough to be rescued. After all, determined rescuers had liberated Javan's father from a monastery.

"I—think such a life might bring me great comfort, your Grace," Ursin finally said, as Javan nearly held his breath. "These past years, I have betimes led something of a contemplative life, such as I have been able, but the chance to do useful work again would be a great gift."

He averted his eyes, as was seemly for a Deryni in captivity, and Hubert nodded, a prim smile on the rosebud lips.

"I trust that your gratitude will extend to exemplary behavior," he said. "Very well. As a favor to his Highness, I shall select a suitable religious establishment and recommend to its abbot that you be admitted as a lay brother, there to spend the rest of your natural days in penance, contemplation, and useful work. With time, I would hope that you might come to be accepted as a productive and welcome member of the community. However, there are certain conditions."

As Javan braced himself for the conditions, Hubert continued. "You will submit to all the regular disciplines of the monastic life, as determined by your abbot and chapter and the Rule of your Order. Because of your unique status, I shall give your abbot absolute authority of life and death, but if you are obedient and humble, you will be dealt with fairly. And of course, you will continue to be tested regularly with *merasha*. Are you willing to accept these conditions?"

Dully Ursin turned his gaze to his unconscious son, to his wife, then bowed his head. The movement stirred the chains on his manacles, underlining his helplessness to decline the offer.

"I accept the conditions, your Grace," he whispered. "I can do none other. And I pray God have mercy on my wife and son, for I can do nothing more to help them. God's will be done."

"Amen to that!" Paulin said.

"Amen," Hubert repeated lightly. "I will not suggest that you might discover a true religious vocation, for we now begin to believe that those of your race are not capable of genuine religious devotion, but you might find usefulness and expiation of your sins."

But neither he nor Paulin would allow Ursin further grace to bid good-bye to his family. With an impatient jerk of his chin, Hubert bade Lior get the wretched Ursin on his feet, chivvying him toward the door.

One last glance over his shoulder Ursin gained, before being marched back down the corridor by Lior and a guard toward his own quarters—though at least he was not drugged again, as had been the usual pattern in the past. Oriel, when they had gone, turned his attention back briefly to Ursin's family, gently depositing the unconscious boy in his little bed set against one wall, then bidding the lady to her bed as well, where he used his powers to send her mercifully to sleep. Outside the chamber, once the door was locked, he faded into the background with Charlan and Guiscard as Javan rounded on Hubert and Paulin.

"I should like to pursue this matter as soon as possible," he said. " 'Tis said that Master Revan winters in the hills above Valoret, emerging in time for Easter. I shall send riders north as soon as the first thaws begin, to seek him out."

"Aye, but first things first, Sire," Hubert murmured. "Master Ursin has asked for a trial of the religious life. Had your Highness any particular establishment in mind?"

"I thought to leave that decision in your capable hands, Archbishop," Javan said neutrally. "Your Grace knows best where an extra scribe's talents might best be employed."

"Hmmm, yes. Not having worked as a scribe before, however, I expect that Master Ursin will require formal training in that regard. There is also the matter of suitable spiritual direction for a Deryni." He glanced at Paulin, then back at the king.

"I think, perhaps—yes, the abbey at Ramos. Your Highness will recall it fondly, I hope. Granted, the discipline is exacting, but I firmly believe that proper discipline is an essential foundation for sound spiritual formation. He can be taken there when we send his family north to seek out Master Revan—unless your Highness wished it sooner?"

"No, that's fine," Javan murmured. "I thank your Grace for this demonstration of pastoral concern, even for your Deryni flock. I pray that Master Ursin may prove worthy of this opportunity to redeem himself in God's eyes as well as with the Church."

Javan worried about the archbishop's choice for Ursin as he made his way back to his apartments with Charlan and Guiscard, and wondered whether he was merely delivering up Ursin to a more speedy death. The discipline at Ramos *was* strict, and a confessor with a Deryni in his hands would have almost unlimited authority to impose whatever penances he felt necessary to save a penitent's soul.

Rigorous fasts and frequent scourging were probably the least that Ursin could expect. And as a vehicle for intimidation, all the more sinister for being couched in the trappings of pious concern, minution probably had no peer. Javan thought he recalled that the Rule did not require that lay brethren submit to minution—but ask Father Faelan whether it had made any difference that the Rule also said that even professed brethren might only be required to submit once. But if Ursin could survive long enough to be gotten out, the risks were worth it.

In his quarters, with Etienne joining Guiscard and Charlan, he outlined what he had in mind, both for Ursin and for Ursin's wife and son. Guiscard seemed mostly overwhelmed by the scope of the plan, but Etienne only nodded approvingly.

"It's daring; it's audacious, but it just might work—if he can stay alive long enough, as you say. It will be a delicate balancing act, though—to leave him in long enough to fall into the routine, to convince them he's not a threat, long enough that the coincidence of his release won't reflect back on you, Sire—but not long enough for them to decide it's time to rid themselves of one inconvenient ex-Deryni."

"That's the part that worries me, too," Guiscard agreed. "Hubert said that Ursin's abbot would literally have the power of life and death over him, but killing doesn't have to be anything overt. They could keep him in solitary confinement and cut his rations so that he slowly starved to death; fasting is a time-honored means of monastic discipline. They could even overdo this minution you've spoken of, without actually bleeding him to death—just take a bit more than normal over a long period of time, never letting him quite recover before bleeding him again, until he finally just faded away."

"I thought that even among the *Custodes*, bleeding was an optional discipline, after the first time," Etienne said. "A kindness to relieve the pressures of living close together and to keep tempers low."

"For laymen, they're not even supposed to be able to require it once," Javan said. "But where Deryni are concerned, even former Deryni, the Rule and the rules are very flexible."

"So I gather," Etienne replied. "And all of this is before even thinking about trumped-up charges or even *Custodes* whim that could lead him straight to the stake." He shook his head. "Oh, you may not have done him any great favor, Sire."

"Given the choice, I think he'd rather have the chance at freedom, even if he doesn't yet realize that's what it is," Javan said quietly. "I don't plan to leave him there indefinitely. Once his wife and son are safe—"

"Best not hinge your plans for him on *their* safety, Sire," Etienne said. "There are other Deryni still captive here, whose safety could be put in jeopardy if suspicion is raised. Unlike Ursin, who was married to a human, Oriel's wife and daughter are Deryni, and Sitric's mother and sister likewise."

Javan nodded. "I'm aware of that. Don't worry. I don't plan to move too fast." He grimaced. "But you and Guiscard had better get moving. The sooner Joram knows what I've done, the sooner we can move things on."

Others, meanwhile, wondered at what Javan had set in motion.

"Why does he want Ursin out of here?" Hubert was saying, both hands supporting his multiple chins as he leaned on the table across from Paulin and Albertus. "He knows that puts the man in our absolute control, to do away with whenever it suits us—unless Ursin isn't really as helpless as he appears. And this business about the woman and the boy—"

"Fortunately, we have several months before action becomes necessary in either regard," Paulin said, drumming his fingers on his chair arm. "Right now, I'm far more concerned about Master Oriel. I don't know whether he knew in advance what Javan planned, but I do believe that the good Healer is becoming a decided irritant rather than a mere aggravation."

Hubert looked at him sharply, though he did not lift his head from his hands. "He's the only Healer still accessible to us," he pointed out. "Think carefully before you consider eliminating him. You've seen those inefficient poseurs who masquerade as court physicians."

"Yes, but I begin to wonder if we might be better off to take our chances with conventional medicine, rather than be subject to the whim of a Deryni. I warned you that the usefulness of our collaborators was coming to an end, Hubert. I don't think you believed me. Oriel gives the king an edge I'd prefer he didn't have, especially in light of what else we begin to suspect about him. If there's to be *merasha* testing, I want one of *my* people to do it. And if there's to be Truth-Reading at court, I want it to be *my* Truth-Readers or none at all."

"Well, we do have the offer of Sitric's services. Rhun has been most generous in that regard. And then there's your Master Dimitri."

"Yes, and even Rhun has been quite candid in stating that the day may be coming when even his own Deryni will become more trouble than he's worth," Paulin replied, ignoring the comment about Dimitri. "No," he went on, clasping his hands behind his head and leaning back in his chair to gaze up at the ceiling, "I do believe that Master Oriel has about outlived his usefulness. And I think that Sitric may be just the man to take care of the problem for us."

It was several weeks before Sitric found the opportunity he had been ordered to watch for. The Princess Michaela's pregnancy had now become a known fact at Court, and Oriel was just returning from his regular weekly visit to check on her progress, accompanied as usual by the knight who was his bodyguard.

Sitric had recruited his own bodyguards in the past few days, for he knew he could not hope to overcome Sir Gavin, subdue Oriel, and rip his mind as ordered, without help on the physical level. The mind-ripping he must do for himself, but human sword fodder could answer for the first and possibly the second requirements.

He had his own men waiting along the route he knew Oriel and Gavin would take to return to quarters—two ready to follow them into the stairwell and cut off retreat and the other three waiting with him in the first landing, all in Haldane livery. He had carefully selected them from the king's own garrison and bound all five to do his bidding, setting in place unshakable conviction that they were thwarting an attempt on Sir Gavin's part to assassinate the king's Deryni. One of them, if he lived, would even remember overhearing Gavin's boast to another knight, whose name he conveniently did not know, that Deryni still asserted altogether too much influence at Court—and Gavin was going to do something about it.

What none of them would remember was that Sitric had further bade them dress the blades of their swords with *merasha*, so that the slightest cut to Oriel would render him incapable of using his powers to defend himself or his accompanying knight. And multiple wounds to either man, even slight ones, would contribute to a fatal *merasha* overdose. Sitric had treated a dagger for himself as well, and kept it sheathed as he waited for his intended victims' approach. He could hear their voices as they came up the stairwell, easy banter that reflected no suspicion that they were climbing into a trap.

What Sitric had not reckoned on was that the king would change his plans that morning and decide to take a newly arrived census report up to his quarters to read before lunch, rather than braving the blustery March morning for his accustomed early ride. Charlan and Guiscard were with him as he headed up the back stair, Charlan in the lead, when sudden scuffling and an anguished mental cry from several floors up spurred all three men into an alarmed scramble upward.

Sir Gavin had acquitted himself well before he fell. One body was crumpled in the stairwell just before they reached the landing where swordplay was continuing, and another man sat wheezing against the wall opposite, blood bubbling from his lips and seeping between the gloved fingers clutched to his chest, a smear of blood on the wall showing where he had slid down it. To Javan's astonishment, both men wore his livery.

Gavin himself lay sprawled facedown in a spreading pool of his own blood, his hand still twitching feebly around the hilt of a broken sword, while beyond him a third man in Haldane livery attempted to fight off two more men, one with a sword and the other with a dagger he had just slashed across the upraised hands of yet another man in a tunic and mantle of dull green. Another man was on the ground behind them.

The green-clad man cried out. In the dim light of the stair landing, it was just possible for Javan to see that it was Oriel, his Deryni aura flaring and then wavering as his attacker turned to point the dagger at him, directing a stream of orangy light between his victim's eyes. And the attacker—

"Sitric, no!" Javan shouted.

Charlan and Guiscard were already launching themselves across the landing, skidding in Gavin's blood, swords ready to strike. Javan was following right behind, the Haldane sword in his gloved fist, desperate to get to Oriel. Snarling, Sitric broke off his attack and loosed a fiery ball of energy at Charlan.

Not even thinking of the consequences, Guiscard struck Charlan aside with the flat of his blade and launched a counterspell, white light swelling from his hand like a silvery morning glory to deflect the ball and engulf it. In the confusion, with Javan moving in right behind Guiscard, Sitric became convinced that the defense had come from the king.

"You!" he screamed, pointing at Javan with the dagger in his hand and loosing another attack.

Chapter Forty

A proud look, a lying tongue, and hands that
shed innocent blood.

—Proverbs 6:17

Instinctively Javan ducked, his free hand upflung and the Haldane sword raised in defense, projecting a protective veil between the two that swallowed up the ball of fire in a crimson flash. Not waiting to find out what else Javan could do, Sitric spun on his heel and bolted for the corridor beyond. In the same moment, Guiscard bowled over both men still fighting over the fallen Gavin and shifted his psychic focus from defense to offense, gathering his powers to stop the fleeing Sitric. In that instant, Javan realized what he intended and reached out to meld his powers with those of Guiscard.

The form of the spell came unbidden, and its power caught Sitric before he had gone a dozen steps. He screamed as he fell, engulfed in a sheet of flames that left of him only a scorched, twitching corpse. In the sudden silence that followed, Javan could hear footsteps pounding up the stairs from the other end of the corridor, and gestured with his sword toward the men sprawled around Gavin, the one leaning against the wall. And Oriel—

Make certain nobody remembers anything! Javan sent to Guiscard, at the same time scrambling over to Oriel to check his condition.

The Healer was doubled over on his knees, his slashed palms cupped and crossed on his breast. Another thin cut on one cheek trickled a thin line of blood down his neck, but otherwise he seemed untouched—except for the chaos emanating from his mind.

"Merasha!" Javan warned, glancing around wildly. "It must be on the swords. Charlan, come and get Oriel on his feet. Make him walk. Don't let him pass out on us. I don't know how much he's got in him. *Guards!"* he shouted at the approaching Haldane men. "Somebody get a couple of battle surgeons! And, dear God, *Gavin!"*

As he moved quickly back to the fallen knight's side, he dropped to his knees in the pool of Gavin's blood and laid down his sword, turning the young knight to raise up his shoulders and hold him in his arms. Others were crowding onto the landing now—more of his men, several taking charge of Oriel—but Javan paid them only vague notice, though he was aware of Charlan moving in to guard his back.

"Gavin, they're fetching a surgeon. Just hang on. How did this happen?" he whispered, clamping a gloved hand across one particularly ragged gash in the young knight's chest and trying to hold the life in—though there were at least three other wounds equally serious.

Gavin rallied a little at the familiar voice and opened his eyes, seeming to draw a little strength from the royal presence.

"I don't understand," he managed to whisper. "They were our own men. We were coming back from your brother's apartments, and they just—attacked us." He coughed weakly and brought up blood, and Javan glanced around futilely. Even were Oriel not incapacitated—and even *he* might die, if there was too much *merasha* in his system—Javan doubted that even a Healer could save the man in his arms.

"I—tried to defend him, my prince," Gavin whispered, though the voice was weaker. "I think I—took out two before they got me."

"Three," Javan whispered. "And you did all any man could ask."

Gavin shuddered and closed his eyes briefly, then looked up at Javan again. "Is it—getting darker in here, Sire? I—can't seem to see very well . . ."

"Oh, God, Gavin, I am so sorry," Javan breathed, bowing his head briefly to hug his face to the dying man's shoulder.

"I am—proud to have served my king," Gavin whispered. He winced and drew a deep, bubbling breath. "A sword, my liege. Give me a cross to hold."

Tears streaming down his face, Javan groped blindly for the sword he had cast down as he knelt. It was slippery with Gavin's blood, and he tried to wipe off the hilt on the side of his tunic before giving it into Gavin's hands.

"A Haldane sword for a Haldane champion," he whispered, helping him bring the cross-hilt to his lips to kiss the sacred relic enclosed within. "And a cross of glory for one who goes faithful and true to stand before the throne of the King we both serve. May He gather you to His bosom, Gavin. May you find peace in the service of a higher Lord."

Gavin found strength to breathe a final "Amen," but in that moment Javan felt the soul slip past. He held the dead man tightly for a moment, shaking his bowed head and rocking back and forth.

Gradually the sounds around him intruded on his grief, and he looked up to see black mantles and crimson, surrounding him in a sea of booted feet. Charlan was still standing over him, Guiscard at his other side, leaning wearily on his sword. A battle surgeon in Sir Robear's livery was crouched beside a moaning and groggy-looking Oriel, examining his hands. Another in *Custodes* habit was standing at Gavin's feet, a medical satchel clutched in both hands, looking genuinely helpless.

"Somebody tell that other surgeon to get Oriel on his feet and make him walk," Javan said, laying Gavin's body down and letting Charlan help him to his feet. "Don't let him pass out. He's probably got a *merasha* overdose. There was *merasha* on Sitric's blade. And everybody be careful of the swords; they may have been treated, too."

He was nearly as covered with blood as Gavin, and he let his gaze drift numbly over the scene. Rhun was out in the corridor with several of his men, inspecting Sitric's body, and the two remaining Haldane men from the fracas were both standing dazedly under guard of Albertus and several *Custodes* knights, hands bound. A *Custodes* priest was giving the Last Rites to the other man, slumped against the wall, who had expired.

"Well, that's very convenient," Rhun said, coming back into the landing to confront the king, glaring at Oriel. "He's killed the only other Deryni at Court. *My* Deryni. Leaves you in an enviable position, doesn't it, Sire?"

Javan looked sharply at Rhun, though he was immensely relieved that Rhun apparently accepted that Oriel had done it.

"Actually," he said, "it rather appears that your Deryni was trying to kill *my* Deryni. Did you put him up to this?"

"Certainly not!" Rhun replied. And he was telling the truth.

That put an interesting slant on the incident. Javan could understand why the opposition would want Oriel dead—and that clearly had been Sitric's objective. But who would dare to give Sitric such orders without asking Rhun first?

"Well, I intend to hear Master Oriel's story before I make any judgments," Javan said, glancing back at the Healer, who was having something poured down his throat by Robear's battle surgeon. "What is that, Master Surgeon?"

"Stimulant, Sire, to counter the sedative effect of the *merasha*. It means he's going to have to weather the disruption part of it pretty much unabated, but it's better than the alternative."

"Well, he obviously isn't going to be in any shape to tell us much until tomorrow or the next day, so we'll have to continue this discussion at that time, my Lord Rhun." He glanced down at Gavin's body.

"Someone had better see about notifying Sir Gavin's family, too," he said wearily. "I want him laid out in the Chapel Royal, with burial in the vaults of Rhemuth Cathedral. And those men—" He gestured toward the two bewildered-looking prisoners. "Robear, take a detail to guard them. I'll want Oriel to question them as soon as he's up to it. I rather suspect we'll find that Sitric had them controlled—though one of them was fighting the other, so maybe Oriel managed to take back control of him. The real question is, who ordered Sitric to do it? Why would he try to kill another Deryni?"

He left them mulling that question while he went on to his quarters with Guiscard and Charlan to change out of his bloody clothes.

Afterward Albertus accompanied Rhun back to his quarters, one of his knights and a battle surgeon in tow. Paulin and Hubert met them just outside.

"Were you responsible for that?" Rhun demanded, when he had admitted them and closed the door. The *Custodes* knight remained outside to guard, but the surgeon stood at Albertus' elbow, eyes downcast and leather-clad arms clasped easily behind his back, beneath his black mantle.

"Please sit down, my lord," Paulin said quietly. "I'm sorry for the loss of your Deryni. Fortunately, we have another."

Rhun froze and stared at Paulin, then flicked his gaze over the others, pausing to look more closely at the battle surgeon, whose face was the only one he did not know. Hubert also was staring at the man, who now was clean-shaven, the brown hair close-barbered after the fashion of a man-at-arms of the *Custodes*, with a token tonsure shaved at the crown.

"Who is this man?" Rhun whispered.

"Rhun, Earl of Sheele, permit me to present Master Dimitri," Paulin said easily, smiling as Rhun recoiled from the dark gaze Dimitri raised to his. "While not a Healer, he does have rudimentary training as a battle surgeon. However, his more valuable skills have to do with interrogation. He has formerly passed as a scribe in my household, but we recently agreed that a change of image might be appropriate. I might add that Master Dimitri came to my employment of his own accord and willingly serves our cause. Had circumstances evolved otherwise today, your Sitric might still be alive, with Master Oriel awaiting burial as well as the unfortunate Sir Gavin."

"You mean, you set Sitric up to murder Oriel?" Rhun muttered. "Why was I not told?"

"It seemed wiser that only those directly involved know of the plan, my lord," Albertus replied. "As it was, your outrage was genuine and the king cannot suspect that you had any part in it. As you yourself suggested, without prompting, Oriel's action in killing Sitric can be seen as an act of jealousy against the only other Deryni at Court. It now places Oriel more in doubt than ever. The king will not be able to keep him long at Court; and when he is gone, whether alive or dead, Master Dimitri leaves us in a position of strength."

Rhun exhaled audibly, obviously keeping his resentment in check, then pulled out a chair and sat.

"I believe I'm owed some explanations," he said, "without *him* present. Master Dimitri, if you will excuse us?"

When Dimitri had gone outside to wait with the guarding knight, Paulin briefly reviewed their suspicions about the king and the recent developments concerning the captive Deryni still held hostage at the castle.

"And Javan wants Ursin and his family out of here?" Rhun asked, when he had heard the background from several different perspectives.

Hubert nodded. "It came out of the question of whether Ursin is still Deryni, and the status of his son, and then it became more an ecclesiastical matter. That's one reason we didn't tell you. And of course there was the added feature that you couldn't reveal what you didn't know. Now that it's cost you your Deryni, you have a right to know. He'll probably want to send Sitric's family as well."

"I should just have them quietly strangled," Rhun muttered.

"There's a better way," Paulin said. "I think we *should* send them with Ursin's wife and child. Maybe by then we can send Oriel's as well."

"If you're thinking to go after Oriel again, you'd better think twice," Rhun said. "If he survives, what's he going to discover when he questions those two men who survived?"

Oriel did survive, but it was two days before he was sufficiently recovered to question the two Haldane men-at-arms. At the insistence of Paulin, he was made to perform in front of the entire Council, who had gathered in the withdrawing room at the rear of the great hall to witness the interrogation. Before that, he had declared himself innocent of any plot to eliminate Sitric as a rival and stated that he had no recollection of lashing out at Sitric with his magic.

"Though I suppose I must have, in self-defense," he concluded, spreading his bandaged hands in a gesture of apology. "Healers are conditioned not to take life, but survival instincts can be more powerful. I swear to you, he and the men-at-arms attacked us without warning, there in the stairwell. They clearly meant to kill both of us, and they did kill Sir Gavin."

He had healed his hands on recovering the use of his powers, and the cut on his cheek as well, but he retained light bandages wrapped around his palms to protect the tenderness of newly healed wounds—and also to avoid reminding his listeners that he could work such magic.

Dimitri noted this from his vantage point against the wall behind Albertus, for he and all the others who had witnessed the aftermath on the landing had been ordered to be present. He had not yet caught any hint of falsehood in Oriel's statements, but something did not quite ring true. He bent to whisper in Albertus' ear as Udaut was ordered to bring the first man in. Albertus nodded and passed the message on to Paulin.

Lord Jerowen was designated to interview each man first, as a representative of the king's justice, while Oriel merely Truth-Read. The first man-at-arms, whose name was Baldwin, related a confused story: of being told—he could not remember by whom—that Sir Gavin was plotting to kill Oriel. He and his fellows had gone to intercept Oriel in the stairwell, where the killing was to take place—no, he did not remember seeing Sitric—but Gavin had proven more powerful a swordsman than expected.

They managed to take him, but only at the cost of several men—and then his captain had ordered them to turn their swords on Oriel after all. But just when Baldwin was moving in with his remaining fellows for the kill, Oriel had seized him, and a great pain had burst behind his eyes, and suddenly Baldwin *knew* that the two men facing him, one of them his comrade, were *not* supposed to kill Oriel, and he must protect the Deryni.

After that, things got even more confused, with blinding lights and more pain, and then hands wrenching his sword from numb fingers and binding him—and he did not understand what had happened. He still did not understand.

The Council stirred uneasily as Baldwin finished. Clearly, he believed his account to be true—Oriel indicated as much as he came forward, and freely admitted seizing control of the man to save himself—but equally clearly, the whole story had not been told. Baldwin himself admitted that there were gaps in his memory that he could not explain, though he swore to the king on bended knees that he had never intended treachery.

He was trembling as he sat back into the chair they had placed for him, craning his neck to watch as Oriel came around behind him. He flinched as the Healer's bandaged hands dropped lightly onto his shoulders.

"I'm not going to hurt you," Oriel murmured as he shifted his thumbs to brace against the back of his subject's neck, fingertips curving around the sides. "Relax now. You won't be punished if you only acted under compulsion."

The man's eyes closed under Oriel's touch, and the Healer bowed his head. After several long minutes, Oriel looked up and drew a deep breath, though his subject did not stir. "Sire, I have no way to prove this to you, but it appears that Sitric approached each of the men involved and implanted certain beliefs and commands that could not be resisted. The crux of the story was that Gavin planned to assassinate me, and these men were to attempt to prevent it.

"A secondary imperative required that, once Gavin had been eliminated, they were to turn on me after all. I believe you will find that the other prisoner has direct memory of having heard Gavin boast that he would kill me—that he was tired of Deryni influence at Court, interfering with the king and subverting his good judgment. I'm sorry, Sire, but that's what the man claimed to have heard. You may verify it when the other man is brought in, before I lay a hand on him. I will leave the room, if you wish."

The involvement of a possible plot by Sitric turned all attention briefly on Rhun, who had been Sitric's master, but Rhun denied any prior knowledge of the plot and stated unequivocally that he had never given Sitric any such orders. Oriel's confirmation of the truth of the statement shifted the focus back to himself, and elic-

ited muttered rumblings among his listeners, some clearly in agreement with the sentiment allegedly expressed by the late Gavin.

"What of the magic that killed Sitric?" Paulin asked when the
subject of Gavin's motives had been exhausted.

"What was it you wished to know, my lord?" Oriel replied.

"What does he remember of that?"

"Bright light, a sheet of fire enveloping Sitric. I—ah—had him
under rather tight control at the time, my lord. I was trying to
prevent his accomplice from butchering me as the *merasha* eroded
my defenses. I—don't think he saw much else."

Dimitri could read that this, too, was true, but again, something
was missing. He told Albertus so, under the faint buzz of comment
that passed among the assembled Council members as Udaut took
the man out and brought in Nevell, the second man.

Nevell's story was much as his comrade's, with the addition
that he did indeed relate the promised story of having heard Gavin
swear to kill Oriel, because of his undue influence on the king.
Oriel's probe revealed that the entire memory had been planted by
Sitric, but of course he could not prove it, with Sitric and Gavin
both dead. One thing that did seem certain, unless Rhun was lying,
was that if Sitric had plotted the murder of Oriel, he had done so
on his own, without Rhun's connivance.

"We certainly have no reason to doubt Lord Rhun's word," Tammaron said, when Udaut had taken Nevell away and Sir Sorle had
taken Oriel out. "I must point out, however, that neither does his
lack of involvement prove that Oriel himself is innocent in this
matter, Sire. Unfortunately, with Master Oriel now the only Deryni
left at Court, we no longer have a check to ensure his own truth-
fulness. Especially in a matter that may reflect on him personally,
we can hardly accept his word."

"I believe Master Oriel is telling the truth, my lord," Javan said,
"but what do you suggest I do? What would convince you that it
was Sitric and not Oriel who instigated the incident?"

The consensus was that nothing would, but in the end Javan
only agreed to keep Oriel under closer supervision in the future,
with Sir Sorle assigned as his new personal bodyguard.

"And for now, I'll have the two men-at-arms kept under house
arrest, as well," Javan said. "I'm convinced that they were innocent
of any deliberate participation, but I don't see how I can trust them
anymore. The next time there's a rotation to one of our garrisons
far removed from Rhemuth, I want them sent out. Robear, see to
it."

"Aye, my liege."

Javan dismissed them after that, returning wearily to his quarters and sending Etienne to report the proceedings to Joram and ask for guidance. Oriel, all but convicted despite his innocence, was moved into quarters directly across the corridor from Javan's, with Sorle in adjoining quarters on one side and Guiscard on the other.

And later that night, while the castle slept, Master Dimitri moved silent as a wraith to take his turn on the rota for guarding the two disgraced men-at-arms.

Javan was heading through the great hall the next morning with his brother and Sir Tomais and his own two aides, pulling on leather gloves in preparation for a brisk early ride, when Sir Robear came pounding down the main stair with Earl Udaut right behind him and headed them off at the great hall steps.

"Sire, I don't think you'll want to take your ride this morning," he said, gesturing toward the doorway that led into the cloister colonnade skirting the garden, and not even looking to see whether Javan followed.

"Go with Robear, Sire," Udaut urged. "It isn't going to be a pretty sight, though. It's as well you've not yet eaten."

Even warned, Javan felt a little queasy as he drew up beside Robear on the far side of the garden, where a nude male body lay facedown in a flower bed. Rhys Michael and the others had gotten there ahead of him, except for Charlan, who had hung back to accommodate his master's slower pace.

"Who is it?" Javan asked, as his brother followed Udaut's gesture toward an open window some four stories above them, where several men were peering down and pointing.

Robear was kneeling beside the body and had turned the face to look at it, sighing and shaking his head as he did so.

"I believe you'll recall the name Baldwin, Sire?" he said.

"Dear God, did he *jump*?" Javan breathed.

"Jumped or was pushed." Robear made as if to lift the body's shoulders and turn it over, then shook his head again. There was blood underneath, for the unfortunate Baldwin had impaled himself on several garden stakes meant to support young plants.

"Well, if the fall didn't kill him, these didn't help," he said, standing and wiping his hands against the legs of his breeches as he glanced up at the window again. "I don't suppose it was any worse than that other poor bastard."

"He's dead, too?" Javan said.

Up in the chamber Baldwin had vacated so precipitously, the

hapless Nevell had found a slower if no less painful way of ending his life. Since he and his comrade had been under house arrest, without access to weapons, Nevell appeared to have smashed an empty wine flask and used one of the razor-sharp shards to slash both wrists almost to the bone and then start on his throat. He, too, was nude. If there had been doubt about Baldwin's intentions, there was none about Nevell's. The broken fragment was still clenched tightly in his stiffened fingers, his blood sprayed all over the room and spattering his white body. The dead eyes were fixed on the window through which his comrade had jumped, the mouth set in a rictus of mad triumph.

"Sweet *Jesu, why*?" Javan whispered, sinking down on his haunches as Guiscard knelt down to inspect the body.

"Perhaps despondency over having lost the trust of his king," Rhun said coldly. He and Albertus had been among the men examining the room and the body when the king arrived, along with a *Custodes* battle surgeon. "These men had no future, Sire, for their liege lord had determined unjustly to banish them from his presence."

"Don't be ridiculous!" Javan retorted, though his cheeks were burning. "That isn't sufficient cause to take one's life—and especially not like this. Robear, do you think this could be something left from what Sitric set, when he took them over?"

"Why not ask if it was something left from Master Oriel's work, Sire?" Rhun went on, not relenting. "If Sitric had set an order to self-destruct, they would have done it before they could be examined for evidence against him. But Oriel was in their minds only yesterday."

"That's absurd!" Charlan blurted. "If they didn't speak out against Oriel yesterday, they obviously weren't ever going to do it. Why would he do such a stupid thing? It serves absolutely no purpose other than to set tongues like yours to wagging!"

"Sire, I suggest you curb this impudent puppy, or I shall be forced to whip him for his impertinence!" Rhun retorted. "Do you dare to defend the Deryni, boy?"

"You go too far, my lord!" Javan warned, lurching to his feet. "Charlan, to me. I'll have no quarreling among my own people. Guiscard, if you please."

Guiscard had been continuing to inspect the body, ostensibly testing at the amount of rigor and examining the wounds, but rose immediately at Javan's summons.

"It wasn't Nevell's idea," he murmured to the king as they headed back down to the great hall for food none of them really wanted. Rhys Michael had left them to return to his own apartments, saying he would have something sent up later. "I wish it were possible for Oriel to do a proper examination of the bodies, but after Rhun's remark, you don't dare order it."

"Why not?" Javan whispered.

"Because if it's suggested that they were forced to do it, he's the only suspect—or you'd better hope he is. Because if he didn't do it—and you and I certainly didn't, or my father—that means there's another Deryni about. Unless it's Sitric's ghost, I can hazard a fair guess, and I expect you could, too."

Javan pulled up short to stare at Guiscard. "Dimitri? *Here?*"

"Well, I doubt he could do it from *Arx Fidei*," Guiscard replied. "And it's occurred to me that they wouldn't have risked Sitric if they didn't have a backup in reserve."

"It has to have been one of the new *Custodes* who have appeared in the last month or so, then," Javan murmured. "But there's been no one to match the face we got from Serafin."

"He had a beard," Guiscard said, suddenly sitting forward. "And he was wearing lay attire. But shave off the beard, and put him in *Custodes* habit—picture it, Sire."

Javan sat back in his chair, suddenly deflated, now well aware where he had seen that face.

"The battle surgeon who showed up with Albertus," he breathed. "He was at the inquest yesterday, and he was even with him this morning." He closed his eyes and conjured up the image—the same greying brown hair, now cut short and tonsured, the dark eyes, always carefully veiled, the sensuous mouth—the tiny indentation in the right earlobe that once had permitted a gold earring to pass through.

"Dear God, what can we do?"

Indeed, as the king asked that question, Dimitri was already advancing his efforts on his masters' behalf, sequestered with Albertus and Rhun and Hubert in Paulin's dayroom down at the cathedral.

"This morning was most illuminating, my lords," he reported, standing before them where they sat before the fire. "Knowing what you have told me of the king, I cannot swear that what I sensed was a Deryni power stirring; but it was very like Deryni. And it came from either the king or possibly the knight he calls Guiscard."

"De Courcy?" Rhun said.

"I would tend to favor the king," Dimitri said, "though I grant you it is possible that both were involved. This supports the impressions I was able to gather from the soldiers Baldwin and Nevell before setting other instructions in their minds. Not knowing to suspect the king, both *assumed* that Master Oriel was the source of the attack. But in fact, neither had any clear memory of the exact moment. Also, Master Oriel had a great deal of *merasha* in him by then. It does not seem likely that he could have focused sufficiently to raise such power."

"It has to have been the king, then," Paulin murmured. "The stories are true, and the Haldanes do have power. They may not be Deryni, but their power comes from the Deryni. And that, in itself, is sufficient reason to see him brought down and destroyed!"

No intimation of this intent reached Javan in the weeks that followed. The "battle surgeon" they thought was Dimitri was no more seen at Court—which tended to confirm that it was he who had been responsible for at least some of the recent unpleasantness—and Javan dared not inquire concerning him. He could only be glad of the man's absence and hope that neither he nor Guiscard had betrayed himself in his presence.

Sir Gavin received the lavish funeral merited by his gallant death in the king's service and was buried with all due ceremony at Rhemuth Cathedral. The suicides Baldwin and Nevell joined Father Faelan in the potter's field by the river. Rhun was allowed to have Sitric buried in holy ground at Saint Hilary's—a *Custodes* priest presided—and reluctantly agreed that the dead man's mother and sister might join Ursin's family when Javan sent them north to meet the holy Revan.

With Oriel well out of sight, rarely venturing outside his room, that aspect of the furore also faded. Javan could no longer make open use of the Deryni's services for Truth-Reading, but at least he had him as a Healer. And when Ursin turned up dead in his bed late in April, the morning after one of his routine testings with *merasha*, Javan took the Healer with him to examine the body.

"There's no mark upon him, Sire," the court physician said, who had been summoned initially when Ursin did not rouse for breakfast. "I give you my word, he was fine last night when I left him. Of course he was groggy from the *merasha*, but he had not even been given his customary second dose. Since your Highness had determined to release him to the care of the *Custodes*, such precautions no longer seemed necessary, just to move him from room to room. Perhaps his heart failed as he slept. This cannot have been an easy life for him."

The man spoke no more than the truth, as both Javan and Oriel knew full well, but when the man had gone, Javan had the Healer examine the body more closely. Charlan was with him; Guiscard was outside with Sir Sorle, questioning the guards who had been on duty. Other than the expected puncture marks in Ursin's forearm where the known dose of *merasha* had been administered, there were no marks upon the body. But when Oriel delved deeper to attempt a Death-Reading, he recoiled after only a few seconds.

"Dear God," he whispered, clutching at his head in stunned disbelief.

"What is it?" Javan demanded.

With a shake of his head to delay answering until he had finished the Reading, Oriel bowed his head over the dead man again, trembling hands set on the cold forehead, then withdrew again, shaking his head as he held out a hand to Javan.

Stealthy footsteps in the night, Ursin rousing from drug-fogged sleep just as three shadow-shapes converged on him, two holding him down while the third jammed a pillow to his face.

Struggling to fight off his assailants, knowing they sought his death, fighting to breathe, body beginning to go into spasms, strength draining from his limbs—and then, just as consciousness dwindled almost to oblivion, respite from the smothering pillow only to have his jaws forced apart and a vial of burning liquid poured down his throat, numbing his tongue and sending paralysis coursing along his limbs and into his brain . . .

As Javan withdrew from the contact, shaking, Oriel was already opening the dead man's mouth, peering down the throat, recoiling again at the concentration of *merasha* still present—far more than enough to kill.

"But who would do this?" Javan whispered to Guiscard, when the body had been removed and Oriel had been sent back to the safety of his quarters with his guards. "And why? He wasn't a threat to anyone. And if the *Custodes* wanted him dead, all they had to do was wait a few weeks, until they got him to Ramos."

He had not disclosed Oriel's findings to anyone outside his immediate circle of confidants, for anything Oriel said would only throw unwanted scrutiny back on him again and underline Deryni abilities that were best downplayed. Furthermore, Guiscard's questioning of the guards suggested that it had taken a Deryni to penetrate the security around Ursin's room. He had not been able to do more than Truth-Read, but the men were absolutely adamant—and telling the truth as they remembered it—that no one had passed them during the night.

"My guess would be that Dimitri's back," Guiscard said, "but we can't even ask Paulin about him without arousing new suspicion. With Oriel discredited, we have no legitimate way of knowing about Dimitri."

The Deryni knight made a special point of scrutinizing as many *Custodes* men as he could in the next few days, sometimes taking chances that might have betrayed him if he had uncovered a Deryni agent, but when he discovered that a *Custodes* party had left Rhemuth the very morning that Ursin's death was discovered, he dropped his investigation. The discovery tended to support their suspicions, but they could prove nothing and ask nothing.

Meanwhile, Ursin was allowed burial at Saint Hilary's, ncar the grave of the departed Sitric, and Archbishop Hubert's expressed regret over Ursin's death even extended to allowing his widow to attend the funeral—though not her Deryni son. No other mourners attended, other than the *Custodes* guards who had been on duty the night of Ursin's death, plus the court physician who had attended him the day before. Paulin himself elected to officiate at the solemn requiem the king had ordered for the repose of Ursin's soul, and spoke almost regretfully of the monastic profession Ursin had intended to make for the redemption of his Deryni soul, now thwarted by his untimely death.

Javan stood far back in the basilica during the Mass with his brother and Charlan and Guiscard and Read the truth of Paulin's words, almost convinced that the Vicar General had had no part in Ursin's death, but he could not bring himself to go forward for Communion at Paulin's hands. Nor did the others. He could tell that it did not sit well with Paulin, but he did not care. Afterward he returned to a testy session with his Council at which everything Hubert said seemed to irritate him. Paulin was not present, but Albertus was.

But overt hostility to the king's ideas seemed to abate somewhat after Ursin's death. Apparently the idea of sending a former Deryni into even a lay religious situation had rankled his great lords more than Javan realized. Concurrently, a clean disposition of the now-superfluous families of Ursin and the slain Sitric began to gain growing approval. Even Hubert's objections to the Revan solution seemed to have died away, and Javan began to hope that perhaps he had gotten past the worst of the opposition.

With winter fading into spring, he sent Sir Bertrand de Ville north to inquire regarding Master Revan as soon as the roads were passable again, while his Council sat in Rhemuth and began collating the writs of disclosure that began coming in as the roads cleared. Meanwhile, he worked mostly through Etienne de Courcy to keep Joram informed of his progress, and had him working at the other end to prepare an appropriate reception for the three women and the boy who shortly would be sent north.

It was late in April when Sir Bertrand returned with word that Master Revan was back at the bend in the Eirial River, offering his new baptism to wash Deryni clean. He had met with the master to tell him of the king's plans, and with one of his captains underwent an icy immersion to receive cleansing of any taint they might have incurred by contact with Deryni themselves, whether or not they had been aware of it. They came away with a blessing—"not my blessing, but the blessing of the Lord of Hosts," Revan had assured them—and Bertrand with the beginnings of a head cold. But royal knight and men returned convinced that the Master Revan's work was both benign and beneficial, and so reported back to the Council on their arrival back in Rhemuth.

"I wouldn't go so far as to say that Master Revan is a saint," Bertrand confided, between swipes at his nose with a soggy handkerchief, "but surely purifying those who have been contaminated by Deryni contact, and cleansing Deryni themselves of their evil, is far preferable to merely seeking out and destroying them. Isn't it better to offer these unfortunate people some hope of redemption? If compassion and mercy can accomplish the same purpose as ruthlessness, is this not preferable, if we say we walk in the example of our Lord?"

It was the basic argument that Javan himself had set in Bertrand's mind before sending him north, though augmented by the young knight's own passion at having experienced Revan's cleansing firsthand. Somewhat to his surprise, the Council seemed to respond to it rather well.

Too well, perhaps. Nothing in the response of any man in the room rang false, but Javan sensed an underlying current of tension that he could not explain. He knew that Paulin intended to test Revan further on Hubert's behalf, but not even the *Custodes* Vicar General raised the objections to Bertrand's enthusiasm that Javan might have expected. He tried for several days to get Hubert alone, in hopes of gaining further insight by a quick probe, but the archbishop always seemed to have others around him. At length, Javan decided that perhaps the royal presence was indicated for the expedition, to ensure that things went smoothly.

He broached the subject to the Council and encountered a vague uneasiness—which simply confirmed that it probably was a good idea to go. The weather was improving daily, and he had a loyal Haldane garrison in place in Rhemuth that should be more than adequate to keep order for Rhys Michael. Also, the thought of an outing was appealing after a winter cooped up in the castle. Nor would it hurt to show the royal presence in the north. It was only about a week's easy journey to where Revan was working, even travelling by easy stages on account of the women and the boy.

The Council's full approval was still uncertain when he adjourned for the day to give them time to consider further, but resistance had been wavering all afternoon. That evening he had dinner with Rhys Michael and Michaela and outlined his intentions with them.

"I shouldn't be gone more than a fortnight," he said, "and most of the potential troublemakers will be going with me. I'll leave you Tomais, of course; and I think it's fairly certain by now that Udaut is our man. That should ensure the loyalty of the castle garrison. And you'll have Etienne and Jerowen and Lord Hildred."

"I can handle that," Rhys Michael agreed. "And I've got Oriel, in case Mika needs help." He reached across to squeeze her hand. "It's months before anything's due to happen, though. You should be well back before that. Who's going with you?"

"Well, Charlan and Guiscard, of course. And Paulin will bring Lior, to make sure his three Deryni really do get 'purified.' That probably means he'll also want Albertus and a bunch of *Custodes* to escort us, but I'll take along a good-size Haldane levy under Robear's command. That should keep the *Custodes* from getting any stupid ideas."

"What about Rhun?"

"I'll take him, too, so you don't have to worry about him. He can ride with Albertus. He'd like to be the next Earl Marshal, you know."

Rhys Michael snorted and grinned. "Not bloody likely. It sounds like good strategy, though. You think they'll really let you go?"

Javan gave him a sour look. "Do you really think I'd let them *stop* me?"

In Hubert's quarters down at the cathedral, the archbishop was asking the same question of Paulin.

"No, I think he's made up his mind," Paulin replied. "Our young king has become very wise in nearly seventeen years of living. I don't think you're going to turn him around. Fortunately, there's a contingency plan already in place."

Hubert glanced at Albertus, sitting silent and slyly smiling beside his brother, then back at Paulin.

"Just what are you up to, Paulin?" he whispered.

"Just never you mind," Paulin replied.

"But the hostages are Deryni—"

"They will be dealt with, I assure you."

"And the king?"

Paulin smiled. "Let him go to Master Revan."

CHAPTER FORTY-ONE

And their king shall go into captivity, he and
his princes together, saith the Lord.

—Amos 1:15

The departure of the former hostages was set for the first week in May. On the third, Holy Rood Day, Javan heard Mass in the Chapel Royal with his household and family, ceremonially handed over command of the castle to his brother on the great hall steps, and joined the entourage mounting up in the castle yard.

Robear had his Haldane levies lined up by fours and stretching back into the practice yard—fifty Haldane lancers with their officers, Haldane livery bright gold and crimson in the morning sun. Albertus had assembled his escort of twenty *Custodes* knights just outside the castle gates, forming a double line through which the royal party would pass—for Paulin had indeed declared himself leery of travelling without powerful escort in these troubled times, especially with Deryni in their company.

More *Custodes* men-at-arms sat their horses in the castle yard, a pair for each of the three curtained horse litters standing at the head of the modest baggage train. A *Custodes* battle surgeon was leaning into one of the litters to check on its occupant—not the elusive Dimitri, Javan was relieved to see, as he swung up on his cream-colored stallion and the man emerged. It had been agreed that all four hostages should be sedated for the journey, but not with *merasha*, which could prove harmful over the five or six days the journey was expected to take.

It was probably a mercy of sorts, for travel in the lurching litters would not be particularly pleasant, even though they were deep and well padded with cushions. Javan could see little Carrollan curled in the curve of his mother's arm, already asleep, just before the battle surgeon drew the curtain back into place. The other two litters held Sitric's elderly mother and his sister, a handsome young woman in her twenties. The hostages also were chained by one wrist to the frames of their litters, lest any seek to escape despite the lethargy of drugs.

They rode out just before noon, lightly armored over their riding leathers, with Javan leading at the head of Robear's lancers and Charlan bearing the royal standard, he and Guiscard flanking the king. Paulin and Lior rode with Rhun and four knights in Rhun's livery, directly behind the royal party. Albertus' *Custodes* knights fell into place as vanguard behind the litters and baggage train.

As they picked their way down the cobbled descent from the castle mount and through the city, exiting the city gates to head northward along the familiar river road north, the people came out to cheer them as they passed, for the king had not ventured forth in formal procession for some time.

Javan knew he looked like a proper king as he rode forth that May morning. The cream stallion pranced and curvetted, sometimes mincing sideways under the bright flutter of the Haldane banner Charlan carried. The surcoat Javan wore over his leather jazerant bore the Haldane lion picked out in rich gold bullion, bright against the crimson, and the hilt of the Haldane sword at his knee caught the light like a thing alive. The circlet of running lions was on his head, rich gold against the sable hair caught back at the nape of his neck in a short queue. The metal plates sewn between the layers of the jazerant made it heavy, but the weather still was brisk. Even under the noonday sun, the crimson mantle collared with black fox was not too much.

It was good to be out under the open sky, good to be riding on a mission that had a noble purpose to it. Javan inhaled deeply of the fresh spring air and found himself grinning as he glanced wickedly from Charlan to Guiscard, glanced back at Robear and Bertrand in warning of what he was about to do, then gave the cream stallion its head to bolt into a gallop of sheer joy. Guiscard and Charlan moved as one with him and six Haldane lancers spurred after to guard him, while Robear held up an indulgent hand to keep the rest back and let the train continue its slow, sedate pace.

The king turned around and came back after half a mile's race, reining back into his place with a grin of thanks to Robear and thereafter settling into the decorum that was expected of a monarch.

That night they lay at a priory of the *Ordo Verbi Dei*, just a few miles short of a *Custodes* establishment. Paulin had offered the hospitality of his own Order, but Javan politely declined. The royal party and their hostages received lodgings within the guest quarters of the priory, whose brethren were greatly honored by the royal visit, and the soldiers camped contentedly outside the priory walls in the mild weather.

This became the pattern of their travel for the next week, travelling in easy stages because of the horse litters and baggage train and staying in monastic accommodations, taking the longer but easier river route rather than striking out directly across country. Each morning, the king and at least a dozen of his knights and lancers spurred several miles ahead for exercise, and to take the edge off their battle-ready mounts, before returning to rejoin the sedate procession of horse litters and baggage only barely started out. Such travel quickly became tedious, but Javan consoled himself with the promise of a faster return journey, once the hostages had been delivered.

The last night before their expected arrival at Master Revan's riverside campsite, Javan shared a bottle of wine with Charlan and Guiscard in the quarters vacated by the Abbot of Saint Mark's for his royal visitor. They had bypassed the comforts of the Archbishop's Palace at Valoret, even though Hubert was not in residence, to press on closer to their intended destination.

"We'll be there tomorrow," Javan said, pouring wine for his two aides, who also had become his closest friends. "What do you think?"

Guiscard turned his cup in his hand, studying its contents, and glanced over at Javan.

"I'd love to interview either Paulin or Albertus alone," he said quietly. "I can't put my finger on anything specific, but they're up to no good. I've managed to chat with a few of the *Custodes* officers, but I think they've been told not to fraternize with the opposition. There's definitely a feeling of two camps—and we're not in the same one they are."

"Do you think we should turn back? We could hole up at Valoret."

Guiscard shook his head. "I don't see what that would accomplish, other than to delay your own plans. It certainly wouldn't resolve the hostage situation. At least we know Revan is on our side. And we do well outnumber the *Custodes*."

"Charlan?" Javan asked, turning his gaze on the other young knight.

Charlan shook his head. "I'm afraid I can't add anything. Just the same uneasiness you're both feeling." He sighed. "But I suppose we'll find out tomorrow whether we're letting our imaginations run wild."

They were on their way shortly after first light, for even leaving early, they still would not reach their destination until midafternoon. It was a bright, crystalline day, brisk when they set out but growing pleasantly warm by noon. Javan pushed his cloak back on his shoulders and began to scan ahead with greater interest.

They arrived at their destination just past noon. As Javan and his aides crested the little bluff that overlooked the bend in the river, Guiscard bearing the royal standard today, Javan could see the scenario spread before them as it had been the one other time he had been there. The crowd was not so large as it had been that other time, when Revan's ministry was new; but at least thirty or forty people were gathered around the still pool formed by the river's bend, in addition to the half dozen or so of Revan's disciples who were always present. Some showed evidence of recent immersion in the pool; others merely listened. A large proportion of them seemed to be women and children.

Revan, too, appeared much as he had when Javan first had seen him: a thin, slightly stooped figure in a robe of unbleached wool, standing ankle-deep in the water, light-brown hair falling around his shoulders, the upturned face shadowed with a beard and moustache that had not filled out appreciably in nearly four years. The graceful hands were uplifted in exhortation to heaven, and the pleasant voice drifted upward on a fresh breeze as Javan let his horse move a few steps closer.

Up on the dry sand of the spit, where his audience sat or knelt, a rusty brown mantle and a hairy goatskin pouch lay discarded beside a figure Javan thought he recognized as the Healer Sylvan O'Sullivan, Revan's familiar olivewood staff thrust into the sand beside him. Several more faces along the front row looked familiar from before—some of Revan's principal disciples. Tavis and Queron were among them.

"It is not enough merely to be purified," Revan was saying to his rapt audience. "Ye must maintain purity, by the example of your lives. Those who walked in darkness must eschew it and embrace the Light. God's grace can bring cleansing to those who truly repent and offer themselves before His mercy. Yea, even Deryni may feel His grace. The gateway to heaven is narrow, but God is merciful to those who truly repent."

He noticed Javan's arrival about then, and though he gave no immediate sign as first Paulin and then Albertus also crested the hill, to draw rein to either side of the king and his attendant knights, his audience soon noticed. Albertus would only be a black-clad knight added to the ones in Haldane livery, though helmeted where the other two showed bare-headed, dark and fair, but Paulin wore the full ceremonial attire of his office as Vicar General of the *Custodes Fidei*, bearing the haloed-lion staff of the Order footed in his stirrup like a lance. The gradual appearance of more armed men behind the king gave further cause for uneasiness, so that a babble of anxious speculation rippled through the company, momentarily drowning out Revan's words.

Before Paulin or Albertus could do or say anything to set things off in the wrong direction, Javan swung down from the big cream stallion he rode and motioned forward the horse litter carrying Birgit O'Carroll and her son. Father Lior followed on horseback, a Deryni pricker already in his hand. The *Custodes* battle surgeon was walking beside the litter and pulled back the curtain as its groom halted the lead horse.

The hostages had not been drugged as heavily this morning, and the human Birgit not at all. Birgit looked younger than the first time Javan had seen her, perhaps revived somewhat by the shred of hope being offered, for Javan had briefed the hostages on what to expect before leaving the abbey this morning.

"Come, my lady," he said, holding out his hand to her. "Your salvation awaits you."

Trembling, she clutched her son closer to her. Then, at Javan's nod of reassurance, she tentatively slid one foot out of the horse litter. Charlan was waiting to hand her down, Bertrand to scoop up the boy and, before he or his mother could protest, deposit him in the red leather saddle Javan had just vacated.

The boy's hazel eyes went wide with awe as he clung to the pommel and looked around him, reaching out one chubby hand to pat a strand of the stallion's mane. The woman shrank back as Charlan set his hands to her waist, and looked almost weak with relief when the young knight had set her sideways in the saddle behind her son. Throughout, Javan stood caressing the stallion's nose, gentling the great beast, his eyes never leaving his charges until he was certain they were settled.

"You surely do not mean to take them down yourself, Sire," Paulin said, obviously scandalized.

Javan gave him a taut, nervous smile. "Who better, my lord? Sir Bertrand will come with me, if you wish. No one else here present has felt the Master Revan's touch—though if any of your men wish to accompany us, to submit themselves for purification, I have no objection."

Put in such terms, the offer did not brook acceptance. A few of Paulin's men stirred uneasily, but a look from Paulin stilled them. Signalling Bertrand that he need not come, Javan set his hands on the stallion's bridle and began walking him slowly down the slope toward the pool, young Carrollan grinning imperturbably, if a little sleepily, his mother hanging on to the saddle for dear life. Just at the bottom, Queron came forward to hold the horse, his message passing in a flash as his hand brushed Javan's in taking the reins.

Tavis is here but blocked, in case Paulin should insist upon testing him. Locally, he's known to have undergone the purification and has become one of Revan's most trusted disciples. Now you're going to have to convince Paulin and the others that it really "took."

Queron bowed low over the reins to cover any betrayal of expression, giving Javan time to cast his glance over the others of Revan's disciples. Tavis was standing not far from Revan near the edge of the pool, the dark-red hair ablaze in the wan sunlight, the water-pale eyes like two holes burned through his head to the pool beyond.

Javan feigned shock as he saw him, for all the Court believed that he and Tavis had parted on bad terms four years before. The Healer also stiffened and then sank to his knees, his handless left wrist clasped piously by the right hand at his breast. Not taking his eyes from the now-kneeling Tavis O'Neill, Javan stiffly moved closer to the water's edge and Revan.

"The prince has become a king since last we met, Sire," Revan said softly, not coming any closer.

Javan shifted his focus to Revan, the grey eyes hard, playing his assigned part.

"Has that man been long with you, Master Revan?" he asked, pointing.

Revan inclined his head. "Brother Tavis came to us several years ago, Sire. He was Deryni, as your Highness well knows, but he humbled himself before the Lord of Hosts and renounced his past. The waters of mercy gave him birth to a new life. There remains no taint in him, your Highness, just as there remains no taint in you."

Turning away slightly, Javan muttered, "He betrayed our friendship. He abandoned me."

"And it was well that he should, Sire, for in staying, he would have dulled the purification that was yours. And now I see that you bring others to be purified as well. Do they come of their own free will?"

Wearily Javan nodded. "They do. The lady's husband was the Deryni Ursin, who came to you last time we met. She is not Deryni, but their son is. It was Ursin's fervent prayer that you grant cleansing to his wife and son."

"I remember Brother Ursin," Revan replied, inclining his head. "But your Highness speaks in the past tense. Has Brother Ursin passed on?"

"Yes," Javan whispered.

"I am sorry to hear that," Revan said. "I shall pray for him. Tell me, Sire, did he keep his purity?"

Javan nodded. "He was to have entered a monastic establishment as a lay scribe, there to offer up his skills in expiation for past sins. I—pray that he has found peace."

"That is my prayer, as well, Sire—and my prayer for his family. Brother Aaron, let us proceed."

At Revan's signal, Queron handed down first Birgit and then her son, urging them on down the slope toward Revan while he continued to keep the stallion gentle. The boy clung tightly to his mother's hand as they went, apparently a little intimidated by the bearded men standing in the water in strange robes. Birgit stopped a few yards from Revan and made him a nervous curtsey, only fearfully meeting his eyes as the boy shifted to hug her around the legs, face buried against her knees.

"Is it true, Master?" she whispered. "Is it true that you bring healing?"

"I alone can do nothing," Revan said, "but the Lord of Hosts is strong and is able to do great wonders."

"Can He take the taint from my son?" she asked, tears welling in her eyes. "Can aught cleanse us from the contagion?"

"Faith in the Lord can cleanse all from all, my sister," Revan declared, holding out his hand. "Will you be washed in the Mercy?"

As she stared at him, swaying on her feet, caught in his charisma but not yet brave enough to take his hand, Revan began to pray, lifting his arms and eyes heavenward as he had that day Javan had come to him.

"O Lord, look with favor upon this, your daughter, who desires to draw nearer to Your divine Countenance yet is assailed by human fears. She has walked in darkness, but Your Light calls to her still. Give her courage to humble herself before You, O Lord, and grant unto me, Your servant, the grace to reach out to her and draw her to Your salvation . . ."

Like all of Revan's prayers, it was calculated to wrench at the heart. Javan let the words stir a response in him as well, after a moment sinking down on one knee in the sand and bowing his head, in example to the one who was the true focus of Revan's words.

She was already under his spell, rapt eyes fixed on his face, lips moving in silent prayer. As Revan began backing into the water, holding out his hands to her, she started walking blindly after him, drawing the boy along. Just before she reached the water's edge, the Deryni Sylvan and another of Revan's disciples moved in quietly to join her, Sylvan picking up the boy and the other man steadying the mother as she waded in.

In that instant, Javan knew the deed was already done, and let himself peer out from under lowered lashes as they reached Revan, now waist deep in the water, and Sylvan put the boy back in his mother's arms. The lad twined his arms around her neck and locked his little legs around her waist, no trace of fear remaining as he peered over his mother's shoulder at Revan. The fear seemed to have gone out of her eyes as well.

"It is good, my sister," Revan murmured, setting one hand on her other shoulder and brushing back hair from the boy's forehead with his other hand. "Have faith in the Lord of Hosts, for He shall sustain you. What is your name?"

"B-Birgit, Master," she stammered.

"Birgit—a beautiful name for a brave and beautiful soul," Revan replied. "And the boy?"

"Carrollan, for his grandfather," she whispered.

"Carrollan," Revan repeated, his gentle smile eliciting a grin from the boy. "The water's cold, isn't it?"

Soberly the boy nodded.

"Well, this won't take long. Carrollan, you and your mother are going to duck under the water. I know you probably think it's a very silly thing, to duck under the water with all your clothes on, but do you think you can hold on very tightly? And my lady, simply lie back when I bid you. I and the Holy Spirit will do all else."

As the boy and his mother nodded, the boy's eyes wide with awe, Revan slipped his one arm farther around Birgit's shoulders, bidding his disciples back off a few paces before raising his free hand.

"O Holy Spirit, descend upon these, Thy servants, and free them of whatever evil may have assailed them," he said, bringing his hand to the back of Carrollan's head. "Give to this woman that peace of mind that can only come from purity in Thy sight, and grant mercy to this child, that his innocence may be restored."

He tipped them backward as he spoke, invoking the Trinity as their heads disappeared beneath the water.

"Be ye purified of all darkness, in the Name of the Father, and of the Son, and of the Holy Spirit, that ye may regain that holy vision of the Light that brings all souls at last unto the Lord."

He was bringing them up again as he and those around him uttered a confident "Amen." Javan got to his feet as Revan brought the two back toward shore, where one of the women waited with a towel. As they all emerged, streaming with water, Javan took off his mantle and laid it around the woman's shoulders, then crouched down to help dry the boy's face. The faint vestiges of Deryni power discernible before were gone, and Javan had no doubt that Carrollan O'Carroll would now react only as human to the test of *merasha*.

He headed back toward Queron and the stallion, one hand supporting the woman's elbow and the other closed around one of the boy's small ones, glancing up and beyond them at Paulin and the others waiting at the top of the hill. Over to the right, he saw Robear sitting his horse beside Albertus' second-in-command, both men staring hard across the bend of the river, Robear standing in his stirrups to point aghast at a line of horsemen emerging over the crest of the next rise. The men were heavily armored and bore the enflamed white cross moline fitchy of the outlawed Order of Saint Michael on their surcoats of Michaeline blue.

"Javan!" he heard someone scream, from back among his own troops.

To his amazement, it was Albertus, urgently wheeling his horse out from behind the *Custodes* line and signalling the royal troops forward.

"Sire, come back, it's a trap! They're Ansel's men! The same who held your brother hostage!"

At that very moment in Rhemuth, further elements of a long-set plot were also unfolding. Rhys Michael had not been at all certain he should convene the Council that afternoon, for Archbishop Hubert had taken exception to his handling of a request received the day before from a factor of his brother Manfred, in Culdi. The prince was still smarting from the public dressing-down Hubert had given him in front of the entire Council, as if he were an errant school-boy.

Afterward Etienne had assured him that it was Hubert who had been in error, not the prince, but Rhys Michael was not eager to give the archbishop another crack at him so soon. On the other hand, the Council was supposed to meet regularly in Javan's absence, to deal with the reports now arriving almost daily from the king's royal commissioners.

Resigned to his duty, Rhys Michael let it be known that the Council would meet as planned, then lost himself in his usual morning exercise and sword drill with Sir Tomais, and with Lord Hildred, who was refining his riding skills. He shared a midday meal in his quarters with his now visibly pregnant princess, Tomais joining them and Cathan serving them.

Sorle and Oriel joined them just as they were finishing, for Sorle and young Cathan had been working on several new lute tunes in honor of the princess. He and his charge had been moved into quarters adjoining the royal suite before Javan left, for Oriel to be nearer the princess as her pregnancy progressed. Except for Tomais, the prince left them to pass the afternoon in gentler pursuits, Michaela stitching contentedly on a christening gown for their expected child, while Sorle played and he and Cathan and Oriel sang intricate three-part harmonies.

The Council rose as Rhys Michael and his aide came into the sunny council chamber, the prince taking Javan's usual place at the head of the table, but in a less ornate chair than the carved throne chair customarily used by the king. He wore the royal blue of the heir with the Haldane device picked out in scarlet and gold on the left breast, but differenced by a silver bordure around the edge rather than the label of a third son he had borne during Alroy's lifetime.

A silver coronet confined the jet-black hair that was a Haldane hallmark, his earring of twisted gold wire just glinting through the hair on the right. He twisted at his signet ring as he sat down—it still bore his old coat of arms—and glanced around the table to see who was likely to annoy him today. With Albertus and Rhun and Paulin gone with Javan, the meetings had been smaller this last week and less formal.

Tomais had slid into his customary place at his master's right, on a stool set just slightly behind him. Hubert sat immediately to Rhys Michael's right, with Tammaron directly across from him, on the prince's left. Constable Udaut was just beyond Tammaron, Lord Jerowen at the far end of that side. Archbishop Oriss' seat, between Udaut and Tammaron, was empty.

The prince glanced idly in Hubert's direction as Tomais slipped an agenda onto the table in front of him, wondering where Oriss was. Odd, but a fair-haired *Custodes* knight seemed to be serving as Hubert's secretary today, seated on a stool directly behind the archbishop with head bent over a sheaf of papers balanced across his knees.

And beyond Hubert was Richard Murdoch, arrogant and surly looking, returned to Court the day before from his seat at Nyford. He and Rhys Michael had quarreled last night, for the young Earl of Carthane had brought his castellan with him to Rhemuth—a big, burly man called Sir Gideon, who had been castellan at Nyford for Richard's father and continued to serve Richard in that capacity—and Gideon had brought far too many men with him to make the prince entirely happy. Lord Udaut had finally intervened, belittling Rhys Michael's objections and ordering Richard's men quartered in the barracks temporarily vacated by the lancers gone north with Javan. The prince hoped they did not intend to stay long.

He noted Lord Hildred on Richard's other side, and Etienne de Courcy beyond him, then glanced back at Oriss' empty place.

"I see that Archbishop Oriss is not present, my lords," he said. "Does anyone know whether he plans to attend this afternoon's session?"

"Archbishop Oriss begs to be excused, your Highness," Hubert said lightly. "I believe he did not sleep well last night."

Satisfied, Rhys Michael nodded and shifted his feet under him to stand. The Haldane sword was with the king, so it could not be laid on the table in token of royal authority, but Lord Tammaron always set the State Crown of crosses and leaves there in its place, as symbol of the king's authority vested in his regent. The prince rose briefly to touch the fingertips of his right hand to his lips, then to the Crown, as a sign of his fealty, then glanced expectantly at Lord Udaut as he settled in his seat again.

"In the absence of the Earl Marshal, the Lord Constable will please convene the Council," he said.

Looking faintly bored, Udaut rose, slowly drawing his sword as he had at every meeting for the past week, as substitute for the marshal's baton that Albertus would have wielded. But instead of bringing it to salute and reciting the prescribed formula, he sidestepped quickly to the left to seize a handful of Lord Jerowen's tunic, jerking him to his feet.

At the same time, so quickly that Rhys Michael hardly had time to blink, blades slithered from other scabbards, Richard

Murdoch overturning his chair to strike Lord Hildred senseless with the pommel of his sword and then confronting Etienne de Courcy, who had come to his feet in a flash but now raised his hands in a warding-off gesture of surrender, not even attempting to resist as Richard disarmed him. Simultaneously, the *Custodes* knight sitting behind Hubert launched himself sideways in a flurry of flying papers to sheathe his sword in the belly of an astonished Sir Tomais, before the young knight's sword could even clear its scabbard.

Tomais' choked cry broke the instant of shocked betrayal that briefly had frozen Rhys Michael to his seat. Survival instinct launched him into action then, throwing himself to the side away from Tomais and at the same time groping frantically for the dagger at his waist. Surely this could not be happening!

But Earl Tammaron was already catching him with an arm around his shoulders from behind, with a speed and skill Rhys Michael had never even suspected, dragging him upright in his chair again with the flat of a dagger's blade pressed hard beneath the royal right ear. Rhys Michael tried to duck out of Tammaron's grasp, hands coming up in reflex to claw at the restraint, but the earl jerked his arm hard across his captive's throat with a whispered "Don't." At the same time, Rhys Michael was aware of the *Custodes* knight reaching a gloved hand across to pluck the dagger from his belt.

As soon as he had done so, Tammaron abruptly released the prince's throat and stepped back, though a hand remained resting lightly on the prince's sleeve, the dagger turning idly in his other hand in warning. Gasping for breath, Rhys Michael recoiled from him in horror, still hardly able to comprehend the betrayal—then whipped his head around at an anguished gurgling behind him to see the *Custodes* knight bending over Tomais, the prince's own dagger bright with the blood gushing from Tomais' throat.

With a cry of denial, Rhys Michael tried to go to the dying man, but Tammaron's hand stayed him. Meanwhile, Tomais' murderer tossed the bloody blade on the floor in a gesture of finality, then bent to retrieve his sword from Tomais' belly, looking coldly into the prince's eyes as he wiped his blade clean on a corner of the dying man's mantle. As Tomais' feeble twitchings ceased, Rhys Michael buried his face in his hands with a sob and turned away, certain they meant to kill him as well.

"I would advise," Hubert said in the sudden silence that followed, "that anyone wishing to share the fate of Sir Tomais has only to offer further resistance. Your Highness, I regret the necessity of having to eliminate your aide in so brutal a manner, for I believe he was also a friend, but I wish you to understand very clearly that what is now unfolding is deadly serious. Now, you will oblige me by drinking this."

As he spoke, he brought out a little silver flask from somewhere in his ample cassock, setting it on the table and pushing it closer to the prince. Rhys Michael stared at it and him with blank incomprehension for several seconds, suddenly fearing what it might contain—and no one could help him. The traitorous Richard Murdoch had bolted the door and then herded Etienne and the groggy Lord Hildred over to join Jerowen on one of the benches along the long wall of the Council chamber, where Earl Udaut now held all three of the prisoners at sword's point.

"What is it?" he managed to whisper.

"Your brother Alroy was well acquainted with it," Hubert said with a smile that contained no mirth at all. "Over the years we have found it exceedingly useful for keeping headstrong princes tranquil and biddable."

"No," Rhys Michael whispered.

"I do not wish to hear that word from you again, your Highness," Hubert said coldly, taking up the little flask and removing its stopper, not taking his eyes from Rhys Michael's as he set the flask back on the table and pushed it toward the prince again. "If you prefer, Lord Tammaron can hold you while my good *Custodes* knight applies more direct persuasions, but I do not think you will find his methods to your liking. Drink it."

The blond knight was now standing casually by Rhys Michael's right side, his sword now sheathed, gloved hands resting lightly on his sword belt, but the prince had no doubt that the man could and would force him to drink, if he did not obey of his own free will. Deciding not to dignify Hubert's threat by giving him a direct answer, Rhys Michael raised his chin defiantly and favored the archbishop with a withering glance, then took up the little flask in a trembling hand and tossed down its contents in a single swallow. When he had set the flask back on the table, he wiped the back of his hand across his mouth in a gesture of utter disdain, then folded his arms belligerently across his chest.

"Thank you," Hubert said, smiling the cold smile again. "Now we shall sit here together for a few moments and await word that our other objectives have been attained."

The minutes ticked by. Rhys Michael could feel his tension unwinding despite his fear, the dull lethargy of the drugged wine slowly insinuating itself into body and mind. Richard and Udaut both pulled chairs from around the table to sit facing their prisoners. Hubert, in one of the most hypocritical displays Rhys Michael had ever seen, lumbered his bulk to his feet and came to kneel ponderously beside the dead Tomais and give him the Last Rites.

After a few minutes, the sound of desultory fighting in the corridors outside intruded on the taut silence of the Council chamber. Hubert rose, his quick breathing telling of his tension as he came to stand with his hands on the back of Rhys Michael's chair. The *Custodes* knight went to the doors at the end of the room and listened with his ear against the wood, the sword that had killed Tomais again in his hand. Tammaron was sitting at the prince's left again, though his dagger now lay on the table in front of him.

Rhys Michael considered trying to snatch it, but he didn't know what good it would do except maybe get him killed—or another of his men killed, for now he did not think they meant to kill him. Besides, the grip of Hubert's potion was now so strong that he did not think he could summon the will even to stand without assistance. He found himself leaning his head against the back of his chair and closing his eyes, even though the posture put him closer to Hubert's profane hands.

He thought it must have been close to an hour before a knock at the door jarred him from the troubled half sleep into which he kept drifting. Hubert had returned to his chair at Rhys Michael's right and now got to his feet. The sound also roused the *Custodes* knight, who had been sitting on a stool pulled close to the doors, sword in hand, his ear set against the wood to listen. Now, as Rhys Michael tried to make his eyes focus, the man smiled grimly and shot back the bolt on the door, though he stepped aside with sword still at the ready as he let the door swing inward.

But the big man who appeared in the opening with a bloody sword in his fist was all too familiar from the day before—Richard's castellan, Sir Gideon, a wide grin splitting his bearded face as he pushed past the *Custodes* knight to salute first Richard and then Hubert with a flourish.

"All secure except for his Highness' apartments, your Grace, my lord," he reported. "We believe that the Healer and Sir Sorle are there with the princess."

"Mika?" the prince whispered, eyes wide. As he labored to get his feet under him and stand, Tammaron was already at his side with a hand on his arm, both supporting and restraining.

"Now, your Highness," Hubert purred. "Harming the mother of a future King of Gwynedd is the last thing any of us would wish. However, I fear for the contamination she may suffer by the continued presence of a Deryni in your household. Perhaps you would care to accompany us as we go to relieve her of this danger."

CHAPTER FORTY-TWO

And the revolters are profound to make
slaughter, though I have been a rebuker of
them all.

—Hosea 5:2

Javan broke into a lurching run, dragging the woman and child with him. Albertus and the *Custodes* knights were already wheeling to circle around to the right and down, where the slope was less steep, apparently intending to cut off the Michaelines at the ford just below the pool.

But the newcomers could not be Michaelines, even though the blond man riding at their head clearly was intended to be taken for either Joram or Ansel MacRorie.

"Saint Michael and MacRorie!" the men shouted, brandishing swords and spears and spurring their mounts forward, the white crosses of the outlawed order gleaming on their breasts.

As the Michaelines who could not be Michaelines began splashing into the river, the horses plunging chest-deep across the ford, Javan pushed Birgit and the little Carrollan into the arms of the nearest of Revan's disciples and dashed for his own horse. Right now, he wasn't sure who the men were, but he knew they were no friends. And the unarmed folk gathered here to hear Revan preach, many of them women and children, were about to be crushed between the two converging forces—and Javan, too, if he did not get back to the protection of his own lines.

"Who *are* those men?" he demanded of Queron, as he struggled to mount from the downslope and the Healer gave him a leg up. "Warn Joram! Try to get these people out of here. We've all been set up!"

He was spurring his horse up the hill then, heading toward his banner, for Guiscard and Charlan and about a dozen of the Haldane lancers were plunging straight down the slope to rescue him. The *Custodes* were nearly to the ford. Robear and the rest of the lancers had fallen in behind them, apparently positioning to back them or contain them, depending on what happened when they met the men in blue.

Except that the *Custodes* knights obviously had never intended to confront the men in blue. Just before they reached the ford, the *Custodes* knights wheeled and charged back into their erstwhile allies, their heavier horses carrying them well into the more lightly mounted lancers. Robear managed to survive the first engagement, but Javan saw Bertrand go down in a roiling confusion of sudden and treacherous combat.

"It's a trap!" Javan screamed as he reached the relative safety of Guiscard and his banner.

Above them, looking down on him, he could see Paulin calmly sitting his horse beside Rhun, flanked by Rhun's four knights. The scope of the betrayal suddenly became very clear. Eliminate both a troublesome king and the embarrassment and possible deception of Revan and his Baptizer cult, and blame it all on the Deryni and the Michaelines.

Fighting to control a mount now fractious with eagerness for battle, Javan weighed the odds and possible intentions of the dual opposition. Surprise now past, the lancers seemed to be more than holding their own with the *Custodes*, but the false Michaelines were even now falling on Revan's helpless followers down by the pool.

"Come away, Sire!" one of his lancer captains shouted. "We mustn't divide our strength."

He was right. Javan dared not go back down. With a grimace of regret, he drew his sword and wrenched the cream stallion around to pull it back on its haunches, circling the sword above his head and then thrusting it in the direction of the treacherous *Custodes*.

"No quarter to traitors!" he cried. "To Robear—and watch your backs!"

But as the cream stallion sprang forward, part of Javan mourned for the helpless folk he was leaving to their fate. Down at the pool where Revan had preached a reconciliation of humans with Deryni, the first of the false Michaelines were already churning through the shallows, leaning down with swords and spears poised.

A venerable old man with a white beard was one of the first to fall, skewered by a Michaeline spear and then trampled under the hooves of nearly a dozen horses as the marauders began butchering their quarry. Javan had thought Revan and the others on their way to safety, but as he looked back over his shoulder he suddenly saw the preacher just at the edge of the pool with several of his disciples, flailing about him with his olivewood staff and even knocking an attacker from the saddle. Sylvan was in the water beyond him, trying to get a child to safety.

Horrified, Javan pulled up slightly and let most of his lancers pound past him. Guiscard and Charlan were also hanging back, but urging him to come on. Revan's followers were scattering, their screams shrill and terrified as the blue-clad horsemen cut them down. Javan could not see Queron or Ursin's family, but he suddenly spotted Tavis running toward the water, where Sylvan was still trying to get children and old folk on their way to safety. Something about Tavis seemed odd.

Then Javan realized that the Healer was still blocked and was trying to reach the only other man who could restore his powers. He pulled to a full halt and stood in his stirrups, for if Tavis decided to use those powers to strike back—

Sylvan was knee-deep in the water, a child in his arms, trying to outrun a horseman bearing down on him with a short spear aimed at his back. Tavis reached Sylvan and tried to push him aside just before the horseman forced his mount between them and buried his spear in Sylvan's chest, also slicing a deep gash in the child's arm. His killer paid, for a bolt of verdant lightning from Tavis' hand lifted him clear out of the saddle, dead before he hit the water; but Sylvan's blood was already blossoming around both bodies like some obscene flower as they sank.

From the shore, swinging at another blue-clad rider with his staff, Revan screamed, "No!" for he had seen the stab of lightning, as had dozens of others. But rather than loosing more of his magic, Tavis now began searching quite single-mindedly for the child who had been in Sylvan's arms, probing the bloody water until he brought the weeping, hiccoughing youngster to the surface by a handful of curly dark hair.

Blood was streaming from a gaping wound in the little girl's upper arm, and Tavis pressed sleep upon her with his stump even as he gathered her to his breast, holding her close with his handless arm while his Healer's hand clamped over her wound, already starting to work on the Healing as he began staggering from the water.

The false Michaelines were backing off all around him, milling uncertainly, for no one had warned them that Revan's hitherto ag-

gravating but presumably harmless scam down by the river really
was a Deryni plot.

But cringing terror was already shifting to outrage in Revan's
followers, as they realized that the preacher had lied to them. Not
all Deryni who came within his sphere of influence gave up their
powers. How much else had been a lie? The great Tavis, whose
conversion had provided such inspiration for so many, was still
Deryni. Deception! Betrayal! The Deryni *were* the scourge of hu-
mankind, and this Deryni must pay—and Revan, for having betrayed them!

Almost all the bodies littering the corridors of the castle wore
Haldane livery. Rhys Michael was cowed and frightened as he was
hustled up the main stair and along the corridor toward his suite.
Resistance was not possible. Tammaron and Richard flanked him,
each with a hand locked around one bicep. The *Custodes* knight
who had murdered Tomais was following them, which made the
prince more than nervous, and Hubert and Gideon preceded them,
the traitorous archbishop vast in his robes of episcopal purple.

The prince was still reeling over what had happened just as they
left the Council chamber. The gentle and soft-spoken Jerowen Reynolds was dead. Udaut and half a dozen guards had been taking the
prisoners away to alleged incarceration when the three made a bold
bid for freedom.

Jerowen had fallen almost immediately in the scuffle, brutally
slain by one of the guards—why had he tried it? He was not a warrior. Baron Hildred had taken a dreadful wound. Almost miracu-
lously—or perhaps it was blind luck—Etienne de Courcy somehow
had managed to dash into a stairwell and escape, Udaut and his
men in hot pursuit. The speed of it all had stunned the prince and
left him sick with apprehension despite the drugs blurring his reaction, for he very much doubted that the bookish Etienne could
manage to remain free for long—or that his pursuers would spare
him, once they found him.

They rounded the final turn leading to his suite, Rhys Michael
stumbling a little as they hurried him along. Ahead, past Hubert's
bulk, he could make out *Custodes* soldiers where Haldane guards-
men should have been—four of them armed with deadly little recurve bows, barbed war arrows already nocked to their weapons,
lounging casually along the wall as they awaited instructions. An
officer and six more men in Richard Murdoch's livery were drawn
up just outside the door.

All of them came to attention as Gideon trotted ahead to speak to the officer, drawing him slightly aside. As they began to confer in low tones, Richard joining them, the *Custodes* knight behind Rhys Michael glided in to take Richard's place on the prince's right, laying a heavy hand on the royal shoulder.

Revulsion made Rhys Michael stiffen despite the drugs that were supposed to keep him tractable, but he knew he did not have the strength or the will to put up any serious resistance. He could not stop these men; he could barely stay on his feet. He briefly considered trying to cry out, to warn Mika and the men inside, but taking such initiative required far more effort than he thought he could summon. His sigh of numb resignation caused his *Custodes* minder to slip deftly behind him and lock his shoulders and throat in the circle of his left arm, a gloved right hand coming in to clamp lightly but firmly over the prince's mouth.

"Not one move or sound, Haldane, or you're out," the man said quietly.

Though conversational enough in tone, the words sent a chill through Rhys Michael's body, for he had heard that voice and those very words before. Utter despair seized him; now he knew the truth of the allegations he had scoffed at when Javan made them—that his abductors had been *Custodes*—for surely the *Custodes* knight now holding him had been his principal keeper during his captivity. It also meant that his abduction had indeed been part of a larger plan of treason whose full scope only now was unfolding.

Ahead, Hubert and Tammaron were moving in to the left of the door, Gideon to the right, as the archers ranged themselves directly in front of it, two standing and two crouching before them. Richard's men filled in crescents to either side with swords drawn—though there was no way that Oriel or Sorle was going to get past the archers. Rhys Michael did not want to watch, but he knew that he must, and that his captors wanted him to watch, and that whatever they did to try to intimidate him, he must remember this when he eventually found a way to pay them for their treachery.

"Your Highness?" Tammaron called, knocking at the door. "Your Highness, it's Tammaron. Is Master Oriel with you? There's been an accident."

It was the one appeal that a Healer could not refuse, and doubly treacherous because Tammaron had never before been linked with the active conspirators.

"Master Oriel, we need your services," Tammaron called again, after repeating his knock on the door. "The prince has taken a bad fall. They think there are bones broken."

The words brought the intended result, as Rhys Michael had known they must. Michaela wrenched open the door. Sir Sorle was trying to keep her from it, sword drawn, and also trying to shield Oriel behind him, for the Healer had sensed the danger. But Richard's Gideon forced the door wider and surged past, engulfing the screaming princess in his bearlike arms as he rushed her out of harm's way and the archers let fly.

Sorle was probably dead before he hit the floor, for three of the first four arrows slammed into him, one of them straight through the eye. The fourth arrow and three of the second flight found their targets in Oriel, who threw up his arms in a futile attempt to ward them off and took one shaft directly through a palm. Two more hit an upper arm and a shoulder—all flesh wounds, so far— but another, buried deep in his chest, looked to be fatal, if only slowly so.

The Healer bit back a cry of anguish as he sank to his knees, his unwounded hand plucking ineffectually at the arrow in his chest. To Rhys Michael's horror—and now his captor did not seem to care if he screamed—the archers calmly nocked to shoot once more, placing their shots with precision, one by one, but only to wound, not to kill. The Healer cried out as each arrow thumped home—one in each thigh, another through the hand already trans-fixed once, upflung in vain entreaty, a final shot to the angle of the groin.

The force of the hits drove the Healer backward, shattering the shafts through his hand as he vainly tried to catch himself, knees bent back under him, back arching with pain. Movement behind Oriel and slightly to one side brought two of the archers bounding into the room with bows drawn to shoot again, the other two cov-ering them; but it was only Cathan Drummond, Michaela's younger brother, weeping and shrinking behind an overturned stool with his arms over his head as he cried, "No! No!"

The two men inside relaxed their draws and seized the boy by both arms, yanking him roughly to his feet and dragging him off to join his sister, whose anguished sobbing could be heard off in the direction of the royal bedchamber. As they disappeared, the remaining two archers eased cautiously around the groaning Oriel and headed off to the right to check the rest of the royal apartment, making way for Richard and one of his men-at-arms to enter.

Oriel was in agony; that much was certain. Even from in the

corridor, Rhys Michael could hardly bear to watch, heartsick with horror, now supported as much as restrained by the arm of his captor around his shoulders. As Richard moved into the room to survey his victim, whose blood was ruining a precious Kheldish carpet, Richard's man set his hand on his dagger and glanced from Oriel to his master in inquiry.

"No, indeed," Richard said softly, but loud enough that neither Oriel nor Rhys Michael could fail to hear. "Master Oriel doesn't approve of the *coup de grace*. I heard him tell my father so."

Rhys Michael bit at his lip, for now he understood exactly why Richard had been given the job of eliminating this particular obstacle to their plans. The Healer's pain-filled eyes drifted dazedly to Richard's, almost all pupil, and it was clear that he, too, understood.

"I only regret," Richard went on coldly, "that the *merasha* on the arrowheads will kill you before you die of your wounds—and my archers were so careful . . . But I couldn't risk that you'd use your foul magic to escape your just reward. For as long as you have, Deryni, I hope you suffer!"

He spat in the Healer's face with deliberate contempt, then stepped clear of the writhing body to head off to the left, out of sight, where the sound of hysterical weeping from behind a briefly opened door suggested that Michaela, too, had seen and heard far too much of what had just occurred.

"Someone had better get a physician in here quickly," Hubert's voice came above the weeping, just before the door closed.

"Mika?" Rhys Michael whispered numbly.

But they would not let Rhys Michael go to his wife—not until he had witnessed Richard's vengeance to the end. Numb with grief and horror, the prince did not even try to resist as his minder walked him into the room and thrust him to his knees between the dead Sorle and the dying Deryni. Even with the *merasha*, it seemed to take Oriel a very long time to die, and just before he slipped into an unconsciousness from which he would never wake, Rhys Michael took the Healer's bloody hand in his and held it to his breast.

"I'm sorry, Oriel," he whispered, before his minder could pull him away. "I didn't believe. God give you peace—"

He was weeping as he collapsed back onto his knees, forbidden to touch the dying man but not permitted to leave. He was still weeping when Oriel finally drew his last breath, and could not seem to stop, even when a royal physician came and led him into another room, now nearly as concerned for the prince's well-being as for that of the young woman going into premature labor in the royal bedchamber.

Heartsick, Javan tried to shake off his last glimpse of Revan and Tavis as he spurred on with Charlan and Guiscard, heading for where the lancers were successfully pushing the *Custodes* knights back on their own line. Revan's followers had turned on both preacher and false disciple like wild animals, once they realized their betrayal, and the bogus Michaelines had stood by and let them tear the two to pieces. It had been over almost before Javan could even comprehend what was happening.

He saw Revan overwhelmed, to be seen no more; and he would never forget the sight of that bloody, handless arm being thrust aloft from within a teeming mass of humanity—and then a blood-spattered, wild-eyed man triumphantly brandishing that arm like a club, gleeful and laughing as he and several of his fellows now turned their battle lust on the blue-clad riders.

It bought them the extermination the false Michaelines had probably intended all the while—a savage killing orgy that cut down men, women, and children alike, for their masters would never risk future dealings with a people who could turn so savage, even in the zeal of a cause they all espoused.

And Javan could spare no men to try to stop the carnage, because the *Custodes* knights must be contained. A shout went up from his own men as he joined them, and the lancers lit into their traitorous opponents with redoubled efforts, making serious inroads into the ranks of the rebel knights despite being more lightly armed and mounted.

Javan saw action almost immediately and found that his past months of training served him in good stead. There was almost an exhilaration to it—laying about him with the Haldane sword, quick and agile on the back of the brave cream stallion; Charlan guarding his back, cheerful and competent, always there when he needed to be; and Guiscard, not far away, joyously slaying any *Custodes* warrior who dared to threaten the Haldane standard or its king.

They were winning, slowly but surely, the *Custodes* forces now reduced by more than half, Albertus himself now in serious peril of being overrun, when new riders suddenly began to appear back on the ridge where Paulin and Rhun still watched—fifty or sixty of them. Many of the fresh troops carried wicked little recurve bows, and their commander rode under the banner of Manfred MacInnis,

Earl of Culdi. He was too far away for Javan to tell whether it was Manfred himself, but the man stood in his stirrups to raise an arm toward Albertus as he drew rein at the edge of the field; and Albertus raised an exultant arm in reply.

"Dear God, now we *are* betrayed!" Javan said to Charlan, as the latter rallied half a dozen lancers closer around the king and they prepared to meet this new threat. As the new arrivals charged into the fray, well armored and freshly mounted, Rhun and his knights also fell in.

The tide was turning. The royal lancers now were well outnumbered. Javan was suddenly fighting for his life in earnest, slowly beginning to realize that he was not likely to get out of this. Manfred's fresh troops moved in well-disciplined units, the archers sweeping in, eight or ten at a time, to fire withering volleys of arrows into the midst of the royal lancers. Half a dozen went down practically in front of Javan in the first pass, and several arrows grazed his horse. Robear went down with eight or ten shafts protruding from his body, dragging a Culdi man down with him, bright steel flashing in his hand just before the dust of battle obscured his end.

All around Javan, rebel treachery was taking its toll. Not far away, beneath the Haldane standard, Guiscard was being engulfed by at least eight men in Manfred's livery, fighting like a madman, an arrow protruding from the back of one shoulder and several in his horse. The Haldane standard faltered but did not fall. The Culdi men cut his horse out from under him, and then Guiscard himself went down, flailing and slashing, bloodied sword keeping at least some of them at bay. He managed to pass the standard to another man in Haldane livery before he vanished under a flashing glitter of blades, but almost immediately Culdi livery overwhelmed that man, too, and the Haldane standard disappeared from sight.

Javan caught a sob in his throat, for he knew the Deryni knight must be dead, but he must wait until later to mourn Guiscard. He was fighting for his own life. The Culdi archers were firing again, and the cream stallion sank under him with a muffled squeal, four or five arrows buried in its silken flanks and chest. Javan landed on his feet, sword still in hand, but now he was hampered by his foot, unable to move as nimbly as he had on horseback. Charlan spurred nearer and tried to pull the king up into the saddle behind him, but their attackers cut down his horse as well.

More arrows were whining through the air all around them, and Javan cried out as he took one in the shoulder and another in his bad leg. Charlan was hit as well, but only once, in the thigh, and he laughed in the grim desperation of a battle going sour as he snapped the shaft off close and kept on fighting, guarding his king's back.

But it was no good. Javan managed half a dozen exchanges with a never-ending succession of assailants, sheer will keeping him on his feet, but soon it was no longer possible to deny his growing weakness, and the unmistakable waves of vertigo, of nausea. To fall to traitors' arrows was bad enough, but *merasha* on the arrow-heads—

Another arrow struck him in the calf, then another slammed into his chest. He felt himself falling, the Haldane sword spinning from numb fingers, and he knew with a briefly blinding instant of clarity that it was a moot point whether his wounds or the *merasha* would kill him first. Somewhere he had lost the coronet of running lions.

Charlan caught him as he fell, letting fall his own sword and weeping as he gathered him in his arms. Time seemed to slow almost to a stop, and he could not seem to hear properly. More arrows bit into the ground beside Charlan, kicking up dirt; but then, all around them, the fighting seemed to die away, though farther off he could vaguely hear the sounds of battle continuing.

"My liege," Charlan whispered, rocking Javan to his breast and not even trying to hold back the tears. "God, what have they done to you?"

Through the narrowing tunnel of his fading vision, Javan could just make out Charlan's face—and beyond him, the dark silhouettes of booted legs drawing near, the swirl of *Custodes* mantles all around them, blocking out the light. He could see Albertus looming over him with bloody sword in hand, gazing down at him in cold appraisal, and another dark-cloaked form moving in behind Charlan, a heavy broadsword held point-downward by the hilt, dripping blood on Charlan's back.

He knew what was about to happen. He saw that Charlan knew it, too, and chose not to acknowledge it. He managed to tighten his fingers on a handful of Charlan's surcoat, wanting to tell him how sorry he was . . .

Above him, the *Custodes* Grand Master merely smiled coldly and gave a nod to the man behind Charlan. Helpless to stop it, Javan watched the sword-hilt rise inexorably in leather-clad hands and then descend in a vicious downward thrust—and felt Charlan's mortal gasp as the blade pierced his back and into his vitals.

"Loyal Charlan," Javan whispered, tears welling in his closing eyes as he felt the young knight die.

And in that same breath, he commended his own soul to God, praying that he might have no better companion when he came before the throne of heaven than the brave knight in whose arms he lay—and that other, so recently gone before them, who even now seemed to welcome them both from within a brilliant light on the other side of the darkness.

EPILOGUE

Our inheritance is turned unto strangers, our houses unto aliens.

—Lamentations 5:2

Rhys Michael knew that his brother had died, long before the first *Custodes* couriers came galloping into Rhemuth with confused reports of an ambush by Ansel MacRorie and renegade Michaelines. Awareness of it intruded gradually through his shock at the brutal murder of Tomais and Sorle and Oriel and then the added and unexpected blow of the death of his son, born far too soon to live and never even drawing breath to cry. He knew it in a deep recess of consciousness never tapped before, but the physicians' drugs kept him numbed to all of it for many days.

They brought his brother back to Rhemuth on what would have been his seventeenth birthday. The pale and obviously grieving Rhys Michael was permitted to receive his brother's body at the steps of Rhemuth Cathedral and to walk in his funeral cortege a few days later—attended on both occasions by two solicitous and kindly-looking *Custodes* priests—but many remarked that he appeared to be in shock. Hence it came as no surprise when the lords of state let it be known that the new sovereign and his young queen were devastated by their double loss and intended to remain in seclusion for some weeks before even considering a coronation date. Meanwhile, the king's Council would carry out the day-to-day business of government.

Later, Rhys Michael would remember only snatches of those days that put paid to his youth. The new king spent the remainder of the summer a virtual prisoner in his own castle, always at least lightly sedated, periodically more heavily medicated when they must trot him out for some official appearance, though these were few. During the more lucid intervals, they made it quite clear what was expected of him and what would happen if he did not comply. From the depths of drug-induced despondency, it sometimes occurred to him to wonder whether this was what Alroy had had to endure, all those four years he had been king. It got worse again as his coronation approached.

They let him be crowned on Michaelmas, his sixteenth birthday—drugged, of course, and led through his responses by an attentive young *Custodes* priest, on whom he was often obliged to lean for support merely to stand. His condition shocked most observers. Rhys Michael, of all the princes, had always been hale and robust, his fair, rosy countenance a dramatic foil for the jet-black Haldane hair. But on the day of his coronation, dark hollows stained the delicate skin under his eyes; his physicians had bled him several times during the preceding week.

His appearance and general lethargy only confirmed what had been said all summer: that the new king's health had been shattered by the shock of his brother's death and might be some time mending. Quite obviously, he would not be able to take up his public duties for some time, perhaps not until the spring. Meanwhile, the Council would continue to rule in his stead.

It was soon after the coronation that they stopped giving him the drugs. They also moved him at last into the new royal suite already occupied for some months by Michaela, far from the rooms where Sorle and Oriel had been so brutally slain. Within days he found his head clearing, his appetite improving, and his general strength increasing. It was heartening to be able to think clearly again, but he also knew what it meant.

Accordingly, his reunion with Michaela was strained. They had seen one another but seldom through the summer, first because she was recovering and then because his state of continual befuddlement made him no fit company for anyone. She had been frightened, he knew, both by their situation and by his condition, and he was certain she remained frightened.

But because he knew *why* the great lords had allowed them to resume at least the outward appearance of domestic regularity, he found himself stiffly holding back from any interaction that might lead to renewed intimacy. The privacy denied them all summer was now encouraged, but he would not touch her. The hours they spent together found each of them occupied with solitary pastimes while sitting in the same room, she at her needlework, he trying to read or, more often, simply staring out the window or gazing despondently into the glitter of the Ring of Fire. They spoke little, and then only of inconsequentials. And late at night, when they lay on opposite sides of the great state bed that had been Javan's and Alroy's and their father's before them, he sometimes heard her softly sobbing when she thought he was asleep.

It took her several weeks to summon the courage to question him about it. They had dined silently in the gentle dusk that makes autumn evenings soft and sweet, and afterward they were sitting in cushioned chairs in front of the fire, sipping a fine old Vezaire port that she knew he loved—though he drank far less than he had done in the old days.

"Rhysem, what's wrong?" she asked.

Smiling sadly, he sighed and rested his forehead against the side of his goblet, closing his eyes. He had been expecting the question for some days.

"I'm a puppet king, Mika," he whispered, though he knew that was not what she was asking. That had been obvious from that awful day their world turned upside-down.

When she did not say anything, he picked up his head and cupped the goblet between his hands. "Someone once told me—and I honestly can't remember who, anymore—that before my parents were married, my father told my mother she was to be nothing but a royal brood mare. I'm told that later he did come to care for her, but I suppose that, in a way, that's what she was. She gave my father five sons in four years—two of them twins, I'll grant you— and then conveniently died within a few months of giving birth to the last."

"Whatever does that have to do with us?" Michaela asked. "I want to give you more sons, but I've never gotten the impression that you wanted *me* to be a royal brood mare. I wasn't even ever certain you were that happy about impending fatherhood—though I think you would have loved our little son, if he'd—"

She broke off and sniffled quietly, bravely wiping away tears with the back of one hand, then whispered, "I'm sorry."

"I wish I could tell you how sorry *I* am, Mika," he whispered. He drew a deep breath. "Neither of us realized, but you *were* expected to be a royal brood mare—or I was to be the royal stud. It's me they're really after; you were just a helpless victim."

"What are you talking about?"

"The great lords," he said, looking down into his cup. "They were Alroy's regents for more than two years, and they kept him under their thumb even after that, partly by intimidation and partly by keeping him drugged. The reason they've stopped drugging me is so that it won't impair the royal stud's performance. I didn't want to tell you this, but you have a right to know."

"Rhysem, you're scaring me," she murmured.

"You *should* be scared. God knows, I'm terrified." He started to take a deep swallow of his wine to fortify himself, then shook his head and set the cup aside.

"I've done a lot of growing up in the last few months," he said, sitting back squarely in his chair. "This isn't easy to say to you, but every word is true, so you'd better listen. Javan told me, and I didn't listen, and now he's dead. They killed him because they couldn't control him. And if they think they can't control me, they'll kill me, too—but not until I've given them what they want."

"What do you mean?"

"The great lords want another regency. As soon as I've secured the succession—probably the traditional 'heir and a spare'—I can almost guarantee that the new king will meet with a conveniently fatal accident." He smiled bitterly. "Just think of it: another twelve or fourteen years of unbridled power for the likes of Hubert and Rhun and the new ones who have come along since the last regency. What kind of a chance do you think our sons would have to rule independently, after a lifetime of indoctrination by men like Paulin and Albertus? Javan didn't fall for it, but I did—and we only had a few years of their lies and deceptions to contend with."

"Rhysem, you can't be serious," she whispered, moving to sink down at his feet and gaze up at him in the firelight, feeling his trembling as she rested her hands on his knees. "Tell me you've made this up."

"God, if only I had," he breathed, shaking his head wearily.

"Well, then, we—we just won't have any children for a while, if that's the way they're going to be," she said indignantly, a look of fierce determination coming over her pretty face. "I love you, Rhys Michael Haldane. I love everything you are. I love your body and the way you make me feel when we're together, and I loved carrying your child. But if that means your death—"

He shook his head, chuckling mirthlessly. "There's one other thing I haven't yet told you. If I absolutely refuse to oblige them, they can't force me; but they *can* force you."

"What do you mean?" she murmured, her eyes wide as she raised up on her knees to stare at him.

"Quite bluntly, my sweet queen, I mean that if I fail to impregnate you, someone else will do it for me. Who's to know, outside these walls? I'm told that there are several eager volunteers."

"Who?" she demanded.

"Rhun and Richard, among others."

"I would rather die!"

"I doubt you'd be given that choice. And if you did succeed, they'd simply drug me up and marry me to some more biddable bride. Rhun's Juliana, probably. And if I couldn't be persuaded to perform with her, another willing surrogate would be drafted to found a new royal line. That would be the end of the Haldanes, even though the name would go on."

"But that's monstrous! Rhysem, what can we do?" she breathed.

"Well, as I see it, there are three options. One, we can actively defy the great lords and possibly be killed. If I die without male issue, that would end the Haldane line and open the way for the return of that Festillic claimant who's been lurking in the wings all these years. They don't want that, of course, so they'll do their best to keep me alive until I've served their purpose. In the worst case, it could go very much as I outlined. Not good for either of us, and not at all good for Gwynedd."

"What's the second option?" Michaela asked.

"We defy the great lords indirectly by refusing to breed an heir, but we pretend that we're trying. That keeps them from drugging me again and gains time for us to maybe figure a way out of this. That can't go on forever, because they know you're fertile, but losing the first baby *might* make it difficult for you to get pregnant again right away.

"Eventually, though, we run the risk that someone else will be ordered to do the honors—which, if it's one of the great lords themselves, provides a veneer of legitimacy for a new dynasty then directed by the great lords in blood as well as power. Of course, as soon as you've produced a few healthy bairns, regardless of their actual father, I become the *late* king and you become a young and beautiful dowager queen. I think they'd probably keep you around, to care for the children."

"How can you talk about this so calmly?" she whispered, tears welling in her eyes as she shook her head. "Those are no choices at all."

"I know." He could feel tears starting to run down his own cheeks as he lightly touched her hair, and he closed his eyes as she leaned her head against his knee, his hand beginning to caress the shining strands.

"You said there were three options," she said after a few minutes. "What was the third?"

He leaned his head against the back of the chair and breathed a heavy sigh.

"We can do what they want: Give them their heirs—and ensure the legitimate Haldane line," he said.

"But—they'd kill you, once we'd done it."

"Probably. But I've thought a lot about this in the last few days. My own life isn't that important, in the great reckoning of things, but preserving the Haldane line is. Despite the meddling of the great lords, the Haldane kings have been good for Gwynedd—certainly better than the Festils ever were. If I have to die to ensure that Haldane princes will continue to rule—well, if one has to die young, I suppose that's a better reason than most. Besides—" He flashed her a brave smile. "We might have daughters first. And we can still delay as long as we dare. After that—well, it still takes time to grow babies, even once they're started. We might have a couple or three years. Maybe that will be long enough to figure out a way out of this."

"Oh, Rhysem . . ." she whispered, and burst into tears.

He let her weep against his knee until her despair was spent, continuing to gently stroke her hair. At length she dried her eyes on the hem of her gown and turned her face to him again. He had never seen her look so unlovely, with her nose reddened and her eyes swollen from weeping, and he had never wanted her so much.

"Well, what do you think?" he whispered, wiping a last tear from her cheek with his thumb. "The decision can't be mine alone. In a way, whatever we decide will affect you far more than it does me."

For answer, she took his hand and pressed it to her lips, then cradled it against her cheek.

"Rhys Michael Haldane, you are my lord and my love and my king—and my life. If it is your wish as well, I hope one day to bear the Haldane sons you must have—even if it means I must lose you."

She kissed his hand again, then gave him a bright, courageous smile. "But I hope I bear you several daughters first. And maybe, before it grows too late, we'll find a way to gain you back a Haldane crown that's free."

INDEX OF CHARACTERS *

AARON, Brother—Queron's alias among the Willimites.

ADELICIA of Horthness—age 8; daughter of Rhun.

AGNES Murdoch, Lady—age 21; wife of Rhun of Horthness, Earl of Sheele, and daughter of Murdoch of Carthane.

AIDAN Alroy Camber Haldane, Prince—deceased infant son of King Cinhil*

AILIN MacGregor, Bishop—Hubert's Auxiliary Bishop at Valoret.

AINSLIE, Lord—a royal commissioner.

ALANA d'Oriel—Deryni wife of the hostage Healer Oriel.

ALBERTUS, Lord—Grand Master of the *Equites Custodem Fidei*; formerly Peter Sinclair, Earl of Tarleton; brother of Paulin of Ramos and father of Bonner Sinclair, the present earl.

ALFRED of Woodbourne, Bishop—Auxiliary Bishop of Rhemuth; formerly confessor to King Cinhil.

ALISTER Cullen, Bishop—Deryni former Vicar General of the Order of Saint Michael; Bishop of Grecotha and Chancellor of Gwynedd under King Cinhil; briefly, Archbishop of Valoret and Primate of All Gwynedd; alternate identity of Camber MacRorie.*

ALROY Bearand Brion Haldane, King—age 16; dying King of Gwynedd; elder twin of Javan.

AMBERT Quinnell of Cassan, Prince—client prince of Cassan, northwest of Gwynedd; father of Princess Anne, who married Fane Fitz-Arthur; grandfather of Tambert.*

ANNE Quinnell, Princess—daughter of Prince Ambert Quinnell of

---

*An asterisk indicates a character mentioned only in passing, possibly deceased.

Cassan and wife of Fane Fitz-Arthur; mother of Tambert, first Duke of Cassan.

ANSEL Irial MacRorie, Lord—age 22; grandson of Camber and a prime mover in the resistance against the former regents.

ARIELLA of Festil, Princess—slain elder sister of the late King Imre and mother of his son, Mark.*

ARION of Torenth, King—age 22; Deryni King of Torenth and elder brother of Prince Miklos.*

ASCELIN, Father—*Custodes* priest at Saint Hilary's Basilica in Rhemuth, replacing Father Boniface.

BALDWIN—soldier of the Rhemuth garrison who "attacks" Oriel.

BERTRAND de Ville, Sir—age 20; squire to Prince Javan before Charlan.

BIRGIT O'Carroll—Ursin's human wife and mother of his son Carrollan.

BONIFACE, Father—deceased former priest and sometime confessor of Prince Javan at Saint Hilary's Basilica in Rhemuth.*

BONNER Sinclair, Lord—age 23; Earl of Tarleton; son of Lord Albertus and nephew of the Abbot-Bishop Paulin.

CAMBER Kyriell MacRorie, Saint—Deryni former Earl of Culdi; father of Joram and Evaine; canonized as Saint Camber in 906; sainthood rescinded by Council of Ramos in 917.

CARMODY, Declan—see *Declan Carmody.*

CARROLLAN O'Carroll—age 4; Deryni son of Ursin O'Carroll.

CASHEL Murdoch—age 17; younger son of Murdoch of Carthane.

CATHAN Drummond—age 12; brother of Michaela and son of Elinor and James Drummond.

CATHAN MacRorie—slain elder son of Camber, father of Ansel and the deceased Davin.*

CHARLAN Kai Morgan, Sir—age 19; formerly squire to Prince Javan and now his aide.

CINHIL Donal Ifor Haldane, King—late King of Gwynedd (reigned 904–917); father of Alroy, Javan, and Rhys Michael.*

COLLOS—alleged brother of Dimitri, Deryni.*

CONCANNON, Father Marcus—see *Marcus Concannon, Father.*

CORUND, Sir—a knight formerly in the service of the royal household, now deceased.*

CULLEN, Bishop Alister—see *Alister Cullen.*

CUSTODES FIDEI—*Ordo Custodum Fidei,* the Guardians of the Faith; religious Order founded by Paulin of Ramos to replace the Michaelines and reform ecclesiastical education in Gwynedd for

the exclusion of Deryni. Mandate later extended to ferret out
and eliminate Deryni by whatever means.

DAÍTHI, Father—a *Custodes* priest at Rhemuth; official King's Chaplain after Father Faelan.

DAVIN MacRorie, Lord—slain older brother of Ansel.*

DECLAN Carmody—Deryni in service of the regents; he and his wife
and two sons slain at regents' orders after he refused to misuse
his powers.*

DE COURCY—see *Etienne* and *Guiscard de Courcy.*

DERYNI (Der-in-ee)—Racial group gifted with paranormal/supernatural powers and abilities feared by many humans.

DIMITRI, Master—Paulin's new Deryni.

DRUMMOND—see *Cathan, Elinor, James, and Michaela Drummond.*

DUVESSA (Sinclair), Princess—dowager Princess of Cassan and mother
of Anne Quinnell.

EDWARD MacInnis, Bishop—age 24; Bishop of Grecotha; son of Earl
Manfred and nephew to Archbishop Hubert.

ELAINE de Fintan, Lady—Murdoch's wife, and Countess of Carthane.

ELINOR MacRorie Drummond—widow of Cathan MacRorie and
mother of Ansel and Davin by him; wife of James Drummond,
by whom she bore Michaela and Cathan.*

EQUITES CUSTODUM FIDEI—Knights of the Guardians of the Faith; military arm of the *Custodes Fidei;* intended to replace the Michaelines.

ESTELLAN MacInnis, Lady—as Manfred's wife, Countess of Culdi.

ETIENNE de Courcy, Baron—a southern lord, secretly Deryni, sent
by Joram to infiltrate the Haldane Court in preparation for Javan's accession; a law lord.

EVAINE MacRorie Thuryn, Lady—Deryni adept daughter of Camber,
sister of Joram; widow of the Healer Rhys Thuryn; died 918 attempting to restore her father from a suspension spell.*

EWAN, Duke—Second Duke of Claibourne, treacherously deposed
from power as one of original five regents of young King Alroy
and slain; brother of Sighere and Hrorik, father of Graham.*

FAELAN, Father—young *Custodes* priest from *Arx Fidei* who becomes Javan's confessor.

FANE Fitz-Arthur, Lord—eldest son of Earl Tammaron, and husband
of Princess Anne Quinnell.

FITZ-ARTHUR—see *Fane, Fulk, Nieve, Quiric,* and *Tammaron.*

FULK Fitz-Arthur—age 13; son of Tammaron, and a junior squire at Court.

FURSTAN—dynastic name of the ruling House of Torenth.

GABRILITES—priests and Healers of the Order of Saint Gabriel, an all-Deryni esoteric brotherhood founded in 745 and based at Saint Neot's Abbey until 917, when the Order was suppressed and many of its brethren slain; especially noted for the training of Healers.*

GAVIN, Sir—age 19; formerly squire to Alroy.

GEORGIUS, Brother—a dying monk at *Arx Fidei.**

GIDEON, Sir—Richard Murdoch's castellan at Nyford.

GIESELE MacLean, Lady—Co-Heiress of Kierney; sister of Richeldis; smothered to death at age 12, at orders of regents.*

GRAHAM MacEwan, Duke—age 14; Third Duke of Claibourne; son of Ewan and nephew of Earls Hrorik and Sighere.

GREGORY of Ebor, Lord—Deryni former Earl of Ebor (title now attainted and in abeyance); father of Jesse.*

GUISCARD de Courcy, Sir—age 29; son of Baron Etienne, secretly Deryni; sent by Joram to infiltrate the Haldane Court in preparation for accession of Javan; aide to Javan.

HALDANE—surname of the royal House of Gwynedd.

HALEX, Father—*Custodes* Abbot of *Arx Fidei* Abbey.

HILDRED, Baron—Master of Horse, loyal to Javan.

HONORIA Carmody—wife of the Deryni Declan Carmody; slain with her young sons at orders of the regents.*

HRORIK of Eastmarch, Lord—Earl of Eastmarch; younger brother of Ewan, elder of Sighere; uncle of Duke Graham.

HUBERT MacInnis, Archbishop—Primate of Gwynedd, Archbishop of Valoret, one of Alroy's former regents; younger brother of Earl Manfred and uncle of Bishop Edward.

HUMPHREY of Gallareaux, Father—Deryni Michaeline priest killed by Cinhil after poisoning Cinhil's firstborn son.*

IMRE, King—fifth and last Festillic King of Gwynedd (reigned 900–904); father of Mark of Festil by his sister Ariella.*

IVER MacInnis—age 25; son of Manfred; Earl of Kierney by right of his wife, Lady Richeldis MacLean.

JAMES, Master—a court physician.

JAMES Drummond, Lord—deceased father of Michaela and Cathan Drummond.*

JASON, Sir—a senior knight loyal to Javan.

JAVAN Jashan Urien Haldane, King—age 16; clubfooted younger twin of King Alroy, whom he succeeded; reigned 921–922; succeeded by his younger brother, Prince Rhys Michael.

JEBEDIAH of Alcara, Lord—slain Deryni Grand Master of the Order of Saint Michael.*

JEROWEN Reynolds, Lord—a law lord and member of Javan's council.

JESSE MacGregor, Sir—age 20; a Deryni adept, eldest son and heir of Gregory of Ebor, though the Ebor title is now attainted.

JORAM MacRorie, Father—Deryni adept and youngest son of Camber; brother of Evaine; priest and Knight of the Order of Saint Michael; now coordinating resistance to the former regents and assisting Prince Javan to realize his full powers and keep his throne.

JOSHUA, Lord—a *Custodes* captain at *Arx Fidei* Abbey.

JULIANA of Horthness, Lady—age 17; elder daughter of Rhun; formerly being groomed for marriage to Alroy, now slated for Javan.

KARIS d'Oriel—age 4; Deryni daughter of Oriel.

KENNET of Rhorau, Sir—nephew of Termod of Rhorau and brother of Sudrey; killed with Duke Ewan's party in 918.*

KINEVAN, Dom Queron—see *Queron Kinevan, Dom.*

LIOR, Father—a senior priest of the *Custodes Fidei*; assistant to the Inquisitor General.

LIRIN Udaut, Lady—age 16; daughter of Constable Udaut; wife of Richard Murdoch and Countess of Carthane.

MACGREGOR—surname adopted by Jesse, son of Gregory of Ebor.

MACGREGOR, Bishop Ailin—see *Ailin MacGregor.*

MACINNIS—see *Edward, Hubert, Iver,* and *Manfred.*

MACLEAN—see *Giesele* and *Richeldis.*

MACRORIE—surname of Camber's family. See *Ansel, Camber, Cathan, Davin, Evaine,* and *Joram.*

MANFRED MacInnis, Lord—Earl of Culdi of second creation; a former regent; elder brother of Archbishop Hubert and father of Iver and Bishop Edward.

MARCUS Concannon, Father—Chancellor General of the *Ordo Custodem Fidei*, in charge of all seminaries and other institutions of education in Gwynedd.

MARK of Festil, Prince—age 16; Deryni posthumous son of Imre and his sister Ariella, and carrier of the Festillic line after his parents' deaths; also known as Prince Marek, the Torenthi form of his name.

MICHAELA Drummond—age 15; daughter of Elinor and James, sister of Cathan; eventually, wife of Prince Rhys Michael Haldane.

MICHAELINES—priests, knights, and lay brothers of the Order of Saint Michael, a militant fighting and teaching Order, predominantly Deryni, formed during the reign of King Bearand Haldane to hold the Anvil of the Lord against Moorish incursions and defend the sea-lanes; suppressed under the Regency of King Alroy and outlawed thereafter.

MIKLOS von Furstan, Prince—age 17; Deryni younger brother of King Arion of Torenth.

MURDOCH of Carthane, Lord—Earl of Carthane and a former regent of King Alroy; father of Agnes, Cashel, and Richard; responsible for deaths of Duke Ewan of Claibourne and Declan Carmody.

NED—a farrier at the Michaeline sanctuary.

NEVELL—soldier of Rhemuth garrison who "attacks" Oriel.

NIALLAN Trey, Bishop—outlawed Deryni Bishop of Dhassa; a confidant of Father Joram MacRorie.

NIEVE Fitz-Arthur, Lady—Tammaron's countess and mother of four sons by him; widow of the late Earl of Tarleton, by whom she bore Peter (later known as Lord Albertus) and Paulin (of Ramos).

O'CARROLL, Ursin—see *Ursin O'Carroll*; also *Birgit* and *Carrollan O'Carroll*.

O'NEILL, Lord Tavis—*see Tavis O'Neill, Lord*.

O'SULLIVAN, Sylvan—see *Sylvan O'Sullivan*.

ORDO CUSTODUM FIDEI—see *Custodes Fidei*.

ORDO VERBI DEI—Order of the Word of God.

ORIEL, Master—a Healer in the forced service of the great lords, particularly Hubert and Tammaron; his wife and infant daughter held hostage for his good behavior.

ORISS, Archbishop Robert—Archbishop of Rhemuth; former Vicar General of the *Ordo Verbi Dei*.

PAULIN (Sinclair) of Ramos—younger son of the Earl of Tarleton and stepson of Earl Tammaron; briefly Bishop of Stavenham before his resignation to head the *Ordo Custodem Fidei*; brother of Albertus (Peter Sinclair), the Order's first Grand Master.

PIEDUR, Sir—a knight formerly in the service of the royal household, now deceased.*

QUERON Kinevan, Dom—former Gabrilite Healer-priest and founder of the Servants of Saint Camber; now working with the Master Revan as a "Baptizer."

QUIRIC Fitz-Arthur—age 11; son of Tammaron and a junior squire at court.

RADAN, Sir—a weapons master at Rhemuth Castle.

REVAN, Master—human charismatic preacher working with a Deryni faction to save Deryni by blocking their powers via a kind of "baptism."

RHUN of Horthness, Lord—called The Ruthless; Earl of Sheele of second creation and a former regent for King Alroy; husband of Agnes Murdoch.

RHYS MICHAEL Alister Haldane, Prince—youngest brother of King Alroy, age 15; succeeded his brother Javan as King Rhys (reigned 922–928); husband of Michaela Drummond.

RICHARD Murdoch—age 19; son of Murdoch; later, Earl of Carthane.

RICHELDIS MacLean, Lady—age 17; Countess of Kierney in her own right; married to Iver MacInnis.

RICKART, Dom—Healer to Bishop Niallan and part of Joram's staff.*

ROBEAR, Sir—a senior knight loyal to Javan.

ROBERT Oriss, Archbishop—see *Oriss, Archbishop Robert.*

SEANNA—younger sister of Jesse.

SERAFIN, Brother—Inquisitor General of the *Custodes Fidei.*

SIGHERE, Lord—Earl of Marley; brother of Hrorik and uncle of Duke Graham.

SINCLAIR—surname of the Earls of Tarleton.

SITRIC—Rhun's pet Deryni.

SIXTUS, Father—elderly priest in Hubert's service.

SORLE Dalriada, Sir—age 25; formerly squire to King Cinhil.

STACIA, Lady—age 12; daughter of Hrorik and Sudrey; Heiress of Eastmarch.*

STEVANUS, Master—*Custodes* battle surgeon at Culdi.

SUDREY of Rhorau, Lady—niece of Termod of Rhorau and therefore a distant cousin of Mark of Festil; as wife of Hrorik, Countess of Eastmarch.*

SYLVAN O'Sullivan—former battle-surgeon/Healer in Gregory's household; now part of Revan's baptizer team; one of three known Deryni with ability to block Deryni powers.

TAMBERT Fitz-Arthur-Quinnell, Duke—age 3; First Duke of Cassan; son of Princess Anne and Fane Fitz-Arthur.

TAMMARON Fitz-Arthur, Earl—Chancellor of Gwynedd and a former regent of King Alroy; father of Fane and grandfather of Duke Tambert.

TAVIS O'Neill—former Healer to Prince Javan; now a part of Revan's baptizer team; one of three known Deryni with ability to block Deryni powers.

THURYN—surname of Rhys; see *Evaine* and *Rhys*.

TOMAIS d'Edergoll, Sir—age 20; formerly squire to Prince Rhys Michael.

TREY, Bishop Niallan—see *Niallan Trey, Bishop*.

UDAUT, Lord—Constable of Gwynedd; father of Lirin.

URSIN O'Carroll—formerly Manfred's pet Deryni; stripped of his powers by Revan; a failed Healer.

WILLIAM of Desse—Master of the Works, Rhemuth.

INDEX OF PLACES

ALL SAINTS' CATHEDRAL—seat of the Archbishop of Valoret, Primate of All Gwynedd.

BELDOUR—capital of Torenth.

CAERRORIE—Camber's principal residence as Earl of Culdi, a few hours' ride northeast of Valoret; now the seat of Manfred Mac-Innis, Earl of Culdi of the second creation.

CARTHANE—Murdoch's earldom, south of Rhemuth, whose capital is Nyford.

CASHIEN—episcopal see to the west of Rhemuth.

CASSAN—former petty princedom ruled by Prince Ambert Quinnell; now a duchy of Gwynedd under its first duke, Tambert Fitz-Arthur-Quinnell.

CLAIBOURNE—principal city of Old Kheldour and first duchy of Gwynedd; seat of Graham, Third Duke of Claibourne.

CONNAIT, The—barbarian kingdom to the west, famous for its mercenaries.

COR CULDI—hereditary ancestral seat of the Earls of Culdi, near the city of Culdi, on the Gwynedd-Meara border.

DESSE—port town south of Rhemuth.

DHASSA—traditionally neutral episcopal see east of Rhemuth, in the Lendour Mountains.

EASTMARCH—earldom held by Hrorik, middle son of Duke Sighere of Kheldour.

EBOR—earldom north of Valoret, formerly held by Gregory, now in abeyance.

GRECOTHA—university city, former site of the Varnarite School; seat of the Bishop of Grecotha.

GWYNEDD—central of the Eleven Kingdoms and hub of Haldane power since 645, when the first Haldane High King began to unify the area; seat of the Festillic Dynasty, 822–904; restored to the Haldane line in 904 with the accession of Cinhil Haldane.

HORTHNESS—Barony of Rhun the Ruthless.

HOWICCE—kingdom to the southwest of Gwynedd; loosely allied with Llannedd.

KHELDISH RIDING—viceregality broken off Kheldour after its annexation by Duke Sighere and King Cinhil in 906.

KHELDOUR—small kingdom north of Gwynedd, now comprising the Duchy of Claibourne and the Earldoms of Marley and Eastmarch.

KIERNEY—earldom north of Culdi.

LLANNEDD—kingdom southwest of Gwynedd; loosely allied with Howicce.

MARBURY—episcopal see in the earldom of Marley.

MARLEY—small earldom carved out of Eastmarch for Sighere, youngest son of Duke Sighere.

MARLOR—barony of Manfred MacInnis.

MEARA—kingdom/princedom northwest of Gwynedd; nominally a vassal state of Gwynedd.

MOORYN—province at the far south of Gwynedd, including Carthmoor and Corwyn.

NYFORD—port city south of Rhemuth, seat of the Earls of Carthane; episcopal see for Carthane.

RAMOS—abbey town southwest of Valoret; birthplace of Paulin Sinclair; convening place of the Council of Ramos, winter of 917–918.

RHEMUTH—ancient capital of Gwynedd under the Haldanes; abandoned during the Festillic Interregnum; restored under Cinhil and Alroy; secondary archbishopric for Gwynedd, junior to Valoret.

RHENDALL—lake region north of Gwynedd; territorial title given to the heir of the Duke of Claibourne.

SAINT MARK'S ABBEY—monastery near Valoret.

SAINT NEOT'S ABBEY—stronghold of the Order of Saint Gabriel the Archangel, an all-Deryni esoteric Order specializing in the training of Healers; located in the Lendour highlands; destroyed by troops led by the Regent Rhun on Christmas Eve, 917.

SHEELE—seat of the Earldom of Sheele, north of Valoret.

STAVENHAM—episcopal see in the far north of Kheldour.

TORENTH—powerful kingdom to the east of Gwynedd; origin of the Festillic line, who were rulers of Gwynedd 822–904; currently ruled by King Arion.

VALORET—Festillic capital of Gwynedd, 822–904, from which springs the primacy of its archbishop.

PARTIAL LINEAGE OF THE HALDANE KINGS

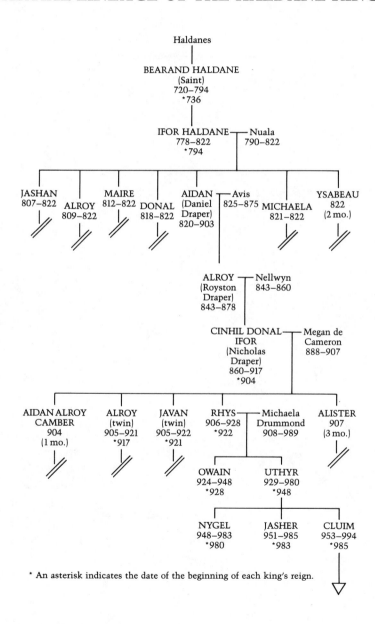

Haldanes

BEARAND HALDANE
(Saint)
720–794
*736

IFOR HALDANE—Nuala
778–822   790–822
*794

JASHAN   MAIRE   AIDAN—Avis   YSABEAU
807–822   ALROY 812–822 DONAL (Daniel 825–875 MICHAELA 822
          809–822   818–822 Draper)   821–822 (2 mo.)
                                    820–903

ALROY—Nellwyn
(Royston 843–860
Draper)
843–878

CINHIL DONAL—Megan de
IFOR   Cameron
(Nicholas   888–907
Draper)
860–917
*904

AIDAN ALROY   ALROY   JAVAN   RHYS—Michaela   ALISTER
CAMBER   (twin)   (twin)   906–928 Drummond 907
904   905–921 905–922 *922   908–989   (3 mo.)
(1 mo.)   *917   *921

OWAIN   UTHYR
924–948   929–980
*928   *948

NYGEL   JASHER   CLUIM
948–983   951–985   953–994
*980   *983   *985

* An asterisk indicates the date of the beginning of each king's reign.

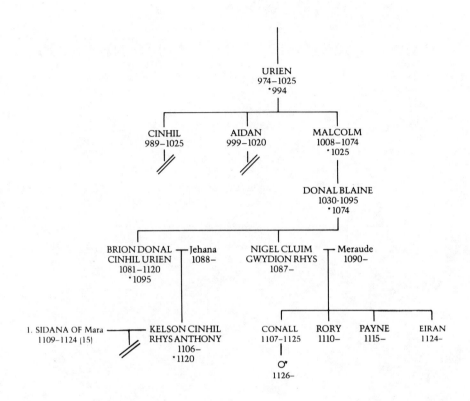

APPENDIX IV

THE FESTILLIC KINGS OF GWYNEDD AND THEIR DESCENDANTS

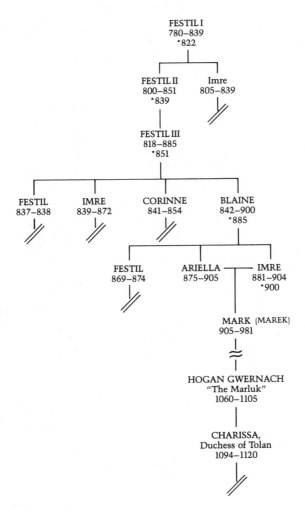

* An asterisk indicates the date of the beginning of each king's reign.

APPENDIX V

PARTIAL LINEAGE OF THE MACRORIES

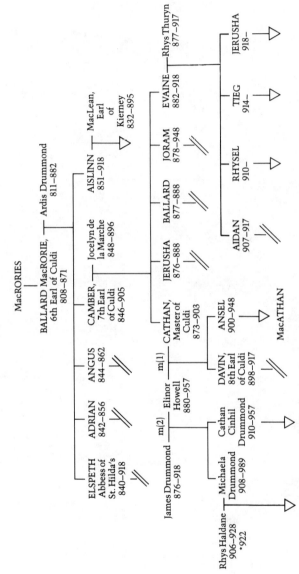

* An asterisk indicates the date of the beginning of each king's reign.

ABOUT THE AUTHOR

KATHERINE KURTZ was born in Coral Gables, Florida, during a hurricane and has led a whirlwind existence ever since. She holds a Bachelor of Science degree in chemistry from the University of Miami, Florida, and a Master of Arts degree in English history from UCLA. She studied medicine before deciding that she would rather write, and is an Ericksonian-trained hypnotist. Her scholarly background also includes extensive research in religious history, magical systems, and other esoteric subjects.

Katherine Kurtz's literary works include the well-known Deryni, Camber, and Kelson Trilogies of fantasy fiction, an occult thriller set in WWII England, and a number of Deryni-related short stories. At least three more trilogies are planned in the Deryni universe, and several additional mainstream thrillers are also currently in development.

Ms. Kurtz lives in Ireland with her husband and son.